# GATEKEEPERS

*The Fog Chonicles*

Virginie Bonfils-Bedos

*To Kat,*

*A lovely friend*

*this book*

*may let you escape*

*the daily life and*

*transport you to other*

*realms!*

*xx Virginie*

Book cover © 2015 Virginie Bonfils-Bedos
Author photo © 2015 Diana Patient

ISBN: 1517478227
ISBN 13: 9781517478223

*To my mother Geneviève and late father Jean-Pierre, whose unconditional love, constant support, and unshakable faith in my abilities gave me the strength to follow my dreams. They are the backbone of all my enterprises.*
*And to my dear friend Diego, who inspired me to write the stories floating in my head.*

# WEEK I

*This is my story. This is how it all started, what I have observed, heard and learned, in my own clumsy words.*

*Yoko*

**Day 1 (Sunday)**

The first thing that hit me waking up was the cold. Nothing new from the previous day, but I just could not get used to it. It was so unlike London to have a long spell of extreme cold weather, staying in the minuses for months in a row. I reached out with one arm and pulled the cord to open the curtain. The room filled with brightness, but glancing through the window I couldn't see anything. I was only staring into whiteness at some kind of fog, a very thick one. This winter was definitely the worst in my twelve years in this town. It was now early March, the weather should have started to be more pleasant, but no. London was clearly in the midst of a mini-arctic phase, during which the ground was still covered by a blanket of snow and people actually slowed down their active pace to avoid a painful fall on their butts.

My name is Yoko.

At the time, I was barely in my thirties, living in a house share in Central London a stone's throw away from Notting Hill, just five minutes' walk on the north side of the park. I moved to London after high school for university, and haven't budged since. The best way to describe myself would be as a 'foreign Londoner' with a melting pot of backgrounds being half French, quarter Italian and quarter Japanese. My first name Yoko comes from my maternal great-grandmother. Apparently this name confused people. Everyone took a moment when hearing it for the first time to try and match the name to my Mediterranean features with no traces of Japanese: olive skin, thick brown locks cut in a shoulder-length bob and almond eyes. The only possible Japanese touch was the deep jet black colour of my eyes, yet that could be Italian too. In addition, I know barely ten words in Japanese and only have a very basic knowledge of Italian. To this day I don't understand why I took Spanish at school, not Italian or Japanese. Teenage rebellion? A wish to conform to my friends? For whatever reason, I missed that boat.

That Sunday morning, fog and cold didn't stay long on my mind because my main focus when waking up was food. I am the grumpiest person in the morning until my continental breakfast and a strong coffee are in front of me. Not enjoying being grumpy, it never took long before I put on my dressing gown and my spotted fluffy slippers and headed down to the kitchen.

When I arrived downstairs, my three housemates were already there. On weekends we usually all woke up at different times, depending on what had happened the previous night. Breakfast all together with Zeno, Rico and Harry was a rare occurrence. For that reason, on that Sunday morning, Zeno decided breakfast together would be a feast. He put on a warm coat over his pyjamas, his bare feet into his boots and headed to the door on a quest to buy fresh *pains au chocolat*, croissants and other treats at the bakery round the corner. Zeno could not have made it much further than the front yard before he was back seconds later, a frown on his face. He looked at us silently, blinked several times and turned back out, only to reappear again after a minute or two, bewildered. Everyone was chatting away at the table when Zeno's staring made us stop. I asked him if he had changed his mind and suggested we could just take some bread from the freezer instead. He didn't reply immediately and just stood there, looking bleached.

Finally, after a long intake of breath, Zeno asked in a shaky voice if someone would accompany him, adding in a whisper, 'I have a little ... thing ... something I'm not sure about.' So I stood up and went to the entrance, picking up my coat and a pair of sneakers on the way, saying, 'Sure, it's not fair for you to go alone.' He held the door open for me and we stepped out.

'This fog is unreal. I can't see a thing! Absolutely nothing!' I exclaimed taking my first step outside.

'Yes ...' he replied vaguely.

'I can just make you out and you are right behind me,' I continued, thinking the lack of visibility was probably why he wanted company.

'Yes ...' he repeated.

'How are we going to go to the bakery? Wait! I have an idea!' I said, taking out my mobile and selecting the torch application. Just as we were noticing that the torch didn't make much difference in showing the way, we stepped out of the fog abruptly and walked right into a clearing in a forest. Yes, a forest. My foot stopped in mid-air for a split second, eyes widening and jaw hanging low. Zeno asked, sounding short of breath, 'We are in a forest, aren't we?' Both feet now on the ground, I stood rooted to the spot. What I was seeing, and not seeing, was incomprehensible. Where was my road and why were there trees ahead? There was no city noise. Instead, birds were singing and the wind shook the branches of the trees. No neighbours' houses, no cars, no road, no other human beings. A real forest. It was unreal! The only words that escaped my mouth in reply to Zeno's question were 'What the hell?' Rude, but a forest? Before coffee!

'That's the 'little' thing I was talking about ... this.' He made a sweeping movement with his right arm. 'I don't know what's happening, but both times I came out, I ended up in this forest.'

'That's not possible. Maybe I'm sleeping. Yes, this is a dream,' I whispered, followed by 'ouch' when Zeno pinched me. 'Well, apparently not,' I continued, frowning at Zeno.

'Scusi, ma ... just to check.' He didn't sound that apologetic to me.

'Right. Let's go back in. Let's get the others!' he said. We turned on our heels. Facing this fog again made me hesitate a few seconds before stepping back in. It was like facing a wall, and my heart was beating abnormally. The need to go back to the others won over the apprehension and we quickly went in. Rico laughed when he heard us opening the door and shouted from the table, 'So now you've both changed your mind?' He stopped when he saw our faces. We must have been looking like bloodless zombies staring into the void.

'Guys, you need to see this,' said Zeno. I just nodded, repeating in a low voice, 'I don't get it.' Rico opened his mouth to speak, changed his mind and closed it. Harry raised one eyebrow and stood up, immediately followed by Rico. They both put their coats on and switched from slippers to trainers, not bothering with socks. Harry left first, Zeno and me behind him, Rico leaving last and closing the door behind us. After a short struggle through the fog, we finally reached the front gate where, again, the fog came to a sudden stop. Ahead of us a few cars were parked and a motorbike zoomed along the road. We were in our good old London. Something was just not right.

'Weird fog! Never saw anything like this. You were right. It was worth coming out to check it out. Look how it ...' Harry started.

'Harry ... this ... this is not what we wanted to show you,' I interrupted.

'I don't understand,' said Zeno first to himself and then to me. 'I think ... I think we are losing the plot. I mean ... ' He turned to Harry and Rico and continued, 'There was a forest, but now, there is no … it was so real! But Yoko, you saw it too? I mean, it wasn't just me, right, you saw it too!'

'Yes, I saw it all right.' I just couldn't stop staring at a couple walking on the pavement ahead. Even though this street had been mine for years, it had never looked so comforting.

'What are you two talking about?' Rico retorted, getting slightly annoyed. 'Right, I am cold and hungry. Let's get back in. Harry, you deal with them, they've both gone bonkers.' Rico turned and entered the fog with determination. Harry looked at us both, taking his time. He clearly believed we were not joking and was trying to pry into our minds to understand what we were on about. As he obviously couldn't, he finally just said, 'Let's go inside.'

Back at the table, everyone was silent. Confusion overcame me. I felt lost and unable to think, vaguely aware of Harry and Rico looking from me to Zeno to the door. Within minutes Zeno popped back out again in the hope that everything was back to normal and no forest was to be seen. On his return, he nodded to me in such a way to indicate that he had emerged into the forest. He asked Rico, 'Could you just step out and tell us what you see? I know it sounds weird but please, do it, because right now I don't know what to believe.'

When Rico came back, he sat down, hunched his shoulders and said 'our street'. That shook me out of my daze. I stood up and rushed to the front door, grabbing Harry's mobile from the entrance table on the way. What was needed was some kind of proof. Zeno arrived by my side promptly, telling me he would not let me go out there alone. I was about to protest, but he had a point: being on my own to face whatever was out there, if not my road, was not tempting.

As we emerged from the opaque, white and thick mist, the view in front of me took me aback despite being mentally prepared this time. The sight was captivating. Fifteen to twenty metres separated us from the tall and rather bare trees of the forest. The ground of the clearing was uneven, a mixture of dead wood, moss and leaves carpeting the space. The scenery was eerie and peaceful, for a few seconds it made me forget its abnormality and felt strangely serene. A crack in the branches and a pheasant suddenly taking off took me out of my reverie and back to activating the camera on Harry's mobile. For the rest of our time there, the forest was only observed and snapped via the screen of the mobile. We didn't stay long, ten minutes at most. When we got back in, I went straight to the dining room area, sat at the table and passed round Harry's mobile in silence to share the photos just taken. The shots showed trees, dead trunks and sightings of birds or red squirrels. It could have been an album of a day out in the country. Harry knew the photos had not been on his device before and Rico just had to look at his face to understand the whole thing was not a prank. Harry then went out and returned shortly with new photos on his mobile following the forest ones, all of our street and of some passers-by.

'Something is really wrong here,' said Rico.

'No, really?' replied Harry.

'Yoko, I think we have a problem,' Zeno said, his jaw clenched.

All I could do was bite my lip, utter something unintelligible and nod. An additional thought had just bothered me: there were no more red squirrels in England. The grey squirrels got rid of them all. So how come the forest seemed full of them?

The four of us lived in a three-storey terraced house, part of a group of eight houses with a residents' parking area in front. Each house looked alike, with a small front garden separating the building from the cars. On the ground floor a large main room served as living room at the front with wide windows and as a dining area with a large table at the back. That room and the adjacent kitchen both had access to the back patio. The ground floor also benefitted from its own lavatory, which was handy for visitors. The first floor had two bedrooms, a bathroom and a small office. My room was the largest one at the front of the house with bay windows. The second floor, just under the roof, was slightly smaller also with two bedrooms and a bathroom. This was a simple house in need of freshening up, but it was a very warm, cosy and much loved home. Having moved in shortly after I lost my fiancé two years before, I considered myself lucky to have found such a welcoming place with people who helped me recover with their kindness and humour. Despite our differences in personalities, backgrounds and habits, we had become very close.

Zenone and Enrico, more often than not known as Zeno and Rico, were two Italian friends from the same home town, a place just a little bigger than a village that they considered the centre of the world. I have never really known if they really believed it or not. They had known each other since their teenage years, being a few years apart in age. They were more brothers than best friends, arguing, hugging and supporting each other. Rico was a talented artist yet to be recognised for his politically incorrect paintings. He was of African origin, slightly above average height, with large eyes, dark chocolate skin and a huge grin when having a good time, that is to say most of the time. He was also obsessed with staying fit and toned for the ladies. He could not yet make a living from his art and Zeno regularly found him odd jobs to help him out, more often than not on some of Zeno's diverse market and trading activities. Rico was a thorough and hard worker, so they both found it a good arrangement. Zeno had his hands in various projects, decidedly a nifty person with good business acumen. To my joy, his latest venture was an Italian olive oil import business, so we had a good selection of it at home. Zeno was tall, 6'3" or 1.92m (I could never get rid of the metric system) and a bit chubby, although it wasn't showing much with his height and broad shoulders.

Harry was the only English one in the house. He was a lecturer in Contemporary European History, with a slightly pronounced posh English accent and a 'typically British' sarcastic sense of humour. He was also quite tall at 1.82m, with a head fully shaved to avoid showing his balding top, and a little bit of a beer belly. Harry acted as the wise man of the house. He called it his privilege as our senior and main tenant of the house. Indeed the rest of us were his lodgers.

The bunch of us, from mid-twenties to mid-thirties, had moved from being mere cohabitants to real friends. We were all independent and lived our separate lives, but we all saw the household as a mini-family with the members both appreciating and respecting one another and, as in any family, shouting at each other yet knowing that the next day we would have moved on. Our mutual trust and respect was put to the test on that foggy day.

'Fine. Let's stop and think here. Let's review.' My head in my hands, I was talking to myself as much as to the others.

'Zeno, when you leave the house alone, you walk out into a forest. Same when you are with me. If the four of us step out together, we end up in our street as usual. Now, Harry, when you went out on your own, you also reached our good old street. This leaves ...' At this point Rico jumped from his seat, rushed to the door and came back shortly afterwards, panting and confirming with a sigh of relief that he emerged on our parking. The next steps were for Zeno and me to leave the house with only Harry and only Rico. Both times we crossed the fog to London. There was only one scenario left to check: going out on my own, which Zeno refused to let me do. His argument was that, not knowing what was out there, he would not forgive himself if something happened to me. I hesitated, the need to know and the apprehension fighting each other. In the end another need won, the need for coffee. I couldn't face anything more without coffee and breakfast, let alone an unexplained forest. So I caved into Zeno's will.

As we sat around the table, a loaf of bread defrosting in the oven, we summed up that it was only Zeno and me together or on our own (theoretically for me) who reached the mysterious woods. Somehow, the two of us were linked to this mysterious forest that had appeared on our doorstep as if by magic. Also, even though the other two housemates were not affected like us, they somehow had the ability to bring us back to our normal London landscape.

And to think we were not even under the influence from late night drinking …

'So, as we're not in London, where are we?' Zeno pondered.

'I think we've established you're in a forest,' replied the ever sarcastic Harry.

I rolled my eyes, yet was unable to smother a little smile, and said, 'Oh shut up. Now is not the time to joke.'

'Does that mean every time you want to go out in London you need one of us?' Rico asked.

'Come on, this is surreal! It must be a bad dream and I'll wake up soon. We'll have a good laugh when we look back on it,' I said and laughed nervously. Rico's question was daunting.

'It isn't a dream,' Zeno said.

'Nope,' Rico added.

'My dear, would you like me to slap you to be sure?' Harry finished, taking rather too much pleasure at the idea.

'Great, guys. Thank you for the moral support,' I said sulkily. 'And Harry, no thank you. Zeno already did that type of check.'

'Sometimes double-checking is good. Anyway, what do we do now?' Harry asked.

'Yeah, what now?' Rico shouted from the kitchen where he was preparing more coffee.

'Maybe this is a temporary time–space glitch and everything will be back to normal when the fog lifts? Maybe in an hour or so, or tomorrow?' Zeno's voice was betraying hope. Hope mixed with incredulity. He was as freaked out about it all as I was. The sooner things went back to normal the better, especially when he referred to this …

'Did you just say temporary time–space glitch?' I asked him.

'Yes, he did,' Harry replied, 'and the scary thing is that no one is making fun of it.'

'Breathe. Do not panic. Just breathe,' I repeated inwardly in the silence that followed Harry's comment.

Rico came back to the living room with bread, butter, jam, honey and Nutella. There wasn't much we could do about the situation, but we could eat. I was trying to rationalise how to react: one option was just to continue as if everything was completely normal; the other was hyperventilation and nervous breakdown. Not keen on the latter, I informed the men that after breakfast I would have a shower and pop out to run some errands. Either Rico or Harry would have to let me out of the house. Maybe it was not necessary and I could reach London on my own, as this scenario had not been tried yet. This trial would have to wait: I had had enough. For now it was some normality I needed.

'No problem babe, I'll let you out,' Rico finally told me. He put his arm round my shoulders and added, 'while you're at it, would you mind getting me some hair gel? I'm running low.'

Breakfast was not a jolly affair. We were mostly lost in our own thoughts until Harry laughed and said, 'Actually, it could be pretty cool.' That got our attention and we all turned to look at him as he elaborated. 'Look, you can be in two places at once. OK, you need one of us to get out in London, but that's nothing, and then at the other 'end' you have an unknown forest and, from the look of it, a wild one. I wonder what it is and what's in it ... I would love to see this forest for real.'

It was not clear whether he was serious, sarcastic, or if he was trying to cheer us up.

'Yes, jeez, I am feeling so lucky right now,' Zeno replied. 'What I would like to know is what is happening to me,' he said, then looking at me quickly corrected 'to us!'

I gazed through the window at the thick fog, and began talking to myself, first in a whisper then raising my voice more and more, carried away by my own thoughts. 'Maybe this is like Narnia and the front door opens to a magical world. Or it's something like in the *Stargate* movie and the house is set on an alien artefact connecting us to another planet and we have powers to transport us there! Or maybe we are thrown back in time. Yes, what if we stepped in the past or the future going through the gate of time, like the time–space thing Zeno referred to before?'

'Here she goes … The craziness inherent in womenfolk has just awakened,' Harry said, shaking his head and grabbing another piece of bread.

'Have you never thought that maybe the guys who wrote this stuff could have used their own personal experience?' I was looking at the three of them, my smile growing. 'You know what, now that I'm starting to think about it in a new light, even though I really, really don't want this 'situation' to be a lasting occurrence, I am getting curious about this forest …'

'No, no, no, no, no! I know you can be a bit weird and wild, but NO!' Rico exclaimed. 'You are not getting curious about this forest. I can see your brain beginning to plot an expedition next. No! Forget it. You don't know what is out there in this forest. There could be monsters. Or cannibals!' Rico slammed his hand on the table and winced in pain.

'As if we could stop her …' Harry said with a lopsided smile across his face.

Zeno had remained silent so far and he too had started to stare at the window. 'Mmmm … I am getting curious too… There could be some interesting things in this forest. Who knows what we could bring back from there? Of course, if our lives returned to normal it would be nicer. Except if we found gold or something. We could even trade some of the wood …' It was typical of Zeno to focus on the business opportunities even in critical times.

'You just have to love crazy foreigners,' Harry noted and smiled.

I was beginning to cheer up and reconsider that morning as a weird adventure. My feelings were undeniably mixed: on one side terrified, especially not understanding what was happening, and yet, unable to contain a certain excitement.

'Yes, Zeno, let's do it! Let's do it! But let's get prepared, right? This is like a mini-adventure: let's pack some food, some water and a rope. And chalk! We need to mark our way. Oh, and do you have a compass, Zeno? Or you Rico? I mean you guys must have something like that, right? I am getting E X C I T E D!'

'Rico, Harry, she's scaring me,' Zeno said, half-alarmed, half-amused.

'Nothing new there. She is a woman, after all. Even worse, one with an eccentric streak. The type you can't just pinpoint as crazy and yet ...' Harry replied.

'Guys, you are not serious, are you? There may be wolves, bears or worse in this forest. You have no clue!' Rico shouted.

'Oh, shut up Rico. What else can we do? If this is temporary, and surely it will be, we must have a quick look before it disappears. We can't miss the opportunity. And if the forest remains, which I don't even want to think about, we would be bound to explore it at some point anyway,' Zeno replied. 'And I don't know why you are getting all upset about it, you are not the ones who will go out there.'

'But I do care. It's dangerous. You know nothing about this forest. Nothing! There could be monsters, dragons ...'

'We'll take the big knives from the kitchen, right Zeno?' I was trying to reassure myself as much as Rico. 'We will also start very small, just around the house, until we are properly ready and armed.'

'The bound-to-be-there dinosaurs will no doubt be terrified at the sight of the bread knife,' said Harry, serious but for a twinkle in his eye. 'You should take the forks, too, so that they think you're after them for dinner.'

'Ha ha! Very funny,' Rico replied, 'but it's true, there could be dinosaurs for all we know.'

Harry rolled his eyes and suddenly changed the subject. 'Would the mobiles work out there?'

'Mobiles?' I exclaimed. 'This is brilliant. We should try.'

'We could also film our discovery with its video camera, even without network ...' Zeno added.

'If it works,' I jumped in, 'we could even have an online video call with you guys and you could see what we see and ...'

'And be there with you!' Harry continued, standing up. His unusual burst of excitement surprised everyone, but it was the push we needed.

'Let's check now, just outside the house.'

When Zeno and I reached the forest, we experienced again excitement, anxiety and fear at the inexplicable view in front of us. This time, what unsettled me most was the lack of familiar sounds. It was unlike anything I had ever encountered. The various countryside and forests visited before, the trips on boats, none had the same sensation of silence. None were so completely empty from the sound of traffic on a distant road, or planes, or cow bells, or the voices of your travelling companions. Never had such a feeling of loneliness washed over me. The daunting effect of this absence of familiar sounds gripped my throat, and it was an effort not to take a step back but a step forward instead. Just one was a start. Little by little, the sounds of the forest became more defined, with the light irregular sound of the wind in the branches and the multitude of birds singing, some beautifully, some less so. The squirrels reappeared and we could distinguish a variety of birds flying and hopping from branch to branch, from tree to tree. Zeno was as captivated as me. My mobile beeped a message from Harry asking if we had received it. The device showed full signal.

'Amazing,' I whispered, immediately making a call to Harry.

'Are you in the forest?' was his opening line.

'Yes. Just outside the house, on the edge of the woods,' I answered. Rico was by Harry, talking to us too, 'Babe, anything happens you both run back inside. You hear me, you just run in!'

Zeno bent towards me and spoke to them, 'OK, let's try a video call. Let's see if it works.' While we were talking, we both kept peering anxiously towards the woods, in case a dragon or dinosaur was making an appearance. We scanned the forest, fascinated but focused, unwilling to be caught by surprise by anything coming from there. We regularly glanced behind us too, in hope of reassurance. The fog was concentrated only where the house was, and even knowing the house was within it, I missed the solace of seeing my home.

The call on, Zeno turned his handset towards the forest and we heard Harry and Rico's intake of breath. The forest was captivating for us all. Its apparent silence took over again, followed by the growing sound of nature. Placing myself in front of the camera, the callers were able to see we really were on the edge of a forest. It was a strange situation: us here, Rico and Harry in the house only a few metres away, without knowing what or where this forest was. It didn't make any sense, but soon this slipped my mind: the scenery, the peacefulness and serenity of it all grabbed me in a timeless feel, and my mind went blank. Lost in observation of the forest in its entirety and in the details within, the surreal of the situation disappeared. I forgot myself, being totally absorbed in the moment.

This peaceful state of mind lasted what might have been a few minutes or an eternity before it was washed out by a sudden tsunami of questions and uncertainties. They went through my head so fast I couldn't make sense of any of them. How could it be? How could this forest be there? Why had only Zeno and I been affected by it and how? What happened and would this forest always be there now? Or how long would it last? Why? How? Why? Then another thought troubled me: if the forest is only here temporarily, accessible from the house for a brief period of time, could we end up stuck in here any minute now?' At this last thought, I gasped and shared my fears with Zeno. His eyes opened wide, he swore, grasped my wrist and we promptly disappeared back into the fog towards the house.

To our relief, the house was still there, the door left wide open by Rico in case we needed to run back in, away from monsters. As we crossed the threshold, I pointed out to Zeno, 'Do you think that whatever creature living in this place could actually get in the house, not just us? I mean, we could now have a wood rat from …

or an unknown type of mosquito, or spiders!' Zeno was quiet for a few minutes, shaking his head slowly before finally saying, 'Yoko, please, let's just deal with one thing at a time. I am still trying to deal with having a forest on our doorstep.'

'Sorry. You're right,' I replied with an apologetic grimace. 'I'll try not to express my terrible thoughts aloud. And terrible they are! It's buzzing like a wasps' nest in my head right now. Plus, really, I don't know if I am terrified, fascinated or ecstatic. I alternate between each every other second ... I keep having new ideas and new things I want to check, or I want to hide under my duvet with a box of chocolates.'

'I know, me too ...'

'I also want to check the back door and if we are still in the forest leaving from that side too? One of us could keep an eye on the fog to make sure it doesn't dissipate and leave us stranded.'

'I'm not sure I want to go back out.'

'But that's my point, maybe the back of the house is normal. Maybe we ...'

'Fiiine ...' Zeno raised his eyes to the ceiling and relented.

As Zeno updated the others, I grabbed two large knives from the kitchen and handed one to Zeno when he joined me. We went out, crossed the white blanket of fog, and came out to the view of the forest. The woods were much closer than on the other side, maybe five or six metres away. It made me feel more exposed and insecure, as any hidden danger jumping out from the depth of the woods would be upon us within seconds. I didn't want to waste any time and planted my knife in the ground to mark where we had to come back in after our circuit of the house. It took us barely a minute to return and confirm that the cloud of fog was covering the whole house. In London, the house was part of a terrace, linked on both sides to other identical houses, so that making the tour of the house would be impossible. This fog and forest had the house as a single unit. The situation was getting even more perplexing.

Back at the dining table, Harry told us that while we were out he had popped out to double-check that the fog was limited to our house. It stopped abruptly on the exact party wall and gates. He realised too how obvious the fog would be to the residents of the houses around and to any passers-by. The fog was so dense our house could not be seen at all.

'Man! Does that mean people will think this is a freak house now?' Rico exclaimed. We were starting to comprehend the forest might not be our only issue, the fog itself was as well. It seemed acceptable to assume the fog and forest were linked somehow, and even that Zeno and I were also connected to both. Maybe we should just move out and let the landlord deal with this unusual problem? Yet, if we were linked to the fog, could we even move? We would have to deal with questions we could not answer, especially if the phenomenon lasted. Our little household would have to make a decision: to talk or not to talk about the forest, the fog, about Zeno and my weird experience, about the mobile photos, the Skype call and about the red squirrels.

'Hang on a minute.' Rico seemed to come out of a momentary torpor. 'What if there are other human beings out there? Would they be like us? Hey, there could be some hot babes!' We all rolled our eyes, but Rico wouldn't stop that easily when thinking of women. 'And I can't even check them out. They would miss out on me, too? That is terrible, man! This is shit!'

Zeno and I just stared at him speechless. Not that we should have been stunned. By now, his obsessions with women (by this read sex), with fashion and with his hair were well established in the household. But really? Even in these circumstances? As for Harry, a smile crept over his face as he replied, 'What took you so long?'

Rico ignored him. He turned towards Zeno, half-joking, half-serious. 'Zeno, you bastard ... I bet they never even met an Italian before ... poor them.' Zeno was not in the mood. He dismissed him by replying that he had a girlfriend.

'She's not in the forest though. She's not even in the same country,' Rico remarked.

'That is not the point. I am not fooling around when in a relationship. Wait! Why are we even having this discussion? We don't know if there is anybody else in this forest. Hell, what am I to say to her about it?' Zeno exclaimed.

Harry intervened, 'Guys, that brings us back to the immediate problem: do we say anything about what is happening here and to the two of you? Honestly, this should be your call,' he looked at Zeno and me, 'as you are the main ones concerned.'

We both simultaneously answered in the negative. It was not a big loud 'no', more a slight shaking-of-the-head no, pronounced in a low voice as if we were not that convinced ourselves by our position. The truth was that we didn't want to be the only two involved. Also, we needed Rico and Harry, and we didn't want them to feel unconcerned. We were stuck without them. This was an instinctive reaction, not one I felt proud of once conscious of it. Harry leaned back in his chair and, understanding our hesitation, commented, 'Yes, you are right. We're entangled in it too.'

'You bet we are! And I say, let's keep it quiet for the moment,' Rico interjected.

'Let's check if the forest is still here in a few hours or even tomorrow,' Zeno continued, 'and let's check if everyone can see the fog, too. We don't even know that.'

I grabbed my notebook and a pen nearby, opened it to a new page and looked up. 'Let's brainstorm!' I said. 'Here is what I suggest. We write down the priority questions and our thoughts on what we should do and then we try to make a bit of sense out of it all.' Without waiting for their reply, I bent over the notebook and began scribbling, reading aloud what I was jotting down. 'What and where is this unknown forest and what/who lives in it, if anything or anyone?'

After a few seconds everybody fired questions and I had to ask them to slow down.

'How long will it be there?' (Rico)

'And can we get stuck in it?' (Zeno)

'Why Zeno and me?' (me).

Harry intervened matter-of-factly. 'My friends, your questions are all very appropriate, but it seems to me we have no way of answering any at this point. Maybe we should stick to questions we can work out an answer for, like, "Could anyone help you, Yoko and Zeno, to get out in our 'normal world' or is it just us?"'

He was right. We should have a practical approach for now and write down what we could check today and tomorrow. That is, if the phenomenon continued. We resumed our brainstorming with renewed focus and selected our points more carefully.

(Here let me make a little *aparté* in the story of the chain of events, to tell you a bit more about me. Being aware of my light personal introduction so far, you might be surprised that by then I hadn't totally freaked out, burst into tears, or gone completely berserk. My state, in truth, was not that far from it all. It was only either a lack of seeing the big picture, or my being a bit of a free spirit, or both, that enabled me to keep it together. First, the existence of the forest was so unreal, so impossible, I struggled to accept it really was there. I knew, but I couldn't accept it. Second, I endeavoured to keep a positive and spontaneous outlook in life, notably in dealing with the unexpected it often brought. After all, I had already lost so much in the past. My belief was that life is a river, one with various currents, sometimes tranquil, sometimes savage. The best way to enjoy the journey is to let you and your boat go with the flow, steering now and then during the hard times, or to seize the opportunity of a better current and a better view. Sometimes you go ashore for a break, to replenish food and energy, before continuing your river journey. That Sunday, life had brought a forest outside my London door and the best attitude was to go with it and work out which way to paddle. Discipline and organisation are paradoxical yet not incompatible with a free spirit: to cope with the current events I opted to proceed practically and with structure, keeping my mind focused and carefully filling my notebook with the notes from our discussion).

By the time we had finished, it was already mid-afternoon. We all felt a bit clearer having jotted down our ideas and set up a plan of action. Annoyingly, when we read them back, our points were succinct and shamefully obvious.

'How could it have taken so long to come up with only these few basic notes?' Rico asked.

'That's because we eliminated every reference to sex and politics you made,' Harry answered.

'Because we crossed out anything long term, to stick to today and tomorrow,' Zeno added, 'as well as anything we have no way of knowing, or that is just too dangerous for the time being.'

We had decided to limit ourselves to minimal exploration for now. Even though one side of me still felt we shouldn't even go out there, it was too unique an opportunity to pass. The idea was to do it intelligently and as cautiously as possible.

So I picked up the list and one more time went through our basic questions and points:

1/ The fog

    A. From the street:
- can everyone see the fog?
- can anyone/everyone else go through the fog to and from London?
- can anyone communicate from outside the house to the forest by mobile or just the people from inside the house?

    B. From the forest:
- can anyone be called on the mobile?
- are the mobiles' signals relying on proximity to the house, and disappearing when moving further away?

2/ The forest

A. Exploration:
- to start with, stick to the surroundings of the house, never leaving the fog out of sight;
- mark the explored territory;
- can something vegetable or animal be brought into the house crossing the fog?
- can any other human presence be found?
- gather a lot of photos! And videos!
- stay on constant video conference with the boys inside the house, with the mobile oriented to watch our back, so they could raise the alarm if something comes from behind;
- go out there prepared (whatever that means!)

B. Preparations:
- buy bottled water, snacks, fruits, grains and almonds for birds and squirrels to capture one (even if Harry says a worm would do as sample. No way would I go digging the earth for a worm. Plus I wouldn't see a difference between worms from here or there);
- get compass, jacket, rucksack, knives, pepper spray, something to mark the explored territory, brooms to scare off animals, electric lamps;
- fully charged mobiles;
- warm clothes, scarf, boots, gloves;
- Rico and Harry must stay in the house during the exploration in case of issues (even if they would not be able to get into the forest);
- Zeno and I must remain together at all times.

A light bulb went off in my head. We needed to mark our way, right? With something easy to set up yet recognisable. 'Let's use the Christmas tree decorations to mark the explored territory!

Not the tinsel, the Christmas baubles. After all, they are made for trees, they are colourful, so easily distinguishable, and it makes it all a bit fun ... The box of decorations has been doing my head in anyway. It doesn't fit anywhere. Rico took advantage of the temporary gap in the cupboard during Christmas to stuff in all his paint tubes etcetera.'

'What? I did it for you! I thought you would be happy that my tools were not lying around in the living room. You know I'd do anything for you, babe ...' Rico retorted.

'Yeah, yeah, yeah, skip it. You know I am immune to your charms and you know you sneakily just spread your painting stuff all round the house,' I said smiling. Rico is really unique. Zeno and Harry laughed. Christmas baubles were a go.

3/ Lead a normal life

- we are not to talk about it to anyone at all, not even families and girlfriends. (The 'it' meant the fog, the forest, the weird situation Zeno and I were in.)
- Harry and I would call in sick from work in the morning, unless the fog had disappeared, so that the four of us were at home and we could explore.

No talking to anyone about it.

We all lived away from our families which would help us keep quiet on the subject. I had no boyfriend, so that one was easier for me than for Zeno. He had a long distance relationship with Cris who lived in Athens. For once the distance would help. As for Rico, unsurprisingly, he was a player. He had been with lots of women but none he would confide in, so there was no issue there. Regarding Harry, well, he didn't seem to have a girlfriend, but who knew? He hardly spoke about his intimate life anyway. Because he was not a talker in general, there was little doubt he would keep quiet about the whole affair.

We had decided that books on exploration and forests, not just Google, would be good for our preparations. We could scribble, highlight and discuss them at the table more easily. Zeno wanted to check the possible animals we may encounter. As far as I was concerned 'glimpsed' would have been a better choice of word than 'encountered': I had no wish to go that far in the forest yet. I felt like just dipping my toe in rather going for a swim. Harry suggested we should hit shops and bookstores before they closed.

'Wouldn't it be a good idea if someone stayed home?' Rico said seemingly slightly uncomfortable. 'I mean, we don't know what's coming next? Maybe the house will move completely to the forest and this is just a transition.'

'Rico, shut up,' Zeno, Harry and I replied in unison. Just then the doorbell rang.

'Well that answers one question: other people can get here,' Harry commented as he stood up to open the door, being the closest to the entrance. The person at the door was here to see Zeno, to give him the positive feedback on the day's business for a new market stall location they were trying. Our visitor didn't immediately talk business though; his first reaction was dismay about the 'fog, or smoke, or whatever that thing is'. Zeno replied awkwardly that it was weird indeed. At this, I quickly scrawled down some possible explanations for the presence of the fog: 'Micro-climate? Technology experiment? Leak under the house?' The last one could work, something like a hot water pipe with vapour escaping from it. It was a bit far-fetched, but considering there was a tangible and visible element, that is the fog, it might be believable. I copied the leak idea on another blank page, tore it and showed it to Rico and Harry who both nodded. Rico told the visitor in Italian, and Zeno visibly relaxed.

Harry indicated to me we should both go out and run the errands now while Rico stayed in with Zeno. Rico commented in a low voice that they would run some tests with the visitor – without telling him what they were up to – to check if Zeno were able to walk out through the fog in the streets with him, as he did with himself and Harry. I silently prayed he would.

While shopping for our mini-exploration and browsing the bookshop, Harry and I were finding it very difficult to believe something was amiss. Everything was so normal around us, it made the events at home too surreal to think they could possibly last.

It was already dark when we arrived at the terraced houses and most of them were lit up. We couldn't see ours or its lights; they were hidden behind the unusual thick fog. We walked through it, carrying our shopping bags as if nothing was different. Due to the weight of our bags, we walked more slowly and both felt the fog's density more than previously. There was a certain resistance to it. The fog also felt warmer than the freezing winter weather of the streets we were coming from. We walked directly to the dining table and dropped the bags onto it. Rico was sitting on the sofa, smoking a joint. He did this only occasionally, but the oddness of the day allowed it. He raised his eyes to us and told us Zeno was in his room. He had gone up after his friend had departed, quite upset. The bad news was, when crossing the threshold together with his friend – under the pretence that Zeno wanted to show him something – Zeno walked out into the forest and the other one to the street. He tried again later holding his friend's arm, but somehow they got separated and ended up in different places. Zeno later explained he had felt some kind of electric shock pushing his hand away.

'So not everybody can enable you to walk out into the London streets, babe,' Rico concluded, puffing at his joint. 'You need either Harry or me to help you out. If nobody else can, this is quite messed up.' Harry looked at Rico then me and commented in a low voice it was indeed quite a dependence and quite a responsibility for all involved. He put his hand on my shoulder, in a comforting and sorry gesture. I didn't have happy thoughts at that moment. Even for a positive person, that was pushing the limit.

I took several deep breaths and very slowly, very calmly, said to myself, 'Don't panic, don't panic. I will not panic!' and to Harry and Rico, 'Maybe tomorrow it will be gone, maybe we just have the evening to get through.'

'We can only hope,' Harry replied.

'Yup,' said Rico.

**Day 2 (Monday)**

None of us woke up feeling refreshed. Unsurprisingly it had not been a good night. The previous evening, Zeno finally came back down attracted by the smell of bacon prepared for the *pasta alla carbonara*. He had managed a troubled nap and looked in a grump. At dinner we went over the events of the day again and again, trying to find an explanation, knowing very well it was in vain. We looked at every single shot of the forest, letting our imagination roam free on what could be out there. Zeno and I were again facing thoughts of the next day with a mixture of anticipation and fear: it was curiosity versus security, normality versus adventure, comfort of the known versus challenge of the unknown. My mind couldn't settle on anything. Also, I was very aware my 'condition' was not clear, not having tried to go out on my own yet. It had been dark when we had returned from the shops, too dark to try alone. That Monday was the day to do so.

Only Rico had a decent night while we more normal people just barely dozed through it, now and then checking the window to see if the fog was still there. It was a ridiculous thing to do as we couldn't see anything anyway; all we saw that night was the time on the alarm clock and the minutes passing by. It compelled me to decide that if the forest was still there on Monday I would follow Rico's lead and have a joint before going to sleep. I didn't smoke, a single puff made my head dizzy, but these were extraordinary circumstances.

Around 6 a.m. Zeno decided he had had enough. He left his bed and walked downstairs to put the coffee on. He tried to be quiet, but Harry and I were awake as well and heard his steps, so we joined him in the kitchen. We put the news live on one of our tablets and sat on the sofas listening and sipping coffee.

My coffee finished, I moved towards the entrance, Zeno instantly following me. We put coats and scarves on, grabbed mobiles, two torches and the knives that were still on the hallway table. Harry joined us before we crossed the doorstep and we stepped out in the fog and into our street. The city was quiet and still mostly in the dark. Only a few cars passed by and one person was hurrying in the direction of the main road, probably towards the tube. We turned back and re-entered the house. We had just closed the main door when Zeno took me by the shoulder to lead the two of us out again. We stepped out into the fog and started walking. The fog was pitch black. While walking, I switched on my torch as did Zeno, but the beams were instantly absorbed by the fog. Abruptly, the soft resistance of walking stopped and heavy rain fell on us. Zeno and I were still in near total blackness and couldn't see ahead, but we knew. The two beams of light were struggling with the rain and we could barely distinguish the trees further away. Our feet were anchored in wet grass and moss. Zeno pulled me towards him and suggested we go back. It was too dangerous to remain in the dark in an unknown forest without being able to see anything. Harry was waiting for us exactly where we left him, in the hallway with his coat, scarf and slippers on. He didn't react when we told him the forest was still there. Only when we mentioned it was pouring with rain did he remark that it hadn't been raining in London.

'Oh great,' I grumbled. 'So the forest doesn't even have the same weather as here. That will make the exploration today so much easier too ...'

No one comes to London for its weather and I was well used to the rain by now. But still, in an unknown forest and a weird situation, being able to stay dry and see clearly would have been nice.

Waiting for the sun to rise to start our forest exploration, Zeno and I had more coffee, a big breakfast and showered. Barbour jacket and never worn rain boots far too big for me came out from the bottom of my wardrobe to finally be used. I added scarf and fingerless gloves, necessary to still use my touchscreen phone and snap a few shots, plus a large hat that would leave my hands free to hold a knife at all times and of course the mobile. In my big cross-body satchel were jammed together bottled water, two ham sandwiches, two chocolate bars, some nuts for the birds and squirrels, a torch, a bell, an emergency kit, a compass, a rope and lots and lots of Christmas baubles. Zeno was in full scooter gear with padded jacket, helmet and boots. All that was missing was the scooter.

'Zeno, maybe we should try to get the scooter in the house later, then see if we can drag it with us in the forest?' I asked.

'Yeah! That would be brilliant! We could store things in the trunk, bring some spare fuel and you could watch my back while I drive.'

Harry jumped into the conversation, 'I'll bring it in while you are out.'

'I'd rather you didn't do that,' I said.

'Why?' asked both Zeno and Harry.

'We don't know yet what could happen if you change something around the house. I wouldn't want us to be stuck out there.'

Zeno turned to Harry. 'No moving the scooter.'

I had difficulties not laughing at the sight of this tall padded up guy, all in black with the helmet and a knife in his hand. He looked like a murderer. It was strangely reassuring. Harry fetched his mobile and started the video call. When Zeno and I walked out into the forest, it was still raining but at least it was daylight.

'Here we are. In the forest,' I said to Harry as we stopped just outside the fog.

'Actually, not exactly,' Zeno corrected me. 'We need to be accurate now. The house is not in the forest, it is surrounded by a forest. We are in a clearing within it.'

I took two steps. The moss on the ground was acting like a sponge and making sucking sounds under my feet. Much of it was covered by large puddles. This time, we couldn't hear any signs of life in the forest. No birds, no cracking branches, no squirrel chatter. The rain was blocking any other sound, and the animals were out of sight. It made me feel uncomfortable and exposed, we had to rely on sight alone to warn us of any danger, and even this was limited. Checking the time for Harry who was in charge of taking notes on the exploration, it already showed 9.07 a.m. I had forgotten to call the office!

'Arghhh no!' I blurted aloud.

'What? What? What?' said Zeno, getting into a defensive position, pushing me behind him and looking right and left with his knife up. 'Where is it? Where is it?'

'Err ... sorry Zeno ... it's only that I forgot to call in sick.'

'Yoko! You can't do that. You freaked me out!'

Providing sincere apologies and feeling bad to have done this to him, we made our way back in so I could make the call under cover. Five minutes later, we returned and the rain was reduced to a drizzle. The sky was brighter too and this was a relief. The forest almost felt familiar now, and yet it was difficult to make a move forward. At that instant, I was scared, more scared than I would have thought. Zeno took my arm and led me on. When we reached the first trees, I picked three Christmas baubles and tip-toed to reach the highest branch possible to attach them. As an afterthought, I undid my scarf and wrapped it around the trunk as well.

'Why are you doing that?' asked Harry who was watching me do from the mobile camera.

'So that we recognise which tree we need to start walking from towards the entrance of the house. Otherwise, once I have put Christmas baubles in different locations around the house, there'll be no clear mark to know where to turn back. We may end up hitting a wall. That won't help if we're in a hurry to get back in.'

We kept close to the edge of the woods by the clearing, the fog always in sight. I was gripping my knife very tightly, walking on the inside towards the house while Zeno was on the outside towards the deepest forest. From within, the forest wasn't as dense as it had seemed and glimpses of sky could be seen above the trees. Maybe because of the weather, maybe because our presence was intruding on the local animals currently keeping at bay, there was very little noise. Only the wind in the trees, our steps cracking little twigs, or our feet getting stuck in the moss could be heard. The intense feeling of solitude was back and my whole being was on alert. At the same time, I marvelled at the beauty of nature, at the peace and purity of the surroundings. Zeno was holding his phone with the camera directed over his shoulder for Harry to watch our backs, ready to warn of any immediate danger. Every five steps or so Christmas baubles now decorated some of the trees' lowest branches. They would be visible from the house when leaving the fog, as well as from a short distance within the forest. It was a start. I wondered if the books on survival in the wild would help. I doubted it really. It would probably not mention harmless English woods, or any alternative of not-to-be-dismissed encounters with dinosaurs or legendary monsters. I told myself to stop thinking about monsters and re-focus before I panicked and made a run for it. When not hanging tree decorations, I took snapshots with my mobile of trees, leaves, mushrooms and any little animals or birds I could spot. Taking pictures of the fog covering the house, it reminded me of a tea cosy, except my own home was underneath it. After thirty minutes, we were on the second tour of the clearing and at last relaxed a little. The baubles had run out, but seeing them hung in the trees made the forest seem more cordial. It added a trivial note to an intense situation. About ten minutes before, Harry had switched off the online call to answer the door. He was meant to call back but hadn't. That was bothering me, not being in touch with the house and us being alone in the middle of nowhere. Literally, we were nowhere known.

Suddenly, we heard a howl. A wolf howl. The suddenness of the creepy sound in the surrounding quietness took my breath away and I froze before identifying what it was. Zeno jumped out and pushed me against the trunk of a tree checking around frantically, his knife raised.

'Sorry Zeno. Sorry. It's my phone. I just received a message. My latest ringtone for incoming messages is a wolf howling.' Though sorry to have scared him, I was touched his first reaction was to protect me. What a good friend!

'I hate your phone. I hate your ringtones. You have ringtone issues. Put the bloody thing on silent!'

'Yes Zeno. Sorry Zeno. I thought this ringtone was funny back then but ...'

Just then another howl interrupted me. This one wasn't coming from my phone, but from the direction of the house. More exactly it came from behind the house. Worse, it didn't sound very far away.

'You must be fucking kidding me! You called a wolf with your ringtone!'

'Funny, usually you swear in Italian.'

'Yoko, shut up.'

'Sorry, I'm nervous ...'

'I know, but please just shut up,' Zeno whispered.

'I think whatever we do next, we are not supposed to run,' I said in a low voice after a few seconds passed of us listening to the silence.

'I am freaking out,' Zeno whispered again. More seconds passed.

'I am petrified, Zeno, petrified. I don't think I can move!' I said in a hushed tone.

'Let's walk back very slowly,' Zeno decided, grabbing my arm and pulling me towards the clearing.

Another howl broke the forest silence. Zeno and I looked at each other and we started trotting to the house. Trotting, not running! It took a lot of self-control. In the clearing, without the protection of the tree, I felt observed by a million round eyes. We finally made it inside the house without hearing the wolf again. Zeno's first reaction was to angrily say to me, 'Change your ringtone!'

'Yes Zeno.'

'I can't believe you didn't think about it before. You should have cut the sound off in the first place anyway.'

'Yes Zeno,' I was still shaken from danger of wolves nearby.

Zeno just looked at me and shook his head, murmuring 'Bloody women!'

Only then did we register that Harry was talking to someone in the living room, most probably the reason for him not calling back. We put the knives on the table in the hallway, covering them with some unopened letters lying around, and then headed towards the living room. The minute we stepped in, it was apparent we had a new problem: three firemen stood facing Harry, who was giving details on the non-harmful leak of steamed water under the house causing the fog. The firemen didn't look convinced. Not that gullible, the London Fire Brigade.

'Have you had tests run on the fog?' one of them asked.

'Kind of,' replied Harry.

'Kind of? Any paperwork asserting it's harmless?'

'For the moment, it is just oral. We … haven't got the paperwork yet.'

'We may need to do some checks to ensure your safety.'

'Of course.'

My thought was that it wouldn't be a bad thing to know if this fog could be harmful.

When he saw us, one of the firemen – the shortest, oldest and chubbiest – turned towards Zeno and me and asked if we lived here too. When we answered in the affirmative, another constantly frowning fireman remarked our clothes were wet and asked if it had started raining outside. The question unsettled us and it took me several seconds to find a suitable reply, that we had been washing the car. Zeno added that we had a water fight. 'Yes,' I continued with a nervous smile, 'we're big kids …' Lying had never been my forte and the man looked doubtful, maybe not convinced that my unease was due to embarrassment only. His colleague began to speak again and created a distraction.

'We have been informed that your house has been surrounded by this smoke since yesterday. Apparently the neighbours were not alarmed at first as it showed no signs of fire, but finally one of them contacted us,' the old fireman said.

'I'm surprised they didn't try to contact us first, we would have told them not to worry,' replied Harry.

'Do they have your number?' the same fireman asked.

'Errr ... I'm not sure ... Maybe ... I'm not sure,' Harry admitted.

'Then maybe, as they couldn't contact you and wouldn't come to a house showing signs of danger, they contacted us. They did the right thing,' the fireman continued.

'Well, thank you for coming and I hope we have reassured you all is fine ...' Harry replied.

'We will put a sign on the parking space to inform everyone not to worry, and that the situation is being taken care of,' I added.

'That would be a good idea,' said the fireman.

During the whole conversation, Zeno had remained silent. As the firemen were on the way out, he spoke for the first time to ask when they would be coming back for the checks.

'We'll try to organise it for this afternoon. The sooner we ascertain the nature of this smoke the better.'

'I'm very curious about the tests and tools you'll use. I've always found science experiments fascinating.' Zeno was up to something.

'You can't see anything, either from this side or the other of the house,' one of the other firemen, who had moved towards the window, commented. 'I've never seen anything like this before.'

We had to avoid more questions; we were not ready for them. We had not worked out enough plausible answers yet.

'Well, thank you for your visit,' I said in my best business voice, determined to end their visit. 'We look forward to your coming again this afternoon to confirm all is safe. Hopefully it will be repaired soon anyway.'

'Yes, thank you for coming,' Harry backed me up.

When they were gone Zeno and I turned expectantly to Harry. According to him they were not suspicious, just concerned about the quality of the air. We should be fine. For now. If the tests turned out safe they would be off our backs. While Harry was talking, Zeno and I started to peel off our jackets, satchels, boots and helmet to get more comfortable. I headed to the kitchen to put the kettle on, followed by the two boys. It was my habit to call my housemates 'the boys'. In return Rico could call me 'babe' without my growling.

'Yoko, we should test the air in the forest too. I also want to buy night goggles and books on the stars and go there by night. We could work out where we are by the stars and if we are … if … Well, I've got to say it … on earth,' Zeno said looking at me straight in the eyes. So that was what he was up to.

On earth? Night exploration of the forest? Zeno's last words resonated in my head. Where else than on earth could we be? As for night exploration, after what had just happened, not a chance! I was about to give Zeno my opinion on his idea, when the heavy steps of Rico rushing down the stairs made us all turn towards the staircase. He froze when he saw us through the open door of the kitchen.

'I heard the front door and I feared you were already out,' Rico said hugging me.

'We have already been out,' I told him.

'Rico, it's mid-morning, of course we've been out,' Zeno added slightly exasperated.

'OK, Rico, here is the deal,' Harry explained to the late sleeper. 'Yoko and Zeno went out but we haven't had a chance to discuss the results of the expedition yet. The door you heard was from three firemen leaving. Before you get all wound up, everything is fine. Some alarmed neighbours informed them about the fog and they came to check. For the time being our excuse was accepted, although they are coming back this afternoon to check the quality of the air and the nature of the fog, which is good for us too. Mostly, I think the issue will be if the fog lasts.'

'Ah ... good. Good ... so ... firemen visitors. Well, if you say it's OK ... So you both went to the forest? So? Any traces of humans?' Rico turned towards us.

Following a thought that came during Harry's de-briefing to Rico, I asked them to give me a few minutes before we dealt with Rico's question. I ran upstairs and dug into my box of ribbons and odd pendants, took a small necklace with a little bell from a soft toy's neck (I wasn't lying to the firemen when I said I was a big kid) and jogged back downstairs. Putting my coat on and shouting to the guys that I would be back in a minute, I popped out into the fog. The fog covered the surface of the front patio up to the wrought iron gate which still existed in both worlds: my idea was to attach the bell to the gate. We would have a warning when people were coming in. Later we could put a proper bell or alarm. Slowly I walked the few steps towards the gate. The front gate was barely visible in the fog and I hit it with my arms, dropping the bell on the ground. It was difficult to see properly and the bell couldn't be found. I took a step forward outside the gate to have another look, as the bell could have rolled. Usually the fog stopped at the gate, with either the clearing or London ahead. This time, the fog continued beyond the gate, a thick white blanket hiding everything from view. Doubt and fear bubbled up inside me. I made an additional step beyond the gate and got properly scared. The fog completely engulfed me. All around me was just white and full of light, like weightless cotton, and total silence was enveloping me. I didn't know where I was, except for the gate left behind and now quite invisible. I stayed there, incapable of moving for what seemed hours but was probably only seconds before managing to turn and run back. Then I hit a wall. I had run back into the wall of the house and it hurt. So great was my relief to see and feel the house that I didn't care. Extending my arms, I felt the door frame a few centimetres from my right shoulder. It became clear I was leaning on the wall between the door and the living room window. I took a side step to the door, pushed it open and shot through into the house.

Harry, Zeno and Rico were immediately on me, much alarmed. I was shaking and struggled to make sense of what they were saying. They were telling me that Zeno had gone out just after me, refusing to let me out alone, but when he reached the forest I was nowhere to be seen. He knew it was not possible for me to have wandered far as he had left the house just half a minute after me. From the edge of the fog, he could neither see nor hear me, and called in vain. Something was unmistakably wrong. He came back to the house in the hope I had changed my mind in the fog and returned but I wasn't there. The boys were extremely worried.

Harry took me by the shoulders and looked at my face. I was paralysed: Zeno had just confirmed that he had reached the forest when I had not.

'Yoko, you're completely white, you're shaking. What happened? Are you OK? Where were you?'

'I don't know … I don't know where I was. There was only fog. Just the fog. I wanted to reach the gates to attach the toy bell … but there was nothing beyond. It was horrible. I … Harry, I panicked. I don't know where I was! I'm scared! Guys, I'm scared!'

It was all just too much suddenly. The bubble burst and the tears broke out. It wasn't sweet pretty tears rolling down the cheek either, it was the whole catching your breath tears, with snorts, runny nose and garbled incomprehensible words. A big ugly Yoko collapse.

They led me to the dining, recently turned brainstorming, table, put a big shawl on my shoulders, a cup of tea in one hand and a chunky KitKat in the other. A large mouthful of chocolate gave me temporary relief. I needed a few more minutes to gather my thoughts and said so. The shaking and the big knot in my throat and stomach were still very present. The waterfall of tears was not far away from my burning eyes either. Trying to fight the grip of anxiety, my face turned to stone and my voice turned mute. Simultaneously, my brain was in full throttle reviewing all the details of my experience out there alone, trying to analyse the situation and to regain control.

'OK, Yoko, take your time. Zeno, why don't you tell us about your morning outing first? I have already debriefed Rico on the firemen situation.' Harry said, peering at me from the corner of his eyes and respecting my need to be left alone in my corner a little bit longer.

As Zeno was going through our earlier tour of the forest, my focus was on organising my thoughts, knowing they would soon have to be shared. So, our little household had made the positive assumption, or wish, that I would be like Zeno and that when leaving the house alone I would reach the forest clearing. We had assumed wrong. From my latest venture out, there was just nothing when on my own: nothing seen, nothing heard, nothing smelled and nothing felt. Was it even anywhere on this planet, or was it just a world of fog? Maybe I was being dramatic and walking a bit further I would reach ... somewhere.

'Breathe Yoko, breathe,' I kept telling myself.

So to discover the truth I ought to keep walking further. That meant going out alone again in nothing land. I wanted to go back into the fog on my own as much as to enter a night club naked! It was ridiculous; I could get lost in there. After a couple of steps beyond the gates and a few seconds' run, I didn't even reach the door and had hit the wall! Exploring further away in the fog, it would be possible to never find the house again and be trapped in the fog forever.

'Breathe, Yoko, breathe. These are thoughts, not facts. Don't panic,' I repeated inwardly.

Thinking clearly required all my strength. It was important not to let fear take over and to focus on how to deal with the latest crisis. I needed to know if the fog really was never ending. I needed some kind of plan of action. First, a rope could be attached to the house to prevent me from losing my way. I had a ten metre extension lead upstairs. Ten metre ... hopefully long enough to exit the fog.

'OK, I'm a big girl,' I murmured to myself. 'I can do it. I can do it alone. Alone but armed with the kitchen knives.'

'Yoko?' Rico was staring at me, worried. I looked around. They had stopped talking and instead of the quick glances they had given to start with, they were now bluntly looking at me with concern. I straightened myself and tried to smooth my face from its deep frown and pursed lips and to force a smile.

'So. Gentlemen. Here is what happened.' I narrated my new foggy and lonely experience, my panic and my hitting the wall. Harry and Rico had more difficulties than Zeno in comprehending the emotional storm going through my head and body. How could they imagine the full extent of feelings to be so completely cut off from the world? Zeno understood this. He looked horrified. He was probably the only person who could get my alarm: He had discovered the forest alone first. To cope and contain my anxiety, I launched into my plans on what to do next instead.

'So what do you think of the ten metre extension lead? Should we try? Please? Could we do a video call too for me not to feel totally alone?' It was a cry for support. They responded positively.

I was at the front door, one side of the lead attached to my belt and the other rolled round Zeno's arm, ready to unroll. Harry and I were already connected on a video conference call, even though we were side by side. Zeno was tense. His role was to follow the lead towards me after a couple of minutes. Rico was hugging me from behind.

'This is crazy, babe. Completely crazy. What is going on? What is happening to us?' Rico exclaimed. His hugging me tight wasn't helping. It made me want to go back to being a little girl and be protected, when I had to remain positive and strong. Knowledge was my urgency. What happened next was a good surprise. I walked past the wrought iron gate out into the forest clearing. I was ecstatic not to be lost in the fog. It was the first time the forest presence reassured me. When Zeno arrived, I couldn't stop grinning. Obviously they all already knew as Harry was on the phone to me and it was a big relief for them as well. I longed to dismiss the earlier experience as a kind of fog 'hiccup', an error of programming. It brought me momentary relief. At the back of my mind though, the matter was not resolved.

Zeno and I walked back in and before anyone could say anything, I said firmly, 'We need to try something else. Sorry guys, but I need to be sure. So this time I will walk attached not to Zeno but to the front gate as minimum security.'

It was with tense faces that they silently saw me leave again. This time it felt much lonelier. Holding the phone tight, I walked through the fog, anxiously looking for the gate. Once there, there was nothing beyond but the white fog. A white nothingness. Harry was talking to me as my anxiety resurfaced. It was the most reassuring voice I had ever heard in my life. It felt like a link to the real world and helped me not to give in to panic. I attached the lead to the gate, stepping out and leaning on the outside of the metal gate while doing so. In the meantime, Zeno couldn't help but come to the gate and arrived there when I was still on its outside. However, neither of us saw each other. We were at the same gate but not at the same location. He saw the knot of lead on the gate, tried to touch it and had to take his hand off immediately as an electric shock ran through him. I stepped back through the gate and onto the front patio, leaving the lead outside. We met on the inside of the gate. This was just too weird! Then with him moving forward, we got out into the forest. We went back through the Fog and he returned to the house while I stayed on the inside of the gates, still in the fog. Then I picked up the lead and moved outside the front gate where the thick whiteness reigned. I didn't want to dwell on the weirdness of the situation just yet. Getting on alone was the only right thing to do. I double checked the quadruple knot securing the lead to the iron frame and walked out into the white unknown.

My connection to Harry was getting worse with each step forward. Moving forward was harder too. It felt as if the fog was getting thicker and thicker. It reached the point when I had to really force my way through, pushing against the fog, struggling to advance. Soon Harry could barely be heard between the cracklings and distant voice. Before long, my phone was only emitting white noise. One metre further and the call was finally lost. It was now a real effort to make any further move. I pushed and pushed against the fog which was like a white thick wall, stopping me and even pushing me back. It was also getting more and more difficult to breathe. Dizziness began to affect my balance. I checked the lead which still had plenty to go. My head was swirling as I struggled to make some kind of mark on the lead to record the distance walked. I realised the urgency to go back fast before I lost consciousness. Nobody would be able to come and help me there. Making my way back, I was feeling very weak, even if little by little I could breathe more easily. It seemed to take forever to reach the wrought iron gate again by pulling on the lead. I detached it with difficulty and made my way home. Still dazed, I bumped into the window first.

The person who invented the expression 'Home Sweet Home' was a genius of emotional intelligence. Being home was entering paradise. I stepped inside the open door to an effusive welcoming committee. Rico was a nervous wreck and before anyone had a chance to say anything, he lunged at me and hugged me so hard I couldn't breathe. This time I didn't mind. His body seemed shaky, he was crying.

'I want to go out. To be in London. To walk around the streets. No, correction: not want, need! Need to roam, walk and drive around. On my own.' These words were all I could utter as the latest events overwhelmed me.

Their anxious faces betrayed that they wanted to be there for me and talk through what had happened. It would have to wait. I needed time to recover and register what I had just experienced.

My break had to be total, them included. They already knew the extent of the fog the loss of signal connection with the increased distance from the house. More details would have to come later. I gently pushed them aside and went up to my room where I changed and threw a few things in a handbag. Harry was the first one to react and came forward quickly when I came back downstairs, knowing Rico or he would have to escort me out of the house to get to London.

'I knew one day you wouldn't be able to live without me,' he said trying to make me smile. It went flat, although I forced a half-hearted smile.

My plan was to put my headset on and pick a lively playlist on my mobile, and then hit the streets with my camera in hand. If it didn't work, a big drive on the busy roads was my next idea. To be in my car during commuter traffic with plenty of cars and drivers on the roads, me safe in my little car, music blasting loud, sounded like heaven. The other options were to treat myself with retail therapy, junk food therapy and friend therapy. I would definitely call one of my good friends who would know how to cheer me up. A little bit of real life was what I wanted, including its hassle and annoying drivers. Getting my 'empty my mind' plans rolling, I headed at a brisk pace towards Whiteleys, the small local shopping mall. Doing so I took out my mobile, selected the correct speed dial, and called my friend Jazz.

**Day 3 (Tuesday)**

The alarm clock indicated 2.31 a.m. I had been back from my evening with Jazz since midnight. We had ended up in a lounge bar dancing to 90s' tunes. It felt so good! I had forgotten how crazy London could be on any given night, Monday included. Now in bed, the house was quiet and dark. Everyone was sleeping. Each of the boys had been in touch before calling it a day to check on me. They were such good housemates and good friends. I was lucky: if the ones I had to rely on to escape the fog had been insufferable, what would I have done?

It was going to be a tough morning later. I had decided to go to the office and live my life as normally as possible while we waited to see if this fog would last. Again I tried not to think of how we would need to adjust our lives if it did.

Anyway, sleep completely eluded me. The episode of being alone in the fog was back in my mind and still too vivid. So now, at 2.31a.m., I grabbed my laptop and started browsing the web. I searched 'house, fog, forest' and quickly dismissed the first results: Cloud Forest in Costa Rica, no; Foggy Forest Photo Gallery, no. After fifteen minutes, this internet search was already the most frustrating ever made. Google not giving me the information I looked for was unheard of. Google always had the answers. Oh dear ... if even that world was collapsing ... I was now frantically typing a combination of words and emotions 'stuck, home, fog, lost, can't breathe'. Nothing. 'Come on Google! Come on! You can do it!' I whispered angrily towards the screen. Though frustrating, the search was strangely therapeutic so I kept going.

Next I did a similar search in French. This time something came up that got my attention. Dated seventeen hours ago on Yahoo.fr, someone had posted that he needed help regarding a thick fog outside his home that was blocking him in. This Frenchman, who signed in as cdr69, was in Marrakech in Morocco to check the renovation work in progress in his summer house. He explained that overnight from Saturday to Sunday a thick fog had covered the house and now every time he went out he was stuck in this fog. He couldn't see a thing in this white mash so he wouldn't venture far: he didn't know the town that well yet and couldn't walk there blind. Also, the fog seemed to get denser as he moved further. He had checked online but nowhere did they refer to this strange weather in Marrakech. He didn't speak Arabic though and he was only checking French and English weather forecasts. He would have dismissed it and just chilled at home for the day but he needed to stay abreast of local information if he didn't want to be messed around by the local builders.

I was cheering silently, throwing my fist in the air and mouthing, 'I knew I could count on Google. I knew it! In Google We Trust!' There was no way sleep would come now. It was huge: we were not the only ones with the fog issue. Most importantly, I was not alone to face fog only on my own. I was riveted and read his notes several times. His experience indicated he was more like me than like Zeno. He had walked around a bit and the fog had grown thicker. I was torn as to whether to wake up the others or not, and I was also still feeling guilty about leaving them so abruptly hours ago. As a few hours would not make a big difference, I decided to let them sleep. Instead, as they didn't speak French, I prepared a quick translation to give them first thing in the morning.

Going back to cdr69's message, nobody had replied to it seriously. He just got a few jokes and a couple of angry comments about wasting people's time. I didn't understand why people could be bothered, until I noticed that a tab opened to another post from him dated Monday morning. It mentioned that renovation builders came in to continue their job. They were surprised about the fog outside his home, his *riad* as they call it locally. Their remarks were rather alarming due to the fact that the fog was limited to his house. He went out and was surrounded by fog again. So as not to get lost, he decided to walk next to the walls up the street, but the walls stopped abruptly at the end of his house. That was definitely not normal. He circled the house, hands against the walls. It should have been impossible: only one facade was open to the street, the rest of the residence was joined to other buildings. As he re-entered the building, panic began. He tried to talk to the workers in vain as they looked at him as if he was mad. He then attempted to leave with some of them and somehow he ended up separated and alone in the fog. Concerned about getting lost, he later attempted to tie a rope to the front door and chanced pushing further. He felt the fog thicken and his breathing getting more difficult. His wife, whom he called repeatedly in distress, thought the joke was not funny. She finally gave in and agreed to go to Marrakech earlier than planned and arrive on the Wednesday instead of the Friday.

'So he is like me, I was right,' I muttered. 'I wonder if she will be able to help him, like Rico or Harry or Zeno with me.' Cdr69 wrote that he thought he was losing his mind. Poor guy. I started writing a reply and realised I shouldn't. We had agreed in the house that we would keep our situation a secret for now. I would talk to them in the morning so we could all agree on how to re-spond to this latest development. I felt sorry for this man, alone in dealing with the fog's sudden appearance. Yes, poor guy.

Lots of questions were bouncing around in my head: if there was another person or place experiencing the same as us, could there be even more? Zeno and I have a forest on the other side, what would it be for him if he had his 'Zeno'? A desert? A moun-tain? Of course these were just new questions with no hope of an answer at present. This was maddening. This was so unreal, so implausible and so incredible.

The sound of my alarm playing 'It's a Wonderful Life' by Ray Charles woke me up at 7a.m. My laptop was open next to me on the bed. I must have closed my eyes and drifted out of this world (no pun intended). It all came back to me within seconds. I jumped out of bed and went to knock at the bedroom door of everyone in the house. All of us gathered in the kitchen to hear the news on cdr69 and the foggy house in Marrakech. The man was like me but without a Rico or Harry to enable him to go to the real world, or a Zeno to go to what we could only refer as 'an alternative place'.

I was pro-contact, maybe out of sympathy for the man, maybe also because sharing information could help us understand the mystery of the fog and the forest. Aside from Rico, who still had reservations, we agreed that today I would post on his forum a simple 'contact me on ...' and provide an email address created for that purpose. Rico's reluctance was based on his anti-government streak, conspiracy theories beliefs and lack of trust in internet security. True enough, involving technology meant we were going out in the open: the web was not a safe place to put any sensitive information. Still it wasn't as if we were on the radar of the secret service.

'They're everywhere. They're watching,' Rico disagreed. 'You post this, they will know. I'm telling you. Within days we'll get a knock at the door and we'll be in for it, man!' Rico was on his pet subject and he was just getting started.

'Shut up Rico!' The rest of us reacted in unison. Even if he had a point, being totally reclusive would mean we stopped learning more about the fog.

'Anyway, if they are on the lookout, the information is already there, the French guy put it out there,' I said to Rico and the others. 'It wouldn't take long before they look for more fogged houses. Yes, 'fogged' for lack of a better word. It isn't as if ours has gone unnoticed. It will be in the firemen's report which is probably accessible to other services within the government. So we might as well make contact, learn what we can and see if that helps us somehow.'

'Whatever!' Rico replied while the others nodded in agreement.

Afterwards it was time to leave for work for Harry and me. It was easier for the other two, Zeno being his own boss and Rico an artist. A quick shower, a smart suit, a wrapped jam sandwich as breakfast to nibble during my walk to work, and I was gone.

My professional life was busy yet without unnecessary stress, thanks to a nine-to-five office job as a marketing communications manager at the London headquarters of a restaurant chain. They were based in Mayfair by Hyde Park. It was a thirty minute journey at a steady pace. I always welcomed the mild exercise and time to myself. Today this personal treat would make me late but would hopefully help me relax. My job was by no means my passion in life. As mentioned earlier, I was just in my thirties, an age when most of my peers contemplate building a career, settling down and starting a family, according to social standards. A couple of years back it looked like I was on track. I had my own place, my own business and a man I loved, but life doesn't usually work out as planned.

Rewinding five years, I held the position of account manager in marketing communications for an international luxury hotel group. My dream, deep down, was not to have a big career with them. It was to set up my own business: a little bakery/salon de thé/bookshop. I loved – and still do – cooking and baking, and watching the pleasure on people's faces when they bite into a dish prepared with care, like a warm soft chocolate cake with a melting and nutty core. At that time Michael entered my life, Michael with whom I would spend the next three years. He was the new manager of one of the hotel's many restaurants, who also hoped to be his own boss one day. Soon, we decided to make our dreams come true and launched our own little shop. We bought both the retail shop and the flat above for our business and home, deciding to move in together at the same time. That meant we were both heavily in debt, yet happy, motivated and optimistic about the future. We agreed that at first Michael would keep his job at the hotel to secure valuable income for the mortgage. The shop did well almost from the start; we had one lovely waitress to help me and good customers. It was hard work but life was good.

Three years ago, Michael proposed. We were to get married within the year when he got sick. The cancer spread at lightning speed and Michael was gone in three months. Seeing him fade away was torture. I couldn't accept my abysmal inability to help him or get rid of his pain. He only wished for me to be by his side, which was so little and so hard. It left me at the end of each day feeling useless, empty, frustrated and angry. I longed to take some of his pain, to alleviate his fears. Every day I had a knot in my stomach and my heart squeezed white both at the sight of his suffering and the idea of losing him. How do you cope with the foreboding and reluctant wait, with the passivity of having no choice, no say in the ultimate result?

I was devastated when he passed away. Friends and family cared for me night and day for weeks, receiving my tear-filled calls and almost force feeding me. The shop's waitress was amazing, taking over the running of the shop for me. When I finally got back on my feet two months later and put my nose in the finances, I saw disaster looming. The interest of the mortgage and other debts without Michael's income were too high for me. First, I sold the flat and put a sofa bed beside my desk in the already cramped tiny room that served as an office in the shop, making one of the lavatories unisex and turning the other one into a shower room. My best chance to keep the business was to cut my expenses and reduce the mortgage. It didn't work, there were still too many running costs for the shop to survive. So in the end I had to close, sell it all in a bad market and look for a job. I was lucky to find one quickly, although I was still financially and emotionally drained. My options were flat-sharing within a reasonable distance of work and close to my friends, or to live on my own far from my work. I thought living alone may not be the best idea while getting back firmly on my own two feet. I had returned to my positive fighting attitude, but loneliness can suck you down fast. It wasn't worth taking the risk. So I turned to Google, typed 'flat-sharing Central London' and found by accident the little gem I was still living in at the time the fog started. Like a new little family, it mended my broken heart and restored daily laughter to my life.

In general my job contented me, albeit without excitement. Back to that Tuesday morning, I loved it with its prospect of normality, of having to focus on something other than the fog.

My phone rang. It was my mother. She had called many times since Sunday without an answer from me. I winced. I had to pick up the call this time as she knew my timetable and was aware it was my commuting time. Hopefully she would not be too inquisitive about my weekend. I took a deep intake of breath and answered the call.

'Hi Mum!'

'Well at last! I was starting to think you were avoiding me!' she said, spot on.

'Of course not Mum. Why would you think that?'

'Because you usually return my calls shortly.'

'Crazy busy weekend. How was yours?' I asked, trying to change the subject to her life and not mine.

'Tedious. I'm afraid I have a request you will not like.'

'You know I'll always try to help. What can I do for you?'

'I need you to come home next weekend.' That took me by surprise and was the last thing I wished to hear.

'What? Now I am worried! What is the urgency? Is everything all right?' This was unlike my parents to make such a last minute request without a good reason, and I couldn't think of a positive one.

'Your sister is coming. We need to have a family meeting. I can't go into details right now but this is serious. We need you to come.'

My sister and I are not the best of friends. We are very different and do not share the same vision of life. She was going through a difficult time right then with her husband and I was sorry for her. Nonetheless, I couldn't help her with anything, and it wasn't her style to involve me in her life. The matter must be linked to my parents then. I had a vision of them being sick and feared the worst. It couldn't be worse timing with the fog and what was going on, but suddenly the fog seemed so much less important than it had been a few minutes earlier. Of course I would go.

All morning I vaguely dealt with emails, in reality barely reading them and just adding them to my to do list for later, whenever that might be. Between the fog and the call from my mother, did I really think I would be doing some proper work that day? Honestly, who was I fooling? At lunchtime, hot Thai chicken soup and bread on the desk by my keyboard, I gave up my attempt to review a presentation for a client's meeting on the coming Thursday. I dropped a few bits of bread in the soup and returned to the Yahoo forum to write to cdr69. There wasn't much I could say without getting into my own experience or the mere fact I had one, so I went for the simplest of messages: '*Mon email est kymsonline@yahoo.com. Ecrivez-moi*' translated 'My email is kymsonline@yahoo.com. Write to me'. Why *kymsonline*? An article read long ago on the value of secrecy had popped in my head when creating the new profile, entitled 'KYMS' for 'Keep Your Mouth Shut'. I thought it very appropriate, and pretty cool actually.

Now all I had to do was wait. It got boring and frustrating within three minutes. I went to my main email inbox – a Gmail one, what else for a Google addict? – and set it up to receive the kymsonline emails directly in there. Like this I would stop staring at the computer screen, refreshing the Yahoo inbox constantly. My mobile would just beep when a new email came in. I finished my lunch and got cracking with the client's presentation, trying not to think of the fog, my parents or cdr69. Thirty minutes on, having checked my phone ridiculously often in case I hadn't heard the all-important beep, I had to concede there was but one thing to do in order to concentrate on work: switch the mobile off. It was a drastic solution, clearly above my ability and strength as a smartphone addict, so I did the next best thing by half-heartedly putting my mobile in flight mode and closing the internet on my computer. Whatever this fog was, I needed my job. I had bills to pay.

Getting ready to leave the office, it hadn't been a totally wasted day in the end and I had achieved some positive work. The change of location did me good too. My life appeared more normal and now I felt I could deal with it all. Jacket on and work computer off, I switched the cell phone back on full reception mode. After a few seconds, text messages popped up and email notifications beeped. There were ten emails in my inbox: four junk, two invitations for dinner and drinks, one funny story and – here my heart leapt – three emails transferred from kymsonline. Only one was from cdr69 and that puzzled me for a second, but when you put your email in a public space, you are bound to get unsolicited messages. Cdr69 wrote the following, translated from French:

> Dear Kymsonline,
>
> You left your email in reply to my posts. I hope you didn't leave your email to make fun of me because this is not funny. This is not a hoax. I need help. Do you know what is happening to me? CAN YOU HELP?!
>
> Best regards,
> Christophe de Roque

So his name was revealed. Christophe de Rocque, quite a posh name. I preferred cdr69, it had more kick to it. His signing with his full name surprised me. I wouldn't have. Maybe it was fake, or maybe it was an automatic signature. His email was brief and direct, the tone a bit abrupt. There again, he wasn't really in the right frame of mind to waste his time in diplomacy and flowery prose, was he? Next I quickly checked the emails from the unknown sender, not expecting much from them.

I was wrong.

One was in French and one was in English, as per below:

> Dear Kymsonline,
>
> I thought I should inform you that French is not my forte and that I used a translation tool for my previous email. In case you speak English, I am sending the original version too. I think it is important you understand my message well, because I may be able to help you.
>
> You left your email address on the wall of crd69's Yahoo forum this morning. I do not know if you did so because you have real interest in his story or if you are experiencing the same situation. I do not wish to leave any message or trace on his forum and would suggest you delete your message as well. If you are indeed both affected by a similar situation, I hope that cdr69 will contact you. I do have some information that will be useful to both of you. Let me just write, for now, that the fog and what lies beyond is real. If you are not concerned by what I am referring to, please dismiss this email as irrelevant and I apologise for the inconvenience.
>
> Yours sincerely,
> Leila

I had stopped walking and stood rooted to the spot.

'Wow.' Not only was 'Leila' a new person allegedly aware of the fog, she wrote she had information. Information! She also referred to '*the fog and what lies beyond*' so she knew that there was more than the fog. That was not divulged in cdr69's posts. He never mentioned anything other than fog outside. So a third person somewhere else had a foggy experience and this one professed to be able to help. I had to tell the boys! My brain had been on overdrive for the past three days, but right then it could have been on Redbull overdose. Calling Zeno to read him Leila's email, I had to repeat it three times before he understood my sentences blurted too fast on the phone. Sadly Harry and Rico's phones went to voicemail. Hurrying back, I typed some possible responses to cdr69 and Leila on my mobile, and hit a tree. I had never realised how painful that would be!

The house was empty on my arrival. I had got less excited about cdr69 while walking. Sure, it was good news that we were not the only ones and I felt sorry for him, but Leila had all my attention. When the boys and I talked in the morning, we agreed to give cdr69 some limited information about our experience with the fog, revealing only that my case was similar to his but not revealing anything about my whereabouts, identity and the existence or exact role of my housemates. In my drafted message, I was to briefly explain that some people could lead me beyond the fog back to the real world. It didn't work with everybody and sometimes you may end up in an unknown place as well. I was not to elaborate further, but this should entice him to open up. We were cautious and would reply we didn't have all the answers if he asked for more. Hopefully he would also share fresh information and shed a new perspective on what was happening.

Drafting a reply to Leila was more difficult. I wasn't sure how to approach it, not knowing what she had experienced, and if she could really help. Maybe she was merely fishing for information. I should really wait for the boys' return to get back to her. I already knew how things would go: Rico would be on the distrustful side, with a comment like 'we'll ask her for information first then maybe we'll say something about us'; Harry would be more level-headed in his thoughts, preferring cautious engagement; as for Zeno, he had already told me his opinion on the phone, that is to write the same to her as to cdr69. We had to give something though, otherwise why would she provide me with any help? Waiting alone in the house, I drafted a reply to Leila. I tried to call Harry and Rico several times, only to reach their voicemails again. I didn't resist long before sending the email. I was so eager for information! Even though I had taken great care to refer only to myself without any mention of the boys, I knew they should have had a say. The second the 'send' key was hit, I was gripped with guilt. Belatedly it came to my mind that using kymsonline@yahoo.com to keep a minimum of anonymity was laughable. It was probably easy to trace its origin via the IP address. Well, what was done was done. There was no going back now on my sent message:

> Dear Leila,
>
> Thank you for your email and for contacting me. I am very interested in your indication that you may have information that could be of help. Like cdr69, I face a fog when I get out of the house. I am also interested in your comment on the reality of it and on 'what lies beyond': my experience is that, depending on the circumstances, either the fog turns into a wall the further I walk into it, or opens up in my normal street, or leads to unknown countryside. I have no idea what is happening and why and I would welcome any explanation and/or advice. I very much look forward to hearing the information you were referring to in your email and I can't emphasise enough the 'very much'!
>
> Yours sincerely,
>
> Yoko

Ten minutes later, I was in my room, tidying and preparing the next load of laundry for a wash, when my phone beeped a new email. It was cdr69 (his real name Christophe just wouldn't stick in my brain):

> Dear Yoko,
>
> I am so relieved! Thank you! Thank you! So I am not crazy!
>
> How did you find the people that helped you cross back to the normal world? Is there a way for me to know who can do it? Or can anyone do it with some instructions? A friend of mine is coming tonight, so maybe she can help? Maybe my wife could tomorrow? Or maybe your people could help me too?
>
> I am feeling very claustrophobic. Nobody believes me but you. You have to help me. Do write more about your fog. Where are you? Are you also in Marrakech? Do you have any idea what is happening? Why me? Maybe we have something in common that would explain why we are going through it? Please, share any information with me. I am going out of my mind here. You have friends, I am alone. Nobody believes me. I am so relieved you contacted me.
>
> Please write more,
> Christophe

Just then, a new email from Leila arrived.

> Dear Yoko,
>
> Thank you for your trust in getting back to me and do not worry about what is happening. There isn't much I can do to help in your situation aside from enlightening you a little. I cannot explain

'why' this is happening, I can only give you some details on 'what'. However, I am reluctant to write it in an email. I would rather we met. It is preferable that I come to you instead of you travelling. Of course I am not asking for your address, but maybe you could give me a location that would be easy for you to get to? I could meet you there. I am aware you could be anywhere across the globe, nevertheless I am happy to travel. This is important.

If you agree to meet, I would recommend that you pick a public location where you will feel safe, yet somewhere we can have a private discussion. I live in the US, so depending where you are I may need a couple of days to get organised. Would sometime towards the end the week be convenient for you? Ideally, we should meet before the weekend.

Also, have you heard from cdr69? I would rather not leave my email on his forum, as I previously mentioned. It was understandable you did so, but I would like to avoid attracting any additional attention. I noticed you deleted yours: thank you for following my advice, it tells me you are taking me seriously which I appreciate. It is also possible you will receive more emails from people going through the same situation if your message was spotted. You may receive some unpleasant ones too. Do not be alarmed, there shouldn't be too many.

Yours sincerely,

Leila

Yes. I definitely wanted to meet her. No doubt about that! I even knew where we should meet: Heathrow Airport. The house was minutes away from Paddington Station, from which the Heathrow

Express train took fifteen minutes to reach the airport. Leila would assume, rightly, that I live in London, but a doubt would remain. Heathrow is only a short flight away from anywhere in Europe. When I thought of Heathrow, something stirred, something forgotten. I just couldn't put my finger on it and dismissed it for now. It would come back. Heathrow was a public place, with lots of cafés and restaurants for a private chat. It was perfect. One thought led to another: would the boys hide and would I meet her on my own? Would one or all of them want to join me for the encounter? Another brainstorming session of the household was really needed. So where were they?

We were around the table, eating dinner. They had all arrived by 8.30 p.m. Rico had had his shower, Zeno had finished three calls in twenty minutes and Harry had helped me lay the table. I had told them about the events of the day. I had feared Harry and Rico's reaction to my having replied to Leila without waiting for them and if they were not impressed they didn't show it much. Harry said that unfortunately there may be situations in the future when we would have to use our own judgement and we had to trust each other. But, if time was not of the essence, I or anyone else should wait for the others. He was right of course. They didn't have a go at me because they could see I was feeling bad about what I'd done.

Like me, they were all more excited about Leila than about cdr69. Also, I must admit my mixed feelings about cdr69. On the one hand I was sorry for him and tempted to tell him everything because I could relate to his situation and what it was like to face the fog alone. On the other hand, the way he wrote made me uncomfortable. I wasn't sure what it was, there was an unpleasant 'bossy' impression of him. In the end, we opted for my being honest and concise: I explained that I was like him, with no answers yet but hoping to meet someone shortly who professed to have information. I added that she would be interested in contacting him too and, if he agreed, I would provide her with his email address.

Switching the focus to Leila, Harry and Zeno were backing me up on the Heathrow meeting, but only if they were coming too. Rico agreed although finding it suspicious she would travel anywhere to meet me. Then Zeno dropped the bombshell. 'But aren't you supposed to visit your parents this weekend?'

'S-h-i-i-t!' was all I could say. Somehow, it had completely slipped my mind. I now recalled the previous niggling thought that there was something important linked to Heathrow. That was it. 'How could I forget?' I said to myself. 'You don't just forget when your parents might be in trouble. It could be very serious!' I would normally never forget this kind of thing. I loved my parents too much. My stress level jumped to Defcon 1. I couldn't imagine not going. Returning to the meeting with Leila, I was working out my options to see her before leaving on Friday to return on Sunday evening. Thursday evening would be ideal: it was now Tuesday and she said she may need a couple of days. It was tight but it could work.

All these thoughts and plans churned inside my head. A silence settled around the table as the boys waited for my suggestions. I could have sworn they could see my brain rotors turning. They agreed that Thursday and Heathrow would be the most convenient, so I wrote to her:

> Dear Leila,
>
> I would be delighted to meet you and I appreciate your making the effort to come to me from wherever you are in the States. I hope you will not have to travel too far for my suggested meeting place which is Heathrow Airport (United Kingdom) this Thursday at 7 p.m. Would that be convenient for you? If so, I will look for the best place to meet there.
>
> I also wish to ask you why you mentioned that travelling is not recommended. I am planning to

travel this weekend and would rather not have to change my plans. This is for an emergency of another nature.

Yours sincerely,

Yoko.

Within minutes, she replied.

Dear Yoko,

It is not up to me to tell you what to do and what not to do. Some things are meant to happen. They happen for a reason.

As you are able to get out of your house and lead your normal life, I assume you have worked out how this is possible. Now, if you need to travel and spend the weekend somewhere else, I would strongly recommend you bring this 'how' with you. I recommend it very strongly. I would rather not get into details online.

Unfortunately I will not be able to meet as soon as Thursday. Would a meeting on Monday or Tuesday next week at 7 p.m. work for you instead? Will you be back?

By any chance, have you heard from cdr69?

Yours sincerely,

Leila

'Hang on a minute,' I thought. 'What she was writing was that Rico or Harry should accompany me to my parents! Really? Most importantly, why?' This was not a good sign at all. Not at all. There was no fog there I would need them for. Unless ... unless it followed me. She didn't say that though, but it was a possible implication from her words. I couldn't bring the fog to my parents, above all if they were already in a serious situation. This is when it hit me: maybe they were facing the fog as well! Maybe it was why they wanted me to go down. Leila would not know though … This was such a mess! Family comes first, above any of my issues. Because of my mother's call in the morning and the urgency in her voice, because despite her recommendations Leila didn't write not to go, and because of the promise made to my parents, I decided there was no stopping me going. Now I needed to convince Harry or Rico to come with me. I looked at each of them puppy-eyed and explained my predicament, hoping one would agree to join me for a weekend in France.

**Day 4-5 (Wednesday & Thursday)**

There isn't much to say about the days prior to my trip. The situation was most unusual and yet life continued as normal. It was surreal. I should have suffered panic attacks at best, and so should Zeno. We did not. Instead, we led an apparently normal life getting accustomed to the presence of the forest beyond the fog. Zeno and I settled into a kind of routine without difficulty. Rico and Harry adjusted easily to their role of accompanying us out in the morning, and in the evening if we had plans in London. Only once or twice a day did Zeno and I pop out into the wild forest, coffee in hands in the morning, beer or glass of wine in the evening. Further exploration, including by night, was postponed to the following week after we had heard what Leila had to say.

The meeting with Leila was set for Monday, 7 p.m., Heathrow Airport Terminal 1, at the Costa Coffee by the arrivals gate. She had suggested that we stop communications until then, except in case of emergency. The wait was very frustrating albeit I appreciated her discretion. It was reassuring to know we would talk in person. I managed to get another little piece of information before we stopped communicating. It was little but valuable: the fog was not toxic. We had assumed it wasn't because we appeared to be alive and well. We had even told the firemen so. Their tests had come back inconclusive and it reinforced our assumption. Their basic tests did not show traces of anything harmful, but they couldn't ascertain the nature of the fog either. When enquiring if Leila recommended us moving out or if it was safe to remain, Leila wrote back that we were absolutely fine and there was nothing to worry about living in the Fog. This little crisis averted, life went on. Most of my social plans were limited. I only kept a few, so as not to cut myself from the rest of the world altogether just because I couldn't access it without help. It was the same for Zeno. His new hobby was planning the future expedition. He had a whole project for the weekend ahead in my absence: watching documentaries on 'How to survive in the wild', 'Secrets

of successful wildlife exploration' and many others. He had already started and was holding meetings at dinner to brief us all.
Even though I was the most assiduous of the attendees, even I
would start to doze after twenty minutes. After all, we could pack
a lighter and matches, food and drinks, so I wasn't fascinated by
how to make a fire from scratch, especially if the purpose was to
roast bugs. Still, I noticed he was getting more and more into the
idea of night discovery and learning to read the night sky stars.
Hopefully he would not be ready for it before a long, long time
had passed. I couldn't let him out there on his own at night, yet
I was not looking forward to night expeditions among the wolves
and the possible dangers of the forest. It would take a long time
to get used to the idea. Another one of his ideas that didn't excite
me much was to get his hands on two guns and some ammunition. It didn't seem to bother him that none of us had shooting
permits. He had done his Italian military service and obviously
he could shoot. Me? I had no clue how to fire a gun. Actually that
was not totally true, I was pretty good in funfairs but it probably
didn't count: I may be able to wait and aim patiently to win a soft
bear; I may not be so poised in front of a live one. Run for your
life would be more like it.

What surprised me was the total lack of news from cdr69. I
did send a brief email on Tuesday enquiring if all was well as he
had not replied to my last email or given any news. I had received
no reply since. Hopefully nothing had happened to him, such as
him venturing into the fog, getting lost or fainting. I checked his
forum and he had taken it down. The decision was his without
Leila's advice as she didn't have direct contact with him. I had not
given his email address before he agreed to do so. My intuition
told me he was the kind of person who required careful handling.
Bar any other tangible information to base my actions upon, intuition ruled.

**Day 6 (Friday)**

On the plane heading to Marseille, I sat next to an enthusiastic Rico who was looking forward to discovering the South of France for the first time.

'Can we go to the beach sunbathing?' he asked excitedly.

'No. It is still winter. It is cold.' My mind was preoccupied elsewhere.

'But is it possible?'

'No.'

'Do you have any hot friends there?'

'No.'

'Are you going to be grumpy the whole weekend?'

'Yes.'

'This is going to be fun!' he replied, not fussed. He knew not to take my morning mood personally.

Watching the clouds beneath me from the window, I thought of the coming Monday. Did Leila really have information? Could she really help us understand? Could she actually help us more? Maybe she knew how to get rid of the fog. If she could, should we? I thought Zeno would not want to do it immediately, not before he had had a better taste of it. What about me? Could I really just go back to my previous life and never wonder if I had not missed the greatest adventure of my life? What about cdr69? What about, maybe, others? What about my parents and this emergency? I checked myself, there was no point thinking about all of this. 'Conjectures about the future will only feed fears,' I mouthed silently, 'so, Yoko's mind, shut up.'

I had had my book open on the same page since the plane took off, forty minutes earlier. Rico was sitting back, his eyes closed, headset plugged in his ears and listening to some kind of hard rock. It was pretty loud and his left hand neighbour kept glancing at him, with a mixture of annoyance and interest. She was about thirty or thirty-two years old and his Italian charm was clearly working on her. I touched his shoulder and he unplugged one of his earphones.

'Rico, I'm sorry I have been grumpy with you all morning.'

'Don't worry babe, I get it.'

'I'm just worried about this trip. You know ... what could happen and why you had to come?'

'I know.'

'Again, thank you for coming. I know you had other plans for the weekend.'

'Anything for you, babe.'

'And I'm sorry you have to play the heartbroken role. When I called Mum to tell her you were coming, I had meant to just say you fancied a break in the South of France. I don't know why I made that up. I lost my nerve when I heard her disapproving silence.'

'She can't be that bad, come on. I know you love her, so it can't be that bad.'

'I do, and she's great. Still, imagine a mix between a tough Italian mama and an inscrutable Japanese princess. Difficult to conceive indeed, though that's what she's like.'

'Tough mama I can deal with. Japanese princess will be a new challenge. Bah, I'll manage. I'm the poor guy whose girl-friend just dumped him, right? By the way, I think she will suspect that excuse being untrue when she meets me. Who would leave me?'

My mother is an amazing woman. She has an iron will, set from an early age and much needed to deny her high society family the marriage they had in mind for her. She chose my father instead, a barrister from southern France. It had been acceptable for my Japanese grandfather to marry an Italian woman for she was a countess. However, a commoner from an unknown town in France was not good enough for their daughter. The support of her grandmother (also called Yoko, hence my name) had proved invaluable. Mum was strong, eccentric, determined, kind and very difficult to approach. She might have rebelled against her family but she still inherited from them the knowledge, or art, of how to master perfect control of her emotions at all times. She could read me like a book, while I struggled to read her. So did my sister and to a certain extent, my father. I knew she would give me the world and give up everything for me, but communication and demonstrating feelings was clearly not a trait of her personality. I was not totally comfortable opening up to her, not because sharing was difficult with her, it wasn't, but because it is difficult to be the only one displaying emotions.

Dad was different. He had a bucket load of charm and he seduced my mother thanks to it. In addition he had intelligence and culture, both precise and broad, making conversation with him a constant source of learning. I was very close to him even if we didn't talk that much on intimate subjects. He was one of those people who put love into everything he did more than in his expressing it. Because it was easy to open up to him if I wished, somehow I hardly ever felt I had to. It was as if he understood everything without me having to say anything. Consequently I barely talked about myself to my parents aside from what I was up to. Mum by sixth sense, Dad by mutual understanding, both knew when I was feeling low or high. Even when I was not talking because I didn't want them to worry – because I loved them and wanted to protect them – they knew.

Right then, watching the peaceful clouds, I had a foreboding that this nice balance was going to collapse this weekend. Something was about to go very wrong, I could feel it. Plus my sister would be there too and that was the worst of all the news I had had that week.

'You are going to love my parents, Rico. Both of them.'

'I don't doubt it. Don't worry babe; everything is going to be fine. I'm here to watch your back.'

'You are just the nicest, Rico. Thanks.' I smiled at him. His self-confidence and kindness were endearing.

My mother came to pick us up at the airport. Dad, although officially retired, was still working part-time as a consultant for the company he had created in his youth. He was always in his home office, jazz music loud on the latest iPod sound system. He loved buying the latest technology, even if it took him ages to work out how to use it. I introduced my mother to Rico who was on his best behaviour. My mum shook his hand and looked at him intently. He was after all one of the people I was sharing my home and so much of my time with. She had longed to meet him and had talked about visiting me in London and in the house for a long time. For whatever reason, it had never happened. It was funny to think they had never met. I was close to an outburst of laughter watching Rico. He was standing straight, very formal, his face serious with a tiny smile, clearly in awe. My mother was a beautiful woman, with big wide eyes set harmoniously in her Asian face, circled by wavy and long thick black hair. He grabbed his bag and mine and silently followed us to the car.

During the drive home, she asked him a few questions about his art, keeping very discreet about his 'broken heart'. She informed him her car was at his disposal if he wanted to roam around the countryside during his stay. She would use my father's in the meantime. After a lot of 'Yes ma'am', 'No ma'am', 'Thank you ma'am', Mum finally told him to drop the 'ma'am' and to call her Eleonora. The ice was broken.

It was a short drive from the airport to the house. My parents lived in a small village a stone's throw away from Marseille. It was an old house, which had seen several centuries before my father bought it to settle the family. It had two en suite bathrooms assigned to my parents and guests and three additional bedrooms sharing a third bathroom. All the bedrooms were on the first floor. On the ground floor, the front door opened onto an old stone staircase, with a large dining room leading to the kitchen on the right and the living room on the left, followed by my father's office. The living area was a spacious room of classic style, more suited to entertaining than family life. The same applied to the dining room. The office, more accurately described as my father's den, was crammed with an old-fashioned partners' desk, books, papers, files and notebooks. Mostly I stayed out of the living room and dining room; when not in my bedroom or outdoors, I lived in the kitchen. It was a cosy room with all the modern technology somehow squeezed in with the old features of a nineteenth century layout. The wood beams gave it a timeless feel and copper pots were still hanging from the walls. It was the heart of the house. I loved this room. I got my love of baking and sharing the joy of food there.

The house had a large terrace at the front, with trees older than the building itself and a pre-Revolution well in working condition. At the back, in a green courtyard, my parents had added a little swimming pool for the hot summer days. The whole property was surrounded by a high old-fashioned stone wall lined by trees both on the inside and the outside. We were on the edge of the village, secluded and protected, and it was for me a little corner of paradise.

It was already past lunchtime when I put my bag on my bed. It had been a relief upon opening the gate of the property to note there was no fog as a part of me feared it was my parents' issue and why they had asked me to come. The reason my visit was necessary hadn't yet been elucidated and wouldn't be until my sister's arrival the next day. My mother had a surprise treat for the afternoon: she had organised horse riding for me. I was thrilled! It was rare these days I practised my childhood passion. She had also gone to the market hall and bought a few of my favourite foods for the weekend. I turned and checked Rico. He was grinning with expected pleasure. For him, the prospect of good food was second best to the prospect of women hunting.

**Day 7 (Saturday)**

I woke up with a start and checked my mobile: 9 a.m. London time. I jumped out of bed, threw open the curtains and smiled at the sight of the blue sky and blazing sun. No fog! No fog! Relief went through me in a huge wave and I grasped how big a burden I had been carrying the past two days. Leila must have suggested I bring a friend as a safety plan, not as a necessity. The fog had stayed in London. Or had it? I quickly texted Zeno to check if there had been any change of situation in my absence. No immediate answer, he might still be asleep.

I left the room with a spring in my step and went to the kitchen. It was too early for Rico to be up yet. However, from the smell of coffee and toast lingering on the ground floor, my parents had finished breakfast already. The sound of jazz from Dad's office growing louder as I walked towards it indicated he was working. After knocking loudly, Dad invited me in, stopped writing and smiled at me. I went round his desk to give him a kiss on the forehead. I was strangely protective of him.

'You look better today, darling,' he said to me.

'I didn't know I looked bad yesterday ...'

'You had something on your mind. Today you are lighter.'

I smiled. We looked at each other. He was not going to ask and I was not going to tell. I could if I wished or needed to, it was enough for me to know this.

I found my mother on the phone in my parents' bedroom, finishing getting dressed as she talked. She raised her hand to indicate for me to wait while she finished organising a dinner or card game or something similar with one of her friends. Same old, same old. I had grown up listening to this type of conversation.

'You were quite preoccupied yesterday,' she said, kissing me when she hung up. She always had cut to the chase.

'Me? No,' I lied.

'Do you have a boyfriend?' Direct and to the point.

'No,' I answered, cringing, as she walked towards me for a good morning kiss.

'You should.'

'Yes, well, I have to meet someone first.'

'Is that what's been bothering you of late?' Here it was, the question.

'No, not really.' I was dumbstruck. I should have said yes. Of course I should have said yes. That would have stopped the questioning.

'What then? Something is clearly on your mind. Your father and I agree you look troubled, although better today.' Again, direct. I smiled to her and attempted to defuse the inquiry.

'Mum, don't worry about it.'

'I am your mother, I always worry about "it".'

'Then please don't. I'm starving ... Shall I prepare a quick breakfast? After that I'll get ready and go out with you. Can you give me thirty minutes?'

'Of course, darling. I'm only going to the market.'

'I know, you always go on Saturday and Sunday mornings. You also know I love the market! Plus I think you have something to tell me as well.'

'I'll wait for you then. I have a few more calls to make anyway. However darling, we can't talk about that something yet. Your sister will.'

My sister Julia was in her mid-thirties, married to a forty-year-old banker from a French aristocratic family. They had a three-year-old toddler named Eudes, an old-fashioned and regal name in France. However, her husband had just had a midlife crisis, or a revelation depending on how you looked at it. He had decided to leave her for his car mechanic, a handsome twenty-five-year old Moroccan man. My sister was, obviously, in extreme shock and her temper was at its vilest.

Julia and I were very different. She had taken her looks from my mother's Asian side and was tall with straight, thick, deep black hair which she disliked and dyed chestnut with amber highlights. She had a lovely eggshell complexion, wide-slit eyes with thick eyelashes and a small mouth with pearl-like teeth. It would have been impossible to guess we were full sisters by looks. Julia and I also led very different lives. I still believed she had a good heart, besides being an over-conventional annoying snob, although it was not easily apparent. She lived her life by the strict rules of the Parisian jet set which she applied to the extreme. Moreover, she judged people too rigidly by the norms of what she believed to be socially required or acceptable in her circle. Needless to say, she rarely invited me to visit her in Paris. I was not close to Julia anymore and she treated me as an alien in her world. I felt sorry for her over the new drama in her life though. Her world was collapsing. If only it could have made her lower her defences and let me in, we might have bonded again.

This positive thinking didn't last as her current mood annihilated it. Dinner was excruciating with Julia being her worst insufferable self. She talked only and continuously about the latest gossip from her circles of friends and enemies. She dismissed every word I dared utter and ignored Rico, only addressing my parents in French. My parents proposed we discuss the urgent reason for the family gathering after dinner in private. She just brushed the suggestion away saying she was too tired and couldn't possibly go through it now. It would have to wait for tomorrow. As soon as was decently possible, I grabbed Rico and announced that I should really give him a tour of Marseille by night.

Once we were out, I said to him, 'Leila was right. I had to take you with me! You will be my key to escape my sister this weekend. Thank you! Thank you! And thank you! She is getting posher – in the negative sense – every time I see her!'

'She is quite cute though. And I can't understand what she says anyway, she only speaks French, even when the rest of you make a point of speaking English for my sake.'

'That is r-u-d-e! Her highly developed obnoxiousness renders her intolerable!'

'You know she uses all this varnish to cope better and hide what is going on underneath, right? Her husband left her for a man. And a younger one too. She is unpleasant, but her situation is bound to ...'

'Unfortunately she was already like that before. The situation is tough, I give you that and I am really sorry for her. She is my sister and despite my finding her so difficult, I feel for her, but it doesn't justify her behaviour. I don't understand how she turned out that way. We have the same parents for God's sake ...'

'Maybe she needs rebound sex to chill this poshness ...'

'Get that out of your mind right now!'

'B ...'

'Drop it!'

We both laughed. Then he noticed a bar in the village with some pretty girls inside ... Ahhh Rico ...

# WEEK II

**Day 1 (Sunday)**

We had not stayed out late the previous night. There was only so much partying one could do in a little village, even one with a surprisingly large amount of young people (proportionally), and we didn't go to Marseille after our stop at the village bar. The next morning, enjoying the knowledge of being in a little haven in southern France, I dozed in bed and woke up slowly. My thoughts turned to what awaited me in London, to my meeting with Leila the next day. I had had no contact with her or with cdr69 for days now. It felt like the whole past week was not real and had happened in another life. I checked the time on my mobile: it was 8.41a.m. in the UK. I noticed two text messages, one from Harry and one from Zeno. Both had regularly texted yesterday to check all was fine on our side and to inform us there was nothing new on theirs. We kept the messages brief and general, without mention of the fog. It must have been daylight filling the room that woke me up. A quick glimpse at the window confirmed I had forgotten to close the curtains. They were wide open and white light was flowing into the room. It took me a few seconds to realise there was light but no sun or blue sky. All I could see between the curtains was fog.

I didn't scream. I didn't cry. I didn't jump out of bed. I just gawked. When my neck began to hurt, I lay back down in my bed staring at the ceiling instead. 'Dammit!' I swore in a whisper.

I dragged myself out of bed, picked up my mobile and made my way to Rico's room. It was early for him and he wasn't going to be happy, but I had to talk to him without delay. If my mother wanted me to accompany her anywhere, I also couldn't without my ally. I knocked twice and receiving no reply entered his dark room. I hoped he was wearing something to sleep in. I went to the window and threw open the curtains. Outside I should have been able to see the beautiful trees of the terrace. I could see nothing but the now familiar fog.

'Rico, Rico, wake up,' I shook him gently.

'Mmmm,' he groaned and then farted. Nice!

Shaking him a bit more vigorously, he finally opened his eyes and drowsily looked at me. It began to smell horrible in there. He had distinctly overdosed on the roasted onions the previous night.

'Cosa?'

'Rico, the fog. It's here.'

'Che ...?'

'Come on Rico, wake up, please. The fog, it's followed us here!'

'Ma nooo!' He bolted to the window with a loud 'Cazzo!' After a minute of staring, he turned towards me and asked, 'Does that mean it isn't in London anymore? Are you the one attracting it? Or me?'

I hadn't thought about that. We both knew that if it followed anyone, it made sense it would be me. I was more affected by the fog than he was. I called Zeno. The phone rang for some time before a sleepy voice answered.

'Zeno, I'm sorry to wake you up, but the fog, it is here now. Do you still have it?'

'No way! Hang on, I'm checking ... Yes! It is still here!' a fast awake Zeno replied.

We were all silent until I asked both Zeno and Rico, 'Do you ... Does that mean ... Am I the one who attracts the fog? Do I somehow ... create it?' Zeno and Rico couldn't answer that. Rico just kept looking back and forth between the window and me, shaking his head slowly.

'She knew. Leila, she knew. She must have known that this would happen,' I murmured. I was still in Rico's room, lost in thought. It had to be me bringing this fog here. Was I cursed or something? I needed to write to her. This qualified as an emergency, certainly. I told Rico I was going to my room to fetch my tablet and write to Leila. He nodded. Reaching the door, I heard him say he was going to get ready and added 'we must go out and check'.

As I sped to my room, I heard my mother coming up the stairs. I was hoping to pass unnoticed, but either the sound of my feet or the glimpse of a movement betrayed me and she called my name. I saw she was already dressed and ready.

'I put the coffee on. Your father and I were waiting to have breakfast with you. I was hoping you would be up soon, it's been a long time since we've had the pleasure of a family breakfast.'

'Yes. Of course. I'll be right down. I just need five minutes and I'll join you.'

'Lovely. Your sister is not up yet, but Eudes is. He's downstairs. Your dad is reading him the paper and Eudes seems fascinated. Your father really has a gift with children.'

'Right ... Yes... I'll be down in five minutes.'

My hurry to get inside my room was apparent and, leaving, I felt the intense look of my mother on my back. How was I going to explain what was going on?

'Later,' I whispered, 'when I've checked with Rico if the fog's effects are the same as in London.'

First, I sent an email to Leila:

Dear Leila,
    Currently in South of France, I woke up with my head in the fog. Is it me? Why didn't you warn me?
    I cannot wait to meet you tomorrow. I do hope you can really help me.
    Best regards,
    Yoko

Despite my alarm, I tried to remain general in my message. She would not give a specific answer either. By then, I really could do with a coffee. For that I had to go to the kitchen, face my parents and keep calm in front of them. I made a mental list of what needed to be done: check if the fog was the same as in London and limited to the house, and venture out alone to see if Rico's help was required to return to this world. At the thought of going out on my own my chest tightened. The prospect of total whiteness and solitude with no vision or sound, added to the sensation of slowly losing the ability to breathe, filled me with anguish. No, I really didn't want to check but would have to. I looked around me for the necessary rope. I started rummaging under the bed and found a box full of wrapping paper and ribbons. Three were new and the labels indicated each was five metres long. Joined together, the length should cover enough ground to have some answers. After a quick getting washed and dressed, I made my way downstairs. My parents were patiently waiting for me when I arrived, although Mum checked her watch and put some more coffee on preparation.

'Bread or croissants?' she asked.

'Bread, thank you,' I replied, moving to the kitchen counter. 'Please sit down Mum, I'll get it.'

I went round the table to kiss both Dad and Mum, took the loaf of bread and sat down. My father had just put down the paper and was looking out of the window commenting, 'They said on the news we should have a sunny day and the same in the paper. Strange. Maybe it will clear later.'

'I went on the terrace earlier and couldn't even see the trees. The terrace has completely disappeared. Yoko, are you OK darling? You look pale?'

'Yes, of course I am fine. Probably just hungry. Would you like some ...' I stopped mid-sentence. I'd just had a thought and the enormity of it made me freeze my movement of bread slicing. What if, as in London, one of my parents turned out to be like Zeno? Like Rico or Harry would be fine, or fine-ish, but what if in bringing the fog I had changed their lives forever in the Zeno-way?

'Yoko? Yoko?' I came back to the present in the kitchen with my father calling me. Mum was just looking at me, frowning. Both of them showed concern.

'I am just ... This fog ... I'm ... intrigued! Can I quickly go on the terrace and see it? It sounds so unreal. I'll be right back!'

At first I intended to attach the wrapping ribbon to the handle on the outside of the front door, and then I remembered that in London it was attached to the front gate, not the front door. I took a deep breath and stepped forward. I knew this terrace by heart and I made my way towards the old stone wall protecting the property from the outside world. Following it until I reached the main gate, I found its hidden key in a pot and I retrieved it easily, knowing each move by heart until the door opened. Fog replaced the streets of the village. The situation was unpleasantly familiar. I made a knot with my ribbon on the outside handle and walked out. I was starting to get the hang of this technique and I held the ribbon tight. Being upset almost took over the anxiety this time. I saw nothing and bumped into nothing. The fog built up resistance and breathing got harder. There was no need to go any further. I knew.

Once back in the house, I didn't return to the kitchen and my parents. Instead, I ran up the stairs two at a time and knocked on Rico's door. He answered within a few seconds and let me in. He was ready, facing the mirror and focusing on his hair. Rico was obsessed with his hair. In fact he spent more time in the bathroom than I did to get ready. Rico was, quite simply, the symbol of the twenty-first century metrosexual. So I told him, first, that his hair looked amazing (sometimes you have to indulge your friends), and second that the fog was THE fog. He didn't show much surprise at either piece of information. He promptly agreed to come out with me sooner rather than later, to get it over and done with before talking to my parents. While he put the finishing touches to his hair, I took my mobile from my back pocket. No message, no email. Maybe Leila was sleeping? I didn't know where she lived and it could be night-time there. If so, hopefully she was an early-riser.

Rico and I were at the front door ready to go out when my mother arrived.

'Rico, good morning! You're going out?'

'Yes, indeed, Eleonora. I fancy a cigarette and Yoko kindly is keeping me company.' I must admit, I was impressed. Rico lied to my mother like a pro.

'I see. Will you have tea or coffee afterwards?'

'Coffee, please.'

'Certainly,' my mother replied, smiling. 'This fog. Most unusual, you would almost think of the infamous London smog, wouldn't you, darling?'

'London fog. Yes. Uh, I mean, smog. Well, London has been free from it for decades now Mum. The smog I mean, not the …' Pathetic. I was stuttering and displaying evident unease. Mum's slightly raised eyebrows showed she'd noticed. Rico had turned his head towards the fog and was trying not to laugh. Right, so now I was officially laughable when lying.

'Very well then honey. Hopefully you will join us at the table later. Your coffee is getting cold. We'll start if you don't mind.'

'Of course not, Mum! Please start. Oh, I'm so sorry ... Mum ... I ... I think I need to talk to Dad and you. In a minute. I am so sorry.'

Mum's face relaxed then, regaining their normal features.

'We'll be here waiting for you, darling,' she added, looking out. 'Quite extraordinary this weather.'

As soon as she left, Rico and I walked through the fog and to the main gate. There the fog stopped immediately and we stepped out in the village. From the outside it wasn't possible to see the fog. It was entirely contained within the limit of the property, hidden behind the stone wall and the thick high trees. The sun was radiant in a cloudless sky.

'I am sure I would still get a tan with this weather,' Rico said. Then he pulled me to him and kissed me on the forehead. 'Let's go talk to your parents. I'll help you explain. Now they have to know.'

When Rico and I got into the kitchen, my mother and father instantly turned to look at us, holding their tongues the way people do when they were talking about you before you showed up. I poured some coffee for Rico and put my cup of cold coffee in the microwave – to Rico's horror. It is tantamount to blasphemy for a full-blooded Italian. I grabbed the piece of bread I had left on my plate earlier and applied a thick layer of honey. I needed a sugar boost. The room was strangely silent. Eudes was eating his toddler food and everyone else was waiting for my next move.

'Mum, Dad, the fog, it is not a normal fog,' I began.

'I agree,' said Dad, 'I've never seen one like this here before.'

'I meant it is more like … a paranormal fog,' I tried again.

'Pardon me?' my mother and father looked at me bewildered and gaping.

That was not a good start. I had to approach this a bit more practically. I remembered in an unusual stroke of genius the good old saying, 'seeing is believing'. Downing my coffee in one go as I stood up, I turned to Rico and nodded. He stood up as well and I told my parents to come with us.

'We can't leave Eudes,' my mother replied.

'Let's put him in front of the television as it will only take a few minutes.'

Our little group followed Rico to the wall and out to the village. Both my parents were quite shocked when they crossed the gate to see they were suddenly under a warm early spring sun. I pointed to the open gate, where only fog could be seen inside. My mother's face was set in stone, only her eyes betrayed incomprehension and something close to distress. My father fired questions at me. I silenced him firmly.

'Dad, not here in the open. Let's go back in.'

'You want us to cross the fog again? Is it dangerous?' Dad asked.

'Oh my God! Eudes! Your sister!' Mum interrupted.

'No, it is not dangerous. We have the same at the house in London. We have had it for a week, haven't we Rico? Come. It is not a conversation for the street, especially in a village. Let's go back in.'

The heavy silence on our return was full of anxiety. My father put his arm round my mother's shoulder. I walked behind them. Rico stayed next to me. Tentatively, I put a hand on my mother's back. She was shivering.

Sitting round the table in the kitchen, I still didn't know where to start.

'Well, OK, here goes. This fog is abnormal. Quite magical in fact,' I said tentatively.

'Magical?' asked my father.

'Well, yes, or something like that. It seems to stick around a specific place, or house, only.'

'How does it happen? Why?' my father continued.

'And you said that you have it in London as well?' added my mother.

'Yes Mum, we have it surrounding the house. Dad, I don't know. There isn't much information to impart yet. Please just listen. Please.'

When I kicked off the explanation, the events of the whole week came flooding out. It was the first time I was telling my story in full, unconcerned about revealing the unbelievable. I was speaking quietly, controlled, as if recounting a banal everyday story. I told them about Zeno and the forest, about the firemen, about the wolves and the thickening fog when out on my own. I explained our discoveries about cdr69, about Leila and meeting her the next day. I informed them of Rico and Harry's help to come back. I admitted trying to hide it all from them both. Next, I confessed Leila's warning and my lie about Rico's heartbroken status, because he had to come and we couldn't give them the real reason. Rico interrupted me only then, stating that of course it was a lie, he would never be heartbroken, 'Why would a woman leave such a man as me?' My eyeballs rolled so much, for one second I feared they would flip backwards. It did make us smile though and that was his aim in saying it (even if, as I suspected, he believed his words). I ignored his comment, as did my parents, to continue the story and finally reach that Sunday morning, with me checking the fog first alone then with Rico. Last, I apologised for having brought it here, if indeed I had. I also begged them to promise not to reveal anything from my narrative to anyone including Julia. Maybe especially Julia. They both agreed with my plea. They dismissed my apologies as unnecessary, considering they were the ones who had asked me to come and had insisted upon it. When I asked them why, they said they would come to that later and it was about Julia.

'What Yoko and I think we need to do next, is control if the fog has affected any of you the way it affected her, or Zeno, or me,' Rico said.

'Oh God, of course.' Dad was looking intently at us both, adding, 'You're sure you're OK?'

'Yes, Dad, we are all OK. All of us, we are fine.'

'What about Eudes? What if he has been affected? How would we know? We can't possibly let him walk out on his own, can we?'

'I don't know Mum. I guess we'll have to improvise.'

Eudes, my lovely dear nephew! I so very hoped he was safe from the effects of the fog. The last thing I wanted was to ruin any of his chances in life. He was a lovely child. I hoped he would retain his good nature and not be spoiled by his Mum's.

It was now almost noon and I was coffeed-up. I had managed to wolf down three thick slices of bread with butter and honey while talking, contrary to good education of not blabbing away with a full mouth (no one seemed to care). Rico had eaten too. My parents had not, but I suspected the fog story had ruined their appetite. Eudes had fallen asleep at the table unnoticed at first, then my father took him on his lap.

'So, when do we start?' Dad asked.

'Huh, if there is no urgency, could I first go to the market before it closes? I had planned a roast chicken for lunch and we need a fresh baguette and another few things.' Remarkable. Even the most extraordinary circumstances would not let my mother falter from being a domestic goddess.

'Of course. It's one of the ways to check. So let's go,' I said with a sigh.

My father disapproved. He wanted to make tests on the fog a priority and said so. He reminded me of Zeno and his thirst for knowledge. On the contrary, Mum liked the routine and structure of her world, especially in stressful times. She could cope with any situation by imposing her normality onto it, by including it in her everyday life. Also in my family, there is no messing with the Sunday roast, whatever is roasting. After we cleared the table, my mother went up to get her bag and my father disappeared into his office. I checked my messages. Harry, Zeno and a few friends had been in touch. The first two had communicated with Rico while I was talking so they were not worried. I wrote back that I was pleased to have gone through 'the talk' and things were now cleared with my parents. It was a huge relief, not just having shared the story with them but having spoken aloud about what was happening.

My sister came down as I was finishing my text to Zeno.

'Mother is weird.'

'What do you mean, Mum and Dad are weird?'

'She was rather dismissive. With all that I have to deal with right now! What are you all still doing here anyway? You're usually at the market at this time. Have you seen this weather? Ghastly. Where did Daddy leave the paper? Be a dear and look after Eudes while I grab a bite to eat. I so need a cup of tea! Is there any almond milk? I hate it that Mother always forgets I only take almond milk these days.' All the while, she was holding Eudes and pushing him towards me for me to take. Absolutely-in-her-dreams. Even though I loved my nephew to bits, I hated how she assumed people would do what she wished without even a 'please'.

I crossed my arms and replied, 'We're going any time now. Mum just went up to collect a few things and we will be on our way. Rico is coming with us of course. Dad will stay in his office as usual, listening to jazz in peace.'

'Good. Will you take Eudes with you? I have a slight headache.'

'No, we are not taking Eudes with us. We are late and will need to rush around. Anyway we looked after him all morning. I am sure your son will be happy to spend a bit of quality time with his mummy.'

'I'll leave him with Dad then.'

Mum had arrived as the dialogue started with Julia. She was looking at me unimpressed by my snappy tone, although I could tell she approved of my position. I quickly went to say bye to Dad. I wanted to warn him Julia was up and that Eudes and she should really remain inside in our absence. Also, if he wanted to check on his own and if beyond the front gate he could only see fog, he should use the ribbon to make sure he didn't get lost in it. My big hope was that Julia and Eudes were not affected by the fog. She was not one I wanted to either reveal anything to, or involve in that new aspect of my life. I still loved my sister and had fond memories of her up to my late teens. This aside, it was difficult to have either time or patience for her lately. In my everyday life, she now felt like a stranger, which saddened me. How did we reach that point?

When we were back from the market, putting a large chicken covered with garlic and herbs to cook in the oven, a selection of vegetables in the tray bathed in the dripping fat from the poultry, it was time to test the fog with the members of the house. It clarified that neither my dad nor my mum was affected by the fog. They could go to the village as normal. Only Rico was able to help me do so. The tricky part was to get Julia out in the fog next, with and without Eudes and without explaining why. It was planned for after lunch.

Just when we sat down at the table, Julia complaining of the meal's lateness, my mobile chirped the arrival of a new email. (Yes, chirped. I had changed animal since the wolf ringtone.) It was cdr69. I couldn't take care of it now as we were at the table. My mother was strict on the rule of ignoring phones during meals. I knew that considering the circumstances my parents would be lenient, but my sister would be most surprised and make a fuss. That was the last thing I needed. So I thought I'd just have a quick glance and reply later.

> Dear Yoko,
> I am in hell. The internet collapsed on us and nobody in this bloody country would come to repair it. They treat us like shit. Customer services are shit. It just came back on and we don't even know how or why. It may collapse any minute again

so I will be quick. What a country! Next thing I will do is sell this bloody house.

Things have been crazy hectic here. A girl-friend of mine came to visit. We realised that when I go out with her, I can go through the fog but not to town: we reach the desert! Then my wife arrived and I tried to go out with her and we ended up in a desert again! A DESERT! On her own she is always in a desert too. Same with my friend, she ends up in the desert alone as well. Isabelle is hysterical. She and Louise have big fights. I love my wife, but let's say Louise and I have a special relationship. Isabelle is not stupid and she understood. Let's call a spade a spade: I am doomed! I am stuck between my 4 ½ months pregnant wife and my mistress of one year who didn't know my wife was pregnant. Isabelle needs me, I love her, but I need Louise too. Lately I almost considered losing myself in that fog.

You mentioned that someone contacted you that could be of help. Well obviously I need help! Isabelle is driving me insane, and Louise is an emotional mess and nags me non-stop. Please hurry and pass on my details to anyone who can get me out of this living nightmare!

The sooner the better!

Christophe de Rocque

'What a bastard!' It escaped me. Everyone around the table turned to look at me. My mother frowned.

'Huh ... Sorry ... I ... Never mind. May I have some roast potatoes, Mum?' I tried to pull myself together, I was fuming inside. This guy was so selfish. HE was in hell! What about his wife? What about this Louise? If I had been any of the women I would have let him stew a bit in his fog, not even helping him get to this desert. What an arse!

I was trying to cool down.

'So they ended up in a desert. Interesting. Quite appropriate geographically,' I thought to myself. My parents remained silent. They were wondering if my message was linked to the fog without being able to ask. I decided to try and give them a hint. 'Just a man I contacted online to have some information about a strange matter. He is not that helpful and not that pleasant either.'

'Never mind him. Eleonora, those potatoes are to die for!' Rico joined in, changing subject for my benefit.

My mother looked between Rico and me and concluded with confidence, 'The world is full of assholes. Let it not ruin our lunch.' My father almost spilled his drink and my sister stared at Mum in awe.

'What is happening today? What is wrong with you all? And in front of Eudes, too! Mother, gosh! How could you use that word?'

'Can I have some more chicken with gravy, please?' interrupted Rico.

'Rico, I haven't even started mine. You can't possibly have cleaned your plate already?' I happily ignored my sister to focus on Rico – easier subject.

'Yes I can. This is so good! Your mother's Sunday roast is fantastic. Eleonora, you are not counting on leftovers I hope. If allowed, I'll have a third helping.'

'Rico you are a pig,' I said, grinning.

'What! Why? I was making a compliment!' He looked genuinely surprised

'Unbelievable ...' I nodded.

My dad was laughing, my mother was beaming and my sister was horrified. The lunch took a turn for the better with everyone in a happier mood, apart from Julia as should be obvious by now. Rico's interruption had been a blessing; he had got rid of the cloud of negativity.

The time to check on Julia's fog status came too soon. Here was the plan: first, I would take Julia on her own with me. We would try with her son afterwards. Julia agreed to a quick walk with me on the terrace under the pretence that I needed to show her something. She only reluctantly obliged. Heading out, she immediately hated the fog and complained it made her feel claustrophobic. I couldn't agree more …

'It gets better once we are out in the village.' I silently prayed that we would indeed arrive in the village. We reached the terrace wall and gate, opened it and stepped outside. After a sweeping glance, I sighed. It was not from relief, it was from resignation. In front of my sister lay the beautiful local countryside of wild grass and savoury herbs, tortuous small trees, scattered rocks and small hills. It was so gorgeous, so peaceful and so missing our village. My sister kept looking right and left and right and left. She finally turned to face me.

'Yoko … What is this? Where are we?'

'Well … I don't really know.'

'What do you mean you don't know? Where is the village? Where are we?'

'Julia, I don't know. It's the fog.'

'What? The fog? What are you talking about Yoko!'

'Well, apparently, the fog can 'transport' some people to somewhere else. We have a forest in London.' That made me recall cdr69's message. He had a desert. It seemed the place beyond the fog matched our location's botany and geology without human habitation.

'What do you mean by "we have a forest in London"?' What forest? What is this fog thing? You are not making any sense!'

'Let's go back and I will explain some more.'

'No Yoko. I want to know now! Where is the village? Where are we?'

'We'll get there later. We just need Rico.'

'We just need Rico? What do you mean "we just need Rico?" I don't need Rico! Rico is a joke.'

'Don't start being a bitch. Rico is my friend, plus, trust me, you don't want to alienate him just now. He can help you.'

'You'd better have a good explanation for it all, Yoko.'

'What do you mean "I'd better"? Do you think I control this thing? Do you think I am having a lot of fun right now? Stop, Julia. Don't get on my nerves. Don't piss me off. Just shut up, OK? Shut up and come back to the house!'

I pulled her back in through the fog and into the house. My parents were in the living room. They were trying to act nonchalantly and were reading, one his paper, the other her book. Rico was drawing in his sketch book. Yet the moment we entered, the three of them looked up anxiously. I think our faces told them there was a big problem before we even spoke.

'Did you know?' Julia shouted. Eudes was sleeping upstairs and I was hoping he would not wake up anytime soon. What was coming was not going to be pretty.

'Yoko told us this morning that this fog was special,' my father replied.

'And no one thought of telling me! Why? Why do you always exclude me from your little group? You always treat Yoko better because she is your favourite!'

'That is enough!' my mother exploded. This was rare and this was dangerous. When my mother lost it, you didn't want to be the target of it. It was deadly, she never missed a shot. Knowing this my sister immediately clamped her mouth shut. Everyone did.

'Your father and I have no favourite. This is a ridiculous, erroneous, and unacceptable assumption. Julia, Yoko did not tell you because there was no reason to alarm you yet. You have enough on your plate right now. Also, we were hoping you would not be affected. Neither your father nor I are, we just have to cross the fog and all the rest is normal. Now, Yoko, Julia, tell us what happened.'

Julia was still steaming, so I talked first. I explained that we reached a wilder countryside than we ought to have and with no village. I then summarised the London situation for Julia, omitting references to Leila or cdr69, just keeping to the details of our house and the roles of Harry and Rico.

'So you see, Julia, all you need is Rico to be able to access the village,' I ended my monologue.

'And after can I just go back to Paris as normal? Divorce my gay husband – this jerk – get as much money as I can for the hell, shame and disease he put me through and forget all about this horrible fog?'

'I ... I don't know.'

'What do you mean you don't know?' Julia said this very slowly, her jaw clenched and the words barely audible.

'I don't know, Julia ...'

I was distracted. Could you escape from the fog?

'Well. Why don't we go out with Rico first so that you can be reassured you can get back to the village?' Julia squinted at me, turned, grabbed Rico by the shoulder and headed outside.

When Rico returned, he was alone.

'We got separated in the fog. I was holding her arm, the electric shock jolted my hand away and then I lost her. She wasn't in the village when I reached it. She was ahead of me so she should have been there. I am sorry Yoko.'

'No! No! No! No! No! Nooooo!' was my spontaneous reply.

'I couldn't agree more,' my father commented.

'She must be in this other countryside now.' I was thinking aloud and wincing. 'She won't be happy ... plus, none of us can go and get her; we have to wait for her to return.'

'This is a disaster,' my mother said under her breath.

'We ought to try again, this time with Rico holding her tighter,' my father added.

'I don't think that will change anything. We tried everything in London. Somehow, we always got separated,' Rico told him.

Julia banged the door shut. She was extremely pale. Rico immediately led her back outside, telling her this time he would try not to let go. Within a few minutes he returned and soon after she did too. She was crying and I felt terrible for how I had been thinking about her all day. I took her in my arms.

'Why is this happening to me? Why? First my husband and his dirt, now this! What have I done to deserve it all. And what am I supposed to do now? I have appointments with the lawyers and the hospital on Monday. I want my divorce. I want to bleed him dry for what he has done to me!'

She pushed me away from her and, between her tears, she sneered and screamed at me, 'This is entirely your fault. You brought it with you from London. That is what happened! You did this … you brought this thing with you, you selfish bitch! You should never have come here. I didn't want you here, I said it to Mum and Dad. I am not even sure you didn't do it on purpose! Maybe you knew, maybe you just wanted to ruin my life even more! I hate you! I hate you!'

She launched at me claws all out, but Rico intercepted her just in time, holding her by the waist from behind. He kept her tight while she attempted to wriggle out of his grip, screaming and scratching his arms. My sister had just gone completely mental. In the family, we knew she could just lose it and turn hysterical, but that one topped anything we had ever witnessed. She looked completely wild and mad. My father stood regally and moved towards my sister. He slapped her without hesitation. She stopped wailing and kicking and just glared at him.

'Pull yourself together, Julia. This is a crisis situation. This type of reaction isn't going to solve anything. Sit down and calm down. Now!'

My father had never raised a hand to us. He rarely even raised his voice. My sister was so shocked she obeyed. She let herself fall on the sofa heavily and just stared ahead, mouth and eyes wide open, stunned. This phase of shock did not last. Soon her face turned rigid and stern and she looked at me with loathing. I shivered and wondered how long she had been carrying this hate with her. Also, was she right? Did it come down with me, or because of me? I should have followed my instinct and not come to my parents. I felt terribly guilty for my sister's pain and not just on the fog, even though I didn't do any of it on purpose. I felt helpless and guilty despite her outburst and unfairness.

Rico walked across the room to me in the heavy silence. He hugged me and whispered in my ear, 'Have you heard from Leila?' I hadn't had a chance to check my mobile since the Julia saga started and told him so in a whisper. Maybe Leila had answered something helpful? I needed to check, so when we separated from the hug, I said with a constricted smile, 'Rico, you are such a good friend. You are right, we could do with coffee. I will go and pre-pare some.'

Outside the living room, I pulled out my mobile from my back pocket and saw the light blinking for a new email. It was from Leila. Thank God!

> Dear Yoko,
> The answer to your question is yes. It is you.
> Please do not worry: you are perfectly fine and healthy and anyone affected is also fine and healthy. Healthier even. Life is meant to be unpre-dictable for us. Your life as you knew it will never be the same but I truly believe you are meant to – and will – open new avenues in the lives of many. You have started something amazing. Otherwise why would it happen? Of course, this doesn't mean it will be easy, or appreciated by all at first; still there is much to learn.
> Do not worry. Do not be angry. This is new and you are in the midst of a transition. That is all.
> I hope tomorrow I will be able to reassure you by my sharing what I know. My knowledge is lim-ited and you may reject some of the things I will tell

you as they are extraordinary. You will get used to
it, you will see. Just, please, do not worry.
    Best regards,
    Leila

'So it is me ... It is me ...' I re-read the email several times.

My mood had slumped. It was a far cry from the kind of excitement I had come to have in London at the thought of discovering of new world, even though my excitement was tainted by
fears. Well, 'world'? I had no clue really. Maybe it was a 'door'
to somewhere on the exact opposite side of the earth as far as I
knew. And as I knew nothing, it could be anything. Leila wrote
'do not worry'. Of course I was worried! How could I not worry?
I was turning houses into foggy interspatial transporters. I was
blocking people out there too and we had no idea for how long.
Actually, that last was probably the worst of it all: my poor parents would be stuck with my hysterical sister for an indeterminate
time. They too were paying the consequences of my visit.

Just as I was winding myself up and grumbling about Leila,
I received another message from her. She seemed to have read
my mind. 'PS I know you must be very frustrated but I really can
only explain all the details face to face. Please hang in there until
tomorrow. Please don't worry. Remember the words of Rumi: "Try
not to resist the changes that come your way. Instead let life live
through you. And do not worry that your life is turning upside
down. How do you know that the side you are used to is better
than the one to come?"'

She really had to stop with her 'don't worry'. She was starting to get on my nerves with this little mantra of hers. After a
quick browse through my memory, I had the vague notion that
the Rumi she mentioned was a poet and a Sufi, a mystical branch
of Islam. She might be a keen follower, but quoting Sufi's wisdom
was not helping me at all. It hit home, yet it didn't stop my finding
the wait and repetitive 'don't worry' most irritating.

I went to the kitchen cabinet, picked up a pack of chocolate, nut and raisin cookies, put a full one in my mouth, and kept the pack firmly in my hand. When in doubt, add a little bit of sweetness to your life. Only then did I prepare coffee and put the kettle on for tea. As an afterthought, I needed something stronger and grabbed the bottle of wine left from lunch.

**Day 2 (Monday)**

I was exhausted, having hardly slept the previous night after a late return from my parents. Too many questions kept me awake as well as guilt over Julia and Eudes' new predicament. My poor innocent nephew had been affected the same way his mother had: my parents and Rico tried holding his hands or even carrying him out to the village, but each had to let go because of this fog trademarked electric repellent. No one could resist whatever it was. When with me or his mother, Eudes ended up in the wild countryside. We didn't have the heart to send him in the fog on his own. He was too young for all of this.

The only positive aspect was that he was not separated from us and stuck alone in the fog, he was with his mother. How we were to explain this to the father, I didn't know.

Julia was sending me long spiteful emails on how I 'ruined her life', 'came for the weekend on purpose', 'planned it all along out of jealousy'; how I was a 'bitch', a 'snake', the 'black sheep of the family'; and how I 'had better sort things out and fast'. She had turned her meanest, recalling and distorting memories of childhood, presenting herself as a victim and me as a calculating heartless sister. She was going too far and was unfair. I hardly believed how her memories and mine could differ so much. Feeling bad and sorry for her, I didn't fight back as I would have in normal circumstances. My parents had been in touch several times and they were very supportive of me. From their odd reactions and silences, it was obvious Julia's presence and current mood were difficult to handle. At least they enjoyed having more time with their grandson Eudes, who unlike his mother was so easy to be around. It was killing me what happened to him because of my visit. What if I had ruined his life?

My parents promised they would not mention details about Leila, Christophe de Roque or anything I had not disclosed already to my sister. It was important to tell her we were meeting a contact with information this week, but it was very hush-hush and anything related to the fog had to be kept quiet. I emphasised the 'hush-hush' as she had a tendency to tweet her life away. She was going to argue when Rico had intervened, 'Well, I wouldn't say anything if I were you until we know more. You wouldn't want your ex-husband to try and use what you disclose online to get custody of Eudes.' That silenced her! It was a good move by Rico and a painful reality punch combined. He had put the pressure on the right spot. She only hated me even more for the imposed silence. At this point, I couldn't tell the difference anymore.

At last it was Monday evening. At the airport, I sat down at one of the coffee tables outside, feeling able to breathe again. In minutes, some light would be shed through the fog. Harry, Rico and Zeno were spread over the mezzanine and I tried not to look to where they were. I had been asking myself too many questions lately and I didn't like that. It didn't serve any purpose except bringing my spirits down, as there was no answer available. Yet. Maybe worse than my spirits, this self-introspection had to stop because three packs of cookies in one and a half days was way too much for the waistband of my jeans. I looked down at my jeans. I didn't need a belt anymore and I could swear there was a slight overflow of tummy fat. At least I could still do them up, but I needed to go back to jogging.

My outfit for the encounter was very plain on purpose: standard jeans, jumper and boots. No jewellery, no accessories, basic make-up. Only a red scarf tied around my wrist stood out. The scarf was our agreed recognition sign with Leila. My winter jacket was hanging on the back of the chair. I was fiddling with my mobile. The boys had suggested using the latest voice recording application to keep all the details of the conversation for them. I would have to leave the mobile on my lap or in my bag left open for the device to capture our voices.

As nonchalantly as possible, I scanned the mezzanine and the people passing for Leila. I noticed a petite woman dragging a small wheelie bag behind her, looking at the name of the café and then screening the people. She stopped at me, lowered her eyes to the red scarf, smiled and pulled out a red scarf from her pocket that she wrapped around her wrist too. She made her way towards me; I switched on the recording app and stood up. We greeted each other with an awkward handshake and sat down. As I did so I put the phone on top of my overfilled bag, leaving it open on the chair between us. We were both struggling not to study each other in too obvious a manner.

'Would you ... like anything to drink? Juice, tea, coffee or ... hot chocolate?' I asked.

'I would love a hot chocolate, thank you.' She had a very sweet and poised voice filled with serenity. A warm smile on her face boded well for her nature.

'I will be right back,' I smiled back at her.

I went to the counter and placed the order for two large hot chocolates. My first impressions of Leila were good. Leila was petite, with middle-eastern features, in her mid-thirties and spoke with an American accent. There was something open and welcoming about her. I found her natural and sympathetic. Of course I could be completely wrong, but my gut instinct was telling me she was a decent person and that I could trust her. The woman had good vibes. It was a relief: it would have been harder to listen and trust her words if she felt wrong. To proceed with caution was still a priority in case my intuition was inaccurate, yet it was a nice start.

I walked back to the table and sat down, putting one of hot chocolates in front of her as well as some of the little packs of sugar I had picked up on the way.

'Thank you.'

'You are welcome.'

'I have been waiting a long time for this moment to arrive,' she said softly. 'This is the start of something very rare. I am very excited.' She had a big grin and was looking straight at me, her enthusiasm shining through.

'You mean the Fog?'

'Yes. The Fog and you. You see, the Fog is as rare as you are rare. From our studies, we believe there should be only seven of you creating the Fog. So you see, to have you in front of me is ...'

'Seven ... Seven like me?' I interrupted her, 'Creating the Fog? Studies? Our Studies? Who is "our"?'

'Right, sorry, as I said, I am very excited,' she in turn interrupted, 'I am much too far into the explanations already. Let's start again. So, the Fog is not a new phenomenon. It is a recurrent one. It happens every 231 years.'

'What? But how do you ...'

'Please. Oh! I thought I knew where to start but there is so much to tell you! OK, let me give you the basics first, before you ask questions.'

'Huh, yes, fine, sorry,' I replied. She laughed.

'I can tell you have learned English here, even if I don't know where you live. You've picked up the British habit of saying 'sorry' for anything and everything! Now, let's start with the Fog. It occurs every 231 years, apparently roughly in the same locations, give or take seven miles, and roughly on the same dates, give or take seven days. Yes, I see you frowned at my second mention of 'seven' and you are right. The number seven is a key number with the Fog phenomenon. I'll explain more about that later. So, we have attempted to study past openings of the Fog worldwide and although we can't be certain because of a flagrant and frustrating lack of records, we expect that for each Fog, there are seven Switchers, seven Crossers and seven Facilitators.'

'Switchers? And what?' I was finding it hard to follow. She had just started and I was already overwhelmed.

'Switchers. The Switchers are the ones who generate the Fog, like cdr69 and yourself. We call you Switchers, because you switch a place into a portal via the Fog. It is a door to another ... world. This is the most appropriate term although not entirely accurate.

I will come back to this later. The Crossers are people who have the ability to travel between the two worlds, unassisted for the newly created one, assisted for ours. Such assistance to cross the Fog back to our world is the role of the Facilitators. This is the only obvious link the Facilitators have with the Fog: they enable Crossers and Switchers to come back. A Switcher on his or her own is ... world-less. Fog-bound only. However, he or she can access the new world if accompanied by a Crosser or the old with a Facilitator.'

I didn't get it.

'Yoko?'

'I am lost. Well, I kind of understand but it is all ... blurred.'

'It is a lot to take in, I assume.'

'Yes. Maybe Leila, I could take notes. Would you mind?'

'No, of course not. Please go ahead.'

I hurriedly pulled out a notebook and a pen. I summarised what Leila had just said:

- Switchers = Fog creator. Need help to access our world (with Facilitator) and new world (with Crosser). Otherwise Fog-bound.
- Crossers = need help to access our world (with Facilitator) or direct access alone to the new world.
- Facilitators = assist Switchers and Crossers to come to our world.

I re-read it aloud to Leila to check I had captured it all correctly and she agreed. Looking down at the open page, I thought, 'So I am a Switcher, Zeno is a Crosser, Harry and Rico are Facilitators. At least now we have names for what we are doing.'

It made sense considering the facts, but all the same my head was swirling. My next thought was of Julia and Eudes. If they were Crossers, they didn't match the rule, how come Rico couldn't 'facilitate' them?'

'Leila, are Facilitators supposed to help any Crossers, no matter what Fog location? And are some people able to access the Other World but blocked until they have the right Facilitator?'

Leila was silent and studying me for a moment before replying.

'We are not sure yet about the Crossers and Facilitators having the same abilities with all the Fogs. I know what is in your mind and I think here you may be facing another issue. I mentioned three categories of people who play an active role with the Fog – Switchers, Crossers, and Facilitators – with seven people in each. Aside from them you have the ones not affected at all by the Fog, that is they cross it and nothing happens, or you have the ones who are completely affected. As an estimate, from the one location we have well documented from the past, not scientifically proven, one out of seven crossing the Fog is relocated. This quota is pretty random, it could be that twenty will not be affected and suddenly three will be completely affected. This is a tricky one.'

'I don't follow you. One out of seven what?'

'People. Relocated. I am talking about the relocation of some of the people crossing the Fog. We don't know how or why it happens to them.'

'You mean, they ... they are sent to the Other World and can't come back?'

'Yes.'

'Ever?'

'Yes.'

It took me a few minutes to gather my thoughts and get the full implications of what she had just said. I was filled with horror for Julia and Eudes.

'Oh no ... No ... no ... no ... no! Not them. Oh my God! My sister is going to kill me!' I murmured.

'Your sister has been relocated?'

'From what you are telling me, yes! She has! With her young toddler son too.'

My chest turned to stone and I found it hard to breathe. I felt like a monster. Leila listened to my brief summary of the weekend. She already knew I had Rico with me. Well, she didn't know Rico by name, but a Facilitator. I didn't give any locations either. Afterwards, she pinched her mouth in an apologetic way and confirmed, 'Indeed, I am afraid your sister has been relocated.'

I was struggling to accept the idea, trying to find an alternative. Leila could be wrong. She had to be! I had another thought and asked Leila why, if Julia was not a Crosser or a Facilitator, I was able to follow her into the Other World and was not ending up in the Fog. She replied that as a Switcher or 'Fog generator' I could follow anyone affected by the Fog to where they belonged.

I was breathing slowly; Leila patiently waited for me to recover a little from the shock. I focused on trying to think clearly. It had hardly ever been more difficult.

'Leila, the Fog, how long will I continue to create it? This 'Other World', what is it?' I asked her after a few minutes.

'The Fog is now with you for the rest of your life.'

'Jeez … So, I will create this Fog wherever I go for the rest of my life?'

'Yes and no. You only create it once a week. What day of the week did you switch your place?'

'During the night of Saturday to Sunday, nine days ago.'

'And at your parents, also from the night of Saturday to Sunday?'

'Yes,' I replied.

'That is what I thought. It seems cdr69 had the same night experience from the date of his first post,' she continued. 'So, for this Fog occurrence, places will only be switched on the night from Saturday to Sunday.'

'Right. Sleepover at friends' or boyfriends' on Saturday is now forbidden for the rest of my life?' I tried to joke but my heart was not in it.

'That would be advisable. Don't stress about it though, wait and see how things evolve. You might be surprised. Things happen for ...'

'Leila,' I interrupted her. 'You are not one of those spiritual gurus, are you? Because, honestly, it has never been my thing. I have a spiritual side of course, nonetheless all this stuff on energies and the like are often too much for me.'

'No, Yoko. I am not a guru or a life coach. I just believe life unfolds on its own and you cannot predict or stop its unfolding. You can prepare yourself the best you can, it will still surprise you. I am sure you are beginning to see that.'

'Hum ... right,' I said, thinking it was easy for her to say, not being the Switcher at this table. 'I am having another hot chocolate. One for you too?'

In truth it was cookie time. After the news that to be a Switcher is for life, I certainly deserved them. Earlier I had spotted the extra-large caramel and chocolate chip ones on display and the largest one was mine. With a bit of luck, the Fog also had calorie burning powers. It was putting me and my family in such deep trouble (to use a polite word); it could at least do something positive for me too, couldn't it? This short break was also agreed with the boys. While at the counter, I took off the red scarf and put it round my neck. It was a signal for the boys: kept on my wrist would indicate I mistrusted her and wanted out. I had almost forgotten, fascinated and shocked by her revelations. That was one more good reason for the cookie break.

I came back and sat at the table with an additional huge cookie for her. She thanked me with a smile, cut a piece and brought it to her mouth. In unison, we expressed an unexpected hum of delight. This little pause in our chat was doing me good. I was in awe of what she had told me so far, even if I had to know more.

'So, Julia, my sister, she will only be free from the Fog when I die?' I continued where we had stopped.

'She will never be free from the Fog. She has been relocated. She will never come back.'

'But if I die and the Fog disappears?'

'When the Fog disappears the door will close. She will remain in the Other World with no link to this one. Right now the portal is her link to this world. When you die, not just this portal but all the others you have opened will close simultaneously. The same for all the seven Switchers. Again the number seven. Aside from seven, the number three is key too, for example the Fog phenomenon occurs every seventy-seven times three years and there are three types of direct role linked to the Fog. The others are either in one world or the other, but not playing an active role with the Fog. At least that is what we have deduced from the information we have gathered and analysed.'

'Seven and three ... Why?'

'We don't know.' She pulled an apologetic face and I wrinkled my nose too at her recognition of ignorance. She continued, 'Those numbers have always carried strong meanings in theology, astrology, numerology and elsewhere. The number seven is said to relate to the collective consciousness, to the seeker of truth, to deeper meanings and even magical forces and esoteric. In the Bible, it is the last day of the Creation, the Word of God, and is continuously referred to as the number for completeness and perfection. In Judaism, seven is supposed to be a perfect number. In the Qur'an and the whole Islamic religion, seven is recurrent as well. I can't get into details, this is a whole other subject. Same for the number three which in the Bible relates to completeness, even if to a lesser degree than seven. It also is a time identifier with past, present and future.' She smiled then, adding, 'Personally, my preferred meaning for three is the one linked to intuition, creativity and new adventure.'

We had reached the limit of the down-to-earth approach and gone quite mystical. Something more tangible had gained my attention and I jumped at it. 'You referred earlier to "we" and "our". Who is "we"?'

'I will come to that later.' She quickly dismissed my question, returning to the earlier topic of conversation. 'I have to warn you, there is a lot we don't know. For example, if any Crossers and Switchers can be helped by any Facilitators; if a door opened by another Switcher can also be accessible by a relocated who is from another Fog which itself has been created by another Switcher. Yes ... There is plenty we do not know. In 1782 they didn't have the internet and the world was not a global village. The information they left us is limited. We have a lot of assumptions that we hope to confirm or correct this time round!' She beamed at the thought. She added, 'So exciting! Such a privilege to be a witness and study it for real. My predecessors were not so lucky.'

'Your predecessors? Leila, come on! Who is "we"?' I insisted, leaning forward, determine to make her explain. She couldn't withhold any information anymore, she had said too much already.

'OK, we are ... I know it will sound far-fetched ... We are a secret community which has been gathering information and travelling the world for centuries in preparation for the Fog recurrences. Since the last Fog closed and up until now, we were mainly researchers and administrators waiting for the next Fog to open.'

'Right ... A secret community ... Of course...' I looked at her deadpan. Had she really just said that!

'I am their members' liaison officer.'

'Uh-huh. Of course,' I commented. I was reconsidering that all of this could be a long bad dream. Real life does not involve secret societies for an average person like me.

'So my role is to liaise with all those who are involved with the Fog.'

'I see ... you are the Fog Public Relations ... is that what you put on your business card?'

Leila was looking at me with such a serious and mildly offended face, I couldn't help it, I got the giggles. It was a typical nervous reaction to all I had just learned and to the improbability of the situation. The giggles wouldn't stop and it reached the point of tears. Every time I looked at her I guffawed. The last point on a secret community was too close to Indiana Jones or the Da Vinci Code to take seriously. Poor Leila looked completely taken aback, uneasy at the attention we attracted. She finally cracked a smile, started giggling herself and that was it, and the two of us burst out laughing.

'Oh Leila. I am sorry, but you must realise, this is such a movie stereotype,' I said when finally calming down a little.

'I realise that Yoko, but it has been my life for as long as I can remember. I ...' Leila replied, wiping a tear from her eye.

'Huh? Even when you were a child?'

'My father was a researcher for them and his aunt before him. I am the one who was picked among my brothers to continue the family tradition. The rest of the family doesn't know. A secret only remains a secret if it is kept as such.'

'Sure,' I reflected on her last sentence, 'although the question is: why does it have to remain a secret? It would have been easier to cope with if the occurrence of the Fog and its effects were known. And my sister ...'

'When so few people have the control to create and access the Other World, it gives them power,' Leila replied sternly. 'Where you have powers, they risk being overused and abused either by the owner or others. There is a whole world to discover, to discover and to protect, along with those who are living in it.'

'Pardon me? "Along with the ones living in it"? You mean to say there are inhabitants in that Other World? Oh my God! Are they ... like us?' I was gaping at Leila now. Could I cope with any more big news?

'They are us,' she replied simply.

'They are us? What does that mean "they are us"?'

'Some of them are my ancestors. Relocated back then. They are the descendants of all the previous Fog occurrences.'

'Oh my God ... Oh my God...' I was stunned.

'We don't know what exactly that Other World is. We refer to it as an alternative world, or a parallel world. The geography is similar to earth. And back in 1782, the night sky and stars matched.'

I had now jumped from fiction to science fiction. 'My life can't get any better,' I thought. 'I am a Fog creator, opening portals to a parallel earth where men might still wear tights. Awesome!' I was having visions of a forest full of people cut out from history books, and not all of them looked friendly.

'Yoko?' Leila shook me out of my reverie.

'Errr ... Yes ... Sorry. Those inhabitants, could they be dangerous?'

'We don't know.'

'Ah! Bugger! Do they know about us?'

'I expect so. The crossing between worlds is a big part of their origins and history. At the last opening, they knew. However we don't know how things have evolved on their side and what information has been passed on from generation to generation.'

'And do they know about the Fog recurrence?'

'Again, we think so, but we can't know for sure.'

'So you think ...'

'We do not have all the answers, Yoko. We are placing a lot of hope in today's technology to learn more.'

'Can they ... can they come through the Fog to the house?'

'Yes.'

'Yes?'

'Yes.'

'Are you sure?'

'Yes.'

'And you don't know if they could be dangerous?'

'No, we don't know.'

'So anyone from the parallel world, possibly dangerous people, could come into our house?'

'Yes. I recommend you lock your doors. Just in case.'

'We have bay windows.'

'You may want to get some sturdy shutters.'

'Great. What if we called the police for protection?'

'Then you get your government involved ...'

'Maybe that wouldn't be a bad thing, considering ...'

'Maybe. Maybe they would respect you. Or maybe when they discover about the Other World and your ability to create the gate to it via the Fog, they will put you in a lab to study you and to understand how you do it, like a golden cage. Or maybe they will use you to open the doors in strategic places. With the very visible fog, it will be difficult for you to hide anywhere once they know. Nonetheless, maybe I am just being negative on the intentions of the government and its respect for your individuality and freedom.'

'You just summarised why we haven't contacted them yet,' I told her, the conversations within the household flashing back.

'Also, you are not the only one involved.'

'What do you mean?'

'I mean that it is not just your freedom and rights. Whoever has been affected by the Fog needs the Fog.'

'Again, what do you mean?'

'I mean that the Relocated and Crossers need you to maintain the Fog so that they can access the house – and they will want that, I expect, as a link to our world. In addition Facilitators and Crossers have to be in contact with the Fog for health purposes. If they don't cross the Fog at least once in seven weeks, they start to develop terrible migraines. They worsen until the sufferer is completely incapacitated.'

'How do you know that?'

'It was noted during the last occurrence.'

'So if I die, within forty-nine days, or seven weeks, any portals I opened would turn back to normal and any Facilitators and Crossers linked to that 'door' would suffer afterwards horrid migraines. Something like a kind of Fog-withdrawal syndrome?'

'Yes.'

'Honestly, is there anything positive about this Fog? Right now, it is more a "plague" than a "power"!'

'Having power is not always easy to carry.'

'I know, I know. "With great power comes great responsibility." It was in Spider-Man the movie.'

'Yoko ...' Leila began but I didn't let her finish.

'Leila, you seem to be a decent person. I think you are being honest with me and this is all quite fascinating. Terrifying, daunting, overwhelming but fascinating. It is all hard to believe, but mostly, the way this Fog works ... I am not impressed.'

'You will be surprised. Actually, I think you are going to love it despite the responsibilities involved. I also have the feeling you have a good bunch around you. My understanding is that you have a Facilitator with you, don't you?'

'Yes.'

'You have a Crosser with you as well, don't you?'

I remained silent. It was like answering in the affirmative anyway.

'Yoko, you have so far encountered a Crosser, a Facilitator, a Relocated ... That should help you believe the rest of what I am telling you. Anything more I should know from your side? It could be important ...'

I wasn't sure about telling her we had a second Facilitator in the house. As I was hesitating, she asked another question.

'Yoko, are they here? Have they accompanied you?'

Her questions took me by surprise. I half-answered her. 'They're on standby if I need them to come right away.'

I picked up my mobile and texted the boys, 'She guessed we are three people affected in different ways by the Fog. Do any of you want to meet her?'

Leila waited until I was done to continue.

'Yoko. I understand that you wish to protect your identities and location. I wish to make you an offer. Our research is available to you. We can help you deal with the new, and later, with the unknown. We are neutral, Yoko, we are not a cult or anything like that. We are more like guardians of sensitive information, information that is too sparse and of which we aim to gather more this time round. We are historians mixed with scientists.'

'You are geeks really.' I was only half-joking.

'Hun? No ... Not really.'

'Geeks are not that bad, you know. Actually geekiness is even fashionable lately.'

My mobile beeped. Zeno had replied that the three of them wanted to meet her. However, they didn't want it to happen there. They were in agreement to bring her back to the house, blindfolded to protect our address. They trusted my judgement if I believed her trustworthy.

Bringing her back home was not a logical choice: we didn't know her, she could be wired or with a location tracker and I didn't want any more guilt on my conscience. On the other hand we needed to know as much as possible. The others had a right to hear the information first hand too. Plus a bit of trust would not go amiss in the mess we were in.

'Why not? After all, she has answers Wikipedia hasn't,' I whispered to myself.

'Sorry?' said Leila.

Leila gasped at my suggestion to go to the 'portal' and meet the others, repeating 'yes' several times with a broad grin. I pointed out to her that coming to the house, she could be affected or even be relocated. Her grin disappeared and she leaned back in her chair. She confirmed that she could and didn't mind. She had prepared herself for the eventuality. She would still continue her work from the other side, focusing on the research and directly experience it as well. She had no other plans for the evening except seeing me; she was staying in the Society's little flat by Paddington Station, chosen for its easy airport access as well as being quite central. It unsettled me a little that she was staying in our neighbourhood. It didn't last. I had passed the point of being surprised.

I received another message from Zeno. He informed me they had left a bag for me at the coffee counter to pick up fast before it created a bomb alert. My mobile screen showed a notification of a message from cdr69. I would check it later. It reminded me that I still had to discuss his case with Leila. I took the bag left for me and went to the bathroom to peruse the contents. There was a note saying 'cash for the cab journey from the station (waste a good half hour cruising around) + Mask for Leila (Rico's)'. I looked at the mask. A lovely pink satin mask with black velvet lining, with the inscription 'Get down and dirty'. Nice ... it wasn't necessary to indicate it was Rico's in the note, I would have guessed. Was he carrying this type of thing in his pockets at all times? Really!

Leila and I headed to the Heathrow Express. She just followed me in silence. As we waited for the train, the boys arrived on the platform one by one, trying to be as discreet as possible. Harry held an evening paper under his arm and opened it as soon as he had checked when the next train was due. Zeno was quite cool, on his mobile chatting away in Italian. Rico was just Rico enhanced: a caricature of the macho Italian man, one hand in his pocket and smiling cheekily to any girl on the platform. The train was relatively full and not the best place to resume conversation on the Fog topic. I sat next to Leila and by way of chitchat asked her if she had had a good flight. She hesitated and fetched her bag, pulling out her flight tickets. The first thing I read was her full name, Leila Al-Safidi, then I noted the airport of departure, JFK airport, New York. I raised my eyes.

'New York? Or its vicinity?' I inquired.

'New York. Manhattan. It is a good place to be anonymous and to access a lot of information. Also a good place to travel from and to.'

'And you travel much?'

'That depends on the ongoing research and leads. We split all the roles, everyone doing some research, analysis etcetera. That said, my main role the past few years has been to prepare for being a contact point.'

We remained silent for the rest of the fifteen minute train journey. Once in the street, I hailed a cab even though our house was less than ten minutes' walk away. Using a page of my notebook, I wrote the first destination that crossed my mind, the Royal Albert Hall, just across the park. The idea was also to repeat the process and change cabs often for half an hour. I reversed the mask to hide the writing and placed it on Leila's face, gave the note to the driver and told him it was part of a surprise hen weekend. The taxi driver just smiled. Not even an eyebrow rose. Good old London cabbies, they have seen it all. You've got to love them. We changed taxis four times, every time with different directions to the driver. After thirty-five minutes, lighter by far more than £30 (that's when you stop loving London cabs), we made it home or almost. The last cab stopped round the corner in a quiet street and we made the rest of the journey on foot, with me helping her walk blindfolded. When we arrived home, a most of the lot's houses already had their lights off for the night. Our house was in a pool of blackness, of course. I led Leila through the Fog. As I opened the door, the house smelled of sautéed onions, basil and tomato, and I could see through the open door of the kitchen Rico was grating some parmesan. Rico stopped when he saw us, wiped his hands and followed us to the living room without a word. Zenone and Harry were already there waiting. A bottle of wine was opened and five glasses on the table, three of them already in use.

I took the mask off Leila's eyes. She looked at the two men in front of her with a wide smile and they came to greet her. She turned to say something to me, freezing when she noticed Rico behind me. I noted her surprise and pre-empted her question. 'Leila, we are four in the house. I am the Switcher, Zenone is the Crosser, and both Rico and Harry are Facilitators.'

The boys were looking at me frowning. It just dawned on me they had never heard those titles before!

'Sorry, but I think you two are way ahead in this discussion,' Harry intervened. 'Maybe, you could fill us in?'

'Ahem ... Over dinner? Because I am starving and the pasta is ready,' Rico interjected.

Zenone was already on his way to pick up the pots in the kitchen. Leila and I unpeeled several layers of warm clothes. I took my mobile and notebooks out of my handbag, in the hope I could just replay the recording over dinner to bring the boys up-to-date. Leila started to fidget at my words and said nervously, 'I should have been more careful. I had been given a little device that creates white noise stopping such recordings. I was so excited to meet you, I forgot to switch it on. Please, you will delete it, won't you?'

'Yes, I will when we finish listening,' I told her with a smile.

When we reached the end of the recording, there was a moment of silence before the boys shared their reactions.

'Wow ...' Zeno said.

'Indeed,' Harry added.

'... Cazzo,' Rico ended.

'I'm sorry but ... would you mind if I go out and check if I have been affected by the Fog now?' Leila asked in an apologetic tone. We realised she must have dying to check from the minute she came inside the house. She had not even raised the subject until now. We all stood at once, everyone agreeing it was overdue. Rico went first to wait for her on the parking lot in front of the house and Zeno went to the forest, to greet her there in case she had been relocated. Both were discreetly on the phone ready to update Harry and me in the house. Sure, she seemed trustworthy and provided us with what seems to be valuable information, but we still didn't know much about this Society of hers, so Rico was also ready to stop her checking our whereabouts.

It took less than ten minutes to try all the combinations and establish Leila was not a Relocated, not a Switcher, not a Crosser and not a Facilitator. She was not Fog-affected. A side of her was disappointed, we could tell.

'So, Leila, what can you tell us about your geek Society?' Harry asked.

'We are not geeks ...'

'You are more adventurer-historians scouring the planet in search of mysterious information on an unknown world. So Indiana Jones. Cool!' Zeno interrupted.

'Neither. Not geek, not adventurer. We are ...' Leila was still not impressed by our vision of the Society.

'A religious cult,' I joked, and said as an afterthought, 'Actually, your Society doesn't have religious doctrines and proselytising, does it?'

'No, we do not. As I said, we are just a mixture of scientists and historians, chosen within the families of our elders. Lately we had to recruit more, but we are very thorough in checking people's backgrounds.'

'What is the name of your Society?' Harry raised a good point.

'We don't have an official name or status,' Leila hesitated. She seemed willing to talk about everything related to the Fog but less confident if not reluctant to discuss this 'Society' of hers.

'You must refer to it as something, no?' Harry pushed.

'Well ... We call ourselves the Society ... Simply.'

'How original,' I couldn't help commenting.

Harry turned to me and added, 'Definitely geeks.'

'Yep,' Rico said with a nod.

'In centuries, you couldn't come up with something with a bit more oomph to it?' Zeno asked.

'Huh ... that wasn't really a priority, I mean ... what is wrong with "Society"?' Poor Leila looked so apologetic, the whole household took pity.

'Oh Leila, so sorry. We are just teasing you,' I told her, putting my hand on her back in a comforting gesture.

'I guess it is a good sign. We are feeling comfortable enough around you to do so,' Harry further reassured.

'Oh! Then, thank you!' Leila replied and laughed.

I looked down at my mobile and remembered the unread message from cdr69.

'Leila, about the other houses switched ...' I didn't have time to finish my sentence.

'Yes, I wanted to tell you about that,' Leila broke in. 'We found more. In addition to here and Marrakech, we found one in Italy. I need to go and visit all these places this week. You guys are dealing with the situation quite well, I hope it will be the case with everyone else too.'

'Where in Italy?' Zeno and Rico asked in unison.

'Rome.'

'More Italians!' Zeno said, smiling.

'It is more complicated than that. The Switcher is an American student temporarily in Rome. There are two Italian Crossers and, so far, no Facilitators. You have two, so it is possible they won't find any around. Really, we need to confirm if a Facilitator from one Fog can help a Crosser or Switcher from another Fog.'

'How do we know they are Crossers and not Relocated, as they haven't been back in our world?'

'Because their nails have gone opaque.'

'What?' The boys and I immediately stared down at our fingernails. I couldn't see if mine had turned opaque or not, my nails being painted taupe. The Italians and Harry confirmed that their nails were now opaque white.

'The three categories – Switcher, Crosser and Facilitator – all seem to have a slight body reaction to being bound to the Fog. It affects their nails, turning them whitish opaque, and their irises turn a lighter shade, for example, from brown eyes to light chestnut.'

'Wow. So me …?' I asked. Leila stood up and came to check my irises, turning my head towards the light.

'You have grey eyes. How did they use to look?'

'Black. Jet black.' I went to the downstairs bathroom's mirror to see for myself. I couldn't really see, so I took my mobile and lit up my face with the flashlight.'

'It's true! They are grey. This is weird!' I exclaimed. All the boys stood up and joined me in front of the mirror and sure enough, their irises had changed. How come none of us had noticed it before?

'So, only the seven people in each of the three groups, twenty-one people in total, have this effect of opaque nails and lighter irises? The Relocated don't?' Harry asked.

'No, they don't.'

'This is why you kept looking at your hands during dinner before you knew if you were affected by the Fog or not?' Rico noted.

'Yes, but I wasn't sure how quickly the change occurs.'

'We can't help you there. We only just noticed it at all.'

'That is a question I will have to ask the ones in Marrakech or Italy,' Leila mused, in a note-to-self manner.

'Ah! Cdr69, I meant to tell you: from what I understand so far, in Marrakech they have a Switcher and two either Relocated or Crosser. One is four months pregnant. No Facilitator as far as I know, but I have an email from cdr69 I haven't read yet. It arrived during our meeting in Heathrow.'

I picked up my mobile, opened the email and read it aloud. I shouldn't have.

> Dear Yoko,
> Where the hell are you?!
> You write you can help, I ask for help and you
> go AWOL on me! This is so messed up. I told you
> about my situation, how horrible it is for me here.
> Don't leave me like this! Either you can really help
> and do something, or fuck off!
> This is a real nightmare!
> Christophe

'OK, he is a confirmed jerk,' I thought. Even if I understood his distress, he didn't have to be so aggressive or selfish about it. While I was quietly fuming at his tone, the boys updated Leila on Christophe de Rocque's situation. When they finished, Leila commented, 'I have the feeling that group is not going to be among the easy ones to deal with.'

'I, for one, will be happy to pass on the communication to your expert hands,' I said.

'Expert in theory only. We haven't had a chance to confirm our postulations and knowledge in practice, not since our ancestors way back,' Leila corrected.

'Still, better you than me to deal with him,' I retorted. 'I don't rate that guy.'

'It would help me if you would still make an effort though,' she pleaded with eyes reminding me of a puppy begging for a treat.

'Why? Aren't you taking over?' I grimaced.

'Because it will be in your interest to ally yourselves with others like you and help each other,' Leila answered. 'We are happy to support you and help you as much as we can, but all of you who are affected should also be there for each other. It wasn't possible in the previous Fog occurrences, what with distance and lack of easy and fast communication. Now you can. You all share a rare experience. Nobody else other than you guys can understand better what you are each going through. Some might struggle to cope and will need someone who can understand them. Once we have checked if the Fog is the same for everyone, you could share responsibilities to switch, cross, or facilitate.'

'Great,' I grunted.

'Yoko, the guys in Rome seem quite nice.'

'Of course. They are Italians,' Rico noted, smug.

'The two Italians are Leo and Dante. The American is Jack,' Leila commented.

'Fiiine. I know, I know … You are right. Let's just hope that this Christophe aka cdr69 aka sore-pain-in-the-butt is a solitary case of antipathy among the Fog people,' I conceded. I decided to change the subject and asked on a lighter note, 'So, what will our wonderful little group with special powers be called? The Transfoggers? The Fogtastics?'

'We have always referred to you just as the Foggies,' Leila stated.

'The Foggies? You are joking!' I pulled a face.

'No way!' Zeno exclaimed. He had been pretty silent so far.

'Ma no, non voglio essere un Foggy,' Rico grunted, clearly unhappy to be classed as a Foggy.

Harry remained silent. As he was the only one who had not commented, I turned to look at him and saw why. He was looking down at his plate, struggling not to burst out laughing.

'What is wrong with Foggies?' Leila asked.

'Sounds like Fogies,' Harry replied immediately, 'like fussy old-fashion oldies.'

'Or Froggies,' I added. 'Which is not something my French side appreciates that much …'

'Or Frosties. And I don't want to be some type of cereal,' Zeno remarked.

Before Rico had a chance to express why he didn't like it either, Leila put an end to the subject.

'Until you come up with something better or that everybody likes, it is and will stay "the Foggies". We have used it for years and it works well,' she said softly but firmly. 'It's not that important anyway, is it?'

'Well, it is for us,' I whispered, laughter simmering in my throat. I just thought it could have been worse, it could have been Foggers, sounding terribly similar to 'F***ers.'

She dismissed me and continued, 'OK, seriously, there is much to do and organise. Anytime soon, some of you will encounter people from that Other World and we need to be ready to meet them, whoever they are, especially as they may not be friendly. I am not even commenting on the attention this Fog is bound to attract in cities and the need to look after the Relocated.'

Harry's contained giggles had been contagious and only Leila was not stifling a laugh. The last point calmed me down. Remembering Julia and Eudes' situation was definitely a kill-joy.

She looked round at us and sighed, 'I am sorry. It is great you are all relatively relaxed and keeping it good-humoured. I need to remain focused. Time is of the essence and we need to get on with it. The Foggies community should get started as soon as possible. The sooner you liaise with each other, the better. We have set up a safe platform for you guys to communicate online. Even though it is late, maybe I could quickly brief you about it? I am afraid I have to be on another plane to Italy tomorrow around noon.'

Unsurprisingly we all wanted to hear what she had to say.

Leila went on to explain what the Society suggested. It was frustrating not to know much about the Society, the people who comprised it, their base and research, but we couldn't expect to know everything in one night. One thing was for certain, before agreeing anything concrete with them, we would demand to know more.

First, Leila explained about their communication device for the Foggies. She had brought in her wheeled bag three high-tech hand-size tablets, set up with the latest protection, secure email and a video conference system for safe communication between users. She would request a fourth one tomorrow for the unexpected Facilitator. She took time to demonstrate how everything worked. The tablets were mainly for use within the Foggies community, although there was a direct link to message or call her. There was a Society emergency contact too, in case she did not respond. In brief, the page appeared pretty much like a minimalist Facebook with six categories: Switcher, Crosser, Facilitators, Society, Relocated and External. There was also a map on which a fog symbol was pinned over England (she explained they had put it there temporarily until they got our location), Rome and Marrakech. On Leila's profile, there was a mobile number with the option to call. I looked up and raised my eyebrow. She confirmed that each tablet was provided with a secure line to call as well. The Relocated page was simpler with two subsections: a currently empty list for names and their mailboxes.

'We won't be able to provide a secure tablet to every Relocated. In any case they will only be able to use them in a portal house with internet and phone signal access, so we are thinking of providing one Relocated network for each Foggy portal, with key contacts for support. The Relocated page will be where you can liaise with them and keep track of what is happening. We will have to work tightly all together to keep a tab on communications and security and be there to support everyone involved.'

'It feels like we are entering a brand new club, or even a family,' I commented slowly, a bit in awe. 'They say you don't choose your family, I presume you don't choose your Foggies.'

'What about the black sheep of the family?' Harry asked.

'What do you mean?' Leila asked, frowning.

'Well, how do you know everyone will follow the security rules and not talk? Every family has a black sheep. If the Foggies are like family ...'

'As long as people use their brains ...' Leila began.

'If they know how,' Harry interrupted. 'Stupidity should be taxed. People would make more effort to think.'

Leila continued, 'As I mentioned, you Foggies need each other. A black sheep would lose any support from you. Imagine a Switcher without a Crosser and Facilitator: Fog-bound for life. Or a Crosser cut out from accessing the Fog portal: no more modern world and migraines. The only ones who don't lose much are the Facilitators, but they would get the debilitating migraines after seven weeks. As for us, the Society is intent on making sure that everyone is OK. We are not forcing you to do anything, we just withdraw our support if we disagree though.'

'How do you do that? I mean, how come you can finance so much research, technology and support? And apparently offer it for free?' a suspicious Harry asked, while Zeno and Rico were playing with their new high-tech toys. I clearly heard Rico asking Zeno if they could also download apps and play together online and on their separate tablets. Leila heard too and chose to ignore it. She focused on the more serious question from Harry instead.

'The Society has been around since the last portal opening in 1782. We have had time to plan ahead with sound investment in the long term to very long term. We have a banking and property branch to support our financial needs and a private university at our disposal for our research. It is very practical for scientific and historical research, or for justifying our travelling and nose-poking activities to the authorities. Of course, only some key people at the university are aware of why we do what we do, or even what we do: the ones who have been chosen by the elders in the Society. We are a very big family too.'

'So, you DO have geeks in your university who set up the whole tablet and social platform, right?' Rico asked, lifting his eyes up from the tablet.

'What is it with you guys and this obsession with geeks!' Leila exclaimed, her eyes round.

'We like geeks,' I replied.

'Yeah, but only the nice geeks, not the arrogant geeks, or the geeks who try to conquer the world, like in movies,' Rico added.

'Thank you Rico, for this clarification,' Harry sighed and shook his head. It had always been strange how those two got on so well and were so different.

'Maybe next time I'll wear glasses, just for you,' Leila said, the corner of her mouth raising just that little bit into a complicit smile.

There was one more tiny detail to go into with Leila. A tiny very important detail.

'So I get why we have to support each other. It was obvious from the start in this house, even if it was pure kindness from Rico and Harry. However, what do you at the Society get in return for helping us and supporting us?'

'Knowledge and peace.'

Harry rolled his eyes, 'Don't tell me you are behind the Miss World competition too?'

Leila had got used to ignoring his sarcasm. She explained further, 'We have some data about the Fog, but most is missing. We also know our ancestors directly witnessed or suffered abuse linked to the control of the Fog. We want to limit it this time round. Perhaps we are idealists, yet this Other World has huge potential; we have already damaged this one so much, our dream is to avoid a repeat in the other one. Both sides of the door could benefit from the openings. The knowledge we are to gain is phenomenal, for example on the air quality, the other animal species and the vegetation. Consider us as the guardians of the Fog and the Fog-affected people. To simplify: if this was a movie, I would say we are the good guys trying to protect the newly empowered Foggies against the greedy bad guys. Why? Just because we love this earth and have faith in people. We are not religious; we are actually a mixed bunch with several faiths or approaches to life. What we have in common is that we all have faith and we are against the damage done to this planet. Imagine, the oceans have a surface bigger than western Europe covered by plastic bags. Whole species are extinct, basic natural resources such as woods are devastated. I won't even get into the wars and how humans treat each other. Maybe the Other World can help save this one. And maybe we can help save the Other World from this one.'

Leila paused, deep in thought, before whispering to herself, 'Yes, we are probably idealists ...'

'What bad guys?' Rico asked. The bad guys allusion had made me shiver as well, even if her speech and her 'Save the planet' crusade were all very nice.

Leila took her time to answer. 'Let's just hope that a Fog will not occur in North Korea. We have limits as to where and what we could do in certain locations, should the doors fall into the wrong hands. Any illicit product or illegal activities could be set up there. Bombs, missiles, weapons storage could be built in that Other World without any one's knowledge, then easily smuggled back into our world through the portal. Relocated children trade, slavery, drugs even, by government or private corporations alike. Let's make one thing clear: your existence will be known. This is unavoidable in this world of global information. What matters is that you are ready to face it when it happens, to face the pressure and that you are protected and in a position to defend your rights and what is right. We want you to know you are not alone. Of course, we are also hoping we can advise and help you make the decision that benefits the whole picture, not just you or someone else. Ideally, you will be independent, notably financially, so as not to be influenced or manipulated. We are not here to rule, but neither should you. For all of this, we have prayed that the Fog would pick wisely the ones it affects. So far, so good.'

Leila's speech left a strong impression on me. Good versus evil; bad nasty people out there; the threat of international drug cartels. It was an impressive tirade. I was feeling very small suddenly, quite insignificant in fact.

The room was plunged into a heavy silence until Zeno broke it. 'Then maybe we should live somewhere high up on a mountain or alone on an island where no one would find us?'

'We should also stop inviting people or letting people come into the house, to avoid relocation?' It was a recurrent thought of mine that I voiced for the first time.

Leila shook her head. 'Hiding is not going to work. Some people know of the Fog, as a legend, a folk tale, or even as a spiritual phenomenon supposed to happen after December 2012. They believe it is true, keeping their eyes and ears open for the unusual and extraordinary.'

'Are you going to tell us that this is what the Mayan calendar was referring to as the end of the world as we know it, predicted December 2012? Come on ...' I had never taken to this story and didn't want to start believing in it now.

'No one really knows what they were referring to,' Leila winked at me. She was messing with me. Good, about time she got her own back.

'Still, if we moved to a remote place which would be difficult to find, we would at least protect the people from being relocated by accident. Plus we would be less visible,' Zeno said, returning to his earlier comment.

'You would think so. However, if one person finds out and spreads the word, the new location would turn into a place of pilgrimage for all those who wish for another chance in life. The Fog offers a new place, a new beginning and a new start. Oh, did I mention it before? The Fog has some healing faculties. The crossing of the Fog heals it somehow. Those who are affected by the Fog don't get sick. Well, they can break a leg, hurt themselves, but they don't have viruses, microbes, or infections. We have data that makes us think that it applies to the Relocated as well. It is as if the Fog cleans you when you go through it, preparing you to be transferred without transferring diseases and viruses too. So yes, the people going through the Fog face the risk of having their lives turned upside down, and it can also improve or even save them.'

'So in short, you mean we need to live our life and let what is meant to happen, happen? I summarised.

'Yes.'

'So you believe in fate?' I persisted.

'I believe we make our own choices in life and that also means we can choose to have faith in life. Call it instinct, sixth sense, gut feeling, vibes, we are all looking for the signs life puts in our path. Afterwards, it is up to you to follow them or not. I think we should. Sometimes we should even choose to let life guide us. By trying to control our lives all the time, we miss the signs.'

'Leila,' Zeno interrupted. 'Are they all like you in the Society? All with this spiritual and inspirational vision?'

'More or less, I presume. We choose to dedicate our life to this project because we share the same idea and approach to life.'

'So you think that maybe I haven't ruined my sister's life by having her relocated? That it is what was meant to happen and I shouldn't blame myself?' I asked, genuinely interested by her reasoning.

'If you need to blame someone, you can blame me. I decided not to tell you about the possibility because I didn't feel I had the right to interfere with your actions or tell you what to do and what not to do. Still, was your sister in a good place in the current world?'

'Not really ...'

'Do you think she could do with a new start?'

'Well ... Yes ... But she would probably argue that point.'

'She will get round it. Anyway, you didn't intentionally send her there. You didn't know. Also, remember, you did not choose to be a Switcher, no more than the others in this house chose their links to the Fog. Whether a coincidence or some kind of selection totally incomprehensible to any of us, it happened; now you now have to deal with it. The same applies to her and will apply to more people after her. Increasingly more people, I expect.'

'What do you mean increasingly?' We all reacted together on that one, although Harry's voice was louder and clearer than the rest of us.

'It is only assumptions.' Leila shook her head. 'There is so much I long to discover and confirm!'

The boys and I looked at each other. We silently agreed we wanted in on the Society's support and knowledge. I held my mobile up and pointed to the Fog. The boys nodded.

'Leila, another thing you may want to know.' I had a little detail for her she might appreciate. 'Mobile phone and internet: they work around the house in the Other World too.'

'What!' Leila cried out.

'Yes, we actually were able to do video conference calls from the forest in the Other World,' I continued. We told her about our experience visiting the grounds around the house and what we had observed. It was limited and I wrapped it up in twenty minutes. Zeno only interrupted once to mention the wolves and ask if they could provide some kind of animal gun with sleeping ammunition.

At the end of my little speech, Leila was on the edge of her seat, taking notes (much more efficiently than me earlier that evening). It was past 4 a.m. and it had been a long evening. Apart from Leila, everyone was fighting against sleep. She noticed.

'Let's call it a night,' she said. 'We have covered quite a lot of ground and it is very late. If you agree I will give the Rome guys a tablet and tell them you are equipped with one too. Would it be fine with you? Would you mind contacting them?

'Of course not!' the whole household replied.

'What about cdr69?' I added.

Leila thought she could be on her way to meet him from midweek if he gave her the go ahead. We wrote via the kymsonline email address to inform him:

> Dear Christophe,
>     Sorry for my silence. I have also had a few things
> to deal with here. As you wrote so expressively, this
> is not an easy situation, no more for me than for
> you. I would appreciate your understanding.

Someone will be coming to Marrakech this week to provide you with some valuable information and some help. Would you agree to meet this person? Your situation will not change though, it will just be informed.

Please let me know if you are happy to receive such a visit and if yes, would you provide me with your address. The meeting will have to be at yours as you cannot leave it. I have just met this person and found it very instructive. I highly recommend you meet her.

Best regards,

Yoko.

The tone of his last message was not pleasant and we ought to mention it, even if subtly. If we were meant to 'work' with each other as Foggies in the future, the man should be aware he could not just lash out at me without my reacting.

It was time to say goodbye for the night. Zeno gave Leila a lift back to the Society's flat by scooter. She said that as we were giving away our address, she was happy to give away hers. So far she and the Society had been fair, even generous in giving us the tablets. We still didn't know if they had ulterior motives or not. We would have to wait and see. More discoveries were to come. Leila and I hugged each other goodbye.

'Leila, thank you!' I smiled, dead on my feet.

'No, thank you. For your trust, for sharing and for welcoming me so nicely into your house. I think we'll get on. Everything will be fine, you'll see,' she replied with a huge grin.

'I hope so.'

'Goodnight, Yoko.' She disappeared into the black of the Fog.

This had been the most fruitful and instructive encounter I had ever had, even though many questions remained unanswered. I closed the door and went to bed. I still had to go to the office in the morning. It was going to be a long, long day.

**Day 3 (Tuesday)**

It was barely mid-morning. I was at my desk on my fourth cup of coffee. A double espresso this time: the previous three single cups just didn't seem to have had any effect. I was getting too old for barely three hours sleep. It was not to be my most productive day at work.

When I called my parents on my walk to work earlier, they put the phone on speaker so that my sister could hear the gist of the explanation provided by Leila. The point on relocation generated tears and screams. I insisted on the need for discretion for Julia's benefit especially. Most of the time, when Julia asked further questions, my replies were that we didn't have all the answers. I didn't want to get into too many details either, trying to keep it simple. When she started to ask about her situation, how she would deal with their disappearance from Paris and what to say to the father, I was at loss as to what to reply. There was no solution to offer, making me feel pretty useless and bad. Guilt came rushing back. I also reminded them that we still had not discussed the serious matter that was the reason for my visit the past week. After some silence, they replied that considering the circumstances, they would rather wait to be sure before telling me. As they had a lot to deal with already, with Julia's presence and distress, I did not insist despite my being worried.

Christophe de Rocque had replied first thing in the morning. He was very excited at the prospect of help coming to him. He dismissed my situation as 'not possibly being as bad as his, except if I was also stuck between an hysterical wife and lover in the same house while fearing for my life'. He was obviously the type of person who empathised that others have a life as well, that even though their problems might not be the same as his, they were still problems ... some stereotypes can be true: there was such thing as the annoying arrogant Frenchman. I decided not to wind myself up, ignored his comment and wrote back that his details would be passed on to Leila. He could deal with her directly from now. Sorry Leila.

Our little household planned another brainstorming at dinner that Tuesday. We also had to work out how best to proceed with what we had learned barely twenty-four hours before. For years we had kept an open house where people could pop in as they wished. Now, if we were lucky and people called or texted when in the neighbourhood before stopping by, we could stop them coming. Today we had to decide: should we let people come in with the risk of them being relocated? Or should we continue to keep our family and friends out of the house? In the past ten days, the people who visited us like the firemen or Zeno's employee, had been unaffected by the Fog. To avoid the postman and other junk mail distributors having to cross the Fog, Zeno had placed a temporary mailbox outside the front gate. I doubted the leaflet distributors would have crossed the Fog in any case, but our postman was a thorough man who enjoyed a good chat. Plus he was a purebred old-fashioned English man who would not be daunted by a bit of Fog, right?

Despite Leila's 'Faith in Life', my point of view was that we couldn't let people in knowing the consequences. It was difficult enough to cope with Julia being relocated because of me when I didn't even know then it could happen!

It was 7 p.m. Rico was in the kitchen preparing more pasta; I was in the living room setting the table and thinking that I ought to introduce more vegetables into my diet. Harry was sitting on the sofa sipping wine and grading essays. The sound of a scooter's engine outside the house indicated Zeno was back. After a few minutes, the front door opened with some unexpected banging and scratching. Upon checking, I saw Zeno was pushing his scooter into our small hallway, leaving only a minimal space on the side for him to squeeze through to get inside. Taking off his helmet, he announced that tomorrow he would explore the forest on his scooter. He advocated my going with him to watch his back and film the exploration. I loved the idea! It would be such a cool way to explore! We both started jumping up and down in excitement. Literally. Harry spoke from the living room. 'Hey, you kids! There are no roads in the forest. Ain't going to work.'

'I've had country tyres put on, and got a full tank. I have even fitted a spare fuel container underneath my legs to be safe. It will work.' Zeno counter-argued. He said to me, 'Knowing you, you won't take time off. So I am thinking of going tomorrow first thing in the morning or early evening when there is still light. What do you think? With the scooter, we will feel safer, see more and wolves won't bother us.'

'Zeno, do you know what is in the forest?' Harry retorted as Zeno and I entered the living room. 'Trees. Everywhere. Forget it. You'll be faster on foot. At best a mountain bike, if you were pro.'

I laughed. 'Give it up Harry! You know we'll do it anyway! Because you are so right, we ARE big kids.'

'No!' Rico shouted from the kitchen. 'I don't like it! Scooters are noisy: it will be like trumpeting to the locals you are there.'

'Exactly,' Zeno said. 'We take the lead and show them some of our technology. Let's demonstrate we have powerful stuff.'

'Good point, although we don't want to intimidate them either,' I thought. 'Anyway, they can't be in the close vicinity, otherwise they would have knocked at the door already, no?'

Just then, we heard a knock at the door.

'Anyone expecting anyone?' Harry asked. No one was. Zeno went to the door, as best as he could with the scooter in the way. I heard the bubbly voice of Jazz saying hello.

Jazz was one of my closest friends. She was a petite and bubbly half English, half Indian woman, with (fake) blonde long wavy hair and caramel-coloured skin. When I write petite, I mean very petite although her exact height remained a mystery as she always wore the highest pair of heels on sale. She bore a constant smile on her face and had gorgeous curves attracting much attention from the men. Jazz was a successful property manager in her late twenties and spent much of her hard earned money on her passions for fashion (especially shoes – obviously) and jewellery. Despite sounding a high maintenance woman, it was only partly true. She also had a down-to-earth and relaxed side, especially in our house. That was one of the reasons why she loved coming round to visit. I loved spending time with her and her impromptu visits. Except now.

'Jazz, hey!' I went to give her a not-so-enthusiastic hello kiss.

'Nice to see you too ...!' She said sarcastically.

'Sorry hon! My mind was just ... somewhere else!'

'Somewhere nice? Man involved?'

I grunted and replied no. She squeezed past the scooter to the living room and sat down on the sofa.

'What's with the scooter?' She asked. I only had to reply, 'Zeno ...' for her to laugh and say 'Who else!' She explained she was in the neighbourhood to meet friends for a drink later and thought she would pop in and check if I felt any better than the previous Monday. I frowned at her words.

'My dear friend, I know you,' she commented as she sat on the sofa in front of Harry. 'You don't party on a Monday. You had something heavy on your mind. Anyway, you look better.' She said as she sniffed the air approvingly to the scent of the tomato sauce coming from the kitchen. Her next question was the one I dreaded. 'It is weird thing outside your house. I couldn't see a thing, just like pitch dark black. Ah! And your trip, your parents, how are they? And your sister, was she bearable?'

Zeno came in and asked her if she could move her car. Jazz just looked at him and asked why, as she wasn't parked on the lot. Jazz never goes anywhere walking with those heels of hers. She doesn't 'do' walking. It was fair to assume her car was outside and it was just Zeno's bad luck that for once she wasn't parked in the lot. Zeno awkwardly explained a neighbour had noticed there was a problem. It was clear to the other boys and me what he was up to: he wanted to test her being affected or not by the Fog. Harry stood up and went out without uttering a word to meet her in the lot should she end up there as normal. Jazz left with Zeno, commenting that we were all weird, or more exactly weirder than usual. Alone in the living room, I started praying, 'Please let her reach London, please let her reach London, please let her reach London ...'

When I heard a high pitched 'YOKO!' and Zeno saying 'It's OK, Jazz. Don't worry, it's OK', I braced myself.

'Yoko!' Jazz burst into the room. 'How did he do it? I walked out with Zeno and we were not in the parking lot. It was dark, but it looked like ... It looked like there were trees. I started to walk to check, but Zeno stopped me and said that it was too dark and the forest was dangerous. "The forest"? What is it all about?'

'You were in a forest.' From the corner of my eye, I saw Zeno and Harry, who had both returned, leave the room to let me explain the situation to Jazz. She didn't appear to notice.

'Well, I know it wasn't the normal parking lot, that's for sure. My heels sank in the ground.' As she said that, she looked down at her shoes. 'Nooo! Look at them, they are ruined. Is that ... grass?'

'You were in a forest, Jazz. It's the Fog.'

'Fog? What fog?'

'The Fog that surrounds the house and the reason why it was so dark when you came in.'

Jazz put both her hands in front of her to indicate stop. She shook her head and said, 'Yoko, you are making me freak out now. What on earth are you talking about?'

'You shouldn't freak out yet. Wait until I've finished talking.'

'Yoko ... now I am starting to be really worried. What is up? How did he do that?'

'He didn't do anything, Jazz, the Fog did. And, the Fog apparently comes from me.'

'You are making no sense! Are you on drugs or something? Have you been drinking? It is Rico, isn't it? He gave you one of his joints ...'

'Jazz, I am going to ask you to walk out of the house and when you reach the gate, if you are still in the Fog, to tie a rope to your waist and walk five steps. Look around to find out if you are on the parking lot, in a forest clearing, or … nowhere. Then come back and tell me.'

'Yoko, is it a joke? Have you lost your mind?'

'I mean it Jazz. It is very, very, very important. Please do it. Trust me.' Because of my seriousness, she stopped arguing. She let me lead her to the hallway. Her face betrayed a mixture of confusion, worry – for my mental health probably – and fear. For one brief instant I considered suggesting she changed shoes, but then they had already been smudged so I didn't bother.

Zeno was at the door already, a knife in his hand. Jazz gasped when she saw it. Zeno nodded at me and I nodded in return. He would look after her if she reached the forest. Harry was back on the parking lot just in case. I opened the door and gently pushed her out, reminded her about the rope if she couldn't see after the gate. She looked at me uncomprehendingly when told not to linger wherever she was. I turned to Rico who had come by me, 'Unfortunately I think she is either a Crosser or a Relocated.'

'Another potential babe in need of my services,' he smirked.

If it turned out she was a Relocated, she would be devastated, not least because she would have to invest in flat shoes.

The boys stayed out of the way while I helped Jazz back to the sofa and briefed her on the situation: she was a Relocated. The whole time, she just looked at me haggard, with a little frown of pity. Either she believed I was due for the asylum, or she thought she was having the weirdest dream of them all. When I finished, she kept silent. I just waited. Only her eyes moved repeatedly from me to the floor and back, otherwise she was like a statue. I waited some more.

'Bullshit.' She spoke calmly, quietly.

'OK then. Try to go to your car,' I told her. She hesitated. She had been out twice already without reaching the parking lot.

It took three more attempts – with me, alone and one of the boys – for her to finally collapse on the sofa, alternately saying, 'No! No! No!' and 'Shit! Shit! Shit!' The guys put out one more plate for dinner and brought down a duvet for the sofa bed. Tomorrow we would turn the office into a small bedroom for her. We had a new housemate. Considering that she was moving from a large one bedroom flat to a single bedroom the size of her walk-in wardrobe, Jazz was not impressed. For now she was still in shock. There were no tears, no explosion and no shouting. I expected that would come later.

**Day 4 (Wednesday)**

The sound of my alarm started me awake. The first thing I saw was my tablet. Groggy, I picked it up and logged in using the password and hidden fingerprint recognition. It was really secure, requiring several attempts in my sleepy state. My inbox showed two new messages, one from Leila and one from 'Leo'. It took my drowsy brain a few seconds to remember Leo was one of the Roman Foggies. The Foggies network had officially started. I didn't have the time to read the messages though as the doorbell blasted through the house. Shortly after, Zeno called everyone down. I threw a jumper on, slipped on my fluffy slippers and went downstairs. Two policemen were attempting to get past the scooter in the hallway.

Later that morning at work, I stared blankly at my computer, mentally reviewing the latest events. I had to share it all with Leila. My Foggies tablet came out of my bag and I wrote:

> Dear Leila,
>
> I hope you are well.
>
> First, I shall give you the positive news. Leo wrote last night via the Foggy tablet you provided. I haven't had a chance to read it yet but will do soon.
>
> Now for the bad news: this morning we had the visit from the police tracking a missing person. Apparently an employee of the Westminster Borough Council, the borough in which we live, has disappeared during his round for the national census survey on Friday last week. The council gave the police the list of all the people this missing man was due to visit that day and we were among them. It seems all the houses before us confirmed he called upon them, or left a note in the mailbox to schedule a visit, but no one after

us. I think you realise what it could mean ... Zeno and Harry were not at home most of the day and evening, Rico and I were on our way to France. We didn't get a note either. We said so to the policemen. They left thinking something must have happened during his route between the previous house he visited and ours. Zeno, once they had left, admitted having thrown away a bunch of leaflets that he thought was junk mail and there could have been a note of his visit among them. It is fair to assume the poor man crossed the Fog to speak with us, we were not home, and he went back through the Fog ending up in the forest. He probably tried to come back and the house being empty, he left a note or notes. He must have been desperate. If this is what happened, now we have a Relocated lost in the forest somewhere who knows nothing about what is happening to him. He may be in danger, or worse, he might have been attacked by wolves. There could be bears too! When the police had gone, we immediately planted a red umbrella outside the fog with a note attached on the stick (we left the umbrella opened for it to be visible and protect the note from the rain). It explains we are aware that the house is a portal to the forest and that we would be home tonight. It may be read by the local people as well as the lost person. Hopefully he will come tonight and stay with us. And what do we do about his family? What to say to them?

This is not all. We have another Relocated, although at least here the situation is more under control. Last night my best friend came for an impromptu visit and she got relocated. Jazz is staying with us. We briefed her on the situation and so far she is holding up.

Leila, I don't think I can do this, have people's lives turned upside down in one instant because of me! Because I create this Fog! I must help them, all of them. I talked to the boys and really, we hope the locals are friendly, for I don't know how we would be able to take care of the Relocated alone in the long term.

Zeno will be back home in the afternoon and will place more notes all around the fog.

Thank you again for coming to see us. It is so good to have you around, we feel less alone. We hope to see you soon again and quiz you for more answers if possible (sorry!). I will keep you updated on the latest from our side.

Best wishes,

Yoko

Just being able to write to someone was such a relief.

Afterwards some colleagues came to discuss a couple of projects and I tried to do a bit of work. I couldn't concentrate. I longed for the lunch break, and when at long last it was noon I went out to buy a piping hot soup and sandwich. Back in one of the empty meeting rooms, I logged on to the Foggy tablet and opened my inbox. There was no new message, just the one unread from Leo. Munching my sandwich, I read:

Dear Foggies from London,

We just met Leila. She told us about the Fog, about how people can be affected, about you in London and that we should contact you directly. She said that some of you are Facilitators and hopefully will be able to help us because we don't have one. She said we should tell you more about us. So I am writing this email on behalf of us all in Roma. This is complicated. Dante and I are friends but Jack is just visiting here.

So, my name is Leo and I am Italian, born and raised in Rome. I spent a year in London as part of a university exchange as a computer game designer so I speak good English (or good enough to get by). I work as a freelance website designer and run a bed and breakfast at the same time. It was my grandmother's house and it is too big for me alone. It is a perfect arrangement, it leaves me enough time for my freelance activities.

Three weeks ago, the B&B was full. The last room available – a small single one – was rented by a by a 21-year-old gay American student, Jack. He had just arrived and was here for six months for fashion studies. Jack was a very nice guest. Then two weekends ago, we woke up and the house was surrounded by a crazy fog. I prepared breakfast for the guests and they all left for their visits or to the airport. Sunday is the day of most departures and arrivals. The cleaning lady was due anytime to tidy the rooms, the house and prepare for new guests. I wanted to go do some work and then get out in town. Except that Jack came back in a state of panic, saying he couldn't go out of the house and almost got lost in the fog. I sat him down and gave him a coffee to calm him down. He is a sweet boy so I told him I would guide him to his university. I thought he was overreacting but when out with him, the Fog was indeed unbelievably dense. Then we walked out of it and were in the countryside. I was stunned and Jack was hysterical. He thought he was going to go mad. He is young, his emotions overtake him quite easily.

We went back in and tried again to go out several times, alone and together. I always came out of the fog into the countryside, alone or with him. On his own, he always faced the fog only. We were freaking out. Now I was also starting to panic. The cleaning lady came and left muttering to herself, upset. I have no doubt she thought we were mad, making her go in and out with us and always coming out on her own in Roma. Since then I have made sure we're as normal as possible when she comes, although she starts worrying about the Fog now. I told her the excuse Dante came up with, about some experiments one of my uncles, a supposedly government scientist, is doing on the house to test an anti-bug 'fog'. It is so far-fetched people have believed it so far. I didn't know Dante could have such imagination.

Ah! Yes, Dante. I haven't introduced Dante yet. Dante is my best friend. He lives close by. I have known him from childhood because our families are from the same area. He is an architect and an intellectual guy, into serious books and philosophical analysis. He can be intense and introverted; yet, he is a fun cool guy when you get to know him better. Anyway, as Dante lives nearby, I called him for help. When he arrived later that Sunday, I explained the situation to him. I didn't make much sense and could see he was doubtful, but he agreed to go out with me. Jack had gone to bed with two sleeping pills. He had decided maybe it was a nightmare and he could sleep it off. He was driving me insane so it was better to be Dante and me. We went out, and both came out in the countryside. It was incredible! I was expecting to be separated, but no! In a way I was feeling relieved to have my friend with me. On the other hand, it was spooky: why with some people it was shock separation while with other it was a trip to the country? And why, for Jack, it was only the fog. What was happening? We were freaking out.

Now of course I know. Leila explained. Jack is a Switcher; Dante and I are Crossers.

What apparently we don't have with us, is a Facilitator. She explained how it works and we are hoping someone will come and turn out to be one. We discreetly tried with all the current guests. No such luck. We don't want to call family and friends, we don't want to relocate people in the process. Leila also said we had to check with you, because you have two Facilitators and maybe they would also work here. I mean maybe they could facilitate in this Fog too, not just yours. That would enable us to go out to Rome. I have opened an account for supermarket delivery. The cleaning lady is not happy about it: The delivery people could be relocated too, so everything is sent to hers and she has to bring it over. The Fog means I will close the B&B for now. Leila said not to worry about the financial consequences. The Society will help. I am not sure yet on that. I don't like being dependent on people I don't know. The good thing is I can work from home, but for Dante it is more difficult ...

As for Jack, he is completely depressed. Dante and I agree: he is a very up or very down type of character. Right now, he is very low. His dreams have been destroyed.

Leila says your Other World is a forest clearing. Not for us: the B&B seems to be in a kind of low trees or high bushes spot. When we pass through the trees and get in the open, the Fog behind us is not obvious to the eyes. Leila says there might be some other people out there, but we haven't seen them yet and I don't think they have seen us either.

I am sorry for jumping from one subject to the next. I am trying to write down everything. Leila told us about the Foggies community and this is a big comfort not to be alone, that others are like us. To be able to talk about what we are going through. Dante and I hope one or both of your Facilitators will be able to help. If you don't mind, could we organise the visit of one of them soon, please?

Please ask any questions you may have too. We can't wait to hear more about you.

Yours sincerely,

Leo

The message was sent to each London Foggie. Knowing my fellow housemates, I would be the only one who would make a proper reply, being the writing freak of the house (hence this memoir). They had all suggested I should deal with the communication. Indeed, Zeno didn't even like writing text messages, Rico hardly even communicated by phone except with his mother and, if Harry was the best writer of us all, he had neither the time nor the inclination as he wrote or corrected essays as a profession. I took a deep breath in and began typing: the house and us, the first morning with the Fog, the forest, cdr69 and Leila, the excitement about the Foggies, the issue about the missing person and so on (leaving out the weekend in France). It took more time than expected.

Browsing the Foggies' page on the tablet afterwards, there was a profile section for each of us to complete with details such as photos, description and languages spoken. Revealing much about me was not that appealing. However, if we were to be stuck with each other for the years to come, someone had to start opening up. It would be an incentive for others to follow. Once an acceptable photo was uploaded and a couple of lines written about me, I checked Leo's. He had also updated his profile and posted two photos. The man looked classically Italian. He had dark hair, chestnut eyes, a stubbly beard and a definite air of cheekiness about him. He was smiling at the camera and there was a sparkle in his smile and eyes. The man had charms aplenty! Hopefully for the Foggies' community, he was as nice and pleasant a man as he seemed to be. I had the same hopes for Dante and Jack, and even for cdr69/Christophe de Rocque: aside from having a jerky side, maybe he wasn't that bad to be around. Then there would be the others, the ones we hadn't found yet. It was similar to starting a new job, hoping very much the new colleagues would be OK, and some even potential friends.

I checked the time and hurriedly closed the tablet. I was late on every single one of my deadlines! This Fog was really taking its toll on my job.

I had finally managed to achieve something at work, albeit only in the afternoon. Walking home, I doubted if it was really of any value, but something was better than nothing. My boss would disagree with that statement I supposed. On the walk home, the boys and I started a conference call using the tablet I had with my headset on, avoiding the video that wouldn't be practical or discreet while walking. I updated them on Leo's email and my reply. None of them had read them. Harry had been too busy with classes; Zeno had never been hooked to emails, messages and social platforms; as for Rico, he admitted he had downloaded a few apps and played with the tablet that afternoon when staying home in case visitors from the Other World came by. The boys all said they might reply to Leo later, only if they thought my email required further information. It was nice they trusted me to have done a good job at it. The Fog affected and troubled us, still we had not changed and the reactions matched our personalities and habits. I would always be the geekiest, most organised and the writer of the household.

My call to Jazz next was a pretext to check on her. She insisted she was fine and had taken a day off, watching movies in bed. As her own boss, she was working from home most of the time, hardly going out by day except for property visits. She was sociable in the evening to a limited extent. She was a loner, picking her friends and outings with care. I wondered if I could switch a place for her with Fog so that at least she had a proper home. There were many flaws in my idea, not least that switching a third house increased the risk of other people being relocated. I had to start keeping track of the houses I switched and when, in order not to miss the forty-nine days until the compulsory Switcher visit, or 'switching maintenance'. It dawned on me I would already have three to visit in the three weeks since the Fog happened. Home here, home in France and next, maybe Jazz's home.

Thinking of the other houses affected, I wondered if the Society had located the four other Switchers somewhere in the world, and with them, more Facilitators, Crossers and Relocated. Leila was very relaxed about us having to live our life normally, yet I, for one, would be upset if relocation happened to me in a random place. Imagine being relocated on holiday on Easter Island, of all places!

Faith.

Leila had faith that life should go on. She believed we were meant to switch house, meant to cross, meant to facilitate, that some were meant to be relocated. Did she believe it was our role or purpose in life and we should let it happen to others too? A part of me agreed it was a good philosophy, another was not comfortable to take the choice away from the people. Now that we knew, I believed we should inform them and, after, if then they chose to cross, it was their decision and responsibility.

We had tried to protect the house, to stop people coming and being affected. Obviously we couldn't control the chain of events: two people aside from Julia had been relocated despite our precautions. At least my parents' property was wall-enclosed and the mailbox was on the outside. No one could just sneak past the fog and accidental relocation was less likely, except for robbers who should not have been there in the first place anyway.

After dinner in my room, watching movies with Jazz, I could hear Zeno and Rico downstairs chatting in Italian about Rico's impending trip to Rome. He had offered to go at dinner and booked a flight for tomorrow evening, all costs paid by Leila. Leo had already written an excited and optimistic email about that visit. Jazz had agreed to keep quiet for now and not talk to anyone about the Fog and its consequences or about relocation. She said she would keep up the pretence of normality as long as she could. Her excuse to her family and friends was a necessary last minute trip. Jazz had been dating someone for a couple of weeks and she expected that this 'sudden trip' would no doubt put an end to it. She had not been sure about the relationship before, so easily put the story in the past. It was the least of her concerns right then. There was a loud knock at the entrance door. The doorbell had not rung. As the boys were downstairs, I didn't move from my bed but was on standby, listening with a sense of foreboding. Next came the call, 'Everyone, please come down!' I sighed and grabbed my home jumper and fluffy slippers. Jazz looked at me inquisitively about whether or not she should join me. She had not changed or left her room much since yesterday and was still wearing the pyjamas I had given her last night.

'No, I don't know what it's about,' I pre-empted her question.

'Do I really have to go?' Jazz asked.

'You are part of the team now, Jazzy.'

She smiled a little at my reply. I was very grateful she wasn't blaming me about the relocation, despite being upset and scared. I was trying to act normal around her and it was hard. I wanted to comfort and cuddle her all the time, and of course I felt at fault and responsible. We walked downstairs, the last ones to arrive in the living room. Three strangers were standing in the middle of the room, with Harry on one side, Zeno and Rico on the other. Everyone turned to look at us when we entered. One just had to look at them, the cast of a period drama in costume, to understand they were locals from the Other World.

My knowledge of eighteenth-century fashion being limited, I had googled it and the gist of the outfits was now on display in the living room. All the non-essential items from that period had been removed, leaving the most practical and simple elements. Nothing fancy, no wig, just an austerity reminding me of the Amish look or Wild West movies. The three visitors looked very proper, even quite classy and exuded cleanliness and sobriety. They were standing very straight, their hats off and held in their hands. Three men, no women. I noticed the three of them were glancing uncomfortably towards Rico and their eyes also avoided looking at Jazz and me directly. Completely the opposite, Harry gave me a head to toe look. I shot one glance down at my clothes and one at Jazz. No wonder the visitors were startled by our arrival and lost their composure for a split second. We were not at our best even by modern standards. Jazz wore a baggy sky blue pyjama top with a big yellow star in front and 'Super Hot Woman' written across it. I was dressed for the night too, in black leggings with a pink T-shirt decorated with a hot chocolate stain. I won't even mention our messy hair. Probably not a sight they were used to from the women in their world. I wondered if Jazz's caramel skin might be uncommon for them too. I shuddered at the thought there could still be slavery in their world. I recalled the anti-slavery movement started in the late eighteenth century in Britain and the Abolition Act dated from 1833. The people crossing worlds would have known the world was changing, but did they apply the same Act?

Harry broke the silence.

'Good evening, gentlemen. Welcome to our house. You must be very curious about us. I expect that you know our ... world is be very different to yours. Please let me first introduce ourselves. I am Harry Baxton, English and lecturer in contemporary history at Imperial College. Here are Zenone Grande, an Italian entrepreneur and, Enrico Scelti, a talented artist, also Italian. This lady is Yoko Salelles, who has a French father and a Japanese-Italian mother. This other lady is Jazz Jones, an English-Indian friend and new resident with us. Please do make yourselves comfortable and take a seat. May we offer you a cup of tea?'

Harry must have rehearsed his little introduction, it was so perfect. I could sense some of the tension from the three men slipping away. For all that it was barely noticeable, it did make a difference. I informed them I would put the kettle on and disappeared into the kitchen, followed by Jazz announcing she would help me. Ironically, the presence of these men had turned the household into an old-fashioned one: the men together in the living room, the women in the kitchen. In addition to tea, we took some cookies out and put them in a plate for our guests. I might as well be good in this temporary role. I did not intend it to last.

When Jazz and I returned with tea and biscuits, the men were sitting in the living room area. Harry stood up and pulled two additional chairs from the dining table. Zeno and he took the seats and left us the space on the sofa with Rico. I could see one of the visitors frowning at Jazz and Rico, then me, before turning his eyes to Harry and Zeno.

'Yoko, Jazz, may I introduce you to Augustus Hoare, sheriff; to Edmund Poff, church leader; and to Benjamin Snayth, mayor. I understand they are the leaders of the local town council,' Harry informed us as we had missed the information while in the kitchen.

Harry continued by explaining we were a house share and what it was. Augustus Hoare raised an eyebrow and enquired if it was a common occurrence for men and women to live as friends under the same roof. His face was a picture of disapproval. I imagined our system may not have been common in his vintage community. He had not directly looked at any one other than Harry even once, giving at best an occasional glance at Zeno or Rico from the corner of his eyes. Jazz and I were ignored in such blatant way, our presence evidently disturbed him. I was very tempted to go by Harry where he could hardly avoid looking at me, but decided against it. Let's have a good start.

When Harry paused and turned round, I nodded to him in such a way to indicate my wish to talk. Let's show our presence was not for illustration only. I launched into an account of how there had been a lot of changes in society and that London was now a very large, cosmopolitan and open city. When I referred to technology, from the way they looked at me, I might as well have been talking Chinese. The church leader – Edmond Poff – twitched uncomfortably; Augustus Hoare fussed with his hat; only Benjamin Snayth seemed to be paying attention without being unsettled. Snayth, the town mayor, was the most engaging of the three. He was smiling even though showing confusion. I made sure to keep a smile on my face too during the whole of my monologue. I pronounced ten sentences at most, just enough to impress on the newcomers that our side of the sofa and the women folk were fully part of the conversation. Under this roof, there would be no dismissing Yoko and Jazz, or Rico for that matter. When I finished, I saw Edmund Poff was ready to speak, but Benjamin Snayth put a hand on his shoulder and made him stop in his tracks. He quickly glanced at the third man, Augustus Hoare, and began his address. He was looking mainly at the men of the household. Only once did he turned to acknowledge Jazz and me. In the split second it took him to broaden his smile, his eyes crossed mine. The brief look was so surprisingly hard and penetrating, I held my breath in shock. It took him only the time to blink before Benjamin Snayth appeared again such a charming man, talking with warmth about their role as representatives

of their small town. The town was called Lil'London. Their ancestors had kept it simple. They announced that Lil'London couldn't
wait to discover all that they had missed on the evolution of the
'Big London'. I remained unsettled by the hardness I'd read in
his eyes for the rest of the council visit. During his account, I
observed the man and the discrepancy between the sensations of
disquiet he had caused with the pleasant person in front of me.
Benjamin Snayth was a good-looking man in his mid to late forties. He was clean shaven with wavy hair, sideburns showing just a
touch of grey and tall with gentlemanlike manners. A few minutes
before he had seemed charming indeed, with a hint he could be
a charmer too, now I had reservations. It almost felt as if I had received a warning. Had it been intentional, to put the woman back
in her place, or he had let his guard down for a brief instant and
had I glimpsed at a side of him that was usually hidden? It took
some effort to bring my mind back in the room and concentrate
on what he was saying.

Benjamin Snayth informed us that they were aware the Fog
was due to happen this year, even this month. They had been
looking for signs of the Fog the past few weeks. It was not as easy
to find as they had hoped, especially not knowing for certain
where and when it would arise. They would not have known for
sure the Fog had started, if not for the appearance of the lost man
coming from our London.

'Ah, the missing Westminster Council civil servant!' I thought.
We had guessed right, the civil servant, James Fisher, had ventured
through our Fog to knock at the door to proceed with his survey
and left a card when nobody answered. He had turned back, only
to arrive in the forest. The mayor filled us in on the rest of the
story. Of course, James Fisher had come back to our door after
exiting the Fog into the forest, knocked and even attempted to
force the door open. He had stopped before breaking in through
the windows: if we were the cause of his misery, we might be dangerous and he shouldn't alienate us. He left notes that day and

evening and tried to find a place close by to spend the night. At some point on Friday night he heard the wolves, panicked and started running. He finally found a tree he could climb and spent the night sitting on a branch, clinging to the trunk. In the morning, he was even more lost than the previous day and incapable of finding the house again. The poor man started roaming in a dazed state through the forest and grasslands until he came upon a path. That was his first lucky break. The second one was that he followed the path in the right direction, reaching Lil'London after an hour's walk. The town inhabitants knew immediately he was neither from the town, nor from their world. James Fisher was received with lots of excitement, celebrations and questions. He was already in a shock when he reached Lil'London and that was probably the last straw. He collapsed in the street and since Saturday evening had been bedridden with fever and cold sweat. Benjamin Snayth took the newcomer and settled him in his home, with the women of his household looking after him.

The arrival of James Fisher confirmed the portal had opened. Lil'London's council organised a search of the area he had walked from. On Tuesday, one of the tree climbers saw the top of the Fog in the distance. Lil'London Council came to call upon us on Tuesday afternoon, yesterday. Unfortunately no one was in. They tried again later in the early evening and again they had no answer. This morning they saw the strange note on the equally strange red umbrella. They decided they would come again after supper, when the man – or men – of the house would relax after a day's work (as it seemed the house was empty during the day, they had assumed the owner was occupied elsewhere).

For some time Augustus Hoare had been looking towards the dining area at the fireplace with a confused air. I used a pause in Benjamin's long monologue to ask the sheriff, 'Sir, it seems something in the house is distracting you. May I ask what is object of your interest? May I be of help?' I surprised myself by how formal my language was. Isn't it funny how you adjust to your surroundings and people?

Augustus Hoare looked at me directly for the first time and said, 'Madam, it is most kind of you to notice. Indeed, there is a sound in the room, inconstant, even with words sometimes. It appears to have its source by the fireplace. Some kind of music maybe?'

We were so used to it, we were not paying attention to the background music anymore. Zeno or Rico had left an iPhone in the docking station inside the fireplace, and forgot to switch it off. Music without instruments would be quite a novelty for the representatives of Lil'London!

'Sir, this is music indeed. Modern music. We have various styles and the one currently playing we refer to as "pop".' I could see real curiosity on his face. He had a nice face. Another clean shaven one with short hair and sideburns. Like Benjamin Snayth, he was quite a tall man with allure, somewhere in his late thirties or early forties, although there was no sign of grey hair there. He was more poised than the mayor, also he was less expressive and warm. Augustus Hoare was also a contrast to the fidgety Edmund Poff who always looked to his companions for comfort, confidence or approval (I wasn't sure which). Augustus Hoare by comparison seemed quite confident, even if somewhat uncomfortable with the situation.

'Sir, would you like to see how it works?' I asked him.

'I should like that,' he answered, standing up.

We walked to the fireplace, the others remained sitting in silence. I glanced at Jazz who winked at me. Turning my attention to Augustus Hoare with a smile, he relaxed a little and gave me what could be the beginning of a smile back. Pointing at the iPhone, I explained as best as I could, 'In the last century, we found a way to capture music on hard objects. We can take images as well, though let's focus on music for now. So the technology used to capture, retain and for lack of a better word "free at will" the music was refined. It got smaller and smaller, until a few years ago thousands of songs and music could fit in this tiny box. You can press some buttons to select the song you want to hear. You can even select them to play one after the other. You may play directly from the tiny box or use speakers to hear them better. With this button ...' I touched the volume key and increased the sound a bit. I could hear his astonished reaction by his instant intake of breath, 'you can make it louder, or quieter.'

Augustus Hoare was fascinated. I indicated to him with a nod to try. He randomly pressed on the screen and a new song began, 'Sexy Back' by Justin Timberlake. Not the best choice of song for the current audience. I stopped the song quickly before they got outraged and selected something classical. Verdi was on top of the list and I put it on low volume. Augustus Hoare did not question my rapid change of tune, more interested in the technology.

'What makes this instrument work?'

'I beg your pardon?'

'Well, our musical instruments work because we play them. This ...'

'Oh! I see. It works with ... electricity. I presume you do not have electricity, do you?'

'I don't think so.'

'Then you don't or you would know. How should I explain? Well, let's see ... Lightning! You have seen lightning in the sky, I presume?'

'Yes, of course.'

'Well, lightning is a natural source of electricity.' I was racking my brains for remnants from my physics classes at school. It was pitifully close to none. So I made a mixture of logic and whatever else was in my head and, blurted the results hoping for the best. It came out something like, 'Some time ago we found a way of re-creating the lightning in a controlled way, using it as a source of energy. It is our modern wood for heating the house, our modern candles for light, and energy for such a musical box.'

Augustus Hoare was transfixed and so were the others on the sofas, including Jazz and the boys: the ones from Lil'London out of wonder and, maybe, awe; the household from the sudden grasp of how far behind Lil'London was with their technology. We knew it already but suddenly it was very real.

'We have many different styles of music. Some of them you may disapprove of, I have to warn you. I think a lot of things in and from our world will surprise you. Some may even shock you. I hope you can be lenient with us.' We were a very different society from theirs and their ancestors'. I feared they would not be pleased by it all.

'This instrument is amazing. I hope to have a chance to study and listen to it some more in the future. I also take note and thank you for your concern regarding our world's differences. Of course we have been expecting discrepancies. At every previous occurrence your world had changed much. It seems nonetheless that the gap is considerable this time, like this trapped music, this unused fireplace and yet warm house, or the lamps with no flame demonstrate. Fashion is also very … different. There will be more, I am sure, on morals, rules and the mixing of people.'

'Does it shock you, the colour of my skin or Rico's?' Jazz asked all of a sudden, with a higher pitch than normal. Her interruption was abrupt. She must have held her tongue for some time until she could no more.

Augustus Hoare's smile and mine froze at her words.

'No, we have coloured people in our town as well. Only, they usually work for us, they are not our friends or on a par.'

'Well, they could be, you know!' Jazz persisted.

'Miss Salelles suggested we should be understanding with your world. Would you be so kind to be with ours too?'

Jazz stared at him with barely contained anger. Rico's jaw was clenched and so were his knuckles. The Other World already had one major flaw for them linked to their skin colour, from their Indian and African origins.

My thoughts went to Jazz as she now had to live in that world. The same reflections were crossing her mind as I deduced seeing her eyes watering. Rico noticed too. He swallowed a big amount of pride and broke the icy silence, 'So, would anyone like some more tea? Biscuits?' Everyone accepted eagerly.

Benjamin Snayth asked what we knew about the Fog. With my being used to recounting the situation by now, I naturally took the role of speaker. I limited my speech to the most basic information: no reference to the Society or Leila, no reference to family, just the key facts.

I mentioned someone with knowledge about the Fog had contacted us. Thanks to this, we knew the Fog occurred every 231 years, that people were differently affected by it and that there could be a local community on the other side. They didn't need to know anymore. The less said, the better, until we knew more about the people we were dealing with on both sides. I was beginning to wonder if this caution was not verging towards paranoia.

For Benjamin Snayth the information provided would not suffice. Always smooth, always using nice forms and flowery language, he was nonetheless most persistent and inquisitive. No wonder he was the town mayor, this charming manipulator was probably the best politician around. Augustus Hoare struck me as a listener, a silent observer. He was the type who didn't speak much but would store every single bit of information and analyse it in detail. The last one, Edmund Poff just appeared nervous, ill at ease, with eyes avoiding contact and regularly checking in with the other two.

They didn't stay very long after my little speech ended. When Benjamin Snayth started probing too much and all he got for an answer was, 'we don't know,' 'we have not been informed,' or 'I wish we could tell you', Harry stepped in and suggested we meet again the next day early in the evening. I interrupted Harry pointing out that tomorrow, Thursday, would not be convenient for me and suggesting Saturday afternoon instead. My thinking was that we needed more time and twenty-four hours was not sufficient. We were not ready, when we should have seen it coming. Somehow it had just been unreal and too fast.

For the first time in the whole evening, Zeno talked and asked if they could also give us some information on the Relocated James Fisher. He was right, our priority was to look after the Relocated.

'Relocated is a funny word,' Augustus Hoare commented.

'Relocated from London to Lil'London. It seems a very appropriate term,' Zeno continued.

'Indeed, it is. We will of course inform you on James Fisher's health and we will tell him of our meeting with you,' Benjamin Snayth confirmed.

'Would you also inform him we would be delighted to invite him to visit us when he is feeling better?' added Harry.

'Of course,' Augustus Hoare replied.

'We will tell him when he has recovered,' Benjamin amended slightly.

'Very well. Thank you,' concluded Harry.

Once they were gone, we all gathered again in the living room.

'Gosh, they are so cool! I will have a ball with my new neighbours!' Jazz slumped on the sofa and added: 'Yoko, please, I really need a drink!'

Zeno went to get his favourite grappa and shot glasses for everyone.

'Those people, they are something. I'm almost scared!' Rico said.

'Benjamin Snayth was the only fairly pleasant one. The other ones ... Well, Edmund Poff reminded me of a slippery weasel and Augustus Hoare of a rigid stern headmaster,' Harry said.

'Man, that Augustus guy is spooky! He has less facial expression than Spock from Star Trek,' Jazz added.

'Next time, I'll give him my uncle's homemade strongest grappa which will shake him up,' Zeno said, finishing his glass in one go and refilling it.

'Hey, now that is an idea, maybe we should give them a spliff or two!' I exclaimed. 'Or I could prepare some special biscuits? I have never done that before. I have always wondered if it really works. They would be great guinea pigs, wouldn't they? With them, we could really tell the difference!'

'Oh Lord ...' sighed Harry.

'Hey babe, if you want some, I'll get you some. That's cool.'

'Yoko, you are joking, right?' asked Harry.

'Well, it was just a silly idea, but now that I think about it ... Yes, I know we shouldn't, but maybe just a little bit.'

'You. Are. Not. Doing. That! This is too serious, Yoko. We need to deal with them properly! Come on! I know you are not reasonable sometimes and have your childlike moments, but you are always decent. That is not.' Harry had stood up facing me. He turned to Rico. 'Your pot is for your own consumption only. Not for poor guys from another world who probably have no clue what marijuana even is.'

'Rico, could I get some too?' Jazz broke in. 'Actually, I might have to open a tab with you. I think I'll need some regularly where I am going.' She waved her glass to indicate to Zeno she needed more grappa.

'Jazz, you are not helping.' Harry rolled his eyes.

'It isn't you who will have to live with those guys!' snapped Jazz. She downed her drink and stood up. 'I'm not happy. I'm going home. Oh wait. No, I can't! Ha ha ha!' She made a grumpy guttural sound, closed her eyes as they quickly got swollen with tears and said, 'Yoko, guys, I am going to bed. I'm done. Ciao.' She disappeared up to her mini bedroom.

I couldn't blame her. Benjamin Snayth might be a hand of steel in a velvet glove; Augustus Hoare felt cold even if intriguing; Benjamin Poff's nervousness reminded me of a trapped rat, scared and as a consequence possibly dangerous too. Not exactly the people you want to spend the rest of your life in the company of. I was ready to cry for Jazz's sake. It was time to call it a day.

'Shall we talk about it tomorrow morning over breakfast?' I suggested. 'Zeno, we could have a little trip around the house after on your scooter? Otherwise we could do it tomorrow early evening as you suggested. We will see if they have set up a watch around the house and what type.'

'I have some early work on a property tomorrow morning. I can't change it this time. Can we do a lunchtime Foggy tablet conference call?' replied Zeno

'Yes. Brilliant. Let's put the tablet to good use,' I said, eager to get a grip on how the tablet worked.

'Fine by me,' Harry said.

'Me too,' Rico concluded.

'Right, I'll be off then,' I told them. 'I must write a note to Leila to update her on this latest encounter and confirm Rico's trip to Rome tomorrow. I will copy all of you guys.'

I kissed each of them goodnight and headed to my room. Closing my door, I heard them go to their own rooms as well.

In bed, my Foggy tablet opened on the community platform, an email from Leila confirmed she would take care of all the transportation for Rico to and from the airports and in Rome. An unknown sound beeped from the tablet, a small panel popped up and Leo's name appeared in what I deduced to be an instant messaging system. It really was a super-trendy tablet.

'Ciao, Yoko. It is Leo here. How are you?'

It made me smile. However, completely sleep deprived, exhausted and in no mood to start online chatting with a stranger, even if a fellow Foggy, I decided to keep it brief. 'Ciao, Leo. All good in Foggy London. I was going to write to inform you that Rico is very excited to come and visit you in Rome tomorrow. Let's find out if he can help you out of the Fog!'

'Fantastico! Thank you, thank you, and thank you!'

'Don't thank me. We don't know if it will work yet and it is Rico who is travelling to help, not me.'

'Right. But I thank you anyway for helping, bella.'

'My pleasure!'

'Ms Yoko, I have to say, you look very intriguing, with your exotic name not matching your look on the photo of your profile.'

'Ahhhh ... I am French with some Japanese blood, hence my name.'

'You don't look French.'

'I also have Italian genes.'

'Really? Where from?'

'Italy,' I wrote, thinking it was not the time to get into my whole life. Cheeky Italian!

'Hahahaha! Where in Italy?'

'North.'

'I see. Mysterious woman. I like that. But you are French, brought up in France, right?'

'Yes, I grew up in France.'

'Where?'

'For God's sake, man,' I mouthed to myself. 'What is this? The Inquisition? I need sleep!'

As it was my first interaction with him, I indulged him and answered, 'A small town not far from Marseille. Actually close to a Roman town.'

'So you are a little bit Roman too.'

'If you push back a couple of millennia, yes.'

'Come on, give me a hint and I will find out which town!'

'Oh really?'

'A few hints and I'll do some research. I'll find out.'

'Is that a challenge?' I couldn't resist. I loved challenges.

'Yes, that's a challenge. If I win, I'll take you out on a date. It may have to be at home in Rome if your friend Rico can't help. Otherwise, London.'

That made me laugh. Unbelievable! This guy was actually flirting with me! He had never met me, just seen one picture and that was enough for him to try using his Italian magic on me. To my shame, it worked. I had a stupid grin on my face ... Opening his profile, I checked his photo again. He did have a little something. Not bad looking at all.

'Deal. If you win you can take me on a date. That's fine. If I win, you give me your family recipe for pizza, bolognese sauce and tiramisu. Your mother's or grandmother's ones. My Italian housemates won't reveal anything and I love cooking, so ... Also, you have only three hints and one attempt for each to find the answer. I'll be generous though, I grant you all the time you need to come up with your answers.'

'Wow, you are tough! My mother would kill me if she knew. My instincts tell me you are worth it though. So, DEAL! Just promise you wouldn't reveal them to anyone else. Promise, but I will win anyway!'

'Don't be so sure about that, but OK, I promise! I hope in any case Rico will be able to help.'

'He will. I have faith.'

'And if he fails?'

'Maybe I would go on a wild adventure across land and sea just to have a date with you.'

'Brave man. I am impressed. By the way, you are aware photos can be deceptive, right?'

'Dear Ms Yoko, I also have Leila's recommendation about you. And my proven Italian instinct.'

'You are too much! But OK, we have a deal.'

'Bring it on!'

I thought for a few minutes and gave him his first clue.

'Hint number1: it has a strong and unusual religious history for France.'

'Ok. Religious history. Not far from Marseille. I'll start digging now. I'm going to win.'

My grin was back. It was so clichéd, but those Italian men, they had a knack for enthralling the opposite sex.

'I am going to go and let you start your search now.'

'Nooooooo!'

'Sorry, I badly need to sleep. And first I need to message Leila about our latest big news. I'll give you the scoop: we have had visitors from the Other World community representatives tonight!'

'No way! So? What are they like? Friendly? What did they say? Please tell me more.'

'It's difficult to define really. Clothes-wise, they reminded me of the people from Western movies, not the commoners of the Far West though: the elite, the ones who were probably the jet set and key people in the town. They call their town Lil'London. I can't wait to see what it looks like. They were expecting us and had been looking out for the Fog. They seemed prepared to welcome us, even though I am not sure they were anticipating such a major culture clash. They knew there would be an enormous difference of evolution, but the difference between knowing and experiencing is huge.'

'I can't even imagine.'

'Our little household was quite a surprise for them too: two unmarried women and three unmarried men living as friends under the same roof, including one of African and one of Indian origin.'

'I thought you were just four in the house?'

'One of my best friends, Jazz (the one of Indian origin), paid me a surprise visit and got relocated. So she is staying at ours for now. As we foresee the role of women to be plainly old-fashioned and kitchen-bound, she is not a happy bunny right now. In addition they may have retrograde ideas on skin colour. I think Lil'London doesn't know who is about to land on them. She is going to rock their world and I don't know if they will like the music.'

'Terribile!'

'Exactly!'

'Hey, you speak Italian?'

'No. Not really. Just enough to order in a restaurant. And some swear words.'

'The essentials. Why don't you speak it as you are part Italian?'

'I think my mother didn't want to start with languages: if she taught me Italian, she would have had to do the same with Japanese. She has a grudge against Japanese. Plus, she tried a bit with my sister as a toddler but my sister was impervious to it, so she gave up on Italian after the first born stubbornly refused to learn. Anyway, I digress. Stop making me write my whole life story! It is late.'

'OK, OK, I let you go. Not willingly! It is nice to get to know you.'

'You are such an Italian flirt.'

'Me? No. I just can recognise a good thing when I see it.'

'...'

'Why '...' ?'

'I just can't believe it. You haven't even met me!'

'And?'

'What if I am a pain-in-the-ass bitch?'

'Then I am not paying for dessert on our date.'

'Scrooge.'

'You will see I am not. You'll have dessert. I'll treat you like a princess.'

'You are incredible. This is bordering the cheesy. I'm going now!'

'Ciao bella!'

'Ciao Leo!'

OK, I admit it, I felt pretty good. It was nice to be chatted up, even if it was online. Maybe I still had it in me. Of course it would have been better if he had not been stuck in Rome. It was a bit sad, too, how easy it was to flatter my ego.

Before my eyes refused to stay open any longer, my email to Leila was quickly written and sent. I described the evening's encounter, updated her on James Fisher, and gave my first impression of the visitors. It was tricky not to express private judgements and to stick to the facts and general observations. I would tell her my opinions later, but it was important she was aware they were only opinions and personal feelings, and thus may be erroneous. To avoid having to retype some details, I 'copied and pasted' a couple of my comments to Leo. I finished by mentioning Rico wished to join the meeting with the Lil'London representatives via a video conference on Saturday afternoon.

By the time I was ready to switch everything off – tablet, light, brain – I had received two more messages, one from Dante, the other Crosser in Rome and, one more from Leo. I gave them a quick browse. Leo's was brief, just 'Goodnight, bella Yoko. I have started searching and I am learning a lot about Provence right now. X ;-)'. Dante's was longer. He was pretty much introducing himself and after two lines I closed the message, deciding to read it the next day. I was in no state to compute anything anymore. I put my head on the pillow and drifted off to the magical world of sleep.

**Day 5 (Thursday)**

Sipping tea in bed, trying to wake up from too short a night, again, I read Dante's message on the Foggy tablet. My laptop was also switched on beside me on the bedspread, an internet page open on the BBC news page informing me of what was going wrong in the world, which included a lengthy English weather forecast. From that morning, I referred to the tablet as the FTab: if it was to play a major part in my day and life, I might as well give it a nickname.

Dante's message, despite being an introduction to himself, was very impersonal, very different from Leo's who had opened up immediately. Dante explained that he was an architect, who had set up his own practice two years previously. He was doing OK, considering how difficult it is to launch a new company and manage to make ends meet. He had several projects on the go and some potential ones on the back burner. His style was eloquent if quite formal. He struck me as an intellectual and I remembered Leo had mentioned his surprise when Dante came up with an original excuse for the Fog. Dante gave the impression of a very neat, academic person. In a way, Leo and Dante seemed to complement each other quite well.

After reading it, I replied with a few lines about me and the household. It was getting a bit boring to type the same stories again and again. It would be an idea to prepare a standard story to pass on to the other Foggies, known and future. That made me think of cdr69, his wife Isabelle and his mistress Louise. There had not been any news from him for some time: what were they up to?

I heard a beep, followed by another, a different one, coming from the FTab. The first one was an instant message from Leo, the second was an email from Leila. I checked Leo's. 'Good Morning bella! Here is my answer to where you come from: Avignon! So, when are we going out on this date?' He had again brought a smile to my face.

'Hello Leo! Good try. It could have been, with its old history and the Pope's palace. Sadly for you, this is the wrong answer. You have two attempts left.'

'Argh! It was very interesting though. I didn't know that in the fourteenth century there were two popes claiming the title and one was living in France, in Avignon. OK, OK, I will get it with the next one ... Hint number 2 please?'

I hadn't given any thought to my hints. On the one hand, I wanted to be fair and give him a chance, on the other, it was a challenge and I wasn't going to make it easy for him. Still, getting my hands on real Italian family recipes sounded good ... Hint, hint, hint ... OK, I had one.

'Hint number 2: the town is on the Via Domitia.'

'What is the Via Domitia?'

'That is for you to find out, signore. Good luck.'

'Not needed. I will win. I want my date.'

'Either that or you really don't want to ask your mother for her recipes.'

'I already have them. I have even improved them. I make the best pizza in town and I do not give out my recipes. I will have the date instead. Ciao, bella.'

'Yeah, yeah, yeah ... Ciao signore.'

Browsing Leila's email quickly, it contained the details of Rico's itinerary. She had copied the email to the boys as well. A quick check on the time informed me I was running late. It would be a quick shower. Soon after, walking to the office, my parents made the now daily call. I briefed them on the visitors and mentioned I would probably know more by Saturday evening. They updated me on Julia, completely depressed and refusing to leave her bed. My parents were caring for Eudes full time. They asked if they should try crossing the fog carrying him, as they didn't see how they could get separated if one of them was holding him in their arms, but I didn't recommend it. What would happen if they did get separated and Eudes ended up alone in the Fog or in the

Other World? Would he be able to find his way back? It was too dangerous. They abandoned the idea.

At lunchtime, as I popped out to get soup and a sandwich, my FTab beeped several times in my bag. There was no such thing as having 'a quick look' at the FTab, what with all the security to log in, but I was fast getting used to it. There was an email from Leila and an instant message from Leo.

'Via Domitia goes from Rome to Spain! Come on, this is a tough hint!' he wrote.

'Indeed, the Romans built the road – or 'via' – Domitia for exactly that purpose, but not all the towns on its path are within two hours' drive of Marseille and with a strong obvious historical impact,' I replied.

'I have never learned so much so fast about France in my life.'

'Remember your own words: I am worth it.'

'That is why I will continue searching and ... win! I have selected a few towns that fit the profile already. I am searching a bit more before I suggest them. This is important, only two attempts left. Apart from this, why are you in London, French woman with Italian and Japanese origins?'

'I followed a green parrot.'

'What???'

'I followed a green parrot.'

'You followed a green parrot, and it led you to London?'

'In a way.'

'I don't dare ask.'

'I wouldn't explain. Yet. Bye bye, signore.'

The exchange with Leo was done while queuing, ordering and paying for my lunch and I put the FTab back in my bag, heading back to work. I enquired at reception which meeting room was free. Having the planned video conference at my desk was not an option: there could be no private conversation there, with the risk of being overheard or interrupted anytime. The small meeting room was free. Most of my colleagues had lunch at their desk, like me until recently. I was behind with every single project in my charge, my work had degraded in quality to the bare average (if that), and I lacked any interest in it whatsoever. It couldn't be long before I received the request to visit the boss's office. Biting into my sandwich, I opened Leila's email:

Dear Yoko,

I am very excited that the local people from the Other World made contact and that they seem keen to establish good relations. Do you think I could join the meeting? Or, like Rico, watch using a FTab camera? We don't want them to know about the Society and, thank you for not mentioning to them that we exist. For us it's important to remain in the shadows, except for the Foggies. Please let me know if you would be comfortable for me to be a secret attendant in the meeting. Also, if you wish, we could meet again this weekend. I will be in London.

For your information, I am in Marrakech to-night to meet with Christophe de Rocque, his wife Isabelle and his friend Louise. He didn't mention his special relationship with Louise. I am pleased you did, so that I know to tread carefully. I will let you know how it goes.

Now for the big news: we have found more Foggies around the globe! We haven't made con-tact with them yet, but there are Fog portals in Nevada and Mexico. We are working on the exact location and contact points. I will let you know as soon as I have further details. Knowing if Rico can help Jack, Leo and Dante in Rome is already going to be a big step. We are all crossing our fingers that he can.

I have to go, time to board my flight.
So exciting.
Best,
Leila

Everything seemed to be happening so fast! Since meeting Leila, Fog-related matters had accelerated and taken over my life. Now, two more portals had been found. It was exciting and daunting: were we all going to get along? It was really like joining a new school and class, with the same people year after year. The Foggies community was getting real and international. North America, Europe, Africa ... I wondered why and how the Fog picked the people and the places. Simultaneously I anticipated we may never get an answer to these questions and more.

It was time for the video conference. Zeno and Rico were huddled together at home. Harry was in his office at the university. First, I updated them on Leila's request to be present on Saturday. The answer was yes, she was welcome to join secretly. They would gladly see her before as well. Harry pointed out that she may have information on who the Lil'London ancestors were, which could come handy. Unsurprisingly, the boys were also very excited to hear about the other portals. Zeno mentioned that with Leila's presence on Saturday, he felt a little bit less overwhelmed by the whole experience. In a way, she was like a specialist and provided back-up from the Society behind her. We discussed some of the points to raise with Lil'London's council. One of them was for Zeno and me to visit their town, take photos and assess the range of the mobile phones. Furthermore, we were hoping to see James Fisher and meet with some of the people in the street. We didn't think these were outrageous requests, but we didn't know the rules of the town: maybe it was a dictatorship or autocracy of some kind. For all we knew, it was even a theocracy.

Zeno and I agreed we would take the scooter out into the Fog that evening. There was no reason why we could take a lamp torch through to the forest and not a scooter. Parked in the Fog, Zeno should be able to take the scooter with him in both worlds, depending on whether he were accompanied or not by Harry or Rico. We would try it all tonight.

Besides the video conference call, I was getting hooked on the little game with Leo. He really tickled my curiosity. He had not given his second guess yet, but I wanted to be ready and worked out the hint number 3. Mid-afternoon, a new message from him arrived.

'Montpellier! Its Faculty of Medicine was established in the thirteenth century and ever since has been one of the major centres for the teaching of medicine in Europe. Plus, it was one of the centres for spice trading and a rare town with rights of its own. And it is on Via Domitia.'

'I am impressed! Montpellier has a very interesting yet mostly unknown history and yet ... No. The town closest to my parents' home is not Montpellier. I wrote earlier that the one I referred to has an obvious display of history.'

'Cazzo! Only one chance left! Argh!'

'Hint number 3: the obvious display of history – the town has several Roman monuments.'

'Yoko, I refuse to accept that hint. All the towns on the Via Domitia have Roman monuments.'

'Fair point. So let me add that some are still in everyday use today.'

'I still think that it is not fair!'

'Leo, I tell you anymore and it would be a gift, not a challenge!'

'You promise you are being fair?'

'Yes!' Unbelievable. I had actually just promised to this guy I wasn't on purpose trying to get out of a date with him. Why?

The scooter trip was fun, though short. Zeno was fully attired with his motorbike outfit, I had a thick coat and thick jeans on, with thigh-high flat leather boots, a little find from a charity shop I loved and which had been on my list of shoes to polish for six months so would be forest-perfect. Zeno was as eager to head out on the 'country scooter wheels' set up by his mechanic friend as he was to have a proper tour of the forest and explore further afield. As for me, the idea of discovering that Other World more, and independently, was exciting. Soon, the indigenous population would show us round. They would only show what they wanted and how they wanted. I was bitterly aware as well that we could only rely on ourselves there. They seemed open and friendly enough, but they were still ill at ease and of unknown intentions. Once on their territory, they could do whatever they wanted, we were at their mercy. For all we knew, they could be plotting to kill us as a danger to their establishment. I brushed these dark thoughts away and focused on the here and now, on the excitement of getting out in the forest with the newly adapted scooter. Since the first week of stumbling upon the forest when leaving the house, neither Zeno nor I had been out in the forest much, aside from little outings, and then mainly to check it was still there.

The forest trip was at best odd, at worst, unpleasant. First, as could be expected, two locals were in a makeshift shed, set up on the edge of the forest. They had a fire lit by the entrance and sat talking to each other, holding old-fashioned shotguns. When they saw us, they were at loss how to react and unsure whether to come forward and talk. We must have been an unusual sight indeed, Zeno as a cape-less Darth Vader, me as a weirdly attired woman. Actually, they probably had doubts that I was a woman, with those high leather boots and puffed jacket. They nodded at us and we waved. My helmet now on, we both got on the scooter and Zeno turned the motor on. The two men stood up abruptly and raised their shotguns, both the stools they had sat on falling back. I waved at them again, pointlessly, as they only stared at us, incomprehension and fright on their faces. The scooter ran smoothly and slowly towards the forest. The startled men stood still apart from their shaking hands. It was not very reassuring as those hands held the shotguns. Next time, I would put on a bullet-proof jacket, just in case. Our little ride lasted ten minutes maximum. The customised wheels did hold on, but, frankly, we would have been faster walking. The experience soon proved to be a pain in the ass, literally. What were we thinking, using a 125cc scooter to drive in a forest? The relevance of the idea had to be reviewed: the concept worked, the practice didn't.

'Harry will be smug,' Zeno said with a sigh.

'At least we made quite an impression,' I thought, 'except if they saw us as the embodiment of the devil riding on his death horse.'

The evening passed like one of our new usual. Zeno and I updated Harry and Jazz on our forest foray and scooter idea failure. We were not going to give up on the motor vehicle idea just yet. It seemed a four-wheeled quattro would have the best chance of efficiency and could fit through the front gate and on the patio. I withdrew to my bedroom early to check for messages from Leila and Rico. He had not arrived in Rome yet and they had plenty to assess, so I was not expecting to hear from them before the next morning. I didn't really want to admit it even to myself, but I also hoped for a message from Leo. A puzzle, how quickly little things or people can be part of your life. Logging in the FTab, the Foggies platform had been updated with the newly discovered fog locations. New names had been added. I was considering if I should or not contact them when a new instant message beeped in. Leo.

'Nîmes. My last guess is Nîmes. Fingers crossed here!' He wrote.

'Well, dear Leo, you have officially a date to plan.'

'YES! I have done it! I have a date with bella Yoko!'

'Congratulations. I will of course check with the others that no one told you anything.'

'Tut-tut-tut. Have a little bit of faith. I didn't ask. This is between you and me. You know, Nîmes is quite amazing: it is a mini Rome! So many Roman monuments and you even have your own coliseum in use! I am not really keen on bullfights though, but I like that the amphitheatre is still operating.'

'Yes, it makes it part of modern life. We have concerts, operas, plays, shows, not just bullfights in it, you know.'

'It is the religious history part I did not really follow. The town is a Protestant stronghold in France, but what does that mean?'

'Until a few decades ago, at least half of Nîmes' population was Protestant. When you consider that Protestantism is a religious minority in France, a country largely Catholic, it is unusual. The Protestants are only two to three percent of the French population.'

'And you?'

'Take a guess.'

'Protestant?'

'Maybe. Difficult to define with my mixed origins, isn't it? Anyway, now you know where I am from.'

'And still I don't know much about you. A good thing I have a date to discover more.'

'A well-deserved one. It wasn't that easy and you certainly did some proper research. I have to say, I am impressed!'

'Grazie, grazie! Hard work indeed, but I learned a lot! Now, ideally I would love to come to London and meet you all and invite you out. Your friend Rico is landing in forty-five minutes.'

'It will work. It has to. Really, how many different types of Fog and Other worlds could be out there otherwise? It doesn't bear thinking about.'

'Yoko, I do hope it will, I really do hope it will. I want to see Rome again. At least Dante and I can go out on our own to the countryside and escape the house whenever we wish, but Jack ...'

'It will work.'

'I will message you immediately when I know.'

'Leo, how is Jack? I received an email from Dante, but not him.'

'He is depressed. He hardly leaves his room and it is a small room, so really he doesn't leave his bed. He told his parents about the Fog. They didn't take him seriously which made his state worse. It is a good thing for us they didn't, who knows what they would do? Still, I am wondering what will happen if they decided to come and collect him.'

'Even more reason to hope Rico is able to help.'

'Even if he does, we will be back to square one when he leaves us and returns to London.'

'First things first, let's hope that Rico can help.'

'Dante and I think that maybe we would need to move closer to you, to London. And take Jack too.'

'What about your house?'

'So far, we don't think anyone has been relocated, so if Jack goes, we could let it turn back into a normal house and then I would just rent it, or sell it.'

'How would you know if someone is relocated within the five and a fifth remaining weeks' period before it goes back to normal? You might already have some you don't know about and then they would be totally stranded.'

'I have cancelled all the room bookings. I don't want the responsibility of anyone being relocated because of me. My money issues are suddenly much less important than before the whole Fog thing started.'

'I have the same concern with the relocation responsibility. Except it is too late for me. I have turned another house and relocated someone there when I didn't know it could happen. In London as well, people got relocated by accident.'

'Like your best friend?'

'Yes ... is it possible that the Fog intends to open portals and intends to be used a certain way, and if you try to control it, it will find a way round it? Like it is alive?'

'It sounds a bit like Leila's theory, but even weirder,' he wrote.

'It does, doesn't it? Quite a fatalistic approach: we are not in control of anything, and another entity might be,' I wrote back, thinking I preferred Leila's approach.

'I think that is pretty obvious, we have no control here. *Ma,* right now, it doesn't matter, I have won the challenge. I have a date with you.'

'You have. Stop boasting!'

'Ciao, bella Yoko.'

'Ciao, cheeky Leo.'

When the instant message box closed, I returned to the Foggies' platform. You could select Foggies either by name or by location. I selected the map and counted: London (United Kingdom), Rome (Italy), Marrakech (Morocco), Skagway (Alaska), Nairobi (Kenya), Carson City (Nevada), Mexico (Mexico). These were more than Leila had mentioned in the morning. It totalled seven locations, that is, seven Switchers. That was it! All the Foggies had been found. I sat up in my bed and bent further over my tablet to read.

Foggies of three locations had been in contact with me, even if my knowledge was limited in Marrakech to Christophe (little by little I would manage not to call him cdr69) and the missing Jack in Rome. I clicked on Skagway, Alaska and saw three names appear: Rosario, Mitch and Tony.

Rosario was a good-looking brown-eyed brunette, with a hint of Alaskan or Native American features from the slightly tanned colour of her skin, almond shaped eyes and long, straight, lustrous hair. Despite the clear don't-mess-with-me personality shining through, there was a kindness in her face which made her seem good-natured. She looked to be in her early twenties. So my first impression from the picture was of a strong yet sympathetic young woman. I breathed a sigh of relief. The picture was taken at a dining table with a white wall behind, bare except for a photo of four individuals on a lake with a mountain background. It was too small to see the details, but I thought one of the people was her. There was no last name on her profile (I didn't put mine either) and she was labelled as Switcher. My fellow counterpart across the globe then.

Mitch, marked as Crosser, looked a bit like Rosario: dark features, dark eyes, kind smile. Even with a short cut, he had a lot of hair pointing and waving in all directions, dishevelled and wild. The picture was shot outside a wooden house and showed him from the waist up. He was tall, fit and slender. My guess was Mitch and Rosario were family because of the shared similar features and eyes. Mitch seemed older, the rough weather and winds of Alaska having already started to leave traces on his face

Tony was slim and strawberry blond. He had short hair like Mitch, but his was better tamed. The picture of him was more posed: businesslike and wearing a suit. It reminded me of the business shots on company websites and brochures. Tony looked in his mid-twenties. He was their Facilitator.

If I was correct in my estimates of their ages, they were all in their early to mid-twenties. They were young to have their dreams for their future shattered. They faced a new life that nothing and no one had prepared them for. They had barely had a chance to experience normality. Were they coping with the novelty of their situation well?

Next, I selected Nairobi, Kenya.

Clare, Mary and Putu were all women. That was a change: so far the majority of Foggies were men. Clare was a good-looking woman in her late fifties to early sixties, with dark skin and cropped black hair. The photo showed her in an elegant suit, smiling at the camera in what looked like her office. Clare was the Switcher. Mary was undeniably her daughter and looked in her early thirties. Same face shape, same eyes, same half-smile, even same haircut. Mary was a Crosser. The third person, Putu, was a young blonde woman, with a shoulder bob and a very white, almost transparent skin. How she handled the sun in Kenya, I couldn't be sure. She seemed more suited to Scandinavia. She looked young, more a teenager than an adult and very frail. The picture was a spontaneous shot of her outside a low-built large house surrounded by children. She was wearing a stethoscope.

Her notes indicated she was a doctor, so she must be more than twenty-five, even if appearing to be only seventeen. Putu was tagged as a Facilitator. I speculated on what her connection with Clare and Mary could be: did mother or daughter call for a doctor when the Fog happened, and Putu went to treat them, only to discover she was a Facilitator? Also, I noted that Putu sounded like a local name. Not that I wanted to be prejudiced or make assumptions, but a pale blonde woman named Putu was most unusual.

The Marrakech tab showed only two names: Christophe de Roque and Louise. Isabelle was a Relocated, not a Foggy, she was not included on the Foggies page. Her status had been confirmed by the nail and irises test: hers were unchanged. I would have loved to put a face to her name. That would come later. Only Christophe had put in any information at that time. From his photo, it was difficult to determine what his height was. The best guess being average. He had grey hair, which surprised me for his age of forty-two. I could tell his age because he had entered his birthday. In fact, he had filled in a long section about himself. It looked like a copy and paste of his CV plus a brief biography, which seemed as if it had been extracted directly from a company profile giving his whole professional background: finance (asset management), studies (an overlong list), hobbies (skiing, squash, tennis, rugby, scuba-diving, hunting, the whole thing). Christophe de Rocque was a good-looking man, lean, with a lot of allure and presence and indisputably very French. I would not be able to define what I meant by 'the French look' but he embodied it. Most French abroad can spot another French person a mile away and with Christophe that would be an easy job. He looked a bit of a charmer too, one of those handsome men who know it too much and play on it. At least, he definitely used on it on the camera. I was pretty sure he did selfies a lot and often practised in the mirror. There again, maybe I was biased by the bad impression he had given me via his emails.

The Mexico and Carson City tabs were empty. Leila probably hadn't had a chance to go and visit them yet.

'OK. Time to connect,' I thought. First, I wrote a little bit about me and the household in the profile section, not much, just what you would tell at a dinner party when first introducing yourself. Afterwards, I prepared a template for an 'Introduction Email' to send to FTab contacts. Those few lines took me over an hour to type, as I approached them like a professional introduction. No matter what some people say, first impressions count. This made me wince, recalling my appearance for the encounter with the Lil'London Council members. The result of my labours was half a page on the house, the household, and how I fitted into it. Most importantly, I invited the recipient to connect: 'We are all in this together. Yes, this is quite an adventure, and yes, this is also a nuisance. It will be easier if we support each other as a community'. My little note was addressed to everyone including Leila. Leo immediately replied with 'Nice one, cutie!' That was a new one, 'cutie'. I am not a fan. A teddy bear, a puppy, a baby is cute, but me – a grown up woman? Best to just ignore.

Just as I was about to switch off the light for the night, I received another message from Leo at the same time as a text from Rico: Rico had enabled them to come back to Rome! So Facilitators could help with any Fog. Leo added that Jack already had a big crush on Rico, his new hunk-hero. The Roman Foggies were over the moon with joy. This was big, huge, great news!

**Day 6 (Friday)**

Friday, at last! I woke up thinking I ought to keep a record of my experiences, as well as the number of weeks passed for each Fog created: it was important not to let seven weeks go by without visits or the Fog would return to normal, that is a non-portal. Some days when my sister was just a pest with me, the possibility of letting the parental home return to normal was tempting. Of course I knew I would never do this to her. When asked what would happen if she was in the house when it 'unfogged' Leila had explained she would just wake up in the Other World, her bed or whatever she would be sleeping having somewhat dropped to the ground. At least it was in theory. So I had to make sure I visited my parents before that happened.

Back at home in the evening, Jazz and I were chatting, a glass of wine in hand. For the rest of the world, she was now supposedly visiting relatives in India. We were in the kitchen, preparing her favourite ginger and walnut brownies to help raise her spirits. Zeno was with us as well, on the phone as usual and picking at some of the stemmed ginger as he talked. We heard Harry barging down the stairs, shouting 'Damn! Damn! Damn!' It was bound to be Fog-related. The Fog was a big swearing inducer. We followed him to the living room without questioning him. He set his laptop on the dining table and the evening news was blasting out. We were all staring at some photos of a lovely resort in Mexico, which then disappeared to show a live image of a foggy mass surrounded by palm trees, ambulances and police cars. There was frantic activity of people in either touristy clothes or official uniforms. Corpses were being carried away in the background.

'Oh shit ...' I muttered to myself.

'Shush!' Jazz prompted.

We stood in the middle of the room, listening to the anchor and watching the ominous images.

'Hang on. I'll select the story to replay it from the start. You need to listen to that,' Harry said.

'Good evening. I am reporting live from a small beach hotel in Cancun, Mexico, scene of a horrific massacre that took place in this usually beautiful and peaceful holiday resort. Last night the hotel, currently closed to the public for analysis due to a local phenomenon, suffered a violent assault by an unknown group who killed anyone in their path. The police and family of the besieged hotel staff received terrified calls that men in the traditional local attire of feather and cloth were attacking them. The police intervened, but only a few people were found alive. None of the attackers were captured. Using the fog to facilitate their escape, they left carnage behind them. The police are gathering evidence and reviewing the resort's security tapes. This was a terrible scene of bloody and mutilated corpses. We do not have details at this point. The police have only informed us that the killing was barbaric with the use of blades, axes or machetes. The count is of seventeen people dead and of ten in intensive care, having suffered severe mutilation. Only five people of the thirty-two members of staff currently on site escaped unharmed, although they are terribly shaken by this traumatic experience.

'The circumstances could have been even more dramatic if the hotel had been open as usual. The hotel owners were currently debating about whether or not to reopen its doors to guests. Indeed, about two weeks ago the hotel had to close due to an unexpected and baffling phenomenon. The Sunday before last, the guests woke up to find their hotel covered by a strange mist. This was even more curious since it was limited to the hotel building and once out of the fog the guests were able to enjoy the beauties they had come to see. However, the hotel manager, staff and guests grew alarmed when the mist remained as the day went on. Many of the guests were at the end of their holidays and left to go back home. The authorities decided that the remaining ones and new arrivals would be redirected to other resorts, while the hotel closed for health and safety reasons. For a week, the origin of the mist was investigated. This investigation proved unsuccessful and neither the origins of the mist nor its nature could be defined. It presents a mild non-toxic radioactivity, otherwise its components are those of mist, or, for a more appropriate term due to the highly limited visibility, fog. The hotel was allowed to invite the staff back earlier this week, with a view to preparing the venue for new guests over the weekend. The police have enrolled the help of specialists to find out if the fog could have been created by the killers to help them carry out their deadly actions. It has certainly helped them escape the police.

'In addition, the hotel is undergoing a 'missing person' investigation, which also started the weekend the fog appeared. The police welcome any lead in the matter. There are fears they could have been taken by the aggressors.'

The news went on to some elections in Hungary, or maybe it was Poland, no one was paying attention anymore. None of us had moved an inch.

'Holy shit!' Jazz burbled.

'We all think the same, don't we?' Harry asked, looking round.

'Yes. The hotel is a portal and the inhabitants on the other side are definitely not keen on tourists,' I said.

'I am changing my opinion on Lil'London. It might be more of a paradise than I thought ...' Jazz continued.

'I don't understand,' Zeno said. 'Why would they kill everyone? They don't even know us? What do they gain by doing that? Why?'

'Maybe they didn't like the fact that the Spanish eradicated their civilisation?' Harry replied.

'Well ... if you put it like that ... a bit extreme, no?' Zeno said, scowling.

'It is terrible. Poor people! Terrible. Just terrible. And the one who switched the house? He or she must feel so awful, so guilty, so crap right now. That is, if the person is still alive. Oh ... my ... God!' My words brought silence. I broke it with another thought voiced out loud. 'Oh no! Now, with the fog in the news, how long before people here make a parallel with us?'

'Yoko, Leila is supposed to be in London already, right? She wasn't in that hotel, investigating aside for the Society, was she?' Zeno exclaimed.

This prompted me to run upstairs to get the FTab to write to Leila for confirmation she was safe in London. She replied within minutes. The Mexico situation was a major crisis. The whole Society was focused on it, including her. She would still do her best to join us tomorrow morning as agreed.

Jazz had been very excited to meet Leila and she was even more expectant now. She was determined to get her hands on an FTab. I tried explaining to her that it was reserved for the Foggies and that the Relocated would get something different, but it made no difference.

'Forget it Yoko. I am always in the in-crowd, not any others,' she said dismissively.

'Jazz, there is no in or out ...' I began but she interrupted me.

'You know what I mean! Come on Yoko, I am trying to deal with it here. It is hard. It is very hard! I ... I try not to think of what I have lost. I try not to ... At least it is not a random person who relocated me, but my best friend. Imagine me stranded with strangers. Yuk! Plus I have the boys to protect me here and it is reassuring.' She looked round at Harry and Zeno and added, with a weak attempt at banter, 'Well ... just a bit reassuring then.' Jazz shuddered when she finished, 'Jeez, this Mexico hotel ...'

'Girls, seriously, this Mexico story, it concerns me,' Harry said. 'It could easily happen here. In our sleep.'

'Harry, you are not going to do a Rico on us, are you? Yes it could happen, but it hasn't so far,' I told him. In reality I was terrified, only attempting to play the big tough kid to lighten the mood.

'Why don't we booby-trap the place? Like putting little bells at windows and stuff?' I suggested.

'I am calling tomorrow to have an alarm set up,' Harry replied.

'It is expensive,' Zeno retorted.

'Life is worth it,' Harry snapped.

**Day 7 (Saturday)**

'Here is the situation with Mexico,' Leila explained the next morning. 'You may have noticed a new addition to the Foggies platform based in Carson City with Adam, Switcher, his wife Sophia, Crosser, and his daughter Michelle, Facilitator. They went on holiday to Mexico three weeks ago and switched the hotel into a portal on the same night you did Yoko. It happened on their last night before their return back home to Nevada. That Sunday when they woke up and found the hotel surrounded by Fog, they just thought they were leaving at the right time. Of course, like everybody else, they were surprised when they realised the Fog was only over the hotel building, but they were leaving so they did not linger over the matter. They were with their daughter and stepdaughter Michelle that morning, so they did not realise that without her as Facilitator they would be stuck in the resort or in the Mexican jungle of that Other World. As they left, they were also unaware that four people had been relocated, or at least we assume the four missing people are Relocated. It is only last weekend, when they turned their house in the suburbs of Carson City into a Foggy portal, that this family realised something was wrong. It became even more obvious when for some reason they headed out without Michelle ... To cut a long story short, only when we met them on Thursday about the Carson City Fog, did we realise that Mexico was their work too. Another member of the Society was still in Mexico trying to make contact with the ones who had switched the house. We feared it would be a guest who had switched the venue. We were right. Now we have a major crisis on our hands! The Koplats are terrified by what they created and the carnage that ensued. They live just outside the city in some kind of modern ranch with horses for Sophia who adores them. The property is not enclosed and the Fog is easily seen once you get on their dirt road. The good news is that they don't have immediate neighbours and the post is left in the mailbox at the start of a mile long dirt road. Plus they have kept a low profile. So far, they don't think the transformation has been noticed. As for us, we found them by satellite images – an arduous task, I am pleased not to be in my colleague's shoes.

'Now, in Mexico, we are dealing with a serious issue. We need to get that hotel empty, even from the police or anyone. They are all placed in danger as soon as they step in. The locals from that Other World can come in at any time. We do not want another massacre from – and of –either side. In five weeks, the place will return to normal. We need to gain time and to keep the place closed for that amount of time. We are also trying to speak with the survivors, which is proving difficult with the authorities. We must find out as much as possible on the locals: we do not know when the last opening in that location was and which civilisation they are based on. This makes first contact difficult. Honestly, our hopes of getting in touch with the Relocated are close to none.

'And last, we must exercise damage control on the spread of information. We do not want the attention to be turned to the other "fogged places" around the world. Like yours. You are right in the middle of town. How long before the firemen connect the dots and you end up having police and other officials on your back? You need to move. Same for the guys in Rome and in Marrakesh. The others are more remote and have gone unnoticed so far: we will ensure it stays that way.'

'How?' Zeno enquired.

'We monitor the information out there and intervene when we can. We have already hacked the fire brigade system and deleted the report regarding your house and did the same for the lab company they used.'

'What?' we all exclaimed.

'You just broke into their system and 'simply' deleted the data?' I was stunned.

'Well, yes, how else would you like us to proceed? We can't walk in and ask them to hand it over, can we? Anyway, the ones who came obviously know, so we have to deal with that.'

'You are not going to eliminate them, are you?' Zeno looked horrified.

'Of course not! We are not THAT type of Society! A little bit of tampering with data is not the same as killing someone. No, we simply think you need to move.'

'Wouldn't it be an admission something is wrong with the house, with us?' I asked.

'Maybe, but it is better than staying here. We are thinking the countryside would be good.'

'What about me?' Jazz asked. Her jaw was clenched, her stare icy. She was not a happy bunny. 'I was actually working on a little idea of my own: selling my place and trying to buy the house next door. Yoko could turn it. I would organise a move remotely of all my stuff and, done! New home!'

'You were working on this?' I was looking at Jazz dumbfounded. She had not said a word to me about it.

'Yes and, trust me, this fog thing's a good way of getting to buy the place. I contacted your neighbours by email and said I was working for a scientific company interested in the nature of the fog as it is a rare occurrence. I mentioned they wanted to analyse the long term possible effects and growth potential of the fog. They do not like it at all.'

'Miss Jones, you should not have done this. This is not ethical,' Leila said, frowning.

'Miss Al-Safidi, I really couldn't care less,' Jazz replied.

'But, really ...' Leila started, before Jazz interrupted, the icy stare fixed on her. Any of the classic Jazz sweetness was gone. Jazz was showing her other side.

'Don't even try. What? Do you think only the firemen will talk? You know very well that once the authorities are aware a similar fog exists in England, they will hunt us down. Not that I have a say, but I would feel more secure in town than in the middle of nowhere if I were the Foggies. Isolation might not be the best protection. Yes, I am using the situation to my advantage to try and make myself a nice nest. Isn't it normal? To manage to buy the house next door, I will have to play on their possible concern with the Fog. I would! This is human of me, no? Still, I will be fair. I won't try to make them sell it to me for nothing, I am just trying to make them sell. You are not in my shoes, so don't judge me. Later today you will meet the guys who will be my social interaction from now on – other than this house's inhabitants and visitors. They are such a jolly lot; when I met them my thoughts were that I might as well shoot myself.'

'Miss Jones, I ...' Leila tried again.

'I. Haven't. Finished! Now. You don't know me. I know I can't control what is happening to me right now, but I am incapable of letting things happen without reacting and without trying to make it the best I can for ME and that is exactly what I intend to DO! What about the other Relocated? James Fisher and any future ones before this house returns to normal as you suggest? Where does your idea leave us? You don't think we keep a link with you? With our families and friends? I do!'

'Jazz, I for one want to make sure our decisions include what is good for you too.' I was looking at Jazz and Leila, then turned to Zeno and Harry and continued talking, getting more and more animated as I spoke. 'I think it's a great idea renting or buying the house next to ours for you, Jazz! Yes of course I would fog it. We could build a wall to hide the Fog from view. Then little by little why not get all the houses on the plot? They wouldn't all need to be fogged of course. Some of us could have a double life, benefitting from both a normal house and the life in our good old world. Not only that, we could then use the parking lot to store vehicles and other tools for transfer to the Other World to make our life better. Maybe even a helicopter for any necessary long journey? Yes! I am dreaming big! Let's keep dreaming: the Society could have an even bigger site, one in more remote countryside, maybe in the UK, or maybe somewhere else in Europe and in the US, where you may even have planes flying between the Foggies communities. And Switchers, Crossers and Facilitators could easily go where they are needed. Thanks to the planes and helicopters and the similar layout of the ground, a Relocated would be able to travel too, if needed. And then maybe we could gather the Relocated in the location best for them and we would not be so disseminated and at the mercy of the World II whimsical locals ... and then ...'

'Hmm ... Earth calling Yoko. Get off your cloud!' Harry took advantage of my need to breathe to bring me back down to reality.

'Leila, Jazz, guys ... I know this is totally unrealistic and financially huge,' I continued more poised. 'I have been told so many times that you have to dream big to reach big. We do have responsibilities with the Relocated and we should try and help as much as we can. We have Jazz and Mr Fisher here. We have Isabelle in Marrakech, alone in a desert with a baby coming soon. Not forgetting my sister Julia and my nephew in France as well.'

No one spoke after I stopped talking, until Leila broke the heavy silence a few minutes later.

'I agree the Relocated are important. As to this idea of using the lot, some of it might be feasible ... But I still think London is not a good idea,' she commented.

'Leila, leaving London means we all need to give up our life,' Harry decided it was his turn to speak. 'As a Facilitator, I have no reason to. I am not directly affected by the Fog, all I do is walk out with the ones who need help to come back to our world. I love my job, I love being in London and do not want to move to the country. Yes, I am delighted I can be here for my friends. It is a privilege to help them without having to give up all I have worked for and all that is my life. Leaving London would mean that. Please note, I am not saying I wouldn't do it for them, just that I don't see why, if it isn't really necessary at this point. Jazz's way of thinking is very attractive.'

'Me neither, I don't want to,' Zeno added. 'I don't have a specific reason. I just don't fancy it.'

'I see ... I guess we will have to find good reasons or an alternative then,' Leila moaned. She had a lot on her mind already and this was one more thing she could have done without.

'How about Yoko's more global idea of getting the whole lot of houses? You said some of it could work?' Jazz asked.

'Well, we could look into it ...' Leila replied.

'I'll get on with dealing with the owners next door this coming week, as well as selling my house,' Jazz persisted.

'I need to present the idea to the Society first.' Leila had not completely given up. 'It is a big budget. It may take time and still leaves a high chance of the authorities getting involved. I guess we could monitor servers and emails of the police and intercept any reference to the Fog ... '

'Can you do this? Really?' Zeno asked, baffled.

'If you have the technical tools and the brains, yes you can. And yes, we can.'

Zeno let a 'Spookyyy ...' escape and his eyes started to glaze over. I could only imagine what would have been Rico's reaction had he been here.

At 6 p.m., in my room writing to Leo, I was recounting that afternoon's visit from Benjamin Snayth, Augustus Hoare and Edmund Poff. This time again, Snayth had done most of the speaking. Augustus Hoare sometimes broke his fellow council member's monologue to complete a point with a few details (more often than not, details that left us uncomfortable). Edmund Poff essentially nodded with vehemence at the description's accuracy of the Lil'London customs and life. Neither Jazz nor I could nod our approbation in return.

Snayth started by giving us an endearing description of their community. A quiet little town where people had learned to get on with each other and attend to their dedicated businesses. The town had its own democratic structure with the council acting as a board of wise men running the town. It all sounded very lovely. However I doubted that this apparently idyllic town had really managed to escape the flaws and pettiness intrinsic to human-kind. Utopia does not exist. Besides this too good to be true pic-ture of Lil'London, the handsome albeit stern face of Augustus Hoare and the total lack of joy emanating from it would kill any enthusiasm for the town. I was trying very hard not to let my cyni-cism take over and put on a charmed face, until they described their method to ensure the survival of the human race on their lands. To enable the city to grow and ensure their future, they had established an efficient system of polygamy starting from an early age, ensuring maximum productivity and use of women's fertility. Those who proved non-fertile were to compensate for this defi-ciency – as they put it – by various means according to their status. Barren women of high standing were to dedicate time to the edu-cation of children. Women of lowest status or coloured women were helping by nursing and tending to the children's care, by alleviating the traditional house chores of cleaning, washing and cooking. The same went for women who had passed the age of giving birth. Jazz was struggling to control herself, jaws, hands, back and shoulders tensed, and I realised I was doing exactly the same.

Meanwhile, the men were hard at work putting food on the table for their wives and children. Their work varied: farmers, hunters, carpenters, blacksmith, doctor ... Everyone had a spe-ciality. The town had a market to sell the various produce and a store which also served as a trading place. They even had a little restaurant, a doctor's surgery and a brothel. Yes, a broth-el! It was managed and secured by the sheriff, currently Hoare, and used by the men whose wives were pregnant or otherwise indisposed. The brothel was used as punishment for the rebel-lious women who had refused to follow the rules or for loose and adulterous women. They had found it much more efficient than sending them to prison, where they would not be of use. This feminine dreamland currently counted about 8,500 inhabitants. The figure brought consternation from our household, no one expecting such a large number. It was an even bigger surprise to hear that they were also trading with another town from some previous portal openings about thirty miles away which counted a good twelve thousand people. Twenty thousand people in a thirty mile radius! I had thought five hundred, maybe a thousand at most. I was imagining a village, a hamlet even, not a real town. Out of nowhere, I remembered reading that social analysts had calculated one percent of the population of any community is psychopathic. So among those eight and a half thousand, there could be eighty-five psychopaths. Now, in a big town you can always have the illusion you don't know them and they get loss in the mass, but there, we were bound to meet them. Some knowledge is sometimes best forgotten.

When I mentioned the size of the local community in Lil'London to him, Leo's reaction was similar to mine. He was immediately curious to see if it could be the same in his part of 'World II'? Would he encounter a 'Lil'Rome'? He confessed he had been online researching some of the local history of 1782 to try and discover who might have disappeared then and if there was any record of a mysterious fog. He had found nothing. Neither had I for London. Either there was no information out there, or the Society had erased references to mysterious fogs in any known literature from the past.

The Society. I longed to know more about them too, their resources and their objectives. They were almost too good to be true, with their generosity and positivity. None of us in the house wanted to become the lab rat of any government or corporate entity, but neither did we wish to rely too much on an unknown 'Society' which could have ulterior motives. So far, their spirituality and idealism did them credit, though to be realistic, they might try to use us as much as any other entity later on. It was one of the reasons, not voiced out loud to Leila, why I didn't want to move to the country under their supervision. No way was I going to move to an unknown area where they would control everything. That was already sorted by the time I wrote to Leo. Leila had dealt with our morning request efficiently. The Society had agreed to consider buying the plot of houses as an alternative to us leaving the house. However, they refused to allow Jazz to buy the house next door ('I don't need their permission!' she had exclaimed on hearing this. 'Even if struggling to get enough money for it, I refuse to be told what I can and cannot do by them!') Their idea was to buy the eight houses in the lot, including the house we lived in. Some would be turned into the portal, the others would be for the Society and any visitors.

I had refused categorically, remaining very laconic in my reasoning except that it would leave us totally dependent on the Society and that was not acceptable. If they wanted us to trust them, they would have to trust us. I suggested the ownership should be divided and went even further, saying that even if they bought the eight houses for our sake, three should be in our household names (Zeno, Harry, Rico and me) – one to remain a portal in which Jazz could live, and two to remain normal. I didn't know what came over me, probably a surge of rebellion in the name of freedom. Everyone in the room, me included, was gobsmacked. Being a business shark was not in my character, yet there I was, negotiating to be given three houses in Central London. It was very gutsy, and I was pushing the limit of the reasonable pretty far. Leila just gaped at me, a smile slowly rising at the corner of her mouth. After thirty seconds or so, she nodded. She agreed to talk to the Society on our behalf. Leila didn't even try to fight against my demands as if she approved of them or of my attitude. That, too, surprised me.

Earlier that evening, Leila contacted us with a counter-offer from the Society. Those guys worked fast! Here was their offer: they would buy the eight houses and put three houses in our names, leaving them with five houses. In exchange, they were expecting the following:

1. Two fogged houses
   One theirs. One ours (for Jazz). I would switch and maintain both. They wanted to use it for their studies and for travelling Foggies. They thought it would be easier if the two fogged houses, Jazz's and theirs, were next to each other, so that they could build a protective partition in the front and at the back of both to hide the Fog from view. If acceptable to us, they would set up high security, with cameras and motion sensors on the ground inside the walls (but not inside our houses).

2. Four normal Society houses
   Two of their houses would be on each end of the terrace for better security, as directly on the street. One would serve as an office for the company set up as per point 4 (also to be used as a front house accessible for the authorities and uninformed visitors and as a mailing address for visitors and friends). On the other end of the terrace, the house would be transformed into a storage facility for goods, vehicles and whatever would be required to explore or trade on the other side of the Fog. Their third house would serve to accommodate visitors in the know, Foggies and members of the Society as needed. The last one would be for their security and IT team.

3. London Fog Company
   The Society was to create a UK company to justify the changes on the lot, focused officially on managing the properties and unofficially on dealing with local Fog-related matters. That company would also liaise with the Society in New York, manage visitors and organise analysis and studies. Last but not least, it would deal with the

exchange of goods and information with the Other World
and be the crisis management centre in case of Fog issues,
either related to this world or World II.

4. Jobs

They suggested Zeno and I could work for this new company. There would be lots to do in terms of gathering
information, trading, liaising and, reporting to and with
the Other World. Relocated settlements and family issues would need to be supervised, plus visits from other
Foggies. As well as being a member of the Foggies group,
all this would need to be dealt with. It would be helpful if
I would accept the post of project manager and liaison officer and Zeno, trader and on-site analyst. It seemed to be
appropriate to our range of expertise and competencies.
It would all look official, with a proper income and travel
opportunities. The roles and hours would be flexible and
negotiable. The Society would also put at our disposal the
means to do our jobs properly. Their goal was knowledge
and liaison with the Other World, as well as to avoid any
more calamities as had happened in Mexico.

They also offered part-time positions to Harry and
Rico. The objective was that both Facilitators would have
this time free should any Foggies require their help to
cross between worlds. Rico being a painter, such a part-
time income would enable him flexibility for his art. For
Harry, the Society understood his wish to continue his
current occupation, so what they suggested was to create
a fellowship for him at their university in partnership with
his, just requiring him to reduce his hours to get more
flexibility. They would be very happy to let him in, too, on
some of the work they had done and planned to do.

In the house, we were all dumbfounded. 'What? Why? How?
Have they really just offered us our own houses AND a job?

Really?' I exclaimed inwardly. Somehow, I was torn between jumping up and down screaming 'Yippee!' and scowling with suspicion, grumbling there must be a catch somewhere. I could only blame myself for being in this situation though: the idea of getting the whole bunch of terraced houses bought had come from my little mouth ...

'Why are you being so generous?' Harry questioned, voicing the question we all had in mind.

'We have been waiting for more than two hundred years for another door to open. We have been studying and researching and have a long list of questions and unknowns. We have many hopes, many unanswered questions. Without you though, we are nothing. We need you. We don't want to force you into anything, just your cooperation. If we work together on the basis of a mutual agreement, some good work will come out of it and it will benefit and please everyone involved. Money is not what drives us. Knowledge is. We are pure intellectuals and scientists.'

'And if we say no and refuse to cooperate, what would you do?' Harry insisted.

'We would try to propose alternatives that would suit you better, but if you persist in saying no, I guess we would have to focus on the other Foggies and just try to protect the London Fog from afar. That would be an unfortunate loss of potential and opportunities, for you and for us. I really believe that. We can help you make your life easier. You will be free and independent: we want a partnership, not control. We are not a coercive entity. It is against our goals and it represents exactly what we want to fight.'

'Yes, you said it before, you are pacific little academics who only want to act for the better good of both worlds,' Harry remarked ironically.

'I know what you are thinking: things like 'too good to be true', 'hidden agenda', 'fake good Samaritans', but why can't you believe that would be possible? Look at Greenpeace, Médecins sans Frontières, even the Red Cross, don't they have the same goals? Don't you realise how fascinating this is for us? We could test the ozone or rediscover extinct animals. And at the same time, we can prevent damaging that World II. Do you think corporations would not find it a unique opportunity to dig up rare resources in the Other World, or even dump their rubbish, toxic or not, there? It is not their world, how many of them would care with their profit-oriented minds? Or terrorist groups: if they have access to that world, would they not take the opportunity to use it for their hidden activities, store arms, develop nuclear weapons, all without control? I mentioned it all before. Knowing the potential and risks, don't you understand why we want to keep the portals quiet and try to use them for the greater good? Not everything or everyone is bad in this world. And honestly, had we wished to, we could already have had you taken and locked up somewhere, blackmailing you into doing what we want by using threats to your families. We haven't.'

That was food for thought. She had a point. Looking round at the others, their faces betrayed they thought the same as me. She continued, 'In fact, we have discreetly protected you from the beginning, ever since we met. We have actually set up encryption on your phones and increased the security on your emails to avoid your being put on the radar of people searching around the Fog. We have even interfered with satellite imaging data.'

'No way? But ...' I exclaimed.

'Don't even ask, we just did. We have great technological means at our disposal. In fact, we have great means in general.'

'Was it really necessary to go as far as that?' Something about her tone had raised the alarm and I was fishing to know what.

'Yes. There is at least one other party interested in you. There is no doubt that party has means too. I can assure you, they are active. And dangerous.'

'Dangerous? How do you know?' Zeno broke in.

'Our representative in Mexico was found dead a few hours ago.'

'HOLY SHIT!' I exclaimed.

'Yes, my thinking exactly. There were signs of fighting and shooting in his room, then he obviously managed to get out to his car. There are signs of a car chase and shootings. The police are now involved. Unfortunately our man got shot and his car crashed.'

'Are you sure it wasn't some local thugs? A robbery maybe? Or even one of those crazy feathered 'Mayans' from World II?' Zeno asked.

'Yes.'

'But ...' Zeno started.

'When he was in the car he sent a quick text. 'Attacked. After Fog information. Pro.' It was definitely a professional job and he or she searched his papers either before or after the event. The killer didn't take any money. He/she didn't have a chance to get their hands on the electronics – tablet and mobile – which were on our agent. The police did. It doesn't matter, they couldn't crack the codes. Thankfully we can remotely erase everything and reset the device to manufacturer's settings. Still, it confirmed suspicions we have had for some time that we are not the only ones interested in the Fog. That someone else has an interest is fine by us, depending on what type of interest. However, the people behind this, we don't like their methods. It doesn't bode well. We are pretty angry to tell you the truth.'

'No kidding ...' Harry muttered.

'This is why we really, really, want to protect you now. We have also placed digital and physical protection on each of your families. We want to be open about this.'

'What about my family?' Jazz asked. She had not uttered a word for some time, just gasped here and there at what Leila was saying, like all of us.

'Sorry Jazz. We have only set up digital protection on communications for your parents and siblings, not a physical one. We need to prioritise.'

'Great ... This Relocated thing sucks. It's like second-rate citizenship. I already know I am going to get fat with all that. I foresee chocolate compensation for my bruised ego. Or ... Actually, Yoko, I need a drink.' Jazz's half-sarcastic, half-serious tone didn't hide well how shaken she really was. She was close to tears. I decided to match her falsely light-hearted attitude to help her hold it together: 'I presume only champagne will do?'

'Yes.'

'Errr ... I don't have any ready. I have Prosecco in my fridge, would that be acceptable?'

'Yes!' She jumped off the sofa and went into the kitchen.

Leila had been listening to the conversation quite stunned.

'Does she have a drinking problem?' Leila asked, serious, 'because drunk people can talk and considering the circumstances ...'

'No,' I replied with confidence. 'She doesn't, have no fear. She will only have a glass or two. She is shaken, she is after a boost or to give her countenance.'

From the kitchen, we heard Jazz shout, 'I can hear you, you know!'

I shouted back, 'It was a fair question!'

The cork popped open and a few minutes later Jazz reappeared, skilfully holding four glasses in one hand, including a full one, and the bottle in the other. She put them all on the table and started pouring into the three empty glasses while Leila continued, 'So, to return to the deal between the Society and you for the acquisition of the terraced houses, I know it's a lot to dwell on. I will email you the details of the offer so that you can think about it and discuss it among yourselves. If you could reach a decision by tomorrow evening or maybe Monday morning, we would be grateful. We would like to get moving as soon as possible. The earlier we buy all the houses, get trees and build the wall, the better we can ensure discretion and protection. And Jazz, sorry, I know you wanted to buy a house, but you could have a separate deal with the Foggies.'

'Yeah. Whatever. Second-class citizens indeed.'

'I have to go now. A pleasure to see and to deal with you, as usual. Thank you for being quite cool about all of this. Trust me, not everyone is that amenable.'

'Among the Foggies?' I asked.

'Yes, but this is a story for another time. Let's just say cdr69 proved to be rather exhausting, along with 'his women'... I must go. I will be in touch very soon.'

All of us in the house, in harmony, closed the conversation with 'Bye' and after a few seconds we all reached for a glass, except Jazz who was already sipping hers.

'Wow!' I uttered.

'I am not even going to mention not having a tablet either,' Jazz moaned.

'A lot of information. A lot to think about,' murmured Harry to himself.

'Maybe you should apply for a job as well,' I suggested to Jazz. 'You could undertake basic spy training online and offer your services to the company. I am sure we could find some information on Google for this!' If she was working with us, she might develop a sense of purpose about being a Relocated. That would soothe her 'slightly' bruised ego too.

What the Society was saying made sense. Leila had convinced me, and they had my vote in favour of their offer. A little part of me still felt that we should simply contact the authorities and rely on them to secure and provide for us and the Relocated. Opting for the official and clear option, we would have less responsibility, plus we would know who we would be dealing with. All the same, how much would the government be open to negotiating, instead of imposing their will for the 'national security' and/or the so-called 'national interest'? Anyway, which government would we turn to? English? Italian? French? No, I didn't trust them to respect me as an individual and the flexibility in my life, which was exactly what the Society seemed to offer. Sleeping on it was a good idea.

For the rest of the evening, Jazz and I decided to have a bit of pressure release and spend an overdue fun nonsensical evening together. We planned a cosy dinner, another bottle and a romantic comedy movie for some laughs. I hoped that getting tipsy would put me to sleep. I was wrong. The second my head hit the pillow, a thousand thoughts churned in my head and fed my night anxiety: why is it that the scenarios of your life are always dramas when trying to sleep, hardly ever comedies? Lil'London's old-fashioned views on women and racism, Mexico and the deaths of many innocent people, the ruined hopes in life of the Relocated, the dead member of the Society, and this dangerous third party who didn't stop at killing, all of this turned and turned in my mind. I hugged my pillow and hid my head under my duvet as if it could protect me from the dangers I sensed linked to the Fog … Even the good news about the house and my proper addiction to exchanging messages with Leo could not lift my spirits.

# WEEK III

**Day 1 (Sunday)**

I woke up hungry and not feeling refreshed. I had not slept well. A big breakfast in bed gave me a lift: thick slices of bread with a generous spread of butter and honey on top, plus both an espresso and a milky cup of tea. A quiet morning with time on my own was needed to gather my strength. Today Rico would be coming back. I was looking forward to having him at home and safe. Harry had been great the past two days, not leaving the house and remaining at our disposal should Zeno and I need to get out to London. In truth, he was behaving almost as usual; he never left the house much. He never talked about girlfriends, never brought his friends at home much. The few, but very few, ones who visited were all colleagues from university. Harry was a great guy, he had a fabulous sarcastic sense of humour, but he lived for his work. If he agreed to the deal with the Society, the Fog would shake his world a little with the travels involved to the other Foggies and the Society university. The latter was right up his alley.

I was enjoying each bite of sliced bread, honey running over my fingers, each followed by a sip of tea. It was a peaceful moment. I didn't seem to have many of these of late. Half-consciously, I was postponing opening the FTab and getting busy. I was also completely overdue in replying to my emails, calls and messages from friends I had avoided, cancelled, or ignored in the past two weeks. Some of them were even close friends and I was feeling pretty bad having to push them away so they didn't come and visit. What else could I do though? I didn't want another case of a friend being relocated. It made me think of the Society proposal: with a house for us next door and unfogged, I could have friends coming again for dinner, tea and so on and act as usual. It would almost be a normal life. With a sigh, my breakfast finished, I logged into the Foggies platform. There were emails from Leila, from Leo and from some of the other Foggies I had written to. The breakfast moment of peace was over.

First, I checked Leila's message containing the offer in writing from the Society. I skimmed through it and there was nothing new in addition to what she presented to us yesterday. Next, I opened Leo's. He was giving a little update from his side, explaining how they were all dreading Rico's departure and returning to their isolated situation. Even though with the internet, they could still be part of our world, virtual presence was not the same as a physical one. If they knew that before the Fog, it was painfully clear to them now. Dante and Jack had also written, the former talking about Rico's visit and how good it was to get access to his architecture practice again. The latter was more expansive, praising Rico's kindness, humour and the quality of his English no end, as well as mentioning that maybe it would be a good idea for him to move to London, close to Rico and the other Facilitator. He could even continue his studies there. Oh dear! Rico had a gay stalker.

Next, I read the messages from Marrakech, from Christophe de Roque and Louise.

Christophe went on explaining who he was (I browsed quickly, his FTab profile had already been a mouthful) and the grand things he was not able to do in Paris while being stuck in Marrakech. 'Thank God for internet,' he added, 'as I could still do some work.'

Apparently, the office would be lost without him and his clients needed his advice day and night. I caught myself judging him and told myself off, 'Stop, Yoko! You don't know the guy. Maybe he is not an arse at all, just a guy who doesn't present himself from the best angle and has an umbrella up his ...' He could be just a normal guy in an unusual situation and that was his way to react to stress. I thought of his pregnant wife and mistress and how he still just thought about himself. Maybe just not a very caring good guy then. I read on, 'I was thinking, Yoko – if I may call you Yoko –, do you think you could send one of your Facilitators to come here and help me out? I would like to go to Paris for a month or two. Plus, I could really do with going back to the office. I need a break from the women. They are just doing my head in. And it will be good for Louise and Isabelle get to know each other. They will probably spend a lot of time together from now on.' He was infuriating! First of all, they were not 'my' Facilitators, but free independent people and cdr69 could ask them directly. Then, 'What about your pregnant wife!' I screamed inwardly. I returned to my original thought, he was categorically a selfish jerk.

I wondered how 'his women' saw the situation. They must have a very different point of view. I opened Louise's message and read. She explained she was a mixed media artist and worked part of the year as a 'GO – Gentil Organisateur' (translated something like 'Kind Host') – for the Club Med, an all-inclusive holiday resort company with venues all around the world. It was her second year in Marrakech, where she met Christophe. Louise went on to detail their encounter in one of the souks or local markets the previous year, their passionate love story (he swept her off her feet!), his unhappy marriage with an emasculating wife (she felt such an idiot), his promises (he was leaving his wife for her) and her hopes (of giving Christophe the love and family he had always dreamed of). To help him, she oversaw the riad's renovations in his absence and in her free time, and couldn't wait until they lived together. Louise's email was a long, a very long intimate account of her relationship with Christophe, most of which was an emotional rollercoaster of her dreams and falling heavily back to reality. I felt sorry for her, if overwhelmed by her unloading so much private information.

'Now he is expecting me to help him cross the desert whenever he needs some fresh air and his wife refuses to leave her room,' she wrote, 'and to keep his wife company as if we were friends! He says that my being a Foggy is a blessing, another sign we are bound to be together. One side of me wants to believe him. He does love me, I know that. He also used me. His wife is pregnant. Pregnant! About five months now! He had told me their relationship was so bad they were not sleeping together anymore. When I met her, it was terrible, we had a bad fight. She accused me of being a husband stealer, a whore, a family breaker. She said all sorts of things. He was there and didn't even defend me or mention that the marriage was in trouble. He just said to her that I was an artist and it was different for and with artists. With her, he was all 'Sweetie, don't be upset, you know I love you'. Her reaction was to tell him to shut up and she would deal with him later. The coward left. He left!!! OK, she is scary, his wife, but he left me alone with her!'

Louise's email demonstrated she had obviously no difficulty sharing her emotions, or her personal life for that matter. My thirst for an insight into Marrakech was well and truly quenched. What was surprising was the very limited reference she made to the Fog and how it affected her. The time the message was sent indicated 3.30 a.m. local time. Louise must have written this when she was down emotionally, or after an argument with either of the 'de Rocque' spouses. The Fog didn't seem her biggest concern then.

The next message was from Rosario in Alaska. From the first line she indicated the email contained bits from everyone in Alaska, written by each. It began with her, followed by her brother Mitch and finishing with a paragraph from her betrothed, Tony.

First, she thanked me for making contact and giving them some details about the London situation. She indicated they had received a similar email from the Roman Foggies. The Alaskan indicated that aside from the need to reorganise themselves when they wanted to go out and Tony having to move to Rosario's earlier than planned, the Fog had not really affected them. They were living in the forest, a good ten minutes' drive from the closest hamlet. When the Fog occurred and they realised something was wrong, they added a gate at the bottom of the path leading to their home and locked it. Quite simple.

Mitch and Rosario were still living in the wooden house they had grown up in with their mother who had Parkinson's disease. They didn't want to put her in a home and anyway Jean, the mother, refused to leave the home she had lived in for more than forty years with her late husband. She had turned into quite a recluse since her illness started and couldn't bear being surrounded by strangers. Mitch was a vintage car dealer, not the like of Ferraris but more the funky type, the ones which make you smile when you see them on the road. The countryside was his true passion and so he also acted as a local guide, organising excursions and climbs in the forest and mountains. Mitch was twenty-seven, Rosario twenty-four. She had decided to return to Alaska two years ago after her studies at Berkeley to look after her mother. On the plane heading back home, she met Tony. Since then, unhappy with the local job market, she had worked hard to create a local travel and event agency. Her company was doing quite well considering the remoteness of Alaska and its small population. Mostly she was happy to be there for her mother and to build a decent life for herself. She had been hoping in the long term she could branch out in Vancouver with Tony, but now the situation was naturally 'under review'.

Tony explained his arrival in Alaska in more detail. He was born and bred in Manhattan, New York, and was still living in the Big Apple when he met Rosario. He had been on a business trip to report on the status of some petrol platform. Tony was working for a major insurance company and had a brilliant career ahead of him at the age of thirty-one. After meeting Rosario on the plane to Alaska, following the encounter with drinks, dinners and more during his stay, he arranged to spend a two week holiday in Alaska. He was hooked, both by the country and the strong gorgeous woman. Rosario was, he said, a woman with real personality and confidence, who spoke her thoughts loud and clear and who had a heart of gold. Within six months he had managed to change his location from New York to the insurance offices in Seattle, making it easier for him to go and visit Rosario over weekends and for her to visit him. Mitch had a pilot's licence and was able to go and pick him up in Vancouver. The little plane was inherited from Mitch and Rosario's father and was essential to Mitch for his excursions deep in the wild, with or without paying guests. Tony was at present in a state of uncertainty. He was visiting for a long weekend when the house was 'fogged'. When he realised his role, later to be known as Facilitator, he put in for an emergency week's absence from work. He had now been in limbo for two weeks. Considering the situation was permanent, it was clear he had to give up his job, find something local and revise his plans for the future. She was worth it and anyway he wanted to be part of this unusual adventure ('He was now a Foggy, wasn't he?'). Yet it was still a lot of change in one go.

For Mitch and Rosario, as they had already mentioned, nothing really changed in their remote life. Mitch had been exploring the wild forest and, apart from slight differences due to the absence of his benchmarks he had left around in the mountains. The one exhilarating thing for him was to go where hamlets or small towns usually were and to see nothing. Just the wild so far. He still had to see signs of local inhabitants.

For Tony, his spirits and momentum were good. As he wrote, he had a lot more apparent changes to deal with than the other two. At least, not being a Switcher or a Crosser, he didn't have to deal with a dual-relocation, just the one to Alaska.

I had one message left, sent by Putu from Nairobi. Clare and Louise had not written, neither had the ones in Carson City. On the Foggies platform, one location was also left blank. It used to be Mexico when the Society first believed it to be the seventh one. It wasn't, so there was still one out there.

'Let's hope we find them first, before the other Fog hunters do,' I said to myself with anxiety. The 'we' had entered my thoughts, I had begun to identify with the new little Foggies group already. Questions about who these other Fog hunters were, why they had killed in Mexico and what would they do to us were leaving me uncomfortable. The sense of belonging was reassuring in the current circumstances, notably as there was no one else to rely on.

I opened the last email and read on. Putu was Australian and had studied medicine in Sydney before settling in Kenya. She explained her move to the African continent was a decision she made at nineteen. For her gap year, she had had travelled around Europe and had thumbed her way around the highways and roads. During her stay in the United Kingdom, she met some young English people whose families lived in Kenya and invited her to come with them for a different break. It was winter, she wanted some sun and so she seized the opportunity. She booked her tickets for a month later, was now broke and did odd jobs in bars and museums to put some money aside. She learned a lot doing this, including to observe. She fell in love with Kenya, the culture, the people, the land. She also felt that she could make a real difference there, more than she would in Sydney. She was planning to be a doctor, to give proper care to people. In Kenya, she felt a calling stronger than anything she had ever felt. It was a calling and a duty. She went back to Sydney determined to get the best qualifications in equatorial medicine and to return to Kenya. She wanted to work both with charity associations and the local authorities to improve health regulations as well as help people.

She was only twenty-eight and it was difficult to make her voice heard, but she was determined to make it happen.

She met Clare and Mary in her endeavours, as Clare was working for the government as a coordinator of international aid. Putu was a psychiatrist, working in one of the main hospitals in Nairobi. They had grown friendly, even if it remained at the acquaintance level. When Mary had a panic attack the morning after the Fog's apparition, Clare called her to help out. Mary was visiting her mother at the time and decided to stay over for the night after a dinner and movie ended late in the night. It turned out Putu was a Facilitator, which was a far from ideal situation for her. She was a very busy woman, her services in high demand. The three of them had agreed she would go and help them out of the house in the morning and in case of emergency. Putu had medical duties and calls at any time of the day and night, so she was not always immediately available for Mary's last minute requests. Over the past two weeks, it had worked. In the long term, she foresaw it would turn out to be a problem, especially with Mary who often took things personally. There were tensions between Clare and Mary as well. They were both uncompromising women. Mother and daughter got along well, but they had had to move in together and that was taking their relationship to another level.

'Altogether,' Putu wrote, 'I consider myself lucky in my Foggy role. At least my task is simple, just open and close a door; for Clare and Mary, life will never be the same.'

I made a mental note: so far, in Alaska and Nairobi where the Foggies had a Facilitator, none of them had mentioned they had moved or contemplated to move. Like us.

While I was reading, Zeno had knocked and suggested 'coffee?' through the door.

'Give me ten minutes and I'll be down,' I replied. It was all the time I needed to finish reading, put a jumper on and gather everything on the breakfast tray to bring it back downstairs. I even managed to send a little note to Leo. I could not resist, he was online. By now, Leo and I had dropped any formality and were both chatting as outrageously flirting friends.

'Miss Yoko, let us not always write about Foggy things. Tell me more about you. Come on, reveal some secrets sides of yourself!'

'Aaah, dear Leo, of secrets I have many. Interesting secrets. Surprising secrets. Very secret secrets. Like everyone. However, secrets should be preserved. The best way for this is Silence.'

'Could it be another challenge? I love it ... You know, I don't even have your last name! It is not on the FTab profile. The secrets ... They are always extremely interesting like all forbidden things. They grow in value when someone wants to protect them ... At the moment you are a whole big secret for me ... But I can feel that I'm getting little addicted and I am about to discover more ... And I think ... Yes ... That you are secretly a little addicted too ... You can't stop.'

As I was reading and grinning like an idiot, while melting on the inside, 'Yokoooooooo!' was bellowed from downstairs. Time to go down and have coffee with the guys. There were serious matters on the table in addition to coffee cups: to accept or not the offer from the Society.

'Got to go, Leo. And no. I won't admit to any addiction.'

'Ciao, bella Yoko. Maybe you don't admit it, but you know ... '

'Beware of what you write, or I may consider I need to detox from you.'

'Noooooooooo!!!!!!!!!'

When I arrived downstairs, everyone aside from Rico was sitting at the dinner table. He was still present via the FTab video conference system. The discussion had already begun.

'What if it doesn't work, having two houses fogged so close? That stresses me out! Why are you grinning Yoko?' Jazz turned her attention on me as I was coming in.

'I'm not grinning,' I replied, trying to put on a serious face. I had not realised my face still betrayed the last chat with Leo.

'Oh yes, you are. Plus, I am staying in a room on the same floor and I can hear you giggling constantly. What is up?' Jazz retorted.

'That is true you have been laughing a lot lately, on your own in your room,' Zeno commented.

Harry was just looking at me with a side of his mouth lifted in a friendly knowing smile, de facto agreeing with the others. I wrinkled my nose not to smile any further, perceiving belatedly this betrayed an admission on my part that something was up.

'Oh! Give me a break. I have just been reading funny stuff. Now, can we focus on the matter at hand?' I replied, trying to cover my previous instinctive reaction.

'Who is he, the author of the funny stuff?' Jazz quizzed further.

'Jazz, you are a pain. Drop it. There is nothing to tell.'

'We'll see. I am not done with you yet. Wait until I get you on your own.'

'That promises to be interesting,' Harry taunted. 'How would you handle a boyfriend with the Fog being there?'

'I would be curious to know!' whined Jazz. 'I have had to give up all my suitors. Not that many of them had real potential, but still, I enjoyed the little string of men wrapped around my little finger ... My dating life is over. So is my social and family life. Argh! I am doing my best not to think about it, but how can I not?'

'Maybe you will fall head over heels for the local doctor in the Other World?' I teased, welcoming the change of subject from me to more general issues. It was half-hearted; Jazz's fate deeply saddened me, her being completely cut off from anyone else from her previous life except for us.

'Very funny! Ha ha!' she snorted in discontent.

'I know what you mean. I am trying to sort it out with my girlfriend. She wants to come and visit. I am not sure how long I will be able to stop her coming. Ever since yesterday, I've started dreaming of this separate non-fogged house. It would be ideal as she could stay. The issue is how long the whole scheme would take to be ready. At least you didn't have a proper boy-friend you loved ...' Zeno cut in, the last sentence addressed to Jazz.

'At least you can have that non-fogged house! All I have been doing for the past week is catching up with friends on Facebook – Yoko don't frown, I thought of disabling all the localisation settings –, on Skype and on Google Talk. I cannot BE with anyone, but in fact, I have never chatted so much on-line with my friends than within last week.'

'Maybe that is the solution, just say that you had to move to Australia or New Zealand or the North Pole due to an identity crisis?' Zeno suggested.

'Identity crisis? Really? Do you want me to give you causes for your own identity crisis?' Jazz gritted her teeth and added, calm-ing down, 'The moving idea is on my line of thought ... It will be difficult when they ask for photos or videos though ...'

'You know, kiddos, you are entertaining. Anyway, our decision regarding the offer from the Society seem pretty set and clear,' Harry said gravely.

We all stopped and looked at him, back to being serious.

'It is the best opportunity for us to lead a life as close to nor-mal as possible,' he continued. 'The Society was right, they could have kidnapped and done what they wanted with us. They didn't even have to inform us of what was happening. They have treated us with respect, at least so far. I have been debating with myself at length, as surely you all have, on why we are reluctant to go to the authorities. As far as I am concerned, I don't want to be part of the government big machine where individuals have very little say in general.'

Just then my FTab beeped. It was lying face down on the table, already an accessory/necessity I was carrying everywhere with me. By habit, still listening, I turned and glanced at the message. It was Leo sending me a wink emoji.

'I knew it!' Jazz exclaimed.

'What?' I replied concerned, before understanding she was referring to the instant grin on my face. There must be a special light in the smile brought by someone you are having flirtatious relationship with, an intangible je ne sais quoi that betrays the person bearing it.

'No doubt,' joined in Harry, with a malicious glint in his eyes, 'something is in the air.'

'Is he from this world or the other?' Zeno jeered. 'Just tell us it is not Augustus, please! I would freak out with him as my "Foggy-in-law".'

'Oh! Leave me alone! All of you!' I did an eye roll, taking the FTab at the same time and closing it. 'Anyway. I agree with Harry. I am not certain of the whys and wherefores of the Society, and we certainly need to stay on our guard with them, even if "so far, so good". Plus, it would enable us to continue to choose the life we want and keep a certain independence. I also love the concept they came up with for the houses' lot. Zeno, Jazz, your turn: what do you think?'

'I don't really have a choice, do I?' Jazz answered first. 'I am stuck in here and I would really, really, really rather you stayed around too!' She crossed her arms around her waist, not as a display of bravado, but of vulnerability. My heart felt a pinch.

The agreement on the offer needed to be unanimous. The decision involved a life together for the long term, so all of us had to make the plunge willingly. Zeno looked around and cracked a smile, 'I quite like the idea of being a spy and explorer. It is pretty cool. I am a man on a mission! I will fill the house with all the trophies and discoveries gathered on my adventures! And if you are not around, who could I share them with? I don't really care where we are. I just want to be with my adopted family.' As he said this, he pulled out a pair of sunglasses, put them on and pouted, making a gun with his hand across his chest. 'My name is Grande. Zeno Grande, Foggy Crosser, New World Explorer, Society Spy, at your service.'

Jazz shook her head, murmuring 'Oh Lord.' Harry gave him blasé glance with a hint of a smothered laugh. As for me, I stood up and hugged him bellowing 'My hero!'

'Hang on guys! It is my turn now,' Rico shouted from the FTab above our laughter. 'I think their generosity is very suspicious and they could be manipulating us into trusting them, to ultimately do what they want. They are probably tracking our every movement and words through the FTab as we speak. In fact we are already in their pockets, trapped. We don't know who they are. They could have a major government or disgusting capitalistic corporation behind them. We are already doomed as far as I am concerned.'

'Jeez, Rico ...' I began. He interrupted me.

'However, there may still be a slight chance that they are not corrupt bastards trying to use us, and indeed have the future of this planet and the other one – if it is also a planet – in mind. Plus they haven't locked us up yet and it SEEMS they are giving us a choice. So my thinking is, they can't be worse than any lying governments or greedy inhuman companies or deluded fucktard terrorists.' Rico stopped a millisecond for breath or for effect, and concluded. 'Plus Leila is cool. And pretty. So I am in!'

We were all quiet. Our lives would never be the same again. This time it was a conscious choice.

'OK ... so ... let the adventure begin!' Zeno exclaimed.

For some time I had looked for something that would cheer up Jazz and change her mind. Going shopping was my best idea.

'How nice!' Jazz snapped, looking unimpressed. 'How fantastically sweet of you! I am thrilled! So, which shopping centre shall we head to? Harrods? Selfridges? Peter Jones? Or shall we head towards my cubicle bedroom and browse the shelves of Net-à-Porter? Amazon? Or even better, eBay?'

'I was more thinking Harrods, or even closer, Whiteleys?' I persisted.

'And how shall we manage to do this?' she sneered.

'Well, I was thinking headset, FTab or phone in front pocket with video camera on as we roam around the shop. We can share comments and choose 'together' what we like.'

'Keep talking!' Jazz's interest was aroused.

'I am thinking a selection of nice dresses, jeans, basic clothes for the Other World, chosen by you and me, thanks to the video camera. Bringing them back here in minutes as the shops are round the corner, you could have a private catwalk session and then I would walk back with whatever does not fit or does not suit us!'

'DEAL! Deal, deal, deal, deal, deal, d-e-a-l!' Jazz was jumping up and down in excited approbation.

'Yes, it is limited, but hey, better than nothing! I have been thinking a lot about it. About how to try and help you stay in touch with your old life, for you not to lose everything.' I was so glad to help her in any way feel better.

Jazz's eyes were getting moist. She was biting her lips to control her emotions. I had brushed an emotional nerve. I went to hug her and led her upstairs. She wouldn't want to cry in front of the boys, however understanding they would be.

It was a lovely afternoon. Harry let me out and I headed for the small local mall, the video call with Jazz on. There were sections in every shop with promotions in which we looked for hidden gems. We got a few new essentials for World II: trekking boots, loose thick jeans and corduroy jackets, thick woollen jumpers and socks. My favourite little find was a red and white checked shirt. When we both tried one, we felt like modern women lumberjacks. We had a good laugh: Jazz certainly needed it and so did I. Of course, Jazz also tried to push me about this FTab correspondent I was messaging and giggling with. Dismissing her comments and questions was a real challenge! I didn't want her to know how Leo was constantly in my mind and how regular were our exchanges, chatting about anything and keeping in touch all day long on any silly or serious occurrences and thoughts we might have. Either a great friendship had started, or I was slowly falling for someone I had not even met yet. It left me a bit unnerved to be honest.

Early evening, I was in my room and chatting online with Leo via instant messanger.

'I can't wait to see you. We will go dancing and you'll show me your moves on the dance floor. I bet you are irresistible when you dance!'

'Stop, you are going to make me blush. You are just being an Italian flirt now. You will be too occupied with the sexy twenty somethings swarming like bees around you, as if you were some kind of sweet honey, to check out the slightly older ones.'

'They are girls, you are a woman. Women are so much more attractive and interesting. Especially elegant sexy women.'

It was a nice compliment. It touched me, as if it was a balm applied to the little wrinkles around my eyes, wiping them away.

'Thank you.'

To change the subject and hide my being troubled, I filled Leo in on what I had been up to that afternoon with Jazz and how we had both felt so much better afterwards.

'You are handling the whole situation very well.'

'I don't really have the choice. Either I cope and be positive against all odds, or I might as well shoot myself. It could pretty much be anyone's motto in life. It is Jazz who is admirable,' I replied.

'Well, some people are stronger than others. They are not as vulnerable and affected by things,' he commented.

'I disagree, everyone is affected by what life throws at them, good or bad. Vulnerability and uncertainty are inherent to mankind and to life. Well, at least for normal people. I guess people with mental disorders may be spared, but they have other issues. The difference between a strong and a weak person, if you have to label them as such, is not the absence of doubts and vulnerability, but the ability to face, accept and get over them faster.'

'That still makes you a tough woman.'

'Not tough. I hope to be a strong, yet sensitive woman. Not tough. You can be strong without being hard and ruthless, you know.'

'I like your approach to life. Without doubt you are strong and sweet. From what I have discovered about you through all the things you write, all the things you do, I think you are a good person.' That last sentence affected me. The guilt over Julia, Jazz and the Fishers was constantly on my mind. Someone new believing in me got my emotions all out. It was time to change subject again. A good thing we were messaging, video chatting. It was funny, how we never got round to suggesting, or wanting, to see each other on video so far.

'There is also news on the Society front and the London Fog. We are moving!' I wrote on, getting on safer grounds

I summarised for him the Society's offer and our striking a deal after some negotiation. I kept the information minimal and he didn't ask any questions on the details. Leo only commented that it sounded great and that he hoped to be invited to visit when in London for our date.

'Well, I don't know when the houses will be bought and everything. It could be weeks, if not months.'

'I doubt it will be months. The Society would not want to wait so long.'

'I am not sure. The Society promised they would give the neighbours a fair deal. Property buying takes time.'

'So that will also show if the Society is true to their word,' Leo commented.

'Yes ...'

'Don't worry, Yoko!'

'I am past worrying, Leo. Right now it is about keeping the boat stable while going with the flow.'

'Not a bad thing. I am trying to do the same.'

'In any case, you WILL be invited to visit, not because of the pending date but as a friend. By now it is pretty clear you are one.'

'I can't wait to see you in person, not by video conference. I don't like it. I feel more self-conscious with the camera in the middle.'

Here was his reason for avoiding the video conference call.

'I don't mind the camera, but I can understand. Leo, I am sorry but I have to go. I still have to contact Leila and let her know our decision. I should have done it first instead of chatting with you, but ...'

'Sure! Of course! Next time we chat, let's put a date in the diary, shall we? For our date! Someone has to come and help us out, so it can hardly be spontaneous ... Sorry!'

'Yes. I will talk to the others and Leila. We need to find a solution, we can't leave you stranded in Rome for too long, that must be terribly claustrophobic.'

'Yes ... We are very grateful to Rico. He is a nice guy. A bit weird, but nice.'

'Spot on. Ciao, Leo!'

'Ciao, bella Yoko!'

When I wrote to Leila that we accepted the Society's offer, she replied instantly that she was over the moon. She commented she very much looked forward to working with us and spending more time in London. She informed me that the lawyers were going to start on the property acquisition right away. Hopefully by the end of the week they would have bought the houses and the necessary refurbishments could start, inside and outside the houses. One of the priorities was to build a higher wall around the area of the whole terrace.'

'By the end of the week? Launch the refurbishments? You can't possibly achieve this by next Friday. First, selling and buying a house takes time and paperwork. Second, you need to get planning permission for any building work and the authorities are tough. It takes time too!' I typed.

'Yoko, don't ask,' Leila wrote back.

'The council is pretty strict on ...'

'Really, don't ask. Just know that nowadays everything is computerised.' She stopped me continuing my message. I was speechless from the implications of what she was saying.

'It is not that bad,' Leila added, reading my mind. 'We will just break and enter, but instead of stealing, we will drop a nice new little folder here and there.'

'You know that each case is individually reviewed and any name you use would definitely remember not having worked on a case!'

'We will have a complete folder, with emails and so on. Someone who doesn't remember would not want to appear like a fool. Trust me, we will do things right.'

'But … but … just the time it will take you to build those files!'

'Our team started the minute you suggested the idea and we considered it viable.'

'I am in awe.' And I really was.

For a few minutes we didn't write. I was gathering my thoughts and she was informing the Society of our decisions. Then I mentioned to Leila that Leo and I had been chatting and that they were thrilled about Facilitators being exchangeable between portals. They were hoping to come to London soon. According to Leila, the sooner the better. The Rome situation, with Jack being rather emotional, to put it mildly, needed to be dealt with promptly. In her opinion, the easiest would be for them to come and join us for good. They were not aware of any Relocated in Rome, the area was contained with scaffolding, and the Society's men intercepted anyone going to the house. However, Leo and Dante know the isolation was not sustainable for Jack. Also the absence of a Facilitator on site made Dante and Leo in the same shoes as any Relocated. So, first Leo, Dante and Jack had to review their options and decide which one they liked best. The choice was theirs.

When I enquired about Mexico, Leila immediately reacted with stress.

'It is hell! Trying to control the flow of information is proving impossible! All we can do is misinform. We provide false data on the Fog and have to conceal the murder of our agent there as a car accident. And ...' Leila stopped for a couple of minutes, leaving me in suspense, 'and we have noticed some parallel misinformation going on. Someone, or some other entity, is promoting an alternative explanation of the events, sometimes even promoting ours. They have potentially killed one of us and now they are backing us up by hiding the reality behind the Fog and murders. This is most worrying.'

'No wonder! Still no idea who/what is behind the killing? Or why?'

'No. They are covering their tracks pretty well. We have a thin thread of a lead. It is minuscule and we have to be careful. They are on to us, too.'

'Any risk for us?'

'The longer the Fog is seen, the more risk there is. One of the advantages of you remaining in London, and one of the reasons why the Society agreed to support your choice, is that it is more difficult to spot the Fog by satellite in a town. Soon the houses' lot will be enclosed and protected from view from the street.'

'So why did you suggest moving to the country first?'

'Easier. Less paperwork to falsify and less hacking, less hassle with buying, less people to deal with.'

'Yes, but in the country it could have been noticed more, as you said.'

'Not with low buildings in the middle of high trees. We had already found the ones we wanted in the Cotswolds, less than two hours on the train from Paddington Station. Perfect. Actually, it is still on the cards. It could help to pass large items and vehicles to World II, such as a helicopter. We could go to pick up your sister thanks to it. We just need to make it cross the Fog, including fuel and spares. Then, at your parents', we would transfer some fuel too. Your sister could settle in Lil'London with the other Relocated and have you around. Afterwards the Fog at your parents can be left to die out. I told you Yoko, we are trying to help. I am conscious I could have prevented your switching the family house and how distressing it is for you. I still believe it was meant to be, but if anything can alleviate your disquiet, I intend to try. You will have to deal with the Fog for the rest of your life, yet now that you have agreed to work with us – pending of course we agree on the terms – we will endeavour to make it as guilt-free for you as possible.'

A huge burden lifted off my shoulders at the prospect of improving my sister's situation and my nephew's. It would not give her back her old life, or Eudes a normal future, but it was still better than being stranded alone.

Leila and I briefly commented on a few other matters, like Rico's return and Jack's possible crush on him. We then chatted randomly on life in London, New York and good addresses to eat in the European capital. I liked her. In normal circumstances we would easily have become friends. I had to be careful this didn't blind me: there is a saying in France, that 'la confiance n'exclut pas le controle' which translates as 'trust doesn't exclude caution', not a literal translation, but the most appropriate one. I wanted to keep myself on the lookout a bit longer.

Zeno came back that evening with a video projector and a DVD collection of the Bourne movies. In no time, the main wall of the living room was transformed into a blank canvas for the movie night ahead. We couldn't go out to the cinema without leaving Jazz on her own, so we brought the cinema home. Rico arrived as we started the third movie. He didn't let us stop it to talk about his trip. Instead, he squeezed himself between us on the sofa, grabbing one of the beers from the side table. As some point in the movie I looked round. We were a good bunch. 'Together, we are going to be OK,' a little voice in my head said.

**Day 2 (Monday)**

'Good morning my new, so intriguing and magnetic obsession! A person I don't know in person and who still captivates all my mind and attention. XX Leo.'

Now, come on, you wake up and read this, wouldn't you feel that it was going to be a superb day? This guy was good. Really good. Moreover, he seemed to mean it. This man had taken so much room in my life, and made it a happy space.

In the office, aware I would soon give in my notice, I was determined to work on my current assignments properly. Time to get a grip and finish what I had started and be proud of it. Call it self-respect if you will, but I had my standards and would adhere to them. Only at lunch did I take a break to finally reply to the Foggies' emails from the weekend. The difficulty was to find the right balance of openness and privacy for the boys and me to trigger a response from them. I longed to meet the other Foggies soon. My new Society job involved some travelling and meeting the other Foggies, so my hopes were well founded.

My phone beeped. It had been neglected of late with my being hooked on the FTab. At least I had taken the time on Sunday to reply to my backlog of texts, mentioning every time that I was just snowed under with various projects and had had to withdraw from social life for a while. I was less present on the online platforms too: I had glimpsed at my Facebook and Instagram account irregularly and given up on the others. Twitter was forgotten for example, what could I possibly tweet about anyway?

'@JazzinLondon to @yokosalelles: foggy as usual today. Have decided to invest in special fog light headset. Miss normal shopping.'

'@JazzinLondon: Don't fret, I am sure the Lil'London will soon open Vintage Shop for your errands.'

'@EtiquetteSavvy: Lil'London people gave me a fox fur today. Not keen on fur by principle. Any suggestion for suitable way of

returning it without hurting their feelings & causing a war between two worlds?'

'@PrincessJulia: Stop saying I am a bitch online for relocating
you. It was an accident!'

Being active on social media was too time consuming and less
attractive these days. Strange how strong habits had evolved so
quickly into something of the past. Somehow it made you wonder
how you fell into it so heavily in the first place. The Fog had been
an instant detox. As an afterthought, considering how much time
I spent on the FTab daily, I had only switched from one platform
to another.

That evening we got news from Leila: they were expecting the
exchange of deeds for all the properties by Thursday! We all decided not to ask too many questions on how they could do it so
fast. For once, we decided to believe in the expression 'ignorance
is bliss'! We had an in-house expert in Jazz, literally and physi-
cally, regarding property deals. We used her competencies in full.
It was even more appreciated as none of us, reading the offer in
the afternoon, knew how to handle it and deal with its subtleties.

**Day 3 (Tuesday)**

When Leila sent the paperwork on Tuesday morning, Jazz disappeared into her room with the stack of printed documents to review them before confirming they were just perfect and could be signed. It took her two days of intense work. Jazz had had to lower her expectations and reluctantly conceded not to buy 'her' house for now. She was still selling her flat: she had been efficient on that project as well and her old home was already on the market. Her move was scheduled for the end of the week. During her hard work on the deeds for us, Rico and I went to hers. With the help of the video conference system of the FTab, Jazz selected what was to be sent to temporary storage. The rest would be sold in an open house auction.

It all felt as unreal as the Fog and the Other World itself. In less than a week, I would have a house with my name on it, a new challenging job and no rent to pay; I would get rid of the last of my debts. This Fog could turn out to be the best thing I have had in my life since ... Michael. When Jazz confirmed the papers could be signed, the relief washing over me made me realise how my past was still holding me back. Blocking my thoughts was not dealing with and accepting my past, some wounds still were not healed. The job offered by the company was also a thrill for me on another level than having more time to understand and adapt to the Fog. When I had set up the salon de thé, my pleasures were not just to bake, to create wonderful treats to share around, but also to be independent. Independence, it seemed, was my real ambition. With the London company created by the Society, I would run the office, as well as the inter-Foggies and Foggies–Lil'London relations. Yes, I would still have a something akin to a partner in the Society, yet here in London and on an everyday basis, I was in charge! Zeno would be my peer, managing the exchange, trading and exploration. We would work together at many levels: he would do some liaising when needed and I would for sure go on World II exploration too!

I had already started working in my new functions in 'inter-world relations' as I put it. 'international' didn't seem adequate somehow. We had received a short social call from the Lil'London Council on Tuesday to organise our official visit to their town. It was a grand affair, a banquet at the town hall on Sunday after church. They had picked Sunday as it is God's day and everyone would be in their best attire after the religious service. We had already discussed with Leila, Dante and Leo and decided not to include the Romans for the first visit. Should a problem occur, we would need them to come and get Zeno and me out. James Fisher, the Westminster council employee, had accompanied them. He kept silent most of the time and looked very pale. When they arrived, Augustus Hoare mentioned that he would first like to settle the matter of the visit and we could then discuss James Fisher's specific situation with him.

Fisher was too nervous to talk when it was his time to speak. He kept glancing at Snayth and Hoare. He obviously didn't feel free to talk, so I intervened, 'Dear Mr Hoare, Mr Snayth and Mr Poff, thank you for your valuable help. What a lovely visit! I am thrilled and very much look forward to discovering your community and town on Sunday. I believe we have covered all related matters, haven't we?' At this point I stood up smiling. 'I shall thus bid you farewell, until Sunday. It is getting late and Mr Fisher and I have plenty to discuss on how to proceed with his move to your world, links to ours and how we can help him.'

The reaction of the Lil'London Council members was immediate. Benjamin Snayth's eyes narrowed, his permanent smile turned rigid. Augustus Hoare looked stern and his frown deepened. Edmund Poff started to fidget and look nervously from one of his colleagues to the next. They had been dismissed and they didn't like it. It was obvious they had hoped to witness our discussion with James Fisher. Well, no! Not on my watch. Benjamin Snayth reacted first. 'Of course. Mr Fisher, we will indicate to the men outside to have you accompanied back to your lodgings after your meeting. I trust you will still join us for supper?' He then turned to me and added with a sweet smile, 'We have prepared a little dinner for the council at mine tonight to further discuss your forthcoming visit to our town. We have waited for you for so long! As our house guest, James is invited to any of our meals.'

I smiled back, giving him the same honeyed grin. He had subtly reminded James Fisher that his new home was Lil'London and that his future and status was in their hands. James thanked Snayth and nervously confirmed he would join them for dinner. He looked as delighted about it as a trapped mouse.

Alone with us, James remained unsettled at first. I sympathised. We were strangers to him and the cause of his current relocated condition. About this, I wondered what he knew about the relocation.

'Mr Fisher.'

'Please call me James. I can't stand this formality anymore. It is so cold,' he interrupted, with a tentative smile.

'James,' I tried again. 'I understand you must be quite ... troubled about your situation. Have they explained to you what happens with the Fog and the people affected by it – the ones who can cross, the one who are relocated and so on?'

'They have. I am in a kind of parallel world with a connection opening every 231 years and for your lifetime. I cannot go back. My only link to my old life is this house and you.'

'Good summary.'

'I have had the time to think it through the past few days.'

'About that, would you tell us your symptoms? We could like to provide you with some medicines? What type of treatment have they provided for you?'

'Herbal stuff mostly. I refused bleeding! Shit, I feel like I am living in some type of backward religious sect. They use the name of God so often. I don't even believe in this crap.'

'Well, at least they've been taking care of you it seems.'

'Oh yeah. They did. Curious lot though. As soon as I started getting better they bombarded me with questions on our politics, our faith, our values, and all kind of things. Then they met you and started asking a lot about women and race. Technology too. I faked illness most of the time, answering vaguely and then feigning headaches and sleep. Until I know where I stand, I am not talking! Who knows what they will do with me once they have squeezed all the information out of me? No way! They don't reveal much either. Except today, I haven't been out of the house much. Mostly I am confined to my room at Snayth's. OK, I'm supposed to be sick, so it makes sense. They are keeping a good eye on me though. I can feel it. I am being s-c-r-u-t-i-n-i-s-e-d! What am I supposed to do?' James Fisher was loosening up and getting more and more animated. Good: it would make him talk and he obviously needed to get a lot off his chest. Bad: we needed to have a proper chat with him and had little time to waste. Jazz had remained in her room during the Lil'London Council's visit, working on the property legal documents. When she heard James Fisher was here and finally alone, probably informed by Zeno or Rico, she took a break and came down. Now she joined in the conversation. 'You are not alone. I am a Relocated too.'

'You are? Thank God! Are there any others?'

'Not that we are aware of,' Jazz replied, 'but it wouldn't surprise me if there were be more of us before long. Apparently it is inevitable. In any case, we are not alone. Yoko, Zeno, Rico and Harry are here too. They are not Relocated but we share a common ground.'

'What about my family? My wife? My children? Could I see them? They must be worried sick! Could I call them?' James Fisher's tone was begging.

'Well, that is the difficult part. Yes, you can call them, but what are you going to tell them? Because your situation is unusual to say the least,' Jazz asked him.

'I would tell them the truth! They would believe me. They know I love them. I always tell them everything.'

Jazz and I looked at each other. This was a moment we had both dreaded; we had to bring him back to reality. There was no way his wife would believe him that easily. We didn't really know what to do on information disclosure either. The Society's policy advised keeping the Fog secret. The less people knew the better. However neither the Society nor us could forbid people to talk. The problems were with the consequences of talking. Once out, the story was bound to spread. Jazz, the boys and I had envisaged the various options and there was no way round it, even with family and loved ones. The breaking of the news was a tricky one. Now I had to present this conundrum to James, interrupting his flow.

'James. Please. Stop. We have no doubt your family love you and you love them.' I had no clue. For all I knew he could have mistresses all over town. Diplomacy was part of the new job. 'Still, you have to analyse the situation in detail. First, you understand that calling them and saying you have been Relocated by a paranormal fog would be equivalent to telling them you have been abducted by aliens. You do realise that, don't you?'

James Fisher was shocked. He had not viewed the situation from that angle.

'Second, let's say you manage to make them come here to meet you: you put them at risk of relocation. Not everyone is affected in the same way. Imagine if your wife is relocated and not your children, they would be separated from both their parents. Whoever is relocated, no one comes back. It is a new beginning along with a rough and tough experience.' I was trying to be both gentle and matter of fact, but there was no kind way of hiding the fact that we were on a knife edge.

'Third, let's say they confide in someone about the Fog, how long before the situation gets out of control, with the government or individuals trying to cross? If the World II feels disrespected or even invaded, how long before tension and animosity rise between them and us? You would be stuck in it. In the middle of it.' Afterwards, I related the Mexico drama and horrid massacre to him. They may not be perfect in Lil'London, but at least they seem inclined to establish good relations with our world.

'Fourth, there is quite a limited number of Switchers, Crossers and Facilitators. If the Fog gets more widely known, we are placed in a dangerous situation. Various people or entities would certainly want to have access to the Other World. Most would not care about us, only wishing to use us, against our will if needs be. Not a direct concern for you. Indirectly, yes it is. If something happens to me, you lose your connection with this house. No more contact with any of us and so, with good old London and the rest of your old World, including your family.'

'Yes,' Jazz pointed out, 'I for one do not want to lose the support, medicine, information, material, trade opportunities, or in general the link to London and earth. It will always be my homeland. You will have unique opportunities in the communities here. Additionally, as the house will still have internet, electricity and all the utilities of the twenty-first century, it can make your life much better. Yours and any other Relocated. You know, depending what you say to your family, you may not lose them altogether. Technology could enable you to stay in contact ...'

'What do you mean? What did you say to your family?'

'Well, my situation is a bit different to yours. I don't have a husband or children and I didn't disappear without trace for a week. When I came to visit Yoko and found myself in the forest, I was made aware of the situation right away. For family and friends, I had an impromptu trip to New Zealand for some kind of business opportunity. Soon, I will inform them of my crazy decision to move there and keep in touch with everyone online for as long and as much as possible.'

'What if someone travels to New Zealand and wants to see you?'

'Unfortunately I will be out of the country then.'

'And your family?'

'That is the toughest. I am distraught at not being there for them when they need me and not seeing them. I am sure they will want to come and see me. I am considering finding or inventing an incurable terribly contagious disease ...'

'I can't lie to my family like that. I just can't.'

'Then don't, but deal with the consequences! Man, sometimes lying could be to the benefit of the ones you love. Do you think being here and keeping them in the dark is not killing me? I don't want to separate my brother or his wife from their infant should they come and visit. That's it! I will not take the risk. I'd rather they lose me than break their family apart. I will lie to them because I love them!'

'You don't trust them. If you did, you would know you could tell them the truth and trust them to decide on their own what they wish to do.'

'How dare you! How dare you! I lie to them because I want to protect them. I don't want to make them choose, I don't want to make them feel guilty about not coming to see me!'

'Maybe they would surprise you if you told them the truth! Maybe you underestimate them! I will tell the truth to my wife and children. And I will trust them to keep the situation secret. I think you are right on this at least and secrecy is best. I will also trust them to decide for themselves whether they want to come and see me or not.'

I intervened, unable to keep my tongue still any longer. 'How old are your children?'

'My son is fifteen, my daughter is twelve. Why?'

'And you are sure that at twelve and fifteen they would be able to recognise the importance of such a decision and their one in seven chance of being relocated?'

He was quiet for a second, then said, 'I have never lied to them before and will not start now. I have always treated them as clever individuals. They are very mature. I believe in honesty!'

'Oh! For heaven's sake!' Jazz exclaimed. 'There is no point in discussing it with you. We just have to agree to disagree. I am going back to work. Bye.' She stood up in anger and turning her back to James as she left the room I heard her murmur to herself 'idiot man!'

'Wait until my sister is here, then the conversation will really be explosive between Jazz and Julia.' I winced as the idea went through my mind. I ought to make sure to be out to run errands that day, no matter in which world. This led me to wonder what type of shops they had in Lil'London. Images from 'The Little House on the Prairie', the TV show of my childhood, flashed before my eyes. Hopefully not.

Returning to James, I explained one of the projects that Zeno had thought of. 'We need to organise temporary accommodation for you. Maybe a trailer to start with?'

'Yes, that would be nice. I don't want to stay at Snayth's much longer. I am getting claustrophobic there. Freaks! I am sorry, they are freaks. I can't stand it! You know, the women, they are all so subdued. Here you would have to drug them to reach a comparable result. Snayth has several wives too. Everyone acts as if they are only doing their duty. There is no joy in that house, I am telling you.'

'We will help you.'

'Thank you. Can I ... Can I call my wife now?'

'If you wish.'

I couldn't stop him, I had no right. Disaster was imminent. I took out the FTab, entered my passcode and applied my thumb discreetly to unlock the device.

He took the tablet and stared at the screen. He took a deep breath in and dialled.

'Would you like some privacy?'

'Err ... Yes, please.'

'I will be in the kitchen.'

I joined Zeno in the kitchen. All the doors were open, we could hear the conversation loud and clear.

James's wife, I presume, answered the call. As James spoke, we followed the alternation of him speaking followed by silences. 'Darling? Honey! It's me!'( ...) 'Oh! My love! I am so sorry. I was detained!'(. ..) 'No, I am fine, but ...' (...) 'There was no phone connection.' (...) 'Well, that is what is incredible. By accident, I crossed a ... A kind of ... F-f-f-fog. Paranormal fog. And it transported me to ...' (...) 'Listen to me! I am not joking. Seriously! I am in another World and can't come back! You know I always tell the truth. Come on, how could I make up something like that? I ...' (...) 'Don't scream at me! It is the truth!' (...) 'I can call now because I am in the house between the two worlds. Shit, honey, I know that sounds crazy, but you have to ...' (...) 'Darling ... Please don't cry.' (...) 'Hang on, someone can confirm what I am saying. YOKO?'

I wanted to get involved in that conversation like cutting off my right hand. I told Zeno to come with me. His answer was no. I grabbed his arm and said that was not a question. The few minutes that came next were not pleasant. James made me speak to his wife, but I only managed to say a couple of words because a loud and angry 'Who are you?' blasted in my ears. I quickly uttered he was telling the truth and passed on the phone to Zeno, grimacing. He said the same, keeping the phone away from his ears, sensibly having learned from my experience, then passed the phone back to James. James was crying.

'Honey. My Love. I know how it sounds. I am sorry. I promise it is true and there is no one else and I love you and the children. I am telling the truth. There is this fog ...'

He stopped talking and looked at the phone. 'She hung up.'

Tears were rolling down his cheeks. He was crying, silently. I felt sorry for him. I could understand he needed to talk to his wife, but what did he expect? He had not thought it through in detail and said too much too soon. He had gone for it totally un-prepared. So did we.

I couldn't help myself and gave him a hug. 'Give it time. We'll work something out. Give it time.'

'How could I be so stupid?' he struggled to say and me to understand.

'Well, maybe you wanted them to believe so much you forgot that sometimes patience is required. Also, some things need to be seen to be believed. Seen or experienced.'

'What about trust!'

'Stop being idealistic and switch to being realistic: you just told your wife who hasn't heard from you in a week that you are fine, but fog-transported into another world where there was no phone reception.'

'Were you listening?'

'Does it matter? Get a grip!' I would not accept him passing his nerves and wife's rejection on us, We had a lot on our plates too. James didn't stay long after the call. As he left, he told us he was drained and would go back to his room and continue to fake exhaustion, if not depression. He managed to get a sleeping pill from me to help him on with this tactic. He would come back and meet Zeno soon to organise his temporary home close to us and the house.

## Day 4 (Wednesday)

On Wednesday afternoon, I placed a video call to my parents. My focus was Julia, although I gave them a short update on the happenings in the house too. My sister was a mess. Apparently she would not get out of her dressing gown and hardly out of bed all day. She just kept moaning and raging. I wanted to tell her that it would not help her predicament, but I couldn't. Part of me understood: it is difficult to fight depression. So I made an effort to be nice and told her I was working on ways to improve her situation.

'Will you be able to give me back my old life in the glamour of Paris?' She asked, half-excited, half-scornful.

'No. That I can't do. From what we know, it is impossible.'

'Then, whatever,' Julia responded, full of scorn.

'Julia, I am really trying here!' I replied, half-sorry, half-exasperated. 'Stop fighting with me! We are in it together sis. I am trying to make things better! Help me out a bit, will you?' I exclaimed. I had not called her 'sis' in many, many, many years and it had just come out of the blue. It shocked me and it surprised her too. Or at least it made her shut up. She just pursed her lips and looked down after a few seconds.

'Easy for you to say. YOU can still get out and have a normal life,' Julia finally murmured, as if to herself. 'I am going now, I am tired,' she added and cut off the communication.

This type of exchange had started in my university years when my sister started to grow apart and to ruin the family equilibrium. Ever since, she had been a thorn in my side with her aggressive attitude or rejection of me, with her disdain. Did I really want her to be transported to England? No. Did I have the choice? No. Did it make me happy? No. What I read and heard somewhere was true. Life was a bitch sometimes. It gave with one hand, took with the other. I supposed the key was to learn to be content with what was left for you to keep. Cope and be happy, against all odds: it really was a good motto Catherine the Great had chosen to get on with life.

On other foggy business, things were moving forward for the Romans. Leila had been active: in parallel to the London acquisitions, the Society had bought the property they had had their eyes on outside London in the Cotswolds. The exchange had already been done. The Roman Foggies were to come to London ideally by Saturday night so that the 'unfogging' process of the Rome house could start as soon as possible. The Romans were to join the new formed Society's company and would be based in the Cotswolds with regular trips to London.

Dante was to be the architect for all building structures in the World II. The Relocated needed housing. They would certainly want as many modern amenities as possible in their homes. It would be hard enough to establish themselves within the Lil'London community. Let them at least have some of our benefits. The Lil'London people would certainly wish to enjoy some of the modern features of our world too. This was a very different opportunity from Dante's practice in Rome, a challenge requiring different resources and imagination. How to make the community of Lil'London jump forward to the twenty-first century, with no prior infrastructure of electricity, modern roads, running water or gas systems either? The more I pondered on it, the more I perceived how exhilarating it could be for a young architect. From what Leo wrote, Jack wasn't sure what he wanted to do. He just wanted to come back to an English-speaking country and have a Facilitator around. Having a crush on Rico was probably a big incentive for him to come to England. He could have gone to Alaska or Nevada in his home country. As for Leo, he was hoping to join in on the exploration projects and develop one of his passions: photography. He dreamed of being the photo reporter of the Other World: he longed to document the excursion with Zeno and me, the Relocated's new lives, the ways of the Lil'London community and how it adapted to our world connection. All in images, with a thorough journalistic approach.

Leo and I chatted a lot those days. A lot. In a period of four days, the count reached above three hundred messages. Still not using the video conference system, we were consciously or unconsciously postponing any visual contact, enjoying how our friendship flourished through the words. It really was irresistible! I now understood how some people could fall for someone via letters. The man was so endearing, I was already attached to him. It felt warm and strange. To confess, one of the reasons I was shy about the video was my fear that I would not be attracted to him in person, and vice versa. It would be such a disappointment! We would know soon, the Romans were coming. Rico was leaving for Rome again on Friday and returning with the three Foggies on Saturday morning. The sale being on the Thursday, our neighbours would not have moved out by then. It was all going pretty fast, but not that fast! They would be out by the end of the following week, which was an express exit really. So Jack, Rico and Leila were going directly to the property in the Cotswolds. The manor had been on the market for some time and was mostly empty, ready to move in. The removal company with Dante's and Leo's belongings would arrive from Italy on Monday the following week. Apparently their furniture would barely fill up the huge house.

Leo and Dante would stay in London for the weekend. Leo had mentioned to Leila that he had friends to see in London and would rather see them before settling in the manor as once there he would get caught up in organising the house and sorting their belongings. Dante had jumped on the bandwagon and said he would first stay in London for a couple of days too. He wanted to buy a few books on old architecture in England to study their methods and how to adapt them. Leo's first catch up for his London visit was me. Immediately after he had dropped his bags in his hotel room (near Paddington Station of course), we were meeting for a lunch date. I was so looking forward to it that I had jumped around in my room with a silly grin when Leo suggested it, before nonchalantly typing back 'Fine by me'. To turn the conversation onto something which would contain my teenager-like momentum, I enquired thereafter on the seriousness of their move to England and how they were dealing with it.

'Isn't it a bit difficult to just let go of Rome and so fast?'

'Well, we haven't really been enjoying the neighbourhood of late.'

'This is still a pretty definitive move. Will you really sell the house?'

'This is the thing: so far, we have avoided, or are unaware of, accidental relocations like the ones you have experienced. When it happens, which is bound to happen if we stay, we will be stuck there for good. We couldn't leave people behind. So I have to let it go.'

'You could still stay in Italy ...'

'We could, but you forget, we do not have a Facilitator. What difference does it make, in Italy or in the United Kingdom, if we have no access to this world? We would rather be based close to you guys, so that life is more manageable with better infrastructure, Facilitators and for group exploration too. I also believe it is better to have one strong team in one strong fort. Also, Jack can't stay, you know. He couldn't.'

'You said before ... He struggles with the whole thing, doesn't he?'

'Actually, he is better now. The prospect of more time with Rico is definitely cheering him up!'

I laughed and commented, 'Clear crush alert!'

'Oh yes!'

'Leo, going back to Italy. When things settle down, later, you would be able to rent a remote villa or similar for forty-nine days and you could still have an Italian holiday and do some exploring at some point.'

'I hope so. One day. For now, I am just looking forward to discovering Lil'London. I never thought I would live a real adventure.'

'Me too! That is exactly as I want to see it, like an adventure!'

'My turn to ask you a question: Leila and the Society? We don't know anything about them. We are using all their technology and structures, will live in their properties, and rely on their protection, even working for them. We will be relying on them for so much more. How can we be sure we can trust them? Have you had doubts?'

'Yes.'

'And ...?'

'After consideration, they seem the best option at hand and the least of all the other perceived evils. Plus, I like to follow my instincts sometimes and have a good feeling about Leila. And she represents the Society. One correction though: we are working with them, not for them.'

'I am with you. I know the risks, so at least I am not going there completely blind either. So far they have shown respect for who we are and what we don't want. I appreciate that and it gives me respect for them in return. I am not sure we would have received the same decency elsewhere.'

'Yes, when I think government, a guinea pig image of myself pops up in my mind.'

'That and a "freak" label.'

'Such a pity. After all, from a certain point of view, we are a rare breed of people, maybe a new type of superhero ... OK, maybe not. We don't actually have super powers.'

'Come again, Super Yoko! O You Super Fog Portal Creator!' Leo played around with me. It was good to loosen up and not take things seriously.

'I need a super attire then! I want a cape!'

'I totally agree. I recommend skinny shorts and tight bustier.'

'How predictable!' I replied.

'Do not undermine Super-Leo!'

'Super-Leo?! Hahaahhhhhahaahahahahhahah! (Sniff. Tears of laughter.) Hahahahaahahaha!' I actually wrote all of this and was really laughing, too.

'Pffffttt. I feel undervalued,' he typed back.

I was so looking forward to meeting him.

In addition to eagerly waiting for my imminent date with Leo and to meet Dante and Jack (I confess it was secondary to the date), I was very curious to visit the Cotswolds manor. It made Leila smile. She was at ours then, visiting to discuss with Jazz some clauses on the deeds and to exchange contracts. She said not to worry, there would be many visits in the future. Everything was well on track. Theirs was a high level of performance and promptness to act and difficult to match. It gave me the blues. What would happen if I was bad at my job? They couldn't fire me, or could they? They could ask another Switcher though? They could ask Jack ... or someone else. Where would that leave me? I quickly checked myself. I couldn't afford to go on speculating gloomily. This was now my life, not just a job, and I wasn't going to make a mess of it. Remembering my words to Leo, we were working with the Society, not for them. In those moments of doubt, headset on, I would choose some strong beat music and go for a jog, focusing my thoughts on whatever positive I could find in the current situation. That Wednesday evening, the night before the signature for the house and after the job offer was confirmed, I went to my room instead. It was too late for a jog, so I got lost in the music, dancing on my own. That day, the spotlights were on new beginnings. The music was to drum a positive outlook into my mind. In truth, a half-full bottle of wine and some chocolate chip cookies came along with me ... Very soon, any doubts, fears, self-confidence issues were utterly forgotten. I am sure Jazz would have joined me, but when I knocked at her door after the dinner she had missed, she was deeply asleep. She had achieved a lot in a few days.

**Day 5 (Thursday)**

Thursday was exchange day. We all showed up, except Jazz of course, at the Society's lawyers in the City and we signed the deeds. It was surreal. My head was surprisingly clear and strong despite the entire unknown and peculiarities in my life since the Fog appeared. Thanks to my friends, thanks to this strange contact with Leo, thanks to the Society even, the temporary blues were gone. Moreover, the job was very loosely defined and would be adjusted day by day to the situation's needs. It was very much the case that it would have to adapt to me as much as me to it. So what was there to fear?

Blues gone and spirit up with new job in the pocket, new house to live in, Leo's date ahead, and geeky addiction fed with the FTab, the future looked better. All I needed now was to exercise: with all the chocolate cookies I had indulged in of late, I could not to squeeze into my beloved jeans. No more postponing jogs!

**Day 6 (Friday)**
Friday was the day I finally emailed my notice to the human resources department. Theoretically there was a full month of work
before being free from my contract. I would do a week only. Leila
had already hinted she would arrange for medical support regarding any claim of being unwell and unfit for work. It would
have been easy to just disappear, but a week would enable me to
finish the current projects. Unfinished business bothered me, as
much from self-respect as for the people who counted on me.

During my last conversation with Leila, we discussed how
the other Foggies were faring. They were all getting accustomed
to their situation, some faster than others. So far, it didn't seem
they had attracted too much attention, aside from the Mexico
drama obviously. It amazed me that the Fog phenomenon and
existence of World II had remained unknown after the Mexico
events unfolded.

Leila had a new worry which she passed on to me: the seventh
Fog portal had been found (well, the Society hoped it was the
original and not a repeat of Mexico and a tourism portal). It was
located in one of the poor suburbs of Jakarta in Indonesia. The
local police were involved with a case of a missing person and
possibly kidnapping. My first reaction was to link it to the ones
behind the death of the Society's agent in Mexico.

'We don't think so, Yoko,' Leila objected. 'It is a possibility,
but we don't think so. Here is what we understand so far. The
same night as you, this little hut or bungalow, whatever you call
it, was turned into a portal. Five people lived together in there:
the two parents and their young son Helo, along with the older
daughter and son of the wife from a previous relationship. They
have all disappeared except Helo, seven years old. From interrogating neighbours, we gathered they saw the mother walking
out of the Fog early that Sunday morning with Helo in her arms,
then both returned soon after to the house. Later that morning,
Helo appeared out of the Fog, playing in the street with his best

friend and neighbour. Since then, no one else from the hut was seen. Helo went back home and reappeared soon after in tears, running to his friend's parents. They went to his home which was empty, and left a note saying Helo was with them. Every day, they went back at different times, sometimes late at night, no one was at home and everything was left unmoved, accumulating dust. It looked as if everyone had gone. We will need to send one of the Crossers with a Facilitator to investigate and confirm our suspicions, which are that Helo is a Facilitator and that the rest of the family were Switchers, Crossers and Relocated. We fear that they got lost, that they disappeared in the Other World and, because Helo is still here and free, that they have no way of coming back. There must be a wild jungle on the other side of the Fog ...'

'Oh no! That is true! The Fog must be difficult to find again if they wander too far.'

'If the Switcher went out alone and ended up astray in the Fog, the others could have gone in search of that person and wouldn't find their way back. What about the indigenous population? What are they like? Honestly, the Mexico carnage has traumatised us. We are praying this won't be a repeat.'

'What are the local police saying?'

'Well, at first they were not taking the case very seriously. They assumed the family had gone on holiday or something and forgot the young child. A bit unconvincing in my book, they would have come back or try to have someone pick him up in that case. Helo is but a child!'

'And now?'

'Now they are giving us a lot of work ... The father of the two eldest was contacted in an attempt to find the whereabouts of the household and he is fuming. He refuses to take Helo in, arguing the child is not his. He claims his ex-partner abducted the two eldest and Helo escaped. He is threatening to alert the media and launch a hunt for the kidnappers. The nice neighbours looking after Helo until two days ago seemed genuinely worried. We have someone there who organised the paperwork for us to have custody of Helo while the situation is getting sorted. The child is not safe, we had to get him out of there fast. Just in time too, as the neighbours received a visit just after from other people wanting to look after him and they were definitely not Indonesians.'

'The other organisation interested in the Fog?'

'Most certainly.'

'What did they look like?'

'An Asian woman, two Caucasian men. Both in their thirties. We have some vague photos as the whole ground is under covert video surveillance. They are not clear: the two men and woman keep their head low.'

'How did they know about Helo?'

'The same way we did, I assume. Monitoring information and web traffic. Analysis of satellite images. Checking of police communications.'

'I thought you were ensuring that key information was contained?'

'We do what we can, but these guys know what they are doing. They are thorough and clear on what they are looking for. We miss the smallest detail and they are on it. This is a big case, we have to intercept as much as possible to stop the media getting involved. The police case escalated and that is difficult to oversee. It is also very difficult to control the parallel made between the two fog occurrences, in Mexico and in Jakarta. That was bound to happen.'

For a moment, none of us spoke, then I asked what I feared to hear.

'And do you manage? I mean, do you have the information under control? Are we ... Are things ...?'

'Honestly Yoko, barely. We had to use increasingly unethical procedures.'

I raised my shoulders, palms open and did a little eye roll. 'What's new there?'

'Wait! Yes, we fiddle with the legal side of things, but we don't fiddle with ethics.'

'Mmm ... OK ... Let's not get into the whole ethical/legal argument. What did you do?'

'We created fog in a very wide area of the slum. We exploded some pipes and had a whole section evacuated. We had to transform some of the pipes to do so and creating the fog was a bit tricky, but ...'

'Wow! That is a big intervention. How come we didn't hear about it? That must have been in the news.'

'Yes, though only in Indonesia. Plus it is presented as a problem linked to old infrastructure,' Leila explained. 'Nonetheless, now we have to maintain this for forty-nine days until the portal closes, one way or another. Moreover we had to have everyone leave and evacuate! We can't stop the police going in unfortunately. They are very involved in the case now. Anyway, this is hell to manage!'

'The emerging countries are more prone to have issues than the western countries. Inequalities seem to spread even when the Fog is concerned.' The remark was more to myself than to Leila.

'Yes. It seems like it,' Leila commented. 'I just hope the family didn't indeed flee somewhere out of fear, leaving the child behind, and is now opening little portals on random Indonesian Islands. That is also a possibility we cannot dismiss.'

Mexico and Indonesia: what a Foggy mess!

That Friday gave me another dilemma, a private one: to tell or not to tell Jazz about my date with Leo. So far I had managed to keep my mouth shut on the flirting between us. Keeping the news of the date quiet was hard, especially considering how excited I was. Jazz and the boys were not stupid and they could tell something was up with me that made me quite giddy. The comments and teasing were often something like:

'So is it your mysterious man again?' (Harry)

'I don't have a mysterious man.' (me)

'Have you slept with him yet?' (Jazz)

'Is he good in bed?' (Rico)

'They are just funny messages! Stop it! Both of you.' (me)

'She hasn't slept with him yet … I can tell.' (Jazz)

'Wow. He is good. He is taming her first. Good tactic.' (Rico)

'Maybe he is gay?' (Zeno)

'Or maybe this is a woman … Wooooaaaaaaahhhhh! Exciting!' (Rico)

'Rico, you have issues … Gimme a break, all of you!' (me)

Or another time, Jazz randomly asked, 'Do you have a photo?'

'For what?'

'Your new guy.'

'Again I don't know what you're talking about …' I feigned innocence, knowing she knew I was dismissing her question.

So here I was, preparing for my date, trying to act normal and hide my eagerness. I had suggested a little gastropub well known for its surprisingly good Thai food. Pub and Thai food is an unusual combination and something offbeat was attractive. The Churchill Arms was close to Notting Hill, at walking distance from home but not too close by. In addition, the weather forecast indicated it would be sunny. If the lunch went well, it would be perfect for a stroll afterwards. I was pondering on what to wear, either jeans and smart casual top, or a little understated dress that would be becoming. Maybe even a slightly sensual one. As my selection of outfits was displayed on the bed to try, Jazz knocked on my door and walked in before I replied. She took a look around at the clothes on the bed, saw the face of someone being caught in the act and closed the door.

'OK. Talk. When are you seeing him?' She pushed some of the clothes aside to sit on the bed and crossed her legs, waiting for me to speak. Jazz had the air of someone who wouldn't budge until she was satisfied she knew it all.

'I have a lunch tomorrow with a friend and I'm working out what to wear.' I gave in half the info.

'Let me rephrase this. You have a lunch DATE tomorrow with someone and you are trying to work out how you are going to play it. Sexy, chilled, casual, or damn hell hot.'

'Err ...'

'The guy with whom you are exchanging messages all the time?'

'Err ...'

'Do you have a photo?'

'No,' I lied.

'Right. I know you. Show me a photo.' Obviously I don't lie very well to people who know me.

'No! Not showing you a photo.'

'Do I know him?'

'No, you have never met him.'

'So what is the problem? Show me a photo.'

'Give it up, I won't show you a photo.'

'But why? I just want to get an idea of what type of person he is so that I can help you choose the right clothes. What is it you are trying to hide? Is he ugly? Is he famous? Is he Augustus Hoare?'

'What? No, no and no! It is just ... It is just that I don't want to make a big fuss about it.' She would meet him very soon and recognise him. It was already difficult for me that he was another Foggy. We belonged to the same restricted group. Forever. These were good reasons enough not to get involved.

'Then why are you finding it difficult to choose what to wear if it doesn't matter?' Jazz was annoyingly good at asking the right questions and getting to the core of things, even if she wasn't always aware of it.

'Because however important the situation I do like to give a good first impression.'

'Mmmm ... OK, I'll let you off the hook on that one, Nutella. Just know you can't fool me. I know there is something you are not telling me. I will work it out.'

'What a suspicious friend you are.'

'Don't go all sarcastic on me ... I will find out. In the meantime: tight black jeans, this tight turquoise top with long sleeves – the colour suits you – and longish earrings with a hint of turquoise as well. Those ones.' She pointed to a pair in the box of earrings I had out on the bed. 'Add your black leather jacket with a white scarf on top. Don't forget black leather gloves. Smart casual, elegant AND sensual. The best for the end: mid-height heels, kind of court shoes, black.'

Perfect. She got it spot on.

'Jazz, you are a star.'

'If you kiss him, I want to know! Bye.' She winked at me and left the room. I was NOT going to tell her if I kissed him, or if he kissed me. Then I wondered if we would. Would it be too soon?

**Day 7 (Saturday)**

So here I was, outside the pub, waiting in the sun and chatting with a friend on the phone. Leo and I were supposed to meet at 1.30 p.m. It was 1.35 p.m. I felt foolish, nervous and excited out of proportion for a meeting with a man I had never even met. I was attempting to lower my expectations by being practical, telling myself that he was probably just a big Italian flirt. I was paying absolutely no attention to what my friend was saying on the phone, lost in my own thoughts and arranging my belt, hair or checking my lipstick in the shop windows. Then a taxi arrived in front of the pub and Leo got out. I blurted goodbye to my friend on the phone, ending the call without listening to her reply and dropping the FTab in my bag. Leo turned towards me and recognition from the Foggies platform photo showed on his face. We both smiled broadly and walked towards each other. There was an awkward moment when we faced each other during which we hesitated about what to do next. He put his hands on my shoulders and kissed both my cheeks the continental way. Then he took a step back and looked me slowly up and down appreciatively, one corner of his mouth lifting, teasing.

'Ms Yoko, you are even better in real life. You exceed my expectations. I am a lucky man to have such a "pen pal" or should I say "keyboard pal"?' I was about to thank him, but he continued, 'Not that you will remain such a pal for long, I hope. Now that I have seen you, I couldn't content myself with just that.'

'Signore Leo! We haven't even sat down yet. Please behave!'

'Well, what can I say, you are irresistible in writing and delicious in person. What do you expect?'

'You are a smooth operator, I can't take you seriously,' I laughed, then went on with some cheekiness of my own. 'Still, as you now know compliments unsettle me I hope you will refrain from saying them out loud. You may however look at me in awe of how amazing I am. Just don't drool.'

Leo burst out laughing and pushed the pub door open. 'A challenging woman! Bring on the banter dear, I am all for it. Just be aware I will challenge you back.'

'That is the only way to enjoy banter, when you have a good respondent.'

At this moment I knew I did not just like the person, his writing style or his way of thinking. I liked the man behind the words. He put his hand on my back to lead me inside the pub restaurant and the contact caused a flash of pleasure to go through me. I was attracted by him. Even if a little voice in my head was ringing alarm bells saying 'Bad idea, bad idea, bad idea. Not good with a Foggy,' but the inclination was already there. I glanced at him while he was browsing the venue, finding his bearings. He was a good-looking man. Not handsome in a top model way with statuesque features, but with a real warmth and charm emanating from his whole person. He had a comforting, serene presence.

After we ordered, he asked me why I was in London because I followed the green parrot. I had forgotten my mentioning this anecdote to him. 'Alice followed a white rabbit, for me it was a green parrot.'

'Give me more than that.'

'When I first arrived in London, I wasn't sure what to make of the town. I went for a walk in Hyde Park and there the parrots were everywhere. They were a noisy lot. I couldn't believe my eyes. They were free urban exotic birds. They should have been out of their element here, but they weren't. I don't know why, I felt I was like them. In that instant, London was home. I only learned afterwards they were parakeets, not parrots. For me they would always be the green parrots.'

Leo and I talked nonchalantly, having a good-humoured conversation, until the main course arrived and that was when he asked, a malicious glint in his eye which should have warned me, 'So, cara Yoko, I know you like a challenge?'

'Mmmm ... Yes I do. Not keen on competitions, just love challenging myself, pushing my limits.'

'That's why you are not really that shy ...'

'I can be shy!'

'Really?'

'Yes. It's just one of the things to challenge!'

'I see. What if I challenged you now, would you do it?'

I looked at him suspiciously and answered, 'That depends on what you have in mind.'

'Well, I thought that would be interesting to continue to get to know each other, but in a different way than chatting or messaging, that is in a challenging way.'

I pursed my lips and narrowed my eyes to display suspicion, although in truth I was curious.

'Again, that depends what you have in mind.'

'Just a little game of Truth or Dare.'

'Gosh! It's been a long time. Continue.'

'Each of us has six truths or dares and you can't pick more than two of the same in a row. And they do have to be challenging. One joker only.'

It was dangerous territory. Reviewing the extent of the danger on the 'dare' in a restaurant at lunchtime, the possibilities were limited to strange but decent. On the 'truth', he already knew the biggest secret I had to protect and for the rest, there wasn't much to hide. I could probably handle it.

'Bring it on,' I said in a deep calm voice as I leaned forward, elbows on the table and folded my hands under my chin. My mind was blank on what truth or dare to ask, so I told him to take the lead and start.

He took his time before he finally asked, 'Truth, or dare?'

'Truth.' It felt less risky on the first round. You can always find a way out of these while you can't of the silly dares. Call it wisdom from bad experiences.

'What type of lover are you?'

So he was attacking with the intimate angle. There were different possibilities to interpret the question, which could help me get out lightly. He seemed to read my mind and he added, 'I mean, shy, wild, aggressive, S&M? Just curious, you know ...'

'Passionate!' I replied, laughing.

'Mmmm. Good,' he nodded, looking falsely serious. On my turn to ask 'truth or dare?' he picked truth. Raking my mind to find a subject not previously discussed and on which I would like to know more, all I could think of was, 'You never talk about your love life. Are you a serial or a serious girlfriends type of guy?'

'I am a serious relationship type of guy. I had my fun in my late teens and early twenties. I am over it now. I have been single for some time. The last one ended from her side. It was tough because I still believed in it.'

'I'm sorry to have broached a sensitive subject.'

'I'm fine. Of late, I have kind of got close to someone else. I like her a lot, in a strange way. She lives abroad. Now it is my turn. Truth or dare?'

I took an in breath and chose dare.

Leo put on an innocent face, his eyes betraying the mischief underneath. 'Baby, sing for me.'

'I can never remember any song's lyrics.' I pinched my nose. Singing in public was not my forte.

'You can always sing the French national anthem, you must know it.'

'You are joking?'

'No. And I don't want some kind of whispering singing, I want the real voice with power singing.'

'Bastardo!' I said, laughing.

That is how I ended up chanting my national anthem loudly, in an English pub turned silent for the performance, a half-full bowl of curry and a two-thirds drunk pint of Guinness in front of me. It was not my most glorious moment. The whole pub seemed to agree on this. Only Leo was clapping along laughing.

'Truth,' Leo took the initiative to say when I finished. 'After such a performance, I would be too scared to dare.'

'And you would be right!' I chuckled. Weirdly, I was having a great time, which I wouldn't admit to anyone.

'Right,' I carried on. 'So, in truth, what is wrong with you?'

'Nothing, I am perfect.'

'I dared you, dear signore, to tell me the truth. You seem to be such a nice guy, but nobody is perfect. Come on, confess. Give me five of your flaws and not the 'barely nasty' ones please, the real bad flaws.'

'Ouch! Your lack of faith in my perfection hurts!'

'Get over it.'

'Fine, fine ... Let me think. Well ... I am a workaholic, flaw number one. I mean, really. I tend to sacrifice my private life to my work. Big time. I just can't stop. When something needs to be done, I have to do it. Now.'

'Well, I will accept it as a flaw, even if you are aware it is also a good sign of discipline and commitment.'

'That depends when you are on the outside and the one being sacrificed ... Flaw number two, I constantly drive over the speed limit.'

'That is not a character flaw!'

'Yes it is! I waste a fortune on speeding tickets. I should have learned by now, but I can't help it!'

'That isn't a flaw.'

'Tell that to the police.' He laughed and added, 'Accept this one and I'll give you a big one.'

I looked up at the ceiling, and nodded.

'So, flaw number three, sometimes I sneakily leave a restaurant or a bar without paying.'

'What!'

'Yeah, I know. Not even because of financial reasons, but for the thrill of it. Teen stupidity which lasts. Once or twice a year, though sometimes I skip a year.'

'Stupidity indeed, secret maybe, but a flaw?'

'The flaw is that I still don't feel guilty about it.'

'OK, that is wrong.' If it were me, I would be eaten up from the inside by guilt.

'I can see you don't approve. I was what you would call a bad boy, you know! Moving on, flaw number four, I snore. Flaw number five, I am convinced no one in the world makes a better coffee than me. I sneer and snap at anyone disagreeing. I am the coffee master. I am the best.'

'I see ... You have delusions of coffee making grandeur. Terrible flaw. How do you manage to live with it?'

'I have no problem with this flaw. It is only difficult for others to accept they are lesser individuals when it comes to coffee making.'

'What about Nespresso and the great George Clooney?'

'I only feel pity for them and for him.'

'Pity?'

'Pity. And disdain. I am sorry for all the coffee lovers out there who will never have a chance to taste my coffee.'

At this point I couldn't keep serious any longer and I roared in laughter. My mobile rang. I was having a good time, hadn't been on a date for ages and a lovely one at that, I was not going to take a call now! It would be rude in the middle of lunch anyway. Leo moved on to my next truth or dare.'

'After the last dare, I am going for truth, thank you very much!' I exclaimed.

'Truth it is. Have you ever had online sex?' he asked bluntly.

'What the ...? How do you think of questions like that?' I blushed.

'Well, I had been wondering that for some time ... Just curious, you know ...'

'Yeah right! You seem very prepared with your questions ...'

'Let's just say I have jotted down a list on the plane of little things I would love to know or see you do.'

'This is not really fair! You have plotted well while I was unprepared.'

'You accepted the challenge! Plus, you are worth some preparation. Now, the answer please? Online sex?'

'Never had the opportunity. Never had a distance relationship with someone before which would make it more likely.'

'Until now. I pick dare.'

I took a moment to register his comments. Did he consider we were in a relationship? The surprise made me lose my composure. I experienced a moment of slight panic. I had not agreed to anything! Thankfully, he had given me a way to pass on his remark by choosing 'dare'. It took me a few minutes to find one, during which I was acutely aware of any details of my body language being observed by him.

'I know! This is your dare: go and ask the chef for a raw bird's eye chilli pepper, bring it back here and eat it all.'

'Cara, that is such an easy dare.'

'Let's see how you feel about it after you have eaten it!'

He stood up and went to the kitchen, coming back a few minutes later with a red chilli, which he proceeded to eat. He didn't have any immediate reaction, but patience was required here. Bird's eye chillies are the strongest ones in Asia.

'So, Yoko, two more truth or dare to go. Which one will it be next?'

'Let's go for dare,' I sighed, fearing what would come next.

'Take off your bra, here and now, at the table.'

I was gobsmacked. He had really prepared his game well. So be it. I looked around. The restaurant was full, including two families with children. Damn. I had been challenged and had to rise to it. Absolutely! Now all that was required was face the dare with aplomb yet discretion. First, I put my jacket on my shoulders. He had not specified the how and couldn't protest. With the jacket on, I slid my arms behind my back under its cover and unhooked my bra. Next, I let my hands slide under my top along my neck to my shoulder and pushed down the straps of my bra down one arm then the next. Last, I slipped my right arm underneath the front of my top and pulled down my bra. One of my family wisdoms, passed on from mother to daughter, is to always, put on nice lingerie, even more so on a date. First for self-respect, second to feel good knowing that underneath whatever you are wearing, you are a sexy kitten. That day I had a lovely plum coloured satin set with black lace and bow on the décolleté. As I folded the bra on my lap, I internally thanked my female ancestors for their tips. Indeed, Leo had pulled out his hand requesting, in a word, proof by handing over my bra. He had seen me taking if off, so I was tempted to say no, but what the heck! At this point, I might as well give it to him. He took it and opened it on his lap. Glancing around to check if our little game had gone unnoticed, I waited for his reaction. He nodded with approbation.

'I like it! Nice! Now I wonder if you are the matching type, with this as part of a set?' Leo looked up with a huge grin.

'Is that the next truth or dare question?'

'No. I will not give up the last one that easily. Anyway I have this feeling you are.' That made me smile, especially as he was right. He gave me the bra back and I put it in my bag, asking him for his choice of truth or dare.

Leo couldn't answer. He had turned red, his eyes were watering, his throat was on fire. The chilli's effects had hit him in full. It was a proper dare after all. It took several minutes for him to recover before he croaked 'truth'.

'So ...' I had no good question to ask. All I could think was, 'Are you that desperate that you had to have a date with a woman on the other side of Europe, who you had never met, just because she looked OK on her profile photo?'

'I am not desperate, I am picky and I had a hunch.'

'A hunch?'

'Yes. I liked the way you look, write and react. I liked your spirit and my hunch was that I would like you in person even more. My instincts are very good. Everything about you is great, so it would be bad luck if I didn't fancy you when we met. I bet on good luck.'

'Unusual way to pick a girl.'

'It worked. I won the bet.'

There it was, blushing again. Always popping up when I didn't want it. So annoying!

'You look so cute when you blush. Now, last truth or dare?'

I was a bit flustered as I muttered 'truth'.

'Truth. Good. I have a simple question for you then. What would you do if I were to stand up now and kiss you?'

The blushing got worse. I was probably the colour of a lobster. I sat inert except for biting my lips and avoiding looking at his face. When I finally looked him in the eyes, he was very calm and smiling, waiting patiently for my answer. I took a deep breath to relax. All in all, my disquiet must have lasted maximum ten seconds, but it felt like an eternity before my self-possession returned. Once ready, I answered, 'I would do nothing and ... enjoy.'

Slowly, Leo pushed his chair back. He stood up and began to walk calmly round the table, his left hand sliding along the edge of the table accompanying his slow motion. I was frozen in my chair, following his move with my eyes only, head slightly tilted up towards him. I wasn't fixed on his face, I realised half-consciously, but looking at his body moving towards me. When he stood by my side, I felt more than saw him bending towards me. A hand tilted my head further backwards, his face leaned towards mine and he kissed me. It was a soft and tender kiss, a giving kiss. Yet a firm kiss. A fantastic kiss. Any tension left me and all I wanted was for it to last. His lips were full, mellow and smooth. I felt my core melt and wanted more, more of his mouth, more of him. Naturally our lips parted and the kiss grew deeper. I must be honest, it tasted of curry. The most delicious curry I had ever savoured. I wanted to hum with pleasure. Maybe I did, I don't remember. His hand had slid down my back, the other grabbing my shoulder and pulling me further and further towards him, into him even. My whole body responded to his touch and I let him take control, pulling me closer. We were both lost in each other, enthralled. It took someone from a neighbouring table to cough loudly to make us part. He straightened up slowly. Our eyes locked, serene, smiling and beaming.

'I should go back to my seat. I wouldn't be able to stop if I kissed you again. It would go down well here,' he murmured.

'No, it wouldn't,' I whispered back.

Leo sat back down and gently took my right hand across the table into his. He began to caress its palm softly with his thumb, making me shiver. The man was turning me on, right there at the table. I was still lost in his kiss. Well, that was only partially true: really, I longed more than his kiss. I wanted him. Judging by how he was looking at me, in a way reminiscent of a hungry wolf, he wanted more too. At that moment, I would not have minded if he planned to eat me alive. I remembered I had one last card to play and decided to play it. 'Truth or dare?'

He laughed. A loud, full, happy laugh.

'Dare!'

'Snatch me away from here.' Suddenly all the people around us were unbearable.

'With pleasure!' he exclaimed.

He hailed our waiter and asked for the bill. I stood up, excused myself, grabbed my bag and headed for the bathroom. After washing my hands I checked my phone out of habit. I had twelve missed calls. They were all from Jazz, Zeno, Harry and Leila. I frowned: that was clearly abnormal. I had only been gone a couple of hours. I dialled the last missed call, right there in the bathroom. Zeno answered immediately.

'Yoko! Where are you? Are you OK?'

'Well, yes.' I was taken aback by how panicky, even frightened, he sounded.

'Thank God! Where are you? Why did you not answer your phone?'

'Well, I was out for lunch, in a restaurant. With a friend ...'

'Jazz told us you were on a date, we know, but we don't know who he is and why you kept not answering.'

I was getting quite defensive now and snapped back, 'I wouldn't answer my phone on a date, would I?'

'Listen! Jack has been taken! He was kidnapped. He was on a train to the Cotswolds and forty-five minutes into the journey, at a stop on the way, he was abducted!'

'What? What! Jack has been abducted? F-U-C-K!' The shock made me swear.

'Yes, at the station. The Society had some kind of protection for them but they couldn't do a thing apparently, it all happened very fast. And we can't get hold of Leo or Dante either!'

'Leo ...'

'Yes and Dante! Leila is with us and ... Wait!'

'Err … Listen, Zeno.' I had to tell him I was with Leo, even if I would have preferred them not to know. It was too important.

'Wait! Yes! OK, Leo just called Leila. He is fine, he is with a friend.'

'Ah! Right. With a friend ... Good ... So ...' I didn't have to tell him just yet.

'Now we just need to find Dante.'

'He said he was doing some shopping, didn't he? Do you think he could have been abducted like Jack? Oh my God! Poor Jack. How did it happen? How is it possible? Abducted!'

'Listen, just come home. Everyone is frantic with worry here. The Society has set up a high security, it the safest place. Actually, maybe we should come and get you?'

'I am not far. I will be with you in five minutes.'

'OK, OK, just be careful, right?'

'Of course!'

'Leo said he would be here shortly too. OK, Leila is trying to get hold of Dante again. What a nightmare!'

'See you in a minute!'

'Just be careful, Yoko. I couldn't bear losing you too! You are in a restaurant? Take a knife with you. Take two knives!'

'Zeno, I will be careful. I am already on my way. Ciao!' The last few words were said as I walked back to the table.

I nodded at Leo and he returned my nod. We both bore a new grave and concerned expression on our faces. Leo put his hand on my back, leading me to the door and saying that he almost went to get me when he heard the news. We went out into the street, him keeping one hand on my shoulder in a protective way. To have him with me was a relief. I was scared. How easy it would be, if I was alone, to just push me in a car and drive off. Leo and I decided not go directly home. We would change cab twice or thrice, and get out in the street next to mine. Leila had already given the address to Leo and had retrieved his belongings from the hotel room when she went there looking for him. In our street, I noticed a few big bulky guys checking us out and the screens of their mobiles, then talking to themselves or most probably to a hidden microphone. Zeno had mentioned the house was under the protection of the Society and I assumed we were recognised and allowed to pass.

As soon as I crossed the threshold of my home, Jazz rushed towards me and hugged me in tears. 'I was so worried! NEVER ignore your calls again! NEVER! You can't do that anymore! Not when danger is looming. Not with the Fog. Never!' she said between sobs. Zeno then arrived and took me out of her arms and into his. I saw Leila from the corner of my eye, who seemed to release a big sigh and said, 'One in, two to go'. From behind me, Leo said 'Two in, one to go.' Arriving together, we said we met in the street outside and recognised each other from the FTab photos. Zeno turned and hugged Leo, to the latter's surprise. Jazz turned and gave him a smile, shaking his hand. 'So pleased to meet you. I feared not have the opportunity.'

'Pleased to meet you too.'

We all moved to the living room where the rest of the household was standing and waiting for us. I was greeted with hugs which almost suffocated me, Leo by a warm politeness. Leila went back promptly to her laptop, turned in such a way I couldn't see the screen. As she started talking to various people, I assumed she was on a crisis management conference call.

Leo immediately started asking questions to Zeno in Italian. It was too fast for me to understand but I heard the names of Jack and Dante repeatedly.

'Guys, in English please. We want to know too,' I asked them.

'Sure. Anyway I wasn't there, Leila could explain better,' Zeno said. Hearing this Leila commented, 'I'm sorry but I can't right now! We don't have much time, we must follow any leads while they are hot. Zeno, please, could you?'

'OK,' Zeno accepted. 'So. When you left your home in Rome, the three of you were accompanied by six guys to ensure your security. Two were in the car with you, as you know, two were on scooters ahead and two in a car behind. They were also there at the airport, with you in the plane and at Paddington Station when you arrived. There, they split: two accompanied Jack on the train and four went with Dante and you at the hotel. Both Dante and you had made it clear you wanted some privacy, so two bodyguards stayed at the hotel to make sure it was secure and two followed you for five minutes, just to confirm you were safe. You were. Should you not have been, they were to stay with you.'

'So what happened to Jack?' I asked.

'His two bodyguards were on the train, sitting in the same carriage. Leila was sitting with him. He went to the bathroom and one of the guys stood up and went up the corridor while he was in there. Someone passed in front of him and next he felt a sting in his neck and collapsed. He had been drugged by a needle. The train was pulling into a station and we assume Jack was snatched out of the toilet and off the train. The bodyguard in the carriage with Leila realised something was fishy when he saw people trying to help his colleague on the floor. He ran to the door of the wagon and saw in the distance two men pushing Jack into a car. Leila and the Society are working on tracing the car's route. It is proving difficult: it was listed as stolen and they took minor roads without traffic cameras.'

'Tonight is Saturday. Wherever Jack sleeps tonight, he will turn it into a portal,' I commented.

'Yes. And we can't do anything about it if we don't find them in the next hours. If they know and are after a portal, what do they have in mind for it? Also, do they have a Crosser to go through it? Do they have Dante?' Zeno asked, turning to Leo, who was white in apprehension.

'Please no! Not Dante!' he whispered, his jaw clenched.

'Even if they don't – I pray they don't – they will have access to the Fog. With no Crosser or Facilitator, they can still try to have people Relocated to gain access to World II,' I reflected.

'They can't control that,' Jazz noted.

'They have one chance in seven to get one,' I reminded her. 'If they make a lot of people cross, someone is bound to be one.'

'Damn,' she replied. 'They would have access to WII. They would enter the Other World.'

'Scusa?' Leo reacted to the last sentence from Jazz. 'World II? WII?'

'The Other World. Jazz has a tendency to give nicknames or shortened names to everyone and everything. Soon you will have one too,' I explained.

'What is yours?' he asked.

I kept silent. Jazz looked at me, waiting for me to divulge it if I so wished.

'Most of the time she calls me Yoko. It is quick and short. Sometimes, it is Nutella.'

'Nutella?'

'Because what is not to like about Nutella!' Jazz jumped into the conversation with a strained smile.

'I see. Fitting like a glove. Especially as Nutella is pretty addictive, too,' Leo commented looking at me, a naughty twinkle in his eyes.

Jazz looked at him surprised, then at me inquiringly. I raised my eyebrows and gave a little laugh, dismissing Leo's comment, 'Ahh ... those Italians!'

I turned the conversation back to the serious matter at hand. 'Are you any closer to finding Jack? And Dante?'

'No news from Dante yet. As for Jack, nothing. They have lost track of the car. This is not looking good,' Leila replied, still glued to her screen.

'No, no, no, no, NO! For Jack, for Dante and for today being a Switching Day. Jack ... He was already in a bad place!' I exploded.

'I am really worried for him. He has big highs and big lows. He will hit rock bottom with this ...' Leo said.

His phone rang. At the same time, Leila shouted 'Thank God!' and turned towards us. 'Dante is at the hotel!' Leo promptly answered. It was Dante. There followed a long conversation in Italian at the speed of light between Leo and him.

Thirty minutes later, Dante had joined us in the house. Zeno prepared coffee and we spent the rest of the afternoon discussing what to do next. We would not switch the Cotswolds manor for now. Although Jack didn't know its exact location, not even the name of 'Cotswolds', whoever had abducted him was bound to keep an eye on locations and extra activity along that train route. The most important issue at hand was how they had come to be on the train. The easiest explanation and usually the right one was that they had spotted the Roman fogged house and spied the comings and goings from it. Leila's recurrent presence and importance might have been noted and they could be tracking her moves. The identity and possible link to the Fog of Rico, Leo, Dante and Leila were compromised. Another problem was that Jack knew about the Society, the London Fog and Foggies' first names. He also knew about the other Fog locations. They had snatched Jack without his bag in which was his mini-tablet so at least the FTab was not a problem. Regarding our existence, Leila was already covering it. She had instructed some guys in the States to double-check that we were non-existent on the web and that names could not be traced on the new property deeds of the houses or on the council survey. The Society couldn't delete our Social Security numbers, instead they controlled their traceability to us. Leila went through the process they put in place, creating separate fake mailing addresses all over the England that a Society member was to retrieve regularly. They created an army of a new virtual Yoko, Zeno, Rico and Harry living in the UK or on social platforms like Facebook. I started to get lost in the intricacies of this huge matrix. How many people worked for the Society to achieve all of this so fast? All could hope for was that they would succeed. I felt a wave of gratitude Leila had found us first.

All the while, I was trying to act as normal possible with Leo, as if I had just met him. It was not easy when from time to time he would put a hand on my back or shoulder, asking if I was OK or if he could help me prepare yet another tea and coffee. It sent shivers up my spine. It was bad timing to be turned on in the middle of a crisis, and yet here I was, blushing at every touch. I felt on display. Surely it was easily discernible to everyone that something was going on between us. Remarkably no one reacted: we were saved thanks to the preoccupations of the situation. I tried to calm my nerves baking a cake.

Another topic of conversation that afternoon was whether or not we should still attend the Lil'London event on Sunday after mass. The conclusion was yes. The small town was bound to have gone through a lot of preparation. A last minute cancellation would have been a diplomatic faux pas. If the 'enemy' organisation were to gain access to WII area, we had to ensure friendly relations with us first. We should even warn them of the existence of that other entity chasing after the Fog portals. That last point was to be discussed with Leila. It would have to be later, perhaps over dinner, for she was still glued to her screen with no sign of being free any time soon.

The whole household and guests were on the ground floor, mostly sitting on the sofas brainstorming. Going to Lil'London the next day was confirmed, and Jazz and I attempted to lighten the mood and raised a fashion issue: what to wear for the Lil'London event? It was trivial and it barely helped take our minds off Jack. It gave us a feeble focus on something else. My ideas were a long skirt, little blouse and waist jacket, and kitten heels, something modern and as respectable as possible for their community. From the corner of my eye I checked on Leo, who was fiddling with his FTab. Jazz, who would be of the party going to the town, wanted us to take out ball gowns and fur jackets for the occasion. I had misgivings about wearing a dead animal on my back. I had not managed to get rid of my fur jacket as it came from my paternal grandmother who I had never met and who I'd had precious little from. Jazz had less remorse: she was against the farming of animals for their fur, but not against wearing it when she was freezing. A complex woman. We were nervous about the visit of Lil'London. It was important to me that on this first official encounter I should emphasise to the local community how good a friend she was to me. I hoped that being a Switcher gave me a de facto social status and that, being my friend, she would be respected.

Jazz and I were discussing the pros and cons of our pre-selection of outfits when my FTab beeped. Checking my messages, I struggled to contain my first reaction which was to glance at Leo. It came from him and read, 'I'm sorry I didn't get more time with you alone.'

As I couldn't stop a smile, Jazz immediately tried to sneak a peek at the tablet's screen, while commenting, 'It's him, isn't it?

When will you let the cat out of the bag and tell me about your mysterious man!'

I winked at her and failed to answer, just turned the FTab slightly so that she wouldn't be able to read. The Society had redirected calls and messages from my mobile to the FTab. It was too complicated to juggle between both and, with my job soon over, it would make sense to keep only one device. It was high time to keep only the most secure option and give in to a sole use of the FTab. Because the FTab received both my old number and Foggies' messages, Jazz had not made the assumption that the secret messenger was a Foggy.

I replied to Leo, controlling my impulse to look towards him, 'I can only hope you will invite me for a second date then.' His reply beeped within seconds.

'Considering how sexy you are, leaning against those pillows, you can bet on it!'

'Wait until you see me tomorrow dressed like a Mormon. You may change your mind.'

'Stop, I am starting to fantasise!'

'About Mormon women?'

'No, on the underwear you may be wearing underneath to compensate!'

'Men! You are all incorrigible ...'

'I would prefer you to wear the ball gown, for sure. You must look amazing in an evening dress. I would still wonder about your underwear, though.'

'I am starting to think you are a lingerie fetishist.'

'No, I just love pretty things on pretty women.'

'I am going to stop this conversation now, before I start blushing uncontrollably.'

'You are even better than Nutella and Nutella is already irresistible.'

I burst out laughing. They all turned to look at me enquiringly, except Leo, who just kept looking down at his screen, hiding his reaction by bringing his hand to his mouth. Nutella is a revered institution for Italians. What a huge compliment! The laugh didn't last long. The thought of Jack came back crashing inside my head and cut it short.

That night, Leo and Dante stayed with us and slept in the house. It was safer until another secure hotel or location was organised. They squeezed into Jazz's room and Jazz shared my bed. Leo couldn't help but raise an eyebrow and sneer when he heard that. So did Rico. Cheeky buggers. It reassured me to have the Romans close and protected under our roof, as well as ready in case something went wrong tomorrow in Lil'London. It was anybody's guess as to what to expect there.

# WEEK IV

**Day 1 (Sunday)**

Since the Lil'London Council visit and the presence of their wardens on the edge of the forest, Zeno and I had put aside any big expeditions in WII. We concentrated on small excursions, mostly to determine the signal range of our mobiles. It proved to be limited to about five hundred metres from the house. The good old walkie-talkie worked better and the latest modern version, the two-way radio, had the best potential for us: it gave us a good eighteen mile, or twenty-nine kilometre, range. We had not tested them to such an extent in the Other World yet. Why no big expedition, you may ask? Well, first, we had enough issues to keep us busy on many fronts on our original planet. Second, we thought we might as well wait for the top notch equipment and four-wheel drive vehicle the Society provided as part of our new jobs. Last but not least we did not want to offend the indigenous population of the Other World: we didn't know how territorial they were or how they would take to us roaming around freely. Considering the current situation, with Jack's newly opened portal last night somewhere unknown, establishing a friendly and respectful relationship with WII was paramount.

Early morning, when she should have been sleeping like us, Leila emailed that the Society was actively inspecting satellite images for traces of a new fog and monitoring communications for reports. They focused mainly on the UK, although it was potentially anywhere in the world. Jack had disappeared on Saturday morning and despite the Society's best efforts, they had no idea where they may have taken him.

As for Jazz, Zeno and me, we woke up concentrating on the day ahead. In an unexpected way, it was a historical event. The first official visit from our world ambassadors to a WII community was of importance. Because of this, I was in turmoil about the details of our appearance and how to make the best entrance. I couldn't decide on an outfit, lacking information on what the women of WII wore.

It was also at the last minute that I wondered if we should bring a gift or contribution to the banquet. Bringing a single bottle of wine or champagne would not do it, a cow or ten would be more appropriate. We had not thought it through well enough! There was but one thing to do and I messaged Leila. She answered immediately that she would look into it. We were to make our way to Lil'London at 12 p.m. At 11.20, the new bell placed outside the front gate, beyond the Fog, rang. When I opened the door in my dressing gown, nearly ready except for putting on my dress, Rico arrived downstairs, sleepy-eyed. We went out through the Fog and the sight baffled us. Three of the Society guards watching the houses were standing by ten supermarket trolleys from Waitrose, the nearby luxury supermarket (thankfully opening at 11 a.m. on Sundays). Some were full of boxes of cakes and various sweet treats, others full of champagne bottles, or brimming with delicacies such as caviar, truffled cheese, foie gras and so on. It was quite a sight! Personally, I couldn't take my eyes off the cakes trolley. I had spotted a toffee and chocolate cake that looked like heaven on earth ... They explained it was the best they could do at such short notice on a Sunday.

'What about the trolleys?' I asked.

'What about them?' one of them answered, a slightly defensive Vin Diesel lookalike guy with an accent from Liverpool.

'You pinched them, didn't you?' Rico spoke my mind.

'Well, we had to find something you could use. We were told you needed a way of transporting them on foot. At such a short notice ...' The huge man looked like a child caught with his hand in the cookie jar. Both Rico and I laughed at his contrite expression and at the contrast with the stern man of a few seconds before.

'Well thought mate! Brilliant idea!' Rico said to him, putting a hand on his shoulder.

'Hey! I could put some ribbons on the trolley to make it a bit more festive!' I exclaimed.

'Yoko, please, no ... Don't start,' Rico retorted, looking slightly horrified.

'Yes! Yes! Yes! Or wrap a nice tablecloth either in or out. Let's make it look nice. I don't want to push a boring shopping trolley down the main road on my first visit to Lil'London!'

'Yoko, they don't know what a shopping trolley is,' Harry remarked, arriving behind us.

We pushed the trolleys towards the house and left them out on the front patio in the Fog. Jazz, wrapped up in the towel and attracted downstairs by the noise, eyed the cakes in the one left by the door. I gave her a clear 'don't you even think of stuffing your face now' stare.

As I went back up to put some clothes on, I asked her, 'How are we supposed to drag shopping trolleys through the forest? And ten of them at that?'

'And how am I supposed to even walk through the forest with my heels!'

'Jazz. Forget the heels. It won't happen.'

'Oh yes it will! I will just get a larger bag, put them in it and slip in them on discreetly when we arrive. Back in a minute.'

'What about the trolleys?' I yelled as she ran up the stairs.

In the end, we had opted for a black tie dress code. Zeno was wearing Harry's suit. If not a perfect fit, it worked well to make him look smarter than I had ever seen him. I was wearing my black velvet 1950s ball gown and cropped matching fur jacket, feeling grateful to my mother for keeping them for the next generation. To complement the dress, I was adorned with pearl necklace and earrings. The finishing touch was long black leather gloves. Velvet would have been more elegant, but I didn't have a pair so that would have to do. I felt like a movie star ready to go on set. Hairwise, it was possible women in WII covered their hair out of the house, as was common practice in the UK in the nineteenth century, so I had looked frantically for a hat that would be suitable. I had none that wouldn't be ridiculous and the same went for scarves, so I gave up and decided that they just had to deal with a bare head. There was only so much I could do without knowledge of their customs and theirs of mine.

When she came downstairs, Jazz was stunning. Seeing her, I was gripped by a mixture of admiration and horror. Admiration because of her guts, horror because of the effect she might have in Lil'London. Jazz was wearing a rich gold and emerald sari, with dozens of gold bangles on her wrist and a gold and emerald set of jewellery on her neck, ears, and forehead. Jazz was in for the kill on that one.

'Oh my God! Yoko! You look amazing!' Jazz exclaimed when I remained mute admiring her. 'W-O-W! You look ... You look ...' Jazz was checking me up and down.

'Like one of the most beautiful women in our world. I agree,' Leo finished, talking calmly and softly. He had arrived some time ago, not making any comment until then. I instantly blushed like a sun-ripened tomato from both Jazz and Leo's compliments. The other boys of the house, as well as Dante, chimed their approval of Jazz and my outfits.

'Jazz, you look breathtaking,' I praised her. 'This sari is sublime and fits you like a glove. You are going to blow them away.

Either that or you are going to terrify them by your splendour. Which one did you have in mind?' I asked Jazz.

'Both! You and I are going to blow their minds, honey!'

A knock at the door.

We all turned towards the entrance and launched into action. Dante, Leo and Leila, who would stay in the house until we got back in case of emergency, went upstairs so as not to be seen. As Rico opened the door, I heard Jazz whispered to herself 'Lil'London, eat your heart out. We are coming!' She turned to me. 'Nutella, I am terrified.' I put my arm around her shoulder and kissed her forehead, telling her in the most relaxed and confident voice I could muster that we would show them what we are made of, we would shine. I was anxious too. To the point it was making me want to go to the loo.

The Lil'London Welcoming Luncheon was the most intense event I had ever been to. Worse than office parties when I was a newbie, drinking too much from nervousness. One thing was for sure, it wasn't fun. From then on, I always sympathised with any politicians, celebrities and diplomats performing official duties. I had not really expected to have a blast, I just didn't realise how exhausting the whole day would be.

The surprises started immediately when we dragged the full and roughly wrapped shopping trolleys behind us out of the house into the Other World. There we came face to face with saddled horses ready for us.

'Glad I have ankle boots on,' I thought. 'New problem: shopping trolleys aren't going to work.'

Zeno leaned towards me and mumbled, 'Yoko! I can't ride!'

Jazz leaned on the other side, 'Yoko! I can't ride!'

'Come on, guys! We really have to face that one, you'll be fine!'

'Well, that is easy for you, you grew up on horses!' Jazz whispered, angrily.

'Oh yeah! Have you seen the saddle on those two horses? Special women's ones, side-saddle type. Guess what: I have never done that either!'

'So what are we to do?' Zeno asked. We were mumbling to each other with frozen smiles to hide from the observers that we had an issue.

'Right, right, Zeno, I apologise for the image, but it's all that comes to mind: ride as if you were mounting a woman. The hip motion is the same.' Zeno laughed nervously and leaned back with a slightly embarrassed 'OK'.

'Jazz, you and I will have to try and settle the best we can and go with the motion.' I then turned to the group of men standing by their horses, waiting for us to move forward. I raised my voice to address them with aplomb, 'Please forgive us, we were discussing a slight problem. We have brought these gifts for the people of Lil'London and it just came to our attention that our method for transport is not adequate for the horses.' As I spoke, I indicated the shopping trolleys with a sweep of my hand.

The Lil'Londoners, eight men, three of whom were the members of the council, turned and peered in the direction I had indicated. Benjamin Snayth nodded to two men, and told them something I couldn't hear. The two men saluted us with a touch of their hats before mounting their horses and galloping away.

'They will come back with the necessary carts for your gifts. The watch will guard them from the fauna until then,' Benjamin Snayth explained.

As 'ladies' the men helped us get on our horses. They were suitably impressed by both Jazz and me. We were very different from the previous times they had seen us and more imposing. I was concerned that if my outfit seemed to be appreciated and even approved Jazz's had more the effect of raising apprehensions. She was already quite exotic for them and she had reinforced her difference. This could be positive, her facing the community head held high, or could also make her acceptance more difficult. I applauded at her for being different and asserting it, yet I worried for her.

People fear what is different, what they don't understand. Fear is dangerous.

It took us approximately forty minutes to reach Lil'London at a casual pace. That located the town about seven kilometres away, so something like five miles. Within fifteen minutes of leaving the house, we hit the road leading to Lil'London. It was gravelled and well maintained. About ten minutes before arriving in sight of Lil'London, we passed by the entrance of a dirt road on the left that Benjamin Snayth mentioned led to his mansion. It made me think of James Fisher, who to my shame had not been much on my mind lately. I had had quite a lot to deal with ... As we got closer to the town, a few locals appeared on the road, going in the same direction as us. Every time, men would take off their hats, some type of round hats reminding me of the Amish or a rabbi. Women would curtsy and bow their heads, looking up at us discreetly. They gave a joyous greeting, but the tension on their faces betrayed a certain anguish underneath. Children were the ones letting go of their restraint, following the horses, laughing and shouting hellos and welcomes and something that sounded like 'Ya-ya-ya!'. To my surprise, a lot of them were sliding. I did a double take the first time I saw this: they were rollerblading! A few of the adults not travelling by carts had shoes on wheels too. I enquired about it to Augustus Hoare, who was riding the closest to me. He explained, not a little proud, that the local people had aimed to be as advanced as possible. When the door opened last, the Foggies and Relocated had endeavoured to keep abreast with novelties and technology in an effort to reduce the gap between the two worlds while the doors were closed. In 1789 a certain Mr van Lede, having moved to Paris in the winter, was missing ice-skating on the frozen canals of his hometown of Bruges in Belgium. He pondered on an alternative and created the 'patins à terre' or ground-skates, in other words, rollerblades. During the French Revolution, part of his family escaped to London. It wasn't clear how the Foggies came to know of his invention, but they considered it would soon become a common means of transport and they ought to bring it across. They adapted it to the unpaved roads with larger, tougher wheels. It became a local hit. Hoare asked me if indeed rollerblading was ordinarily practised in our world. I replied that we had so many various means of transport now, it was merely one of them.

'It is trendy,' I said to his satisfaction. 'You were ahead of your time.'

What I didn't say was that I was a clumsy oaf on those types of wheels.

Lil'London reminded me of a small English country town, with cosy identical houses along a main road and tiny side streets leading to other cosy houses. It was the caricature of the old traditional English architecture. When we arrived, people were gathered along the main road and slowly a roar of clamour and hoorays grew. It reached its climax when we got into the main square of the town, in front of the church. I was trying to appear very dignified and to avoid wiggling in the saddle in search of a stable position – which got lost when I turned to speak with Hoare. The best way to describe the attire of the people of Lil'London would be a mixture of Far West town, Amish and, for the wealthier men, male characters from a Jane Austen book. The difference of wealth and status was obvious, classes very distinct in the quality of their fabric and on their location: the nearer to the square, the higher the houses and the wealthier the people. I looked around. Zeno was clearly uncomfortable and maybe even in pain from the horse riding. Jazz seemed OK, though she gripped the pommel of her saddle with such strength her knuckles were white.

On the square, I saw with horror a stage set up on the opposite side of a church. The two other sides of the square, between the podium and the church, were lined with tables on which a large amount of food was waiting. We dismounted and were led to the stage, joined by Benjamin Snayth, Augustus Hoare and Edmund Poff. Since we had left the house, our little group had talked very little. Now on stage, the cheers quickly calmed down and a heavy silence followed. Benjamin Snayth was looking at the crowd which was looking at Jazz and me, with a mixture of bewilderment and expectation.

Benjamin Snayth took a step forward and began his speech. He greeted the crowd first and expressed how excited he was to be part of this historic moment. Then he lost me. It had dawned on me that we were on a podium, in front of everyone, and expected to speak. Stage fright kicked in. Plus I had no idea what to say! Glancing to my left and my right, Zeno was staring ahead at the crowd, and Jazz was focusing on the wood of the stage. I wished Harry were there. He would have been perfect to make a speech here, being a man, eloquent, able to express himself in an appropriate old-fashioned turn of phrase. I tried to calm down and review the situation. Jazz should not make the speech: it had to be the Crosser or Switcher, not the Relocated. I noticed James Fisher on the right, at the foot of the podium with a group of wealthy people that looked like a family. Already, Jazz had special treatment being on stage. What about Zeno? Zeno was a man, so that would be good in relation to the obvious predominance of men in the hierarchy of power in Lil'London. There again, Zeno was not a public speaker. Really not. Reluctantly, I acknowledged that it was also my new job to deal with the whole inter-world relations.

'Damn!' I muttered. From the corner of my eyes I saw that Zeno glanced at me. He had heard. He frowned slightly in an attempt to enquire if everything was OK. I responded by tilting my head slightly up and giving him a small tense smile. He returned to observing the crowd, and I returned to thinking of the speech ahead. 'Why on earth am I so unprepared? I should have seen it coming!' I berated myself inwardly. 'Think, Yoko, think!'

How long did I spend pondering on what to say, what not to say, or how long to say whatever I would find that I could say? It seemed like only a couple of minutes before I was shaken out of my thoughts by Benjamin Snayth raising his voice a touch louder. 'Folks of Lil'London, let me introduce you to Mr Zenone

Grande and Miss Yoko Salelles, who have opened the door between the world of our ancestors and ours once again!' Clamour and applause welcomed his last sentence. I noted that Jazz had been left out of Snayth's introduction. That was quite insulting: true, she was not a contributing factor to the door between the two worlds, but he could still have acknowledged her in one way or another.

Zeno and I took a step forward. He bowed. Inspired by the women on the road, I did a little curtsey, yet kept my head high and straight. To be taken seriously, I had to appear as powerful as possible, almost royal. The silence returned and all eyes turned to Zeno. I could feel him getting more and more distressed. He glanced towards me, lips slightly pinched and something akin to terror in his eyes. As for me, I really regretted not asking for a toilet break before going on stage.

I took a deep breath, made another step forward, and spoke to the crowd before me. 'People of Lil'London, it is an honour to be among you today.' Every head turned towards me, a look of surprise, if not shock, on their faces. Quite a few heads turned between Zeno and me as if watching a tennis match while I continued, 'My fellow Crosser, Mr Zenone Grande, my dear friend and newly transferred here, Miss Jazz Jones, and I wish to expressed our gratitude for such a warm welcome today. The gathering in your lovely town of so many to greet us is truly appreciated. As the door opener, I have been chosen by my peers to speak on their behalf and to serve as intermediary between our two worlds.' Pause. Deep breath. Smile. 'So far, so good,' I reassured myself.

'Zenone Grande will also act as an ambassador for our world, although on different grounds. His aim is to share with you the new tools, trades and practices developed in our society since the last opening.' Pause. Deep breath. Smile. Head up and back straight. Look at the crowd regally and try to think of what to say next. My tone and wording surprised me. I must have picked that up from movies.

'People of Lil'London, it is also a pleasure for me to introduce my dear friend Jazz Jones who is now part of this world. She is like a sister to me and her joining your community is binding me even closer to the causes and future of this land.' I paused to let the meaning of my message sink in. 'Jazz is a sister to me. Mess with her and you mess with me. Mess with me and you are jeopardising your link to the portal and the future benefits you can get from it. Clear?'

I turned to Zeno and nodded, a very visible, clear nod. I then turned further back and did the same to Jazz. She had tears in her eyes, she knew what I had just done. I am not sure a proper ambassador would have done this, to make it so personal, but I didn't care. She really was like a sister to me. I turned back to the crowd.

'As for me, I feel privileged to have opened the door and be here in front of you today. I look forward to discovering you, your culture and traditions, as well as building strong, positive and en-riching links with the world I come from. It is a great honour for us.' As I uttered the last few words, a few men discreetly brought up additional tables and set them up at the bottom of the stage in front of us. From the corner of my eyes I recognised the Waitrose boxes in several carts being dragged onto the sides of the square. That was my escape route from the stage!

'We wished to express our pleasure at being here today by bringing a few treats from our world. You will find on the tables below the stage a small selection of delicacies most appreciated in our London. We hope you will enjoy them too.

'May this day of festivity be the start of a long, fruitful, friend-ly and enlightening relationship between our two worlds.' Then I couldn't help it, I had a 'Miss World' moment and concluded, 'May peace be with us all.' I swore Jazz stifled a giggle with that last one.

Anyway, I looked around at the crowd, gave them a big wide smile, adding a low head bow for the show.

Cheers exploded. I took two steps back to return to Zeno's and Jazz's level. The members of the council were all smiles and clapping, even though the smiles seemed more politically correct than real. I felt a bit faint. Jazz came towards me, 'Thank you, Nutella. What you said, for me ...'

'Jazz, stop. I meant it all, but now is not the time. You are ready to cry.' To make sure she stopped, I started to walk towards the side of the stage. I had a frozen smile plastered on my face. There really were a lot of diplomatic smiles these days. The fleeting thought that maybe I should practice fake smiling in front of a mirror came and left. I had another thought occupying my mind that gave spring to my stride: finding the bathroom!

In the hours that followed my leaving the stage, I was led round the main families of Lil'London, shaking hands, being introduced to such and such, meeting many wives and children. Then we walked among the crowd, stopping from time to time to nod and smile, or to accept bunches of flowers and gift baskets. Zeno, Jazz and James Fisher didn't leave my side. As often as possible I made sure they were the ones receiving the presents. It was so totally unreal, I felt I was floating in a dream. One tiny side of me was enjoying the attention and sense of importance. The bigger side was unsettled by the excessive attention and reverence. I feared the responsibilities linked to it: Zeno and I were just the ambassadors, not the one answer to all their questions. After all, it was a big accident, a random occurrence that we were the ones here. I noted that some of the gifts were definitely for women – crocheted hat, apron and so on – and others for men – hat, old-fashioned cravat. So at least information had spread there would be a man and a woman, information or gossip, either from the members of the council, the watchmen, or even James Fisher. About the latter, I managed to grab him on the way down the platform and made him stay with us. 'From now on, you stay with us and walk by Zeno's side. You too will play a role in the inter-world relations.' He beamed and tagged along happily. Benjamin

Snayth was less impressed. James Fisher had been staying with his family and having close access to a Relocated was an asset for him. If he got Fisher in his pocket, he could have his own source of information on our world, his own special pawn.

After touring the town, we finally got seated at the table of honour. Being close to toffee cheesecake pie, I thought of all those who would taste such cake for the first time … lucky guys. As for us, we were presented with a large variety of dishes, samples of their best cuisine. Meat was the main ingredient, such dishes as jugged hare, boiled rabbits, calves' heads, roasted pheasants, legs of mutton and spit-roasted larks. There was also as fricassée of eggs and pickled mackerel. I forgot many others. The choice of soups and broths (green pea soup, mutton broth and scotch barley broth) and of pies (lamb pie, sweet chicken pie, minced veal pie, fish pie) seemed endless. Then came an array of puddings and cheeses. I was so stuffed after the first three dishes I couldn't even have more than a spoonful of anything else. A pity, their almond cheesecake and pound cake were yummy. Nothing close to our cheesecakes and pound cakes, but surprisingly good nonetheless. In fact, everything I tried was delicious, if definitely different. I was very curious to find out how to make and bake such a wide variety of dishes, except for the calf's head. I had no curiosity about that one recipe. I managed to give most things a try, but when they brought the head in front of me and sliced off one of the ears, I struggled not to pull a face. That ear stared at me from my plate for the rest of the afternoon.

The festive meal we were enjoying was special. Without doubt, especially in poorer households, the daily menu would be far less interesting fare. The conversation during the meal was relatively effortless. Tasting each other's specialities gave us an easy and neutral subject of conversation between us and Augustus Hoare, Edmund Poff and Benjamin Snayth, along with their respective wives, Clémence, Maud and Barbara. More exactly, I should say some of their wives: they were the head wives, running the household and supervising the other wives (except for Poff, who had Maud only, maybe because of his obvious insecurity). The wives were very subdued at the table and talked little. Mostly, they observed. Maud Poff, wife of the church leader, had an open and warm face. Her smile seemed genuine. She tucked in happily in every dish and shared the odd friendly comment with Clémence Hoarc. Those two seemed be at ease with each other, with less decorum between them than with the others. This made me think they may be friends in real life, outside official occasions. Barbara Snayth on the other hand seemed a bit annoyed by the complicity of the other two women. At some point she made a snappy comment, or what appeared like one judging from the immediate reaction of Mrs Hoare and Mrs Poff. They both immediately stopped talking, their faces turned stern and they stood straighter. They glanced at Mrs Snayth, with exasperation from Maud Poff, with anxiety from Clémence Hoare. The latter was a frail woman, slightly younger than the others, in her early twenties. She had an innocent face and a gentleness in her demeanour, albeit, watching her, she betrayed a certain unease. At some point, I saw Maud put a hand on her forearm in a calming motion and Clémence Hoare took a deep breath. It was a simple, natural gesture between friends. None of them had been looking at each other. I wondered what dynamics and stories were behind the front put up by the people seated at this table. Maybe I would never know, or maybe I would learn too soon.

The ride back in the early hours of the evening seemed to last forever. With the vast amount of food I had consumed, I was drowsy and felt like a big sack of potatoes on horseback. Zeno and Jazz were worn out too. A wave of relief went through me that the day was over. I couldn't wait to get back home, take off those shoes and dress, then pop an aspirin and digestive tablet. At least to keep a cool head I had refrained from drinking. On this it was worse for Zeno: not only didn't he pace himself foodwise at the start and thus had been caught by surprise when more and more came his way, he had also drunk too much. As a woman trapped in a tight dress, I could not eat much from the beginning, which helped me. Again as a woman it had also been much easier to decline the numerous offers of more wine.

On the way back a large cart accompanied us, carrying the various gifts gathered during the visit. When we arrived in the clearing, Zeno whispered to me he had put aside a cake this morning to give to the watchmen as they had missed the festivities. Zeno always had a kind heart.

'That's a great idea. As soon as our official escort is gone, let's go back out and give it to them,' I replied.

'Does that mean I have to stay dressed like this a little longer? Argh!' Jazz replied, looking at her wellies. She hadn't had an opportunity to put her heels on.

'Jazz ...' Zeno and I said in tandem.

'Yeah, yeah, I know, I know. But after I'll go directly to bed and will sleep till tomorrow!'

'You've read my mind!' Zeno replied.

'Same here!' I chimed in.

We started laughing until we realised we were still not alone. One of the men with us transferred the contents of the carts into some of the shopping trolleys in the clearing and pushed them through the Fog. In the meantime, Jazz and Zeno by my side, I went to thank the members of the council who had accompanied us back.

'Mr Snayth, Mr Hoare and Mr Poff. Words are not enough to express our pleasure for the warm welcome we have received in Lil'London today. Thank you.' I had rehearsed this little speech during the journey back. It was strange to hear myself talk in such formal way and with an unnatural British accent. I began referring to it as the WII Speech Effect. After an afternoon of being treated like a queen, I should rename it as the WII Posh Effect.

Shortly afterwards, we were back out. We brought the rest of the trolleys in through the Fog to return them to our world and ultimately to Waitrose, their rightful owners. The watchmen were thrilled when we gave them the banoffee pie. They wouldn't stop bowing and grinning. It was touching. We had had such reactions all afternoon, but there in the forest, with us so smartly dressed and just those two and their little hut, the situation was more personal, more intimate.

When finally home, I stripped off my dress, put warm pyjamas on, my favourite fluffy spotted slippers on my feet and sank into the sofa, a big pot of tea close at hand. Jazz and Zeno did the same and we were joined in the living area by Leila, Harry, Rico, Dante and Leo.

'Guys, I am sorry but I won't last long,' Jazz said, after a big gulp of tea. 'I am knackered. I'll drink this and then go and collapse in bed. Dante, Leo, are you staying here or can I use the bedroom?'

'You can use the bedroom,' Leila replied. 'We have secured a new hotel for them both.'

'Thank God!' Jazz exclaimed and disappeared further into the sofa. From then on, she went mute and escaped five minutes later. She had drunk her tea at the speed of light.

'Zeno, you start?' I was hoping to sip a bit of tea first, but my hopes didn't last long.

'Nope. Fire away.'

I sighed heavily. I was so weary, the day seemed blurry. I proceeded to give them a little account of the visit. Between questions and descriptions, it took just under an hour and three cups of tea. Leila was taking notes, so that I wouldn't have to write everything from scratch when writing the report for the Society. Consciously or not, she was subtly reminding me that from then on, I was to keep a written track of my visits to WII and of anything relevant to the Fog, Foggies and inter-world relations. Reports … there is no escape from administrative tasks. Ever. In any job!

I asked Leila if there was any update from Jack and his new portal, theoretically opened last night. Unfortunately, the answer was no.

'What will happen when they learn in Lil' London that Yoko is not the only one who creates doors?' Leo had asked a very good question.

'I don't know ... I will be toppled off the pedestal, presumably. Plus they may try to play on both sides for their best interests. Not that we are asking for anything, but we have much to offer. I just don't know, I can't think anymore. I am beat.'

'Did they look scared?' Leo continued.

'Some of them. It's only natural, don't you think?'

'Yes. They don't know you and the changes the door is going to bring. Our society is very different from theirs, this is clear to them already. Different and unknown. Exactly what raises fear in most people and communities,' Leila remarked.

'Well, how encouraging! This is going to be so much fun,' Harry commented, being his sarcastic self.

'In any case, Yoko was brilliant. She handled it with brio. And the speech, I was so relieved that she took care of it. That is really not my field!' Zeno told the others.

'It confirms the Society was right in trusting her to do a great job. We are pleased to have her on board,' Leila replied to Zeno.

'I am here, you know,' I reminded them.

'I think she looks the part too. Lots of dignity and charm. And gorgeous,' Leo joined their conversation.

'Thank you, that's ...' I began.

'I had never seen that dress. Quite a statement. I wonder how it can fit in her wardrobe,' Rico continued.

'Errr ... Helloooooo!' I said, wondering if they were having fun with me. 'I am just here!'

'Ahhh ...Yoko, Yoko, Yoko ...' Harry and Zeno said, shaking their heads and smiling.

'Right, I know what you are doing. Stop teasing me! You know compliments unsettle me. Not working guys, I am too tired to care, or react.' I stood up and stuck my tongue out at them. 'I'm drained, I am going to bed. See you in the morning.' I kissed everyone good night and left. It was not yet even 9 p.m. I called my parents and gave them a summary in minutes. I couldn't keep my eyes open anymore. That night I slept a good twelve hours which was unheard of. In the morning, I was back at full steam, ready to face the world. Or two worlds.

## Day 2 (Monday)

Walking to the office through the park, I thought long and hard about how irrelevant this job was in my life now. Of course I could just drop it and I knew the Society would find a way to back me up, but this unfinished business would bug me. This was a point of self-respect, as much as respect for a company who had, after all, treated me right and sorted me out when I needed it. Really though, I couldn't wait to be out of this job now. My mind and my heart were just not in it anymore.

It soon proved to be the shortest and most unpleasant working day of my life. As I dropped my bag under my desk and before I had time to sit down my boss called me into his office. Immediately, I saw it was not going to be a pleasant meeting. As a boss, he was OK. I never particularly warmed to him, nor did I have anything against him. He was one of those people who, like a standard piece of furniture not standing out enough or ugly enough to be noticeable, was just part of the room, one not paid much attention to. Neither enthusiastic nor depressed, he didn't usually display much emotion and lacked presence. Mainly he just acted as an intermediary between his subordinates and his superiors. That day, he looked different: he was obviously upset and it was directed towards me.

'Yoko. I did not appreciate your taking days off without much of an explanation.'

'George. I am sorry to have upset you. I did explain I had a family emergency and ...'

'What family emergency?'

'My sister has a rare predicament and ...'

'What predicament?' Gosh he was cross! He had never used such barking tone before. I struggled not to let it get under my skin.

'She ... can't get out of her own home. She is suddenly unable to face our world and cannot step a foot out of her house. This is very distressing for her and for her infant obviously and the rest of the family. She is falling into a deep depression and we fear for what's coming next.' I had managed to keep my voice level and even better I didn't even lie!

'I see. Well, next time I would appreciate a bit more information. It doesn't justify your lax attitude to your schedule and work lately.' He had calmed down a notch.

'It has been a bit of a rollercoaster. Her situation is long term, hence my giving you my notice.'

'What notice?' The look of shock and surprise did not bode well. Some information had not been passed on yet.

'I sent my notice by email to Human Resources last Friday,' I replied softly.

'I haven't been informed! Why wasn't I informed? And you didn't think it appropriate to inform me directly too?' The barking tone had returned.

'I copied you in to the email.' I defended myself.

'I didn't see it. You should have come to talk to me! We need to talk about that. You can't leave, not in the middle of the campaign project ...'

'I need to, I am afraid. In fact, I wanted to start the handover this week. I wish it to be my last week.'

'WHAT! NO!' He had screamed those words and I winced. The whole office must be wondering what was going on and would now be clustered behind the door trying to work out who was killing whom.

I gathered as much steel and confidence as possible to appear immovable, and said, 'I am afraid this was not a question. I cannot stay any longer. Friday will have to be my last day. I will do my best to pass on all my ...'

'GET OUT!' My boss was standing up, his face red, his fist clenched, leaning forward on the desk. 'G-E-T! O-U-T! I want you to pack your things and leave, NOW!'

'George, there is no reason to get so upset. I ...' The strength of his reaction took me by surprise. I knew that my leaving so fast was an inconvenience, but nobody is irreplaceable and someone could certainly take over my activities. I was taken aback and intimidated by his rage.

He went on yelling, 'I am fed up that people think they can do as they please around me! As your boss, I deserve respect! This is not acceptable that you don't consult me in your decisions at work and, just tell me what you are doing as if I don't count at all. IT'S NOT ACCEPTABLE! You want to go, Go! NOW! And don't come back! We don't need this bullshit. You think I don't have enough on my plate without having to deal with your little problems and your sister's? *It is too difficult. I can't combine issues at home with work ... boohoo.* Rubbish! You just can't deal with responsibilities! With your pretty smiles and stuff, you don't really give a shit. We'll be better with someone else. Someone committed. Really you are full of shit. GET OUT OF MY SIGHT!'

I was looking at him open-mouthed. He glared at me and I stood up. I wish I could say that I was looking at him with my head high, but no. I stood up awkwardly, biting my lips and raising my eyebrows in discomfort and backed out, shaken and feeling pretty ill at ease. Some colleagues were looking at me with expressions ranging from the sympathetic, the inquisitive, or the disapproving. Others avoided looking in my direction altogether. At my desk, I started packing my things in the foldable shopping tote always in my handbag. There was all kinds of non-important stuff I had developed an odd attachment for. I was in shock, not sure if I felt sad or relieved. The scene with George left a sour taste in my mouth. A few colleagues popped their heads in asking what was up. I opted for an abbreviated explanation.

'I gave in my notice last week and said to the boss I needed to leave this Friday. It didn't go down well.'

'You are kidding? You are leaving? No!'

'Well, I have a few personal problems to handle.'

As I made my way out of the building carrying a big load in my handbag, the foldable shopper, and a large box, someone tapped on my left shoulder. I turned expecting a colleague and saw it was one of the Society's bodyguards.

'Can I help with all of this?'

'What ... How, how long have you been standing out here?' I asked, baffled.

'Since you got in.'

'Did you follow me this morning?'

'Yes.'

'I didn't see you ...'

'You couldn't have, you seemed completely lost in thought,' the man said matter-of-factly.

'True,' I acquiesced. 'Shouldn't you keep your presence discreet?'

'Yes, although I have been there for some time and I don't believe anyone is on to you. So, seeing you had a lot to carry, I thought I might as well offer my help. Where are we going?'

'Home. I have been dismissed.'

'You are OK?'

'Yes, I'm fine. It is just five days early.'

'Cab?'

'Sure.' Next came the loudest whistle I had ever heard and a car stopped on the spot in front of me.

'That's pretty cool,' I thought.

We didn't speak in the cab. When we reached home, I hesitated before going in. Harry was at work. If Rico was out as well, then I would not be able to get to London again until one of the two returned. Jazz would be home though. The thought made me sigh. Aside from yesterday's visit to Lil'London which was far from relaxing, she had not been out of the house for a couple of weeks now. She was starting to act like a fish in its tank. It would do her good to go for a walk in the Other World, staying in mobile phone range. Just the two of us, not far from the house and we could also have a little chat with the watchers from Lil'London. After thanking Phil the bodyguard I entered the house. Jazz was in the kitchen preparing a pot of coffee. She had probably drunk a good litre already, she was immune to it.

'Hey! What are you doing here? Shouldn't you be at work?' she exclaimed, giving me a big hug, then turning to pick up a cup for me and pouring some of the thick liquid into it.

'I've been dismissed. My boss didn't like my attitude.' I told her the rest of the story and she laughed.

'So you're at home for a week! Cheers to that!' And she clinked her coffee cup against mine. Despite all her apparent good spirits, I could tell she was really down. The relocation was weighing on her.

'Yes. I have a full week of 'funemployment' ahead! Let's start immediately with a little break. Would you come out with me? In WII, just for a walk and a chat in the woods? I'll let the boys know we are out in case of an emergency and we will keep in mobile range.'

'Errr ... OK ...'

'Let's take some coffee and biscuits or some cake for the watchers outside as well. That would be nice.'

'That would be an idea. Let's make some new wonderful friends who can introduce me to some of their male friends over dinner and I will meet the man of my life there and live happy in WII ever after.'

'Drop the sarcasm, Jazz.'

'Why?'

'Because if you do I will prepare my special almond and chocolate chip cookies with toffee chunks on top. A special batch just for you.'

Jazz stopped sipping her coffee for a few seconds and looked up at the ceiling, as if deep in thought.

'OK, you win.'

'Great! Let's get ready and go!'

I wrote a group message to Zeno, Rico, Harry and Leila to inform them of the latest regarding my job being over, and that

Jazz and I were popping out to the forest. While I was about it, I couldn't resist replying to a short message received from Leo during the taxi journey. It was a one line message: 'Charming Yoko, may I invite you for another date soon? The sooner the better! Baci, Leo.'

'With pleasure! When & Where?' I grinned typing my simple reply, a little knot of anticipation gripping my stomach.

The FTab beeped a new message few seconds later. 'My diary is clear. Pick your day.'

'How about tomorrow?'

'What a good choice! May I suggest dinner?'

'Dinner it is. Looking forward to it. Now off to prepare some cookies.'

'Cookies? I love cookies!'

'Really? Maybe I could prepare a tiny bit more to bring you some?'

'YES! Although not the sweet dessert I already had in mind, it will complement it very well.'

'I am not even going to ask what was on your mind. You are a man, it is not difficult to guess.'

'Wise woman.'

'A good thing you are not in charge of the menu then.'

'Are you playing hard to get?'

'I am not playing. I just am.'

'Well ... Then it has even more worth to it. XXX'

I prepared the cookie dough and Jazz prepared some grilled vegetable, ham and feta sandwiches that we ate while the biscuits baked. When these were cooling, we changed and we finally went out in the cosy afternoon. I used one of the baskets from the presents received the day before to carry a batch of biscuits, some cheeses and a bottle of wine for the two Lil'London watchmen.

The watchmen welcomed us with warmth, despite being quite intimidated and not talkative. I handed them the basket and they opened their eyes wide, repeating endlessly 'thank you'.

Their excessive humility made me feel uncomfortable. They kept their heads bowed most of the time and would hardly look at us. When they finally stopped thanking us profusely, they looked at each other, agreed on something unsaid, and one of them disappeared. We heard a few yelps and the man returned with an adorable puppy in his arms. He, or she, was the cutest ball of light grey and white fur. The man came to me with eyes cast either on the puppy or on the floor and handed me the little dog. It was minuscule and must have been three or four weeks at best. The other man explained the little dog was a female wolf cub. They had found her in a small hole by the Fog, in a dire state close to death. Now the cub was mine. It was a lovely gesture! I couldn't refuse the gift, despite the many reasons I could think of for doing so, such as the uncertainty of coming weeks, months and years, my other priorities and even the training requirements.

'How do you care for a wolf? Was it like taking care of a dog? Shouldn't it be wild?' I thought with concern as she snuggled in my arms.

'This is a lucky puppy,' Jazz commented.

'Why is that?' I replied. The little bundle was nipping at my fingers with her minuscule, yet painfully pointy teeth. She had adopted me already and I was melting.

'She will be spoiled and loved and will end up sleeping on your bed,' Jazz continued.

'She will not sleep on the bed,' I said firmly, tickling the cub on her tummy.

'What do we bet?' she persisted.

'Mmm ... Maybe sometimes it will happen by accident. So I will not bet, but those will be exceptions.' This wolf puppy was so cute!

'Yeah right!'

'Only on special occasions.'

'Yeah right!'

'Anyway, you can say whatever you want, I don't care. Just look at this adorable nose of hers!'

'Hun-hun ... Mmm ... Maybe she will sleep on my bed ... When you are away and I am looking after her ...' Jazz was playing with the puppy in my arms too. I thanked the two men warmly. We didn't stay long after this, as conversation proved difficult with and for them. They really were in awe of us.

Jazz and I didn't walk far. Mostly, we focused on the little wolf cub. We attempted to use a scarf to make a collar and lead, giving up quickly. We were not walking so fast that the puppy could escape far. It would take us seconds to grab her back. We laughed and laughed at the cuteness and clumsiness of the cub on the ground. However thrilled I was to have her, I offered her to Jazz who needed the company more than me. She declined, saying she was more a cat person and it had been a gift to me. She added it would reflect badly on me in Lil'London to have given a gift away.

'What name are you going to give her?' Jazz asked, as I called the puppy 'Little One' for the nth time.

'I don't know. I am still trying to get a grip on the fact that I have a wolf to look after,' I replied, pensive. I stopped walking and reflected. I always take naming seriously, even for a teddy bear.

'Moneypenny?' I suggested. Jazz grimaced and replied, 'I know you are a big fan of James Bond but NO. And don't give me names from movies the like of Indiana Jones either. Pick something nice!'

'You are no fun! I am not going to call her Gucci, let me tell you.' Hearing this, Jazz punched me gently on the arm, pursing her lips.

'How about something from Star Wars?' I exclaimed. 'Given our inter-planetary circumstances, it would fit the movie spirit, no?'

Jazz didn't even reply, just rolled her eyes.

'Fiiine ... How about Scheherazade? Madame Bovary? Marilyn? Beyoncé?' In the silence all you could hear was Jazz and me giggling with each other.

Raindrops hit my face. Big fat drops. I looked up at the sky. Further away thunder was in full blast. The wind rose and the trees started to shake frantically.

'Oh my God! Don't tell me we are going to be hit by a storm!' Jazz shouted above the noise of lightning close by. I could hardly hear her. The weather had turned abruptly on us. I bent down to pick up Little One but she was nowhere to be seen. The light in the forest had darkened fast. I heard a scream on my right and ran towards it. The scream was almost human though it was undeniably Little One and could be either pain or fear. Within seconds, I saw Little One squeezing herself against the trunk of a large tree, an angry boar facing her. I grabbed a piece of wood from the ground and started shouting at the boar, shaking the stick at him. He just switched his aggression to me, and then moved his body in an angle between Little One and me, ready to attack either of us. I had heard boars could get pretty nasty. It crossed my mind I would be better off than the puppy in case of an attack. Jazz appeared on the other side of the tree, distracting the boar for an instant. I jumped forward to the wolf cub, scooping her up with one hand while continuing to wave my piece of wood at the boar with the other. Jazz had started screaming from the moment she saw the boar, frozen in fear. The boar was now eyeing both of us, considering, I hoped, that he was outnumbered. As calmly as possible, I told Jazz, 'We are going to crab walk slowly away from him. Don't let him out of your sight!'

It wasn't necessary. Noise from behind us made the boar run. One of the watchers, alarmed by the screams, was rushing towards us. Rain was pouring down heavily as he accompanied us back to the clearing. We were all completely drenched by the time we got back inside the house.

'A boar and a storm. And all we wanted was a little walk around. What a wonderful world!' Jazz exclaimed. 'Jeez! The change was so sudden!' I had been surprised too.

'The little one, I am going to call her Simba,' I said.

Jazz fluttered her eyes for a few seconds, computing the information, then asked, 'Why? Isn't it a lion's name? From Disney?'

'Yes,' I explained, 'and in the story it is during a storm that the young lion reveals its strength, and bonds with its peers. He also had a wild boar as a friend, and maybe later the cub will, who knows?'

'I like it!' Jazz approved.

'So Simba you shall be!' I told the cub solemnly as I held her in the air in front of me. She was shaking and dripping, nonetheless trying to lick my face. I spoke to her as I moved towards the stairs. 'Simba, I am Yoko and this is Auntie Jazz. You are OK now, we are going to look after you. Now, time to get rid of these clothes, grab some towels and dry us both.' I took her up to my room, then quickly went down to prepare a small bowl of watered milk. After that, I gave her a big pampering, some cuddling and she fell asleep on my lap. That's what you call bonding!

Later, back downstairs, she wouldn't leave my side. Every time I moved to put her sleepy body on a blanket on the floor, she would yelp and drowsily come towards me. I dropped a line to Zeno, asking him if he could bring back some puppy food on his way back and informed the others of the latest addition to the house.

'Jazz, do you realise I will never be able to take the wolf out on my own?' I worried.

'True! The Fog!'

'The poor thing would not even have a tree to pee on if I take her alone.' Jazz made a grimace as I said this.

'Where do you think it would go, the pee, in the Fog?' she asked.

'Some kind of third planet that would soon be a shithole?' I replied.

Even though we laughed, it was unsettling. Could the Fog and the Fog only be yet another world? What could live in it?

Leila looked exhausted and drained on a video call that afternoon. She was not the bearer of good news. First of all, Jack was still not located nor a new door spotted. This was very worrying and frustrating. All that could be done was to continue the search.

The situation in Indonesia was even more unsettling. In the first hours of the morning, the Fog had disappeared. There was only one conclusion according to the Society, the Switcher had died. The seven-year-old Helo was on his way to London via plane, road, train and many detours to avoid a repeat of what had happened to Jack. Officially, he was joining some distant relatives in Chile. Unofficially, he would join the Society country mansion with Dante and Leo, not the Cotswolds mansion which was back on the market, but a new venue also remotely sited in woods and protected from view. It was even closer to Heathrow Airport, in the Harrow/Amersham area, so easily accessible by trains or tube. Of course, I understood the need to protect a seven-year-old but I was still, uncomfortable that Helo was being taken away from his country and culture, I did a little search online to try to ensure that he indeed had no other family who could look after him. I used the Google page translator, as Indonesian is totally incomprehensible to me. Insofar as I could make out, Helo was alone in the world. Poor child.

In Mexico, the hotel was now definitely closed and blocked from access by anyone at all. The Society didn't want to risk having any more massacres. More difficult was handling the police and families. Grief stricken at the loss of their loved ones, people were asking questions and demanding answers. The Society was coming across more and more evidence that an organisation, or something similar, was tracking information about Fog-related events and people linked to it. Were they linked to Jack's kidnappers? Most probably. The immediate issue was to work out who they were without revealing our identity or leaving traces which might allow them to track us down. It was an online cold war, Leila explained, each protecting their defences and each launching some kind of side attack to make the other party make a mistake and betray themselves.

The only purely positive news was about the terraced houses in London. Our previous neighbours had left their houses earlier than planned, undoubtedly due to the 'fog scare'. The basic renovation work was planned to start tomorrow in all the houses bar the one we currently lived in, which Jazz would have at her discretion once we moved out (including any changes she may wish to make). A higher protective and screening wall would be built around the parking area in front of the group of houses first. The Society planned to do it all at an intensive pace and expected to have the work complete within two weeks. Jazz and I sneered.

'In London? Two weeks! You are dreaming. That would be unheard of!' Jazz commented.

'We are in a hurry. The sooner it is done, the sooner we can move our focus onto the Other World, not only this one.'

'Well, good luck with that!' Jazz commented dismissively.

I said nothing. I even wanted to take back my earlier sneer. Considering the achievements of the Society so far, this new accomplishment was not past them.

I told Leila about Simba and how moved I was by the kindness of some of the Lil'London population towards us, even if their deference was unsettling.

'That is nice. I just wonder, have you tried to take her for a walk yet?' Leila asked.

'Yes, why?'

'Where did you end up?'

'Well, the forest of course.'

'Were you with Jazz?'

'Yes. You are wondering what would happen if I was on my own, don't you?'

'Well, yes. I wonder if, with the wolf on her lead, you'd end up in the Fog or the forest.'

'Well, I will try. And if I cross with a Facilitator? We will have to wait for Zeno or Harry to come back. Wouldn't it be nice if Simba could cross with us?'

'I doubt it. If it doesn't work for humans, why would it work for animals? That is something I don't think we've ever tested, the fate of another being that would not be human.'

'I hope you don't intend to do some weird testing on my little wolf?' I asked, half-joking, half-serious.

'Nothing I wouldn't do on you!' Leila teased.

When finishing my conversation with Leila, Simba was looking a bit unsettled and making some mini yelps in her throat. We had given her milk mixed with water earlier. She was probably hungry. I was wrong. Simba sniffed around and peed. A newspaper was on the ground for this, but I was not fast enough to put her on it. At her age, they have just one minute from the conscious need to the action. Time to start her training! I asked Jazz if she could go out of the house just beyond the Fog and wait there for her, even though I would put her on a lead. Jazz pulled a face. 'Rain, remember!'

'What are big umbrellas for?'

'Stubborn idiots?'

'Or brave people not scared of water?'

She sighed, stood up, put on her rain boots and wrapped up. We both picked up large umbrellas. I attached a scarf around Simba's neck as a collar and a used rope from one of Zeno's messy drawers for a lead. I also took a rope for me to attach at the gate, in case I ended up in the everlasting Fog on my own. I did indeed reach the limit of the house and faced the Fog, but Simba was not with me. She had got separated somehow, as always happened with the others.

I called Jazz on her mobile while making my way back home.

'Hey you!' Jazz said. I could hear the worry in her voice. 'Where is Simba?'

'She isn't with me. I thought she was with you!'

'What? No! I kept calling her to make sure she wouldn't wander, but she never showed up!'

As I quickly returned home, Simba was waiting for me on the doorstep. She was crying and yelping, walking right and left by the door frame, just not stepping out into the Fog. I had not wanted to attach her to the lead too tightly and she had managed to get free of it.

'So Little One, you got scared by the Fog, didn't you? Ah ... Well ... You were probably confused between my going through to one world and you going to another.' I patted her and led her inside.

That Monday was also when the Foggies really started to communicate. Checking my FTab, I had messages from Alaska, Marrakech, Carson City and Nairobi.

From Alaska, Rosario, Tony and Mitch wrote that they were very grateful for the opportunity to make contact with other Foggies as well as having their freedom respected by the Society. Rosario suggested a general conference call with all the Foggies as soon as possible. The objective was to make a proper acquaintance by seeing and talking to each other 'in person'. The idea was brilliant! I noticed they had not copied the message to the other Foggies, making their suggestion to me only. It made me wonder if the Society had mentioned I was willing to work full time as 'liaison' between Foggies, Society and the two worlds. It was exciting, the prospect of those important responsibilities, of something I was so personally involved in. It reminded me of my time running the salon de thé. A wave of sadness came over me, as usual when thinking back to those days. I sighed. Simba seemed to notice my reaction and moved from her place leaning against my leg, to come inbetween my feet, giving two ticklish licks on the foot in passing. I looked down and she was sitting there, her head looking up towards me, making small yelping sounds in her throat, mouth closed. I leaned over and caressed her tiny head, talking to her.

'I am OK, don't worry. Just a sad thought. It is gone already.' Simba had only just entered my life and already she brought me comfort.

Cracking on with the new job, I did a search on Google, my internet hero, to calculate what times could work for everyone for a video conference call. It was quite a tricky thing to accommodate everyone and to find a decent hour for everyone to connect. In the end I suggested 6 p.m. London time on Wednesday, the day after tomorrow. It made the following times for the various Foggies:

Alaska (GMT-9) so 9 a.m.;

Carson City (GMT-8) so 10 a.m.;

Nairobi (GMT+2) so 8 p.m.;

Marrakech (GMT) so 6 p.m.;

London and the UK country mansion (GMT) so 6 p.m.

Should Leila and/or someone else from the Society in New York be joining, it would be 1p.m. for them. I wrote the day and time suggestion to Rosario, mentioning the option that a Society's representative could join. I didn't think it was necessary for the first encounter, but it was important to check everyone's preferences.

Next I braced myself and opened the messages from Marrakech. At the top was a message from Christophe de Roque with a string of replies and exchanges from his wife Isabelle and his mistress Louise. Interestingly, Christophe de Roque in his first message moaned about being stuck in Marrakech as Isabelle had burned his passport and hidden his credit cards. Isabelle had replied to this email saying he was a jerk, a womaniser and she was cursing the day she married him. She didn't have a choice in relying on him because of this 'bloody Fog'. For the sake of his unborn baby, if not hers, he should he make an effort and not abandon them in a lonely house in the middle of nowhere, that is a desert. The destruction of his papers was just a way to help him see reason. The message was both angry and pleading, a strange mix of need, lingering love and hate.

Louise also blamed him for putting the two women in such circumstances, saying she loved him but refusing to accept how he had lied to her. In her message, she berated herself for loving and believing him, rather than directing her anger against him. She also believed he should remain with his hysterical control freak know-it-all wife, just because of the baby the 'cow' carried (her words, not mine) and because she still loved him and wanted him by her side. I had a bit of difficulty following the strange logic and the whirlwind of emotions exploding over there. It seemed that, despite the mess he had created, both women were still very much attached to cdr69. They hated him, or themselves, or both for it. Isabelle and Louise also laid the blame and hate on the other woman. I wondered what happened when they all met in the kitchen by accident.

Despite their tragic situation, I must confess reading the emails from Marrakech was also entertaining, in a soap opera kind of way. The increasing level of insults and animosity between the women and the pleading for Christophe's support had a comic streak besides being painfully real. After three emails Christophe had stopped writing, only the women were jousting with words as their weapons. Most certainly avoiding each other and not talking much, they were offloading on this email thread.

There wasn't much to reply to and I didn't want to meddle, especially by suggesting we send a Facilitator. So I opted for a laconic answer with a 'thank you for getting in touch' and expressing how indeed difficult and complex their situation was. I suggested they participate in a Foggies video conference, an idea from Rosario, on Wednesday at 6 p.m. local time. I also asked if they wished a Society representative to join or not. I clicked 'send' with huge relief.

Two done, two to go.

The message from Carson City was two-fold. The first part was from Adam Koplat, whose writing revealed him to be an eloquent, educated and knowledgeable man. His message was polite, charming and businesslike. It was very matter of fact, asking us for further details on our household, our thoughts on the Society and giving some practical information about him, his family and what happened in Mexico. Nothing new for me in his message, as Leila had already briefed us on them. In the second part of the message, his wife Sophia was more personal, explaining that she was a nurse when she met her husband at a friend's dinner party. She recounted how she had taken a break from the hospital where she worked when pregnant and set herself up as a freelance after the miscarriage. She wasn't actively pursuing it though, as she was more focused on the social requirements of her husband. He was apparently a top notch lawyer in Nevada and she had high ambitions for him and their family. She went on to explain that the Society representative they had met – she didn't mention a name, Leila or not – said I would be working with them full time, notably as a liaison agent. She thought it was such a brilliant role. She suggested that maybe she should approach the Society for such a job as well. She asked a lot of questions on how I intended to proceed, if I had a special approach, what were my credentials and so on. She used lots of sweet words and mellow compliments, so many that it wasn't natural. There was a need present in between the lines, a wish to belong, to be important, to matter. The third person from Nevada, their daughter Michelle, didn't get in touch. Adam wrote a few lines about it, explaining she was adjusting badly to the situation. She didn't want her father and stepmother to rely on her, especially Sophia with whom there was tension. Michelle wanted her freedom of movement back and she hated the new reliance her family had on her. Her status as Facilitator gave her new powers in the house and made her stand up to her stepmother more.

My answer was brief, that I would love to share more information about London and we should all benefit from this type of introduction. I repeated Rosario's suggestion of a global Foggies video conference and the possibility of a Society representative participating. The proposed time and date was Wednesday, 6 p.m. London time, 10 a.m. their time. I signed and sent it.

One to go and then of course Leo and Dante. I was keeping the easy (and yummy) ones for last.

I opened the messages from Nairobi. After a quick browse through, my initial reaction was of concern. It read:

> Dear Yoko,
>
> Thank you for your message and for getting in touch. We were quite reluctant at first to use this tablet. We are not fond of technology. In any case my mother is not good with electronics and computers baffle her. We are suspicious of the Society as well. In my work as a psychiatrist and my mother's work as a Human Rights Advisor with the Kenyan government, we have learned that, sadly, people who really have the better good of humankind in mind are extremely rare. We are still debating about being linked to any organisation. Having observed the wonders in the unsoiled World that is beyond the Fog, we feel it is our duty to protect it from this World. Except other 'Foggies.' there is no one else with the same special bond to it. Considering what our kind has done to our planet so far, we doubt we can rely on anyone from here, from planet earth.
>
> Nonetheless, as we are not alone in having access, we would be interested to read your views, compare notes on what is happening and how you would expect things to develop.
>
> Best regards,
> Mary

It wasn't my role to convince her that the Society was pure and clean. I wanted to believe so, yet I had no proof, no certainty on the matter. My reply was just similar to what I wrote few minutes earlier: a suggestion of video conference call, maybe joined by a Society representative, Wednesday, 8 p.m. for them.

Now the London boys. I sent the briefest message to both Dante and Leo: 'Ragazzi, free Wednesday 6 p.m. to join a video conference with all the Foggies across the globe? Trying to organise it all now. Also wondering if you think having Leila attend it would be good. Please, let me know. Baci! Yoko.'

I received an immediate response from Dante. This time he beat Leo's usual split-second reply. 'Fine by me, bella.'

'Great, thanks! How do you like London?'

'Not in London anymore. In the new place. Forty-five minutes from London. Big. Great architecture and layout. Nice potential! Our stuff has already arrived. You should come and visit soon!'

'I have no doubt I will. Both for pleasure and for work!'

'Ciao bella, got to go. Hi to Jazz!'

'Ciao Dante!'

I picked up Simba and placed her on my lap using a rolled up sock to play. With my other hand I took snapshots of the cub from the FTab and send one to Leo.

'New puppy, gift from the Lil'London watchmen. Her name is Simba. Isn't she adorable?!'

The reply was prompt.

'Breed?'

'I am not sure. I am not knowledgeable in ...'

'Looks like a German shepherd. Nice! So they offered you a puppy. Women, so easy to please!'

'Hahaha! It's more a thank you, I think.'

'I bet she'll sleep on your bed. Lucky her!'

'She will not! Except on rare occasions.'

'Yeah right. So if I want to have a chance to come near you now, I have to be nice to the dog first?'

'Well, not really a dog ... But if you don't pass the Simba test you are history.'

'Ouch!'

I spent some time in my room on Google again, researching wolf cubs and what they would eat at a few weeks old. Simba was asleep on a blanket on the floor by my side. Their food was similar to a dog puppy, which meant regular bottle feeding with goat's milk or canine milk replacer. I was going to have short nights for some time, with feeding every four to five hours. Soon I would introduce puppy kibble to her diet, soften into mash, three to four times a day. Just one difficult week of broken sleep to get through. Apparently they eat within minutes, so that shouldn't be too bad. My heart melted at the sight of the little bundle asleep at my feet. She had a soft snore. Hopefully it wouldn't grow to full stereo sound with age. I sent a text to Zeno to ask if he could bring a feeding bottle and two bottles of goat's milk. He said yes, not even asking questions. Then I went online and ordered canine milk replacer and kibble for later. I was starting to think of food for me too and I went downstairs to discuss the dinner menu with Jazz. I had my head in the fridge scanning the options when I received another message.

Leo.

'What are you doing tonight?'

'Sleeping?'

'Fancy dinner with me?'

'Aren't we seeing each other tomorrow?'

'Yes. I am just trying my luck to see you today AND tomorrow.'

And here it was back, the silly grin and warm feeling inside.

'Very greedy man.'

'What can I say? I keep thinking about you, but seeing you is much better than thinking of you. Nutella is addictive.'

'Mmmm … Smooth! Very smooth!' I was not ready to admit his cheesy words worked on me.

'I mean it.'

Was it possible that after two weeks of messaging, one lunch date and a GREAT kiss, I was already so smitten? Undeniably, I was. I didn't like the idea. It was too fast for me. Yet I really, really, really (I can't emphasise it enough) liked the idea of seeing him tonight. I looked down at Simba. It was her first night with me. I couldn't do that to her. Duty called.

'For tonight, I am afraid not. I have responsibilities now you see. I need to organise wolf-sitting when I go out. As I live with various people, it won't be a problem, but this is Simba's first night in ... Plus, I have the feeling I need to learn to say no to your cheeky side.'

'Not a problem, I understand. It was worth a try! A domani, bella.'

The rest of the evening went fast. Simba seemed to understand the characters of the house already: Yoko the mummy, Jazz the softie auntie, Harry the strict uncle, Zeno the one to go on adventure with, Rico the one to harass. She was exhausted when I took her with me to my room for the night. I set up a blanket on the floor by my side of the bed, switched on the alarm for her midnight feed and got into my bed. As I leaned over to switch off the light, she was sitting there on the blanket, looking at me with sleepy eyes, humming low her wish join me on the bed. I caressed her head and left my arm hanging for her to sleep against. I turned the light off. Within seconds she had two paws against the bed trying to jump on. She was still much too small and the bed much too high. So she started crying slowly. I put her back on her blanket in the dark, with a soft 'No'. This we repeated several times, before she just couldn't hold off sleep anymore.

**Day 3 (Tuesday)**

I woke up with paws on my chest, being licked all over my face. I took Simba and held her away from me to stop her licking. 'So, not too small to get on the bed after all,' I told her. The pillows still had the marks of where Simba had slept. I thought, 'Damn. First night and Jazz has already won! Mmm ... Maybe I just won't tell her.' I put her back on the floor, while I got up and grabbed my dressing gown. I then saw how the puppy had got on the bed during the night, as she repeated it in front of me. She had jumped on the bed cushions left at the foot of the bed, and from the cushions onto the bed.

'Simba, you clever girl! Nice one! I better watch out: you could be too clever for my own good.'

After Zeno accompanied me to WII for a quick walk with Simba, I dedicated that day to writing notes for my ex-colleagues, to speed up their takeover of my projects. It may be something I didn't have to care about anymore, but I had my pride. I also wanted to send messages to selected people in the company to explain my sudden departure in a neutral tone – I did not want nor need to be angry with my ex-boss, there was no point. Spending the day working for my previous company was as much a kind of closure as the right thing to do, I believed. It was relaxed work with regular breaks with Jazz, Rico and Simba and a great lunch together.

Mid-morning, I exchanged more messages with Leo. Our date was planned for that evening.

'8 p.m., perfect,' Leo wrote. 'I would have loved to be a gentleman and come and pick you up, though it is best to meet somewhere else, no?'

'Definitely don't come to pick me up! I would be grilled for details by everyone!' I thought, so replied, 'Agreed. Where are you staying?'

'A hotel between Notting Hill and you. Eight minutes' walk.'

'That is precise.'

'I checked.'

'You checked? Scary! Are you a stalker?'

'Absolutely! Let's meet at the small shopping mall next to you? It is five minutes' walk for me, three minutes for you.'

'Sure. There is a nice restaurant on top.'

'Then let's meet there. Ciao, bella Yoko.'

'Bye Leo.'

I had a hot date and was very excited by it. It didn't escape Jazz's notice at lunch.

'Talk woman!' Jazz was smirking at me. 'It's that man, isn't it? Your mysterious messenger you have a crush on? This is a rhetorical question, by the way, you are blushing so much it couldn't possibly be anyone or anything else.'

'Nothing to talk about.'

'You are boring.'

'Yeah, yeah, yeah. Could you look after Simba tonight?' I knew she would guess why, yet I had no choice.

'Ahhh. This is it, you have a date. Are you going to go for the full pampering and wax, too?'

'I don't wax.'

'Stop playing with words. I just know what you are up to, you naughty girl.'

'You are the one thinking about it, I am not!'

'You are not, rrreally?'

'Whatever. The point is, can you look after Simba?'

'I am so jealous ... I would love to be a naughty girl too. I feel like I am getting cobwebs down there. It could do with a good dusting!'

'Argh! Too visual, thanks!' I put my hands on my ears, laughing. Jazz always had some 'interesting' figures of speech. You should have heard the ones she used to define the lower part of male and female bodies.

Over lunch, the household discussed the upcoming work on the houses, the move and how life would get simpler, even for

Jazz who would get her own space. Work had already started and the terraced houses and their grounds were inaccessible to the public. As these days we were not receiving any friends anymore, either ignoring or declining their requests to visit, it didn't bother us. Soon we would be able to have family and friends over again in the new unfogged home. The Society would build a partition wall hiding the fogged house, now Jazz home, the Society's fogged house, and the storage house for trading between WI and WII. The three houses were at the end of the terrace houses. The wall would have protective gates on wheels, able to open wide to let vehicles in and out, and high plants in easy-to-move pots. Visitors coming to visit our non-fogged house would be none the wiser. Jazz had already told me she would organise the best room for me in her house for Saturday nights. There would be a room for me too in the Society's house. My dear friend was grateful to have a house she could consider hers. She insisted we all had a set of keys. The house would always be open to us to visit her, stay over, or just pass on our way to the Other World. She also insisted on paying rent, which we refused.

So, as a consequence, Rico, Zeno, Harry and I had the two houses in the middle. After thinking about how to work out who would live with whom and failing to decide, we opted for joining them into one and creating a large open space on the ground floor. We were to continue to live together with much more room. Rico was ecstatic: the big house would have eight bedrooms and two studies for four people. Already we agreed the two studies would be for guests. Then each had one bedroom plus a spare room to arrange as they wished. Of course Rico was to turn his into a studio. Harry was to have his own home office. Zeno and I were not sure yet. I very much intended to turn it into something special for me, even if I was still undecided as to what.

As agreed, the last three houses were for the Society: a security house, including IT; a visiting Foggies' and Society members' house and the Society office.

Either working full time or part-time with the Society, we would have constant access to the Fog and Jazz. No risk of Fog-withdrawal effects. When we wished, we were to entertain and have friends at home. 'And girlfriends,' I said to myself, when from my room I heard Zeno upstairs in a heated discussion. From the small pieces of the conversation I could make out, he was talking to his long distance girlfriend Cris, defending himself for keeping her out of London. She was not taking this well.

'I can't blame her. I would be fuming in her shoes,' I thought. I was trying not to listen, but it was difficult. It must have been a Skype conference call for me to be able to hear her. I couldn't make out what she was saying, but how she was saying it was pretty clear. For the sake of his relationship, Zeno must have wanted the houses to get renovated fast to invite her over as soon as possible. How he was going to explain the changes to the houses and his new job, I was not sure. It seemed a minor issue in the scale of current events.

Half an hour before the date, I was still trying to decide what to wear, a knotted mix of excitement, anticipation and fear in my stomach. What level of cleavage could I go for without it being too much? How come I had had all day to plan ahead and was still running late? And now my FTab rang. Mum.

'Hi darling. How are you?'

'Hi Mum. Good, thanks. You? Sorry I am on my way out, can't talk for long. Running late already. How are things going at home? How is Julia?'

My mother remained silent.

'Mum?'

'Yoko please, will you soon be able to get her to England?'

'I can't promise you anything, but we are working on it.'

'Please make it fast.'

'Mum?'

'I don't know how much longer I will be able to hold it together before I throw her food tray in her pouting face!'

'Mum! What's got into you? You NEVER lose control!'

'I am close! Today at lunch I had to count to fifty in my head, eyes closed, gripping the table, to stop myself slapping her.'

'You don't slap! You always say you are against such uncontrolled acts of violence, that a punishment should be pondered and thought through!'

'JUST GET HER OUT OF THIS HOUSE!'

'As soon as possible Mum. I promise! As soon as humanly and foggily possible!'

'Don't joke with me!'

'I am not joking Mum.'

'Good. Because I can force you to come and have a taste of what it is like here, you know!'

'Yes Mum.'

'Right, I don't want to make you late. Call me tomorrow, will you?' my mother said, calming down.

'Yes Mum.'

'Just remember: be a good girl and save your parents. I love your sister, I am sorry for her situation, but she is driving us insane.'

'I love you Mum. Tell Dad I love him. And Julia.'

I made it to the restaurant at 8.10 p.m. After the call I hadn't had any other choice than to pick something, anything! So I rummaged through the pile of clothes on the bed, covered my eyes and, sticking my arm in the middle of it, I grabbed the first garment: a little sexy dress with leopard prints and a cowl neck, slightly hugging the body in all the right places. As it was a touch too dressy for the occasion, a pair of black kitten heels shoes would be better than stilettoes. Downstairs, I called to Harry or Rico closing my coat quickly so they wouldn't see what my outfit was. Jazz must have blabbed though, as they all arrived by me with cheeky faces.

'Let us see the date outfit,' Rico said.

'Jazz!' I turned to glare at her, sitting on the sofa with a magazine.

'They trapped me into talking!' She replied with fake outrage.

'What? How? Did they threaten to hide the Nespresso machine? Did they hide your favourite boots?'

'Ha ha ha! No. Rico said he would prepare his family lasagne recipe whenever requested if I would give them an update on the mysterious guy who makes you grin at every message. You can't say no to that.'

'Tsssss ... You sold me cheap. You should have thrown in Zeno's tiramisu too for a top deal!'

'Damn!' Jazz said.

'I'll remember the boots idea for next time,' Harry pointed out, as usual looking serious. You had to know him well to spot the slight upward lift of his mouth to known he was having fun. 'In the meantime, Yoko, open the coat and show us what the lucky guy will get. Except if you are naked, then don't open it.'

'What? Open anyway, especially if you are naked!' Rico interjected.

'Absolutely!' Zeno added.

'Your deal is with Jazz. I never promised anything. Here is a hint though ... Animal print. Byyyyye!' I winked at them, patted Simba and put her in Jazz's arms, grabbed Rico who was the closest to me and headed out dragging him behind me.

When I arrived at the restaurant, Leo was already seated at a table in the furthest corner by the bay window. I left my coat at the cloakroom and walked towards him. He stood up by the table the minute he saw me. I felt very self-conscious on my way there, his eyes detailing me up and down. From his smile and the look in his eyes he approved. I hesitated about what to do when reaching him: 'Hi' and a kiss on the cheek? A proper kiss and a hug? I stopped in front of him, and offered a smile and a 'Good evening, signore'. Leo shook his head slowly, his eyes not leaving mine. He took hold of my waist, drawing me towards him in one swift movement and kissed me. Hell, that guy could kiss! I felt like an ice cream under the blazing Italian sun, melting completely in his arms. When we broke apart, he kept me held close and whispered in my ear, 'Good evening, beautiful Nutella'. He then took a step back, letting his arms slide until he rested one hand on my lower back and pulled out the chair for me with his other hand. I was more than a little flustered, trying my best to appear poised. A waitress came the instant we were seated, giving us the menu and explaining the specials of the day.

'I couldn't understand a word she said,' I whispered to Leo when the waitress had left.

'Me neither,' Leo murmured back.

'Shall we go wild and go for the specials even though we haven't a clue?' I replied enthusiastic.

'Which one? There seemed to be four or five?'

'We can't just say meat, there must be several these days. There is usually one fish special and one vegetarian. How about you take the fish special and I take the vegetarian and we share?'

'Fine by me. I am a carnivore though. Shall we have a meaty starter? Or maybe you are really a vegetarian?'

'I have thought about it on a regular basis. Always a passing thought.'

'Thank God. Meat for starters it is! Meat balls, tapas and chicken skewers to share?' His concentration was deep in the menu as he spoke. I like a man who enjoys his food. Somehow it is synonymous with being a lover of life. As long as the man is a life/food lover and not a voracious man, who acts as if he desperately needs to fill a hole, a gap, and an insecurity. Leo was a gourmet, this I knew already from our lunch. To share a good meal with someone you enjoy the company of, now that was the real treat!

We placed the order with a slightly puzzled waitress. As we had deduced, there were vegetarian and fish dishes in the specials of the day. Of course it was also possible that if we couldn't understand her, she couldn't understand us either and we may end up with steak and fries. Who cared, as long as it was good! I didn't have my mind set on anything particular for dinner and obviously neither did he. At least not for food … My insides were churned by the man seated in front of me. To resist or not resist? It was only the second time we had met face to face, just the two of us. It was only two weeks since we first exchanged messages. Apart from the Fog and what we wrote to each other, I didn't know anything about him. Additionally, we were going to work together and were bound for life by the Fog. Too fast, too complicated, too slippery a ground, concluded the analytical and wiser side of my brain. The emotional, passionate and – yes – the horny side was screaming, 'Hot man alert! Hot hot hot! Yes! Go and have fun, lucky woman! E-N-J-O-Y!'

Wise versus Passionate. Such a conundrum!

Leo and I talked about many subjects during the meal, from our families and my late fiancé to my former tea shop. Although not flirtatious, it was nonetheless obvious we were into each other. We kept leaning towards each other, drinking in each other's words, engrossed in learning more about each other's life. Being with him was so natural; so was his holding my hand across the table. When the waitress reappeared with the dessert menu, I announced my surprise for him. The previous day when cooking with Jazz I had prepared additional cookies for him who seemed keen on it. They were wrapped in a nice little bag with ribbon, the way I used to do it in my shop.

'Your dessert is sorted, if you wish.'

'I would love that. Not here though. Chocolate cookies: do they go well with champagne?'

'How deliciously decadent!'

'Then, may I invite you for a glass of champagne to accompany them? I noticed a bottle in my fridge which would do perfectly.'

'In your fridge?'

'Yes, my hotel fridge.'

For a second there I stopped breathing and felt a constriction in my chest. Heart pang. He was inviting me to his hotel room for champagne and cookies. Just champagne and cookies? Most certainly not.

It was a full blown war between Wise and Passionate.

Wise lost.

'What a lovely idea! I shall accept with pleasure, signore.'

Leo smiled and signalled to the waitress to bring the bill. Even though it was a date and by upbringing I was inclined that the man would invite me, I picked up my bag and looked for my wallet. I do not like to assume I am the guest unless explicitly told so.

'Yoko, when you are out with me, it will always be as my guest. A guest of honour. I am old-fashioned in that regard. It is a way to thank the women for the effort they put in to look so beautiful and pampered for us.'

'An Italian gentleman. Thank you.'

'My pleasure.'

'Then, while you settle this, I will disappear for a few minutes to powder my nose.'

I stayed a little while staring at myself in the mirror. I had not been intimate with another man since Michael's death, a little more than two years ago. I had had opportunities which never seemed worth the hassle of a relationship, or even a fling. Now it was a bit daunting. Did I still have it? Is sex like a bicycle, you never lose the skill? Do you just have to get back on the saddle and go for it? I looked at my body's shape underneath the dress. Was it still OK?

'Ouch!' I told my reflection in the mirror. 'I am not sure I want this nearly perfect man to see me naked today or any other day. I bet he is more used to women in their twenties.'

A slender middle-eastern woman came out of a toilet booth. She stood next to me to wash her hands and glanced at me. Drying her hands, she said, 'I noticed both of you in the restaurant. I think he really likes you and not just for your body. Don't worry about it.'

'Oh ... Thanks. That's very nice of you to say.'

'Don't mention it. We women always belittle and question ourselves. We shouldn't. Have a great night!' Her little speech worked wonders. Sometimes it takes the kindness of a stranger to set things right. I would just have the best night, maybe just champagne and cookies, maybe more.

'Let's see what happens!' I murmured. 'Let's chill. If I want to have sex with a charming Italian man, I will have sex with a charming Italian man. And it will be amazing!'

So chin up, head high, I made my way back to the table where Leo was waiting for me, collecting my coat in passing. Seeing me ready to go, he stood up and came towards me. He took me by the arm and we walked out of the restaurant, out of the shopping mall and towards his hotel. From the corner of my eyes, I noticed someone I hadn't paid attention to earlier that evening: my bodyguard, Phil. I had completely forgotten about him. I wondered where Leo's bodyguard was, as he most probably had one too. When asked, he replied that he had requested him to be off tonight. I left Leo for a few minutes to go and talk to Phil.

'Phil, I should have asked for you to have the night off. I forgot, I am sorry.'

'No worries, I am pleased to keep you safe.'

'Well yes, but this encounter is pretty private, including from my friends or the Society.'

'I see. I am here to protect you, not to report on who you are meeting or your activities. If asked I will not lie, but I won't volunteer the information otherwise.'

'Thank you Phil, I really appreciate it.'

'If it's OK with you, I will stay to protect you. I was on duty for Jack. Nothing will happen under my watch again.'

'Of course. I understand.'

I had no guarantee Phil would not tell Leila or someone at the Society. It was my fault. Too late to worry about it.

'I think you will need even more champagne now,' Leo said when I put my arm back in his.

'A bottle for two, it should be fine.'

'I intend to take my time and savour it.' As he said this, he leaned over and kissed me softly on the neck. It felt like a soft caress, making me tingle nicely.

In the hotel elevator we were joined by another couple who looked like they had been arguing. We went up to the third floor in silence and then walked out. As the doors of the elevator closed, the couple began arguing again. Leo put his key card in the lock and pushed the door open to let me go in first. Almost as a second thought he stopped me on the way and dragged me towards him. Putting one hand behind my back and one behind my head, he kissed me. Leo had incredibly soft lips. So far his kisses had been tender, but this one, this one was ardent. We stood there, half in the corridor, half in the room, my being more and more pushed against the frame of the door as he leaned increasingly against me. When our hands were starting to play with the coats and to ruffle each other's hair, he finally stood back.

'I couldn't hold back any longer, I had to kiss you the way I have wanted to kiss you ever since seeing you outside the pub.'

'What took you so long?' I asked him, still enraptured in the bliss-effect of his kiss.

'Public decency. Same reason I have just stopped. There must be cameras in this hotel corridor. These days, you can't avoid the eyes of Big Brother.'

He invited me in with a large gesture of the arms, came in after me and closed the door. The room was the classic high standard hotel room, with a king size bed and furniture in pastel colours. I walked a few steps inside, Leo behind me, his hands on my shoulders. A shiver of excitement went through me.

I undid the belt and buttons of my coat, which he took and put over his arm, caressing the base of my neck with his other hand. He went to put the coat on a hanger and then moved to a large piece of furniture on the opposite corner to the door, and also opposite the bed. The bottom part of it was the fridge. Leo took the bottle of champagne from above the fridge, two champagne glasses and a little plate for the cookies. He put them on the desk along the wall and proceeded to open the bottle. I retrieved the cookies from my bag. It was strange, the everyday gesture of putting biscuits on a plate, here all dressed up in an unknown hotel room with a sexy man. The cork popped and the bubbly gold liquid filled the glasses. Leo went to the bedside table, pulled out his phone and plugged it into a stereo system. The sound of chill lounge music flowed in the room.

'Nice touch,' I said approvingly.

'Thank you,' Leo replied, back by my side. We clinked our glasses, eyes locked, and both took a sip. I broke eye contact to turn and pick up a cookie with my fingers. Turning back, his eyes were still fixed on mine. We were both smiling, cheeky, sexy smiles, or at least I hope mine was as much as his. I raised the biscuit to face level, slowly moving it towards his lips. He slightly parted them and bit a small piece. He didn't let me retrieve my hand but held it in the air with his other hand, took the biscuit out of mine back onto the plate. I took one more sip of champagne before putting the glass down. He brought my fingers that had held the cookies to his lips and started to lick the chocolate off the fingers. My heart thumped louder and faster. A wave of desire washed over me, accompanied by a slight dizziness. Leo bent slightly to the side, put his glass down, grabbed my waist and pulled me towards him. I slid a free hand to the nape of his neck and we fell into another passionate kiss. From then on I lost track of time. How long did it take for him to let go of my waist and grab my buttocks? My hands soon slipped to his front and fiddled with his shirt and buttons. Shortly afterwards I was caressing his bare chest, firm and lean. The kissing had not stopped. Our bodies were glued to each other and there was no doubt of his desire for me, his body reacting to its contact with mine. He let his hands move down to the hem of my dress and started pulling it up and eventually off. I was wearing stockings. Hold-up stockings, to be precise. I never found tights pretty to look at, nor practical to take off in front of a man. I wore stockings more often than not, even just for me, to make me feel good. That night, it proved not to be just for me.

'Mmmm ... Nice!' Leo hadn't even looked. He had just felt the stockings lines when pulling the dress off. As he said so, he began walking backwards, drawing me towards the bed. When he reached it, I let go of the grip of his hand and sat on the bed. I languidly peeled the first stocking off, straightening my leg horizontally while sliding the soft fabric off my foot, and casting the lonely stocking aside. Leo stopped me before I repeated with the other leg, indicating that he wished to do it. He had the gentlest touch and I could tell he was taking great care not to rip it. I just had time to appreciate how considerate a man he was before he lifted me up and put me further up the mattress. He then climbed on the bed above me. I pretty much felt like the prey of a dangerous animal, a prey who willingly gave herself up. I was ready to beg him to eat me! I most probably did ... I was submerged by desire and pleasure.

Pleasure. The pleasure got more and more intense, passionate, deep and shared, both of us relishing to give as much as to receive.

**Day 4 (Wednesday)**

I walked back home in the early hours of the morning, confident that Phil was close by, yet kindly sparing me the embarrassment of showing himself. I preferred to go back home rather than stay the night, avoiding doubling the walk of shame with the return of shame, when too many questions would be asked too soon. Right then I was happy. I felt like a blooming flower. I just wanted to keep this for me, to protect it. I wanted protect myself, too.

When I got home, Simba yelped from my room. I was surprised Jazz had not taken her into hers. She explained later that not only was she unsure of the time of my return, but also Simba kept going towards my bedroom door. I put her makeshift lead on and we popped out in the Fog for a few minutes for her to have a quick one outside before we settled for the night. Simba didn't seem fussed by the Fog this time. I stayed close to the wall of the house to be safe, on which she had a little pee. Then, we were off to bed.

Waking up, Simba was again on my bed. There was a wet area on the blanket as well. Nice ... My first reaction was to stroke her. It should have been to put her down on the floor and tell her off, but there was no point at her age: she was so young, lessons must be given when the act was just done. Second night, second time the wolf slept on the bed with me. I still wasn't going to mention it to Jazz!

It was already 9.30 a.m., rather late for a weekday. I had only had five hours sleep. Simba jumped off the bed via the cushions and went towards the door. I put a jumper on and opened it, Simba following me towards the stairs. I wasn't expecting her to manage going downstairs on her own yet, but she surprised me by slowly yet surely walking down alone. Instead of the front door, as I thought she would, she headed to the dining area where Jazz, Zeno and Rico were having breakfast.

'You woke up late. Coffee?' Jazz asked.

'Hi guys! Yes, please,' I replied. Zeno had grabbed the sock ball for Simba and started to play with her. Rico was observing me suspiciously.

'You had sex last night,' Rico stated, then continued eating.

'What? Rico!' I shook my head trying to dismiss his comments.

'Ooooooooooh! Now we are talking!' Jazz exclaimed, looking between Rico and me. 'Is it true?'

'Unbelievable! I just woke up ... Rico, why on earth did you say that?' I exclaimed.

'I can always tell. You know I am an expert on such matters. Sex has no secrets for me,' he answered. Jazz and I did an eye roll. Coffee was now a must, not only to wake up but to handle Rico and face the questioning I knew was to come.

'I heard Simba when you came back ...' Zeno started.

'Oh! I am sorry! I ...' I'd hoped that Simba's yelp had been discreet enough, obviously not.

'... And considering the time, I would say Rico is correct,' Zeno finished his sentence with a huge grin.

'For God's sake, guys. I haven't even had coffee yet!'

'No coffee until you talk!' Jazz announced, crossing her arms in a firm determined gesture.

'Yeah right,' I said, standing up and beginning to walk towards the kitchen. Next thing I knew, I was attacked by Zeno who grabbed me and put me over his shoulder, and sat me back down at the table with a firm hand to keep me there.

'No, no, no, Nutella. You stay here and tell us more about this guy. All our love lives being a mess right now, we will compensate with yours,' Zeno said.

'It is not that interesting ...' I began.

'Yes it is!' Rico interjected.

'Well, you can keep the details for me later ...' Jazz suggested with a naughty smile.

'We reserve ourselves the right to request details if we deem it necessary,' Harry commented, 'or if we need to ascertain this guy is not an asshole, a player, a jerk, or a spy.'

'A spy? On the Fog? Come on!'

'Yes. The timing seems to be a bit too convenient,' Harry continued.

Rico was looking at him, brows furrowed and then murmured to himself, 'Why didn't I think of that?'

'It is all very well that the Society is there and provides body-guards and security. They can't deal with the emotional elements, the everyday life and the doubts. Friends can. And with the Fog remaining a secret, at least for now, we will need to rely on each other much more,' Harry had got all serious saying this. He now offered a reassuring smile. Jazz broke the silence that followed.

'Yeah, yeah, yeah, we are like a Fog family now. Veeeeery good,' she said waving the matter away and turning back to me. 'Now, start talking and give us the juicy bits. I am just going to hop to the kitchen to prepare a new pot of coffee. So speak loudly.'

My date last night they knew about, what I had to protect was Leo's identity.

'Fine, I will answer some questions, but at my discretion. What is it you want to know?'

'So who is this guy?' (Zeno)

'Right. Well ... We got in touch via an acquaintance of mine, online at first. I saw his photo later and I thought that not only was he charming in his messages, he was also good-looking.' I spoke slowly, choosing my words carefully.

'You didn't tell him about the Fog, right?' (Rico)

'I didn't break the news to him, no.' That was true, he discov-ered it himself.

'What does he look like? How tall is he? Is he English? How old is he?' (Jazz, coming back in the room)

'Do you also want to know at what time he was born?'

'I wouldn't mind. I could do a proper and accurate astrological profile. Anyway, so?' (Jazz)

'Not British; taller than me, I guess; no idea how old, I would say around my age or slightly younger; dark hair, chestnut eyes, chiselled face, lean body, sexy. Happy? Can I enjoy breakfast in peace now?'

'Hang on, so he could be younger than you?' (Jazz)

'Yes.'

'One bad point.' (Jazz)

'No, no, no. I disagree! You go for it, Cougar Girl!' (Rico, unsurprisingly)

'What nationality?' (Harry)

'Italian.'

'The best!' (Rico, nodding his approval)

'Maybe we know him?' (Zeno)

'There are only hundreds of thousands of Italians in London ...' I really didn't want to go down that route, or next they were going to ask what his name was.

'What is his name?' (Zeno)

'Good try, but that is more than I want to reveal.'

'What does he do? You know, it would be easier if you would just tell us the story instead of us having to ask every single basic question!' Jazz seemed enthusiastic and exasperated simultaneously. Winding her up was quite entertaining to watch.

'Yes, I know it would be easier, but you are the ones who want to know while I don't particularly want to talk. So where were we? Ah! His profession. He is ... an entrepreneur.'

'So is he good in the sack?' (Rico)

Everyone looked at the ceiling and sighed in chorus.

'Most importantly, are you sure he is not with you because of the Fog?' (Harry)

Well, in a way Leo was. We had met because of the Fog, even if not in the sense Harry had asked. So to answer that one correctly without big revelations, I needed a slight twist when phrasing an answer.

'I really believe his interest in me is for me, not for Foggy matters.'

'I just want to know if he was good in bed because, you know, you haven't had someone for some time, so ... I don't want you to be disappointed, babe.' Rico was sulking. Put like that, his interest was touching. Still, I was not going to give him details.

'Look, I had a great time, OK?' I conceded. Rico finally smiled and I blushed.

'When are you seeing him next?' Jazz asked, standing up again as the smell of coffee coming from the kitchen indicated it was ready.

'I'll do it.' I stood up faster than her and made my way to the kitchen, Simba nibbling at my slippers. An strange bell rang in the house.

'This is the bell at the entrance to the parking lot.' Harry was up and going to the door. I followed him.

'I had it set up for post and couriers needing a signature, so that no one comes close to the Fog. I am sure it is the express delivery of puppy supplies I ordered yesterday – some food and a few things for Simba.'

'Good idea on the bell. It could be either your parcel or mine. I ordered something too!'

'You are so kind to have thought of Simba. You really didn't have to buy anything.' I was talking to his back, as he was promptly heading out grabbing a jacket on the way. I followed him quickly before I got caught in the ever-present Fog on my own.

'Well, I was ordering some books for me when I received your text. Buying food for the cub wolf is a little welcoming present ... I did check too: puppy food should be fine. They are kind of cousins, after all. Hey, talk of the devil!' He bent down and patted Simba who was catching up with us in the parking lot. I must have left the door open and Simba followed. I couldn't help but marvel at this bundle of puppy cuteness and energy.

I stopped in my tracks: Simba was an animal of the Other World, not of this one. She shouldn't have been here. I picked her up and held her in front of me. She was paddling her little legs, trying to reach my face and lick me. Harry signed for the parcel and walked back to me.

'So, Simba, want to see what I got for you?' Harry asked the cub.

'Wait a second, Harry, Simba probably needs to do one or two businesses,' I said to Harry as we began walking back to the house. I put Simba on the ground and without fail Simba did what she had to do. My mind was elsewhere.

'Yoko, you are looking disturbed. I assure you mine is only a small little welcome gift,' Harry commented.

'Ah, yes. Can't wait to see it. Sorry, thinking of something else. I am a bit puzzled, I'll explain inside.' We started walking again. Simba slowed us down as she lingered behind, intrigued by a leaf, then a puddle, then a thread, then a cork and finally we made it home.

'So, Yoko, let's go back to the subject at hand,' Jazz said as we re-entered the living room.

'Well, I think I have a new subject now,' I replied.

'Does it still involve sex?' Rico urged.

'Rico, we know you have a perverted mind, but some days it really comes out stronger than others,' Harry snapped. Rico grumbled and started sulking again.

'Here is my new puzzle,' I began, indicating the wolf cub. 'Simba is an animal from WII. So like people from that world and the Relocated, she should be stuck in that world, shouldn't she?'

'Yes,' answered Zeno and Rico together. Harry had a brief frown then his eyes widened as he realised what I meant and what he had seen. I continued, 'So how come just now Simba crossed the Fog and came to join us two in London? Not only did she come to London, she came on her own! And yesterday we could go out in the forest with her.'

'Bugger! She is a Crosser. No! She is more than a Crosser: she did it alone!' Harry said to himself.

'Damn!' Jazz exclaimed.

'Cazzo!' the Italian men agreed.

'What does that mean? Yoko, does that mean it IS possible for someone from World II? Relocated could come back? Could I ...' Jazz started. I interrupted her in the middle of her question.

'Jazz, I don't know. Please don't get too excited.'

'But ... It is possible!'

'I have no idea! Listen, none of us can access both worlds like that. Now the question is, can she go to WII on her own too, or is she some kind of wolf Crosser reversed ... Shall we try?'

That morning we tested many combinations. Harry accompanied me to London and we renewed the experience. She followed us on her own. I then did the same going with Zeno and Jazz to WII. Again, Simba made her way to us alone through the Fog. Then Harry had a thought. 'What if she is only coming wherever you are, because you are the leader of the pack?'

'Or her adopted mother,' Jazz rectified.

'Whatever.' Harry dismissed her comment as a non-important detail to Jazz's annoyance. He continued, 'Shall we try? With you going in the Fog alone and calling her?'

This meant taking the risk that Simba could be lost in the Fog on her own. I didn't like this eventuality, but Harry's idea was interesting and I couldn't dismiss it. We had already tried with Jazz when I went out on my own and Simba would not leave the house. At the time, Jazz was calling her, not me and maybe Simba had got confused.

'If we do that, we should take a treat for her, mashed bacon or something, to attract her back with in case she gets lost.'

So we tried. I didn't believe Simba would end up in the Fog with me. I was more curious to see which world she would appear in, Jazz being in one and Harry in another. Zeno and Rico were at the house too, ready to intervene with puppy treats. I was on a call with each of them waiting to hear where Simba had showed up. Inevitably, what I had ruled out was what happened: she turned up by my side in the Fog. Simba had adopted as me as the one to be followed everywhere. I appreciated the compliment and it bonded me even more strongly to the cute fur ball, but how did she do it?

Simba's case was a high priority as a Foggy point to elucidate and there was no one else to ask other than Leila. She had mentioned they had not studied the case of animals crossing between worlds, so I assumed she didn't know. After a brief chat with the rest of household, we decided not to mention Simba specifically, but just ask questions about people and living creatures – having the crossing capability from WII to our world. Leila replied in the negative.

'It would make sense that if some of us can do it from this world, some in the Other World could do it in reverse,' I said. I didn't refer to animals, not wanting to arouse suspicion.

'Well, from the information we have gathered, it is impossible. Of course we do not have data from all the doors, but we have been pretty thorough. At the last opening, they spent a lifetime trying to pass people and animals from World II to our world. No success. On the other hand they were able to relocate animals in the same ratio of one in seven. We have never found any records of animals being Switchers, Crossers and Facilitators, the like of fogged dens, kennels, or otters' dams. Of course, if is it a nest in a tree, or an ant hole in the ground, that would be difficult to find. I am not even talking underwater. We have doubts have Foggies, but we can't rule it out.'

'I wonder ... What would happen if I were to sleep one Saturday night in a submarine?'

'Interesting. Maybe we should ...'

'No! That was a theoretical question!'

'Still ... A thought-provoking idea.'

'Anyway,' I was keen to change the subject from fogging a submarine. 'I would have loved it if you had evidence that it would be possible to go between the two worlds unassisted. Like someone travelling on his or her own and on his/her own accord.'

'Like someone choosing which world he would go to?'

'Yes.'

'A kind of Super-Crosser. Well no, it is extremely unlikely. That would be fascinating: that would mean the Fog could be controlled by the mind. And things would not be so irreversible. Sorry to disappoint. That can't be.'

'Uh-huh ... On another matter, the conference call tonight between the Foggies, as it is the first one, the majority was against involving the Society. Sorry.'

'Not a problem. I trust if there is something relevant, you would let us know.'

'Well, I would have to discuss with them what can and cannot be disclosed. By the way, the FTab, it is a Society device. I presume it would be very easy for you guys to monitor everything anyway?'

'Yes, we could. I am not aware that we do and I want to believe that we don't. It would be against our ethos.'

'I want to believe that too.'

My mind remained preoccupied by Simba and what we had just discovered. I had a new idea and I didn't want to talk to anyone about it before I put it to the test.

The work around the houses being in full swing, construction and demolition noises were deafening. The work was concentrated on both ends of the terrace. Around our house and the one next door, which I was to Fog soon, the main change was the setting up of a wooden wall, lined with tall trees and flower bushes on wheelie pots. It was the first thing the Society had set up when the neighbours left, to protect the Fog from view. The greenery made this plank wall much less of an eyesore and less conspicuous, both for now and for the future when we had visitors. Their being on wheels would enable the opening of the walls like large gates when vehicles or other large items needed to pass to the Other World. Now the builders were working on raising the larger outer wall and renovating the other houses in concert. The place had been swarming with people all morning when we were doing the tests with Simba. This burst of activity was a good thing, it made our wanderings in and out less intriguing for any observer. However, it had reached a ridiculous level now; it was completely packed out there. The optimism of the Society that the building works would be finished in two weeks looked to be well founded: each room in each of the houses must have had a team of ten working on it!

Simba, Foggy video conference, building work, none managed to shatter the bliss of the previous evening's memories and the constant exchange of messages between Leo and me, like teenagers with a massive crush on each other. We were going to see each other again after the conference call at 6 p.m. as Zeno had invited him and Dante for dinner afterwards. We would not have the opportunity to see each other alone together for some time: the property near Harrow was ready and the Romans were moving in the next day, Thursday. Dante was very keen to go and settle down as soon as possible and Leo couldn't provide a good (official) reason not to. Rico and I would go and spend the night on Saturday to have it switched.

Dinner would be challenging. I would have to take my eyes off him and be natural. At least I knew I would behave; I wasn't so sure about him ...

That Wednesday I also dropped a note to the Lil'London watchers to organise another visit to their town on Thursday. It was time to establish proper inter-world relations and get down to business, as the saying goes. Zeno and I also wanted to negotiate the setting up of a house for James nearer to the Fog. Dante had worked on some plans for a simple structure, but local knowledge and practice would be helpful, so a cooperative project seemed to me the best way to start. The following week, we would introduce Dante and Leo to them. Having more Foggies around would increase our security: Lil'London would be aware that should anything happen to us, more people could come to the rescue. This had been a point raised by Rico, who even for Lil'London had managed to find a possible conspiracy theory, that some of the small town inhabitants, opposed to us or to advance a cause, could take us hostage or do us harm. Annoyingly he had managed to alarm me, hence my wanting to show Lil'London we had back-up.

The day went by preparing the Foggy community's first live introduction, working on dealing with Lil'London, flirting with Leo, and avoiding the knowing looks from Jazz and the boys when I giggled reading his messages. We had to wear noise-cancelling headsets all day, but the mood was light-hearted. Jazz cornered me in the kitchen at lunchtime to ask for further details about my 'wild' night and about the mysterious man. I kept my mouth shut except for telling her just how excited, happy and smitten I was. That was pretty obvious.

'It was about time, my Nutella, that you finally met someone who makes you lose your head romantically!' she commented with a wide smile.

Regarding Simba, her surprise crossing that morning had led me to speculate: if she could follow me to whichever world I was in because she wanted to join me, could she also lead me to whichever world she was aiming to go to? Or, put differently, if she thought we were going to a certain world, could she lead us there? Then I wouldn't need Rico to go to London and Zeno or Jazz to access the forest and Lil'London. I would only need to find a method of training her to lead me where I wanted to go. While I remained silent on Leo's identity, I failed to keep my reasoning to myself on Simba's potential. It concerned my friends too; Simba's ability would make me less dependent on the boys and, as it would for me, it would give them more freedom.

To verify my theory, the only plan was to be patient: each time I went out with Zeno and Jazz, I would tell the puppy 'forest'. When going out with Rico and Harry, I would repeat 'London'. I would reiterate the name of the walk accordingly when reaching the destination. It would be a long process, Simba was young. I pondered that the cub was about four weeks old and found in the Fog. She may not be the average wolf cub. It was mere conjecture, but her ability may result from being born the night the Fog happened. Birth in the midst of the switch and in the Fog might have made her part of it, gifted to criss-cross between worlds and Fog as she wished? A fine balance of time and place transforming her into a unique being. That was an idea I should keep to myself. If it were correct, others, being true to mankind, would strive to re-create her abilities with other animals, or worse, people.

'And who knows what the consequences could be,' I said to myself. That was one secret the household had to keep.

Harry, Zeno, Rico and I were seated together on one side of the dining room table, the FTab facing us. It was 5.55 p.m. and we were ready for the video conference with the Foggies around the world. Dante and Leo would join it separately from one of their hotel rooms, so that the rest of the Foggies did not feel undermined by London joining as a large group. Helo being too young to participate and Jack missing, we expected a total of fourteen Foggies to join, a third of whom were in London. The others were divided between four locations. It was important this first video conference did not appear as an exercise of power. Isabelle and Jazz may join as well.

At 6 p.m. all the Foggies were connected. The screen was split between six squares, each displaying a group of callers. The image was of the best quality, easily revealing how nervous everyone was. All but one group showed excitement about this first visual contact.

The one group which didn't was the Kenyan one. We soon learned why. Clare and Mary had decided their access to the Fog was an amazing opportunity for them to go back to the roots of what society should be and what Africa was really about. In their WII they had encountered a local tribe who viewed their presence as an embodiment of one of their legends. They were welcomed as special and their presence was accepted immediately. The tribe spoke some kind of old Swahili, a language that both Clare and Mary spoke fluently in its modern version. The ecologist and idealist mother and daughter were enchanted. They had no wish to start spoiling the Other World with anything from our world, only to study it with care. They also had misgivings aplenty about any type of organisation that could use their gifts to access WII. So, although they appreciated the Society's generosity, they had decided to withdraw from any dealings with it. For emergency purposes, they would keep the FTab. That was it. They announced they did not want to be part of the Foggies community either, or any community from this world in relation to the gift they had received. They had been sent to another world for a reason that was pure and they would respect it. Only their link with Putu, for her friendship and also for necessities and medicines, would be kept. Putu had agreed to visit them twice a week, as a necessity for her to stay in contact with the Fog, and to check on them and their potential needs. Clare owned the house: as a consultant she could work from home and minimise her meetings and outings to a bare minimum. Clare was not sure yet how she would get organised, but assured everyone she would find a way.

Putu respected Clare and Mary's choice, and wished to continue her life as it was. She was aware that as a Facilitator she could be useful to other Foggies around the world, but her mission was to help people in distress in Africa. The young doctor, with an open, warm, yet determined face, put across to us that she had a calling. Her duties were with the children and the poor in Africa who needed medical help. She would stay in touch with the community without taking an active part in it. The three women had joined the online call to express their decision in person. They were going to contact the Society next to inform them. However, they still had to rely on the Society – unfortunately, according to Mary – to keep them hidden and for the FTab. They hoped their link to the Society would remain limited to this. The women also hoped they could rely on our discretion and respect for their decision.

Before they quit, I asked if they would stay a few more minutes to hear my briefing on the missing Foggies. It was important they were aware that real dangers existed for them in the worlds out there. In both worlds in fact, as Mexico, Jakarta, and Jack's abduction proved. It wasn't necessary; the society had updated them on all of it. For Clare and Mary, it had confirmed their mistrust of our modern ways. For Putu, as long as she kept her visits to the Fog minimal, she felt the danger was limited. The parting words from Clare and Mary were, 'Goodbye and good luck.' Putu remained with us, silent for the rest of the call.

Thus participating online were:

- the Alaskan-based Foggies: brother and sister Mitch and Rosario and Tony her fiancé;
- the Moroccan-based Foggies and a Relocated: Christophe, Isabelle and Louise;
- the Nevada-based Foggies: Adam and his wife Sophia (not Michelle, the daughter);
- The UK-based Foggies: Zeno, Harry, Rico, Leo, Dante and me.

The fourteen people introduced each other in turn, by groups, each with personalities and dynamics shining through the screen within seconds.

Immediately I warmed to Mitch, Rosario and Tony. They were positive, full of energy and seemed to handle the situation by simply getting on with it. Yes, they repeated the Fog was not changing much for them, apart from Tony who had to quit his job and needed to adapt career and life aspirations to this remote part of the world. Mitch was only missing the long walks with his dog, half-German shepherd/half-wolf, when in the Other World. That made us all tick here in London. Everyone looked at me, waiting to see if I was going to make a comment or not about Simba. It was premature. Simba had only entered my life a couple of days before and my feeling was that the less I talked about her the better.

The couple from Carson City were more complex to work out. Sophia was all smiles, immediately launching into talk of being happy to help anyone who needed it. I had suggested a weekly video conference and everyone agreed. Sophia commented she was about to mention this. Behind her smile, she looked frustrated. Her attitude was a bit too honeyed for my taste. It gave her kindness a lack of naturalness. Michelle was not with them on the call. Adam explained she had a night out with some friends and wouldn't change her plans, even if she thought the FTab was cool. Adam was a jolly extrovert character who kept making positive remarks. However, his observant eyes and the analytical nature of his comments revealed a deeper intelligence behind his tendency to work at keeping everyone's spirits raised. The only ones who looked as if they could do with such help were the Marrakech crowd.

Christophe seemed in higher spirits than he had in his messages. He was using his French charm very well. He was a handsome man seen there on screen. I could understand why he got under the skin of both his wife and mistress and remained there despite his vacillation, selfishness and obnoxious tendencies. He struck me as someone who could put on his best face when needed, even if he was prone to mood swings. Isabelle seemed to have her heart in the right place, yet was not the easiest person to deal with either. Her comments were direct and steely, if not aggressive, when she disagreed. For example, she was fuming at the dropping out of the Kenyan Foggies. She took it as a selfish unreasonable attitude on their behalf and was vehement in saying so. At the same time she was displaying some genuine warmth towards all of us and thanking me profusely for organising the call. I emphasised it had been the Alaskans' idea. 'Maybe, but you did it. It is nice to know you will be a coordinator and are open to the ideas of others too, giving credit when it is due. It would be seriously hard work otherwise.' Isabelle's comment came just after Sophia suggested she would love to organise next week's call. Somehow it felt that Isabelle was backing me up behind her compliments. I thanked both of them and proposed to set up a minimum of one weekly email update from each group, at the latest the day prior to the call. In addition, they should send me their suggestions for the topics to be discussed and I would set an agenda. Sophia responded that it was a great idea and she had just been about to submit it. It was very brief, but I was certain I saw Rosario roll her eyes at Sophia's comments. The three from Marrakech each sat separated by an empty chair, Christophe being in the middle. The last person to appear was Louise. She was bubbly and charming at first, excited to be introduced to us all and it showed. She had an easily read face, one of those people who express all their emotions explicitly with their body language, an emotional person and highly sensitive. When Isabelle sighed loudly in exasperation as Louise was introducing herself and explaining how important it was for her to be in touch with nature, Louise's features immediately closed off, hurt. It pained me to see she was one of those whose raw emotions make them take things too personally and who are unable to brush off the unpleasant. That must be so hard to live with. It reminded me of Julia, even if Julia doesn't have the same joie de vivre to offset it.

The agreed time for the next video conference call was for a week from now at the same time. Until then, all the Foggies in attendance (except Putu) were to jot down the ideas and thoughts they wished to share and be taken into account. Christophe couldn't contain himself any longer and asked when another Facilitator could visit them in Marrakech. It was the wrong move. Isabelle snapped, 'First we need to sort out how you are going to close your business deals and sell the Paris flat, then you can go and do it.' Christophe shut up and dropped the subject. To steer away from the sudden and general unease and, to avoid ending the first call on a bad vibe, I broached the topic of Lil'London. Zeno and I mentioned a bit more of what we had witnessed there. We stayed on general impressions. It felt as though we were all eager to finish by then. Rosario spoke up just as we were beginning to say our goodbyes.

'There is something we haven't mentioned.' She looked preoccupied. Everyone waited for her to speak. 'I understand some locations may have two Crossers and/or two Facilitators, although apparently not two Switchers. In Jakarta, we are not sure who is who, aside from Helo as Facilitator. Another Facilitator would not have disappeared in the Fog, so I don't think that there was another one there, except if he/she got spooked and is hiding somewhere in Indonesia. Anyway, my point is that we have a Foggy missing. We have a Facilitator unaccounted for.'

All the participants to the call now looked lost in deep thought. She was absolutely right. I had just assumed that the last Facilitator had gone missing in Jakarta, but she had a point, a Facilitator could not get lost in the fog ... Making assumptions was never good. Either we had a Facilitator on the loose in Indonesia, or a Facilitator was still to be discovered somewhere in this world. Logically it should be in Marrakech or in Rome, but it could very well be at any other Fog venue, including London. Also, it could be anyone. This gave Christophe de Roque and Louise hope. After all, even if she had not commented on it after his request was dismissed by his wife, she too must wish to escape the Marrakesh house and affiliated WII.

There wasn't much we could do about it. We had no way of tracking who could be a Facilitator, only wait. So far, all the Foggies of one given location had a type of connection, so it seemed logical that the last Facilitator would somehow be linked to a group as well. Could it be Simba? I dismissed this last idea. She wasn't from this world and her abilities were different. On another thought, should the Facilitator have already crossed the Fog, one had to hope he or she would come back before seven weeks had passed. Otherwise, that person was going to start suffering pain. Within three months it would be excruciating.

There are three rules for the average person's survival. The Foggies have a fourth:

1. You cannot live three minutes without oxygen;
2. You cannot live three days without water;
3. You cannot live three weeks without food;
4. You cannot live three months without Fog contact, after that your life is pure pain.

When the call ended, Dante and Leo wrote separately they would arrive in thirty minutes. That would leave me enough time to tidy the few notes written during the call before going to the kitchen to help Jazz. Dinner was simple. Jazz swore by English food when she had to cook, so we had shepherd's pie on the menu. My contribution to the meal was crème brulée for dessert.

Dante and Leo arrived an hour later. Dante, when it came to getting ready and going out, was like Rico: a metrosexual who could spend hours in the mirror checking if a shirt is better than a T-shirt and which half should hang out of his jeans (as was apparently trendy). When the boys didn't show up, we lowered the temperature of the oven to minimum, popped the cork of a bottle and shared our impressions of the other Foggies. They were similar.

Leo's behaviour was perfect all evening. He greeted me with a warm hug, then did the same to Jazz. The whole night he would only look at me when I talked and vice versa, though when we did, even for serious comments, a smile crept onto his face. At the end of dinner I felt proud we had got away with it. He only had one tiny lapse, a little moment when he let go of appearances, safe in the knowledge his action couldn't be seen. Saying good-bye at the door and hugging me goodnight, he put one hand on my shoulder, the other on my ass. I had my back to the open front door. Rico, who was to facilitate the passage of the Romans to London, had gone out ahead and was having a cigarette on the threshold. Leo, noticing Rico was facing the Fog so that the smoke would stay outside, took liberties taking my backside in both his hands. Leo messaged me ten minutes later when back in his room alone. I was back in mine too and we started texting about whatever nonsense smitten people chat about. I always marvel at how interesting all this balderdash seems at the time. Rico knocked at my door.

'Can I come in?' he asked as he knocked.

'Sure, Rico, come in!' I replied, typing quickly to Leo that Rico was here and that we would chat more later.

Rico closed the door behind him and sat at the bottom of the bed, waiting for me to finish my typing. He looked very serious and more silent than I had ever known him.

'Your affair is with Leo, isn't it?' he asked.

'What? Why do you say that?' I was stuttering. If he was still unsure, my face of a monkey caught in the act of stealing a banana was the confirmation of his suspicions. I had betrayed myself so easily.

'The way he grabbed your ass,' he replied, deadpan.

'But how did you ...'

'I had finished my cigarette.'

'Oops!' I pulled a guilty face. I was sitting cross-legged on the bed and looked down at my bare feet. It gave me a couple of seconds respite from embarrassment as I noted my toe nails did look good in an orange nail polish.

'He hurts you, you tell me and I'll kick the shit out of him!' Rico announced in a slightly aggressive tone. 'I am like your bro. Nobody is going to mess with our little Yoko! Not under my watch. Well, not in this world.'

I was quite touched now. He looked so sweet with his genuine care; I leant forward and put a hand on his knee, saying thank

you. He carried on, 'He seems like a good guy. I am just concerned! With this Fog and all. Him being a Crosser and you both
having to work together, it is bound to complicate stuff.'

'Yep.' I knew what he meant. It was already heavy on my mind.

'If he turns out to be a player, you tell me. I'll deal with him.
OK?'

'Yes, Rico.' I was now struggling to keep a serious face. I
was a grown woman without a brother, I wasn't used to this
protective streak from a man towards my relationships. Rico
was adorable, I was moved, but I had to work hard at taking
him seriously.

'Thank you, Rico. It is good to know you are covering my
back.' He nodded once and I added, 'Now, do you think you can
keep the information to yourself? I want to see where it is heading
and how we will handle the next few days at least before informing the others.'

'Of course babe! My mouth is sealed!' I looked at him doing
the zipping gesture on his lips. It was not him breaking his word
that concerned me the most, it was him letting a comment slip,
or giving a look, or making a gesture revealing the information
by accident.

'Ah well, it wouldn't be the end of the world if the others learn
who the mysterious man is,' I thought after he left and shuddered
at the unpleasant idea. For one thing, I would never hear the end
of it from Jazz that Rico knew before her. Talking of the devil, Jazz
knocked and entered.

'Come in,' I said as she sat on the bed.

'Right. No more beating around the bush. You had wild glowing sex last night with a mysterious stranger. I am your Best Friend.
I have the right to have details and I demand them!'

I looked at her with my best 'as if' face and a lopsided smile.

'Bully,' I replied to her order, then ignored her falsely offended look and picked up Simba, putting her on my lap and gently
playing with her.

'I am not! I am a friend using her rights when hungry for info: feed me.'

'Jazz. No. Not yet. I am not ready. Seriously.'

She breathed heavily, accompanying the exaggerated sound with a real smile. She stood up and came to kiss me goodnight. Jazz patted Simba, saying, 'It was worth a try ... You won't get away with it for long, though.' Just then my FTab beeped and she added. 'Tell him if he hurts you, I'll kill him.' She left.

It seemed Leo had a lot of potential death threats on his head!

I wrote to him, 'Rico saw you at the door. He knows. He won't say a thing, but I need to warn you, if you make me cry you will have to face his wrath and a few punches.'

'First, I don't make cute women cry. Second, I have been practising martial arts since my teens. I even taught it.'

'No way!'

'Yes cutie.'

'First, I am not cute. Babies are cute, dolls are cute, puppies are cute, but I am not. Second, now all is clear, your martial arts explain the hot lean body!'

'What explains yours?'

The text messages spiralled slowly towards more hot chatter.

Before sleep time, I took Simba out, curious where we would end up. Earlier tonight we had gone out with Zeno to WII and Simba had accompanied us without a problem. I had repeated several time 'forest, forest'. Tonight I said 'Fog' and remained beside the house in the Fog. It was unfair on the wolf to expect her to already know what to do, so instead I had to be patient. The last thing I wanted was so confuse her by rushing her training and be impatient.

**Day 5 (Thursday)**

My sleep that night was horrible. I tossed and turned all night with nightmares of being chased by some bulky guys in modern outfits in the WII forest. They were not trying to kill me but I felt like a hunted rabbit. Well, at least how I imagine a hunted rabbit feels. I woke up with my chest constricted by anxiety, teary eyed and Simba licking my face. I didn't usually have bad dreams. I took Simba out by the house wall for her more urgent needs, followed by a strong cup of coffee. It was 6.30 a.m. and no one was up. The house was quiet. It would have been lovely if I didn't still feel unsettled by the dream. To get my head busy on something else, I drafted a letter to James Fisher, saying he may come anytime to discuss his situation. We wanted to try and help as soon as possible to settle it as best we could. The coffee must have shaken me awake at last, as I had a good idea: to prepare a parcel for him instead of just a letter and add one of our two-way radios and some spare batteries for him, telling him I would switch it on between 11 a.m. and 12 p.m. if he wished to contact me. I should provide similar radios to the members of the council as well and wrote as much to Leila. The Inter-World Relationship & Trade Civilian Office was officially launched by my unilateral and lonely decision. I toasted this by raising my coffee cup and asked Simba if she was proud to be part of the team. She didn't seem to mind.

Later, after breakfast, shower and the usual, Zeno and I popped out and went to the forest to give the parcel to the watchers. One of them immediately got on a horse and galloped off to Lil'London.

Leila called me on the FTab mid-morning excitedly. 'We have found another Fog! East of London in an area called Essex! It must be Jack!'

'Oh my God!' I stood up abruptly from the dining table. 'That's fantastic! Are you ... Can you ... Go and get him? Can you do that?'

'We are working on it. We are setting up a team of private security men, well, mercenaries really, to go and get him out. If he wants or needs help, that is.'

'Of course he does!'

'What! Maybe whoever abducted him thinks we are the bad guys and wanted to rescue him. Or they may have convinced him they are the best to deal with Fog matters. We must keep an open mind.'

'True. Although I think he would have contacted us to say he was all right, wouldn't he?'

'How? He doesn't have the FTab anymore. He has no way to contact us.'

"I didn't think of that. When is the "maybe a rescue, maybe not" mission?'

'As soon as possible. Later today or tonight if we can.'

'Great! How did you find them?'

'Ah … We had to take some risks there. We lowered our defences and went for a direct and open search via satellite and scanning any official, and potentially unofficial, communication.'

'Can't you do all of this in secret?'

'Of course we do. What we were looking at was not the Fog, though, but people looking for the Fog. By being more in the open, we hoped to lure them into tracking us and it worked. We had set up some traps behind our exposure, subtle ones, appearing more like an accident than done on purpose. There were pitfalls, the main one being that allowing an open door also meant they could get in.'

'This doesn't sound good!'

'It isn't good. We got the Essex location and now have to react fast. However, while we found something from them, they might have found something from us, they might have found you.'

'Or the mansion … They could have found the other property.'

'The place hasn't been switched yet. For security we are selling it and are already looking at alternatives. That just leaves you.'

'Maybe it is time to move,' I thought staring at the screen. I had no wish to move. It would start a vicious circle: every crisis would mean moving. 'Hell no!' I concluded inwardly.

'Before you mention it, I just don't like the idea we would have to move every single time there is an alert. We are building relations here with the other communities and the Relocated. They need to know they can rely on us. Moving all the time betrays instability. It beats the purpose of the exploration, trade, discovery and so on on positive grounds.'

'I know.'

'You are building defences around the terraced houses like a fortress, right?'

'We are, but there is only so much we can do ...' Leila began. I interrupted her.

'Correct me if I am wrong, and this is nothing personal, but it will always be "only so much as you can do". Now, if we are to remain here, could the roofs of the two future fogged houses which will be turned be adapted for a helicopter, as was planned in Harrow? Could you do the same thing on two of the unswitched houses? If yes, it could be an escape route for people from both worlds.'

'Should be feasible. Illegal but feasible. I'll have to talk to the architect to check if the roofs can be flattened and reinforced with pillars underneath.'

'Then maybe instead of a mansion somewhere you could buy more houses on our street, spreading the Society and defences further and inconspicuously. I know London is very, very, VERY expensive, but if you could, your defence and strength can be concentrated here.'

'I will talk to our board.'

'I will talk to the other London Foggies here. And Leila?'

'Yes?'

'Please do let me know about Jack and how things are evolving, will you?'

'Yes, of course, I will do.'

'Thank you.'

After hanging up the call, I sent messages to every London Foggy and Jazz telling them there were updates they ought to know. I asked if we could chat online in fifteen minutes as a matter of urgency. They all replied that they were available, except Harry. He was teaching. In the meantime, my reminder beeped: it was 11 a.m. and time to switch on the two-way radio. Within seconds James Fisher talked.

'Miss Salelles?'

'Yes. Please call me Yoko.'

'Thank you so much for the walkie-talkie. This is great!'

'I thought that would give us direct communication, independent of the Lil'London people.'

'Yes!'

'Now, let's discuss your living arrangements, your family and how you want to organise your life in Lil'London. We are happy to help, either as individuals or through the Society. You will have to be in charge of your own life, but you are starting from scratch in an unknown place with total strangers with, let's say it, strange habits. At least strange for us. We want to provide you with all the help we can. We are as new to it as you are and you will need to be patient and lenient. We can only say we will do what we can ('Gosh! I sounded like Leila!' I thought.) James, are you still here?'

'Yes, yes, I am. I hear you clearly. Any help is fantastic. And of course I understand. I have two things in mind: first, moving out of here and being able to have my own clothes and food. Second, I want to sort things out with my family. I would like to see them.'

'Home: we have some ideas on how to build your own place. Food and clothes: we can help. Family: this is trickier. Do you want to see them in person, or would an online conference call do? Like Skype or something?'

'Maybe I could start with Skype?'

'Would you like me to contact them to organise it, or …?'

'Could you? Could you do it? Maybe you would get a better welcome than I did!'

'I can always try. I would need your wife's number and email address.'

James gave me his wife's details. I made a note in my notebook to call her after my chat with the London Foggies. It was already looking like it would be quite a full day. My new job had well and truly started.

The London Foggies, that is Zeno, Rico, Harry, Leo, Dante, and extended to Jazz, were thrilled Jack's Fog was located. However, the welcome for the news was shadowed with worry.

'So we do not know what 'they' know about us?' Zeno asked.

'No, we don't. They may be none the wiser, or we are in trouble.'

'Is the FTab still secure?' Leo's question was a practical one, a good one.

'Leila assured me it was. It is information from their own data pool they could have accessed, not the network.'

'I wonder who they are and what they want. Not knowing who we are dealing with is starting to irritate me,' Harry said, sipping a cup of tea like the classic stoic Brit he was, far from appearing irritated.

'I think we will know soon,' Rico jumped in. 'I have the feeling things will accelerate from now. It is like war, man. We had the hidden, secret hostilities and now it will all come out in the open and the two sides will reveal themselves in battle.'

'And why is it a good thing? Because I kind of like it when the war is not in my face,' Jazz intervened. My opinion was mitigated: I wanted to know the adversary, but not with a gun levelled between the eyes.

'At least you know who and what you are dealing with,' Harry said, his eyes on me – was I so easy to read? – concluding, 'but I am not sure which is best, either.'

I broke the other news: 'The immediate consequence of the information leak is that the mansion project in Harrow is dropped. Personally, I think that it would be a good idea to let some time pass before they look for yet a third one. In the meantime, my suggestion is to set it all up here and concentrate all the protection here as well. After all, the new house complex should be ready soon. We can share with Leo, Dante and, hopefully soon, Jack. We each have a spare room in the new larger house, or …'

'How about you take Leo in your guest room, I'll take Dante,' Rico cut in, looking falsely innocent.

'Err … No … That… is not really what I had in mind! To finish my sentence, … or Leo, Dante and Jack sharing one of the Society's houses. Maybe the office could be somewhere else.'

'Or I would totally have you!' Jazz exclaimed.

'Thank you. I know you already have a bed for me. The only thing is, living during the week in a non-Fog area, I can go in and out to London as it pleases me which I am aware is not nice to remind you of because you can't.'

'And any Crosser can visit you too, without needing a Facilitator to leave and return to our world,' Rico added, giving a fleeting look at the screen and, I guessed, more specifically Leo, not Dante.

'Well, thank you Rico,' Zeno said, with a little frown at Rico, wondering why he was stating the obvious.

'That is very kind of all of you,' Leo commented. 'I am sure that the Society will sort something out for us like they did for you – in the neighbourhood hopefully. You know, I really wonder what type of money they have, because all this must cost a fortune!'

'Yes, it seems they have never ending pockets full of gold.'

'Yeah … One day you should sit Leila down and start probing more about the Society. I mean, they are very nice and everything …' Jazz didn't think it necessary to finish her sentence with words. She was right, her frown and pout sufficed.

'Indeed, the Society is definitely a bit Foggy,' Harry said, austere but for sparkly eyes. It was a good pun.

'Ha ha ha!' Jazz was not amused.

I remarked to myself that even though both Harry and Jazz shared a sarcastic streak, Jazz's was unrestrained, more the 'in your face' sarcastic type. Harry was more on the poised, almost cold sarcasm, for which you mentally wondered 'was it sarcasm?' His was also more the cynical type. They had known each for years and got on fine. All the same, now, living in the house, a few signs showed that Jazz found Harry difficult. She was an expansive character, openly expressing her opinions loud and clear, while Harry was harder to read, with a quiet strong presence. She bantered, he did not, yet his control and cool made you feel he won any verbal joust. When he did reply, it would be the final word, a cutting one.

So yes, Harry was starting to grate on Jazz's nerves. 'Please let the building work finish on schedule!' I begged inwardly. I didn't want to be in the middle of a clash between those two, stuck under the same roof.

It took a large over-sweet cup of milky tea and some deep breathing before I managed to brace myself and call the wife of James Fisher. This was not an experience I was looking forward to.

'Mrs Fisher?'

'Yes? I am Ann Fisher,' the woman answered cautiously. She sounded tired and her voice betrayed the heavy load on her shoulders.

'Hello. I am a friend of your husband.'

'He is not here. He buggered off,' her voice had hardened.

'Actually, we talked before. He passed the phone to me the other day ...'

'I don't have time for this!' She had instantly switched to yelling.

I could tell there was very little time before she hung up on me, so I jumped in and talked as fast as I could. 'Wait! Your husband has a condition. He cannot come back to you and the condition could spread to you or your children if you visited! That's why he hasn't contacted you before, why he is concerned about your coming to meet him and when he was ...'

'And the bullshit about supernatural fog?' Ann Fisher interrupted me, with a barely controlled high-pitched voice, on the verge of a scream.

'Mrs Fisher.' I was trying to adopt the calmest, most professional voice possible, to appear credible and trustworthy. 'Your husband's situation is serious. He is in a Foggy state. This is a new predicament, undisclosed to the general public. What is happening to him is unexplainable and we have no control over it. His life has changed for ever and believe me he is deeply unhappy. He hasn't betrayed you, been disloyal to you, stopped loving you, abandoned you, or as you put it, buggered off. He thinks of you all the time.'

'Really? Because it all sounds like bullshit to me. Are you a doctor? Where is he? Why didn't anyone call me, his WIFE, to tell me what was going on?'

'No one called you because he was not able to talk to us for several days. The first time we finally could talk, his first request was to call you. We can't tell you where he is because it is highly sensitive information and no, I am not a doctor. I am a representative of the ... institution. The institution which is trying to help him get back on his feet and deal with the new situation he will be in from now on.'

'Yeah, right. Still sounds like a lot of nonsense to me, but OK, I am willing to go along with it and listen. Now, tell me, what are his symptoms?'

'His symptoms?'

'Yeah, his symptoms!'

I hadn't prepared for that question. The simplest was to continue to stay as close as possible to the truth.

'Well, the first few days he had high fever, shivers, cold sweat and he felt he was hallucinating. He was found by some people in a remote location with no phone. It took some time before we got to him.'

'Is he better now?' She sounded as if she was mellowing a bit. Her tone had some anxiety in it. I was getting through to her at last.

'He still has ups and downs. I would say the worst is how to deal with his situation psychologically. He misses you and the children terribly. Your husband, from what I have seen, is a good man.'

'That is what I thought. Well, maybe. Maybe he is.'

'Would you like to meet me and discuss things? I could also set up a video call with him, like Skype, during our meeting?'

Ann Fisher took her time to reply, mulling over my proposal.

'Yes, I would like that,' she eventually replied.

'When would be best for you?'

'Today?'

'I have an important meeting in the afternoon. Would early evening be suitable for you?'

'5.30 p.m.?'

'Perfect, ' I replied.

I quickly reviewed my options regarding the meeting's location. My preference was for a meeting at a short distance from the house. I felt safer with the whole bunch of bodyguards nearby. So I suggested meeting in the lobby of a hotel close by, which had a quiet little lounge bar. We could sit in a corner and have the chat and conference call. If the meeting and call were fruitful, she may want to see the Fog. Seeing is believing, as they say, and in this case my instinct was telling me it would help. If so, using a cab for the journey and a mask for security, she would be introduced to the Fog.

Zeno had arrived a few minutes into the call and had taken Simba out. The newspaper on the floor trick was starting to work and Simba's wet accidents indoors were more controlled now. Coming back, he gave me a note from the Lil'London Council confirming the meeting in the afternoon at their town hall. We were going to make a special entrance today on Zeno's new cross-country motorbike, a request to the Society which was delivered to him in the morning. Its original purpose was a faster and more comfortable means of transportation (Zeno was still sore from the previous Sunday's horse riding). One of the benefits was the demonstration of our technological advancement to the whole town. So far only the three members from the local council who had visited the house had had a glimpse of it. The motorbike was a statement to the locals that we had a lot more to offer than they could imagine.

I worked on a list of matters I wanted to review with them. The main points on my agenda were:

- The Relocated: where would James Fisher and potential future ones settle? What would be their status? What help could Lil'London offer for their acclimatisation to their new lives?
- Lil'London: what was their economy, their structure and rules, their decorum?

   (We needed to know what was illegal, or considered offensive. It was important to respect their laws and customs, as far as we could. Possibly they would evolve with our arrival, but neither the Society, nor I, wanted to force anything upon them. We had no right to do this. In my view, we should demonstrate what we had to bring to the table and what they would gain from us, establishing a strong position, and let them come to us but not impose anything. In relation to customs, I had bought a pair of rollerblades and had to start practising. I was postponing the inevitable one day to the next.)

- Trade: Where did their interests lie? What they would like from us?
- History: What did they want to learn from us? What could they tell us of theirs?

Via Leila, Harry had ordered fifteen books on British history focused on the last three hundred years. Four were to go to James Fisher, giving him something to discuss with locals. Six would go as gifts to the members of the local council and their head wives.

The rest were for each of us in the house to read, to be able to answer the questions bound to be asked by people in the Other World. Harry laughed at me saying that we would be his worst students! Indeed, Rico had looked at his, sneered and said 'No way! Have you seen its size? Forget it, I'd rather watch movies.' Zeno looked at his, looked at me, turned on his heels and ran out of the room screaming 'Noooooo!' Jazz looked at hers, looked at me, looked at hers, looked at me and said, 'I feel punished for something and I don't even know why ...'

I had also ordered a few books on diplomacy and negotiation, as well as on other communities living some type of old-fashioned life in our modern world, such as the Amish. That was for me. The books received the same treatment as rollerblading practice. I would start tomorrow.

My outfit for the second visit to Lil'London was a long wide skirt. A woman in leather trousers would have been shocking to Lil'London. Making an entrance didn't have to go along with creating outrage. At last the weather seemed to have understood it was supposed to be spring. The cold had lifted suddenly in the past three days. I didn't need a big coat anymore and settled for several layers: shirt, cardigan, jacket, pashmina and thick motorcycle gloves. I also put boots on under my long woollen skirt and some detachable protection for my knees and elbows (cross-country apprehension). Last but not least, the helmet. Zeno, as usual, looked a vision of black leather, with black helmet and black visor. We were all set. We pushed the bike from its parking space in the fogged front patio to the forest of WII. We had to push the bike in the worst areas of the forest too. The books, notes, two-way radios monitored by Jazz, and bottles of water went in a rucksack. Zeno put our two guns in his. Yikes. I really hoped we would never need them. Contrary to him, I had no training and wasn't in a hurry to get any.

As I turned to kiss Jazz goodbye, Simba escaped her hold to join us. I patted her head and tried to explain that she ought to stay here. I was already fond of the little one. She needed an appointment with a vet to check everything was fine with her. It would be tricky to avoid the question of her origins. That was a matter for the Society. I sighed: everything was so much more complicated when a whole side of one's life is to remain secret. It must be the same for a spy's life: a good chunk of it must stink!

Thanks to our previous trip to Lil'London and the directions of the watchmen, we made it to Lil'London without getting lost, and on time. Our noisy entrance had the expected effect of making everyone gather around us – although at a distance – with wide-open eyes and gaping mouths. We parked on the main square, took our helmets off and saluted the crowd with a broad grin. Some bold children escaped the hold of their parents and came running towards us, looking at the motorbike in wonder. 'What type of animal is this? Is this dangerous?' A tall blond boy asked. He must have been fourteen or fifteen years old. A young man really.

'It is not an animal, it is a machine. Like a tool created by man to help travel faster,' I told him.

'Ooooh ... Is it dangerous?'

'Only when it is ... awake. It is sleeping now so it is not.'

'Can I touch it?'

'I would rather not. You could wake it up. Also it has travelled fast, so it is very hot. You could burn yourself.' The young man couldn't taking his eyes off the motorbike, fascinated. The adults, as I noticed when I glanced around, were more in awe. I turned back to the young man.

'Maybe you can help? Would you be able to look after it for us? Make sure no one bothers or touches it?'

'Yes!' The young man beamed with pride at my request.

'You don't have anything else to do? Your parents will not mind?' It wouldn't do to antagonise his parents.

'It is fine. Jonas will ensure your property remains undisturbed.' A man with a deep voice spoke behind me. I turned and was face to face with a tall and muscular man, the leather apron of a blacksmith covering his front. His sight made me think of Jazz: if Lil'London had many men like that, Jazz may end up liking this town very much, after all. His face had a weather-beaten look, which probably came from the work he was doing with constant fire and heat, not from wind and sun. He had long dark hair tied in a ponytail and piercing blue eyes. The young one, his son by deduction, had the same blue eyes. The father moved next to Jonas and put a hand on his shoulder.

'Thank you. This is very kind of you both,' I said.

'You are welcome. My name is Barnaby Sparrow.' He bowed his head as he introduced himself. 'And this is my son Jonas.'

'Zenone Grande and Yoko Salelles,' I introduced us in return. Zeno finished peeling off his gloves and the rest of his protective gear.

'This is made with metal?' Barnaby Sparrow asked.

'It is indeed,' I replied.

'Interesting.' Neither Barnaby Sparrow's nor his son's eyes left the bike.

'Would you like me to explain how it works afterwards, if I have a chance?' Zeno joined the conversation with a smile.

Barnaby Sparrow looked at Zeno. His eyes shone at the idea and he nodded.

'Then I will,' Zeno decided. 'Hopefully we will have time today. If not, we will arrange a meeting with you for another time.'

'Thank you. We appreciate your offer and are grateful for your kindness and time.' Barnaby was clearly delighted at the thought and his son could barely contain his excitement.

I had noticed for some time Augustus Hoare and Benjamin Snayth standing in front of the town hall, waiting for us to come in. Edmund Poff was talking to his wife on the side, disagreeing with something she was saying. He looked up and saw me looking their way. He kissed his wife tenderly on the cheek and joined the others. Maud Poff made her way towards us. I heard Barnaby Sparrow behind me say, 'Jonas, go get a chair and a jug of water. You are to remain here until Miss Salelles and Mr Grande come back.' The sound of someone running followed the answer of 'Yes Father!'

Maud Poff was carrying with her a large basket full of flowers. She was walking with a welcoming smile and once again I noted the energy and warmth radiating from her. She was not what I would call a beautiful woman, yet a spark rendered her more attractive than her average looks would suggest. With light chestnut hair and a pale complexion, her face was serene. She was in her late twenties although she could look like a teenager when laughing. I wondered if they had beauty creams in Lil'London, or if they just didn't bother in such a small community. On second thoughts, they probably had. Women just can't help themselves, it is in their nature. I greeted her with a smile.

'Mrs Poff. How lovely to see you again.'

'Mrs Salelles, the pleasure is all mine. It really is. My husband mentioned you would be meeting today and I thought maybe you would enjoy those freshly cut wild flowers from our fields?'

'What a wonderful thought! How lovely of you. Yes, certainly, they will brighten up our home very nicely.'

'I am pleased.'

Maud Poff added, keeping her charming smile and lowering her voice so that it was but a whisper, 'I took the liberty of leaving a little something at the bottom of the basket ... Just for you to see and ... to know.' She then swiftly continued, back in a normal voice, 'Well, I do not wish to hold you up any longer, I am sure that you have much more important things to talk about than our wild flowers, even though they are beautiful.' Maud Poff bowed her head, bade me farewell and withdrew. My curiosity was aroused, although it would have to wait until we got back to the house. It was time for the meeting.

Augustus Hoare looked the most stuck-up I had ever seen him. Benjamin Snayth seemed to have just eaten some bitter lemon and had a forced smile, and Edmund Poff was uneasy, looking down twice at the basket before quickly casting his eyes away. His wife must have informed him of what she was up to. After the first greetings, the walk to the meeting room was made in silence. Zeno and I sat at on the long side of a large polished rectangular table in the Lil'London Town Hall. It was a lovely room, relatively small, with the table taking up most of the space. Panels of dark wood covered the walls, ceiling and floor and the table was made of the same stock. The smell was amazing, like being in a vintage carpenter's shop. We could have easily seated sixteen round this table, we were six. Benjamin Snayth, Augustus Hoare and Edmund Poff were sitting opposite us, with one of their scribes at the end of the table, the entrance door behind him. Behind the three members of the council were four large windows from which the square could be seen, where we had made the speech the previous Sunday. The church was opposite us. The sky was a bright blue, the air was warm and I thought of what a nice day it would be for a walk in their countryside. A young black woman, no older than fifteen and dressed like a maid with apron and little hat, served tea and biscuits within minutes of us being seated. When she left, the meeting started.

'Miss Salelles, Mr Grande, thank you for suggesting this meeting. We were planning on contacting you to organise something similar,' Benjamin Snayth started.

'Then, like you, we believe in the need to establish the foundations of the future relationship between the two worlds,' I told them, 'the earlier, the better.'

'Indeed. We ought to inform you of how our community works and what we might hope you would avoid doing out of respect for us,' Augustus Hoare added, straight to the point. 'This "thing" you arrived with might be your usual way of travelling, but you should understand it is new to us. Maybe in the future you could refrain from introducing elements from your world that may trouble, shock, frighten, excite, or in general disturb the members of our community and confuse their minds, at least until you have presented it to us first?'

'Sir,' I replied. 'We understand your request. However, our mere presence is likely to trouble, shock, frighten, excite, or in general disturb your community, isn't it?' I held my ground. 'I believe you have been expecting us for more than two hundred years and with us expecting changes and differences. We will respect your rules and laws, but we cannot change who we are and how we think. It will be difficult to run everything past you first, as everything we do, we are, we own and we use, is modern and different from you. Even if we did manage to do as you asked, just the way we talk and our ideas are likely to unsettle your peers.'

Augustus Hoare's eyes had narrowed to a slit. Benjamin Snayth lay back in his chair and took a deep breath. Unsurprisingly, Edmund Poff was wringing his hands, head bowed and focusing on an empty space on the table in front of him. Surprisingly though, before his head was completely bowed, I had a glimpse of his face. He seemed to be trying to suppress a smile. I thought I must be wrong.

'Of course. Of course,' Benjamin Snayth spoke next. 'We are just asking you to be considerate and to minimise the impact of the culture clash. We only have the best interests of our people at heart.'

'And we shall respect it. As much as we can,' I emphasised. 'As you may have noticed during your first visit, this is not my normal attire. I am aware the other would shock sensibilities here. We do try harder than you may think. Now, shall we move forward to the urgent matters at hand?' Augustus Hoare was still the image of a reproving headmaster. Benjamin Snayth was a bit taken aback that I seemed on the verge of taking the lead in this meeting. Edmund Poff had his head bent so much I could not see his face. Zeno was comfortably in his seat observing it all, holding his FTab on the table in such a way that I guessed he was filming the whole exchange. Prior to coming here, he had mentioned he would let me deal with the diplomatic elements of the visit, only intervening to back me up or add some clarity if necessary. 'I want to make sure they see us as a team,' he had explained. 'I will conduct the trading and economic negotiations for us, but not the diplomacy. That's for you.' Our aim was to present ourselves as organised and clear partners.

'Our primary concerns are the future of the Relocated and how they are to join your community by having a specific space, a role and way to make a living,' I kicked off. 'We are considering how to help them and you integrate some of our modern technologies to improve your everyday life; how to organise a relationship that would benefit us both and on equal ground.' I saw Benjamin Snayth was going to speak and I quickly added, 'We have brought for you some books we thought you might find of interest, on the history of Britain in the past three hundred years.'

Edmund Poff's head lifted up swiftly, his face lit up and he exclaimed, 'Excellent, excellent! Do you have them here with you?'

'Yes,' I answered, slightly perplexed at Poff's ecstatic reaction. Zeno took the books out and handed them over to the council members.

'Excellent! Excellent!' Edmund Poff repeated as he held one of the books, excited like a kid in a candy shop. Benjamin Snayth took one look at the cover, smiled in a constricted way and put it back on the table beside him. Augustus Hoare opened the first page, then put the book down, keeping a hand on it. He interrupted Benjamin Snayth just before the latter had a chance to speak. 'Did you give any of those to anyone here?'

'No.'

'Good. I would appreciate if you don't. Not yet,' he concluded.

'Why? Because information is power?' I shouldn't have said that, it was not very diplomatic of me. It had slipped out before I could stop myself. Now it was out and Augustus's rigid posture, clenched jaw and dagger-like stare was telling of either internal outrage or fury. I wasn't sure which one. Also, I wondered what was worse for him: that it had been said by a woman? That I may be right? Or that I had said aloud something best left covered with a blanket of apparent good intentions for the community's sake? Benjamin Snayth gave me a quick glance which reminded me of a snake assessing the size of its prey. He then slowly put two hands on the table and in a voice louder than usual, cut the heavy silence.

'Miss Salelles, you have misunderstood us. We only wish to avoid any turmoil in case anything in the book appears indecent for our people.'

'You see me reassured,' I pronounced solemnly. I struggled not to raise a dismissive eyebrow and thus smear the delicate veneer covering the sarcasm in my reply. It was probably still too apparent. Augustus Hoare's mouth and nostrils were so tightly pinched it was a wonder he could breathe. I decided to ease my tone for the rest of the meeting. That was not the start to aim for! I wasn't here to antagonise, especially having no right to judge. I repeated this mentally several times.

'Ireland is free!' It seemed Edmund Poff had been oblivious to the whole exchange. He had his nose buried deep in our history book, cheerful. 'So Ireland is finally independent?' He was obviously waiting and hoping for confirmation.

'Most of it. Except Northern Ireland which is part of the United Kingdom,' I answered.

'What is the United Kingdom?'

'The United Kingdom of Great Britain and Northern Ireland.' I explained the real name behind UK.

'That is the new name of England?' Edmund Poff seemed confused.

'Let me see.' My knowledge of the details of UK history remained shamefully basic in my opinion, despite the many years I had spent in the country. 'Great Britain is composed of England, Scotland, Wales and some little islands around it all. To this you add Northern Ireland and you have what we call the UK.'

'But ... the King ... Is he still ... English? Do we still have a king?' This came from Augustus Hoare, his voice betraying real concern. The tension from the three men in front of me, waiting for my answer, surprised me. 'Why do they care?' I wondered. 'They have never set foot in this country. They have had no news for 231 years. They can't possibly have any allegiance or national spirit, can they?' I was underestimating the weight of traditions and ancestry. Edmund Poff's reaction to the Irish news had been the first clear hint of it.

'Queen. The head of state is a queen. And yes, she is English-born, but most of all she is British. She reigns over the citizens of the UK.' I added to myself, 'And the Commonwealth, including Canada and Australia.' It would be too much to explain just now. I wasn't even sure they knew about Australia. I needed stop postponing my studies to the next day, they were urgently needed. Right then, the easiest was to return to the matters at hand for the meeting.

'I trust you will find a lot of information and surprises in these books. I look forward to discovering your history too.'

'Excellent, excellent! Yes! Here is the copy of *Lil'London Tales*.' Edmund Poff handed a heavy book to me a little ceremoniously, standing up with his hands holding each side of the book. I noted it was not a manuscript.

'You have a printing machine?'

'Yes. This is one thing my ancestors insisted upon. The family has been in charge of the library, texts and printing ever since. We have a little house by the church dedicated to it. Maud helps me ...'

'Yes, thank you Edmund.' Benjamin Snayth interrupted Edmund Poff, exasperated. 'We will talk of those little pastimes of yours and of your genealogy anon.' Edmund Poff sat back down, his ego slightly bruised, but still looking at me eagerly. He was like a new person.

'Thank you Mr Poff. It will be interesting to discuss it further sometimes. It sounds very interesting.' I told him and meant it. I was starting to warm to the little man. When he talked about his hobby and history, there was a genuine passion and suddenly he was a lively and open person, not the shy, indecisive one we had first met. I continued, looking at the other two members of the council. 'Shall we talk about the settling of the Relocated?'

'There are only two and one seems to live with you, so it hardly seems to be an issue. As a matter of fact, we are wondering why there aren't more?' Benjamin Snayth asked.

'While we get organised with the novelty of the Fog, we have blocked access to it to avoid accidental relocation,' Zeno explained.

'Accidental? Why don't you just to let people know not to cross if they don't want to be relocated?'

'It's a bit more complicated than that. For the moment only a very limited number of people know about the Fog,' I informed them.

'Knowledge is power, I presume,' Augustus Hoare commented, his poised and cold attitude graced with a sneer. It was not becoming, but he had a point. I smiled.

'It is. Although, in this case, we are protecting ourselves as much as we are protecting you,' I explained. 'Within a few days thanks to our technology seven billion people on the planet could know about the Fog. You would risk an invasion by anyone dreaming of adventure, wishing to escape the authorities, hoping for a new life, or searching for spiritual answers. You would have to face those wanting to use your natural resources, or dump their junk in your back garden. On our side, we would lose our freedom; on yours, you would risk being colonised. Both would be overwhelmed. Our governments have weapons strong enough to destroy your whole planet if they saw it as a threat. You will read this in the history books: mankind even went to the moon, Mr Hoare, so imagine! We are not trying to gain power by retaining information; for now, we are trying to protect all of us involved from being eaten by bigger fish. By gaining time, we are building a better foundation to deal with the changes and be ready for the future.'

There was a lot to process in my speech and the council took a few minutes to do so.

'I find it hard to believe that seven billion people exist on your earth.' Augustus Hoare was the first to speak again. 'Let alone that information could reach them all in a couple of days. As for your claims you went to the moon or could destroy a whole planet ...'

'Read the book. If you do not believe it, I will show you images, or even movies. Now regarding the seven billion people and news, just give me one minute.'

I took the two-way radios out of my bag and called Jazz. She replied instantly.

'Yoko? Are you OK?'

'Yes, thank you Jazz.' I looked at the three men in front of me. They had stopped breathing and were looking at the radio with eyes wide open. I continued, 'I just wanted you to say a little hi to the members of the council, as you couldn't join us today.'

'Oh! Certainly. Hello everyone! Mr Hoare, Mr Snayth and Mr Poff, I presume?'

'Thank you. I'll let you go now,' I told her.

'OK. Roger that.' Jazz signed off the call and so did I.

'So, now, you understand that communications have changed pretty drastically since sending a letter by a courier on horseback. This gives you an idea how easy it is be to reach anyone on the planet (I wasn't even going to start on internet, media or any of the social platforms) and tell them about the Fog.'

'I see,' Augustus Hoare barely said and proceeded to stare at the wall behind me in deep thought.

'Have you informed your queen about us?' Benjamin Snayth enquired. I could tell from his body language he was agitated. I had provided a lot of information to digest, not the least the threats they were under if, or more accurately when, the Fog became widely known. It was hard on them … So much for mellowing my tone. Despite his question taking me by surprise, it helped me relax and refocus on being friendly first and foremost.

'No, we have not informed the Queen. You don't just 'inform the Queen' these days. You inform the government, probably the Home Office.' I had said the last sentence more to myself than to anyone else.

'So, have you informed her Home Office?' Snayth persisted.

'No.'

'I am afraid to ask why,' Augustus Hoare said, displaying a real gift for self-possession. Benjamin Snayth knotted his hands tightly, eyes concentrated on the middle of the table. If I had to take a guess I would say he was calculating how what I had said affected his policy for Lil'London and how to proceed next.

'We want to know where we stand first,' I continued. 'We also fear what they might do to us: we do not want a life to be spent in laboratories, analysed, probed and tested, only to be moved to various locations depending on their requirements for places to fog.'

'I don't understand,' Edmund Poff said, frowning as he looked up from the history book.

'Me neither,' Benjamin Snayth said.

'I am the one who creates the doors between the worlds once a week,' I clarified. 'It happens anywhere. A Switcher is also the one who keeps them open in the long term. We fear a government will want to use this power. I don't mind helping them, or you, I just don't want to be used and abused. I want to do it of my free will, not by force.'

'So do I. So do us all of us linked to the Fog.' Zeno had said very little until now. Here he intervened with a firm, grave affirmation as clear support.

'Messrs the members of the council, what we are hoping for is mutual respect between Lil'London, the Relocated and us. Same in our original world. However, the balance may be more difficult to achieve there than here. Also, what happens in our world will have strong repercussions here, much more than the reverse. This is why we tread carefully.'

'Thank you.' Augustus Hoare had a deep voice and spoke with measure. His last words had been pronounced slowly, with a care and simplicity which emphasised he meant every syllable. When I turned my head to look at him, in truth a bit startled, he did not smile but gave me a slight nod. I returned him the courtesy. The man was rigid, stern, stiff, outdated (for my world), but he seemed to be true to his values.

At last we discussed the present and future Relocated and how they would be part of the local community. Benjamin Snayth was promoting their settlement around the town. Snayth offered to lease them some lands to build their property. I thought, not kindly, it was a good way for him to make a profit out of the Relocated situation. In the end, we agreed on two possible locations, one by the town and one by the forest. The one near the forest was freehold. The one by Lil'London would be designated freehold with some compensation for the town or landowner, depending on to whom it belonged. This would be for the council to determine. When I told them we would provide the materials and architectural plans through our network, Edmund Poff mentioned that the parish would provide men to help for the building work. On the integration of the Relocated in their society, we broached the issue of how they would make a living and take part in everyday life. It was too early to determine for certain. In all probability it would be linked to the trading and integration of the modernity brought with them. That would need time, and to be sorted on a one-by-one basis.

'How about the medicine? We could really do with an upgrade there,' Poff was getting more confident in speaking his suggestions and ideas. 'Are you aware that our ancestors had the theory the Fog could cure ailments?'

'Yes, it does. The Fog cures elements that are alien to the body causing an imbalance, like viruses. It would not repair broken or damaged bones and the like, or so we think. We wish to study this in more detail.'

'That would also be a cause of massive inflow of people through the Fog, wouldn't it?' Hoare asked.

'I beg your pardon?' I was startled not by Hoare's question, but by his quick grasp of the implications in our world of the Fog's healing capacity.

'If everyone knew about the Fog, wouldn't they come en masse to try and get cured?'

'Yes. I presume they would.' As I said this, my mind went into overdrive. The image of queues and queues of people hoping to get whatever was wrong with them cured by crossing the Fog, despite the danger of relocation, was overwhelming. For seven billion people, all with various ailments in a lifetime, it was really, really daunting!

It was my turn to be the listener while Zeno talked about trade and enquired what would be of interest for Lil'London as a commodity. The small town had very little, or none, of some of our basic products like coffee, sugar, pepper, spices. These were exotic and rare for them, as import was close to non-existent. The council was of course after metals difficult to come by, like copper, silver, gold, as well as textiles and glass. They were all so easily accessible for us. To start with, we could even just get a retailer discount store card and get everything in bulk from there. Zeno was taking notes frantically, commenting every other sentence with 'not a problem', 'si', 'can do'. The trading would at first cover the labour for building James Fisher's house. Afterwards, the Relocated – James and Jazz for now – could make a business and a living out of it, Zeno being the intermediary. He also put forward the idea he would love to explore WII and would require some guidance, offering to pay or trade for it. Lil'London had its own money. We knew this since the first meeting as Snayth had first introduced himself as a banker in addition to mayor. They were also often doing plain exchange of goods, either based on common practice for their worth or having agreed between themselves the value of the items.

Listening to Zeno and Benjamin Snayth discuss goods, markets, everyday and luxury items, was like witnessing the creation of a practical bond between the two worlds. The excitement of those two was fascinating. It was more real, more palpable than my diplomatic foreign affairs activities, even if both were necessary and concomitant. Edmund Poff was now lost in the history book. He was clearly the intellectual of the town. Augustus Hoare was listening to the exchange between Snayth and Zeno, not one emotion betrayed on his face. From time to time he would turn and look at me with expressionless austerity. I gave him a brief smile intended to be warm and he would nod lightly before turning back to watch the two men's discussion. When it was time to go before I got late for my next meeting, my brain was turning to mush. As we left, Hoare asked to be provided with a two-way radio (which he referred to as the speaking box). It was an idea I had had already, and more radios had been ordered in the morning, so I happily agreed to his wish.

When we walked out, Jonas was sitting by the bike, his back straight and telling some sort of stories to a younger crowd of children sat around him on the ground. As we came closer, we heard he was revisiting a legend of dragons and mythical beasts, the bike having replaced the horse as loyal companion of the fighting knight. Hearing us, he stood up promptly and was about to send one of the children fetch his dad. We stopped him, we would not have the time to show them how the bike worked that day. Jonas looked so disappointed that Zeno quickly added that if he and his Dad were to come on Saturday after lunch, he would give them a private demonstration by the house. Jonas immediately agreed and looked around him beaming. Next, putting Maud's basket on the bike wasn't simple. Zeno recommended we put the flowers in the rucksack poking out and that I leave the basket behind. This was impossible not knowing what Maud had left underneath the flowers and the members of the council watching us leave. Zeno finally had to put the basket in front of him and secured it with a rope. It was not comfortable for him and I appreciated he trusted me enough not to insist.

I reflected on the bike journey back. The first inter-worlds relations meeting had been relatively successful, aside from an awkward start. I had to try and be less feisty next time and to remember this was not personal, just professional. Be that as it may, they ought to know I stood firm on my beliefs and positions. They had had a glimpse of the real me, and me them.

Snayth. The man had displayed his mayor side as a strong politician so far (quite a self-interested one, I found) and now the banker was coming out. I had not forgotten the steely look he gave me the first time we met. It had hinted the person was more calculating than he would have led us to believe. Since then and after today, I was more and more forming the opinion that Snayth would be the difficult one to deal with, possibly the sly one. Hoare was tough and inflexible, but at least he was upfront and not deceitful. Poff surprised me; I couldn't work him out anymore. I had seen him in another light today and liked what I saw. I might have judged him too soon, too fast. He had also helped me understand this community had lived with the knowledge of another world somewhat adjacent, and had kept more traditions linking to us than I might have expected. Another meeting was set for the following Monday. We planned to hold them regularly, at least once a week and more if necessary.

As we arrived at the edge of the forest and turned to get onto the path leading to the clearing which had been cleared of branches and trunks by the watchmen of Lil'London for easier access, Zeno slowed down. It took just one minute, yet it might have saved one of our lives as an arrow flew right in front of us, barely missing Zeno. Zeno didn't waste any time in checking where it might have come from. He accelerated and we zoomed dangerously through the forest right to the house. I was stunned, hardly believing that what we had witnessed for one second could have been an attempt to kill us.

'Could we be mistaken, Zeno?' The adrenaline was leaving my body and I felt a bit faint.

'No. It was an arrow. Someone clearly shot at us,' he replied.

'But … But … Why?' I blurted.

'Yoko, go to your meeting. I will go and inform the watchmen. We need to find this arrow.'

'I can't let you go alone! What if it is one of them?'

'It is not. Both of them were in their shed when we arrived. I looked. Go!'

'But …'

'Let me handle this. Your meeting is important too,' Zeno said.

'Zeno, don't mention it to the others, yet, OK? Especially Jazz. I don't want her to freak out.'

'We'll talk about it when you come back.'

Ann Fisher was emotionally draining.

She was a petite lively woman, borderline hyper, in her early thirties. She had had her son (now fifteen) at the age of eighteen and her daughter (now twelve) at the age of twenty-one. She and

James were high school sweethearts and eventually married at twenty. Ann was already pregnant with baby number two. Theirs is a so-called mixed marriage, James being of white English background, Ann of Jamaican background. From the start, it was clear there was no messing around Ann. Why is it I was never confronted with easy-going, quiet, non-confrontational characters these days?

We had a quick chat at first and then we skyped James. He was at home with Jazz and Zeno, who had briefly summarised for him the outcome of that afternoon's negotiations for the Relocated. He was upbeat when he answered the online call. The first few minutes, Ann was ecstatic – and loud – to see her husband. Soon he was crying, telling her how much he loved her. Things turned a bit more complicated when James asked after the children. The boy had taken the disappearance of his father very badly. Ann preferred not to share with him the feeling of betrayal and abandonment she had had when she thought her husband had left them. The daughter too was in a very poor state. She was, I learned, suffering from an acute case of bacterial meningitis, one that was getting worse alarmingly fast with the stress the girl was going through since she 'lost' her dad. At this rate, the infection could do irremediable damage to her nerves and brain. I had a case of conscience and jumped into their conversation.

'James. The crossing cures bacterial infection. Completely,' I reminded him.

James did not hesitate before saying she ought to cross 'it'. What followed was a weird explanation to Ann Fisher of how we could save her daughter and the risks involved. I knew not to just talk about supernatural Fog again, considering her reaction when her husband first mentioned it, so I used a different approach: a mysterious medical discovery! To make it brief, I told her that we had a way of saving her daughter, but it was extremely confidential and she was to keep it a secret from everyone. Inspired, I explained it had come to our attention recently that some particles had the power to cleanse the body of any infections. However, there was a risk involved, as one in seven of the patients had to be sent to a distant location as a side effect. The body could no longer process life in the modern world with all its pollution and so on (in other words, I lied). Not everyone had this side effect, but when they did, they couldn't come back. This is what had happened to her husband. (I was surprising myself how easily I was distorting the truth into some believable rubbish.) Their daughter might be cured without side effects although there was a risk that what happened to her husband might happen to her too.

Ann Fisher listened to me intently, then asked, 'Could I go with her? If she was sent, would I be able to go with her?'

'Nobody can say prior to receiving the treatment.' I was trying to sound professional. 'And if you do, you would also run the risk of being separated from your son.'

'Could he get the treatment as well?'

'Yes, of course, you could all cross … I mean, pass … Have the treatment.'

'And James would be in this other place, if she has to go and not me?'

'Yes, he would.'

'Then, let's do it. Whatever can save Maisie.'

'Are you sure? I mean, you really understand the consequences? You may end up separated from your children.'

'But the treatment would get rid of any viruses. My daughter would be cured. The children's welfare will always come first to me. They would be with their father.'

'Your son doesn't have to. You could just have your daughter do it and only if she is relocated would you need to.'

'Yes …'

James had been listening all the while, nodding. I could tell he was biting his tongue to let me do the talking. When I finished, he asked me to explain to his wife how different life in the new community was. I told her there was another small community there, very traditional in their way of life and thinking. The newbies would live every day like them, but when needed they could come to a communication centre with phone, internet and so on. Things may develop from this rustic life, although nothing was defined for now. So life was quite simple, it was also quite an adventure, with lot of potential. James added he would set up a business there and he might need her help. He also said that when Maisie had gone through the treatment, whether or not she was relocated, they would need to discuss the family's future, him being away for good. Ann nodded, then said to him, 'I'm sorry I shouted at you, the other day. I should have known you wouldn't do that to us, betray and leave us. Not willingly.'

'My love. Of course I wouldn't. Don't worry, I understand. You couldn't have known. I love you.'

The scene was touching. Witnessing the love and sorrow in both of them reminded me of Michael. I loved him so much. I didn't think I could ever love someone again. Not like that, not with the same passion in my flesh, tenderness in my heart and care in my mind. I thought of Leo, the charming Leo, and how he was tickling my senses and arousing my desire. Still, I felt my heart was sealed up. Maybe because I was scared to love and lose again, maybe because I had had my one love, I didn't know. The FTab beeped. It had beeped messages several times already in the background during the online call. It brought me back to the present and the company. Shaking away the memories, I asked Ann Fisher when she and the children would be available to come for 'treatment'. Tonight was not possible as she needed to get Maisie out of hospital first. I suggested Saturday morning and she agreed. It would also give her time to think things through. It was a big decision to make.

As soon as I left Ann Fisher at the hotel, I checked the messages received on my FTab. The first was from Leo, asking me for another date the next day, Friday. I agreed without hesitation! The next message was from Leila, updating me on the situation east of London. All she wrote was that the rescue mission had started and she would keep me informed by the minute. A third message was from Harry to let me know he was on his way to Essex, within a twenty-mile radius of where they had located Jack. Harry was to help to get Jack back to our world once they'd retrieved him. The Society didn't want Harry on the rescue site as they would not risk either his safety during the confrontation, nor for him to be taken by the other side, so the timing would be crucial. Should they break in and have to leave urgently, without being able to get Jack, Jack would have to hide in the Fog until they could return. Harry had mentioned that with one remaining Facilitator unaccounted for there was the possibility the kidnappers had this person too. Harry's idea was far-fetched: how would they have discovered the Facilitator? However, it was a possibility not to be dismissed. The waiting had started, with hopes that all would go swiftly and smoothly. I feared for Jack. My understanding was that he was a nice yet fragile person. That wasn't an evening for a fragile person.

Returning to the house, the first thing I saw on the floor by the side of the staircase was Maud Poff's basket. Empty. The past hour with Ann Fisher and the thought of the arrow which could have killed us had made me forget the basket and its mysterious contents. The flowers were in a vase on the centre of the dining table. Jazz was at the table too, typing away on her laptop. Simba had been jumping at my legs from the moment I crossed the threshold. I bent down to play with her a little, talking to Jazz, 'Was it you who took the flowers out of the basket?' I asked.

'Yes, they were losing their mojo.'

'Was there something else in ...?' I started.

'In your room. I put it on your bed. By the way, Mr Fisher is behind you, on the sofa. He was waiting for you.'

I had totally forgotten that too. Of course, he had come for the video conference call. He didn't have the choice, after all.

'Mr Fisher. Sorry, I ...' I turned to speak to him

'Not a problem. Didn't we say you would call me James?'

'James it is.'

James nodded and said, 'Thank you for your help today. You've been amazing. You've saved my daughter.'

'Not yet. Why didn't you mention her condition earlier?'

'I ... I don't know. It's too personal. I wanted to talk to my wife and ... and I thought they were lost them to me. I don't know. I thought maybe you wouldn't understand, if you take her approach of just having to cut the ties.' He nodded towards Jazz.

'I am here you know! Rude! I will just ignore you too, then, shall I?' Jazz snapped. 'Actually, I think I will just disappear into my room.' With this she unplugged her laptop, put it under her arm and left.

'You are misjudging Jazz, you know,' I said to James when she had gone. 'She has a heart of gold, even if she can seem to be as hard as nails on the surface. That's her way of dealing with the situation, suppressing her emotions to cope better.'

'Will it really cure my daughter, this Fog? Because I was pretty unwell after crossing it.'

'From shock maybe? Its healing powers seem to be common knowledge for anyone familiar with the Fog. Even today, the Lil'London Council referred to it. So, based on this, yes, it will help your daughter.'

'One out of seven is relocated ... Maybe my family will be able to join me then. How many people have crossed and haven't been relocated so far?'

'In London, two that we know of. I would think it unlikely that the three of them would cross and relocate. Also, would you really wish that for them? Would you advise your wife to cross and your son too, if your daughter were relocated? That is a tough call to make.'

James Fisher remained silent. It was a difficult decision for sure. I invited him to lunch on Saturday. If he stayed afterwards, he would meet with a certain Barnaby Sparrow of Lil'London and his son. It would be a good way to have a little get together at home with people other than the members of the council from WII. After he left, I went upstairs, Simba at my heels. She followed me at a snail's pace, each step being a mini-challenge to her. When she was all grown up, it would be a piece of cake. I waited for her at the top of the steps to congratulate her on her achievement, and knocked at Jazz's door to let her know about the visits on Saturday.

'Who are the Sparrows?'

'Barnaby is a blacksmith, I think. It's just a guess. He looked like one and had a blacksmith's apron. Jonas is his son. The father looks clever and the son daring. It will be nice to have a different perspective on Lil'London, don't you think? They're coming to have a good look at Zeno's cross-country bike and I already have it in mind to invite them inside for coffee. Now James Fisher will join too.'

Jazz asked what was going to happen with James's daughter. She had heard the first part of the conversation, I remembered, but didn't know the details. After I told her, she shook her head. 'Poor man. Poor girl. I'm not sure, aside from the Fog curing her, what to wish for either of them: relocation or no relocation. The father wouldn't be alone, but robbing the daughter of a normal life ...'

'Me neither. I don't know. What do you call a normal life? Everything is relative. The folks of Lil'London have a normal life in their eyes. So is the life of the Inuit in Alaska, for them.'

Zeno was not at home. Jazz told me he was in WII, she didn't know what he was up to but expected he was exploring the forest. It was easiest not to talk about the arrow. By then it felt like a blur, and I wondered if it could have been a fast bird, flying low. Instead, I gave Jazz the latest news about the operation underway to get Jack back. As I left her, my FTab beeped. I gave it a quick glance and smiled. Leo was asking if I would like pizza for tomorrow. He had made enquiries and found a reputable place just ten minutes away by cab.

'Your secret admirer? Or dare I say, lover?' Jazz glanced at me, looking mischievous.

'Mmmm ... Yes,' I replied, turning and going to my room.

'And this letter on your bed. Do you have a secret admirer in the Lil'London too?'

'Yes. Today, flowers, tomorrow, a goat!' I teased her.

'Ha ha ha! No really, Zeno told me the flowers were from Maud Poff. Just wondering what's up? You have a secret informer in the place already?'

'I wish! I have no idea what's up. I didn't even know what was hidden in the basket, just that there was something. I will go and read this letter now.'

'I have put the book from Lil'London on your bed too. I guess that's one more book for me to read?'

'Yes.'

'I am so excited ...'

In my room I chose the mysterious letter as a priority over the *Lil'London Tales*. Ripping it open, I inwardly made a note to myself that they had paper for writing, envelopes and books. The whole machinery for it would be quite valuable. I unfolded ten sheets. A quick glance at the last one confirmed it was signed by Maud Poff. Her handwriting was small with elegant and clear lines. It reminded me of manuscript letters seen in museums. Before beginning, as the letter was long and should receive proper attention, I decided to make myself comfortable with a pot of tea. I put on a comfy cardigan with large pockets, picked Simba up and stuffed her in one of the cardigan's pockets. It gave me a pang of tenderness, seeing how cute and little she was, not complaining one bit but adapting to everything so naturally. Then I hopped downstairs. I was excited. It was bound to be interesting, my first letter from another world.

The letter proved a little strenuous to interpret. It made me both smile and frown: smile about its old-fashioned style, out-of-fashion even; frown because I was sometimes unsure of the meaning behind the words used. Indeed, Maud Poff addressed it to Miss Salelles and surprisingly wrote it in old French. Her unusual turn of phrase was baffling, either incorrect or just unknown to me. She opened by expressing how delighted she was that the long awaited reopening of the door between our two worlds had occurred. Their whole community had been expecting the occurrence, without any certainty it would actually happen. They also did not know where. Maud then mentioned that she had read in the archives of Lil'London there had been times when no newcomers had arrived for about seven hundred years. That made me think. It could easily be that the Fog had not been found, as it was in a remote place not affecting many people from our side, but it was worth asking Leila about it. She added that she had found me charming and admirable. She had high hopes that my role as dignitary would refresh and shake up Lil'London. Maud continued that she was sorry to use the subterfuge of the flowers to pass on this letter and hoped not to have shocked or inconvenienced me. Her wish for secrecy related to the council who would disapprove of her actions. They would react with criticism towards Edmund and the rest of their close family.

'Much is to be done on so many levels, including, I am mortified to write, for women. I have heard from my spouse, Edmund, how differently you acted as a woman from the way women in our community would have done during your encounters with the members of the council. A woman of Lil'London would have been compelled to show humility. This is why I hope you will not judge my boldness in writing to you too harshly. Women are not equal to men in our world and are required to display respect in all our dealings with them. Only behind closed doors may we voice our thoughts and often men choose to silence us even then. Men are our masters, protectors and shepherds. We are to respect them. They will respect us if we deserve it. I thank God every day to have been blessed with a husband who respects me and has gladly opened new horizons to me. You may have noticed that

Edmund presents slightly differently from his peers on the council. He supports me in having interests that others would find too unusual for my sex and he accepts whims and confrontations most men would castigate me for. I am aware he does not approve of this letter, but nonetheless he kindly let me do as I wish.

It has come to my attention that you have much to bring to our town and our people and not just in science and trade. I fear some will try to control your influence on our ways of life. Edmund has informed me of his intention to introduce you to Lil'London's past. My intention is to enlighten you on a subject he could not possibly allude to in the official annals: the stories behind the people. I have read the practice of politicians is to know well the other parties involved. Lil'London has waited too long to waste time. I would not pretend to give you a perfect portrayal of Lil'London and my humble writing is flawed and partisan. My dear husband would inform you best. Be that as it may be, my darling Edmund is too reserved, despite his longing to communicate freely with you. From this letter, I hope you will understand you have an ally in him and in me for you to open the minds of our peers.'

I read how Edmund's father was in charge of the church and of the archives of Lil'London. It was a hereditary privilege and charge, transmitted every generation to the eldest son. From the age of seven, Edmund's father started to teach his son English, Latin and the verses of the Bible. Edmund spent much time studying the curves of his father's and forefathers' handwriting of and he struggled. Many times, his father went into rages; many times, his mother wiped his tears and asked him to try harder, but Edmund was very slow. One Sunday, his favourite day as he did not have to study, Maud's parents came to visit after mass to discuss some matters with his father and she accompanied them. She was 6 years old.

'Your father talks strange,' she said to him. He just looked at her, wondering what she was on about. He had seen her around of course at the Sunday services in church, but never had they spoken.

'When we all have to be quiet and listen to him. Your father talks strange. Why?'

'He speaks Latin.'

'What is it? Why?'

He replied once he understood what she meant. Finding it difficult to explain, Edmund went to get his Latin book and showed it to Maud.

'You see, he is reading text written in this old language.'

'Why?'

'Because the Bible is in Latin.'

Maud seemed to ponder on this one, then asked, 'Do you talk Latin?'

Edmund hesitated. 'A little bit.'

'Can you say something to me?'

'Assiduus usus uni rei deditus et ingenium et artem saepe vincit.' Edmund savoured the look of wonder on the little girl. He looked up and said, 'It means "Constant practice devoted to one subject often outdoes both intelligence and skills."' The sentence had a bitter taste, his father repeatedly said it to him when he struggled over his texts. He found it difficult to recognise letters and understand words. The next sentence from Maud shook him out of his reverie.

'Why do you speak Latin and we don't?'

'Not everybody needs to learn Latin.'

'Can I learn Latin?'

'Why do you want to learn Latin?'

'I want to understand.'

'Girls don't learn Latin.'

'Why?'

Edmund couldn't answer the little girl's question. He wasn't sure why girls didn't learn Latin. He had only heard his father say it to his sister and took it as a fact. Maud persisted, 'Would you teach me Latin?'

Edmund just looked at the little girl, bewildered. How could he, who struggled so much to learn every day, teach her anything?

'Pleeease!' a tenacious Maud begged.

'I can show you,' he said hesitantly.

He ran to his father's study, retrieved his old Latin book and ran back. Both children sat in a corner of the church hall and he started showing her the words. For the first time, showing her what he knew, how it worked, and answering her simple questions, he enjoyed the Latin sentences. When Edmund struggled to answer a question or gave a long explanation, Maud would turn it into a simple image that she would understand and more often than not she was spot on. He started seeing Latin as simpler to understand than he had previously. (Reading Maud's letter, I thought that Edmund was suffering from dyslexia. Maud's practical approaches must have simplified the texts and rules for him and, helped him feel more confident, finally overcoming his blocks.) After an hour, they heard Maud's parents calling for her. He had a surge of fear: 'Don't tell anyone I have been showing you Latin.'

'Why?'

'Girls don't learn Latin. I think they would be upset with both of us.'

'If I don't tell anyone, will you continue to teach me?'

'I will,' he answered on an impulse, wondering afterwards why he had said yes.

'When?'

He thought a little.

'Would you be able to meet me in church for thirty minutes every day?'

'My mother would like it if I went to church every day. She says we need to pray daily.'

'We could study in a corner of the church.'

'God would not be upset that we are in the church and we do not pray?'

'If we read the Bible in Latin, we are reading His words. He would be happy I think.'

She pondered and agreed. She would come to church every day and learn the Bible in Latin.

'How come you know how to read?' Edmund asked, suddenly realising that she had known the alphabet already when he had showed her the letters.

'You promise you will not tell?'

'I promise. Then we have to keep each other's secrets.'

'My brother explains to me every night what he has learned during the day.'

Edmund was amazed by the little girl now running back to her parents. Her name was Maud and she wanted to learn Latin. He had never wanted to learn Latin. He had never asked to do it. It had been imposed on him because he needed it for his function as an adult. She didn't need it, but she had learned to read and write already and now she wanted to learn Latin. He considered that she would probably not go to school for another year and then she would receive the basic education he had seen his sister receive. His older sister knew less than him. Girls didn't need as much. Maybe the adults were wrong, though. Maud seemed to need more and she found ways to get it. Edmund was happy that evening at the dinner table. He thought of what he would show Maud the next day in Latin. He also thought that some of the practical images she had used for Latin could be used for English, too. That night he took his books out and they didn't seem that heavy. Something had lifted in him. He felt less alone. He had something to share and someone to share it with.

Edmund and Maud's friendship grew over the years. At first she went to church for just the thirty minutes, but as months and years passed, their bond grew stronger and stronger. Both parents became aware of the uncommon friendship. A childhood fancy, they thought. They could see it benefitted them both, the children seemingly more stable and focused. Edmund achieved excellence in his studies and Maud got less wild and annoyingly inquisitive. He still lacked confidence with other children of his age. Edmund was less articulate and comfortable in society than at home or with her. His father noticed his introverted nature, as well as the books from his study that went temporarily missing, first on Latin and later on French, history and science. He knew the books were for Maud. He liked the girl and later the young woman. She had a sharp mind and he valued intelligence, but it didn't suit a girl. She would sometimes join the family for tea after school and he could see her listening to him talk of the other world and memorising as much as she could. Sometimes she would murmur something and Edmund would bend his head slightly to listen to her. Edmund's father soon understood she was asking a question or making an observation and Edmund would repeat it aloud for her. His father would then comment to Edmund and see her nod or frown, depending if she agreed or not. He remembered, she must have been twelve, when she had asked a question directly, bluntly. He had had to put her in her place, telling her that matters of history and science are not a concern for womenfolk and she should focus on what suits her gender. He had had to tell her off for her sake and his own daughters'. Maud had never again asked a direct question on a sensitive subject. He accepted her presence and their little game because she seemed to stimulate his son. It irritated him though, he wished for his son to be stronger on his own. Soon, he would have to create some distance between them. His boy was now 17 and she had just turned 14. He wanted his son to wed one of the Snayth or the Hoare daughters. He had tried to push Edmund to approach them at the dances, but Edmund and Maud were inseparable. Edmund, who surprised everyone as a good dancer, would only do his duty and invite the girls from the council families to dance once, then he would return to Maud. When Maud was dancing or laughing with her many friends, he would just stand watching the crowd or her. Edmund's father was wary of this. His son had grown into a man and for some time, he had been looking at Maud as a man looks at a woman. It would soon be time for her to marry and start looking after her husband and a family. This friendship had to stop.

After tea, Edmund's mother observed Maud as she played with the dog in the garden. Edmund was sitting nearby with a book. Other children and teenagers were running around too, some hers, some cousins', some neighbours'. She was proud of her son. He had turned into a very bright young man. Although he was reserved, without much presence in public, he had a depth and thirst for knowledge equalled only by Maud's. Like his father, he knew the Bible by heart. He was ready for his function as the next church leader. However, he had a humanity that was different from his father. In his friendship with Maud, she was an equal. She could not express it properly, she lacked the concept, but in her heart she knew he would never be a man who would act as a master to a woman, but would seek a partnership with whomsoever he would marry. She looked at how Maud came and sat on the bench by his side, how he stopped reading, how she said something and he smiled looking at her in the eyes and how, after a nudge from her shoulder to his shoulder, he went back to his book. Edmund's mother stared at the two youngsters in the garden, silent and so comfortable with each other. The mother could not see how they would not remain together. 'God, please help them always be so happy together,' she prayed. She added in a low voice, to herself, 'I will try to help you, my son. I will try to talk to your father.'

Edmund and Maud were wed one year later in the summer. Their union was not a scandal per se, as everyone had known of their friendship for years. The misalliance still deeply annoyed the Hoares and the Snayths. They had hoped the tradition of keeping unions within the decision-making families would be respected. Maud was the daughter of the miller, who was reliant on the Snayths for their vast crops. The Snayths had their own mill for private consumption, so they could very well expand theirs and dismiss Maud's family mill. As it would affect many businesses by ricochet, there was a tacit agreement they would not do so: it created a dependence of Maud's family on the Snayths. Benjamin and Barbara Snayth's attitude towards the Poff couple betrayed their feeling that Maud was not one of theirs. They were barely polite, slightly dismissive with Maud and condescending to Edmund (after all, he had married beneath him and was totally inadequate to deal with the affairs of the town, even if they had to admit that as church leader and historian, he was the best the town had ever had. A pity he was such a recluse.) Maud and Edmund had been happy as husband and wife for the eighteen years up to Yoko and Zeno's arrival. Like anyone, they had had their own troubles, like Maud's difficulty bearing children. The twins were born seven years into their marriage, which was late for a woman in Lil'London. Anne and Charles (or Annie and Charlie as their parents called them) were benefitting from their parents' open minds on equal education and from their vast learning. They were now 9 and fluent in English, Latin, French and Italian – or at least the old versions of it – and pretty good at maths, too.

Maud had never managed to have more children and after many miscarriages Edmund asked her not to try any more: he feared for his wife's life, that one of the miscarriages would be fatal. They started planning their intercourse accordingly. It made the couple even more different from the rest of the wealthy families of Lil'London. Children were precious, they represented the future of the community, and social pressure urged married couples to have large families. The wealthiest men would take a second or third wife when the first one grew too old or proved unable to conceive, in order to continue to extend their family and consequently, their power. Some had expected Edmund would do so. Some, the ones who understood the couple better, had only dared hope it would be so. Edmund was not interested in sharing his life with anyone other than Maud, his children, his books and library and his printing machine. He had faith in God and would fulfil his duties in the church with care. From the pulpit he would talk well, although never looking at the crowd but lost in his beliefs. Yet faith in knowledge was the strongest of all. The Poffs had less wealth than the other members of the council. Much less wealth. They had the power of the church and the Word behind them. His revenue came from a small part of the levy paid by outsiders coming into town for commerce and from the town tax. Augustus Hoare and Benjamin Snayth also both had a share. Edmund had land, but land was not a rare commodity in their world, its value was mostly in its proximity to the town and its fertility. On this, Snayth had the best of all.

I reached the end of Maud Poff's letter with sadness. Maud had captivated me with her story and the humanity behind it. Another world, same people. Social pressure, family dramas, individual struggles and money were omnipresent. Sure, the society structure and priorities were different, but not the people.

Maud finished the letter mentioning she had intended to write about all the members of the council, but she'd got carried away with her own story. It was probably for the best not to put in writing the details of her opinions of others. Would it be possible to meet up instead?

I was very keen to hear what she had to say. I would have to try and find a reason to have a private meeting with her. 'Something related to the church?' I thought. 'Some questions on the history of Lil'London?'

I checked my watch: I had been reading for a good hour nonstop. The light on my FTab was beeping, notifying me of messages. I vaguely remembered hearing it earlier, but absorbed by the letter, I forgot. I had several messages from Leila. 'Jack, I had forgotten about Jack!' I realised, avidly opening the first one. It was timed close to an hour earlier. Leila was informing me the rescue mission was not going as well as they had hoped it would. They were facing strong resistance from the house, which had now turned into a siege. There had been shooting. The Society had intercepted calls to the police and delayed transferring them for as long as possible. It couldn't be for long. The Society had to move in soon before the police showed up.

The second message was not the bearer of better news. The Society rescue team had finally managed to break in and raid the house. There were wounded from both sides. No dead, thank goodness! Unfortunately, the raid had no concrete results. The inhabitants and defenders escaped, and Jack was neither in the house nor in the immediate Fog around the house. They had called for Dante and Leo urgently to check if he was in the Other World. That would mean that the other party had either a Facilitator or a Relocated. Leila mentioned the last option was that Jack had escaped on his own in the Fog and feared coming back in. If so, I may need to go and scan the Fog world. Just as I was finishing reading her last message, Leila called.

'Leila, I just read your message. Terrible! Of course I am coming!'

'No need.' She sounded weary and tired.

'But ...'

'He is on the other side. In the Other World.'

'How do you ...?' I began.

'One of our men got relocated during the raid. He was able to accompany Dante and Leo, a protection in case the others had been able to set up some kind of operation there. His training and experience came in very handy: he saw the tracks. One of heavy boots and one of trainers being dragged along, both coming out of the house and going through the forest. We can conclude the new Relocated took charge of Jack when the house was raided, bringing him to World II. Our mercenary, Leo and Dante got shot at shortly after they came out of the Fog in the Other World. Our guy was in front and protected them. He got hit in the chest, a good thing he was wearing a bullet-proof vest. They retreated. It is an ideal sniper situation out there: there is nowhere to hide getting out of the fog. We couldn't take immediate action. Getting organised proved impossible in the end as the police showed up. We may control calls, we don't control their radio. We had to make a swift exit. Our man, Nick, has a geological map of England and the coordinates of your house in Lil'London. He is a pro. He went out of the house, walked round it in the Fog and crawled out under cover of night. He will try to find the other two and get Jack back if he can. If he can't, he will shadow them. In any case, he will make his way back to yours. This is such a mess. Can we come to see you tomorrow morning? 9 a.m. OK?'

'Sure, come over. See you in the morning,' I told her, thinking of Jack lost with a dangerous man. It could have been me. 'Poor guy,' I repeated inwardly. Depending what Zeno had found, I would tell her about the arrow in the morning as well.

Simba was sniffing around. I stood up quickly to put her on the newspaper left in my bedroom for her, then thought better of it, quickly went down and out in the Fog around the house. Just in time too. I thought the sooner she learned to do her needs outside the better and she seemed clever enough to learn fast. Going back to my room, I stopped by Jazz's on the way. She was on the phone and broke off her conversation with her parents for one second, signalling to me not to speak so that they would not be aware of my presence. They believed her to be travelling in south-east Asia. Jazz had deep tired eyes, red from crying. The situation was taking its toll on her. We really ought to get her to Lil'London more and find her an activity there: she couldn't possibly remain stuck in the house all the time. I could tell, too, that she had already started to gain a bit of weight. This was unlike her and not a good sign.

After dinner, Zeno and I told the others in the house about the arrow incident as we were coming back. Zeno also updated us all on his going to the forest after I had left to meet with Ann Fisher.

'We found the arrow,' he told us. 'I spoke with Hoare on the radio. He came immediately. Sadly there is no way of identifying who shot at us from this arrow. With him and his men, we went through the forest to find where the archer had waited for us. We found it. It wasn't helpful, there were no leads or clues there.'

'So we have no way of knowing who or why?' I asked.

'Not at present. Hoare will organise patrols going through the forest day and night from now on for our protection. It will not happen again.'

'You can't be sure of that! Oh Yoko! This is terrible! Someone tried to kill you. Or Zeno. Or both!' Jazz exclaimed.

To both our surprise, even though we took the episode very seriously, Zeno and I also both decided not to make a big deal out of it and to continue our dealing with Lil'London as before. Zeno told me that the reactions of shock by the watchmen and outrage by Hoare could only be genuine. With patrols going through the forest, it would now be highly unlikely there would be a repeat. Of course, we would have to be extra cautious nonetheless. Zeno also decided to let the council of Lil'London, and anyone else they encountered, know that they had guns. It was a good deterrent against any attack: if anyone attacked us and missed, we wouldn't. Or Zeno wouldn't. Because of our relaxed attitude towards the incident, Harry, Rico and Jazz didn't comment for long. It was obvious it had been a blow to their morale and they were upset about it. It was put aside, but certainly not forgotten.

'I think I will have nightmares tonight. We can't even wear bullet-proof jackets to protect us against that thing! Or can we?' I asked no one in particular

'I can bet you're going to Google this the minute you are in your room,' Zeno said to me, winking.

**Day 6 (Friday)**

Despite the thoughts that troubled me before I drifted into dreamland, it was the best night's sleep in a long time. So much so I felt guilty when thinking of Jack and the loneliness and fear he must be going through.

As for Nick, the Society's latest Relocated, he gave Leila an account of that first night spent in the Other World by two-way radio. She repeated his account to us. Nick was a mercenary with experience in various dangerous countries, situations, or natural environments around the world. Still this was different. No one really knew what, or where, World II was, and if it had unknown creatures and dangers. He even had to smother a side of his brain thinking of vampires and werewolves. When he realised he could not track Jack and his captor in the dark without switching on a torch that would betray his whereabouts, he decided to climb a tree to rest for the night, away from any prey he could think of and the ones he didn't want to imagine. There may be danger up there he was not aware of, but he had to weigh up the situation and the tree was the best he could think of. So he roped himself to a branch and tried to sleep, remaining conscious of each noise in the night. He patted the map in his breast pocket hoping it was correct. At least he had an understanding of his whereabouts if the map really was accurate. In the morning, he hunted for clues of Jack's and the other guy's whereabouts. There were traces on the ground where the man had positioned himself ready to shoot. He also found an area a bit further on where they had spent the night, Jack apparently attached to the trunk of a tree. The other man was not to be found and Nick thought he must have been on a branch too. Jack was the one leaving most of the tracks and everything indicated the Relocated from the other party was a professional like him. That professional must have decided to be less noticeable because Jack's tracks disappeared suddenly. What would he have done in their shoes? Nick explained to Leila. 'Knowing I would be tracked, I'd need to either lose them – easy on my own, less with Jack – or hide him, go back, hide or confuse the tracks and let some time pass.' Nick was on his own and not in a strong position. He could be watched, was an easy target and ought to be on his guard. Nick decided to disappear. He would make his way to us, making sure he was not followed.

Despite all of the bad news and events of the day before, I had woken up serene. There had been good moments on Thursday, and these were the points to concentrate on. Due to Maud Poff's beautiful letter, I had a brand new opinion of her husband. It was subjective of course, she was writing about the man she loved. It confirmed nonetheless the glimpse of him that surprised me at the Lil'London Council meeting. Edmund Poff was not the fidgety insecure weasel anymore, but shy, eccentric, introvert, at ease only with his family, books and studies. A reclusive passionate book-worm. I made the decision to go and hear him preach next Sunday and it hit me: that was it! It was how to meet with Maud Poff in pri-vate! I just had to express beforehand that I would be delighted to meet with the leader of the church after mass to discuss local faith in and history. Hopefully, the other two members of the council and their wives would not crash the encounter with the Poffs, so that I could have a private and instructive, gossipy even, chat.

Now I only had to get in touch with Edmund Poff to coordi-nate it all. The two-way radios requested the day before would be delivered today. My idea was to prepare three parcels, one for each member of the council, with radios, user instructions and a time for interaction. In the long term we ought to find a way to block their radios on a specific frequency, so they could not lis-ten to my conversations with Zeno or others. For today, allocating a specific frequency individually to the members of the council would do it. James as well. Eavesdropping was to be controlled for now, to be eliminated soon. I wrote to Leila about the need for two-way radios blocked on separate frequency. I would keep a record of which one was for which person. James would have to return his old one

Aside from messages to Leila, the flow of exchanges with Leo had not dwindled since our night together on Monday. They were getting cheekier too. By which, I mean saucier. I couldn't wait to see him again tonight, just the two of us, for dinner. I needed to check with Jazz if she could look after Simba for me.

I was buzzing with energy and ideas for the day ahead. I had a quick shower, pulled on some comfortable clothes and walked downstairs. Here I was in my temporary office. Jazz was already at the dining table, in dressing gown and slippers, cup of coffee nursed in her hand, jug of coffee (already down to half-full) on the table. She looked terrible. As I sat down in front of her, she looked up with a weak smile, 'Do you need me to go out with you for Simba?'

'Jazz, are you OK? You look like you haven't slept a wink.' She was pale, her eyes were hollowed, puffy and with heavy dark circles underneath. She had most likely cried all night.

'I am good. Let me just put some clothes on and we can take Simba out.' She stood up and went upstairs. My high spirits dampened, I found myself feeling very selfish. I'd got excited about my new life, new home, new goals, and new challenges, all without being totally cut out of my previous life. She was in a completely different situation. She had not found anything to get excited about, she missed her family and friends and was right now dealing with the sale of her beloved home. Finding something exciting for her to do in Lil'London was urgent, before the low mood turned into total depression. While she was getting ready my FTab beeped a message's arrival. Leila had already been active and efficient: the two-way radios would be delivered by courier within an hour, with a manual on how to use them and a note on which ones were blocked on specific frequencies. The Society had also got me a 'master' box linked to the radios with red lights allocated to each frequency, with lights that lit up when in use. The magic box was already set up for me, so all I needed to do was to keep track on who had which radios/allocated frequency. I would take extra care.

Jazz was back down in no time. She had also chosen easy comfortable clothes, donning a pair of jeans, a jumper and thick shoes.

'Jazz, come on, talk to me,' I said when we were out. She cradled her cup of coffee in her hands, holding it against her chest, lips pursed. She didn't answer me.

'Jazz, I can see you've been crying.'

'I am just a bit emotional, that's all.'

'I am so sorry! Because of me ...' My sentence remained unfinished as she interrupted me.

'Stop saying that. You know I don't blame you. It isn't your fault what is happening. You don't control any of it, including my being stuck here.'

'I am also sorry because I can't help you.'

'You do. You are taking the best possible care of me. My relocation could not have happened with a better person by my side.'

We were silent for a few minutes, looking at Simba playing in the grass. The forest was so peaceful, so calm. Cold, too. Jazz took a few sips of coffee and said, 'I've sold my house. Next, I will organise the move. Hopefully your house will be ready next week and I'll be able to settle in this one. Then my old life will be over. All I'll have left of it will be the house and you guys.' With that last comment, she burst out crying. A big, loud, messy cry. Within ten minutes, we were both in tears, sitting on the ground with cold damp butts, hugging each other and Simba climbing all over us to ease away our sorrow. We shook ourselves out of our big sobbing girly moment when Jazz attempted to sip from her mug: there was no more coffee. In Jazz's world, coffee was like chocolate the damsel in distress: it was essential to the healing process and to move forward.

Rico was in the kitchen preparing a new pot of coffee and we could hear Zeno on the phone in the living room, jabbering in Italian. Harry was already at the university.

'Hey babe. Jazz. Early morning walk with Simba?' Rico asked not looking at us. He didn't notice our red and puffy eyes from the tears, engrossed in his breakfast preparation. It must have been a workout day from what he was making, separating egg whites and yolk for an egg-white only omelette. Rico took his training very seriously, as his athletic physique proved. Jazz and I tried to disappear quickly to her room, but he added, 'The tissues are in the left drawer.' He still hadn't looked at us. He was good! Maybe he understood women more sensibly than we thought.

'No thanks, we are fine now. We have decided that today is the day we will find something for Jazz to do in Lil'London. Something she will love. Something she can throw herself into and get excited by.'

'Shoe business?' Zeno suggested, as he entered the kitchen.

'Pastry shop?' said Rico.

'No. I thought of a coffee shop and I don't want to do that. I want something different, something a bit wild. I want it to be fun. I deserve to have a bit of fun. I haven't had any for some time,' Jazz replied.

'You miss your nights out, don't you?' I said, remembering how crazy she could be on a dance floor.

'Yes, being drunk with music,' she sighed, 'and not just with music.'

Rico, Zeno and I looked at each other. I could have sworn we had the same idea at the same time. Zeno nodded for me to start.

'Jazz, how about you create your own then? Open a lounge bar with a dancing area?' I suggested, rather excited by the idea.

'What are you talking about? Do you see me shaking my booty with the likes of Hoare under a disco ball? Really? Come on Yoko!' Jazz waved away the idea with a dismissive hand, while checking how long was left for the coffee to be ready.

'Think about it,' Zeno intervened for me.

'You could have the ground floor of the house set up with a bar located in the current kitchen,' I continued. 'You'd just have to open a large window in the wall. You would need to keep a little kitchen for basic bar stuff. Then our dining room could be the drinking area with a few tables and sofas, the living room a dance floor surrounded by comfortable sofas too. The house is fogged, so you can keep electricity and … television!'

'You could even have movies or TV shows projected that people can see from the drinking area and bar,' interjected Zeno.

'And private parties,' I added.

'Would you play house music? And rap? If you play rap I'll be a regular. Hell! I could even DJ on special nights?' asked Rico.

Jazz was looking at us, first sceptical, then the idea seemed to take shape in her head. Her face started to lighten up.

'Me … launching a trendy bar between two worlds … This is quite cool. I won't have many customers though – James Fisher and me.'

'And the Foggies. And the families of Relocated – the ones who know. And some of the Society's members maybe?' I said.

'There will be a few curious people from the Other World too. Especially with the television and movies,' Zeno said.

'I could dedicate the first floor to television and movies. We'd have three rooms there: one room for general screening, one for private screening. I could also keep what is my tiny room now as my office and have my bedroom and a guest room upstairs, which you would use Yoko. Then of course, there might be more and more Relocated ones later.'

'Historical movies could prove to be a hit with the Lil'London folk,' I thought aloud.

I was getting more and more animated by the idea. So was Jazz. She was a brand new person in comparison with the one I cried with minutes earlier. Her eyes were sparkling. She was back to being her bubbly self.

'And in the afternoon, I could be a coffee shop!'

'I thought you didn't want to do this?' Rico asked. He was a bit taken aback she had changed her mind so fast.

'I didn't, but now it makes sense. It is good for business to open to a larger public and longer hours too.'

'And are you going to do the baking for this coffee shop?' I teased her. Baking was far from her favourite activity and not her best talent either. She usually stayed with the basics.

'I may need your help there,' she puppy-eyed me.

'It would have been a pleasure, but I may struggle with time,' I replied. 'I'll do as much as I can.' I was sorry to say this, especially as I love creating in the kitchen. It was true though, but I couldn't see myself having the time.

'I will give you a few recipes and teach you how to prepare them. With your late night opening hours, you won't want to be in the kitchen early in the morning. You will need a minimalist selection of delicious food rather than a vast choice. Plus, you wouldn't cope with it in the long term. Quality rather than quantity will be your trademark.'

'Yes, yes, yes! I like that idea! Simple basic things and that is it. OK, I have got work to do. If you want me, I will be in my office in the room next door. Make space on the dining table, I am coming!' With this last enthusiastic comment, she hurried out of the kitchen, up to her room and within a few seconds ran back downstairs laptop in hand. I only had had the time to grab a couple of cups and poured in the freshly made coffee. Rico went back to his omelette which was now sticking in the pan, Zeno returned a call he hadn't answered and I joined Jazz in the dining room. It was about 9.30 a.m. and everyone had a smile on their face.

I had just sat down and taken two sips of coffee when the doorbell rang. I frowned: people did not come to the house unannounced anymore. Leo, Dante and Leila were not due to drop by this morning. I hoped it would be James Fisher or someone from Lil'London, as anybody else would be at risk of being relocated and we were not ready for more of them. Not yet. We would have to face that situation eventually, but the later the better. Zeno beat me to the door and I was right behind him when he opened the door to one of the builders working on the lot. I winced. He should not have been there.

'Hi! A courier came for you. I know we are supposed to leave it by the mailing box, but it's a big parcel and the area was cramped. I didn't want it damaged, so I thought ...'

'You shouldn't be here,' Zeno told him.

'I know. We were told not to come to the house and stick to the building site, but the parcel could have been damaged. So, I thought ...'

'Thank you,' I interrupted him, certain an inkling curiosity on his behalf was also involved. 'This is very kind of you. In the future, just give us a call on the buzzer, the one set up near the mailbox and we will come, so you don't have to. Thank you again,' I was trying to be optimistic, even though we had to check where he would return to.

'Zeno will walk you out,' I finished.

'That's OK, I ...' the man started to say.

'No, no, please let me,' Zeno cut in, already moving past the door and putting his hand on the man's shoulder to indicate it was time to move.

I saw them disappear into the Fog and waited. One minute later Zeno made his way back, the builder behind him. The man's confused and pale face revealed he was a new Relocated.

'Do come in,' I opened the door wide for the man and it was my turn to put my hand on his back, not for leading purpose this time but for reassurance. In the main room, Jazz looked up and saw us. She considered Zeno, me, the man and stood up.

'Let me handle this,' she said to Zeno and me.

'Jazz, that's OK, I ...' I began, but she interrupted me.

'Yoko, let me. It makes sense, I am one too.'

'There is still the possibility he is a Crosser, you know.'

'Remotely.' She turned to the builder. 'What is your name?'

'Tom. Thomas. Thomas Jameson.'

'Hello Thomas. I am Jazz and this is Yoko and Zeno. They live here and now I do too. I had no choice but to move in because of the forest you have just seen.'

'You see it too? What is ...' Thomas Jameson didn't have a chance to finish.

'Yes, I do. Now, let me explain what is happening. Let's sit over there, in the living room and have a chat.'

'But I need to go back to work.'

'I think you may want to listen to me first, then you will want to call in sick. Come.'

After checking what he wished to drink, I went to prepare a big mug of milky sweet tea for Thomas Jameson. Jazz was still going through her coffee pot. Zeno had gone back up in his room, talking on his mobile (although not before asking me to call him when Jazz was done). When I got into the kitchen, Rico was eating his breakfast, standing up against the counter.

'I heard. I chose to let you handle this one. It's good Jazz is speaking to him.'

'Yes .... She can be a bit abrupt sometimes though.'

'Yeah, but she will tell him they are both in the same shit. That is good.'

'It didn't work that well with James Fisher.'

'Stop Yoko! You can't do it all, you know.'

'Fine, fine! I get your drift. I have loads of other things to do anyway.'

'Me too, I am working on some awesome ideas for a painting right now. Actually, do you need to go into town?'

'No. You need to head out?'

'Yes, to the studio. Babe, you call me if you need me, OK?'

'I will do,' I acquiesced.

After this, Rico washed his dirty dishes and headed up to his room, stomping up the stairs. He always made as much noise as a mammoth running up and down. A good thing he slept later than everyone in the morning, he would wake a sloth. I picked up the large parcel brought in by Thomas Jameson, balancing the cup of tea on top with difficulty. I handed the cup to a Thomas Jameson deeply concentrated on Jazz's words and sat down at the table. Then, my headset on, music playing loud in my ears, the outside world disappeared for me. I didn't want to listen to what Jazz was telling him. Rico was right, I ought to take a step back on that one and let her proceed as she wished.

I reviewed the contents of the parcel: twenty two-way radios, half with blocked allocated frequencies labelled and half open to receive any signals. In addition, the parcel contained a 'magic' box with at least fifty small red bulbs, fewer than ten of which were labelled to match the ten blocked radios. A long list of instructions came with it, to be read in detail, whenever the days stretched to thirty hours.

To the tempo of indie music, I went into full organisation mode. I created a new folder on my computer labelled 'Foggy Business' in which I added sub-folders to be filled soon – Foggies, Relocated, WII Diplomacy, Trading, Society, Reports, Operations & Admin and the last one, for me, Personal Notes. Then I sorted out who would have which radio and, for the blocked ones, allocated a designated frequency to them. Poff, Snayth and Hoare in WII, as well as James Fisher and now Thomas Jameson, would have blocked radios. The open ones would go to our enlarged household, to Leila, Leo and Dante. The numbers had gone down fast. Five left for the limited batch, two for the other batch.

After reading the summary instructions for the manual, I started typing an explanatory letter to the Lil'London Council members with terms as simple and clear as possible, googling photos to illustrate my words. When done, I would just print the document in duplicate copy and put each in their respective packages. The Poffs would have a separate note about my wish to visit on Sunday.

The letter was taking more time than expected. I regularly cast an eye towards Jazz and Jameson. So far, only Jazz was doing the talking. The man was listening attentively, his whole face pinched in concentration and, maybe, incredulity. He was a big guy in stature. Tall, I would say 6'1" or 6'2", with big bones, big shoulders, big arms and big legs. He was a bit heavy on the weight too, taking up quite some space in the room. He was also the antithesis to small and dolly faced Jazz: once his builder's helmet was removed, he revealed a shaven head, with ears and eyebrow piercings, completed with arm and neck tattoos. It was full of prejudice, but this big guy was scary.

The light on my FTab indicated a message. I had not heard the usual sound due to the music resonating in my headset. The new message was from Leila enquiring if we had received the radios. I confirmed she had done a great job as usual and took the opportunity to update her on the Thomas Jameson situation. I checked my watch: Jazz had been talking for a good hour already. Did it always take that long? Leila was online and switched to instant messaging while my thoughts wandered to Jazz. My eyes skimmed Leila's words, not registering their meaning. I only landed back on earth when I read that the Society team was attempting to link mobiles and the box to transfer the radio communication onto the mobile. That would extend the communication with World II to a much wider range in this world. Following a sudden flash of inspiration thinking of 'mobile', I wrote to Leila we could get mobile homes for the Relocated! They really needed a fast and instant accommodation solution, an upgrade to trailers. I googled it and punched the air. There were plenty of choices that could be bought and delivered on the day, thus Fisher and Jameson would have a temporary solution from tonight. We could get generators or even solar powered energy in addition.

'I can't believe we didn't think about it sooner!' Leila commented.

'I think we were focused on the long term, not the fast solution, but yes, I can't believe it either,' I replied

'So simple.'

'We are not used to simple anymore.'

'So true.'

'We should catch up soon.'

'Lunch? And you get to meet the new guy?'

'Deal!' she finished.

Once the parcels to Snayth, Hoare and Poff were finished, with a special note in Edmund Poff's, I lifted the headset off my head, stood up and moved towards Jazz and Jameson. Listening in, Jazz was talking about the issue of catering for her lounge and the theme nights she had already thought of. She was working on ideas on how to best mingle Lil'London people and ours. I coughed to attract their attention.

'Yoko!' Jazz jolted in surprise. 'Sorry, I didn't see you standing there.'

'Not a problem. You were quite caught up in storytelling,' I smiled. She looked bright and happy after her long speech. Jameson, on the contrary, had not lost his intensity.

'I'm going to make a phone call,' he said, digging into his pocket for his mobile phone.

'Of course. Just ... I don't know if Jazz mentioned: it may not be a good idea at this point to mention the forest. Well, you have just received some quite hard-to-believe news. Someone else who hasn't seen the forest may find you ...' I tiptoed round my suggestion not to call.

'I must call Mum,' he snapped.

Now that was not what I expected. I had feared he would call one of his 'mates' to come and check us out and that we would end up having a whole gang being relocated somehow and they would turn into bandits in the Lil'London area. I had the whole bad Western movie scenario happening in my head already. I really needed to control my vivid imagination.

'Your mum! Could it wait because ...' I began.

'She needs to know that ...' He cut me off.

'... Jazz and I need to go out and maybe you would like to come with us and meet the watchmen of Lil'London?' I continued as if he had not interrupted me.

That stopped him in the midst of his dialling.

'How long will we be gone? And could I call her right after?' he asked, hesitantly.

'Say, fifteen minutes?' I told him.

'OK.'

'What are we going out for?' Jazz asked.

'I have some parcels for Lil'London Council members and I want to continue training Simba a bit.' Jazz nodded. She knew I was talking about teaching Simba to understand 'forest' and 'London' for her to help me cross in the future. I was convinced it could work within weeks if I persisted and was consistent.

As we walked back from dropping the parcels with Simba, I shared the idea of the mobile homes with Jazz and Big Tom – the nickname just came into my head. It seemed to fit him like a glove.

'How are you going to get the mobile homes into World II?' Jazz questioned.

'We are going to open wide the new front patio gates, drive the mobile homes in the Fog as close to the house as possible and pray that when a Relocated and Crosser drive them out again it will be in WII.'

'New front gates, you mean the wooden wall?'

'Yes. They are well thought through, as they open wide. Plus whatever plants are put in front of them are on wheels.'

'So you mean that tonight I will sleep in a mobile home in an unknown forest in an unknown world next to a supernatural Fog?' Big Tom asked. It was the first time he'd spoken in an assertive voice in front of me. He freaked me out. He had a deep controlled voice, the kind of voice psychopathic murderers have in horror films, talking sickly and sweetly while planting a knife in someone's gut. At least that is how I felt when hearing it, a sensation reinforced by his eyes narrowed on me. I wanted to run inside the house and lock the door.

'Errr ... Yes,' I uttered weakly. It was the truth and he had summed it up pretty well.

'Are those guys dangerous?' he asked Jazz and me.

'I don't think so,' I replied.

'They are weird.' Jazz replied. I shot her a look meant to say 'please don't start stirring!'

'Will you give me a gun?'

'No.'

'Why not?'

'I don't have a gun for you.' I didn't completely lie. We had two guns thanks to Zeno, but they were for us, not for him.

'Fine. I'll get one. I can get one for you both too. You want one?' He looked deadly serious. Gang images came rushing back.

'I'll get you a two-way radio,' I told him, switching subject. I hesitated to inform him that mobile phones worked in the vicinity of the house, but he broached the issue himself.

'What about mobile phones? Do they work over there? I guess not.'

'Signal is obviously a problem,' I replied, 'but as long as you are by the house, it works.'

'So what about the gun? Shall I organise one for you?'

I was going to say no, then I thought better of it. If this guy had dodgy connections, not only was it better to be in his good books, but also they could come in handy in the long term. Something could go wrong with the Society and then this would be another kind of help. Just in case, right? Also, if this guy were to hang around the house with a gun, he would know we were not harmless either with us having guns too.

'OK, we will. Just, there is no rush. In the meantime, we will give you big kitchen knives.'

'OK, love. Now, time for my mum.'

Big Tom walked into the living room and let himself fall on the sofa with a loud whooshing sound. He took out his mobile just as it rang. He checked the caller ID and answered, 'Hi mate! (...) No am at the house behind the planks (...) No I can't come back now (...) Yeah, I understand but am dealing with some stuff (...)

Serious stuff (...) I'm sure he is pissed off (...) Just tell him I said he can go to hell (...) Mate, gotta go (...) Yeah, well, I don't give a shit.' And he ended the call.

Big Tom was such a smooth talker. Jazz and I had sat down at the table to do some work during his call. We were not trying not to listen in when Big Tom placed his call.

'Hello Mum! How are you doing today? (...) I just wanted to check how you are. You're playing Bingo later with your girl-friends, right? (...) Ooooooh! That is sweet of him to invite you out for lunch. You be careful though, you know what men are like (...) I know you're 76, but I'm looking after my Momma (...) Now, Mum, don't you worry OK? The thing is I have to go for a few days on a building project in another part of the country, OK? So I will not be coming home tonight (...) Emergency work, Mum, all good (...) No, don't worry Mum, I will get some fresh pants over there (...) In the north, Mum (...) Yes, go and get ready, make yourself pretty. You are going to break some hearts again (...) Me too Mum, I love you.'

This was adorable! The man was so sweet with his mum! Now I wanted to offer him some milk and cookies. It looked like Big Tom was a softie, just a bit rough around the edges.

'I still wish I had a gun asap,' he said and his rosy image as a cuddly soft bear crumbled.

'Errr ... Let's see tomorrow or this weekend,' I commented.

'What now? What am I supposed to do?' Big Tom asked, play-ing with his mobile.

'Well, honestly, I don't know. I mean, maybe you want to see Lil' London later?'

'Yeah. Sure. Whatever.'

I was definitely asking Zeno to look after him as soon as possible.

'But I can't talk about it, right? That world, I mean. For safety reasons, mainly yours, because we depend on you, right? To keep a foot in this world, right?'

'I am afraid so. Yes,' I replied.

'I can't leave my mum alone. I am the only one looking after her.'

'Well, has Jazz told you that you could tell her, even ask her to come through the Fog to see you, but there is the risk she may be relocated too?'

'Yeah, she has. I am going to think about that.'

He fell back on the sofa, staring at the ceiling. He was thinking about it, I presumed.

Jazz was looking at me, smiling from above her opened laptop. She was delighted her speech had had the outcome we hoped for, that is him not revealing the Fog (yet). I tried to refocus on what I had to do next, the key supplies that would be of interest for WII and, the type of business and activities that could be allocated to the Relocated. I struggled to concentrate.

'Big … Mr Jameson?' I called Big Tom from the dining table. As he was in the process of thinking, I might as well add a little subject to his personal brainstorming.

'Just Thomas love,' he answered, keeping his eyes closed. The ceiling had stopped being inspiring.

'Thank you, Thomas. So, another point you may want to think about is what your assets would be over there. For a job or something.'

'Will do.' He had not budged, nor opened his eyes.

I hoped I would finally be able to do some work. Not that I wasn't sympathising with the man, I was! Only, I was learning to accept that sometimes care and support was all the help I could offer. Talking with Jazz in the morning had made me realise every Relocated would face similar issues: where to live, what to do next, how to say their goodbyes, or not. So I decided to put together some ideas of potential activities for them in WII, with Zeno as a link to this world when trading was involved. A few obvious projects were:

- Shops, such as a grocery, a delicatessen, an ironmonger: we needed to beware of disrupting the local businesses. Flour was already the lifeline of several families in Lil'London, as described in Maud Poff's letter. Killing the local source of income of the locals was not a good idea. The solution might lie in giving exclusive distribution rights, in exchange for … Other Worldly original goods?

- Specific trades and support: construction with modern materials, support for anything transferred from our world, such as telephones, radios, iPods and things (not that I thought that many of them would have iPods, but it was just an example);
- Bicycle and modern rollerblades shop: would that help over there? (That reminded me I ought to learn to rollerblade better);
- Retail shops: fashion, toys and so on?
- A restaurant: Jazz was opening a coffee shop/ lounge bar, would that count as a restaurant?
- School: teaching history, modern English, maths? Would they need it?
- Mechanics: that would imply we would send cars and motorbikes there, which was borderline possible. Fuel would be an issue, especially in the long term. Ecologically, that was a big no-no!
- Farmer: with modern farming techniques;
- Bookshop: that would be a nice idea, yet again, would that create an issue for the Poffs? Plus, I was pretty sure we would face the ire of Augustus Hoare. Especially if among the stock were men's magazines. Talk about shaking a red cape in front of the bull;
- Furniture: now that was a good one and seemed harmless enough;
- Pharmacy!

The last one was of importance. Such a project required someone with experience, or at least someone with basic knowledge and training. I went online to check if the Open University website for distance learning and adult education would provide medical courses. In doing so, I realised it would be an amazing source of teaching for the Other World inhabitants especially as the Relocated competencies were random. With no control on who was sent there, who knows what they could do on the other side. Of course, I very much adhered to the philosophy that everyone has something to contribute, but it doesn't mean it would necessarily be useful there, in Lil'London.

The next thing I wanted to look into was how to maximise the quality of life in WII and bring in some modern amenities. Aside from new vehicles like cars and motorbikes for the long term, mountain bikes could work. Then there was the matter of electricity. We could provide a lot if they had electricity: light, for one thing, but then heating, technology, cookers and music too (certainly not their priority, but a nice treat for the Relocated). The list was long. The best way to provide it without plants was with solar panels. Even windmills or watermills involved a larger structure while solar systems could be a stand-alone power system for individual use. Self-sufficient energy power for all, I liked that. Furthermore, there was the matter of water. They were close to the Thames, so the source would be no problem, only its transportation. The catalogue of ideas, questions and practicalities for life in Lil'London kept growing. At least Jazz would have a fogged house of her own, with internet, TV, electricity and the benefits of our amenities at her disposal. I glanced at Thomas Jameson and thought of James Fisher and both of their families. I felt helpless again and motivated to stop having this feeling.

Time flew by until lunch. Mulling over the Relocated situation led me to call my parents to check how they were faring in the South of France, the answer being 'badly'. They reported that my sister had moved into bed almost full time, alternatively dragging herself round the house in her dressing gown, moaning. Eudes' father had called their house to complain he hadn't seen his son in weeks. He was threatening to take Julia to court for their son's custody. Well, he could if he wanted to, that would not change anything. Of course, we could not tell him that, or why. They had lied and told him she was not there. He didn't seem to believe them, rightly so. The last thing they needed was for him to show up at the house. They had been keeping everyone at bay from the Fog, which was easily feasible thanks to the house's enclosure. It was frustrating for my mother who loved entertaining at home. My parents were also limiting their outings together out of guilt at leaving Julia stranded alone at home.

The only positive input I was able to give them was on my sister's health. Dad and Mum had finally told me Julia's worries and the reason why I had gone to theirs that weekend, ending up fogging the family house: she had suspected her husband of having had extramarital affairs before the current lover, on several occasions with unprotected sex. She was obsessed she had got a sexually transmittable disease from him and had got herself tested. Her GP confirmed her fears, she had hepatitis C. It is the most serious form of hepatitis, a virus which is the source of many liver diseases and often liver cancer. This type of hepatitis can be treated, but generally it cannot be cured. Hearing this, I realised if hepatitis C is a virus, it should be cured by the Fog. I explained to my parents the body cleansing and healing effect of the Fog – for whatever reason I had never told them! – and suggested they have Julia do another blood test. It would be a bit complicated, they would have to take the blood themselves and bring it to a laboratory, finding an explanation as to why the person couldn't come, but it was worth it. They promised they would talk to Julia that minute and organise it all with the support of the family doctor. He was a friend and could bring the blood sample to a lab to be tested.

Zeno returned when I was in the kitchen preparing a simple meal for Jazz, Leila and me. He was looking grim, so I decided to treble the portions. On the menu was sweet potato mash, grilled chicken breast, mixed leaf salad, cheese, bread and the remnants of my last batch of shortbread.

'Yoko, you didn't answer my calls,' Zeno greeted me as he entered, grumpy. 'I called several times about an hour ago.'

'Sorry! I was listening to music while focused on my work, then on the phone with my parents. I saw your missed calls when dialling their number and thought I would call you afterwards. I forgot, sorry.'

'Cris has booked a ticket.' He cut my apologies short. 'She arrives Monday. We had an argument on the phone all morning. She can't come here, Yoko.'

Cris, the long distance girlfriend. I was wondering when that would resurface. So far, Zeno had managed to stop her visiting by promising he would go and see her. It would have been too good to be true that he managed to keep her at bay until our new house was ready. No doubt she smelled something was fishy in London and was coming to check the facts in person. I would have done the same. So now Cristiana was on her way over and, with her, wild explosions were coming too. Cristiana was Spanish born, currently living in Athens. Zeno and she had got together the previous year when she lived in London. It was already a fiery relationship back then. Cris was intelligent, fun, but jealous in the extreme. Any girl friendly with Zeno, laughing with Zeno, or even just looking at Zeno was suspicious. He was a pretty chilled person, with a relaxed attitude with people, including women. Distance was making things even worse, as she was not able to go over each of Zeno's friends and new encounters with a fine toothcomb. Basically, she had to trust him and that is exactly what her jealousy struggled to do. She even had misgivings about my friendship with Zeno! It almost felt a privilege she tolerated me at all.

'What shall I do?' Zeno pleaded. 'Help!'

'How would I know? I really can't tell you what to do. She is unpredictable.'

'Dai! Gimme ideas!'

'I don't know … Tell her that you have an old childhood friend over, staying in your room.'

'She would still want to come. And then she would be surprised not to meet him – because it would have to be a 'he' not a 'she' obviously.'

'Do you have any friends she hates and wouldn't want to meet?'

'All my female friends.'

'Jeez. What about your mum?'

'She is accepted, yet still competition in love and attention.'

'Not an option then … What if you tell her you are using your room as storage for a new market stall project and sleeping on the floor in the living room?'

'She would still come to the house, checking and trying to get the gossip from you guys on what I have been up to.'

'For God's sake! Say you are leaving on a trip on Sunday!'

'Well, I used that excuse before and it's too late for that one.'

'I give up.' I turned back to my sweet potatoes and started mashing them with energy. Leila said she would be here at 1 p.m.

'Pleease! Heelp! … Mmm, OK if I join you for lunch? This mash looks good!'

'Sure, I was counting on it the minute you arrived. I made enough mash for two days, I think, not enough chicken though.'

'I have some. I'll take them out and pan fry them to finish it off. I have more greens for a big salad too. I saw you took only one pack out.'

'Perfect!'

Zeno started helping in the kitchen and we remained silent for a bit.

'So, Nutella, any more ideas?'

'Yeah, just tell her the house suffered a fire …' I began.

'Let's keep it realistic here!' Zeno interrupted.

'… And you didn't want to tell her so as not to worry her,' I continued. 'You're staying in a hotel right now. Dante and you can exchange rooms for a few nights and … basta.'

'Hey, I like that!'

I stopped my mashing. 'Zeno ... Why don't you should just tell her the truth? She is your girlfriend, isn't she?'

'Cazzo! Are you crazy? Cris will never accept I have a parallel life! Plus, JAZZ lives in this house.'

'And?'

'She hates Jazz.'

'What a surprise.'

'Jazz keeps pushing her buttons: every single time Cris and I meet Jazz, Jazz is all over me to wind her up!' Zeno exclaimed.

I laughed. That would be Jazz all right. She had nothing against Cris especially, but her jealousy was something Jazz found ridiculous and she couldn't resist playing on it. Not fair on Zeno, but quite a show!

'Moving to the hotel. Dante or Leo. That is an idea. Not bad, not bad ...'

'Oops. No, no, nooooo!' I thought. 'Not Leo! An exchange of rooms with Leo is not a good idea at all. Too weird! ... Although ... Practical ... No, no, no. Better keep things slow a bit longer. However ...'

'Yoko?' I was deep in thought when Jazz called me from the other room. Zeno was far away too, most probably planning how to set out the lie to Cris and organise the room exchange.

'Yes Jazz?'

'What are we having for lunch?'

'Roast chicken, sweet potato mash, big mixed salad, cheese, shortbread, coffee.'

'Yum yum! Need any help?'

'We're good.'

'Is it simple? Should I take the recipes down for the "J-Lounge"?'

'So that's the name, is it? "J-Lounge"?'

'Not definite yet. I'm working on it, but I quite like that one.'

'When are we seeing Leo and Dante next?' Zeno asked.

'Maybe you should call them to arrange something?' I replied. It wasn't for him to know that Leo and I had a date that night.

'Maybe we could invite them for dinner?'

'Tomorrow? I am out tonight.'

'I need to see them before, to organise it all and check if swapping is fine for them. Which one would you rather have in the house? Dante or Leo?'

'Leo,' replied Jazz. 'Dante is nice, but Leo is more lively and chatty. Don't you agree, Yoko?'

'Well, as long as one of them doesn't mind helping you out, they are both fine with me,' I replied to Zeno.

'OK, good, I'll contact them after work,' Zeno concluded.

Lunch was a bit awkward, even if lovely. Awkward because Big Tom joined the table but hardly talked. Was he a man of a few words, or were his monosyllabic replies a consequence of the shock of his new relocated status? His mobile rang several times; he checked the caller ID and never picked it up. After the fourth call he put it on silent. Due to Big Tom's presence among us, Leila and I didn't talk about foggy business. Instead, we gave him further details about Lil'London, the Fog, how we aimed to help them to be independent while still keeping a link with the good old London. Jazz then took over and started talking about the various ideas she had for her business. As with James, we all instinctively avoided giving up information on other Foggies or the Society until we knew more about who we were dealing with and how they would handle the new situation. Leila explained she was working for a type of charity which helped unusual cases and the Relocated would benefit from its support. After lunch, Big Tom returned to the sofa and closed his eyes. Within minutes he was snoring. This guy worked in mysterious ways. Leila and I went to my room to discuss a few things, while Jazz stayed downstairs at the dining room table, browsing the web for furniture idea for her 'lounge'. Zeno called Leo and Dante.

Leila and I spent most of the afternoon going through updates: on the renovation of the houses which would be ready in a
week's time minimum; on Lil'London Council's fears of the disturbing influence of our modern world on their well-oiled system;
on my new insight into the Poffs (I didn't share the letter with her,
just mentioned it); on Big Tom, the Fisher family and my ideas for
the Relocated. It was a good meeting; it reinforced my positive
opinion of the Society. Working with Leila was easy, I got along
well with her, could laugh with her and she took into account my
ideas and suggestions, as well as hesitations. It would never be that
democratic if I had to deal with the mammoth structures of the
state. Plus, which state would that be, exactly? I was French, not
British, even though I was living on British soil. Which country
would I have to pledge allegiance to? Most of the time I was trying not to over-analyse the situation and deal with the matters at
hand that day, trying to just go with the flow. Some days, it was
more difficult than others, but with practice I was getting better
at it. So, after a good chat with Leila, the load weighing at the
back of my mind was slightly lighter and again I felt happy to have
the Society behind me, despite its occasional illegal manipulation
of information. I was a firm believer that governments were just as
dodgy anyway, only they had the facility to adjust the laws to make
it appear more legally acceptable.

On her side, Leila was adamant we needed to find a way to
protect the Foggies in WII. When I told her about the arrow barely missing us, she blanched.

'You need to learn some self-protection skills until we find a
way to get you protected,' she said.

The rest of the afternoon was spent transferring music from
my MP3 to my FTab so that I wouldn't miss any beeps, or buzzes,
or rings while working with music. Zeno told me he had spoken
with Leo who was not available either for dinner tonight. Both
Leo and Dante had had a good laugh at Zeno's expense, but they
were happy to help. Dante from the start said he would prefer it

if Leo made the swap, as he had laid papers all over his room: research on historical building practices, self-sufficiency solutions, fast and easy structures, plans, transportations of materials, basic instructions and so on, and he was not keen on moving it all.

'Leo didn't appear the most enthusiastic,' Zeno commented, 'but after a little hesitation, he said he would be delighted to help. I think they probably enjoy the liberty of not needing anyone to get out of the Fog. They are nice guys though. I like them.'

'So Leo will move in on Sunday,' I noted as casually as possible.

'Yes. He and I will swap rooms. In a way it's a good thing, you will get to be more familiar with another Crosser. He is a nice guy, I am sure you will get along.'

'I don't see why not,' I replied noncommittally.

'I had a little chat with him. I think we'll be a good partnership. He is quite like me, creative with business. He is good with technology where I am not. I can see him managing stocks and creating online businesses to commercialise the Lil'London stuff in our world as folk, traditional, historical-style products. We could even be green-labelled or craft, what do you think?'

'Sounds awesome.' I was only half-listening, taking in the news that the man I had just met and dated was going to move in one floor up.

'How did I manage to put myself in that situation, exactly?' I asked myself inwardly. 'And how are we going to keep it all under wraps? And … Oh no … Rico … He will never manage not to let a comment slip. Dammit.'

'You're OK? You look like you bit a lemon.' Zeno said and I realised I was grimacing in line with my inner reflections.

'I am good. Just overwhelmed at the magnitude of the task ahead of us.'

'Yeah. I know what you mean.'

'It's thrilling and daunting at the same time.'

'Tell me about it. In addition it is time to call Cris now.'

'Good luck!'

Leo wrote that he had spent the whole afternoon with Dante, helping him check what materials were available in the UK for Dante's ideas. The big winner was solar energy. That would teach me to work solo: I should have liaised with them and would have spent less time searching online for information on solar panels. The Society must have pages and pages of suggestions and plans as well. Leo was still with Dante so we couldn't message each other easily. He briefly wrote he had booked a table for 8 p.m. at a little pizzeria, a ten minute cab journey from his hotel and slightly more from home. I confirmed it was all fine by me. Aside from the date, he referred to Zeno's situation and his moving to the house on Sunday, apologising profusely for it.

He wrote, 'It's not ideal, I know. With all that is going on, we both agree that our involvement is best kept quiet for now. Not that I am not proud like a lion to date such a hottie charming bella! Do you think Rico will be able to keep the secret? Will you be able to keep your hands off me? I will bring a pair of handcuffs, so that I can attach myself to my bed at night and don't turn into a midnight visitor to your room below. The trouble is that I will be at the mercy of anyone visiting my room … '

Such a cheeky bugger! I laughed out loud and indulged at length in indecent thoughts too. We would have to be extra careful. It may be ridiculous to some, this reserve and longing to protect my privacy, especially from my closest friends. I just wanted to know where I stood with him first. With so much happening in such a short period, a bit of self-protection could not go amiss.

In the time I had left before getting ready for my date, I replied to messages from other Foggies. I had received three separate ones from Marrakech: one from Christophe, asking if someone would at least come and stay for a week, so that he and Louise could escape and breathe a bit in Marrakech. Without his passport he was stuck in Morocco, but he didn't have to be stuck in the house. He wrote that he 'understands the bitch [his wife], but she has no sympathy for my situation either and the two women are driving me insane'. I had heard the same story for weeks now and so it sounded like 'same old, same old'. Isabelle also wrote, asking if it would be possible to organise some kind of medical assistance for her pregnancy. She wanted to start preparing for a home birth with regular visits from a midwife she would get to know and feel comfortable with. I passed on the idea to Leila immediately. Last, Louise wrote about the desert. She sent a collection of pictures. They were beautiful. She had obviously ventured out and snapped sunsets, dawns, the odd animal prints in the sand. The photos that amazed me the most were shots of the Fog amid the dunes, a thick cloud over the house where they lived. Sometimes it was on top of a dune, sometimes at the bottom, sometimes on a flat surface. It depended on the wind and the movement of the sands. She had taken the shots over the past few weeks. The Fog would change colour at dawn and sunset, always sparkling in the light. It was magical. Louise wrote that taking those photos was helping her to accept the situation, because of the beauty of the colours and wilderness. Notwithstanding this, she felt lonely. She would love to have a community in the desert, like we had Lil'London, even though it scared her that one day someone from there could knock at the door, because they could be unfriendly as they were in Mexico. All she longed for was real contact with that world.

News from Alaska was excellent. Mitch, Tony and Rosario were adjusting pretty well to the Fog. With the help of the Society, they were building a little house at the bottom of their driveway close to the entrance. The little house would officially be the home of Tony and Rosario and would serve to give a normal front to the group. Jean, the mother, would be moved there when she needed to be seen by a nurse and so would Mitch when he wished to be out of the Fog. They had two-way radios as well. Their life would be close to normal except on Saturday nights, when Rosario had to make sure to sleep in the old house to avoid 'fogging' the new one. Tony was now studying books on gold mining and other precious minerals which could be found in Alaska. If the geological layout was the same, he planned on using recorded old and modern mining locations to ensure his family had a steady income with Mitch doing a bit of digging. It would ensure they wouldn't have to rely entirely on the Society. They would have to control the inflow of gold put on the market to avoid attracting attention. If necessary, he would travel to other countries during the week to make the exchange. The Society wasn't ecstatic about the idea, yet had no objection. His contact at the Society said they would only withdraw their support if what a Foggy was doing or promoting was against their deontology, beliefs and practice. They would not force anything upon them; they would make recommendations and objections if they disapproved, but all they would do is withdraw support and contact upon conflicts of interest.

'Good to know,' I thought. They had a good attitude.

Simba and I were getting really close now, and she was always by my side. I hoped she would be fine tonight when left alone and would not whine. Zeno would look after her, not Jazz. I was trying to get her used to being looked after by various people. Big Tom was outside in the forest of WII in his mobile home, powered by a generator that could last three days. He had asked for some baked beans, bread, butter, a couple of beers and a book, a thriller or crime story, to pass the time. We were very happy to oblige and he withdrew into his temporary home. Leila had told me in the afternoon they were already monitoring his calls. I didn't want to know that, even if I was, in truth, reassured. Against my own will, I was warming up to the evasive ways of the Society. 'Note to self,' I pencilled in my personal notes, 'do not lose track of your own values'. So I told Big Tom that we had to monitor his line, to check if he let slip some information and be ready to cover up the damage.

'Expected so,' he replied.

'All good then,' I responded and was happily guilt-free.

Before closing the door, I added, 'Oh! I almost forgot: there are wolves in the forest. You are not a sleepwalker, are you?'

'Nah. Anyway, tomorrow I'll have a gun.'

At 7.45 p.m., showered, pampered and – hopefully – looking sexy and irresistible, I made my way out to hail a cab to the restaurant. I was looking forward to a chilled evening with a charming man who I really liked. Well, maybe more than just a chilled evening. Let's be blunt: I wanted him! I had years of a quasi-non-existent sex life to catch up on! Phil and I had agreed that when possible I would let him know my plans so he and his team could organise my protection the best they could. He would be at the restaurant tonight. I was pleased it was him again who was in charge of my well-being tonight. I had got used to him.

I arrived there slightly too early and went directly to the reserved table, ordering a bottle of San Pellegrino water. I put the FTab on silent, crunched a grissini and perused the menu. All the pizzas looked so good on paper, the choice would be a hard one to make. From the corner of my eye, I glimpsed Phil coming and negotiating a table by the entrance. He had the delicacy to sit with his back to us so that he wouldn't observe what happened during dinner. Also, seated by the door, he would not miss our exit. I wasn't expecting him to be inside: was he just doing his job looking after us, or could he not resist the temptation of pizza tonight?

Leo arrived shortly after me. I was deeply engrossed in the menu and didn't see him coming. I got startled by a sudden presence by my side and a hand on my shoulder. As I looked up, he bent down and gave me a long tender kiss. We broke it when it begun to get more intense – decency obliged – and he went to sit down in front of me, a big grin on his face. A waiter was immediately by his side, handing out a menu and asking him what he would like to drink. Leo glanced at the sparkling bottle of water already on the table and said we would check the menu for their wine or beer.

'Funny, I have never had beer with pizza in an Italian restaurant before. I always go for wine, usually Chianti.'

'Then we should order beer tonight. One classic would be Peroni. Not the best of our beers, but it works well.'

'You are the Italian one, you know best. You take full responsibility for that one.'

'You are Italian too.'

'A quarter only.'

'Only a drop of Italian blood suffices. When it is in your blood, it is in your blood.'

I laughed. It was cut short by the arrival of a tall man who cast an imposing shadow on the table. He was looking smart in a dark grey suit, impeccably cut and fitted, with a gorgeous tie which was undoubtedly Hermès. The man had a perfect haircut with jet black hair and a dash of grey on the temples, along with a welcoming smile. His bright eyes were fixed on Leo. He politely glanced at me once without a word, only addressing my date.

'Sir, I apologise for interrupting your evening, but there is a matter of the utmost importance I need to discuss with you.'

'I am afraid this is not the …' Leo began.

'It would be best not to delay,' the smartly dressed man insisted. His attire did not match the setting and he received quite a few looks from the other diners. Without doubt his forty-something good looks were also appreciated by the women in the room. He talked with aplomb, in a confident, elegant and tranquil voice. 'I can see I am interrupting a special moment with your girlfriend, or partner, or wife and I apologise for the intrusion. However, the matter cannot wait. Maybe we could go outside to discuss it.'

'Sir, I will not leave this table. I do not know what you are talking about and whatever it is, you can say it in front of … Nutty,' Leo replied firmly, pouring himself a glass of water.

'Nutty?' I thought. 'Did he just call me Nutty?' It took a couple more seconds before I understood. Leo had not wanted to give my name and used my nickname, albeit abbreviated. 'Great,' I said to myself. 'How long before this 'Nutty' takes over 'Nutella' for good.' This man not knowing my name was good idea though.

We didn't know what he wanted, but the odds were strongly on the Fog. I fought the urge to glance at Phil. I wanted to let him know we may be into trouble. Time for a toilet break and urgent messaging.

'Dear, don't worry, I will leave you two minutes with this gentleman and go to the ladies.' I stood up as I said so.

'I'm afraid I need more than two minutes,' the man in the suit said. A waiter arrived, asking if we needed another seat and I took the opportunity to disappear, saying to Leo that the simplest is often the best and I would have a margherita pizza. In the bathroom I quickly sent a message to Phil telling him we had an unexpected visitor at the table. So far we did not know what he wanted, but it was possible he was not here alone and maybe we should have him checked. I knew Leo also had a bodyguard with him, so I wasn't really scared. After Jack's abduction, we were just more cautious. I did a quick search on the FTab and selected the voice recorder. I was not sure what it would pick up from my bag, but it was worth a try. I returned quickly to the table, not wanting to leave Leo alone to deal with this man. As I arrived, the waiter was taking notes. Leo was making his choice, slowly chit-chatting in Italian with him. When he saw me coming back, he finished placing the order and the waiter left. The man in the suit waited patiently, in control of himself. He had Chinese features, but his accent was definitely born and bred American. He also combined the poise and self-control generally given as attribute to Chinese businessmen, with the energy and natural smile of the American. The man just glanced at me with a hint of annoyance tempered with a dose of polite graciousness as I sat down.

'It seems, Miss, that Mr Lumbrosi will not part from you tonight. Thus, may I kindly request to join you at the table?'

'It seems, sir, that your question was rhetorical and does not call for an answer. You have been by our table imposing yourself for some time already, without even introducing yourself,' I snapped back. This man knew Leo's last name. I didn't like that and could tell Leo didn't either.

'You are absolutely right. A boorish omission on my part. My name is Ingis Chen.' The man bowed as he said this.

'Chen,' I thought. 'It sounds Chinese indeed, but 'Ingis', where is that from?'

He was looking at me expectantly. My turn to give a name, I presumed.

'Mr Chen, you may call me Nutty.' Leo smiled at this, but the smile didn't last as Ingis grabbed a chair from a neighbouring table and with no further ado, sat down at the table.

'Well, Nutty, Leo – if I may –, please call me Ingis,' the man said with a wide smile. He hailed a waiter.

'I will have a glass of your finest Prosecco, thank you,' he requested. Leo and I glanced at each other. I could tell that Leo, like me, was both annoyed and intrigued by the encounter.

'Leo,' Ingis said. 'I would like to talk to you about your Roman house. It appears to have suffered a strange fate of late. It seems in a bit of a Foggy situation.'

'Is it? My house is going through refurbishment right now, if this is what you mean. In any case, why do you care about my house?' Leo replied on the defensive.

'Leo, please. We both know your house is more than under refurbishment.' Ingis turned towards me and asked, 'Do you know about Leo's house's fate of late, Nutty?'

I looked at Leo. I wasn't sure what to answer to this.

'I hide nothing from Nutty. You can talk freely in front of her,' Leo intervened. The waiter arrived with the glass of Prosecco and two large bottles of Peroni. Leo poured some in my glass then his.

'Then I shall,' Ingis Chen commenced. 'Leo, I know Jack has created a Fog around your house. I know you have the ability to cross this Fog and reach another earth. I know your friend Dante can do it as well. I know you got in contact with some people here and they sent a certain Rico to enable you three to leave the house and come here to London. It appears that you have some connections in this city that are very helpful. You even have some technology to rely on. I have some names, but very few details. I would be interested to know more. Maybe we could reach some kind of understanding?'

He was going for straight to the point!

'Did you make the same offer to Jack before he was kidnapped?' Leo asked, his whole being as hard as nails.

'An error of judgement on my part. We noticed that your little group was being strongly guarded and we couldn't approach you. My team saw an opportunity later, and they seized it. We mean Jack no harm.' Ingis Chen was being reassuring and charming. Well, he was trying. It did not work that well with either Leo or me. I decided to keep quiet and not say a thing. I would rather he didn't know how involved I was in the matter. Considering his lack of interest in me since his arrival, he didn't know that I was a Foggy. The best would be for me to act as if my only link to the Fog was Leo and the only thing I knew came from Leo. So all I had to do, really, was to keep my mouth shut. That wasn't going to be easy.

'So, why isn't he free and among us right now?' Leo asked.

'Because he is Fog-bound,' Ingis Chen replied, unfaltering.

'I believe we tried to help him out of it recently,' Leo retorted.

'It wasn't necessary. As I said, no harm was done to him. He would have contacted you, if he had had your numbers or emails. He didn't,' Ingis Chen calmly replied, taking a sip of Prosecco. Mr Chen was Zen.

'And his parents, why didn't he call them?' Leo persisted.

'He didn't want to alarm them. They are not aware of the Fog, I believe.' He had a point, Jack had no means of contacting us.

'I just don't get why you took him like that in the first place.'

'We didn't, and still don't, know who the men around you all were, and if they were there for your protection – which would have been a good thing – or if they were guarding you from escaping their grip. We couldn't take the risk of losing you all, we had to act. We did.'

'And when you interrogated Jack ...' Leo began.

'Discussed things with, not interrogated,' Ingis Chen corrected.

'He told you he was a free man, right?'

'Yes.'

'So why did you shoot when we came to try and help to free him from his captors?'

'We didn't know who you were, did we? It could have been anyone attacking us.'

'Who is "we"?' I asked. I couldn't hold my tongue, it just slipped out. Ingis Chen turned towards me.

'Leo must trust you a lot, Nutty, to share such unbelievable information with you, and for you to believe him, except of course if you were in Rome too. Have you been together long?'

'Long enough, obviously,' I replied. 'But you haven't answered my question: who is "we"?'

'Me and my team. This is such a breakthrough occurrence and large enterprise that I couldn't possibly handle it on my own.'

'They are well armed, your team,' I said.

'Yours too,' he replied, smiling at me.

'Beware, Yoko,' I thought before I replied. 'Not mine, thank goodness. A good thing Leo doesn't have to face what is happening alone.' As I said this, I looked at Leo, straight in the eyes, with as loving a smile as I could. If I had to play the trusting enamoured girlfriend, I would take this opportunity to make sure he was on the same wavelength. 'So far, Ingis Chen acts as if I am only a side character in it all. Let's keep it that way,' I tried to make him understand.

'Are they the best team, though? What do they offer, Leo? And why? I can bring you much and for the greater good.'

'For the greater good? Really?' Leo sneered.

'Absolutely. Personal benefits and the greater good. They can easily be combined.'

'That's OK then. We are thus reassured.' Again, I slipped and jumped into the conversation.

'Nutty, you strike me as quite cynical. Do you not think it possible?'

'Maybe it is. It is certainly rare,' I retorted. Ingis Chen simply smiled at me and turned back to Leo. I had just been dismissed.

'How do you know about the Fog anyway?' Leo enquired before Ingis Chen had the chance to speak. The man closed his eyes and laughed. Even though it wasn't natural, it still sounded nice with his voice.

'A blend of family myth and chance. Stories of the Fog have been in the family for centuries, originally as a well-guarded secret of the Chinese emperor. By the beginning of the last century, the whole notion had been dismissed by my family as fantasy, despite papers in our possession dated from 1551 and signed by the emperor, supporting control of a temporary door opening to an unknown land. It was a state secret only a few knew about in his time. After hundreds of years, it turned into a legend, the legend of a state secret. No such Fog to an unknown land was ever recorded in China. For us, it turned into a family tale and was recounted to children. Each new generation dreamed about it in early childhood, with its potential for adventures. We all grew out of it. That is until one year ago for me. My sister Dao is fascinated by the divergences and similarities of how people approach spirituality and energies around the globe. She is a researcher in that field for an American University and last year she came across an old Native American man, half senile and speaking to himself, reciting an old American Indian oral story. He referred to a mysterious Fog, opening to new lands and where only a few could go and even fewer would come back. This, of course, immediately triggered a reaction from my sister. She tried to find out more, but no one seemed able to help in the Indian reservation. She didn't find any reference to it in any Native American documentation she could lay her hands on either. From experience, she is aware that tribes worldwide have a stronger oral history tradition than a written one, so not finding any records was hardly surprising. She repeated the story to me: she was amused and intrigued, but that was all, she didn't care about it much. What I focused on was a detail the old Native American had uttered: that the Fog would soon be upon us again, that the time had come. My sister dismissed it as the ramblings of an old man. As improbable as it seemed, I couldn't shake the idea out of my mind. The potential was ...' Ingis Chen stopped in mid-sentence. He was lost in his own thoughts for a brief time, before focusing on Leo again.

'May I ask, Leo? Do you know you are in a unique situation, being able to cross between two planets? It could make your life difficult, or it could make it amazing. I will make sure it is amazing.'

'You are too kind,' Leo replied in an offhand tone.

'I am not. I can make both our lives amazing,' Ingis said, with a tone that reminded me of a persuasive salesman offering a once-in-a-lifetime bargain. 'Mine, yours and, Nutty's by extension. We would add value to this world and the other. What's not to like?'

'What's the catch?' I interrupted.

'Exclusivity. I want exclusivity,' Ingis Chen replied.

'You mean you want to have the exclusive rights and access to the Fog?' I asked, to make sure I understood him right.

'I want to have the exclusivity of your services, or abilities linked to the Fog. Any benefits from that Other World come from it.'

'I have an idea of how you and I could benefit, but I am curious, how do you think you could add value to both worlds?' I continued.

The waiter came with our pizzas, two margheritas. It was a perfectly timed service: eating would stop me talking. Ingis Chen should do the talking! As I added chilli oil to my pizza, I established it was the worst second date ever. The Fog was really not helping my romantic life, and having a possibly dangerous man crashing the dinner was throwing oil on the fire.

Despite his smooth voice and talk, I was not convinced by his sweet words. After all, in addition to Jack, a man also got killed in Mexico. The thought of danger brought me back to Phil. I hadn't checked if he had replied to my message. I put down my fork and knife and was about to grab the FTab, when I realised it may not be the best idea. They had not seen Jack's, but the latter might have described it. He shouldn't see I had one. So I bent over my bag and foraged in it a bit, making space so that I could get a glimpse of the screen without taking it out. Leo told me later that caused the first obvious facial disapproval from Ingis: his eyes and lips narrowed at the sight of me checking something in my bag and taking my time with it. It required a bit of time to unlock the device. Phil had replied. Twice. The first message said that his colleague had noticed the new arrival and his escort: at least six men and a large people carrier. Phil had called for back-up. The second message confirmed back-up had arrived: a fake couple in the restaurant and three teams of two in adjacent streets. Total: ten. I gave an inward smile of relief and dropped the tablet back in my bag, returning to my pizza. Ingis Chen and Leo had been silent for the minutes it had taken me to read my messages.

'Sorry. Please continue,' I told them, falsely apologetic. Why on earth would I apologise to the man who was crashing my date, would potentially try to abduct us and most probably ruin my chance of having sex tonight? Just when I was starting to get my libido back, too.

I tried to refocus on what Ingis Chen was saying. 'The two worlds can complement each other. We are running out of drinking water, the Other World isn't. We are running out of space for agriculture – or we destroy the forests that give us oxygen to have more, the inhabitants of this other planet aren't. I can go on with the list for some time. Most importantly, I believe it can help on a superior level: do you know what the biggest problem for mankind is? The source of all the other issues, water, food, fuel, ozone, poverty and everything else? Overpopulation! Seven billion. We are seven billion and growing at an accelerated rate. That is not sustainable for this planet. On the other hand, the Other World is raw and under-populated.'

'How do you know this?' Leo asked, as he drank from his glass.

'The emperor's very limited document referred to 'unpopulated' world. Jack confirmed this.'

'So you want to pass on the overflow of people from our world to the other one,' Leo summarised.

'That is one of the solutions. Imagine if we managed to reduce the population by one billion. I know you are going to say it is unfeasible, but why not? All we need is organisation and persuasion. The other solution is, of course, to expand the reserves we need in this world by drawing from the Other World. More lands for agriculture. More water, more natural resources, more of everything. That Other World can save our world and mankind.'

Leo and I looked at each other. Ingis Chen's argument may have some truth in it. These ideas had already been discussed with the Society, except that they didn't seem to want to implement them on such a grand scale. He did. Was it a bad thing?

'What about the Other World? Aren't you running the risk of damaging one to save the other?' I asked.

'We have learned a lot about how to extract, cultivate and look after earth better. We can apply it all there. Anyway, nothing is ever perfect, Nutty.'

'It wouldn't really work, though, would it?' Leo interjected. 'The Fog is only opened for a lifetime. It is a temporary solution to any of our problems. We need to sort out solutions here with what we have here, if we want a long term and real answer.'

'Hence the need to transfer people there,' Ingis Chen persisted.

'So you want to save the world, all out of the goodness of your heart, do you?' Leo persisted.

'I sense a lot of mistrust from you, Leo. Let's be honest: I am not an idealistic man and I am involved because there is a phenomenal personal gain here. It just so happens that it also benefits everyone else in the long term and I am truly glad about that. The Fog perspectives are on a scale beyond anybody's understanding. Its repercussions are major. It connects everything together, the opportunity between the two worlds, and the solution to our race's issues and limitations here. Furthermore, I can get very rich in the process and you too, Leo. So ...'

'You don't strike me as poor now,' Leo sneered.

'I have ambition. Besides, if not me, someone else would do it. Your supporters, for example.'

'And what is it you do, exactly?' I inquired, changing the subject from the Society.

Ingis Chen turned towards me and replied, 'I run a big corporation.'

'Focusing on what?' I asked.

'I am not sure it is relevant.'

'I am interested,' I persisted.

'Now is not the time.' He was brushing me aside, turning back to Leo. It got me even more determined to know.

'Well, if you are not ready to answer our questions, you should go. Now was not exactly the right time for us to have this chat either,' I snapped at him.

Ingis Chen froze for an instant and turned back to me, leaning in an observing pause.

'I can see why you like this woman, Leo. Cute and feisty. All right then! The corporation runs factories and their associated relevant trading. We invest in people. A lot of people. In China.'

'Made in China label?'

'Precisely.'

I thought of all the little things I was buying for almost nothing on eBay. Little dresses, spare batteries, mobile headsets, cheap earrings, cheap bags, cheap shoes and so on, all directly sent from China. I wasn't even counting the 'Made in China' label on what was bought in stores. How many of these were from his factories?

I always thought that they needed the jobs there, but looking at Ingis, it now added another dimension. I didn't dislike the man, he had a captivating presence and charm. Being open and direct about his ideas, he called a cat a cat and I liked that. I was on my guard nonetheless. It was, after all, a big sales pitch and potentially ruthless. Moreover, I was already committed to the Society with whom I felt comfortable.

'OK, you have explained the Why and the What. Now for the How. How do you expect to control those big operations?' Leo changed subject. It was a good question.

'Ah! That is the tricky part. Well, at the beginning, we will have to be quite harsh to get things done. It may not please everyone, but you don't achieve anything without making a few waves along the way. What is important is the end result.'

'I bet you are a Sun-Tzu adept, aren't you?' I commented. No one answered.

'How, Mr Chen?' Leo pursued.

'Ingis, please. I could sugar-coat it, but I think you deserve better. So, on the 'how.' I practice the good old 'a means to an end' saying. Sometimes to cure you need to put alcohol on a wound and it hurts.'

We all remained silent for a moment. The man had ambitions. He wanted exclusivity in the access to the Fog and then he would control the exchanges, the locations and the dreams or nightmares of people. He would play a key role in international politics, in diplomacy and in conflicts, just by choosing the locations of Fog portals. Rare products would be less rare, cultures could be doubled. The balance of power for whole economies and countries would be affected. And this man would control it all. Now I couldn't be sure the Society was as pure as they said in its motives and it definitely was not always in its practices, but they had showed respect and trust towards us. They never demanded nor took as they wished. They didn't strike me as having selfish ambitions and thirst for power. This man, Ingis Chen, was another story.

I spoke my mind, 'So, in brief, your goal is to get rich and while doing so create a beautiful Utopia by joining two worlds in one, in which each will sort out the other's problems. To attain this, you aim to get your corporation to gain control of the Fog 'business' and rule its use, access and key politics both for your personal gain and the greater good of mankind. It so happens that to achieve this your corporation may turn into an autocracy, with you at its head. You would soon have as much power and influence as the president of the United States, with decisions affecting the internal affairs and economy of every single nation on this planet: seven billion people. Leo would accessorily support you in this accomplishment, should he decide to accept whatever offer you are here to make. Well, it better be a good one, because the moral price sounds very high.' As I spoke Ingis Chen's face had become harder, colder and set with an unpleasant dagger-like stare directed on me.

'You present me as the big baddie in one of those stereotyped Hollywood movies,' he hissed. No more nice guy. Then he corrected himself and retrieved a more diplomatic tone.

'First, I wouldn't take the decisions alone. I would have a board of advisors. You used the image of the US President, so remember he is not acting alone. He is surrounded by many specialists and advisers. Leo and the ones linked to the Fog would be very much involved of course. Second, maybe it has escaped your notice, these days people's trust is not placed in governments. These are humongous structures struggling to follow and adapt to the changes of our times. They are old, antique diplodocuses that lack flexibility and speed. Trust in public institutions, or private ones for that matter, is at a low point too. No, these days trust is more in business people, in active and reactive major groups. Why? Because we are running with our time and we have no frontier. We have to take into account the voice of the people: on the inside, to avoid strikes and lousy work; on the outside, to satisfy our clients and potential ones. We efficiently juggle economic, political, social, geographic interests or we die. So I am asking you, aren't we the best to deal with the new challenge appropriately? Why choose anyone else less competent?' he retorted, his smooth voice as hard as steel.

'Why not indeed?' I replied. 'You state your case well. Yet I cannot help dreading the monopoly of one group and one only. Discretionary power has too often led to abuse of power in the history of the world. If only one person or entity is running the show, there is no balance of power. Additionally, between all these interests you mentioned – economic, political, social, geographic, and so on – if two are conflicting, which one would you give the priority to? The people? Really? Call me cynical, but you are a business, not a charity. I am neither saying your group would turn into 'Stalin & Co', nor that you do not care about people. Just that, if as you put it the impact of the Fog will be beyond anything we can even imagine, its running should not be in the hand of a business only, let alone a single company.'

'Anyway, what if I like the alternative offer better?' Leo interrupted. He was looking at Ingis Chen with a severity unseen on him before.

'We would make a counter-offer,' Ingis Chen said, his tone still of steel.

'And if I still decline?'

'Where there is a will, there is way,' Ingis Chen replied. There was no more pretence of civility now.

'It almost sounds like a threat,' I said to myself, then commented aloud, 'You mean something like 'I will get what I want, by your own accord, or not?' Now, remind me, you want us to feel secure working with you because …?' Despite knowing I should stop antagonising this potentially dangerous man, I couldn't help myself.

Ingis Chen just squinted at Leo, ignoring my last comment. The corner of his mouth crept up slightly, as if amused by my comments. His look of confidence and ruthlessness was alluring. He had a dangerous appeal that was captivating. Scary too, this man would not let go. Maybe I should have kept my mouth shut.

The meal had finished long ago. The beer and water drunk, the Prosecco glass doubled and drained, the discussion seemed at a standstill.

'So, would you like to hear my offer, Leo?' Ingis Chen asked.

'Right now, no. As I said at the beginning of the evening, you didn't pick a good time,' Leo answered.

'Let's set up a better time and place then, shall we?' Chen suggested.

'Send me an email and I'll think about it.' It was obvious Leo wanted rid of him and was not intent on giving Ingis Chen satisfaction.

'I do not have your contact details, Leo ...' Ingis Chen discounted Leo's closed attitude.

'And yet you managed to find me,' Leo snapped back.

'It was not easy. Luckily there was a little lapse from your protectors this week. Maybe you are not that safe with them, Leo?'

'What shouldn't I be safe from? Is this a warning?' Leo spoke slowly, his tone low.

'Information only,' Chen replied with a confident smile.

'Yeah, right. Give me your card, maybe I will be in touch.' Leo retorted. He had gone slightly red containing his anger. I became aware of how much he disliked or distrusted Chen.

Ingis Chen considered Leo for an instant, then took out a card holder from his inside pocket. He picked a few cards and selected one. Leo looked at it, and then handed it to me, asking me to put it in my bag. There was only Ingis Chen's name, last name, mobile and email address on it. Leo gestured to the waiter by writing in the air. Nobody spoke within the few minutes it took before the waiter arrived. When he did, Ingis Chen announced that it was on him as he had interrupted the meal and he took the bill. Leo's response was an immediate no. He clearly didn't want to owe anything to Chen, who did not pursue the matter except to say he would pay for his drinks.

'Now what?' I thought. 'We just leave and go? Will he try to stop us? Follow us? Take us?'

Ingis Chen answered my questions with his next remark.

'So, Nutty, an intelligent woman like you, I presume you told someone about me when you were rummaging in your bag earlier, didn't you?' I didn't deem it necessary to answer. It wasn't a real question.

'Leo, Nutty, I bid you farewell. I look forward to seeing you again soon. Leo, I trust you will be in touch. I am sure you will want to sort something out. The support behind you may even find that I have good things on offer.' Ingis Chen was back to being amiable. If it wasn't for the Fog business, I could have fallen for this charismatic man.

As he turned to leave, he added, as if as an afterthought, 'Indeed, you must be aware that Jack is not alone in that other land, protected by a member of my team. It would be in both their interests that we work together to ensure they return to us safely.' With this last sentence, he bowed and left the restaurant, passing by Phil who was bent over a book, sipping water. Phil gave a brief glance at Ingis Chen as he passed by and turned a leaf, seemingly absorbed in his reading. Leo and I remained at the table in silence. It had definitely been the worst and strangest second date ever.

**Day 7 (Saturday)**

8.30 a.m. was much too early in the morning to be awake after barely four hours sleep. I was sorting my laundry from the drying rack. A sleepy Zeno had just walked down to prepare coffee. Harry followed minutes later.

'No! It always happens!' I said, tired and grumpy. 'Guys, I hung some clothes and underwear to dry yesterday and now I have a tank top and one bra missing. Where is my top? Have either of you taken it by accident?'

'Don't you want to know about your bra as well?' Harry asked.

'I kind of have an idea on that one ... I just want my top back.'

'Ooh-oooh! And where did you leave your bra then?' Zeno asked.

'Zeno, the bra was on the dryer. It has disappeared. Do you really think I want the bra back after whatever use someone may have put it to? We all know who is the pervert in this house ... Mmmm, on reflection, I don't want the top either. You never know. Forget it!' I said to myself.

'Wild guess: you haven't had breakfast yet?' Harry asked.

I grunted in the affirmative. Harry just took me by the shoulder, led me to the dining table, pulled out a chair and told me to sit. Within minutes Zeno put a fresh mug of coffee in front of me and I could smell bread toasting from the kitchen. The day was starting to look a little bit better already, despite the memories of the previous night.

Leo and I had a major issue about the previous night. The meeting with Ingis Chen was too important not to mention to everyone at home. However, if we wanted to remain discreet regarding our dating, we couldn't say we were together. Leo could hardly say he was alone for dinner, everyone knew he was out with 'friends'. On my side, I was supposed to be out on a date.

Phil and his whole team knew Leo and I were together and there was little doubt the rest of the organisation was informed too after the restaurant emergency. So, leaving the restaurant we decided to have a conference call with Leila and share what happened and what had been said. We agreed to meet her in another hotel bar. It took us forty minutes instead of ten to get there to make sure we were not followed, driven by the fake couple members of the bodyguard back-up. During this impromptu tour of west London, Leo and I settled we would 'omit' to give the name of who was with him. We would keep that information with the Society for now. If the others asked what happened to his friends, he would just brush it away with a 'don't worry about that' or something similar.

Updating Leila took some time. I had hoped the FTab recording of the conversation would suffice: we had no such luck. The quality was too bad, the device being in my bag and the background noise of the restaurant too loud. Leila listened to Leo and me briefing her without interrupting us even once. We were trying to keep to the facts and relate only what had been said, failing. I had misgivings about his approach on the management of the Fog and use of its potential. He still raised some good points that were rather attractive. It reminded me of the Napoleon syndrome. He was (and still is) a popular dictator. Napoleon did aplenty to restore the country, some even say he saved it after the Revolution despite his despotism and nepotism.

Still, we had strong reservations. As the saying goes, the road to Hell is paved with good intentions.

'So finally we know who else is involved. Well, they haven't confirmed they are the same as the Mexico ones … I am fairly certain it is them,' Leila said.

'So what's next?' Leo asked.

'Well, it seems he didn't convince you to drop us to go work for him just yet. Am I correct?' Leila asked.

'Correct,' Leo and I answered simultaneously.

'So, next is whether to contact him or not. Either you or us, if you agree to give us his details. If you think we should, we may. Open dialogue is better than hidden war. In truth, one doesn't stop the other, it would at least open opportunities for negotiation.'

'Agreed. Nutty?' Leo turned to me.

'Agreed. Don't start calling me Nutty,' I answered.

'Oh! Nutty! It suits you though,' Leo persisted, teasing me.

'Yeah, yeah, yeah. Don't go there,' I nudged him.

'Shall I leave you two alone?' Leila commented with a cheeky smile.

'Sorry, I … err … So … open dialogue is good. Plus that would enable us to get Jack out of wherever he is and avoid any more gunshots at your people,' I blurted in one breath.

Leo nodded at me and I gave Leila Ingis Chen's card. I had already pencilled its details in my FTab during the car journey.

'Leila, please keep us updated about him, will you?' Leo requested.

'I'll make sure that you are both in hidden copy of any written correspondence. Any dialogue I will brief you on too.'

'Thank you. In addition please remember Ingis doesn't know Nutty is Yoko, or who she is and what she can do Fog-wise. He just thinks she's my girlfriend,' Leo reminded Leila.

'Not a problem. Yoko is your nutty girlfriend,' Leila replied, her cheeky smile back on.

'Ha ha! Very funny!' I laughed, all the while thinking, 'Wait! Does she think I am his girlfriend? We are only dating!' I had to clarify this.

'Leila, you know. We are not … I mean, nobody knew we were going out on a date last night. Nothing is …'

'Not to worry, I know nothing and say nothing. It is late now. Time to go. Tomorrow, Saturday, I will be on standby for the meeting with James Fisher and his wife. Just let me know if you need me to come over.'

It was very late, she was right. I was drained. Leo was drained. We looked at each other after Leila had gone. We were still surrounded by the team of Society bodyguards and the situation totally lacked intimacy. We decided to go back to our separate beds – because of Ingis Chen. Leo had already been moved to another hotel and Dante had been removed from his and directed to yet another one. Leo and I had a clumsy goodbye kiss and I made my way home.

At the dining table sipping my coffee on Sunday morning, thinking about the previous night, I didn't delude myself: it wasn't only the lack of breakfast that had made me grumpy, the events of last night did.

Thomas Jameson – or Big Tom to me – knocked at the front door shortly afterwards and joined us for breakfast.

'So, what is the plan for today?'

'Today you are going to meet another Relocated, James Fisher. You may also be interested in witnessing what is going to happen.' I told him about James's wife coming with his two children, about the healing process of the Fog, and about the couple's decision to take the risk of having their daughter go through the Fog. I also informed him that he would meet some people of Lil'London afterwards, in the person of Barnaby Sparrow and his son Jonas. Big Tom seemed to like the idea of meeting local inhabitants of WII. He even gave me a smile. Yippee, the man was warming up to us!

I couldn't take my mind off the previous night and the encounter with Ingis Chen. It was frustrating not to be able to share it with the boys and Jazz, even knowing it was a consequence of my predilection for secrecy. They had to wait for Leo to tell them over dinner. To compensate, after breakfast I set up my laptop on the dining table and wrote down my personal notes on Ingis Chen. I heard Big Tom call his mum, chatting away about this and that in a kind soft tone, then call one of his 'mates' and check how long it would take to get him two guns and a shotgun. He added the latter as an afterthought. I decided to act as if I had not heard anything.

I heard a noise at the door. So did Simba who jumped up and went to investigate with a low growl. We had mail: the members of the council all sent thank you letters, in which Edmund Poff's expressed his delight at my joining that Sunday's service. He invited me to join them for lunch with the family afterwards. The members of the council must have consulted among themselves as well: they informed me in a fourth official letter that the council had organised three horses to be at our constant disposal with the watchmen. I wondered if it was a thank you gift or an invitation not to use Zeno's motorbike in to Lil'London. Zeno would not be ecstatic at the news: he loved horse riding much less than me.

Mid-morning, my bodyguard Phil called to inform us that a woman was at the entrance of the terraced houses with her two children asking to see me. Ann Fisher, with her son Owen and her daughter Maisie, had arrived. The Fisher Fog-crossing was the first of its kind, a controlled and voluntary crossing, with the involved aware of the consequences of their actions. My wish was that Maisie would be cured of her ailments without being relocated. Nothing was that straightforward with the Fog.

I brought tea to the Fisher family outside. They were twenty minutes early and had to wait for James Fisher's arrival at the house. The mother was very nervous, the children very curious and excited. When James Fisher arrived, I took Maisie by the hand and walked with her into the house through the Fog. She was weak, that was easily noticeable, yet she was strong in her determination. She didn't falter when she saw the Fog and stepped in. Once inside the house, her reunion with her father was touching: they fell into each other's arms and cried. Harry had prepared tea and biscuits for everyone and I found myself examining the girl for signs of better health. Within minutes she was less pale, livelier, and fuller of energy than the frail little being of earlier. Could the Fog have healed her so fast? James commented on it too. The mother was still outside, waiting anxiously. It was now time to go back to her, if we could, or more exactly, if Maisie could.

Harry, Maisie and I made our way out, my holding Maisie on one side and having my arm passed under Harry's arm on the other. In the middle of the Fog an electric shock I knew the meaning of separated me from Maisie and Harry. We stopped and looked at each other. Maisie tried to touch me and she could. I asked her to let go a second and Harry took my arm, without shock. It was only when I was linked to both Harry and Maisie that we got separated. I had to choose who to walk with next. It was new having such a choice. I asked Harry to go back in and continued with Maisie. We both emerged into the forest of World II.

'So this is real!' Maisie gasped.

'Very.'

'Wow. Super cool!'

'Maisie, I am sorry. You have been relocated.'

'Like Dad?'

'Yes.'

'I can't go back?'

'No.'

Maisie was looking round at the forest in silence. It was a lot to take in for a teenager.

'Maisie, are you all right?' I asked, worried.

'I guess so. I feel good.'

'You understand your life will not be the one you might have dreamed of. There are lots of new possibilities though.' It was difficult to know what to say. She was so young. All her dreams for the future were now smashed.

'I am fine. I haven't felt so good in a long time. I wasn't sure I'd make it, you know? Now I will. And I'm with Dad.'

She inspired respect in me, she had such good attitude. I smiled and put a hand on her shoulder.

'You know what, Maisie, I think you're right. You will be just fine.' Her reply was a big smile and a slow nod.

'Shall we go back in?' I continued. 'We need to inform your dad and your mother, too. This will be a shock for her. You are now back on healthy ground, but she has still lost you.'

Her smile faded and her eyes glazed over. She nodded again, more pensive this time. She grabbed my hand and we headed back to the house. James Fisher took the news with mixed reactions: delighted that his daughter was safe, that he would have her with him, but concerned that she was a Relocated and separated from her former life, dreams and prospects.

'I will take care of you, Maisie-bee. We will be together. Oh my God, your mother ...' he whispered as he hugged his daughter.

'Poor Mum. We must tell her nicely,' Maisie replied.

Maisie and James wanted to tell Ann Fisher themselves, so they called her instead of my going out with Harry to break the news. Her wailing on the phone was heartbreaking. I got from the conversation that Ann was torn between crossing the Fog and taking the risk to be relocated with her daughter and husband but possibly being separated from her son. She hesitated about sending her son as well. Should he cross first and take the risk of being relocated? What if she wasn't after when crossing? She didn't know what to do and nobody could advise her on what was best. Owen Fisher took the phone from his mother and talked to his dad. I could only guess what was happening and what he was saying. James Fisher's expression betrayed both apprehension and hope. He asked to speak again with his wife. All he said was that he loved her. She was the love of his life and would always be, whatever happened.

When Owen Fisher arrived, he let himself in his father's arms. They had not seen each other for about three weeks now and he had thought his dad dead. The Fog had had a rollercoaster effect on the life of their family. Owen Fisher still had Ann on the phone and told her they would go out the three of them, hand in hand, the father between his children, to face the Fog and see what would happen. Either Owen would come out on the other end to his mother, or he would remain with his father and sister, Relocated as well. I didn't share my thought that he could be the undiscovered last Facilitator. The odds were not in favour of him being a Relocated. To not leave Ann Fisher on her own, both Harry and I went with her. After ten minutes, James Fisher called his wife back. Both Harry and I had already guessed that Owen was in WII. Three Fishers had been sent across. Ann Fisher was the only one left. This time, she just listened to her husband jaw clenched. There was no crying. Her face set in a determined expression, she walked towards the Fog. Harry and I lost a couple of seconds catching up with her and we disappeared in the white thick mist.

Their reunion inside the house was very emotional. Ann Fisher was – how to put it? – unrestrained! She threw herself at her husband, simultaneously crying and laughing, expanding her arms like a mother hen opening her wings to gather her children around the two of them. It was loud, it was touching, it was intimate and we had no place there. Even though we were at ours, Harry and I ended up huddled in the kitchen, joined by Jazz and Big Tom, eavesdropping to know when it would be acceptable to come out. Zeno was out in the forest, working on the bike and bringing tools and parts to show the Sparrows. He was also trying to keep out of the way; Rico was away in his studio.

Before we realised what they were doing, husband and wife were out of the door to test the Fog effect on her. They returned within what seemed hours when it was merely seconds, their faces crestfallen. Ann Fisher still belonged to our good old London. In one morning, the woman had been cut off from her family. She was now alone in her world. James, Owen and Maisie had a new life to create, without her.

If we thought she was unrestrained before, we had seen nothing yet.

Jazz and I had tears running down our cheeks for them. We did not turn towards Big Tom when we heard him sniff back his tears. Harry was more efficient, in the most classic British way. He put the kettle on, chose eight of our mismatching mugs and set them on a tray. His face a closed book, he pushed us gently away from his cupboard, selected his favourite Earl Grey tea and a box of chocolates. When tea was ready and poured, he walked to the living room carrying the heavy tray, the rest of us in tow, and set it all on the table. Gently, he knelt by Ann Fisher who was crying sat on the floor in the middle of the room, her family clustered around her. Harry put a mug of tea in her hand – a very white and over-sweet cup of tea. She raised her eyes to him and nodded, swallowing her next wail and sniffing back her tears. Jazz, Big Tom and I all grabbed a mug and gave them to the other Fishers, then returned to grab one for ourselves. We joined them sitting on the floor. No one could or dared speak, only Ann Fisher, the one whose loss was the most apparent that day, could break the silence. When she did, it was in a feeble, broken and hardly audible voice.

'What am I going to do now? I can't be without you all. I can't. No.'

'Look. We are here, Mummy,' Maisie said. Ann looked at her daughter and gave her a weak smile, caressing her cheek with her hand. In the same feeble voice, in such strong contrast with the violence of her previous emotional explosion, she replied to Maisie.

'My darling. You are looking so much better already. That is the most important thing. You will live. I don't care where. But … all of you, gone, and me alone.'

'Mum, we are here. We can still see each other, spend time with each other. Look, we are doing it now,' Owen said to his mother.

James gave Harry and me a look, letting it slide to Jazz and Big Tom, before saying, 'We will work something out. We can talk every day, maybe even Skype every day. And visits, we will have visits.'

Now I understood the look James had given us. It was one of hope, hope that we would help them make it work out one way or the other. My heart went out to them and I was determined that yes, we would! Harry and I heard Zeno coming back in and I went to the kitchen, signalling him to come and join us. I updated him on the Fisher situation and he was shocked.

'The poor woman ...' Zeno gasped.

'I know.'

'We have to help somehow,' he continued.

'I agree. We must make sure she has access to the house and to them.'

'Yes ... It will be the same for all the Relocated when families are involved. What about Thomas?'

'I don't know. Jazz hasn't told her family. Big Tom doesn't seem to have either.'

'Big Tom?' Zeno raised his eyebrows as he asked.

'Err ... Yes. It fits him like a glove, don't you think?'

'Actually, it does. Talking about Jazz, she never mentions her family. Is she OK?'

'She seems to be OK. She has her ups and downs. She's got us, she has the house and – thank God – her 'lounge' project. This project of hers may end up being key for the Relocated: it will be the perfect meeting place for the Fishers.' A solution was already taking shape for the Fishers, for any Relocated. Well, as long as the numbers didn't reach the Ingis Chen aim of millions.

'Wakey wakey, Yoko.' I vaguely heard Zeno calling me out from my reveries. It seemed to happen a lot recently that I got lost in my drifting thoughts.

'Huh?' I replied.

'Sorry to be quite practical now, but it is already 1 p.m and the Sparrows are coming in an hour. Should we eat?'

'Yes, sure. I was thinking homemade burgers and oven fries, something quick and fast. OK for you?'

'Fine by me. I am going to prepare a big mixed salad with lots of stuff in it.'

The main bell of the parking ground rang, at the same time as my FTab. I answered the latter.

'Miss Salelles?'

'Yes?'

'Hi! Phil asked me to let you know that three additional mobile homes and generators have just been delivered.'

'Wow! That was fast. Thanks!' He hung up. I informed Harry and Zeno, who went to get them through the Fog and to WII, Zeno driving them one by one. Leila explained afterwards she thought James might want to stay around ours, so she organised another mobile home for him and two additional ones as they might as well plan ahead for any potential Relocated. They were hopeful that Nick would make his way to our house in no time and would also need a place to stay. Good thinking!

During lunch, Jazz explained her lounge idea to the Fishers and Big Tom. They loved the idea! It motivated Jazz even more, as she told me later. She was not doing it only for her now: it might be even more important for the other Relocated. I suggested that the lounge being the meeting place between husbands and wives, more would be happening in her private TV viewing room than watching movies. She should plan for that, even if that made her uncomfortable. Moreover, Zeno and I briefed the newly Relocated about the arrival of the mobile homes. I didn't talk about Nick from the Society. They would wonder where he came from and I didn't want to start explaining about the second house, then Jack, then his disappearance and so on. First, it was sensitive information. Second, they had had enough for one day. The Fishers asked if they could stay together for another hour after lunch, to put their heads together about their situation and what would need to be done with Ann's work (she was working part-time and would continue so she could have more time for husband and children), their house (she would sell it and move into something smaller and closer) and the official explanation for the children's disappearance (they were joining their father abroad).

Zeno headed out to be in the clearing of WII when the Sparrows arrived. They would come for tea afterwards when the

Fishers had gone their separate ways. That family had too much on their plates to mix with the Lil'London people that day.

I was clearing the table with Jazz before joining Zeno. Harry had gone to his room to do some work. Rico was still in his studio as far as we knew. Simba had had a lot of excitement all day and a lot of short popping in and out for her needs, but no proper walk. I had not paid her enough attention and felt bad about it. I would make sure to do so when going out to meet Barnaby and Jonas Sparrow.

Jazz wanted to look her best, as I had I told her that Barnaby Sparrow was hot.

'Jazzy, I don't even know if he's got four wives already,' I said, raising my eyes to the roof.

'You're joking! As you don't know for sure, he remains a potential single hunk. I will be looking at my best, until proven he is not available. That … is … it.'

'OK. Got it. Whatever makes you happy, hon.' I winked at her and was heading towards the door when she stopped me.

'Wait a second, you! Not … so … fast.'

'What? What have I done now?'

'Your date. How did it go?'

'Ah. That.' With all that happened today, I forgot she was bound to ask questions.

'Yes, "that"... So?'

'Terrible. It went all wrong, I'm afraid.' I almost smiled at her shoulders slumping. That wasn't fun gossip, plus she was probably disappointed for me.

'It can't be that bad. What did he do?'

'Nothing. It's complicated.'

'Already if he does nothing that is not a good sign, especially when last time he did plenty from what I understand.' Clever girl, fishing for information.

'Well, indeed, nothing happened and considering how complex things are with the Fog …'

'But you like him! I can tell you like him! Give yourself a break, Yoko, you haven't met anyone you like for so long. You're not going to give up that easily, are you? Soon you will all have that big house next door and you will be able to have a proper double life, with the best of both worlds. That includes a man.'

'You don't even know what happened! What if his situation is complicated too? What if it's all a big mess?'

'Has he been in touch since yesterday?' she asked, crossing her arms in front of her, businesslike.

'Yes. But with all that happened this morning, I haven't had a chance to reply and ...' Jazz interrupted me with a firm 'Do it now.'

'Come on Jazz! We are on our way out. I'll do it after.' In truth, I had planned to do it when she was leaving for her room. I didn't want to do it in front of her. I wanted to take my time.

'What did he say?' Jazz was in full inquiry-mode.

Leo wrote he felt robbed of his Yoko-time. He was looking forward to seeing me again tomorrow for dinner, but he longed to touch me and kiss me and have me for him and him only, to play with me a lot more.

'He said he would like to see me again,' I summarised for Jazz.

'Aaand? Will you?'

'Maybe.'

'Yoko! Do you want to? Yes or no?'

'Fine. Yes, I want to. It's just ... What happened last night, it makes me think that maybe I need to focus on getting my life a bit more 'normal' first. You know, a bit more organised. Then I will be able to squeeze a man into it.'

'Squeeze? SQUEEZE INTO IT! Have you lost the plot? Relationships – and intimacy – are one of the best things in life. They are not to be 'squeezed in'. They need to be cajoled, nurtured and placed on a pedestal in your life!'

I sighed. She snapped her fingers at me several times up and down in front of my face.

'Get a grip woman. Get out there and get a nice man. Get some too! At least one of us will get good sex. He was good sex, right? Write to him.' She was now standing proudly, hands on her hips, in a don't-mess-with-me pose.

'Oh for heaven's sake! Yes, he was. It is just … You have no idea how complicated it is! But OK, I will try! There, happy now? Can we go?'

'Reply to him that you fancy the pants off him?'

'What? No!'

'Yoko, r-e-p-l-y t-o h-i-m!'

'G-i-v-e m-e a b-r-e-a-k I w-i-l-l r-e-p-l-y w-h-e-n I a-m r-e-a-dy! OK?'

Now we just glared at each other. We were on the edge of an argument and I couldn't believe it was about my sex life. She threw her hands in the air, over-accentuating how exasperated she was or exasperating I was.

'Whatever. I don't see how it could be that complicated anyway. Just give it a go and have fun, that's all I am saying. It is not as if you would have to see him every day, like a work colleague or something. Wait? It's not one of the bodyguards, is it?'

'No,' I said. 'Worse,' I thought.

'See, so all I am saying is, have a go at it and have fun in the process. If it doesn't work out, it doesn't work out and you can just put it aside, move on and not see him again.'

'Uh-huh … Thanks … I'll think about it. And I'll write to him.'

'Good. Now, hop, hop, hop. I have a hunk to see.'

'I just need the loo and I'll be right down.'

Mostly, I wanted to take the toilet trip as an opportunity to be alone for a few minutes and write to Leo. To Leila I wrote a quick note suggesting she come later today when Leo and Dante would be there, for brainstorming on Ingis Chen. We had to inform the other Foggies as soon as possible. I next wrote to Leo a warm message apologising for not replying earlier, hardly having had any time alone. I added that I agreed with him and so wished for private time with him. It was true, that night in his hotel bedroom was still bringing a big smile to my face. However, Jazz had put her finger right on a nagging fear: because of the Fog bond, I was concerned what would happen in the future. Me, Switcher, him, Crosser, we were bound to be in each other's lives until death. What if a relationship between us turned sour?

Jazz didn't comment on how long I had taken in the loo, but first thing she did was glance at my jacket pocket where the FTab was poking out. Our little chat had dampened her spirits somewhat and she looked a bit sombre as we walked out. However, the look on her face was priceless when she saw Barnaby. I knew he would be her type! I knew it! The closest I had seen this look on her face was during the Gucci sale when she saw a bag she had been drooling over on for months at a third of the price. The sight of Barnaby was definite woman eye-candy. Well built, tall, strong, he even had a nice mane of hair dancing in the wind. He wore a blousy white shirt held to his trousers with a pair of braces, sleeves turned up revealing strong arms. He came to greet us harbouring a pleasant smile on his chiselled face, complemented by a powerful stride and a firm handshake. The man was a woman's magazine model.

Jazz whispered in my ear, 'No wedding band' before putting on her best alluring smile.

'Doesn't mean a thing, dear friend. Another world, remember?'

'Shut up. Don't ruin the magic.' And that was it, she was lost to me, or Zeno, or anyone for the rest of her time in the forest. She was all intent on getting friendly with her new neighbour, as she put it so warmly to the Sparrows.

That Saturday night, in bed and totally exhausted from the rollercoaster of emotions I had gone through that day, I mulled over how they were all linked and entangled with my new job: the Fishers, and my duties to the Relocated and their families;

the Sparrows; the expectations, hopes and fears of the people of Lil'London; Leo, and more broadly the relationship with the other Foggies. I looked back to my office years thinking maybe it wasn't that bad. I didn't have to work at weekends, plus I could leave the work-related stress and responsibilities at work. However the responsibilities of the Fog and my role as mediator between two worlds hit me hard. This was not just a job, this was my life. There would be no holidays, no break, and no way of separating the professional from the personal.

The afternoon with Barnaby and Jonas Sparrow had gone very well. For two hours father and son focused on the motorbike with Zeno and Big Tom. The four men bonded over the mechanics. After that, the team switched to beers and crisps on the sofa. It was very much appreciated by the Sparrows, who looked at everything in the house with wonder. Jazz and I had left the men long ago and gone back inside. At first, Jazz had been acting like a bee buzzing by the honey pot, wanting her share. However, she is a clever girl and read the signs. She reluctantly left the men and their toy alone when it seemed best.

'Here is my plan,' she told me. 'I'll be charming and friendly. I am opening a door. Then, I'll try to get as much info as possible: first and foremost, if he is available, then, how old and how many are his children. Because, I have this feeling some could be too close to my age.'

'Possible.'

'Disturbing.'

'Another World, another ...' I started saying.

'Don't! I know. It's annoying! You don't fancy him, do you?' Jazz asked me, eyeing me suspiciously. I reassured her.

'No, I don't. I agree he is great looking, but I find him a bit too "cold handsome" for my taste. A bit dark. I need more warmth. Best is "charming handsome".'

'What the hell is "cold handsome"?'

'Well, it's like in a museum. The statues, they are perfect, beautiful, works of art to be admired, not something I would like to touch and feel. In short, I am not moved.'

'You are weird. I am finding this guy pretty warm. More, he is hot!'

'Yep, he is, but I am not moved. Too perfect.'

'Too perfect! No wonder you have sex issues.'

'You don't get it. I like the little imperfections that make the person more human, the little faults, the non-symmetries bringing out the uniqueness of a face, defining a personality. Little things, like someone having a different walk because they broke a leg some time before, or a scar on the jaw from sports. Of course, if a jaw-dropping man comes along I will say 'Wow!' and might fancy his fit body – I did talk to you about Barnaby, didn't I? – but for me to be interested in addition to being attracted, the person needs to charm me, to intrigue me, to seduce me. I like to interact with a personality, see it on a face.

'Nope. I am happy to go for the demi-god. Hot body does it for me.' Jazz winked at me.

The best is when you have a good balance of both. Take Leo for example. I looked at him during the evening, while he recounted 'his' encounter with Ingis Chen. Charm, tick. Obvious (bantering) personality, tick. Good looks, even if not top model, tick. I smiled at the thought. I could add kindness, consideration, humour, sweet and so on, but that was something different from what we had talked about with Jazz. So I looked at him and I liked him. He was attractive and interesting. The naughty thoughts forming in my head were interrupted by Rico.

'I don't understand. It was just you and this Ingis Chen? Were you not with ... friends?' he asked Leo.

'Obviously this is not something I would talk about with friends who don't know about the Fog,' Leo replied.

It proved a real struggle to fight my urge to give Rico a 'shut up' stare. I had forgotten that Rico knew my date to be Leo and from the tone of his voice, he was wondering what was going on. He asked me later, when we had two minutes alone in the kitchen, if I was seeing someone else.

'Rico, we couldn't say we were together now, could we ...' I told him.

'So you were there too!' he exclaimed, though in a whisper.

'Yes, I was there. But Ingis Chen didn't know who I was. We didn't lie to the others, we just omitted ...'

'A white lie is still a lie, babe. I hate this crap. Knowing. Well, no, I like knowing, but not being able to tease you and all,' he sighed heavily.

I would have explained further to him, but Harry arrived.

When Leo and Dante left, we all gathered for a last drink in the living room. We had drunk quite a lot that night; Zeno had lavished his homemade do-not-ask-questions-on-its-provenance grappa on us. I was dozing on the sofa after a quick trip to the forest with Zeno for Simba. Doodling on a piece of paper, I was thinking about Leo. Maybe I should just go with the flow and see what happened. Who else was there for me anyway? Someone not involved with the Fog was even less of a good idea. Lil'London people? It would be even more complicated.

Something popped into my head: Lil'London history book! I couldn't arrive tomorrow and meet Edmund without having read at least the first chapter. It would have to be over breakfast, as right then I was not in a state to register anything. This last thought made me drag myself up off the sofa, say goodnight to everyone and go to bed. Jazz was following behind me, tipsy, struggling a bit with the stairs. When she said good night, she hugged me tight and said 'You know, Leo and Dante, they are not bad. Pity neither of them is my type. Dante is a bit too skinny and Leo is less than 1m 85. But they are nice, they are nice ... Maybe if your guy doesn't work out one could be for you?'

'Goodnight Jazz.'

Simba settled next to me on the bed.

# WEEK V

**Day 1 (Sunday)**

The plan was a leisurely breakfast in bed with the *Lil'London Tales* for a read. It was Sunday after all. Aside from taking care of Simba's needs, I didn't have to go out before 10.15 a.m. to attend Edmund Poff's sermon at 11 a.m. Ideally, I could squeeze in a good two hours on the *Tales*. That would be a start.

Just before my alarm went off at 8.00 a.m., the front doorbell woke me up. The doorbell should not have rung on a Sunday morning so early. Simba was up and licking me, wanting to play and go out, so I put on my dressing gown. The weather was starting to warm up at last and it was less difficult to get out of bed. Outside my door, I heard Zeno's door closing and Harry's opening. I raised my voice slightly and told them I would take care of it. Harry hesitated upstairs a few seconds, caught between curiosity and hangover, before opting to go back to bed. Zeno came down and followed me, looking the worse for wear. He indicated he had his gun in his dressing gown pocket with his hand on it, just in case, an after-effect of knowing about Ingis Chen. Simba was half-whining, half-growling at the door, seemingly growing into the role of protector of the house.

A man put a gun straight between my eyes when I opened the door. He swiftly moved in, grabbed me by the shoulders, and closed the door behind him. Pulling me towards him in one fast move, the man held the gun to my right temple. He stopped Zeno pulling out his hand out of his pocket where the gun was with a brief 'don't even think about it mate!' to which Zeno instinctively raised his hands up palms open.

'Names!' the man commanded.

'Zenone,' Zeno replied, eyes moving nervously between me, the gun and the man.

'She is Yoko?' he asked.

Zeno hesitated, then said yes.

'Name of your bodyguard?' The man asked me.

'Phil,' I replied.

I felt the man's tension leaving him, as if he was starting to relax. The shock, adrenaline and fear I had just experienced had drained away my hangover. My mind was suddenly clear and I understood what was happening.

'You work for the Society, don't you? You are the one who was relocated during Jack's rescue?' I asked him. Now it was his turn to hesitate.

'Please take your gun off my head,' I asked as gently as possible, considering the circumstances. The man did and let go of me.

'Shit!' The man said, looking down at his boots. Simba had just peed on his leg.

'Well, that'll teach you. Never put yourself between a puppy and its path to the big outdoors. So, now, can you please put this gun away? It makes me feel uncomfortable,' I asked.

'What is wrong with you? Barging in into people's houses like that! Are you nuts?' Zeno yelled at the man.

'So sorry,' the man apologised in a very British fashion. 'I had to be sure you were who I hoped you would be.' He looked in his early thirties although he could be late twenties. It was difficult to tell with his stubble and tired lines. He was about ten centimetres taller than me, with closely cut blond hair on the side and greasy front forelocks falling on his face. His piercing blue eyes observed everything in one glance, they seemed to note every detail.

'Whatever,' Zeno grumbled unimpressed. 'I need coffee.' He turned his back to us and went to the kitchen. He was obviously very upset. From what he told me later, Zeno was both in shock and annoyed that he had not been able to protect me.

'What's your name?' I asked the man while indicating he should take his jacket and shoes off.

'Nick.'

'Are you hungry?' I asked him. I tried to smile and be nice. I was still very tense from having a gun against my face. I had never had a gun aimed at me before and the adrenaline was still pumping through my whole body. I was not feeling particularly friendly towards him.

'Well, I don't want to ...' Nick began.

'Intrude? Jeez, I think you've gone beyond that,' I interrupted, then checked myself. 'Sorry. We had a bad start. Let's start again. I am Yoko.'

'Nick Baker. Nice to meet you.'

'So, tea? Coffee? Food? I am afraid the full English breakfast is not my speciality, you will have to wait for Harry on that one.'

'Tea would be lovely. Food as well. Anything,' Nick answered with a smile. It showed a different side of him, much more engaging

'What have you been eating since Thursday?'

'Basically, nothing. The odd animal. I didn't want to waste time, or attract attention with campfires. I would have been here quicker, but it was imperative I made sure I wasn't being followed.'

During this exchange, I had led him to the kitchen where Zeno was preparing coffee and had put the kettle on. He had been listening.

'Do you know if Jack ... I mean, have you seen him, or them?' I asked.

'No. I just saw the signs he was with one of the other guys before I lost them. When it wasn't clear who was hunting whom, I followed my orders to come back here. I had all the information given to the team during the mission preps, in case one of us was sent across.'

'So the Society had prepared you for the eventuality of being relocated? You went to the rescue knowing that it might happen to you?' It was the decent thing to do, informing him. Well done, Society! What I was wondering was, why did they take the risk?

'Of course. We were prepared for this eventuality,' Nick answered. 'We all knew what was involved. Part of the job and part of the thrill. Though nothing prepares you for what you feel when you come out in a brand new world, and you realise this is it, you can't go back.'

'Why? Why did you do it?' Zeno asked.

'Because I believe in it. I fought for my country in many ways because I believe in its values. I am English and proud of it. In joining forces with the Society, I am still following my beliefs as an individual and British,' Nick said.

'But … the Society is not British. It is not a national entity, as far as I understand,' I cut in.

'No. It isn't. You see, for me, it's like an international sporting competition: you represent the national interest, but what drives you is the spirit of the sport. In the Society, we are a community from many countries: we represent them, we make sure no one is forgotten, but what drives us is the belief in what we do.'

'That is an unusual comparison, an international sporting competition,' Zeno commented.

'I was a professional boxer. National team. International level,' Nick replied.

'Ah! That explains the athletic physique, but not how you go from boxer to Society mercenary,' I asked him.

'Injury. I pushed too hard. So I joined the army, again for my country. And I wanted to do something with my life. What brought me immense satisfaction when boxing at high levels was how it inspired people, young ones who got mixed up with the wrong crowd, to get motivated to do something for themselves. At those levels, people are brought together. In the British army, we represent your country, but these days we don't fight to defend our country, we protect and promote values. We intervene to pre-empt, safeguard, and help – at least in principle. It is not as simple in practice, I got very frustrated. I don't know how, but the Society found me.'

'You're quite an idealist, aren't you?' I asked him, knowing pretty well that that was what the Society had seen in him.

'I have a quote for you,' Nick replied taking the mug of steaming tea: '"What are we holding onto, Sam?" – "That there's some good in this world, Mr Frodo … and it's worth fighting for."'

'The Lord of the Rings,' I smiled. 'Tolkien. Quite suitable for our situation.' 'I'm not a hippie, but I have found my way to fight for peace and love. Please don't quote me on that, I'll deny it,' Nick said with a grin that made little dimples in his cheek. He looked barely out of his teens then.

Zeno had mellowed a bit. The three of us were sitting at the dining table, sipping tea and coffee. I grabbed from the fridge and cupboards a selection of cold cuts and cheeses, as well as bread, butter and a leftover of tomato salad from the previous night. Nick prepared himself a big sandwich inside a sliced half baguette, piling in everything with a generous amount of mustard and ketchup. There was a moment's silence while Nick chewed and I took the opportunity to call Leila and inform her Nick had showed up here. When I hung up, Nick had finished his sandwich and Zeno was preparing another cup of tea for him. I had more time to look at him. He was filthy, he smelled and needed new clothes.

'Would you like to take a shower?' I suggested.

'I would love to have a shower! Are you sure you don't mind?' he said after swallowing a cookie and grabbing another one.

'Of course not!' I replied.

'I'll give you a pair of chinos and a spare T-shirt,' Zeno added, returning with more tea.

'Thank you. Very kind,' Nick replied. He looked genuinely appreciative. Minutes later, I led him to the bathroom with a spare towel together with a handful of hotel mini shampoo bottles and soaps. I would have to jump in the shower just after him and get ready myself. I didn't want to miss my important engagement in Lil'London. Oops! I still hadn't read the *Lil'London Tales*!

When Nick was done with his shower, I was in my room next door sorting out what I would wear that day, laying it all on my bed. I heard him come out of the bathroom and opened my door to give him the clothes Zeno had pulled out for him. I was greeted by a quite a sight: if I thought Leo was lean, Nick was displaying an Olympic-like body! It was proper eye-candy. I caught myself staring too much. Now, a fit body had never been what drove me to be with someone, on the contrary men too focused on their physiques made me run away. Vanity is not that attractive for me. However, right then, the muscular torso and arms, still wet with droplets of water running along, made me gulp. Nick had a large tattoo on his upper arm of the rampant English lion.

'Here we go. Some clothes for you,' I handed over the bunch of clothes, refocusing my eyes on his face.

'Thanks. Shall I go back in the bathroom to change? Does anyone need it?' Nick asked.

'Actually, I need it. Do you mind changing in my room while I use the bathroom?'

'Sure.'

Jazz picked that moment to come out of her room, just when Nick entered my room and me the bathroom. She took one look at him, one look at me, raised her eyebrows, and with a huge grin on her face she turned on her heel and went back in her room. Great. Now she thought Nick was my mysterious lover.

Before leaving for Lil'London, the whole household met downstairs. Leila had arrived earlier with a spare bag for Nick and they had had a discussion while I was getting ready, the outcome of which soon became apparent. Leila and Zeno had been plotting behind my back about my going to Lil'London to the Poffs on my own. They didn't like the idea that I was so vulnerable. Zeno had already told me he was against it after the arrow incident, and insisted on accompanying me. I had refused. I needed to be alone with the Poffs, especially with Maud. I also wanted it to be a private visit, not an official one. Zeno and I should be seen as separate individuals, so that personal relations could be built with the people there. His afternoon with the Sparrows the day before comforted me on that idea.

Leila and Zeno came up with an alternative solution. I had Phil as a bodyguard in our world, I would have Nick in the Lil'London world. First, the Relocated of the Ingis Chen team was out there somewhere and to be reckoned with. Second, there had been an attack against Zeno and me already in WII. Even though the locals of WII had welcomed us relatively warmly, there were obvious reservations and apprehension in the little town. Only one hate-filled person could put my life in jeopardy. Last, they felt that my travelling accompanied by a guard would suit my standing as an ambassador, or something similar. There wasn't much I could do to protest after all that. Nick promised he would not intervene in any of my activities and meetings, only stay outside or at a distance when I was with anyone. His only goal was to ensure my security for now.

'What do you mean "for now"?' I asked.

'Well, things are bound to evolve. We are only fumbling and adapting as we go along, aren't we?' Leila replied and added, 'There, some cookies direct from Alaska made by Mitch and Rosario's mother. Chocolate and nuts, sent via our rep there on their request.' I resisted the urge to open the pack and have some now. It would be a nice treat to share tonight when I was back.

'Nick, do you horse ride?' I turned and look at him.

'No, but I'll learn,' he replied without even blinking.

'Fancy starting today?'

Nick just looked at me and said, 'As you wish. Where you go, I go. I am yours.' His eyes were smiling, his face was dead serious.

'Jeez,' I heard Jazz murmur next to me. 'The Society knows how to pick them ...' I gave her a slight push with my elbow. Leila had heard and chuckled. Nick too, probably, but his eyes were not moving from me. 'Please,' I prayed. 'May you not turn out to be a creep. Please, please, please.'

I had decided to take Simba with me. Once we were ready to go, I chose a bag to put her in during the ride. Leila caressed the puppy's muzzle, commenting how fast she was growing. I nodded and said that soon she would turn a few heads when walking her in London. Leila started.

'What do you mean, in London?' she quizzed. I realised I had slipped up. I was so fixated on keeping secret the fact that Simba was able to be a Facilitator for me, for which I was training her daily, that I forgot not to mention she could cross between the two worlds. As I began stuttering an explanation, Harry took over, explaining that Simba could apparently accompany me depending if I was with a Facilitator or Crosser. He didn't mention she could walk out on her own and go to either world, or help me do the same (which remained to be proven). From Leila's stare at the dog and heavy silence, the information provided was big news enough.

'Animals from WII, like people, can't cross to our world. At least we thought they couldn't. There is no record anywhere of that. Very interesting ...' She didn't finish her sentence, she was lost in thought.

'Are animals able to cross from this world to the others?' Nick asked.

'Some did. We assumed it was the same one out of seven rule in average. They couldn't go back though. They were relocated.'

'Could it be that animals also have Switchers, Crossers and Facilitators then?' Zeno asked. I had already had this conversation with Leila. My mind was more on Simba and how special she was and how lucky I was.

'No. Well, we don't know everything for sure, but we found no trace of such an occurrence anywhere,' Leila replied, then asked, returning to the subject that currently mattered to her, moving her stare from Simba to me, 'I wonder how she can do that. This is quite unique. Have you noticed anything else?'

'Like ... What?' I was trying to avoid answering her question by asking one myself.

'I don't know,' Leila responded.

'Well, I'll keep an eye on her. It will be easy, she doesn't leave my side. I think I'm definitely her mother substitute now.'

'More like the leader of the pack,' Harry corrected. 'That's how wolves and dogs operate.'

'Right. Yes. Anyway, I am afraid we really have to make a move now.' I was eager to drop the subject and leave. It was my first time not wanting to be late for church.

Attending church has never been my strong point. Not that I didn't find beauty in the service, the architecture, the words, the serenity, or the faith. I did. I was just quickly bored by it. Maybe I had an attention span deficit disorder, but after twenty minutes on a good day I started day-dreaming, or on the bad days inventing scandalous stories about random people spotted in the congregation. Unfortunately, considering the circumstances and the unusual audience, it was not a good day. My attention was specifically drawn to Barbara Snayth, all pampered and looking quite haughty in the private family booth, surrounded by husband, children and other women whose outfits indicated a high social status. Other wives, I assumed. My imagination started to drift on how it would all work in their household. I wondered how many murders between wives occurred each year in this world.

I asked the Poffs about polygamy afterwards. Maud Poff was openly against, Edmund was more considered in giving his opinion, uncomfortable at first. The more time I spent with them and showed him I was not judging but curious, the more relaxed he was with me. Maybe the wine helped: I had brought a bottle of champagne and a bottle of Bordeaux. They definitely enjoyed both to the last drop. As a guest, I didn't want to make my hosts feel uncomfortable. It was clear that even though Edmund Poff disapproved of the local status quo, he wasn't inclined to get involved in promoting change. He had stood his ground at a personal level and this was already an achievement. Maud was more of the activist. In another time and place she would have been a strong and dedicated supporter of women's rights.

The basic status of the women in Lil'London was simple. Their duty was to have children; their role to raise those children. They were not supposed to be intellectual (unlike Maud), to challenge the system (unlike Maud), or to dedicate themselves to something other than the family and good running of the house (unlike Maud). Maud's controversial opinions and actions, although she tried to be subtle in their expression and practice, were frowned upon (I liked Maud).

'My biggest fear growing up was that we would miss the opening of the door to the Other World. My biggest hope was that in this Other World, women would have more recognition,' Maud told me.

'In our world, we refer to your hopes as women's rights.'

'Women's rights? Yes. Rights. It is a stronger word than recognition, isn't it? I am part of the lucky few, I have recognition from the most important person to me, my husband. I still have no rights.'

'My dear, please. You know how you get when you start on these women matters,' Edmund started.

His wife interrupted him. 'Oh darling! But don't you see how some of us are hardly better than their own servants. The only differences are the clothes they wear and the food they eat!' Maud had learned to remain composed even when you could feel the passion behind her words. She was even smiling. Only her voice betrayed her anger. There was hard steel in it mixed with determination. I thought the other members of the council had no idea what was coming their way: the woman who would strive for change the most, the one they should beware of most, was not me.

We were reaching what I had hoped to be dessert but was yet another main dish. It was served by a young woman who Maud and Edmund treated with kindness and always with a thank you before she left the room. The young woman was nervous and kept looking at me. It was strange to have such an effect on this poor young one. She spilled a few things and dropped some cutlery. The Poffs were nice about it. A good way to know the heart of someone is not how they treat those of equal standing, but those from the classes below, that is when there are classes within a society. From this, I appreciated the Poffs had good hearts. I changed the subject from women's rights by apologising to Edmund Poff for not having had a chance yet to read the *Lil'London Tales*, overwhelmed as I was with the arrival of new Relocated and the issues with their families, among other things. He nodded that he understood and commented that they had been informed indeed that some kind of strange homes had been set up near our house and that James Fisher had moved into one with a young man and a young lady who the council assumed were family. He also referred to Big Tom as a man of large stature and unusual allure. Edmund indicated the door to the kitchen, where Nick was (actually, Nick was outside by then, but none of us knew. He had finished eating long ago and was sitting under a tree where he could keep an eye on me through the windows.)

'That young man, Nick Baker, does not fit the description.'

'Indeed. He is not the 'unusual' man. He arrived this morning. He is also a Relocated. Nick is my personal attendant.' Referring to Nick as my personal escort was very strange. I couldn't lie to myself, it made me a little proud.

'So you are now six Relocated from London,' Maud said. I did a quick calculation – the three Fishers, Big Tom, Nick and Jazz – and agreed.

'I also understand that the Sparrows came to visit yesterday and spent quite some time with your ... May you remind me how you call your modern vehicle?' Edmund asked.

'Motorbike.'

'Motorbike. What a strange name ... So Barnaby Sparrow and his son came to visit and met some of the new Relocated. Benjamin wished he had been informed, as you might have guessed. Maud mentioned it to me.'

'Informed of what?' I asked, on the defensive.

'Informed that you had started to receive callers, informed that there were new Relocated to whom he should have been introduced first and foremost, especially before Mr Sparrow,' Maud said before Edmund had a chance.

'Yes, I noticed from Mr Snayth's reaction,' I sighed.

Benjamin Snayth and his family had come my way at the end of the preaching outside the church. I was with Maud Poff waiting for her husband to join us. A few steps away from us, Benjamin and Barbara Snayth detached themselves from their little group and walked towards us. There was slight but palpable tension in the air, from Benjamin towards me, but also between Barbara Snayth and Maud Poff. I heard movement behind me and turned to see Nick moving closer and eyeing a stern Augustus Hoare, who was now approaching as well. His wives and the rest of his family remained behind. The focus from the men turned from me to Nick, before returning to me. Snayth spoke first, 'Miss Salelles, what a pleasure to see you among us today. It is an honour that you wished to join our prayers to God with our little community and not to your usual church. What a pity Mr Fisher didn't accompany you with ...' My usual church? What usual church? If they knew ...

'The pleasure is mine, Mr Snayth,' I said before he had a chance to finish his sentence. If I could avoid getting into the subject of the Fisher family, it would be better. I wanted to leave with the Poffs as soon as possible.

'Will you be returning to your home for luncheon, or may we invite you to join us in our humble abode?' Snayth continued.

'Mr Snayth, how very kind of you. I thank you for your invitation, which I must decline. I am already otherwise engaged.' They would know later I was going to the Poffs, avoiding to mention it now only enabled me not put Maud on the spot there and then. I should not have bothered as Maud said, 'Indeed, Miss Salelles did us the honour of accepting an invitation to come and discuss the *Lil'London Tales* with Edmund.'

Hearing this, August Hoare gave a little nod of approbation. Barbara Snayth's eyes narrowed on Maud, and Benjamin Snayth had a wide fake smile.

'How lovely,' he commented unconvincingly, then remarked, 'Miss Salelles, it came to our attention that a few new people have arrived from the portal?'

'Yes, you have been informed correctly.' No need to give details, I didn't have to justify anything.

'Maybe it would be a good idea to introduce them to us as representatives of Lil'London before anybody else.' So that was it. Snayth and Hoare did not like being robbed of their prerogative to meet the new Relocated before the Sparrows. I fought the urge to look up at the sky and roll my eyes. It was like being back in the school yard. I decided to dismiss the first sentence and only reply to part of their comment, 'Certainly, we ought to organise a meeting between you and the newly arrived from our World. Shall we convene a day and time next week? Would Tuesday suit?'

Snayth and Hoare agreed. Maud Poff believed her husband would happily make himself available to join them. The meeting would take place in the town hall. I then turned towards Nick and conveyed with a look he should come to be introduced. Nick made a move forward but remained just slightly back, his shoulder behind me, not in a withdrawn manner, more a protective one.

'Mrs Snayth, Mrs Poff, Mr Snayth, Mr Hoare, may I introduce you to Mr Baker who just joined the community of people relocated here.'

They all greeted each other, the men shaking hands, then Nick Baker returned to his place behind me. It was obvious he didn't think his current priority was social niceties. Edmund Poff arrived a few seconds afterwards and Maud indicated that it was time to part company. Edmund looked at Nick with curiosity, then inquiringly at Maud when Nick started to follow us. Maud Poff discreetly asked me if she ought to add a cover at the dining table and I replied in the negative. I wanted an intimate lunch, just the three of us, as we had planned. I aimed to drop the formality for once.

Back at the dining table, I asked Edmund Poff if he was also bothered that the Sparrows met Big Tom first.

'Miss Salelles, I believe the council aims to oversee the exchanges and novelties linked to the gate for the benefit of the whole community. We have some grounds to want to be the first informed and regulate the interactions, at least at the beginning. It is important to set up a good foundation. Be that as it may, I think that your ways are not our ways, Miss Salelles, and we ought to accept this. I don't believe you acted in disrespect of our habits and customs. On the contrary, you seem inclined to want to be accessible to everyone. It is very democratic of you. It will take time for both sides to adapt.' When Edmund finished, Maud looked at him with both pride and love.

'Thank you, Mr Poff. Please will you call me Yoko? Our ways are indeed more relaxed and I am not used to such formality in private conversations. On your comments, I appreciate your honesty. I am glad you understand that we meant no harm. Mr Sparrow displayed curiosity about the motorbike and we just thought that it would be nice to spend a couple of hours satisfying this curiosity.

You see, the metal he forges and the metal used for our vehicle are quite similar. It was only natural that he was inquisitive. We want to help introduce our world to everyone without distinction.' As I said this, I knew it was untrue. We still had quite a lot of work on that front of 'equal rights for everyone'. As George Orwell said in *Animal Farm*, 'All animals are equal, but some animals are more equal than others' and the same still applied in the big complex farm that is our planet – and theirs. In truth, the Relocated had more rights, more priorities than others for us. Maud intervened, cutting off my vague recollection of the distant read.

'My dear, I would also take into account the rationale behind Benjamin's and Augustus's convictions. Augustus is an altruist; his concerns are for the moral and social balance of our community. His ideal would be to introduce all the goods and modern tools of your world, yet keep our mentality unchanged. Benjamin is more practical, or self-interested: if the council is the first to know and supervises all the relations with your house, he may seize opportunities first, gain exclusive rights or monopolies, increase his influence and continue to rule here, economically and politically unhindered!'

'Maud! You shouldn't ...' Edmund Poff exclaimed

'Speak like this in front of Yoko – may I call you Yoko too? Why, Edmund? Out of solidarity for the council or our little community? I haven't criticised its work, have I? I am only pointing out some personal motivations behind some of its actions,' Maud defended herself.

'Talking like this in public, in front of Miss Salelles ...' Edmund tried to speak again.

'Yoko, please call me Yoko,' I interjected nicely. It destabilised him.

'Well, I ... I ... Talking in front of Yoko like this is dangerous, Maud. You are protected because you are my wife, but you have read enough to know that going against the system, any system, has negative consequences. Moderation ...'

'I know, I know, moderation is best. You are always so wise, my dear husband – one of your most irritating qualities, though such an endearing one.'

They really were an earnest couple. I just had had a glimpse of their complicity, respect for each other and, yes, care. Maud threw me a glance and smiled. We had clicked (sometimes you meet someone and very quickly you just know you are going to get along, that this person would find a nice little place in your life). The lunch went on to more trivial topics afterwards. We were on the equivalent of British soil, so evidently we had to talk about the weather. In detail.

They gave me a tour of the house, and I spent a bit of time with their twins, Annie and Charlie. They were bright and outgoing children, who loved playing with Simba. They asked me if I would bring books for children as well. I promised to do so, then checked myself and added that I would if their father didn't mind. Edmund seemed grateful for my consideration. I didn't say it out of diplomacy, I said it because I cared. Maud told me that the Snayths would certainly invite me for lunch on Tuesday, as Barbara Snayth would want to have me as a guest, not least now that I had been at theirs.

'How lovely!' I replied, mimicking Benjamin Snayth. Maud burst out laughing.

'What if I suggested organising a lunch between the wives here for you, thus we would beat her to it? She will only dislike me a tad more for it, but a tad more wouldn't make much difference anymore,' Maud offered.

'Maud ...' Edmund sighed.

'Maud, I wouldn't want to create any problems ...' I began and didn't have time to finish.

'Do you know how nice it is for me to have a chance to make Barbara feel she can't completely rule the social life of this town? Please, I'm begging you now.'

'Very well. As you wish,' I replied, albeit knowing I should remain neutral. 'Thank you for organising it all. Maybe I could return you the favour and you could join me for tea later in the week? Thursday afternoon perhaps, if it is convenient for you? I am sure you would enjoy being shown the house and have a glimpse of how we live.'

This could prove invaluable. I was going to suggest Monday and then changed my mind. I had to be careful not to start showing too much favouritism for her before even meeting the other wives. I also thought, but didn't say, that her visit would create the opportunity for her to fill me in more on the townspeople in private. It was important to stay open-minded and to remember she was challenging some of their ideas, so she was also not the most objective. I ought to hear the others' point of view before making my own conclusions about them, with information and opinions taken from each side.

Nick pulled a face getting back on the horse, which didn't stop him being much chattier on the way back. He told me he had been fascinated people-watching in the church. During lunch he had observed the comings and goings in the house, and the children playing outside with old wooden toys. He liked it so much better than children indoors in front of the television or on a computer. There was something healthy in the life he saw. He was aware it was a privileged household and wondered if the others in Lil'London also breathed out happiness and serenity. Simba and he had spent all the time during lunch together and they had bonded quite well. Still, Simba left him as soon as she saw me, welcoming me as if I had disappeared for weeks. Now she was deep asleep in the large opened bag, nestled on the little blanket and toy I had put at the bottom for her.

'Nick – can I call you Nick? Thank you for looking after me today. It was nice to know you were there.'

'Yoko – can I call you Yoko? I hope to look after you for a long time. Your ability is rare – and precious. It is an added bonus that you have a good heart from what I have noticed and heard. It doesn't hurt that you're pretty to look at too, as I will have to check you out all day.'

'Thank you ...' I was unsettled. Was this just a passing comment or was this professional mercenary flirting? I never could recognise any signs!

'You are welcome.'

I wondered if he knew about Leo. Probably not, he was in the forest when the meeting with Ingis Chen happened, when the dating between us had become common knowledge in the Society. That led me to think he needed to hear about Ingis Chen. Nick Baker listened to the story intently. Afterwards, he asked, 'And you said it happened on Friday night?'

'Yes.'

'I wish I could protect you in both worlds. This is going to be so frustrating. Phil is the best though, you are in good hands there.'

We went silent for a while, then he spoke again, 'Yoko, do you love horse riding?'

'Yes.'

'Bugger.'

I laughed and said, 'I promise, sometimes we'll go by motorbike.'

'One each?'

'I don't know how to ride them. You'll have to drive for me.'

'So I'll get to take the lady on a ride! This job is looking better and better.'

He WAS flirting. Oh dear! This could be trouble.

When we got to the house, Big Tom and the Fishers greeted us outside. They were bunched around a makeshift wood-cutting area, devising a little treat for tonight: a forest barbecue on a campfire. Big Tom was in charge of cutting the wood, James Fisher would do the cooking, his son Owen would play guitar and Maisie wanted to roast marshmallows for everyone over the fire. Food was provided by Ann Fisher who wanted photos of the evening in exchange. I suggested Skype video, but James said Ann wasn't ready yet. She feared she would burst out crying and that would ruin the night. They invited Nick to join them, who declined. He had already agreed with Leila this morning to have dinner with all of us.

The evening went better than I had feared, even if it was somewhat awkward, as seemed to happen more and more to me lately. Zeno had packed a big bag to move to Leo's hotel room, Leo had arrived with another big bag with all his belongings, so as not to leave anything that would betray Zeno's little scheme. I couldn't make up my mind whether to be happy or unhappy about Leo moving in. I was just very confused. To summarise:

1. The man I was dating and really liked and, with whom the relationship was secret from the rest of the house, was moving into the room on top of mine.
2. The person I wasn't sure it was a good idea to date, because it was too much too soon with the unclear scenario of our life ahead bound to each other by the Fog, would be on the other side of the ceiling I would stare at all night.
3. The guy I fancied the pants off and almost desperately wanted to have passionate sex with was moving a short flight of stairs away.

   I was pretty much caught between potential true romance and potential disaster. Or, as before, just Lust versus Reason. Usually, I take a step back to think and put a distance between me and the issue. Distance was now non-existent.

Jazz had been invited to join the Relocated lot outside for dinner. Despite not being keen on the campfire experience, she conceded it was good to meet the others sharing her fate. She really needed to get out of the house. The other news was that Leila had left a message for when Nick and I would return. She had been called to Nevada urgently and would not be there for dinner. I introduced Nick to Leo and Dante who had not met him yet and suggested to Nick that maybe he would want to join the others in WII, as Leila was not here.

'I would rather stay with you, if you don't mind. I'll join them tomorrow. It's not every day you meet so many Foggies together,' he replied.

'Cazzo, I still can't get used to this "Foggies" thing,' Rico said.

'I can't blame you,' Nick said. 'Surreal and so real at the same time.'

'I think,' Harry corrected, 'Rico is referring to the term 'Foggies' not the Fog phenomenon.'

Nick frowned and looked surprised. 'Really? Of all the things happening right now, is it the term Foggies that bugs you?' he asked Rico.

'Yep. And the fact that I can't see what their chicks look like.'

Nick eyed Rico stunned, Zeno and I just ignored the remark as a Rico-ism and Harry murmured '15, 17 year old max, I don't give his mental age any more years than that.'

With Jazz and Leila absent, there was a large majority of men around the table: the usual ones – Zeno, Rico and Harry and, that night, Leo, Dante and Nick. On the female side, just me. We chatted about the day's events and activities: Leo on building up an organisation around Zeno's ideas, Dante on his progress for housing the Relocated (he talked at length, losing me fast) and of course we briefed them on our trip to Lil'London. Leo asked Nick what were his first impressions of Lil'London.

'I think I will like the simplicity of the lifestyle, though will hate the claustrophobic village-thinking of the community.'

'I think some individuals are worth getting to know,' Zeno commented. 'Take Barnaby Sparrow for example, I like him. Bright guy. Big Tom might surprise us, too.'

'Because they showed an interest in your motorcycle?' I teased.

'The Poffs are nice, too. Have you met them?' Nick added and his question was addressed to everyone but me.

'Yes,' Zeno said.

'We just met Edmund Poff,' Harry said, including with a swipe of the hand Rico as part of the 'we'.

'Dante and I haven't yet been in the WII here,' Leo noted. There was a certain restlessness in his voice. He had mentioned this to me before, in private. He was quite keen to go there, see the town and meet the people of Lil'London. Dante was keen as well, especially to check their architecture. It was getting urgent to introduce them and I ventured, 'Maybe it's time. The number of Relocated is increasing and they are expecting it to continue. Plus Jack and Ingis Chen's man are out there, so I am keen on preparing them for the fact that there are more Foggies than us.'

'What about Ingis Chen? The council members will know about him if the other guy appears. We don't know what he would say. That could weaken us,' Zeno said.

'They need us for the door as much as before. It may on the contrary strengthen our position if they start to appreciate that Ingis Chen's purely businesslike approach to the Fog, his attempt to grab a share and monopolise markets by whatever means, is less good for them,' I replied.

'You forget his good intentions, my dear,' Harry mocked.

'Oh! Forgive me! Lil'London will love the idea that Chen will overflow our excess population on them, you're right. To come back to my point, I think that when we introduce the Relocated on Tuesday, you should both join, Leo and Dante.'

Zeno approved my proposition. Leo and Dante grinned, the former whispering 'at last' the latter murmuring 'sono pronto!' They were both ready.

Leo then looked at me and said with concern in his voice, 'What about Chen's guy? He could show up here anytime. He is dangerous, he didn't hesitate to shoot at us!'

'He doesn't know where the house is.'

'He'll find it,' Nick said.

'How?' we all asked in unison.

'The same way I would have done if I hadn't known where to go. The geographical layout being the same, I would have gone to the river, to the Thames. Any community of any civilisation tends to gather around rivers and estuaries. Lil'London is by the river, isn't it?'

'True. It's not far from it,' I replied.

'There you go.'

'But he wouldn't know if we were inland or by the sea?' Rico protested.

'We are creatures of habit. He would go towards where the core of London started. That would have been the natural reaction of the previous Relocated. It is also the closest from the Essex house location.'

Harry interrupted Nick, 'Well, that is not exactly the case. They mostly gathered close to where the previous opening was. It is at least ten miles from the City of London.'

'Nevertheless, in all probability, there would be the odd fisherman on the way who would indicate to him where to go.'

'Indeed,' I thought. 'There were other communities besides Lil'London: the council had mentioned there was more than one town. Had they informed them we were here?' I grabbed my notebook and wrote down to enquire on Tuesday when I saw the council next.

Leo cut into the dialogue between Nick and Harry, who were nit-picking on exact mileage and locations, 'Anyway, my point is the man is dangerous. What would happen if, or when, he finds the house? At least it's good to know Yoko has protection!'

'Leila delivered an alarm system this morning. I will set it up at first light tomorrow around the house, in the forest. And yes, Yoko has the best protection. I will not let her out of my sight outside this house, or even in this house.' Nick said the last sentence looking straight at me, face set in a serious professional expression, yet his eyes betrayed the cheeky touch of his remark.

Leo picked up on it and frowned slightly, quickly hiding his reaction by taking a sip of his wine. Rico turned to look at me, raised an eyebrow then he too grabbed his wine glass and took a sip. As if things were not complicated enough ...

'I am going to have cookies for dessert and hot chocolate. Upstairs,' I told them.

Except Nick who was a newbie and shook hands round, we all parted with warm goodnights, Leo and I included, making sure no hugs and goodnight kiss lingered longer than would have been expected. Thus I went to bed early with a steaming hot cup and a few biscuits, determined not to think of Leo in the room above mine. Replying to unread Foggies' messages and updating them on the latest from London was overdue. I didn't feel I had the strength just then, and made another plan for the evening, which was to engross myself in the *Lil'London Tales*. I finished the cookies in five minutes, the hot chocolate in ten, and fell asleep on the book within fifteen.

The Tales were much, much, much more accessible when told by the Poffs. I love history, but reading this was going to be an ordeal. I was still only a few pages into the introduction.

**Day 2 (Monday)**

After I woke up and took Simba out into the forest with Nick, who had been downstairs in the house working on the alarm system, I took my cup of tea and toast to my room. I didn't really want stay downstairs and bump into Leo first thing in the morning. After a shower, with tight jeans and fitted top on, a hint of mascara and my hair done, yes. In my dressing gown with fluffy slippers and face looking all creased from sheets and pillow, no. I had already endured Nick's reaction and that was enough.

'So you're one of those,' he said after looking at me.

'What?' I grumbled.

'Bed worm.'

'What!' I grumbled louder.

'You can tell by the hair, among other things.'

'So sweet of you.' I was already not at my best chatting before tea or coffee, so was he asking for trouble? 'You just talked yourself out of breakfast,' I grunted.

'What if it suits you?'

'No.'

'What if I prepare you breakfast, would that help?'

I considered that one for a brief second before grumbling 'yes'. He put the kettle on and we popped out to give Simba her walk. I didn't aim to stay long and the rain in WII confirmed my decision. Or maybe I was just not in a chatty mood, especially with the line Nick took.

'I noticed yesterday evening you popped out with Simba saying "Fog", today "Forest". When going to London, you say "London"?'

'Yes.'

'Why not just 'walk' or the like, as people do with their dog?'

'It's just. Well. She can go to both worlds, you see, so I like to warn her where we are going, in a way.' I am such a terrible liar. Nick looked at me in such a way. I could have sworn he knew I was up to something.

'What a dedicated dog owner you are, to make sure she is not traumatised.'

'You're being sarcastic, aren't you?'

'Me? Nooooo.'

I dismissed it. I still hadn't had tea and coffee, so my main impulse was just to bite anyway. Better avoid that.

'Wolf,' I told him instead.

'Sorry?'

'Simba is a wolf. Not a dog. Stop saying she is a dog.'

'Right. Dog. No problem.' Nick laughed. 'They told me to tread carefully with you in the morning.'

'Huh?' I turned and looked at him suspiciously.

'Your housemates. They said that you need feeding first thing in the morning.' I must have looked dangerous, because he quickly added, 'They said it in the nicest possible way! They adore you! They just told me so that I don't take it personally and make things worse! No, that's not what I mean ...'

'Omf!' I grunted. 'Drop it! Let's go back in.'

The first sip of tea immediately calmed me down and I relaxed a little around him during breakfast preparations before going back upstairs. This time, I opened the FTab first and not the *Lil'London Tales*. The Foggies messages had waited long enough. The last one received was the first one I opened. It came from the Koplats.

In Nevada they were in the midst of a double crisis. First of all, the relations between Sophia and her teenage stepdaughter, tense for years, had got worse. The Fog had woken up the dormant volcano and turned it into a live explosion.

I had learned from the various emails Sophia sent during the week – quite formal ones and, to my taste, trying a bit too hard to be endearing – that the couple had met four years ago and been married for three. Sophia wrote that from the start Michelle was cold with her and refused to hold her hand, or obey the simplest requests, like washing her hands. She would only listen to her father. Adam kept saying it would get better after the wedding when Michelle would understand that the situation was permanent and Adam would not go back to her mother, his ex-wife Penny (they had separated five years before Sophia and Adam met). She was a journalist, travelling around the world, which is why Michelle lived with her father. It didn't improve with the wedding, it got worse. Michelle entered her teenage years at that time and turned insubordinate and irreverent. 'At least before, she wouldn't answer me back!' Sophia wrote. I felt sorry for her, it must be such an uncomfortable situation to be in, caught between the man you love and his daughter who can't stand you. From what I read, the feeling was mutual.

With the Fog, their relations had turned venomous. Not only did Michelle resent the Facilitator's duties, she was angry at the prospect of losing her freedom to leave home on her eighteenth birthday. She told them her best years were ruined and so was her wish to escape far away, like her mother. She could not have friends staying over, or parties, or visitors. She couldn't talk to her boyfriend about the Fog, have him at hers ever and her father didn't want her to go to his unchaperoned. In the new circumstances, both Adam and Sophia were the enemies and Michelle was turning more bitter and rebellious every day. The parents were concerned about what Michelle might do next. Poor girl though, robbed of her dreams and of the joys of a teenage life! They are not always fun years and you certainly don't need the Fog to make it gloomy. Hopefully she would not do a runner or moan to anyone about the Fog.

Up to that morning, this was the main worry within the Fog situation in Carson City. From then on, Native Americans added to it: the Koplats' house in World II was surrounded by American Indian warriors, with a large camp from which the American family could hear the WII natives chanting. Michelle was not the only one anymore who wanted to leave the house and go far, far away from Nevada.

That Sunday morning email had been sent by Adam Koplat. He explained they had been considering escape route options. Even though Leila was on her way, they were already packing to go to a hotel. They had a week ahead of them before the next fogging night and thus a week to get organised. They had ruled out the American continent: Native Americans in the north, Mayans in the south. Africa did not appeal to them, even though the WII tribes in Kenya seemed peaceful and welcoming. They dreaded to think of what had happened to their peers in Bali and dismissed Asia as a consequence. Russia was an option, but there was the language barrier in this world and the other. Adam Koplat had Jewish Russian origins, but spoke Hebrew, not Russian. However, his wife and daughter spoke neither. That left Europe. So they had in mind either to join us in London, or to stay at Leo's Roman guest house for some time (they didn't know the Italians were gone and the house had been closed off). Their immediate goal was to leave, the rest would get organised later. That was Adam's plan, yet he faced opposition: Michelle didn't want to go anymore, saying they were cowards and she didn't want to leave with them, she wanted to be alone, away from them and if they were going, she could and would stay. Without Michelle, the parents could not step into our world. They were stuck.

Leila had gone there to calm everyone down and give them some support in whatever they decided to do. She was hoping to convince them not to flee but make contact. In the end, she arrived after the events.

The Native Americans knocked at the door just when Michelle had locked herself up in her room and Adam was looking for a hammer to break in. The good news was that they did not have any imminent attack in mind and had sent emissaries to gauge who was within the Fog and who they would have to deal with. They knew about the Fog and were expecting it, although an exact time and place were unknown. The emissaries spoke some odd kind of old English. Sitting on the floor of the Koplats' sitting room, drinking green tea which they liked very much, they recounted why.

In what we know to be 1782, although the WII Native Americans did not refer to a specific date, their calendar system being different from ours, they were already aware of the Fog and its opening a door to another land. It had happened once before, a long time ago, and their oral tradition had carried the stories of the unusual years of the Fog from one generation to the next. What they were not expecting in the eighteenth century was the arrival in their world of the English-speaking white men. They had heard that in the past different tribes had crossed and had to learn to live together, but not from such a different culture, not of guns, not of women with strange attire, not of fair hair and not of the dangers of alcohol. They knew they should have an open mind, but how could they welcome the white men with open arms when they learned of the invasion and massacre of their ancestors' land by them. Blood was spilt on both sides. Little by little, as the Native Americans of World II came to realise they could not get rid of the Fog or the white people, they realised the wisdom of their ancestors in learning to live with each other. In that Other World, the white minority and Native American community mixed together over the centuries that followed. Some Native Americans crossed too, bringing and blending new tribal traditions. All agreed that if their Indian language remained the principal one, English should be taught at least to the key leaders and shamans so they would be ready for the next opening.

This was when the emissaries asked Adam about the Native Americans in this world, about this tribe or that one and Adam fell silent. Sophia could hardly breathe. They kept thinking about the events in Mexico and how we assumed the WII locals had killed everyone out of fury that their civilisation had been wiped out on our planet. It was Michelle, who had come down unseen during the Native Americans' speech, who answered, 'There are very few Native Americans left on our side, I am afraid. The world has changed a lot since the last opening. This whole land is predominantly white and speaks English. Not for long maybe. There is already another change happening: soon everyone will be Hispanic and chatting in Spanish.'

Obviously the Native Americans had no idea who the Spanish were and probably didn't care. They understood very well, however, that their own had been cast aside totally by the white people. The process had already been witnessed over the period of time the Fog was open, hence their decision to keep learning English. It was still an obvious shock to them.

'You know, at least we think Native Americans are pretty cool!' Michelle added. 'We like them and their spiritual approach is very *in* these days. I am sure you are going to be a hit! That is, you would, if they knew about you. Because they don't, because we have to keep our mouth shut and it's a fu ...'

Adam interrupted his daughter, he wrote, because the Native Americans kept looking at each other with incomprehension on their face. He asked them if they could read English and they said yes, some of them could. He suggested getting them a few books, so they would have an idea of what had happened since they last knew of America and the rest of the world. As with the members of Lil'London Council when they first showed up, the Native Americans kept looking around at the big pristine house, so different from their tepees. Michelle prepared a plate with an assortment of food and if their taste buds were surprised at first, delight soon followed. They looked and inquired about the light, the Venetian masks on the wall and asked Adam what was his role in his world. Reading this, I realised the council had never asked me. They probably couldn't conceive that I could have a job. Actually, they had not asked Zeno either.

Adam explained as best as he could what a lawyer was. It was too difficult to get into his speciality, mergers and acquisitions, or even financial law. He kept it simple, saying he was to help people know and apply the rules of the community properly and be in agreement. Adam noted the Native Americans seem to understand, nodding and looking serious. It was quite a sight, he wrote, those American Indians with make-up on, some with feathers in their hair, some without. They didn't have the whole feather headgear like in the movies, Adam explained, but it was still very impressive to see. He also mentioned that there were big silences, as no one really knew what to say next.

In the end, they were invited, the three of them, to join them at their camp that evening for the celebrations of the gate opening. Michelle froze, which Adam noticed from the corner of his eye. He thanked God silently that she could not join them, a point he indicated to the Native Americans. He added that she had another engagement and would not be home. If something happened to them in the Other World, he wanted her somewhere the American Indians could not go to.

Adam and Sophia were faced with a practical and cultural issue during their encounter with the Native Americans. The American Indians had brought a gift, a complex mask which seemed to transform itself into five different other masks: it worked in such way that the outer mask opened up to reveal another mask, the second mask opened up to reveal a third and so on. It was very ingenious and a beautiful piece of painted and wooden artwork, yet the immediate problem was to reciprocate the gift. Adam knew from reading on Native Americans that gifts should be exchanged.

'What could we possibly give them?' he murmured to Sophia.

'We need to give them something?' she replied.

'Yes, but what?' Adam confirmed.

'I don't know.' She was beginning to panic.

Sophia stood up and went to the kitchen. She came back with a wrapped parcel the size of a shoebox and handed it to Adam. She explained it was a selection of three large pots of jam – strawberry, apricot and blueberry.

'They don't have jam, do they?' she enquired in a whisper.

'I have no idea,' Adam replied and he handed the gift to the Native Americans. They were a bit surprised by it, not knowing what to do with the box. Adam showed them they ought to open the wrapping. They did so, making sure not to rip it. They then opened the box and took out three delicious looking pots, staring at them bewildered.

'Those are jams, which we hope you will enjoy,' Adam explained. 'Do you know jam? This is pretty sweet.' Adam turned to Sophia and asked her to get an opened pot from the kitchen for them to try, with three spoons and plates. When she came back, he served each a spoonful. They tasted, smiled and nodded, looking very pleased.

'We like sweet!' said one of them.

Adam felt as if a huge burden had just lifted from his shoulders, as if a test had been passed with success. The feeling was not shared by Sophia. Not at all. When the Native Americans left, Sophia turned to Adam with anger and burst out that it was ridiculous. It was crazy. She would not step one foot out in WII and in the Indian camps. They should just move where they would not have to deal with any of 'those indigenous retarded communities' such as to join the Alaskan Foggies, or where the community was a relatively civilised one, as in England.

'You don't know if a community is not going to show up tomorrow in Alaska. And you don't know if it will be a nice one. At least we don't have the Mayans.'

'We should have gone long ago. It was crazy to stay here.'

'Do you want to be on the run your whole life?'

'What?'

'You are a Crosser for life, darling. You can't run away from it.'

'But, Native Americans!'

'I'd rather one Native American who is upfront than being attacked one day by an unknown person. Don't forget we have a lot to offer to them. Who knows, we might start a jam business soon.'

'This is ludicrous. Do what you want, I am not going!'

'Yes you are! We can't afford to antagonise them!'

'I am not going. Actually, I am leaving right now.'

'How?' a honeyed voice asked from the kitchen and Michelle appeared holding a can of Coca-Cola and crunching an apple. 'Because you need me for leaving and I agree with Dad, so I won't help you.'

'You're only doing this to spite me! You are such a bitch!' Sophia exploded. Michelle sneered with a half-mocking smile, and crunched her apple.

Adam spoke, in a low, anger-contained voice, 'I will not accept your referring to my daughter like this. You might have your issues with her, but I will not accept this type of language.' He turned to Michelle and added, 'And that goes both ways. Understood?'

'Yes Daddy. Of course Daddy. Whatever you say, Daaaddy,' Michelle replied with a hand gesture clearly meant to express 'whatever'. Sophia stood up and walked upstairs to the main bedroom, slamming the door behind her. Michelle's sneer grew.

'Go to your room,' Adam sighed.

'But I didn't say anything?' Michelle retorted in mock surprise and feigned innocence.

'Enough, Michelle! Go to your room!'

Michelle remained for a minute or so, facing her father and crunching the rest of her apple, before she went up to her room. She walked slowly, defiant. Adam let himself down on the sofa. He picked up the FTab and began writing to Leila and to Yoko. Sophia had to go that night, Adam wrote. She had little choice. The most difficult task was to reason with Michelle. She had the most freedom of them all and they needed her. It scared him and, at the same time, he was glad his daughter was neither a Switcher nor a Crosser.

I took the time to read the long message in one go. Due to the time difference, it was the morning here in London but the middle of the night for the Koplats in Nevada, so I wasn't expecting any feedback on the encounter until mid-afternoon at best. I very much hoped everything had gone well, both with the Native Americans and at a personal level, too. It seemed Christopher, Isabelle and Louise were not the only ones with family-related trouble in our little Foggies group. It took me a few seconds to realise I had too, with Julia.

While reading, I had been vaguely aware that the house was waking up and getting more lively. I could hear the sounds of steps, of wardrobe or room doors opening and closing. The noises I heard from above me indicated Leo was up. Time to get ready, have a shower and continue dealing with my emails afterwards. I wrapped myself in a towel, slightly opened my door and checked no one was outside. It was an absurd thing to do in my own home. Maybe I just didn't want to be face to face with him because it was awkward … Or because part of me would want to just drop the towel then and there.

Thirty minutes later, showered and dressed, I made my way downstairs. The plan was to prepare the next Foggies online conference and its agenda for Wednesday. We had to discuss Ingis Chen, the Koplats, and many other points. I thought we should also start setting up some kind of Foggies way to work together. We were dependent on each other, so we needed to find a way to make it work in the future, to make us strong and united. Who knew what we would have to face soon in either world.  It would be a challenge with us being so different and dispersed, but we ought to try. Why was I doing this? Why was I turning into the hub, the organiser of the coalition between Foggies? I had asked myself the obvious 'Why me?' question. My first answer was that someone had to do it. The second was that I was a good project manager, and so it might as well be me. I couldn't stand by and watch the situation slowly develop into a disaster if we were not getting more solid as a group. It was all very well to take in what was going on and go with the flow, one had to maintain the boat. We all had a role to play in this. I wasn't a leader, and didn't have any wish to be one, but I was motivated that we could be team!

As another cup of coffee would help boost my motivation even higher, I went downstairs to the kitchen. There were cables and screens everywhere with Nick in the middle, on his knees setting things up.

'Nick, coffee?' I asked him.

'Yes, please.' He looked up, gave me an once-over and commented, 'Looks like you're bright and ready for the day now.'

'Yes, thank you.'

'If I could request that you warn me ten minutes or so before you step out into the forest, that would be most helpful. I'll need the time to tidy a little. Wires could be dangerous, people trip on them.'

'Sure.' We had been walking to the kitchen during the exchange and coffee was on the go.

'By the way,' Nick continued. 'Where could I set up command-control?'

'Huh?'

'Well, I need a place to set up the operations,' Nick said as if it were evident. I thought back to the electric mess on the floor in the living room and on the dining table. I remembered the radio magic box we had had since the weekend: by itself it was manageable, with the rest it was not.

'I don't know. How about we build a cabin outside?'

'It defeats the purpose. I need to check from the inside. If the cabin is being attacked first, then I can't do anything for you.'

'But ...'

'It needs to be inside, Yoko. Sorry.'

'You're going to have to talk to Jazz. You see, hopefully by the end of the week only Jazz will live here and the others and I will be next door so Jazz will organise this house.'

Nick looked at me and frowned.

'So you won't be living here anymore? What a pity! I will miss the sight in the mornings. It's quite something.'

'Don't you start!'

'I like it, actually. It's entertaining how grumpy you are waking up.'

Just then Leo arrived downstairs. He looked from Nick to me, obviously having heard the last sentence, scowled and said, 'Enough coffee for one more?'

'Yes, of course! Would you like something to eat too?' I grabbed a cup and a plate.

'Oh yeah! I'm ravenous!' Leo replied.

'So, in the meantime, where should I put the controls?' Nick asked again. 'Let's rearrange a corner of the dining room at the back and set things up there. Then it will be up to Jazz.'

'Good. Also, we are going to have a bit of a problem with our mobile homes.'

'Yes?'

'We have electricity with the spare generator for now, we have solar panels to set up, but we need access to water. We also need to empty our sewage somewhere. In the short term we can move the mobile home further away and empty it, but soon we will need to dig a proper septic tank that will be used for the future homes too. The most urgent is access to water.'

'I guess we can try to link you to the house? I mean, I don't know if that would work, to connect you to our water system? Otherwise, can you drive to a source to replenish?'

'Driving is an option, but there is no proper road through the forest and mobile homes are no cross country. Sooo ... Next we also need to build a path to the Lil'London road. We will need one anyway.'

'It raises a question though,' Leo cut in. 'If we connect a new pipe from World II and plug it into the water system, first, would World II actually get some water from World I and second, would that diminish the amount of water you get in the house for World I?'

It was an interesting question and we put it to the test. We plugged a hose to a join in the water pipe of the downstairs washroom and Nick pulled it into the forest. When turned on, water gushed forth, to the joy of Simba who barked around at the flow out of the hose and tried to play with it. So water got through. From the flow of water running from the kitchen tap, we also knew that our supply at home was not diminished for normal use.

It felt good in Leo's company. We were out, just the two of us, with Nick back inside turning the water on and off, speaking to us by two-way radio. Leo and I were acting like two good friends and it felt natural, we joked and bantered constantly. I was aware that we were not alone, what with the Lil'London watchers, as well as the Fishers and Big Tom in their mobile homes. I enjoyed the simplicity of this friendship, yet I was still drawn and attracted by him. 'I am so confused,' I thought. Yes, I liked him and being with him, but now was just such a wrong time – too much going on and to deal with. When Nick joined us again, Leo was immediately a little more distant, either not to show a warmth that could be revealing, or because he didn't yet know how to act with Nick. It was interesting to see them together with me, both protective, Leo in a considerate and warm way, Nick with a quiet strength, imposing yet contained. Both decent alpha males, only one had the Italian charm, the other the English poise.

We were soon joined by the Fisher family and Big Tom, attracted by the noise of Simba playing with the water. In no time, Owen and Maisie were spraying water on each other and Big Tom was talking to Nick about guns. Leo said he would call Dante and Leila to plan for the road and septic tank work. They would prepare ideas and projects for Tuesday when they were to be introduced to the Lil'London Council. The Foggies would thus go and attend the meeting with clear roles and objectives: Dante, the architect; Leo, the commercial structure coordinator; Zeno, the trader and me, the Inter-World Ambassador, as the guys put it. That made me laugh and cringe both: it added a book to the list of my necessary reads: *How to be a Diplomat for Dummies.*

These thoughts reminded me of all the tasks set for today: create a draft agenda and team work for the Wednesday's 'Foggies Board Meeting' or FBM, as I labelled our video conference call. Nick and Leo joined me back inside, Nick to work on the surveillance system, Leo to work with Dante. Inside, Jazz was talking with Rico. They told me Harry had gone already and Rico wanted to know if he could leave or if he was needed.

'I will only be gone two or three hours, babe. I'll be back early afternoon. I want to do a big training session. I had a gelato attack this weekend.'

'Ahhh ... ice cream. I go nuts for that,' Jazz commented.

'No problem, Rico. I have some work to do here,' I told him. Leo said he would go with him to meet Dante and kissed me on the cheek. Rico gave me a kiss on the forehead after whispering in my ear, 'If there's a problem with him, you tell me!' and hurried out with Leo.

'Coffee?' Jazz asked around. I passed on it, I had had my dose for now. Nick looked round and asked if he could prepare himself a cup of tea. Soon everyone settled into their own tasks, each in an area of the room. Jazz was doing some searches and making notes on interior designs and bar management, regularly asking my opinion.

At the set time, I switched on the two-way radios and sure enough, Edmund, Benjamin Snayth and Augustus Hoare were on. They were not very talkative, more stunned. It was a brief chat: we confirmed the visit tomorrow and the lunch between the wives and me. 'And Jazz,' I added, which made Jazz wrinkle her nose. There was a brief silence before they confirmed that of course Jazz was welcome. They asked how many horses we would need for the journey to Lil'London with the Relocated, a number which created another silence.

'That many? In such a short time?' remarked more than asked Augustus Hoare.

'Yes.' My answer was simple. They would know the details soon enough.

After the call, I put my headphones on, the FTab on vibration and got down to work on my draft.

After a couple of hours, when getting hungry, I decided it was time for a break and reviewed my notes for the FBM:

SUGGESTIONS

- Facilitators need to be accessible at least one week a month to those Switchers and Crossers without one;

  (To avoid the ones without going insane! I may not be a fan of Christophe de Roque's ways, but I wouldn't want to be in his shoes not having a Harry or Rico around);

- Facilitators need to be given holidays regularly.

  (They are not our slaves! Yes, it means some Switchers and Crossers would have weeks without access to WI, but one has to be fair. The most important days will be Sundays anyway, as the rest of the week, Foggies could stay in an unfogged house).

- Foggies need to set up a shared 'location' calendar (so that we can organise the Facilitators, their holidays, but also the venues that may need to be re-switched and by whom);

- Switchers must refrain from 'fogging' new locations, unless the Foggies board agrees by a majority. (Should something happen to a Switcher, the others would have to take over the fogging of this location afterwards, for the sake of any Relocated there. So it is important that everyone is consulted first except if the fogging is unavoidable or by accident);

- All Foggies must keep a record of key entries, to share at the weekly Foggies Board Meeting.(It is crucial to know what is happening in one location, where the problems lie and with whom, should we have to go and interfere);

- Anyone who acts in an immoral, unethical, self-interested way at the expense of other Foggies or Relocated, or in any generally unacceptable way may be cut off from the board's support by unanimous vote.

(This would mean exclusion from other Foggies help: that person would then be alone, either stranded in the Fog for a Switcher, or stuck in the WII with no access to the WI facilities for a Crosser. It is more complicated for Facilitators: they give us our liberty of movement back, but get theirs restricted in exchange. Their only need of the Fog is to have regular access to avoid the debilitating migraines. Their potential gain is to be part of the select few having a key role in the exchange with WII. This might not cover the loss of freedom for some, like Michelle. The tricky point for this suggestion is that its implementation is morally difficult and pretty ruthless. It is, however, a strong incentive for a decent line of conduct by all. Big discussions will ensue on that one for sure. There again, we can't afford to have one of us jeopardising the whole group);

- Each other's identities, locations and roles must be kept undisclosed, unless agreed by those concerned.

(If it doesn't jeopardise the group, we may disclose information about ourselves depending on the circumstances, like the Relocated, families etc., but we should not reveal the others' secrets freely. After all, we are not even supposed to give a friend's mobile number without the friend agreeing, so information on Foggies? No.)

## QUESTIONS

- Will the Foggies be a for-profit or non-profit group?
- If we are a for-profit group, how do we control it? Should some get richer than others depending on the location, but then, the Foggies in the poorest location can move to richer ones and it never ends ... Or do we set up a common

pot and we all share the profits with an equal distribution and share the rest for the Relocated? That would give us independence from the Society, with whom we would then be more like partners or consultants? What about the new houses then? ARGH!

- If we are a non-profit group, what happens to the benefits from trade? Charity to the Relocated? We then completely depend on the Society?
- What do we do about Ingis Chen and his corporation?
- I need a cup of tea. With cookies?
- What about taxes? Are we going to have to pay taxes? Of course we will. There is no avoiding British taxes, whatever organisation we are in or create. ARGH! Again.

Reviewing these notes, a headache was budding at all the implications behind organising the Foggies group. I thought it would be good for us to have some independence and be a separate structure, with the Society as our advisers and sponsors if or when necessary, but that also meant a big administration job. Yuk-yuk-yuk! Definitely time for tea and biscuits. I checked the time, it was already past 1 p.m. Forget tea and biscuits, it was lunch break.

'Jazz, Nick. Lunch?' I asked and turned to see Nick was not in his corner.

'He's been popping in and out all morning. I think it is about the camera angles or locations or something,' Jazz said.

'Ah ... What do you fancy for lunch? I am not in a mood for cooking. Maybe a sandwich? Baguette sandwich? I have half a baguette in the freezer, I can take it out, defrost it in the oven, put cream cheese, ham and grilled vegetables in, back in the oven to get it all hot? What do you say?'

'I say "bring it on!"'

'OK, I'll prepare some more for Nick as he will probably come back soon.'

'And cheddar? Can you add cheddar?'

'OK.'

'And onions?' Jazz added. I winced. She was going to go through the whole fridge item by item. She was in one of those moods.

'How about you pick what you want in your sandwich yourself? That way you can't blame me if it's disgusting?' I suggested.

'All right then.' She rolled her eyes.

We both went to the kitchen and Jazz began on her favourite subject. Men. Actually maybe second favourite after shoes, although in her new current circumstances, shoes seem to have been relegated.

'Do you think Barnaby will be there tomorrow?'

'I don't know. Maybe.'

'Are there a lot more hot guys like him in Lil'London?'

'You'll know soon. You should have plenty of curious people who will come to your lounge.'

'Music is going to be a problem. I am not sure the Summer Hits playlist is going to do it for the Lil'London folks.'

I laughed and replied, 'Maybe you have to expand your horizons and get into Scottish reels and Irish music and their tap dancing. What's the name of it again?'

'The Irish thing?' she frowned.

'Yes.'

'I don't know. I think it is just called Irish Dancing.'

'I will have to Google it,' I replied.

'And what about Leo? He is quite nice, Leo? Totally your type,' Jazz said, not that casually.

'I don't have a type.' My whole body closed off, as it does when someone referred to something intimate about me. My inner sanctum had high walls.

'OK. You don't have one type. You have several types. And he is one of them,' she persisted.

'And your point is?' I tried to elude her real question.

'How are things going with your other guy?' Jazz would not let go.

'Dunno,' I replied, keeping to the evasive approach.

'Have you seen him since that fiasco night?'

I had to be careful on what I would reply to that one. I was thinking about my answer when she continued. 'I don't know why I'm asking. I know. I live in the same house, I know what you are up to with your days. Have you been in touch at least?'

'Yes, we have. I am still confused and not sure. Anyway, about Leo, last I knew you were telling me it wouldn't be a good idea to go out with another Foggy.'

'Yes, I know, but a Foggy is better than nobody.'

'Jazz … I am neither a desperate case, nor desperate!'

'There again, you also have Nick. I'm not sure if he is one of your types, but he's not bad, the boxer.'

'Thanks,' Nick replied, who had returned unnoticed.

'Ah! Errr … Sorry! Didn't hear you come in,' Jazz stuttered, blushing.

'I move silently. Part of the job. Anyway, you are mistaken, Jazz, I am not "not bad". I am an unforgettable experience.' Nick did not lose any composure while speaking. Only a spark in his eyes betrayed cheekiness, and I noticed because he was looking me straight in the eyes while he said this. I felt myself blush and to my surprise, a certain longing stirred up as well. 'That's no good. No, no, no!' I said inwardly. 'I can't start being turned on by Nick. He is my bodyguard, for God's sake! He will stick by me and my every move in World II. It's even worse than Leo!'

I quickly turned and focused on the contents of the fridge, telling him what was on the menu for lunch and asking if he wanted to join Jazz and me, which he did. All the while, I was thinking there must be something wrong with me: I had to stop being attracted to the men who would create the most complex relationships. Also, he was probably just about 26, maybe not even that. What was I, a cougar?!

Rico returned as I was preparing lunch but refused the baguette sandwich idea.

'Babe, I am on protein diet after training. You know that.' He prepared himself a six egg-white omelette with a can of tuna. It looked pretty disgusting, and it was. Nick looked at it unimpressed.

'Rico, even when I was a professional athlete, my diet was more balanced than that. There are nutrients in the egg yolk as well,' Nick told Rico.

'All the chemical stuff they feed to the hens goes in the egg yolk. It is shit. I am not eating it.'

'You know, tuna's not that great either these days,' Nick commented. I smiled. It was not recommended to get into that type of discussions with Rico. His diet and his training were sacred, as Rico's next sentence proved.

'Don't want to know. This is my routine and I am not touching it. I have been doing it for five years. It works. Look at these muscles. Look at these abs.' Rico flexed his arms and lifted his T-shirt. No doubt, it worked. It didn't mean it was healthy, but it definitely worked.

The afternoon passed quietly. I continued working on a 'code of conduct for Foggies' but didn't add much to the morning entries I had jotted down. Mainly I read some documents from charity organisations and other non-profit structures to get inspired. Then I finally read the emails from Alaska and Marrakech. Rosario, Tony and Mitch didn't have much to say, aside from their managing to live a normal life and enjoying their time. Tony and Rosario were settling in nicely in the pre-fabricated house they had installed at the bottom of the path leading to the family house. They were now starting to renew and amend their plans for their wedding. They planned to add a layer of rough cut wood cladding around the pre-fabricated house to make it look both fun and old and to increase the heat insulation against the Alaskan cold nights. Once it was all finished, they invited us Foggies to go and visit. They added that they would be delighted if Leila and I would join them for their wedding. They had decided to move it forward and to organise it on a Friday instead of a Saturday. It didn't seem a good idea to fog the wedding venue with all the guests in.

The only negative point in their message was about Mitch. Rosario worried for her brother. She wrote, 'He was a loner before, never managing to make a relationship last more than four months because sooner or later the appeal of the wild would be stronger and he would just disappear for weeks. What woman wants to come second after the mountains! Now I am concerned he will turn into a recluse. He is such a great guy with a big heart and good looking too. I don't want him to be a hermit. I want him to meet a nice girl, have children, and be happy. He would be a great dad. He loves children. He wasn't a great one for going into town and socialising. There aren't many women around down here, so if you don't make a bit of an effort ... With the Fog, it will be even more difficult for him to meet a woman and have a normal life. Yes! I am concerned!!!'

I didn't know much about Mitch. He didn't write often and was very laconic when he did. Mainly, Rosario wrote for them all, in a determined, strong style, full of confidence, with many words in capital letters and a plethora of exclamation marks.

The messages from Marrakech did not bring anything new either. Christopher was moaning about his wife Isabelle and his mistress Louise, and about wanting to go out in the markets of Marrakech, eat their delicious food, and relax in their hammams. His opinion of the town had turned more and more positive with the passing days and him not being able to go there.

Isabelle was relieved that the blood tests organised by the Society came out well. The pregnancy was going without issues and she was grateful for the Society's support. She totally ignored the request of her husband except to repeat he was a jerk and she was glad to have burned his passport, driving licence and ID card. We could send a Facilitator if we wanted, he could not leave the country, the 'LYING CHEAT' (quoting, including the block letters.)

Louise, she concerned me: she was clearly down. It was high time to ask one of the Facilitators to go and help. It was overdue. As we were the closest to Marrakech, it made sense for either Rico or Harry to go.

About to return to my research on setting up a Foggies community, a new message arrived on the Foggy platform, one from Kenya. Clare had sent it to everyone. She was in a state of panic: her daughter Mary wasn't back from the bush and she couldn't cross to go and get her. If that wasn't enough, Ingis Chen had just left, having showed up on her doorstep out of the blue. She had refused to open the door, even though at the time she didn't know who he was. In her anxiety about her daughter, she couldn't care less about any visitors. However, when she opened her FTab to request some help, she saw his name and read about him. She needed help. She wanted back in the Foggies. Who could blame her! I replied to her with everyone in copy, suggesting we should have an emergency Foggies conference call. The Foggies were turning into an operational structure already.

At 6 p.m., all the accounted Foggies were connected to the conference call. Rico, Harry and I were at home in front of the FTab camera, the device plugged into a larger screen so that we could see the others participants better. Leo and Dante were also plugged in, from Dante's hotel bedroom/office (messy, if I may say, with papers everywhere. Here was one who could do with a proper place to work). Leila joined as well due to the emergency situation, from and with the Koplats.

It was an eventful call. It lasted for a couple of hours, too long to relate in detail and better summarised from the easy to the intense:

1.  The Foggies Charter
    I did not present my notes, only mentioned what I was working on. I may have talked further on the matter if the

subject hadn't been raised at the end of the call and we all had had enough. It was put down as a matter to discuss on Wednesday.

2. The Foggies conference calls

   Considering the latest news about the Native Americans and Ingis Chen, everyone thought it would be a good idea to remain open to more than once a week. So it was settled. There was a time of the week – Friday night, 6 p.m. – when I used to go out for drinks with friends or to the cinema. Now I would be on a video call.

3. Zeno's absence

   As everyone except Zeno was present (besides Helo, but he was just a child), his absence was felt. He had written a short email explaining he couldn't make it due to a personal issue with the visit of his long distance girlfriend. When repeated, his comment that she didn't know anything about the Fog caused silence. The secrecy was difficult for everyone. Secrecy was a protection for us. Yet it had a price. Zeno was facing the bill right then.

4. Mary's disappearance

   This was the first object of the call, the one that mattered the most in the immediate circumstances, the one that brought Clare to tears within seconds of her being connected. Her daughter had disappeared, in a place she saw as a purer replica of her homeland, without all the distortions and pollution of the modern world. Without its politics, its traffic, its pettiness, its waste, its greed for money, its corruption, its racism, its prejudices. She believed it was the Africa from before colonisation. In the end though, she had never lived in the Africa from before colonisation and knew nothing of its workings, so even this comparison was idealised and thus flawed. In WII, aside from the local tribe who were apparently friendly and welcoming, there could have been other tribes not as nice. Mary could also have made a faux pas with the friendly tribe and turned them into dangerous cannibals. Plus, there was of course the jungle and its unpredictable dangers. Although Mary was travelling in a specially equipped Range Rover (a parting gift from the Society) and she had a two-way radio as well, when with the tribe she was out of reach. Clare was praying that she had just lost track of time, was out of range of radio contact and engrossed in her studies of the tribe. Her distress was fuelled by the realisation she had no means of helping. She couldn't even go and search for her. She felt suddenly very much alone. She only had Putu to link her to the modern world. Now, it wasn't enough anymore.

Leila reassured her that a team was already outside hers. They had kept a local contact that was waiting, ready to come in when/if she wished. Zeno, despite his absence, had already volunteered in his message to go and help. Mitch also volunteered to go, saying that the landscape was for sure very different, but he was used to the wild and had good training for survival. He would read it up on his journey to prepare.

'Do you know how to follow tracks?' Clare asked.

'In my forest, yes,' Mitch replied.

'But not in the jungle or the savannah ...' a teary Clare murmured.

'We will try to give them a quick preparation, as much as we can,' Leila said in the most reassuring voice she could.

Mitch would go to Kenya via London and would arrive tomorrow, Tuesday. There Zeno would join him to go to Kenya. Zeno leaving for Kenya to disappear in their WII immediately worried me. Mitch too, but especially Zeno. His curious mind let loose in the wild jungle ... Gosh, he would probably want to do an excursion by night.

5. Update on the Native Americans

   Even though the situation had not developed much yet, the subject was fascinating and we all wanted to know more. Adam and Sophia, who hardly had any other choice, had made it out at sunset and were presented two horses to trot the few metres separating them from the Native American camp. Adam had managed to convince his daughter to go and spend the night with friends. She was adamant she would not go at first, but her father traded her leaving the house that night for a shopping trip and an upgrade of her prom dress. Probably not the best parenting practice, it still worked wonders.

   On the visit to the Indian camp, Adam loved it, Sophia hated it. He had to taste some of their mysterious elixir, she had to taste some disgusting dodgy home-made drinks. He witnessed the traditional dancing by the fire, she had to endure a remake of Hollywood movies with drums worsening the headache she had had all day. He was fascinated by the chanting and the spirituality in their welcome, she was concerned that anytime they would take their tomahawks out and cut off their scalps. He felt high and moved by the experience, she never once relaxed from focusing her thoughts on the knife she had in her large coat pocket.

   Adam Koplat had thought long and hard about what to bring them as gifts and had gone out to buy a selection of items he hoped would please the American Indians and give value to their encounter with him and his wife. He gathered a selection of mirrors and carpets; he packed food such as rice, lentils, pasta, boxes of exotic fruits and vegetables, pots of jams and honey, and he got Native American jewellery for the women of the camp, as a special treat. Leila and the Society helped assemble it all promptly, not a small feast on a Sunday. All was put on a wheelbarrow, ready to go. Adam also took his gun, just in case.

Sophia Koplat's only positive comment was on the fur blankets and amber or turquoise silver jewellery they received in exchange. She pointed out during the video call that considering how Michelle had been with her, she would not have any (apparently Michelle had been eyeing a necklace and a ring). Michelle said she had not expected anything from her anyway, but it was also her dad's. The two started to row and we changed subject fast.

6. Ingis Chen

Leo repeated again the events of the night when he had met Ingis Chen, and, once again, omitted my presence. That made me feel uncomfortable: it was a big lie by omission and not a good way to start relations with the other Foggies. When the others referred to the personal relationship getting in the way of the interests of the group, I made up my mind. I wasn't ready for this. Maybe that was why I had wanted to keep it a secret, in addition to my being a private person by nature. Moreover, I had to admit it, at least to myself, I was scared by how fast it had grown. He was great and I did like him. Having him around was so natural, I didn't want to lose it. Nonetheless, the more I felt myself getting attached, the more I wanted to pull away. So my decision was to suggest we settle first into the new situation, the new home, and the new everything and, then, see how things developed between us. I wanted to gain time and postpone having to make a decision.

I had reached my conclusions by the time Leo had reached his. Clare then took over telling her story of Ingis Chen showing up on her doorstep.

'So he actually crossed the Fog?' Rosario asked.

'Yes, he did. He took the risk of being relocated,' Clare said.

'Or he's a Facilitator, don't forget there is one unaccounted for. I for one cannot forget that,' Christophe said.

'Actually, he already knew he was not at risk. He had the Essex house fogged, remember.' Harry pointed out.

'How do you think he discovered my house? How did he find Leo?'

'I don't know,' Leila answered. 'We can't be a hundred percent sure. Only Ingis Chen or his crew would know. It could also be that we missed someone reporting it, or a satellite noticing something. We are looking into it. The most important thing is that he knows.'

Leo was adamant that Ingis Chen's motivation, along with his methods, was unacceptable. Adam started to speak, hesitantly suggesting that it would do no harm to hear what Chen had to offer, but Leo cut him short, 'It would be like planting the seeds of bad weeds among the flower bed!' Leo exclaimed.

'Right, I have a favour to ask you all,' Louise interrupted. 'Do you mind if you can talk that tiny bit more slowly? My English is just OK. You speak too fast.'

'Actually, yes, for me too. It is always that little bit more difficult not talking face to face,' Dante added.

Everyone replied 'Of course,' 'So sorry,' 'We will'. It was a beneficial interruption: it enabled us to change subject to a less explosive one. The matter was not sorted, though.

7. The Foggies location imbalance – and my personal guilt
I don't remember how it came up in the conversation that Leo and Dante were to settle in London. The Foggies were all unhappy about it.

'We should have been informed before!' Christophe said. 'We all ought to know where the others are!'

'Yes! You should have told us!' Adam insisted.

'Ma ... At first we didn't want to say too much before knowing you more. Then ... Then time passed,' Dante replied. Leo kept silent. He was hiding another secret about London.

The reactions of the not-London-based Foggies went from mildly troubled to very upset that we were more than a third in one location. Rosario, Mitch and Tony were concerned that if something happened in London too many Foggies would be affected. Christophe, approved by Sophia who was frantically nodding, was concerned that it created an imbalance of power in favour of the London location in the Foggies decision-making. I fought the urge to tell him to 'get real'. I screamed inwardly, 'For God's sake, what "Foggies decision-making"?' but kept silent, using this as practice in restraint for my role as an ambassador. I liked his next remark even less.

'Next thing we know you will suggest Foggies should only stick to each other, then some of you will get married and make Foggy babies,' Christophe snorted.

'Ahhh that would be so romantic!' Louise said.

'You would say that, wouldn't you?' Christophe spat. The two started arguing.

'Hey! Watch your mouth! I will have a Foggy baby soon,' Isabelle interjected.

'No you won't, you will have a Relocated baby,' Louisa corrected. The argument switched to include the three of them.

Rico was looking at me, raising an eyebrow with a complete lack of discretion and I didn't know where to look. I turned my eyes towards Jazz, who was not on the camera but on the sofa, half-reading, half-listening. She mouthed 'Nick?' and winked at me. No moral support there …

'Well, we are bound to get more closely bound together, that is true,' Adam commented. 'It will be important not to have personal relationships clouding the general well-being of the Foggies as a group, whether it be friendships or romances. A good thing we are all adults, or mostly (he shot a glance at his daughter). No whimsical teenage crazy love decision there.'

I focused on attempting not to blush. Thankfully for me, Michelle changed the line of conversation by asking, 'And what about the young one from Indonesia? Where is he?'

8. Helo

Now Helo caused another heated discussion. The others knew the Society was looking after him, they didn't know he was in London too, increasing the disproportion of Foggies in town. To Christophe and Louisa's anger, Helo was a Facilitator who could help them and hence should be in Marrakech. Leila defended her decision on the ground that he was a child, had gone through a traumatic experience, and needed some time to adapt to his new circumstances. The Nevada Foggies took the side of the Moroccan Foggies: Helo could be looked after in Morocco as well as in the United Kingdom. 'The Society has no more rights over Helo than they have over any of us,' Tony said from Alaska.

'That is true,' Leila said. 'We claim none. We just didn't want the child to face any more disruption in his life. I am not sure joining a household where there seem to be quite a few issues unsettled is best for the child.'

'That is not for just the Society to decide,' I said, taking the side of Christophe and Louise for once. 'If it was me in Marrakech, I would want to have him with me or nearby. Also, Isabelle will have a baby and Helo's presence could be good for both. It could give a sense of family.'

After some more discussion, it was decided that Helo would go to Marrakech. The Society had already found a nurse with paediatric skills within its membership willing to risk crossing the Fog. She also would be able to help

Isabelle with her pregnancy and birth, and support Helo's transition to his new life. Isabelle approved and added that she had no fear Christophe could go anyway, as he didn't have any identity papers anymore. This caused a new row between the husband and wife. Theirs was a very public feud.

Everyone had had enough; it had been an exhausting virtual meeting. As for me, I was ravenous. My stomach was growling in a very embarrassing way. We ordered a pizza, put two bottles of red on the table, and were determined not to talk about anything serious.

**Day 3 (Tuesday)**

I slept like a baby. It was bliss. Sadly I had a headache when opening my eyes due to the wine from the previous night. It was strange, I didn't have that much. We had tried one of the bottles offered by the Lil'London people and it was not to our taste. We couldn't even finish the bottle. I was positive a good shower and coffee should clear it all. It was getting a bad habit those evenings with too many bottles opened. Dinner the night before was just between Rico, Harry, Jazz and me. Informed we had an important video conference, the Relocated stayed away, including Nick. I asked him before the conference how he would control the video surveillance in these cases when he was kept out of the house and he told me he had set up a feeder in the mobile home as well. Everything was running smoothly. For once, I woke up without Simba licking my face like an ice cream. She was whining a little though. I checked the time and it was late, nearing 9 a.m. Everyone had to be ready to leave by 10.00 a.m. Today was the introductory meeting of the London-based Foggies and Relocated with the Lil'London Council. Zeno would be missed again. I was concerned to have to hurry people and shouldn't have worried. Everyone was so excited, nervous, or organised that, coming downstairs twenty minutes later, they were all there ready to go, drinking coffee in the living room and discussing the morning ahead. Jazz and I shared again some details about the people and town (we had already answered lots of questions over the past few days). Leo had come back late from Dante's, and looked a bit grumpy despite his enthusiasm to finally discover the forest, the town and the inhabitants of WII.

At 10 a.m., mounted on the nine horses provided by Lil'London and with four men on horseback escorting us, we departed. Our little group looked quite an eclectic bunch: Leo, Dante and me for the Foggies, and Jazz, James, Maisie, Owen, Big Tom and Nick for the Relocated. We all had various ideas of what would be appropriate to wear and different approaches to riding. Some looked relatively confident, others utterly in pain.

Nothing much happened at this meeting. It was rather a non-event. We all gathered in the meeting room, the members of the council introducing themselves to our group as a whole, then I presented the newcomers individually to the Lil'London officials, which didn't include Jazz and Nick. In this reverse presentation, I gave a little description of their activities in WI and how they happened to have crossed. The Lil'London councillors listened in silence for the Fishers and Big Tom, until I reached Leo and Dante.

'You mean to say, you are also "Crossers"?' Benjamin Snayth asked, surprised.

'Yes, we are,' Leo replied.

'How many Crossers are out there? I thought it was very rare,' Edmund added, unusually for him, speaking in public.

'Can Crossers only be Italians?' Augustus Hoare asked.

It took me a few seconds to realise that indeed, so far, they had only met Italian Crossers.

'No, not all Crossers are Italians. There are four more in other continents. There can only be seven though,' I proceeded to summarise for them how the Fog and Foggies worked. It was necessary to give them further details about us. The mercenary from Ingis Chen's corporation was on the loose in their world and we had to warn them. They could find and help Jack if they knew.

So I talked.

I talked about the rules of seven for the Foggies and for the Relocated. I explained the disappearance of Jack due to a third party involvement. Approaching the matter carefully, I mentioned we aimed to negotiate some agreements and put an end to the disagreements. They limited their questions to clarify unclear points and I limited my explanations to a strict minimum, keeping the information provided to a need-to-know basis.

When I stopped, I started to regret the wine from last night. The little headache was reforming at the back of my head and I was craving sausages.

'So, Messrs Lumbrosi [Leo] and Bopani [Dante], will you be working in accord with Mr Grande [Zeno] for exchange and trade between our two worlds?' Benjamin Snayth asked.

'Yes, but we all have different specialities, so we will complement each other and work as a team,' Leo replied.

'Yes, I am an architect. I have a few ideas for the Relocated. If I may ...' Dante took out his drawings and sketches and launched into a description of his projects to the bemusement of the council members and the fascination of the Fisher teenagers.

Nick bent towards me and whispered in my ear, 'You are not introducing me? Am I your little secret?'

I chuckled and replied in a low voice, 'They have already seen you and Edmund knows you as my "escort". I will stick to that.'

'So I am your escort boy. I like it.'

Augustus Hoare had noticed the little exchange and was looking over at Nick and me. Dante still in his monologue in the background, I presented Nick to Augustus Hoare.

'Nick Baker, my ... protector.'

'I see. Yes, I am pleased you have proper protection with you. It is only suitable and from what you just said, necessary,' Augustus replied, nodding to Nick as a form of greeting.

'Absolutely. It is a privilege to be Miss Salelles' ... escort,' Nick said, returning Hoare's nod.

Jazz and I had to leave to attend the women's lunch. A good thing Leo and Dante were there with the Relocated as well, they would keep an eye on things. Well, Leo would, Dante would probably keep talking about the architectural drawings he had prepared. He had a fan in Edmund, who offered to take him to the library to see what they could find on architecture and design there. Both Augustus Hoare and Benjamin Snayth were looking at their fellow councillor confused: he had switched from a shy nervous man uncomfortable in public, to an eager man, boosted by intellectual curiosity and shared passion.

There was only one point I managed to raise that was not directly linked to the presentation of the new people to the council, which was the existence of other communities living in the England of World II. It was all very well we were establishing friendly relationships and some basis for settlement and trade with Lil'London, but we shouldn't dismiss the other communities in the vicinity. There was an even bigger town with 12,000 inhabitants, plus the odd random hamlets. All of them should be informed of the Fog, of us, and of Jack and the Relocated from the Chen team. I asked the councillors if they would be kind enough to organise a meeting with representatives of both towns and any other groups of people known by Lil'London. Benjamin Snayth didn't look excited at the idea. He had probably worked very hard so far to keep to himself information of our whereabouts, or even knowledge of our presence. I added that we could get on the road and look for them ourselves, but that it would save time if they would help. We would greatly appreciate this and I was certain the communities would too. I insisted that it was even more urgent now that the mercenary and Jack were on the loose in WII, as they may encounter someone from another village or town, who might be misinformed or protest about having been kept in the dark. Augustus Hoare agreed with me and Snayth had no other choice but to concur. After discussion, we settled for trying to have this important meeting the following Monday. With a proud and happy expression, Hoare concluded with, 'I shall inform you by radio on the condition of this affair.' In our world, this guy would be a geek, I was sure of it.

I left with Jazz having the uneasy feeling of unfinished business. We ought to have had a proper conversation about the mercenary at large with Jack to ensure we had their support. So far, it seemed in their interest to be on our side. The mercenary was a Relocated: he couldn't help them access our world and they needed us for this. I should have asked that at least they wouldn't kill Ingis Chen's man. I didn't know what their practice or rule on that was. I doubted they would though, he was still a possible asset and source of information.

My headache grew more intense.

The lunch with the Lil'London Council wives involved many wives: only the one for Edmund, Maud; Benjamin Snayth had four: Barbara (early forties), Jane (mid-thirties), Joan (early to mid-twenties) and Margaret (early twenties, at best); Augustus Hoare had two, Clémence (mid-twenties) and Elizabeth (early twenties). Maud was heading a table, I was sitting at her right with Clémence on my right. Jazz was on Maud's left. Barbara was opposite Maud, on the other end of the table. She had a place of honour due to her rank, and she clearly made the best of it. So the little lunch Jazz and I expected was not a small do, with nine women around a big table and ages varying within a twenty year range. As a westerner I was more used to many ex-wives and only the one current wife. In all honesty, this lunch would have been a total bore if not for observing how the women acted and interacted. Observation was fascinating, conversation was dire: decorum ruled. First of all, even though the lunch was at Maud's, Barbara was determined to lead the discussion. She alone could contribute more than a sentence or ask questions on the choice of subject. Actually, no one could really ask questions. Two of them, Elizabeth Hoare and Margaret Snayth, tried to ask us about what women did with their days, if women were receiving the same schooling as men, or if there were many unmarried women our age in our world. Needless to say, they were silenced by an ominous stare from Barbara Snayth. Should I answer truthfully, those were topics prone to casting doubt on the role of women in their community and Barbara knew it. She was the doyenne of the little group and acted as such. Mainly, she talked. She talked about the importance of the Lil'London Council, the importance of the routine and balance of roles in their community, the importance of their well-oiled system of support between women for the education of children. She talked about the focus on respect and values, which she hoped had remained in our world as well. A lot of blah-blahs delivered with a certain hauteur and preaching tone.

As a consequence, I didn't have a chance to speak much and Jazz even less. Worse, Jazz was barely acknowledged until mid-lunch when Maud intervened after looking tenser by the minute, her smile increasingly frozen and exasperated.

'Miss Jones, hopefully you do not consider that not having children will stop you from being included in our little town as an honoured new arrival. We can, of course, learn to be flexible in our customs,' Maud said out of the blue. Barbara shot Maud a most displeased look, but could not reprove her. She was the hostess.

'Certainly Miss Jones will have ample opportunity to settle here and raise a family,' Barbara commented, adding to Jazz, 'I will be delighted to help you. I have been known to have quite a talent as a matchmaker.'

Jazz's facial reaction was priceless. She displayed a mixture of incredulity, shock, fear and struggle to contain herself and her words, which were without doubt 'what the heck!' I coughed, an action that helped her recover her senses and she finally gave her best fake smile at Barbara Snayth and replied, 'Dear Mrs Snayth, how very kind of you to offer your help! I don't really know yet how I will settle here. I do have some ideas … (There Jazz back-tracked, as it might not be good to talk about her lounge bar right then). Of course your very generous offer to help is very much appreciated. Thank you.'

I had discreetly tried to indicate to Jazz with a slashing gesture of the hand at plate level it would be best to stop talking. The less said on Barbara's thoughts on matchmaking for baby purposes, the better.

'And here it begins. Time for the women to rise,' I heard Clémence Hoare whisper next to me. Her deep assured tone surprised me as much as the strange sentence. I glanced towards her. She saw me look at her and gave me a lovely smile. She was such a sweet fragile little thing that one. She glanced at Maud. She must have quoted her friend.

After this, Jazz tried to make herself as small as possible, literally hunching her shoulders and shrinking in her seat. To Maud's credit, she only occasionally and subtly intervened despite Barbara taking over during lunch. The good news was that as Barbara wasn't hosting, I didn't have to return the invitation and ask her to mine. Not yet. It was bound to happen, though I didn't want to think about it and increase my headache. The bad news was Jazz would not be the only one she had thought of matchmaking for. I suspected there were plans for me in there too. There were probably not many single men in a town focused on procreation, so either she had in mind to make us someone's third or fifth wife, or she would try to marry us to her teenage sons. I took a glass of wine, focused on my breathing and tried to calm down from the rising revulsion at the thought. When lunch was over, Jazz and I mounted our horses and were escorted back home, Nick by my side and a local man on the horse behind. Not talking, Jazz had compensated by drinking. With too much of the local ale and a full stomach, she made an interesting sight on the horse. At home, she went straight to her room and disappeared until the next morning.

It was late afternoon and the others were not back yet. Rico was not home, so I was alone with Nick. Well, almost, there was Simba. As I wasn't sure what would happen today, I had left her with Rico, who said he would look after her until 2 p.m. when he went to the studio. Poor girl had been left home with newspapers all over the floor to protect it from her.

I decided to take her out for a little walk in the forest with Nick as he wouldn't let me out of his sight. I would take this opportunity to have a friendly talk with the watchmen. So I pulled on my jeans and my walking boots, and wrapped myself up in a comfortable jacket with a tightening belt. The weather was getting better, I would need to go and do some clothes shopping soon for summer clothes suitable for Lil'London. Forget shorts, light spaghetti strap dresses. I would have to cover a bit more flesh over there.

Nick was waiting for my call from his mobile home as he had to come pick me up. He came immediately and we made for the door with my wolf. I walked out first and crossed a few steps through the Fog before realising I was in London. Not the forest, London. I stopped dead. That was not possible, I was with Nick, and shouldn't be there. Besides, I could not walk out to London without Rico or Harry, or … Simba! I looked at her and she wagged her little tail. I looked behind me, no Nick.

'Simba, why are we in London?' I asked her.

Tail wagging.

'Did we go out too fast?' I asked again.

Tail wagging.

'Did I say "London" to you? I don't remember … Did I say "forest" or "London"? Tell me, is that it?' I persisted asking.

More tail wags. Now also with paws down and backside up, ready for play.

'Did you read my mind that I wanted to do some shopping? You did, didn't you, you good girl!' I took a rolled up sock out of my pocket and let her grab it, then pulled it so she had to fight for it.

I must have said 'London' to her, I couldn't think of any other explanation. So the training worked! I was ecstatic: it worked! The builders were looking at me as if I was mad. I quickly made my way back. I had to see what happened with Nick, and didn't want Phil or anyone of the Society to see me out there on my own. Plus, I didn't have my purse with me for the shops anyway.

Under cover of the Fog, I did a little happy dance and punches in the air. Laughing out loud, I picked up Simba and did a little dance with her in my arms. My mobile rang. Nick.

'Helloooo!' I answered in a light tone, trying to sound nonchalant.

'All good?' he asked.

'Yes, I don't know what happened. I must have walked out in front of you too fast and ...' I replied.

'No, it's me, I was just about to walk behind you when the alarm beeped on the surveillance system,' he said. 'I'm sorry, I know that means you were stuck in the Fog and it's not pleasant. I hope you didn't venture too far before grasping I wasn't with you?'

'Uh-huh ... Don't worry. I'm fine.'

'Aren't you coming back? Shall we still go?'

'I'm at the door. What was it, the alarm?'

'A lone wolf. I am not a specialist, but I am surprised they are coming so close to the house, the watchmen and the camp, in general.'

I was back in and we switched off the call, continuing our chat in person.

'I don't know. Maybe it's linked to Simba. The mother?'

'Possible.'

'I don't have to give her back, do I, Simba? I can keep her?' After what just happened, I had no desire to give her back, ever. For all that, I had less right than the mother and the wild.

'I don't know. Now that she has adopted you and smells of you, her mother would most likely shun her anyway.'

Selfishly, I really hoped so.

I put Simba back on the floor and repeated to her: 'Forest. Forest, Simba, forest.' It would raise suspicions if we came out in London again. During the walk in the forest, Nick and I were silent at first. I kept thinking of doing more tests with Simba, alone and with others, to see where we would come out. After a few minutes, I started to relax and take in the forest around me, the smells, and the sounds. It was so peaceful. It was like regenerating energy.

'Nick, did you grow up in city or country?'

'City. I am London born and bred through and through. Never been in the country much back then, except for the odd weekend. After I joined the army, I was mostly out of town, for training.'

'Not the most relaxing way to discover the countryside, then.'

'No, definitely not. I will enjoy it.'

'Yes? That's good to hear.'

'I'm a bloke, but the cracking of the branches and leaves under my boots, the birds and distant sounds of animals, even the wind in the trees, yes, I like it.'

That made me smile and join in the good mood. 'And imagine, after this long walk, we'll get to go back home, take our boots off and treat ourselves to a cup of tea.'

'Homemade biscuits too?'

'I still have some left ...'

'I am in!'

We went back to walking in silence. He only interrupted it minutes later when we came across a fallen tree. As we walked towards it, Nick said, in such a soft low voice I wasn't sure if he wasn't talking to himself, 'An intriguing world, a magical forest and a lovely woman to look after. I have a good feeling about this job.' I didn't comment. When we reached the large trunk, before I had time to react, he lifted me up on it by swiftly grasping me by both hands on my waist and putting me up there. He followed me up. Simba, still on the ground, started to make her in-throat yelping, louder and louder. It was my way out of a moment which was getting a bit too romantic when it shouldn't be.

'We should pick her up, we don't want her to attract wild animals. It happened once before. It wasn't my best moment.'

We walked for a good forty minutes and on the way back stopped to have a little chat with the watchmen. They were having ham and bread with ale and offered us some. I only accepted the bread, I was holding Simba in my arms and couldn't put her down. For such a small puppy, this walk had been an exhausting adventure and she wobbled with tiredness, incapable of walking any more. Nick had a slice and a small goblet, and we listened to the men talking about the weather, the best traps to catch rabbits and what we thought of their forest. They also informed us that everyone had returned from Lil'London and were back in their 'homes on wheels' or inside the house. I couldn't wait to get back home and tell the boys, Leo and Dante included, about Simba leading me to London. I would ask them to keep it between London Foggies for now.

Leo and Dante were in the dining area, both hunched over the table covered by various sheets. As Nick and I drew near, we saw the documents were a mixture of architect's plans and maps.

'We are going to build a road!' Dante said, brimming with excitement.

'And the Relocated will have the choice for their home either by the Fog or along the road,' Leo added. 'If they want to live in Lil'London, an exchange would have to be made between a Lil-Londoner house and a Relocated. I guess this is their system of integration. We said this was a point to raise with you. They also wish to have a dedicated area by the Fog, for trading and other matters with London and our original world.'

'I could bet that one is from Benjamin Snayth,' I said.

'The one and only,' Leo replied.

Dante looked at Leo and me, then down at his documents, and said, 'I have a lot of work to do. Leo is on coordination requirements and wishes from the Relocated, but I have to work out what is possible and how. I can't wait to have a proper office!' As he rolled or folded his documents, Dante kept glancing at me or Leo, but never holding his gaze.

He knew.

And they say men don't blab.

What bad timing, now that I had decided the best course of action was to put things on hold between Leo and me.

'Anything else happened that I should be aware of? Were you stuck in the Lil'London town hall all that time? Surely, they let you have something to eat?' I asked.

'Yoko, may I make myself a cup of tea and steal one of your biscuits?' Nick interrupted, putting his hand on my shoulder. Leo flinched.

'Of course Nick. It's part of the country walk ritual! At least I think ... I am not an expert.'

'Would anyone else like a cup too?' he asked around.

The three of us accepted. Nick left for the kitchen and Leo answered my questions.

'We got out of that meeting room quite late. Discussions on houses and roads lasted for some time, especially between Edmund Poff and Dante, who he invited to visit the Lil'London library tomorrow with him. Snayth and Hoare were looking extremely bored. Snayth was all sweet with the Fishers, a bit condescending also if you want my opinion. I wonder if this is because they are, well, mixed-race children. As for Big Tom, he remained silent almost all the time. All he asked at some point was if he could join their boxing club. Guess what? Augustus Hoare is the one who replied in the affirmative! He said they followed Broughton's rules, whatever that is, and that Big Tom was welcome to attend their encounters and participate, should he adhere to the rules and practice. Apparently Big Tom had spoken to Barnaby Sparrow about this last Saturday. Sparrow had told him that he and Hoare were boxers and the sheriff was overseeing the 'club'. This is THE hobby of Big Tom, so he wants in.'

'Good for him!' I replied. 'He's found something in common with some of the locals, that's great news.'

Nick, returning from the kitchen from where the kettle was boiling, heard the last sentence.

'I'll want to join as well! If Big Tom is any good, he alone would be an interesting match. Hoare is pretty well built too. I am a bit less fit after my injury, but I can still throw a good punch. So I'll definitely go, if you let me have any free time Yoko.'

'Just let me know when you need it and I'll plan to either stay at home or stick to good old London.'

Nick nodded. I turned back to Dante and Leo, the latter looking a bit sullen.

'And lunch?' I asked, following up on my enquiry of the day.

'Lunch was served in the ballroom/banqueting room of the town hall. Pretty much like the council room, except bigger. A bit less than twice the size, I would say,' Dante said.

'It was a buffet of dishes I had never heard of before. I don't know what I ate, but it wasn't bad,' Leo said.

'How long before someone opens a Pizza & Pasta restaurant in Lil'London? Who wants to bet it'll be a hit?' Dante commented.

'It depends,' Nick answered. 'If an Indian or Pakistani crosses first, they might beat the Italians to it and set a curry trend.'

'Sushi, on the other end, might take longer to take off there,' I reckoned, choosing a biscuit.

Dante left. Nick went back to his den. I was alone with Leo. We were both sitting at the table nursing our cups of tea and the silence was awkward.

'I really like you, Yoko.'

'I like you too.'

More silence.

'Yoko, you want to click the "pause" button, don't you?'

I was looking at my tea cup and couldn't raise my eyes. I smiled, but it was a sad smile.

'Too much, too soon, too fast. Yes. It is complex right now. I'm sorry, I am a bit overwhelmed, even scared sometimes, by all that is going on and how to deal with it all. But I do like you, really. I would love something to happen. Just not like this, in this mess.'

'I know. I understand. I said "pause", not "end".'

'Thank you for understanding, for not being mad at me.'

'That's OK. I have a plan.'

'You have a plan?'

'Oh yes! I have a plan.'

'Is it a secret plan, or can I hear about it?'

'It is secret, but I can tell you. You won't be able to tell.'

'I won't "be able to"?' I laughed. 'OK, so tell me.'

'I am going to flirt with you and seduce you – publicly. I am going to court you, nice and slow. I am going to grow into your official suitor and won't let anything, or anyone get in my way and when you are ready, we will be together. I am a patient, determined man. Not only that, I have the advantage of knowing that you are attracted to me and some of the things that make me react. In fact, you are already in my net.'

I burst out laughing. He smiled and continued, 'Nutella, it's a pause. Wait and see what an Italian gentleman can do when the woman is worth it.'

'What if ...' I began.

'What if I have to face another suitor? Na ... This is a fight I will win. Nick might be a good boxer, but come on, an English versus an Italian, Naaaan ... I will fight and win.'

'It wasn't what I was going to ask,' I smiled and tried again. 'So, what if ...'

'I get bored of courting or meet someone else? That won't happen. No!' he interrupted, and finished his sentence with a large horizontal slash with both hands.

'You seem pretty sure,' I remarked, head turning slightly and raising my eyebrows.

'I am. Because I know. Sometimes you just know.'

What do you say to that? It was both flattering and intimidating. We looked at each other a bit longer, smiling. We were going to be fine, I thought and felt a rush of relief and tenderness for him. I really did like him. Then I thought, 'Hang on. "Fight with Nick?" So he believes Nick is really interested, not just being cheeky? For God's sake!'

'So, tell me more about your day,' I moved on to another subject. 'How did the Relocated deal with it all?'

Leo was silent for a while, then he replied, 'Well. They are dealing with things pretty well, all things considered.' We talked a bit and then he left me with my thoughts, parting with just a caress on my cheek.

**Day 4 (Wednesday)**

The previous night, under cover of darkness, I went out on my own with Simba again. Instead of Fog, I told her 'forest'. I was feeling drained and impatient to try more with her and double-check my theory. It worked! It really worked! I could see the layout of the trees under the moon, I could see out. I was not in the total darkness of the Fog at night. I didn't stay more than a second before retreating back out of the Fog. Nick had set up video cameras, most probably with night vision. Simba was on a lead, at my feet and I pulled her back too, telling her she was a good girl, a very good girl. Back inside, I waited an hour before heading out with Simba, this time saying 'London'. I felt this bubble of freedom, of something important and couldn't resist. I had some concerns it was too much for such a young puppy and it could confuse her. There was a risk of her losing the gift she had, still I had to try. I had to. Simba led me to London, to the almost finished building site of the lot. I took a brief look and again withdrew back behind the Fog to avoid any of the cameras. Simba was a Double Facilitator. I had already grown fond of her as a companion, now she was even more valuable. As valuable, she would need protection. We would protect each other from now on.

I went to bed early and woke up early. Zeno was downstairs, sitting at the table drinking coffee when I got there.

'Hey you! Welcome home! Did you miss us already?' I went and hugged him.

'Sneaked out to check how it all went yesterday. Told her there was an issue with one of the market stalls, to sort before the markets opened.'

'All good with Cris?'

'...'s OK.' Zeno was very dismissive in his grumbled reply, which meant it was not that OK.

'Want to talk about it?'

'No.'

'I am here if you want to whenever you need to. So, here are the updates.' I told him about the events of the previous day and finished with my big news: Simba's special gift.

'You are kidding me? This is huge! Yoko, this is big!' Zeno had stood up, pushing his chair backwards which nearly fell on the ground.

'I know. She is so young, I just hope it will continue. I am beside myself!'

'That's it, I am getting a dog!' he exclaimed.

'Should we try to see if it works with you first? Like, now? She needs to go out for a pee, so.'

'Yeah! Let's do this!'

We wrapped up and I told Simba to go to 'London'. Sure enough, she led Zeno and me to London and started to potter around. I was aware that, should anyone from the Society be out, they would notice the absence of Rico or Harry with us.

'This is awesome! Oh Simba, I love you, you schmooozzy-mushhhyyy-swishyy koshishishishishisis ...' Zeno was on his hands and knees, playing and kissing the puppy who loved it. Thankfully there was nobody around, it was too early.

'Now, Zeno, would you like to try on your own?'

'What a question! Yes!'

I picked up Simba in my arms and we walked back inside. We fed Simba first and waited ten minutes before Zeno headed for the door with Simba, saying 'London' twice, as I had done. Simba kept looking at me and seemed reluctant to go. Within a few minutes, Zeno returned as he had left with her in his arms, looking crestfallen.

'Forest. It didn't work.'

He headed right to the kitchen to prepare himself another jug of coffee. I bent down on my knees to pat Simba who was all over me, yelping with joy as if she hadn't seen me for a long time.

'She is young. She probably just wanted her 'mummy'. Don't worry. I am sure it will pass,' I told him.

'I smell coffee?' I heard Leo say from the stairs, his steps getting closer.

'Yes, new pot in preparation,' Zeno replied, his eyes meeting mine and looking at Simba. I shook my head and he understood.

'Ciao everyone!' Leo said when he reached us. I heard someone else coming down and recognised Harry's steps. The house was coming alive. Jazz joined the little group shortly afterwards and came to the kitchen with the words 'I can smell coffee!' We might have a slight coffee addiction in the house ...

'Nutella-Bella, have you ever had some Italian biscuits called 'brutti ma buoni'? They are my favourite and with coffee. Mmmmm.' Leo brought his hand to his mouth in the international gesture and sound for 'delicious'.

'Err ... No. What is it?'

'A bit like a hazelnut meringue, crunchy on the outside, chewy on the inside. I'll make you some just for you. You keep cooking us little treats, time you got some back,' Leo replied with a broad grin. Jazz looked at him with wide eyes and murmured to me 'Nutella-Bella? What the ... Did I miss anything last night!'

I shook my head to her and replied to Leo, 'Hazelnut meringue? Feel free to use my kitchen whenever you want. That sounds exactly like my kind of biscuit!'

'Consider it a breakfast date. Let's say tomorrow?' Leo replied as if we just struck a deal.

Zeno, Harry and Jazz were looking quite amused and Leo excused himself to go and dig out his grandmother's recipe.

'Well, Leo seems to have moved from the general Italian flirt to the more targeted flirt,' Harry said, sipping his coffee.

'Interesting,' Jazz said to herself.

'Maybe he is just getting more relaxed now that he is settling into London with us,' Zeno suggested.

'Exactly,' I nodded, jumping on Zeno's comment.

'Interesting,' Jazz repeated. She was looking at me with eyes half-closed. I felt like a lab rat under scrutiny. I stood up looking for an escape, 'Breakfast, anyone?'

The morning passed fast. I continued working on my proposal for the evening Foggies Board Meeting. Mitch would be in London by then, but would not be joining us at home for the occasion. We had decided that we would maintain the separation, so as to not make the others feel further overwhelmed with the large group the four of us from the house, the two Italians and now Mitch would make. I also wrote a message to Leila, asking her for an update on the Society's information, position and actions regarding Ingis Chen. Late morning, most of us all gathered round the FTab to read the new email received from Clare in Kenya:

Dear Foggies,

I am so relieved! Mary is back. She returned an hour ago. She is very very sorry about the worry and stress she has caused. She will join us and tell you all that happened tonight, but I wanted to let you know the gist of it as soon as possible because I was so touched by your immediate response and help. She was stuck at a tribal wedding and her radio ran out of battery. The wedding celebrations lasted several days and she didn't want to leave in the middle and risk offending the locals. I know that Mitch has already left Alaska and will be in London soon. We are sorry he made the trip for nothing.

Also, Ingis Chen tried to contact me again. I was given a letter from him by one of the Society guards protecting the house. He regretted not having access to me directly. He wanted to know if he was able to help in any way and if I was aware that other Foggies existed. He also hoped I was not a prisoner in my own house, either because of the Fog or because of anybody. A friendly letter, yet thanks to you we know there is another side of him. I am looking forward to discussing tonight what should be our line of action with him.

Again, sorry for the inconvenience we put you all through because of my daughter's disappearance and thank you for your support.

Warm wishes,

Clare

Zeno had long gone back to Cris. Half of him would welcome the news of not having to face the jungle with Mitch with only basic preparation, the other half would be very disappointed. I for one was very glad! Harry suggested we should all, or at least Crossers and Switchers, get some training for survival in any situation should something similar happen in the future.

Big Tom joined us and entered saying, 'I'm sorry to disturb you. A parcel should arrive for me soon. It's a special delivery and they are not going to leave it in the mailbox. I don't want them to cross the Fog though. And it is a fragile parcel. I don't want just anyone handling it.'

'Well, it's your lucky day, Rico is away in his studio, but I am working from home this morning,' Harry told him. 'So I will be able to go and pick up your parcel. Just tell them to ring the bell by the mailbox.' Big Tom was fidgety and uncomfortable. He wanted to say something, but didn't seem to know how to begin. Finally, he announced, 'I know you didn't really want me to have a gun, but … I have to. I need to feel a bit more secure. Actually, I wanted a shotgun but thought that one could wait.'

He looked round. We had nothing to say, we understood how he felt. Reassured by the lack of an outburst from anyone, he went on, 'I got you two guns. Yeah, I know the Society can probably provide this stuff for you. Heck! It could be good they don't know everything you've got, right?' Had he read my mind?

Harry turned towards me, 'Yoko, you should learn how to shoot.'

'I have Nick. He would do the shooting, right?'

'What if he is not around for whatever reason? What if he is blocked somewhere and you need to defend yourself?' Jazz asked. 'I want to learn how to shoot too.'

'Absolutely. Nick may not always be by your side,' Leo said, adding 'hopefully' in a low voice that everyone could still hear.

'Fine. I will learn how to shoot!' I exclaimed. 'I have always wanted to for fun, not to shoot at people. I don't think I could pull the trigger at someone even if it was required.'

Big Tom had got the other gun for Jazz. 'Women. It's a man's job to protect them, but a little bit of self-help is good thing too.'

As soon as I had a chance, I told Harry, Rico and Jazz separately about Simba. They all had the same reaction of surprise and excitement. From telling them stemmed the tests with each. The results were the same every time: Simba didn't want to go without me and when carried in someone's arms both she and the carrier would just end up where they would have without her. The only anomaly being, of course, that she should not have been able to follow Harry and Rico into our London, but we didn't even flinch at this anymore.

Doing the tests with Simba, I had a chance to see the outside of the terrace again in the morning. If I thought that it was busy and chaotic with workers the past few days, I'd seen nothing yet. It was now completely frantic. The last house on the left when entering the parking lot, which had been set aside for the Society as a kind of warehouse, had been stripped already and was now being filled with materials and tools for building houses and roads in World II. Dante and Leo were hovering around this 'warehouse'. Leo was focusing on the planning of what should go where and waiting for Zeno to help out. Zeno would need a great deal of the storage as well for the various trades and he and Leo would need to work as a team there. Considering Zeno's lack of organisation, Leo would have to compensate a lot in that regard. On the other side of the lot, the houses were almost ready for their new occupants and use. It was the last sprint towards being completely set up. Everywhere, cables and satellite dishes, solar panels and other electronic and high-end technology devices were ready to be installed.

'I foresee a zillion TV channels,' I thought, 'and a total lack of privacy.' I made a mental note to check every hole in the house for cameras and bugs. I wanted the house to be off the grid. My next thought was more positive: with all this technology, we should at last have a power shower, an upgrade from the renowned poor British showers. The plan was that we would move in on Saturday: our new house would be sparsely furnished with the minimum so we could add our own little touches. So exciting!

Joined by Phil, I went out to do a shop for a proper lunch as Leila and Mitch would be there. I wasn't wandering around the town much these days. Once we moved into the big house, some of the good life in London would return. Mainly the past few weeks I had remained around the house, which was pretty much like a secure village in my mind. Before entering the supermarket, I put Simba inside my large tote bag. It wasn't the first time I used this trick to get her into non-animal friendly places and she snuggled in nicely. It didn't have much room left, so purse and FTab had to go in my pockets. She was getting that little bit heavier every day, my little one. Soon she wouldn't fit it, or would be too heavy anyway. As I was pushing the trolley along the aisles, I felt my life was almost normal, aside from having a wolf cub in my bag and a bodyguard checking onions behind me.

'Miss Nutty. What a pleasure to see you again,' a man said appearing by my side in front of the apples selection. There was no need to turn. The voice was unmistakable. Besides, who else would call me 'Miss Nutty'?

'Good morning, Mr Chen. You surprise me, I wouldn't expect you to run your own grocery errands.'

'I don't. Although the smell of roast chicken from the counter over there makes me believe I've been missing out.'

'Then are you here for market research, or did you just happen to see me come in and thought you would say hi?'

'Something like that. I couldn't miss the opportunity to talk to you again.'

'How lovely of you.' I still had not turned to look at him and was slowly walking down the aisles, choosing my apples with care. I settled on a bag of Golden Delicious and finally looked at him.

'You look tired, Mr Chen.'

'I am just back from abroad. Literally. I landed a couple of hours ago.'

'Maybe you should have a nap.'

'It was more interesting to see you.'

'I have a lunch to prepare. I am afraid chit-chatting with you is just not possible now. So if you will excuse me,' I began pushing my trolley forward towards the dairy aisle.

'I will walk with you,' Chen replied.

We walked. Ingis Chen offered to push the trolley for me. I refused. I was trying to concentrate on my shopping list, the one I should have written and hadn't. Ingis Chen's appearance made me forget everything. After we went through the whole cheese aisle in silence, Ingis Chen spoke. 'Has Leo thought about what we discussed?'

'Yes.'

'Have you?' Ingis Chen asked, slowing down. As I didn't answer, he added, 'I assume that if he trusts you enough to share the situation with you, your opinion matters. Maybe you are the one I should convince first.'

'You can do better than easy flattery, Mr Chen.'

'Please call me Ingis.'

'How did you find me?'

'It was simple, really. I assumed that the little pizzeria we met in was a local of yours. And if you live in the area, you shop in the area.'

'So you had the supermarkets covered.' It was so obvious it made me feel dumb. Annoyed, too. This little game of cat and mouse was starting to get on my nerves. Time to reverse the tables.

'Mr Chen ...' I started.

'Ingis, please,' Ingis Chen interrupted.

'So.' I paused, took a deep breath in and continued in my best businesslike tone. 'I understand you are very eager to get your hands on the Fog opportunities and create a big new Chen empire but, Mr Chen, you can't. Despite your wish to have a share of it and participate in what is coming next, you will nonetheless have to review your plans. You do not have the choice. We are not convinced by you and without us you have nothing. You see, de facto, we are the 'Keepers of the Door' and you need us. And by us, I don't just mean Leo and me, or Jack and Dante. I mean a bigger group, those who have a direct link to the Fog, those who have a direct say on how this link will be used.'

At this point, if Ingis wished to say something, he stood no chance. I was on a roll. 'Now, the good news is, we might – MIGHT – listen to your offer. So, open dialogue is a possibility. Today, all I am asking is that you be patient and back off. Because honestly, our lives have just been turned upside down, we have a lot to deal with and we don't need any more pressure right now. Certainly we don't need yours.'

I smiled to him – a big, bright, fake grin – and asked, 'Now, can I finish my shopping alone? If I forget something and my dish is ruined, I'll be pretty mad and I'll blame you.'

I didn't get an immediate reply, just a stare (looking back, there was a lot more staring in my everyday life than before – stares, frowns or raised eyebrows).

'I shall wait expectantly for few more days,' Ingis said, 'for the pleasure of seeing you again, Nutty.'He bowed his head, turned on his heel and left, looking straight ahead of him. I was facing the French stinky cheeses section. It seemed appropriate: despite their stink, they were a must on the cheese board. Just like Chen would now always be around. I picked a very ripe Camembert and moved on to the next aisle.

We were having coffee outside after lunch, sitting on the dining table chairs brought out for the occasion, and looking out to the trees by the forest clearing. Dante and Leo were walking in and out of the forest, hands and arms gesticulating in all directions. They were explaining something to the Relocated who were following them like a herd. It was either about the roads, the houses to be build, or the septic tanks. While Jazz, Zeno, Mitch and I were enjoying a nice April day, with the warm sun making the moment very relaxing, Leila was with us virtually on a video call. Zeno was enjoying it less than the rest of us, he looked pretty gloomy to me and had been during the whole lunch. He was not supposed to be there, but he had showed up around 12.30 p.m. without giving any reason. He made a good show of enjoying the company and meeting Mitch, but his heart was clearly not in it. There was Cris trouble in paradise. As for Mitch, he seemed a really nice guy. Tall, lanky and wiry from outdoor activities, he was friendly and helpful. He observed a lot, not in a calculating way, more an in-depth understanding way. You couldn't help wondering what it was he was seeing, noticing, gathering, especially when his focus was on you. He talked little and when not looking at you it always seemed like a part of his mind was somewhere else, in his mountains presumably. They would have to wait a bit longer for his return: both Zeno and Mitch had discussed the Kenyan trip with Leila and had decided to go despite the emergency being removed. It would be a short trip, just about five days, with one day training in modern Kenya before crossing to the big wild.

Soon we were looking up at the sky, observing the tele-guided small helicopter Nick had received from the Society. It looked like a fancy toy and I had to bite my lips not to ask for a turn to play with it. I would have been rebuffed. The helicopter had the latest video camera set up underneath, with a radio signal sending the images back to the house. It had the power and signal capacity to fly all the way to Lil'London and back broadcasting. It was one more step of less privacy in this world.

I welcomed the relative peace after an argumentative lunch. I had disclosed my encounter with Ingis Chen and Leo got upset, 'He is stalking us! It is unacceptable!'

'Phil was with you, right?' Nick overrode him.

'I think he will be off our backs for a couple of days now. In any case, his reasoning for finding us was pretty smart. We should have thought of it. And yes, Nick, Phil was with me.'

'We should set up a tracking device on you,' Phil said, to which Leo nodded his assent.

'I am sure you can track the FTab, can't you? Isn't it suffi-cient? It definitely feels sufficient to me, the one being tracked,' I replied.

'If you are captured, we need to wipe the FTab clean. So no, it would not be enough. Also, the tracking device on you would have to be traceable in both worlds, so I could monitor you wherever.'

'I don't like the idea. Already, we are losing a lot of privacy ...'

'You have plenty of privacy, there are no cameras inside the houses.'

'I very much hope so! This is not Big Brother. There shouldn't be cameras inside the house!' I retorted. That was the last straw; there would be no tracking device on my body. I decided to just dismiss the matter for now, knowing from Nick's face that it would come up again.

Instead, I switched subject and asked Leila if the Society had made a decision or had more information regarding Ingis Chen. Leila had verified what Ingis Chen had said to us and it was correct. He was running a large number of factories in China and was present on many selling platforms: in bulk for retailers across the globe, directly to customers in online shops, or to labels as a direct product or by-product. His corporation was selling fashion, accessories, technology, toys, kitchen or home tools, or anything that could be produced in man-powered factories. Following our position to keep in touch with him, the Society had opted for not contacting Chen for now. They wished to keep a low profile and just observe from afar. As long as we kept them informed of our arrangements with him, they always preferred to remain in the shadows. It was also a good way to keep protecting us unhindered. I put these thoughts – and the work on the evening Foggies Board Meeting or FBM – to one side. For now I was enjoying coffee in the sun, with the old and new people in my life and felt good. Mitch had said something a few minutes ago that struck a chord and I realised our good fortune to be a good group together. He had said, 'I love my mountains and I love being able to retreat on my own or with Rosario, Tony and Mum only. Yet sometimes like now, here with you all, it is nice to share the same unearthly experience.'

This FBM should have been a pleasant one. The crisis over Mary's disappearance had been averted, and Mitch and Zeno had bonded well. As a whole we were getting used to each other and coming to appreciate how we should rely on each other. I was right, we all realised the importance of being a team and working together. However, my mistake was to fail to see some of the cracks in the Foggies group. Unknown to some of us, the most unhappy Foggies, namely Christophe, Adam and Sophia, had stirred up a little storm with the some of the other Foggies, Louise, Adam, and even Clare and Putu. Their issue was the controlling influence of the London Fog, due to their dominance in number and apparent special relationship with the Society. Clare and Putu said that they were extremely grateful for everyone's immediate reaction to help Mary, but, returning to the Foggies, they wanted a better balance of power and independence from any external structure. Louise's position was the weakest. It became apparent very quickly that she was mainly supporting Christophe in his demands. Christophe and Adam's point of view was that if we were to all work together it should be on equal grounds. It was unacceptable that so many people were in London and none of the others had been kept informed. Should anything happen in London, it would have created chaos. The Society had taken sides there too, in their eyes. Both of them, although insisting they were indebted to the Society for its generous support, wanted a balance of power as well. They felt that Ingis Chen could be the missing element to counterweight the Society's monopoly with us. Leo lost it when he heard this, reminding them of Jack's kidnapping, of the death of the Society's agent in Mexico (although it was not yet confirmed that it was Chen's work), and of the dangerous way of thinking the man had. They agreed this was not the perfect choice, but the man knew about the Fog, and working with him was also the best approach to control him. The virtual FBM went on with Leo shouting at the screen in Italian, Adam banging his fist on the table with what sounded like Hebrew swear words, Christophe was trying to scream above the other two in French that Ingis Chen was a successful business man, and that Leo must have communist prejudices. Sophia remained silent, until she said that maybe the Foggies should split in two: one group supported by Ingis Chen, the other by the Society. My feeling was that it would be the worst that could happen. Rosario jumped in, expressing the opinion I had kept to myself (as the London Foggies were already in a bad light, I barely dared make a sound, fearing to alienate them further. Instead, I was racking my brains to think of a solution.) Rosario expressed his view that splitting would only make things worse, as then each group would be more dependent. Rosario suggested that instead we should work together to find a solution acceptable to all. She suggested that Sophia and I work together for the coming days to sort something out, representing both schools of thought: with and without Ingis Chen, as well as how each of us could bring something to the group on an everyday basis.

The FBM left a sour taste in my mouth. All the Society had been trying to do far was help, and in London we certainly had not tried to dominate the Foggies. Of course, I agreed to work with Sophia. Neither she nor I showed much enthusiasm. It was the first time there was a clear split between us, not linked to some personality clash but to the Foggies' future line of conduct. To the Foggies' future.

After the FBM, I took Simba out with Jazz before heading to bed and collapsing. It had been another long day.

## Day 5 (Thursday)

The day started as usual. It would not end well.

I woke up, took Simba out, had coffee with the boys (Jazz was not up yet), laughed at Leo's open flirting, blushed at Nick's subtle cheekiness, had some breakfast, dressed and got ready for another day of Foggy business. I was at my 'desk' that is the dining table, trying to think of how to sort out the new problem between the Foggies, when Zeno burst in.

'It's over,' he grumbled. He grabbed the empty coffee pot, shook it angrily to check what was left and headed towards the kitchen. It could only be about Cris. When he returned with a fresh pot of coffee, I tried not to look at him with a sad face, not to say 'sorry' or display excessive compassion. Isn't it always difficult to express empathy when someone has relationship trouble without being intrusive? His whole face was closed and upset. Jazz was finally up and also at the table, plainly trying not to look at him as he didn't seem in the mood to speak. Nick, headphones on and focused on the screens of the security control, seemed oblivious to the new drama in Zeno's life. Leo was out with Dante, Harry was at work and Rico was unsurprisingly sleeping (it was 9.30 a.m., early for him). In the end, I couldn't ignore that Zeno was suffering. He was my friend, one of my best friends.

'Time for some comfort from a friend?' I asked, standing up and walking behind him, giving him a hug as I did. I added, 'I'm going to make you a full breakfast. You need more than coffee this morning.'

'Not hungry,' he answered as I stepped into the kitchen.

'OK then,' I replied. I knew Zeno. He said he didn't want anything, but he would eat if it was put in front of him. Instead of cooking and to respect his decision, I pulled out a large plate and put a couple of apples, pears and bananas on it, along with a few croissants, and brought the lot to the living room setting it up on the table in the middle of Jazz, Zeno and me. As I put it down, I picked up an apple, crunching it on my way back to the kitchen to prepare some tea for myself. I was done with coffee for the day. Back in front of my computer some minutes later, Zeno was eating a banana and dipping a croissant in his coffee. He looked better. Mission accomplished.

'Good timing to head off on a trip. I'm pleased to have a change of horizon,' Zeno said.

'When are you off?' I asked him.

'Heading off to the airport in a couple of hours. My bag is packed and waiting in the entrance.'

'And your other belongings? At the hotel? Shall we gather together whatever you left in the room while you are away and bring it to the new house for Saturday's move?'

'Already organised. Leo said he'll take care of it when he moves back into the room later today. My stuff will be returned here shortly.'

Mitch and he were not planning to be gone for long, they would be back on Tuesday next week. I would be worried sick in the meantime.

I worked all morning on finding a solution for the Foggies regarding Ingis Chen and, when I couldn't bear thinking about the problem any longer, on preparing 'my floor' in the new house. That was the fun part of my day. The new house was, obviously, double the size of the current house share. The top floor was slightly smaller, but had been renovated with a mezzanine created from the attic space, so everyone had the same space and share of the house. The ground floor was now a large open area with, on the one side, a big American kitchen and dining area, the kitchen having the option to be closed off when desired with a sliding panel moving up and down, and a large living area on the other. The wall dividing the two former houses had been replaced by four strengthened columns with a special inside armature, marking the transition between eating and living spaces. On the two floors above, the dividing wall had been kept, with the only change being a single staircase and large door between the two sides. In effect, that meant I had my

own floor, with a bathroom and three rooms (previously the equivalent of my current room, Harry's and Jazz's). On that morning, I was
toying with the idea of having one large bedroom (mine), one home
office/library/studio/spare bedroom, and one, the smallest room,
turned into a very large walk-in wardrobe. A dream finally realised!

Just before lunch, I decided to go for a walk with Simba before
eating. I needed some fresh air. Jazz was in the middle of a call
and Nick was playing with his surveillance helicopter, synchronis-
ing it with his control system and checking the picture quality. It
was a good opportunity to test again if Simba could lead me to
the forest, just her and me. I put my boots on, slid my two-way radio and FTab into the pockets of my jacket and grabbed a bag to
put Simba in when she got tired. I thought of picking some wild
flowers for the house as well.

That was a mistake. Not the flowers, but the wandering
around in the forest on my own. I was feeling too comfortable
and secure in both worlds, protected by Phil or Nick and trusting
the Lil'London friendly welcome.

So here I was, wandering in the forest, checking my compass
regularly, alone. After ten minutes or so, a wave of vulnerability
went through me. I had never been on my own in the forest before. It was such a lovely day, I brushed it away as ridiculous. Still, I
called Jazz on the radio and she only had a chance to say hi before
Nick took over.

'WHERE are you?'

'I went for a walk with Simba.'

'Phil says you are not in London.'

'I am in the forest ...'

'How did you get there?'

'Well, you were busy with the helicopter. I didn't want to bother you. I just thought ...'

'It is my job to protect you! This is more than a job, this is my
duty. Tell me your location, I am coming! You are valuable, you
can't just do what you want ...'

'EXCUSE ME?' He had just wiped away my guilt. I could bloody well do what I wanted!

'Oh! Don't you start! You know what I mean! I am not trying to restrict your freedom, just trying to protect and to look after you. This is not just about you anymore, this is about the Fog and all the people that are linked to it and need you for it.'

I had stopped walking and had picked up Simba to avoid her wandering away as I was concentrating on the call. I put her in the bag as I listened to Nick.

'It is also about you. I am getting to know you and I wouldn't forgive myself if something happened to you. So no, you can't just go out for a walk in the forest without telling anyone. I am not saying you can't roam around on your own, but we need to be in the vicinity and ready to intervene.'

'I AM in the vicinity.'

'I have no idea where you are, so you are not in my vicinity. Give me your coordinates.'

'Give you what?'

'The coordinates, your location, where you are.'

'No idea. Let me check.'

I heard him sigh, then heard a crack behind me. Turning, I vaguely saw something come towards me and I blacked out.

What I had seen was a fist coming to say hi to my face. I gathered this from my painful jaw when waking up. It took me some time to come to my senses and note my being tied to a tree next to Jack, with a woman I didn't know standing in front of me. There was no doubt she was the mercenary from the Chen Corporation from her clothes, her weapons and Jack's presence by my side. We had all assumed she was a man. Had Ingis Chen led us to believe the mercenary was a man too? It didn't matter anyway, from her stern face fixed on me and from my situation she bore no kind motives to me. Next to her was my two-way radio, my bag and Simba. She had zipped up the bag just enough to keep Simba inside, but letting the puppy breathe. Her little muzzle was popping out and she had her low throat yelp which meant she was unhappy.

'I gather your name is Yoko,' the woman said.

I didn't think it necessary to confirm it.

'So, what I want to know is what role you have with the Fog? The man, Jack, wouldn't tell me. Annoying wimp, the only thing he can do well is to keep his mouth shut when I ask him to speak. Everything else is a waste of time and space.'

'I don't think it is in my interest to tell you anything,' I replied.

'I think it is.'

'Well, I'll tell you I am a Relocated, I have no strong value for you and you may want to dispose of me,' I grunted.

'I already know you are not a Relocated. Otherwise, whoever was speaking with you on the radio would not have mentioned you were too valuable to walk around without protection.'

Any of the replies I wanted to give her were rude, so again I didn't bother to comment.

'So, Yoko, tell me, who were you talking with?'

'Don't you know how to use a walkie-talkie? Check for yourself.'

'You think you're funny do you? The radio fell when you dropped it and lost the channel. Give me a name and channel. Now.'

I was trying to think. What was the best thing to do? Was I supposed to tell her? Not tell her? For: maybe Nick had some kind of way to track the signal if she spoke to him. Against: there were bound to be some cons, but just then I couldn't think of any, or think in general. My jaw hurt and I had a headache. So the pros won and I gave the woman the right channel.

She picked up the radio, selected the channel, but didn't switch it on.

'Not the right time yet,' she said. I wasn't sure if she was talking to him or to me. The next question was clearly addressed to me.

'Now, again, what is your role with the Fog?'

I looked at her then lowered my head. This one I didn't want to answer.

'It's a cute little puppy you have in your bag. You wouldn't want him to suffer, would you?' She said with a sneer.

'Bitch!' I screamed inwardly, clenching my jaw which made me wince at the pain.

'What difference does it make that you know what I do?' I asked, trying to gain time to think.

'Just answer.'

'I am a Crosser,' I bluffed, fearing that Jack would betray my lie with a surprised look or something similar. He showed no reaction whatsoever. He kept looking in the distance, as if his mind was way off. Saying I was a Crosser was the safe answer: that made me complementary to Jack. It was better she didn't know she held two Switchers. She just nodded and I decided to play some of my key cards.

'I spoke with Ingis Chen yesterday. We are working on some kind of agreement between him and us.'

'And next you will tell me you and he are best chums?'

'No, next I will tell you that as we are in contact you might not want to do something that goes against his interests, that harms us, or to retain us much longer.'

'What guarantees can you give me that you are telling the truth?'

'How would I know his name if we were not in touch with him? I could also have told you that we have a good relationship with the locals here, that all the Foggies ... I mean the ones linked to the Fog, have become a tight group working together and that in reverse you are alone here, so you may not want to alienate us. Ingis Chen can't help you here. He has as much power here as he would on Mars. But we can.'

'Really? So why are you negotiating with him?'

'Because he knows about the Fog.'

'And because I have Jack. And now I have you too.' She pulled out something from her pocket. My FTab.

'Make it work. Your fingerprints I got, but the password, no,' the woman said in a menacing tone.

'Now how could I, you have tied my arms and hands to the tree.'

'You have a voice, tell me.'

'No!' I snapped.

'Puppy!' she snapped back.

'Go to ...' I began.

'Really, you'd rather I didn't read your personal emails than save your puppy?' she interrupted.

I smiled and said, 'I have a few secrets. Personal ones. But so be it, I will give you the code. Of course you are aware that, like any mobile device these days, that will also pinpoint our location, right?'

That last point made her hesitate. She stopped to think and I took the time to better observe her. She was dressed in what looked like all black military clothes. She had laced up walking boots, a black vest under her multi-pocket jacket, and you could see she was fit. She was definitely a good-looking woman, lean and tall, with strong Asian features and high cheekbones. My first impression was that she was Chinese. Her skin was relatively clear, so I would say she was from north-west China, maybe close to the Russian border. She had long straight hair tied in a ponytail, but instead of the expected jet black, it was platinum blond. The whole sight would have been striking, especially in the forest, but my being attached to the trunk of the tree made it more frustrating than anything.

'What's YOUR name? To be honest, so far in my head I have called you "the bitch" but maybe we could do better,' I asked the mercenary woman. It was my way of trying to make a connection. It was not the best approach, I had reached my limits and my jaw was on fire.

She actually showed the beginning of what could have been a smile.

'I don't mind being called bitch. I prefer that to being a pussy.' She nodded towards Jack as she spat the last words. 'Name is Ushi Tsou.'

'Chinese?'

'Yes. What about Yoko? Asian name but look … Greek? Lebanese?'

'French.'

'You don't look French.'

'I am a quarter Italian.'

'What's with the name?'

'I am a quarter Japanese.'

'And you live in London. Life these days.'

'Tell me about it. I am stuck in a forest in another world with a menacing woman, attached to a tree trunk with a jaw hurting like hell.'

She had another one of what could be called a smile.

'Right. Enough with the small talk. Back to business. We'll put the tablet aside for now. First, tell me about Ingis Chen.'

So I told her in brief that we were looking into finding a way to deal with his presence on the scene. The relations were now more on the diplomatic side, less on the kidnapping side. She switched on the radio and tuned it to the right channel. Immediately, Nick's voice came up.

'Who's on?' he asked.

'The new "friend" of Yoko and Jack.'

There was a short silence. Maybe Nick was processing that he was dealing with a woman.

'If you have hurt her in any way, I am going to kill you.'

'I doubt you could. Now, who are you?'

'Someone who is very pissed off. You …' There was some noise on the line and some angry voices and then Harry came on the line. I could hear Jazz say, 'Let me talk! Let me talk to that bitch!'

Ushi Tsou pulled the radio away from her ears, eyebrows shooting up as she looked at me. She turned the volume up. 'Good afternoon. My name is Harry. I am a friend of Yoko. May we talk to her and ensure she is all right?'

Ushi Tsou looked at me and nodded. She pulled her gun out and pointed it towards Simba. I raised my voice loud so that they would hear me, 'Hi Harry. I am OK. Jack too. Although aching from being tied to a tree,' Ushi Tsou shook her head and I said to her, which could be heard by everyone, 'Oh come on Ushi, where else than the forest could we be!'

'One more word or hint, Yoko, and I am shooting it in the head.'

'Then you would have no threat left.'

'Really? What about cutting little pieces of you here and there? Just a thought: I have four hands at my disposal.'

She had blocked the emitter when saying this. She pulled out something from a rucksack unnoticed before and came towards me. She stuck a piece of fabric on my mouth and nose and soon afterwards I passed out. Although it hadn't smelled of chloroform, it must have been something similar.

I was out for some time. She may have regularly put me back to sleep, I wouldn't know. When I reopened my eyes, the sun was fading and the sky was getting dark fast. Again, it took me some time to gather my wits together. I could hear yet not see Ushi Tsou, so I called out about my need to go to the bathroom. She untied me, but all the time I was doing my business, the muzzle of her gun was on the back of my head. I was pleased it was a simple business. A very unpleasant experience. Afterwards, as she reattached me, I tried to chat with her.

'So did you speak with Harry? Has he confirmed that we are now negotiating with Ingis Chen?'

'Yes, that is what he said. One-sided story, so for me it is all just talk. No proof.'

'I don't understand what you want by just keeping us here. It is not in your interest to act for Ingis Chen instead of us anyway.

He is of no help for you here. Surely there must be something you want to bargain. So, what is it you want?'

'I am in business.'

'OK, so what did Harry offer?'

'The only thing they could offer: help to settle me down here, to get me the best life possible for a Relocated. Even, maybe, to work with your little group.'

'And ...'

'And now I am going to check what the counter-offer is.'

I was confused. What was she talking about? What counter-offer? Had she found a way to access people in London? It meant she was still close to the house, a good discovery as I would be more likely to be found by Nick.

'Are you speaking with Ingis Chen? How?'

No reply.

It was almost totally dark now. I could barely distinguish a shadow against another tree three steps from me. Jack. Only now did I understand that he must have been drugged earlier when he was so silent and out of it. This time he seemed more awake and he shook his head when I asked about Ingis Chen. 'Right,' I thought. 'Let's try again.'

'Or is it someone else? Someone else is interested in the Fog and wants to have access to us.' Jack nodded vehemently. The Tsou woman was still ignoring me. She had stopped moving and aside from a slight noise from time to time, I would have wondered if she was still around. It sounded as if she were sharpening her knife.

'So, Miss Tsou, you have another radio or something for them too?' Silence. Maybe I should just return to referring to her as 'the bitch'. It was too fitting to dismiss.

Jack shook his head in the negative again. That didn't make sense, how could she get a counter-offer from anyone in London without radio or mobile or some means of communication? That would mean there was another fogged house? Could Jack have fogged another place last Saturday and the Society didn't find out? And the people of Lil'London didn't find out either?

Or maybe...

'You are negotiating with local people, aren't you?'

Silence. Big nod from Jack. Bingo. I was finally getting somewhere.

'Well, if you do, it doesn't change that it is in your interest and theirs that we all have a positive base to work on together. Kidnapping is not a good start, let me tell you.' I continued, 'You wouldn't want to have the communities you need both here and across the Fog against you, now, would you?'

I heard her move, with steps coming towards us and saw her – or more exactly the dark shape of her in the almost non-existent light – squat before me.

'You talk a lot. You must be thirsty.' She stuffed the top of a bottle in my mouth and turned the bottle over. Water poured into my throat and all over my face and top. I tried to swallow as best I could. When she pulled out the bottle, I coughed and tried to catch up with my breathing. As soon as I was about to give her a piece of my mind, she stuffed some kind of food in my mouth. It felt like meat, but I wasn't sure what it was exactly. It was nondescript and disgusting.

'Chew!' she said. 'Food is a luxury here. This is all you will get.'

I spit the thing out. She sighed. Next, I had a cloth on my mouth and nose and I was gone.

My last thoughts were that 'Tsou Bitch' sounded like 'You Bitch'. Definitely a very appropriate appellation.

**Day 6 (Friday)**

I woke up shivering. From the light, it was early in the morning. I was cold, my top was also still wet from the spilled water. April in England and World II were the same, the days may be warmer when in the sun, but the nights were cold. I was not dressed for this. The novelty in my situation was the gag I had on. Glancing at Jack asleep, he had one too. I looked round, Ushi Tsou was nowhere to be seen. I couldn't hear anything either, aside from the sounds of the forest. She was probably sleeping hidden nearby. In fact, I was really hoping she was nearby. I didn't want to be in the forest left tied up to a tree as very easy wolf-prey. And where was Simba? I drifted off.

I woke up again. The sun was much higher. Feeling unwell, I was shivering and feverish.

'MmmMMMmmMmmMMMM,' Jack emitted, doubling his attempts to attract my attention by tapping his feet on the ground. I focused on him. He was tied to a tree trunk on my left and he was closer than last night. I gave a cursory look around: we were not in the same location. My head hurt, I felt drowsy and my mouth and throat were pasty. Jack, with a jerk of the head, indicated towards my right. There in the distance I could see two shapes, two people talking. One was Ushi Tsou, I could tell from the ponytail, and the other I couldn't discern very well. It would have been difficult to recognise anyone them in the distance, and with my head pounding, I probably wouldn't have recognised them even if they were closer.

I was in a daze. I wasn't sure if I slept again and how long it was before she was back with us, but when she was, she took one look at me and said 'Shit!' I might have soiled myself as well, I wasn't sure. I am very glad not to remember.

When I woke up again, I was in my bed. My jaw was sore, my head hurt. It took me a few minutes to remember what had happened and to note I had no shivers or fever. I looked at the time: 6.44 p.m. Then a ball of fur hit my face and I got licked to excess by Simba. I laughed and hugged her tight. I had feared Tsou Bitch might have let her loose in the forest and Simba was lost. When I stood up and left the bed, I was dressed in my best pyjamas. I had a brief moment of hope that Jazz was the one who had put them on for me. I had so far managed to protect my housemates from the sight of me naked. It was a brief thought, it was not that important anyway. My clothes were nowhere to be seen, but my FTab was on its charger. I put a cardigan on, slippers on my feet, picked up Simba and headed downstairs. I was hungry, both for food and information. Harry, Jazz, Nick and Big Tom greeted me with exclamations and hugs downstairs, then filled me in on what had happened as I piled food on the table.

When the first radio connection was severed the day before, Nick immediately went on a tracking mission. The first thing he did was to activate the location signal on the radio. He had put one on each radio as a security measure. Unfortunately, it was linked to the radio signal. It only worked when the radio was on, so they couldn't find me. Ushi Tsou was a professional and she kept moving. She was good, not leaving many traces behind. I don't know how she did this with us being sleepy and like dead weights, but she did. They had finally managed to track her down when she contacted them again today at lunchtime. Jazz, Big Tom, the Fishers, Leo and Dante had had back-up. The Lil'London Council had gathered people fast and teamed Foggies and Relocated with locals, including Hoare, Snayth and the Sparrows – not Edmund, he was not that efficient in the forest, apparently. Jazz regretted not being teamed up with Barnaby Sparrow. Big Tom had got there faster. They hunted Ushi Tsou down and when they arrived she didn't even make a move to run. She was standing between the two trees Jack and I were attached to. Jack was awake, I wasn't and looked in a bad state. Apparently I was sweating profusely and mumbling incomprehensible words.

The Lil'London councillors wanted me to go and see their doctor. Nick was adamant I would not go anywhere but back home. The other Foggies present all agreed, hoping that crossing the Fog would help me get rid of whatever was affecting me. It seemed to have worked: I felt absolutely fine except for my jaw. I checked in a mirror and there was a massive bruise on the bottom left hand side of my face. Jazz said she had put tons of arnica cream on it, although it was too late. The bruise would be there for a couple of weeks. The only thing I could do now to look less beaten up was make-up.

I told them about my conversation with Ushi Tsou. Jack, now sleeping in Zeno's room, had relayed part of it when he was not drowsy himself.

'Do you know who this person was? The one she was talking to?' I asked them.

'No, we don't know who he or she is. Ushi Tsou hasn't said a word since we found you all. She's in the Lil'London prison,' Nick said, upset. 'I wanted to get hold of her but they wouldn't let me. Her contact could also be the person who shot that arrow at you!'

'Where would you have put her anyway?' Harry intervened. 'We couldn't have locked her up here.'

'But I could have interrogated her. Now I will have to do it in the presence of their local authorities, namely Augustus Hoare, sheriff of Lil'London. Have you seen the guy? I doubt my technique to make her speak will be approved.'

'Maybe we will have to go for a different approach, like enticing her to speak instead of threatening her,' I suggested. Not that I liked the woman, but we had to find out who was the person she was speaking to.

'From what we gathered talking to Jack, it could be either an individual from Lil'London trying to get direct access to the door, or a representative from one of the other communities,' Harry said.

'But we're seeing them on Monday next week!' I exclaimed.

'They have less room to negotiate as Lil'London got there first and are the closest. With Jack or you, they could have had one of their houses fogged on Saturday night and have their own door to our world,' Harry reminded me.

'Gosh! That's true! That would mean that somewhere around London some poor people would have faced waking up with their place fogged and with me in it?'

'Yes. Or worse, it could have been a hotel. So, completely random!'

'Imagine if it was Buckingham Palace! And the Queen got Relocated!' Rico laughed. 'We would definitely not be anonymous anymore ...'

'That isn't funny.' A stern patriotic Nick snapped. 'And we would all be in a big mess, especially you, Foggies.' We all looked down at our plates and he continued, 'Tomorrow I will go and have a little chat with Ushi Tsou.'

'First, let me talk to Ingis Chen. I want him to know we have her and get him to make her talk to us, IF she still feels she owes him anything.'

'She hit you,' Nick said, looking down at my jaw. From his face, it was obvious he meant to give her hell for it. He was making it personal, I was under his protection.

'Do you want to speak with Leila, Zeno and Mitch? In Kenya?' Harry addressed me. 'Zeno was frantic when he heard what happened. He couldn't believe it was when he was on a plane and couldn't do anything. He was actually booked to come back tonight, but we found you first.'

'And Leila: she looked really, really angry. If you think Nick looked mean, you should have seen Leila. She kept saying, 'If anything happens to Yoko ... If anything happens to Yoko ...' Jazz commented.

'She also said it about Jack, but there is no doubt she is a friend of yours,' Harry added.

Of course I wanted to speak to Leila and Zeno! Mitch, I knew less and it was not as important to me to speak to him, even though I was grateful for his concern. The other Foggies had

had the conference call at 6 p.m. as planned. I had just missed it. Mostly, the topics of conversation were around the abduction and our security. Jack and I were now safe, but for too many hours the Foggies had lost two of their six Switchers.

Despite having slept so much the past two days, I didn't last very long and went to bed early. I typed a few notes on the forest abduction and snuggled in bed with Simba. I was also quite relieved: Jazz had been the one undressing me. She also said she had done a big wash of all my clothes, because they were really filthy. Inside and out. Yuck!

**Day 7 (Saturday)**

Nick was not a happy man. 'And what am I supposed to do now? I mean … I knew it was a part-time job, but really, you could spend all your time during the week in London and what am I going to do in the meantime here? You are my priority!'

'Nick, don't be a grump. Phil is in exactly in the same situation in London.'

'Mmm … Yeah … Not exactly stuck in another world though, is he?'

'I am talking about the job.'

'Again, I bet the highlight of his day isn't to go on a forest walk with you, even if it would make men envious in both worlds.'

'Nick, out of context, I would almost think you are flirting.'

Nick put on his cheeky one-sided smile, half-closed his eyes and looked at me like a cat with a saucer of cream. I saved myself and didn't let him banter back by saying, 'Right, I am going to have a coffee break.'

Nick was helping me carry down my moving boxes full of clothes and various belongings, all thrown together directly from drawers and wardrobe. Jazz was in my room, helping with the packing. Big Tom was helping with Zeno's. Leo and Dante, helped by Rico, were crossing the Fog with boxes. Harry was overseeing the move to the new house. It was just next door and yet, because of the Fog, it was a complicated affair. Nick followed me into the kitchen, where we were joined by Leo, Dante and Rico, always up for a coffee break.

'Maybe now you will reconsider wearing a tag or device that would help us find you if you are in trouble?' Nick asked as I handed him a cup.

I hesitated. I didn't like the idea of being monitored 24/7.

'What if I want some privacy? I mean these days you can be tracked with your mobile and so on, but you can at least switch it off or disable the GPS if you want to escape from the modern world.'

'We can make it non-intrusive. It doesn't have to be an implant. For you, I am thinking an ear-piercing. Something discreet on the back of the ear for example and, if you really don't want us to know where you are, you can take if off.'

It didn't sound too bad and after my experience with Ushi Tsou I conceded that being traceable was a minor limit to my freedom in comparison with being kidnapped.

'OK, I'll do it. The earring, it's small, right?'

'I'll make sure of it,' Nick said and he pulled out his phone from his jeans back pocket, disappearing into the living room.

Leo turned towards me, extended his arm and put a strand of hair behind my ear.

'It will give you a little punk style, the one piercing there. I like it.' He stopped smiling. 'I am glad you agreed to it. I was worried sick!'

'He was,' Dante commented. 'He was white as snow and ready to kill someone. Really. I think you have two bodyguards, Yoko, and one is getting very personal.'

'I have to watch out for the other one though ... I find he is getting a bit too relaxed doing his job,' Leo noted.

I kneeled to pat and play with Simba. She was my secret weapon. I had decided that she and I would go into training. I would learn some self-defence and she would learn how to protect me too and how to beware of firearms and poisons. I wanted her to be as ready as possible to face hostile situations and anyone that could harm her as well as me.

'OK, guys. Coffee break is over. Shall we get on with it?' I suggested. There was still much to be done and the soonest it was over the better. We all had loads of other things to do.

We got back into a rhythm and worked in silence through the morning, each lost in our own thoughts. I recalled my phone call to my parents earlier that morning. Jazz had contacted them when Tsou Bitch got hold of me and again when found. They would be eager to talk to me. My sister picked up the phone first. 'Yoko! Are you all right? Are you hurt?' she exclaimed.

'I am fine. Just a few bruises.'

'We were so worried! And helpless. This nasty Fog ...'

Good to know she was worried. She did sound as though she really was worried and that touched me. It was rare that my sister showed any concern for me.

'Don't worry, I'm back,' I told her.

'I also have some great news: I am cured! Maman said that it was the Fog that 'cleaned' me. At least this damned thing has served one purpose. Maman also said that you would try to bring me to London, so that I am not stranded here?'

'You are cured! That's great news! Such a relief!'

'Yes. What would have happened to Eudes if ...? So, is it true, I am going to get out this hole?'

'You grew up in that house, remember?' I was surprised by Julia's language. She was always so proper and controlled. I liked it though, that she was letting go a bit.

'The house in the village, yes; the house in the middle of no-where with potential cannibals lurking behind the bushes, no.'

'You are exaggerating. Human beings are too rare in that Other World for them to fall into cannibalism.'

'I have no wish to be abducted and used as a breeder either.'

'Fine. I get your point. Well, the terraced houses are almost finished here. Actually we are moving into the new house today. So next will be the attempt at helicopter crossing. We will need to get a pilot able to cross first.'

'What if no one can fly the thing?'

'You'll have to wait until I learn.'

'Very funny.'

'That wasn't a joke.'

My parents were relieved to speak to me and upset about the whole situation. I had withheld quite a lot of information from them, on Ingis Chen, on the mercenary, on Mary in Kenya and

Zeno's trip and much more. I was trying to tell them just the minimum, so as not to worry them. They still didn't know much, but they now knew for certain they were not kept fully informed so they worried. They were being parents.

Jack had woken up early and had now vacated Zeno's room. For the time being, Jack, Leo and Dante would stay in the Society's spare 'visitors' house'. Leila had also reminded us of our side of the deal: we were to fog the house on the other side of our old house, now Jazz's. Jack and I would do it together. So, for my first night of having a new home, I would not sleep in it. That was to be the rule for the rest of my life to protect my everyday abode: Saturday nights would be spent either in an already fogged venue, one due for renewal, or one to be fogged.

Jack was recuperating from his ordeal relatively well. The previous day he had contacted his family to reassure them. I wasn't there, still asleep in my bed, but was told there was much crying and laughing. He faced another problem: he had not told them about the Fog and didn't want to. The boys had come up with an excuse that could work, that he had gone on a field trip, got lost without bags, phone and money in a forest and it took a week for him to get some help. They were so happy to hear from him, they didn't press him for details, especially as he also said he didn't really want to talk about it and relive it all. They would ask later, he knew it, and had to work on his story. While the move was under way, the Society had arranged for him to be seen by a doctor, to go shopping for new clothes and essentials for home, and to have a little tour of London if he wished. Anything to brighten his first day of freedom.

On the same day, in Lil'London, things started to get busy for the Relocated. Jazz soon left the house and joined the little community as they were choosing the location of their future homes, main road, septic tanks and other facilities. Jazz was beginning to accept that just as the Foggies didn't choose each other and still formed a kind of clan, so did the Relocated. She was sorted homewise, but she belonged to their group and should join them for such big decisions.

From tomorrow, with a new non-fogged home, life would be almost back to normal. We would live in London, be able to have visitors, go shopping, even just look out of the window and see what the weather was like. Normality was all relative, of course: our reality was certainly unusual and we had our problems, but so what? It is well known if you have health you have the most important in life, on this we had a pretty good boost to our immune system thanks to the Fog.

Mid-afternoon, the move done, lunch enjoyed in the sun, I was ready for the next step: unpacking. Nick had gone to Lil'London's prison to interrogate Ushi Tsou with Augustus Hoare. He was frustrated that she had been 'grilled' by the locals first. He had had no choice in the matter, he had to wait to be called upon to interrogate her. I was in the new house when Jazz called to inform me Maud was at hers. Within seconds I walked the few steps leading to the movable wood partition hiding away the Fog around Jazz's house. This light wall was well conceived, with large rectangular plant pots screwed to the bottom making the whole ensemble less of an eyesore. Simba was sniffing the plants with disdain. Not wild enough for her. As I crossed the Fog and entered the house with her, I realised Rico might be needed to get me back home. The Simba 'trick' didn't always work, no doubt because she was so young. Also sometimes her need to go out would come before my wish to go somewhere specific. It is well known too that young ones don't always pay much attention to what Mama says ...

It was weird to be back in the house knowing I didn't live there anymore now. Weirder to think of it as Jazz's house. It would take some time to get used to, it was still home. Jazz and Maud were in the living room and so were the Fishers, Ann included. Maud was subdued as she witnessed the display of affection mixed with sorrow between husband and wife, conjointly with the way the children were hugging their mother and answering her anxious questions. She had obviously not realised the impact of being Relocated was not just to get used to a new community and life, the hardest was the loss of the loved ones. The latter was the biggest challenge of them all, for the ones who had crossed and the ones left.

'Maud, it is nice of you to visit. Shall we have tea outside? It is such a lovely day.' I was eager to give some privacy to the Fishers, which Maud understood immediately. Jazz helped me out by suggesting that we go ahead and she would bring tea and biscuits outside.

'I am sorry to call unannounced, I wished to check you were recovered. What a dreadful time you must have had! I do not understand what this woman had to gain from holding you captive. Why hurt you as well?' Maud asked looking at my bruised face.

'I was not really cooperative,' I replied.

'Still, what kind of women would do that? What kind of women is she, anyway? There should be no such thing as a soldier woman. It goes against nature.'

'I am surprised to hear you say that. Why shouldn't women be able to fight?'

'Women are not made to be in battles ...'

'Who says?' I would have none of it. It wasn't to defend Ushi Tsou's choice of life, only if Maud was going to defend women's rights as she wished, she had to realise it had to be all the rights, not the ones she chose.

'Maud, women have evolved to be sailors, soldiers, state presidents, scientists, doctors, surgeons, professors and more,' I listed. 'They have claimed and won the right to abort pregnancies.' This caused a look of shock and sharp intake of breath from Maud. I persisted, 'to have a career, to wear mini-skirts and even to enter English private clubs. You cannot pick and choose: once you give women the right to be equal to men, they will challenge traditions and shake prejudices.'

'How could we abort? Life is so precious! You just have to avoid ...' Maud began.

'I am sorry Maud, things have changed a lot and I am sure that even in your smaller community you are aware that it is not always simple between men and women. In our world, when it is possible to abort what is seen as a mistake, or the result of a rape, it is bound to be the choice of some. I am sorry to have approached the subject so abruptly, it was inconsiderate of me.'

A still shocked Maud put her hand on mine in a reassuring gesture that was maybe more for her than for me. 'No, no, please don't worry. I think a lot of things will surprise me in your world. And you don't have the same need of children that we have.' She stopped, reflecting for a second and I sipped some tea. After a few minutes she spoke again, in a subdued and unsure tone.

'You talked about men and women being equal? I would not have … This is not what … what I would like is for women to be more recognised. To have a voice. To be taken into consideration.'

'Yes, you want them to be treated with more consideration, as intelligent human beings who can make their own decisions.'

'Yes, exactly.'

'So, like men do.'

'Well, I guess.'

'This means you don't think women are inferior to men.'

'Of course not! Ahhh … I see … If we are not inferior, and neither are we superior, then we are equals.'

'Exactly.'

'I see. Then, yes. Still, there are things that women can't do as well as men, surely.'

'Like what?'

'I … don't know. I would need to think about it. Ah! For example, what happens when a woman is in her certain period. She can't possibly be as productive?'

'Medicine helps a lot these days. In truth, I am no feminist and would be the type to drop everything and any career for my family. And yes, as far as I am concerned, during that 'time of the month' I am certainly less efficient. However, I appreciate having the choice, at least in our western world.'

'Western world? Is that what you call your world? And what is a feminist?' Maud was looking at me fascinated, if not a bit confused. I had bitten off much more than I could chew for a simple teatime conversation.

'Gosh Maud! Both are very complex issues. In brief, feminism is the social and intellectual movement fighting for the rights of women, sometimes to the extreme. The western world is not our entire planet, but a way of referring to those countries whose culture and civilisation share the same European roots, culture and influence. That is a very, very succinct explanation, though in essence that's it, as far as I understand.'

'Edmund and I have started reading the history book you gave us. Well, Edmund more than me. I only have a chance to read it when he is busy with his duties. Sometimes I find it hard to believe it all. It doesn't mention the western world or feminism. Maybe in another book?'

'Or much later in the book.' I was racking my brains to find a way to change subject. Soon, either she would ask a question I couldn't answer (I'd rather not, my ego can be hurt like anyone else's), or we would broach a subject we should really not talk about at this stage. Like the suffragettes.

'Why 'western'? For Europe and America, I presume?'

'Well, yes.' For the sake of accuracy, I added, 'Although culture-wise, it would also encompass Australia and New Zealand and other old colonies.'

'Isn't it far south and populated by some tribes? I know some Europeans left to settle there, but 'western'? Really?'

I proceeded to give her the little information I had on the British colonisation of these lands. My knowledge was limited on that area of the planet. It is not a standard subject in French schools.

Finally, after half an hour of rambling and, to my shame, searching the internet for a Wikipedia summary, Maud had a general and vague idea of the Commonwealth. I had to refuse to talk about the rise and collapse of the British Empire. It was too much for me for that day.

'I am sorry Maud, I can't do it. My knowledge of British history is French. I would hate to provide you with erroneous information.'

'I wish I could attend one of your classes on the subject, even if it involved mingling with children to learn the basics.'

'You wouldn't have to. We have courses for adults as well. There is always so much to learn.'

'What a wonderful idea from your people! Courses for adults! I so wish ...'

I was about to say that she could register online, when of course I realised how incongruous this comment would be. It planted a seed in my mind though: if we could find a way to give her and others access to a computer and explain how the courses worked, they could register to online adult classes. I foresaw many problems with this idea: the Lil'London Council would have no way to monitor what was being learned and no one could predict the consequences of their online access to our world. Would they be traumatised by what they saw? My first thoughts were on Hiroshima and Nagasaki, the numerous death camps from China, the Nazis, the Soviets or more recently ex-Yugoslavia. What about the genocides in Africa? Our world was tough and there was quite a lot we should be ashamed about. Well, we were, although with pretty short memories, more often than not stopping at our national borders. After she had gone, I decided to look into online classes in the future. I might have had a knack for creating my own problems.

I took the opportunity of her visit to ask her a question that had been troubling me, which was why no one from the council had asked what we were doing for a living in our world. She replied, 'Because we need you. If you were a maid, we would rather not know: it would trouble the men to depend on a maid as the key element of our future. When we saw you were bright and not belligerent, we considered ourselves lucky. At least some of us do. It would have been better if you were a man or a more malleable woman, of course. Especially for the like of the Hoares and the Snayths.'

Maud left with a gift from me for her children, the whole collection of the Grimms Tales.

'They will be thrilled. Would I enjoy reading them too?' She looked at the big heavy book with brimming eyes.

'Yes, I believe you would. It plays with your imagination. Like entering and living in fairy new worlds.'

'Yoko, aren't you living such a fairy tale then? You have entered a brand new world.'

'It looks pretty real to me. Nothing imaginary like the contents of these books.'

'Maybe it depends how you look at the whole experience. Maybe those books were more than a story once, maybe they were real too? Our world could be in it for all we know.'

I laughed, even though she could be right.

In the evening, we all dined together in the house. Everyone linked to the Fog and present in London gathered around the table: Harry, Rico, Jazz, Leo, Dante, Big Tom, all the Fishers including Ann, plus Nick and I. From tomorrow the newly fogged house next door would be the official meeting point for visitors, trading, Relocated business and so on and this house would be Jazz's. Tomorrow, the materials and compact machinery for the Relocated housing would be sent through the Fog. So that night, a page was turning, a period was ending. Five weeks already. Five weeks of fumbling and adjusting.

Everyone was excited about the building work, the move and organising our new lives. We didn't even talk much about the interrogation of Ushi Tsou. There was not a lot to be told. She was a professional and stuck to her basic story. As expected, she had been obeying orders when she took charge of Jack in WII. She had to bring him by the following Saturday to the location of another house in London, where Ingis Chen would be able to take back control of the situation. Compass and geographical map in hand the task should have been easy. However, the presence of Nick was a blow as she could not afford to be followed and the back-up plan spoiled. She took alternative routes, met some locals and one of them was interested in striking a deal. For her, the choice was simple: help from Ingis Chen via an open door, help from locals for a secure settlement and to advance her position in WII was another. By playing on both with Jack as her asset, she could try to increase her position even further and get more. She had underestimated how organised and protected we already were.

Her two last cards were her link with Ingis Chen and the name of her local contact.

'I couldn't make her talk,' Nick said frustrated. 'The rest of her story was nothing else than expected, but the interesting stuff, the valuable stuff: nada, niente, nothing.'

# WEEK VI

**Day 1 (Sunday)**

My body was moving. No, someone was shaking me. Someone was shaking me awake. I grunted and opened one eye. I was in an unknown room, the person shaking me and calling my name was Jazz.

'Huh … Jazz? What? Stop… Why… Why are you shaking me?' I asked in a croaky sleepy voice.

'Thank God! You are awake! I was so worried! You were like in a coma or something. You wouldn't wake up!'

'What are you talking about? What time is it?'

'It's 1 p.m. I've been calling you on your mobile, knocking at your door, calling your name, shaking you, nothing did it!'

'1 p.m.? Weird. I never sleep that late … And you couldn't wake me up?' I now remembered we were in the Society's house that was to be fogged and turned to check at the window. The thick white blanket of the Fog was visible through the opened curtains.

'Yes, yes, yes, the house is fogged, but why couldn't you wake up?' Jazz enquired, still anxious.

I grabbed my mobile on the bedside table and checked my phone. 1.07 p.m., sixteen missed calls.

'You called me sixteen times?'

'I was worried! It is so unlike you to sleep late like that. You see, two Switchers in the same house overnight on a Saturday, we don't know how that works. Anyway, it wasn't just me, the boys called too. I had to stop all of them, including Nick, from coming to check up on you. For your privacy ... You know ... In case you slept naked.'

'Well, I am awake now. It was out of the ordinary, but I am fine. See? It was probably just some much needed sleep after the Tsou Bitch episode,' I said and added as an afterthought, 'What about Jack, is he awake?'

'Not that I am aware of. I could have missed him, he could be in a different world to mine.'

'I don't think I will ever get used to that type of sentence.'

'Do you think we should check? By the way, be careful where you step, Simba couldn't hold it until 1 p.m. She made me worry about you too. She was yelping in distress by your side when I got in. I could hear her from outside.'

I had been puzzled before, now I was concerned. Being a light sleeper, a phone ring and a puppy howling by my side would always wake me up. I put my slippers on, opened the window to get rid of the smell in the room, went to the bathroom and picked up the necessary to clean Simba's mess. The house had already been provided with the essentials for guests and the sooner I cleaned, the less the smell would settle and linger. I asked Jazz to wait two more minutes while I took Simba out just outside for a quick pee. That proved a good decision.

Jack was sleeping soundly. We knocked at his door and there was no answer. We were hoping he was awake and out somewhere in London, but as we pushed the door open, he was lying in bed, eyes tight shut.

'So here we go again,' Jazz said, going towards the bed to shake him awake.

'Wait Jazz. Do we have to wake him up? We know it's possible as you did it for me, so maybe we don't have to and can let him have a good sleep?'

'I am not sure … I swear, Nutella, this deep sleep is just not normal. You were like dead. I was about to check for your pulse.'

'Let's check his pulse.' I didn't know what took me to say this, having no clue how to measure if a pulse was normal or not. I was satisfied to feel a slight throbbing under my thumb.

'Not dead.'

'I still think we should wake him up. The two of you sleeping like that, that's not normal. I think it is linked to both of you being Switchers and under the same roof on a Saturday.'

'Come on Jazz, I'm fine, aren't I?'

'I'm going to wake him up.'

She shook him. I shook him. We both shook him. On our call, Rico came to shake him. Leo and Dante came and we carried him out to bring him to our new big house for a doctor to come and check him. Jazz remained behind, muttering, 'I knew it. I knew it wasn't normal, I knew it.' Once in our house, his pulse started to quicken slightly. We tried to wake Jack again, calling and shaking him more or less gently. Finally, he opened an eye, confused.

'I don't think it is a good idea that two Switchers stay together on a Saturday night ever again,' Jazz said on video call. We were downstairs in our new modern and shiny living room. Jack was sipping a hot chocolate with a big cardigan wrapped around him. He was still groggy from sleep.

'Or maybe the drug Ushi Tsou gave us has a lasting effect?' I retorted, trying to de-dramatise the event as a non-event, just a temporary big scare. I wasn't willing to have a new negative in my life.

'Still, I wouldn't dismiss it, Yoko,' Harry said. 'I recommend that we inform all the Foggies of this. Too much unknown with the Fog. We can't take a risk.'

'Yes, Yoko, I agree with Jazz and Harry. We need to let the others know and, don't you try this again. Better play it safe,' Leo commented.

'Fine, fine. Duly noted. I will do it, inform the others and Leila too.'

Finally people stopped fussing. It was already mid-afternoon and I was famished. After a quick snack, I went up to unpack my belongings and start owning my side of the first floor. I didn't want to admit it to the others, the event perturbed me than I had let them know, thinking the deep sleep was indeed abnormal. Jack had only come out of it when taken out of the house. What would have happened if he – or I – had been left to sleep?

That night, I was apprehensive going back to bed. I feared not waking up. Anxiety stopped me sleeping until the early hours of the morning.

**Day 2 (Monday)**

Newtonsee was the other town of WII's England, and was bigger than Lil'London with approximately 12,000 inhabitants, located on the estuary of the Thames. I had gathered a general picture of the town from talking to Maud and browsing (far too quickly) the *Lil'London Tales*. 'Town' was a big word for it: there was a core of a few houses and community structures, then many buildings dispersed on the land in the vicinity. I had at first wondered why they all stayed close to the town and didn't claim more freedom from its rules, trade and class structure. Human nature remained the same in that Other World: if a family had children, they wanted the children to play with other children and in the long term marry and have a family, so they needed social interaction. As for the inequalities in social status, they had escaped the whole Karl Marx theories: classes were a normal feature of their society. Furthermore, the sins of greed and power, or greed for power, are unavoidable with mankind.

Lil'London and Newtonsee had a love-hate relationship coming from mutual dependency and rivalry. It reminded me of the relationship between England and France, the best loved enemies whose interests and pasts have been intrinsically linked for centuries. Lil'London was, of course, by the River Thames, but Newtonsee benefitted from the wider sea. While Newtonsee had access to the forest, Lil'London had mastered it better and controlled the trade of crops. Marriages between the two towns were frowned upon, except, of course, for economic reasons.

There was also the odd hamlet with a few groups of individual farming families gathered together to present a stronger front to the towns. I wondered if some of them would be present at the big meeting planned for today.

Shortly before we set off to Lil'London, Jazz and I were in her kitchen having coffee when Nick came in from the living room. He was adamant: I had to take a gun even though he would be with me. He added that Leo, Dante and Jazz, who were coming with us, had to be armed as well.

'I would probably manage to kill myself by pointing the gun in the wrong direction. Forget it!' Jazz laughed at the idea. 'I'm taking my pepper spray.'

'Pepper spray? Does it still exist?' Nick said looking dubious.

'I can test it on you if you want. We'll see if you will still dismiss it!' Jazz replied grabbing her bag and starting to rummage for the spray.

'Jazz, drop it. Anyway, by the time you found it in your bag you'd be done for,' I said shaking my head.

'Right, Jazz, you will have a taser and will keep it in your pocket, ready at hand,' Nick told her in an uncompromising tone.

'I don't want your fuc … Oh! The nerve!' she exclaimed. 'He just left the room! I can't believe this guy is bossing us around. I am taking my pepper spray and that's it. Who does he think he is?'

'Our security specialist? The one who knows what he is talking about?' I replied.

'Don't you start! Anyway YOU could do what you want, you've got the guy wrapped round your little finger.'

'Huh? No I haven't! I am just not as big a pain in the ass as you are.'

'Oh, come on! Between Leo and him, you can have your pick. By the way, which one do you prefer?'

I ignored her question.

'So?' She persisted.

'Jazz, forget it, one is a Foggy, the other is my relocated bodyguard. No picking.'

'You are no fun.'

'Whatever.'

'What about the other guy?'

'Who?'

'Well that answer is the question.'

I only then realised she was talking about Leo, although she didn't know she was.

'No time.'

'You really are no fun!'

'Thanks. How about you take the pepper spray AND the taser? Like that everyone is happy?'

Jazz looked up at the ceiling and hunched her shoulders: 'Fiiine. I still think you should have a bit of fun. Nick is the hottie and Leo the cutie. Maybe you should try them both and keep the best?'

'Go and get ready, we are off in thirty minutes.'

'You should have a cat, not a dog. You already act like an old lady with cats.'

'You continue like that and I'll train Simba to leave a very personal gift on your mat every morning.'

She laughed and made for the stairs. I shouted to her from the kitchen, 'And she is a wolf, not a dog!'

I would take the gun, even though shooting myself in the foot by accident was likely. At least if I waved it around in a dangerous situation it might be scary. I would also take a taser. It had the benefit of being an unknown weapon over there and a good deterrent for anyone seeing its use.

The Relocated were not given firearms by the Society. I guess Jazz had special treatment because of her 'running' a Fog house. They didn't know Big Tom had his own weapon and I didn't tell. There was a general taser distribution for all, alas with no demonstration on how to use them. We lacked volunteers on that one.

I grabbed Simba's bag for the horse ride and another bag for my notebook, tablet, gun, hairbrush, spare tights, basic make-up and various unnecessary things I always carry in my bag, like most women. Simba was growing too fast to fit everything including her in one bag now. I also put on the brand new electronic earring Nick had had delivered earlier that morning and the wireless invisible earbud which had been the additional bonus, connecting me to my tablet-phone.

The meeting took place in Lil'London Town Hall and we were pretty tight around the table. On the Foggies side, we were Leo, Dante and me, Nick keeping watch outside the door. Jazz was there too, unofficially representing the Relocated. The council wondered about Zeno's whereabouts and I just told them he was travelling. On the local side, there were of course Benjamin Snayth, Augustus Hoare and Edmund Poff. The new people were the ones I was the most nervous about: would they be aggressive or welcoming? There were only four new faces in the main room. Three men ranging in age between 30 and 45 years old and one older, displaying a luxurious white beard. I recognised the style of the bearded one as Jewish, with his side hair swirls, hat and dark long coat. He was a Hassidic Jew (or so he explained later). He introduced himself as Ariel, son of Chaim, and looked like Father Christmas to me with his open face and soft eyes with a joyful glint. There was intelligence in them too, and he seemed to be observing people right to their core. Ariel Ben-Chaim was the rabbi and mediator for Yerushaleim, the Jewish village and only Jewish community, as far as they knew, in their world. It was created 231 years ago, named after one of the Biblical appellations for Jerusalem to symbolise it would be their new land of God. They had since grown to about a thousand inhabitants.

I wish it would be possible to know how many people had crossed the Fog between 1782 and 1846, when the doors closed. It seemed a lot of people had been Relocated despite any record of the Fog. Could the Society of that time already be active in controlling information?

The three others were the councillors of Newtonsee. In their roles they were a mirror image of Lil'London's council. Jack Chester, a straight blond hair and fat forty-something, with a big hawk nose and a strong presence, was the mayor. He was one of these heavyweights who could either be a jolly big softie, or a ruthless tough guy. Just then, he was in restful observant mode, so he could turn out either way. Hugh Ashby was the sheriff. He didn't seem the jovial type. He was tall and skinny, bony even, with deep-set hollow eyes. In London you might have wondered if he were a drug addict, or at best anaemic. The clothes just fell off him as if too big, when they were a perfect size. He was the youngest of them all, somewhere in his early thirties. Last was Walter Makepiece, the church man. By the end of the meeting I had inwardly amended his name to Makepeace: he was always trying to keep everyone at peace, even though no one was arguing.

We were in that room for hours, only managing to escape to go to the room next door when lunch was served. The lunch break was also a real turning point in the discussion. Most of the morning was about introducing people, what had happened the past five weeks with the Fog, as well as our relations with Lil'London. The representatives of Newtonsee and Yerushaleim, aside from a brief description of their occupation and town activities, mainly listened and absorbed information, asking occasional questions. However, in the afternoon the talks moved to the main point: the relationship of the other communities to the Fog and the end of Lil'London's exclusive link to it.

'So, what type of agreement has been made between Lil'London and you, Messrs Lumbrosi and Bopani?' Jack Chester asked casually in a surprisingly deep voice, while pouring himself some local brandy.

Leo glanced at Dante, then at me, and replied, 'We do not have anything in writing. It's more like a gentleman's agreement. Or in this case, gentle'woman': our mediator and representative to discuss these matters is Miss Salelles.' He turned to me, 'Yoko, if you will?'

I took my time, observing first the reactions of the men in front of me. Newtonsee's mayor Jack Chester was totally composed, just sipping his drink and only readjusting his position slightly, leaning back in his chair to face me. The sheriff, Hugh Ashby, was erect in his chair and turned his head abruptly to look at me.

'Really? Why?' the sheriff asked, frowning and squinting.

'A woman? Oh! How wonderful!' Walter Makepiece exclaimed.

'Because I drew the short straw,' I replied dismissively to Ashby. 'Anyway, there is indeed no written or set agreement. We are very much working together on an ad hoc basis to respond to the immediate requirements and needs of the Relocated and to define how we could add to Lil'London's community life.'

Edmund and Hoare nodded at my comment. Snayth was tenser than normal.

'And what are the immediate requirements and needs of the Relocated?' asked Chester.

'A home,' I said.

'A road,' Dante added.

'And acceptance,' Jazz overbid.

There was silence around the table, until Sheriff Ashby cut it with an abrupt question. 'I guess the point is will you trade with us on the same terms as you deal with Lil'London?'

A direct question called for a direct answer, so I provided one. 'Yes. We have no reason to exclude anyone from the benefits of the Fog and access to our world. We want to help, learn and be open to all the people here, as long as they treat us decently and fairly.'

'What if we do not?' The mayor Chester asked.

'Then we will not liaise with you, and you will not benefit from the Fog and all it has to give. It would be a pity. You will soon learn that the way our world has evolved may be beyond your imagination.'

'But then you would put your Relocated at risk.'

Jazz interrupted me and retorted aggressively, 'Trust me, you don't want to mess with us. Our means of retaliation are beyond what you could imagine too!' As she was seated next to me I was able to nudge her with my foot, but she dismissed me completely and continued, 'If you were behind Ushi Tsou supporting Yoko's kidnapping, it will not go down well, I am telling you. As you can see, she was hurt and that is not something that will pass easily.'

I stared at Jazz a bit scared by such an outburst of anger. Chester burst out laughing. 'The women of that world of yours, they seem to be something to reckon with! Maybe they are the most terrifying weapon of them all.' The last sentence was pronounced looking at Dante and Leo, who actually nodded in acquiescence, the traitors!

'We did not have anything to do with Ushi Tsou and we regret that you had to go through this ordeal.' Walter Makepiece was the one to answer Jazz's question. 'We wish we could have helped you when you needed help. Yoko, are you faring better? You seem to be dealing with this very positively.'

Everything about his demeanour made me think he would have been a hippie in the sixties. Instead of a history book, I should offer him the Dalai Lama's writings.

'I have a balm that works wonders on bruises. I would be delighted to make some for you,' Ariel Ben-Chaim suggested after I confirmed that I was feeling much better.

'I would be delighted. Are you preparing your own medicines?' I was curious about his proposal.

'I am also the physician for our little community,' Ben-Chaim replied humbly.

'And an excellent one, I must say,' Edmund joined in. 'Ariel has a very interesting collection of books on matters of medicinal concoctions and analysis of the human anatomy. You even have copies of treatises by Galen and Ibn-Sina, don't you Ariel? Fascinating reads. Fascinating!'

I knew little of Galen and Ibn-Sina as precursors of modern medicine, but I liked the way those two seemed to get along. I had grown to appreciate Edmund more and more and the *Entente Cordiale* between the two men was to Ariel Ben-Chaim's credit.

'I shall be curious to see your laboratory, if that is the correct word. Would it be possible?' I asked Ariel Ben-Chaim.

There was a brief hesitation in his eyes before he nodded and replied that he would be honoured by my visiting.

I had taken five blocked two-way radios to give to the representatives. It was a good way to make them feel they had a direct link with us as well. I gave one each to Jack Chester, Hugh Ashby, William Makepiece and Ariel Ben-Chaim, dutifully writing down their dedicated signal channels. They would have a limited use for it though: they were more than thirty miles away from the house and the radios had about an eighteen mile range. I explained these limitations to them and how the machines worked. They were mesmerised when I demonstrated how the radios functioned by calling Nick. Yerushaleim was also out of range, being twenty miles from the Fog house, but it was a short distance to travel by horse to cover the missing two or three miles to communicate with us, so Ariel Ben-Chaim was less disappointed than the other three.

Unfortunately the good mood I was in at the prospect of discovering the physician practice and laboratory was ruined by the intervention of Benjamin Snayth who reminded the Newtonsee councillors that for the sake of the balance in their world it would be important to focus on gaining from us only what they couldn't have already, that is they shouldn't use us to get a better deal on what Lil'London was providing. Chester leaned back in his chair and looked Snayth straight in the eye with obvious dislike. 'That would go both ways, Benjamin.'

'Great,' I thought. 'We are right in the middle of two bickering towns. That promises to be a fun ride.'

As I was leaving, Edmund took me aside and thanked me profusely for the books I had passed on to Maud for their children.

'They devoured them all evening yesterday and wanted to read again at breakfast. As it is not allowed, they have never eaten so fast to be able to return to their books.'

'I am delighted they are enjoying their gift.' I meant it.

'You are a kind woman. I think you will do some good here. I am afraid it will not be as easy as we would hope. Prejudices and fears are difficult to change and overcome.'

'Thank you, Edmund. It is nice to know we have your support.'

'I trust you will find Ariel's community interesting although very difficult to approach.'

'That's for certain. I am not Jewish and my knowledge is limited about their traditions, although it is known they are very close to people who don't belong to their religion.'

'This hasn't changed in your world then?'

'No. It is their strength, yet also what alienates them to the other communities. Sometimes.'

Edmund broached another subject when accompanying me to the horses.

'The radios, could they also be used between us?'

'Yes.'

'Could I call Ariel, for example?'

'Yes. All you need is to know his signal range and to learn how to use it. You will need to ask him if he is happy to share it with you. Also, you will both need to come and see us so that we unblock the use of the channel between you two. To avoid anyone eavesdropping in each other's conversation, we have blocked the lines to only allow conversations with us.'

'I see.'

'Maybe this could be done when you are coming to pick me up on Wednesday to go to Yerushaleim? I can exchange both your radios with new ones, unlocked between both of you, for Mr Ben-Chaim? Only if he agrees, of course and you both have to be aware that any of your conversations could be heard by us, him, or you.'

'I will talk to him.'

We were back home at 5 p.m. We just had time for a cup of tea before the first of this week's Foggies board meetings. Louise had arrived in London during the afternoon from Marrakech and she was lovely and full of energy. She was a far cry from the emotional wreck seen on the screen the past few weeks. She was bubbly, happy and planning a whole tour of London in the days to come. She was staying with Jack in the Society visitors' non-fogged house. She may do him good: she had already enrolled him in night-time parties with some friends of hers in east London. My gut feeling was that we might not see much of her. At least, she was attending the FBM with us, plus wanted to see Lil'London and the forest.

The conference call was focused on Nevada and Kenya. Adam, Sophia and Michelle, with the help of the Society, had decided to rent a little flat in town where they could escape and have a normal life whenever they wished. They would consider later if they intended to buy or not. To their friends, it was officially to give Michelle a bit more independence, but in truth it was big enough for all of them to stay. The non-official side of the story was that Michelle had made a big scene that she ought to be able to have her boyfriend visit. At first the idea was to build a house closer to the entrance of the property, as Mitch, Tony and Rosario had done in Alaska, but in the end they didn't want to take the risk of any of Michelle's friends wandering around the property and coming across the Fog.

The Adams were also getting used to having Native Americans on their doorsteps, regularly bringing them food. They had installed a system to indicate when they were in: with an extension, they had placed a lamp outside the house, which they could switch on or off at a flick of a button. When on, it indicated they were at home and available. The American Indians would turn up usually within two hours and they would discuss history, culture and trade. Adam and Sophia, with the support of the Society, were trying to find descendants of the tribe and anyone who would know about the Fog. Sophia was now considering creating a traditional Native American artefacts and catering business and had started discussions with the Indian community in Carson City. She also thought that the American Indians would provide cheap labour to create all sort of artisanal products in exchange for goods. Sophia wondered if it was how the Chen empire had started. Her line of thought was not my favourite! Then again, working with her to try to find a middle-ground position towards Ingis Chen, I had been pleased to note that they had reservations about him and that she was not inflexible in our discussions.

In Kenya, Mitch and Zeno loved exploring the wild on both sides of the portal. As Clare and Mary had told us, the countryside wasn't much different in WII when away from the populated area and into the Rift valley. They were to return home the next day, although both confirmed they wanted to go back for longer, whenever they could. As for Mary, she was living in a pink bubble, more and more in love with her bushman. She was positively glowing and talking in the most romantic terms about her beau, to the point it was getting cheesy. Clare never commented or expressed an opinion on the matter. In my book, that meant she was not over the moon about the whole story and would rather Mary came back home. This was not the ideal match a mother might dream of for a daughter.

I updated everyone on today's meeting and encounter with the representatives of Newtonsee and the Jewish community. The last point triggered Adam Koplat's attention.

'Jewish community? You have a Jewish community! That's amazing. I bet they've kept all the traditions and books. I would be very curious to know of their origins and how they have evolved. I'm sure they would be interested to hear how we have evolved in this world too ...' Adam stopped, lost in thought.

'Dad! You are not thinking of going to London, are you? Just when I'm starting to like the Native Americans. I need you here!' Michelle looked deeply unimpressed.

'You could come with me?' From Michelle's face, it wasn't going to happen soon. Good luck to Adam on that one.

When I updated them about the possible effect of having two Switchers in the same house, no one spoke for some time afterwards. We didn't like the implications of something new and unpleasant linked to the Fog, something else which couldn't be explained. We didn't know if it was the Fog that had made Jack and me so comatose and, if it had occurred because we were two Switchers under the same roof, could one of us not wake up at all next time?

Last, I told them that Sophia and I were making progress. I was still anxious about the idea of having any partnership with Ingis Chen. In any case, it would have to be flexible and ad hoc and I had no real clue how we would get organised. Yet Sophia's reaction today and Christophe's at the last FBM made sorting relations with Ingis a priority. I didn't want the group and allegiances to split. As I read long ago in *The Three Musketeers*, 'l'union fait la force', or 'there's strength in numbers' as the English saying goes. Sophia and I agreed about this. We had to start somewhere, and that was not a bad beginning. The next step was to contact Ingis Chen to hear what type of deal he had in mind. We needed this to define further our position towards him.

'Christophe is a sweet, beautiful bastard.'

Louise was drunk. We had gone to a pub where she had mixed her drinks with a fast effect on her mojo. She was back to being an emotional wreck, alternately laughing and crying.

'I love him, the bastard. Maybe I should just pick a guy, sleep with him and get Christophe out of my system. That guy over there, he looks good. Quite a hunk. I'll go talk to him.'

'Oh dear,' I mumbled, attempting too late to grab her arms and reason with her. She was gone.

'She's entertaining,' Rico said. 'She has a few hot friends too.'

Louise had gathered a couple of her girlfriends to join us on that Monday night. They were on the dance floor, swinging to eighties music. I just longed for my bed, even if it was just past

10.30 p.m. I suddenly felt old. Rico was ogling them, plotting a suave Italian move. Really it was more a shark attack.

Leo and Dante were smirking, looking at Louise blabbing at the table where two guys were looking at her, obviously unsure how to react.

'Maybe you should go and get her?' Leo suggested.

'The thing is, I don't know her. I don't know if she does that all the time and would be annoyed if I go to "rescue" her when she doesn't want rescuing.'

'I meant for the men's sake. They are the ones who need rescuing.'

I grunted and made for the bar, but was grabbed on the way by an ex-colleague.

'Yoko! Oh my God! How are you? You look amazing.'

I looked terrible, with my lack of sleep and not having bothered to put any make-up on.

'Hey! How nice to bump into you!' I lied.

'So pleased to see you. I didn't have your mobile number.'

'Oh … Really?' I was trying to gently free myself from his grip, looking right to left for a get out.

'Well, we should have dinner sometime?'

'Uh-huh. The thing is, I have a busy schedule ahead, and …'

Just then Phil arrived behind him and Leo behind me.

'Time to let the lady go, sir,' Phil said, putting his hand on the man's shoulder.

'Yoko, is this man bothering you?' Leo flashed a murderous look at Neil.

'Everything is all right?' Rico appeared by my side, checking my ex-colleague up and down. 'Want me to kick his ass?'

'Wow, guys. It's OK. I know him, he is an ex-colleague of mine.'

The man, his face white even in the poor light of the club, disappeared without further ado. I retrieved Louise from the table with the two men who shot me a grateful look. I felt totally depressed. I had just had a glimpse of how my dating life had hit rock bottom. Now a man couldn't approach me anymore without the threat of being rugby tackled to the floor and questioned. Maybe I should consider following Louise's lead and have one more drink.

**Day 3 (Tuesday)**

My spirits were lifted. I had galvanised myself having prepared a few notes, showered, downed two coffees, one croissant, and walked Simba. I was ready. Time to call Ingis Chen. Phil called as my fingers were hovering over the FTab ready to dial.

'Yoko, fireman at the door.'

'Is there a fire?'

'No, he says he is doing a routine call, following up on some fog. He has been here before, he says.'

Bugger! One of those firemen.

'Can you get rid of him?'

'I already tried. The guy is persistent. He's investigating as it appears a similar fog has been spotted east. He's like glue: if we don't let him in, he says he will have to come back with the police and a court order. Not sure he would get one, but we don't want to attract attention.'

'OK, hold him for ten minutes while we close the gate to the Fog and stop the transport of materials around here. I will confirm when you can let him in.'

I went out of the new house, had the gates around the fogged houses closed and asked anyone on site to disappear inside. Then, I gave the go ahead to Phil to let the fireman in. It was unusual to see a lone fireman in his uniform. The fact that he was alone intrigued me.

'Hi! How do you do?' I greeted him.

'Good morning. Sorry to bother you without notification first.'

'Not a problem. How can I be of help?' I almost said 'officer' and stopped at the last minute. How do you address a fireman anyway? Do they have a title? The fireman in front of me was the one who had been dubious about our excuse for the Fog weeks ago. A bad sign.

'Well, I've heard rumours that another house just to the east of London has had a similar Fog situation to yours. It seems to be under control now, but I tried to find information online only to hit a blank. I remembered that we haven't checked the status of yours and we need to update our files, so I came to pay you a visit.'

'I see. Unfortunately, I cannot help you. The house is under wraps while it's being restored and access is denied in the meantime.'

'Is the fog still here?'

'Well, I haven't checked recently.' I had not checked in the past minute I'd been talking to him.

'Have you had the fog tested again?'

'Not personally, no.'

'Did you notice any strange phenomena linked to the fog?'

'What do you mean?'

'Something abnormal? Even people missing?'

'People missing? Like, lost in the fog? Really?' I was doing my best to appear incredulous at the question. In reality I had a little bubble of panic rising in my throat.

'I mean anything unusual that may have happened at the same time the fog appeared?'

'I am afraid you are not making much sense.'

The line of his mouth thinned ever slightly and his eyes squinted. We faced each other. I was trying to look nonchalant and uncomprehending. I had to work on my naive look.

'So, where do you live now?'

'Just here.' I pointed to the house behind me.

'Nice. The compound seemed to have undergone quite a change in the past few weeks.'

'Work being done on one of the houses is disruptive for the whole terrace. It was the perfect opportunity to upgrade them all.'

'I guess. Do you mind if I go and have a look through the planks?'

'Be my guest, but I am not in charge of the works and house. It might be frowned upon.'

I let him go first and followed a few steps behind. He tried to peek at the junction of the planks under them and looked at the height suspiciously. They were as tall as the houses themselves. No point asking for a ladder.

'That's an original scaffolding partition.'

'Is it?'

The way he looked at me, he had no doubt I was aware it was. On my side I had no doubt he knew something was not as it should be with this fog. It was time to dig for information too.

'What did you mean by missing people? You saw the fog, hardly big enough to miss someone in it, don't you think?'

'Forget I mentioned it.'

'That was an odd comment, though.'

'Listen, if you think of anything and wish to share some information with me, you can call me on this number.' He took out a small notebook, ripped off a piece of paper and scribbled his name, number and email, then handed it to me.

I took the piece of paper and started walking towards the lot exit.

'Would you be able to give me a number I could contact you on if needed?' he asked.

I hesitated, but couldn't think of a reason fast enough to refuse.

'Do you have another piece of paper?'

He pulled the notebook out of the pocket it had returned to and opened it to a blank page. I wrote my first name and my mobile number. I had a bad feeling about this. If he knew about missing people, who was he referring to? Jack? Nick? Ushi Tsou? They had all disappeared from that other house, though no one should know about it. If he did, how did he know and what did he know? The minute he was gone, I called Leila. The call went directly to voicemail. I hung up, went back inside my house, indicating on the way that the Fog doors could be reopened. The first thing I did was to drop Leila an email, making sure to copy his name and details. Hopefully they would be able to track down any electronic information he had via his email or text messages. It would reveal more about him and what he knew. I wasn't even feeling guilty that the Society would hack into his private life and snoop. My values were not what they should be anymore. Ah, well …

I was back at my seat, phone in hand and ready to dial Ingis Chen. I was still agitated, so treated myself to a couple of biscuits and a hot chocolate. After two or three sips, I made the call to his mobile.

'Ingis Chen's mobile,' a woman's voice answered.

'Hello. I would like to speak to Mr Chen please.'

'Mr Chen is unavailable at present, may I take a message?'

'Sure. Please tell him that Nutty …' I didn't have a chance to finish my sentence as the woman asked me to hold and within seconds an easily recognisable deep male voice addressed me.

'How nice of you to call, Nutty.'

'Good morning, Mr Chen.'

'Please, call me Ingis.'

'Uh-huh. So … as I mentioned to you when we last spoke, we'd like to hear about what you may be able to offer. Could we meet to discuss it?'

'Certainly. I am at your disposal. If you are free, may I invite you for lunch?'

'Yes, I am. Shall we say 12.30 p.m.?'

'Perfect. May I suggest a lovely venue?'

'If you don't mind, I would rather pick the place. I will think about it and let you know at noon.' I wanted to leave him as little time as possible to fill it with his people. I would fill it with 'my people' first!

With Phil's help, I picked a restaurant in Mayfair, by day the hedge fund centre of London, by night a quietly trendy area among the jet-setters of the capital. The restaurant was on Berkeley Square, which would be busy at lunchtime. I was there at 12.00 p.m. with Phil and some of his team spread around inside and out. I made the call to Ingis Chen and waited. He was there at 12.15 p.m.

'I work in the area,' he said as he sat down. 'I like it round here. I might buy a building to serve as an office, with a flat for me when in London. It is an easy guess that I will be here often.'

'Maybe. Anyway, on Fog and Other World related issues, we have decided that we would consider any offer you make, and possibly go into some kind of partnership with you. However, it would be under our terms.'

'By 'we' you mean …?'

'The group of us linked to the Fog, like Jack, Leo and … me.' As his future point of contact, he was bound to dig and work out I was linked to the Fog anyway. It's better to be in control of the information out there.

'So, not only are you involved with Leo, you are linked to the Fog, too. What do you do?'

'It doesn't matter and I am not involved with Leo.'

'Really, you two seemed …'

'We are not involved. Let's get back to business. There is no point in your going to Kenya and talking to Clare and Mary, or to any other locations where you might find the Fog. We are all part of the same group, working as a team.' The last point was an overstatement, although he didn't need to know that.

Ingis Chen remained silent and focused on me. He looked deadly serious and his usual charm was turned off. He obviously didn't appreciate being robbed of the opportunity to get some of the Foggies on his side.

'So here is how we Foggies work,' I proceeded. 'We rely on each other and make decisions together. We need each other. Being cut off from the group is to be cast adrift. That is a pretty harsh fate for anyone linked to the Fog as it means either being in a Fog prison or suffering a debilitating headache. Regarding your links with us, I suppose it would be on the commercial side, to set up trading opportunities and to use your business *savoir faire* and networks. In any case, we will not be part of your team and work for you. On the commercial front, we don't have set ideas of what we want to do. We have to see how things evolve. But we know what we don't want: you taking over and getting your involvement with us out of proportion. So whatever our relationship with you, if any, it will develop little by little, on an ad hoc basis. Take it or leave it.'

Ingis raised an eyebrow without the hint of a smile. I continued, 'Knowledge of the existence of the Fog and what it can do ...'

'Or what you can do,' Ingis Chen cut in. I ignored the interruption.

'... what it can do and how we are involved, must remain secret. So now, knowing this, are you interested?'

'I don't feel I have much choice. You present it as either take it or leave it and you know I would never leave it.'

'I have no doubt you will always try to get more and won't drop your grand ideas. We are feeding you a salad when you want a burger, knowing you will remain hungry for more. Just keep in mind that at least you have a salad. Try to steal the bun and we'll cut out the food supply.'

'I don't eat burgers. I'm a healthy eater.'

'Whatever. You'll get steak if the partnership works.'

I never thought I'd hear him grunt. He did.

I asked Ingis Chen what he knew about the Fog and I filled in a few blanks. He had gathered how the Fog worked and the role of Switchers, Crossers and Facilitators from Jack, as well as the ratio of the Relocated from the people crossing the Fog. Jack had disclosed the gist of it and I wasn't going to blame him. At least Jack had remained vague about the Society – maybe he didn't know as much as we did and we knew little. Ingis Chen asked me about Yoko, the other Switcher in London.

'Jack told us about Yoko. It is you, isn't it?'

'Yes, it is me. How did you work it out?'

'Once we found the house and searched in vain for information concerning its residents, my team used the old-fashioned way to investigate.'

'Which is?'

'Ask the neighbours. We learned that Yoko was not the Japanese looking woman we expected, more the Italian type. Are you at all Japanese?'

'Partially.'

'Why "Nutty"?'

'A nickname. I don't want to get into it.'

'Very well. What should I call you from now on?'

'Yoko.'

'How could I contact you, Yoko?'

'Here is my number. Before you try, do not waste your time, you can't trace it.'

'Will I be allowed to see where you are based? I know the area, but I would be interested to see the place.'

'Maybe later. Tell me about Ushi Tsou.'

Ingis smiled. His mobile vibrated, he took it out, checked, and indicated he had to take this call. He answered with his name, listened for a minute, said 'bye' and hung up.

'So you met Ushi,' he stated.

'Yes. She left her signature on my eye.'

'I was wondering. How is she?'

'Tell me about her first.' Remembering I am a polite girl, I added 'please' a split second later.

'Ushi is part of the special team I have put together. An excellent recruit. Clever, well trained, gorgeous and the least emotional woman I have ever met.'

'Did your team know they could be relocated?'

'Yes. I am not sure how much they believed it until Jack fogged the place and Ushi was transferred. I would be quite keen to talk to her.'

'I am sure you would. She is in prison right now. The people on the other side did not appreciate her treatment of Jack and me.'

'Prison won't hold her long.'

'I'll pass on the message to the local sheriff. Do you think she is still loyal to you?'

'I would have to talk to her to know. My having a business relationship with you should help, as I will be able to use her as my representative, if you allow me, of course.'

'I guess it depends for what.'

Lunch did not last. I was back home early afternoon, longing for a nap and for the return of Zeno and Mitch later. I missed my friend. In the meantime, I should pay Ushi Tsou a visit and see what I could glean from her. I feared it wouldn't be much and couldn't be bothered to do the journey to Lil'London. Instead, I went to visit Jazz. I messaged Nick as well to let him know, should he have news from Ushi Tsou, and in case I decided to pop out into the forest.

Jazz was at the dining table with Big Tom. They were browsing a catalogue of bar furniture, debating pews versus lounge seating and which one would both create a warm ambiance and also be space efficient.

'Ah! Yoko. Great! Come and help!'

'Jazz, I have no clue.'

She looked at Big Tom and murmured something. He stood up, picked up a big box on the side and took out bottles two by two. Soon a vast selection of vodka, whisky, gin, Malibu, Kahlua and more bottles lay on the table.

'Testing time! I need a proper selection for the bar. Chop chop chop, Nutella! Plus, I am sure after a couple of glasses you will have lots of ideas for the lounge.'

She prepared a Bellini at 3 p.m., crushing ripe peaches, just for me. I thought a light Bellini to celebrate a job done in facing

Ingis Chen was acceptable. Just a small glass, then I would write a few notes on the lunch meeting.

Two hours later, I woke up on her living room sofa. The Bellini had knocked me out. Big Tom was on the sofa opposite, snoring loudly. It was probably what woke me up. It sounded like a helicopter was in the room. Slowly, it dawned on me that there really was a helicopter. The house shook a little and Jazz came running down the stairs screaming my name.

'Yoko! What the heck!'

'I think you have a helicopter on your roof.'

'They could have warned us. I thought there was an earthquake!'

'Let's go upstairs and help the pilot down. Whoever is flying this thing is nuts. Thank God it didn't miss the roof! That could have been messy.'

The pilot refused a Bellini and opted for a cup of tea and some biscuits. She was waiting for orders to fly again or not, depending if she had been relocated. We did our routine tests inside and outside the house. She had not. It was impossible to say if she was disappointed or not, though I was: as the pilot was not relocated, Nick would have to learn to fly somehow and that would take time. My sister would have to wait. I checked the calendar, there were less than two weeks before the Fog at my parents needed to be reactivated. I dreaded the confrontation with Julia if I went bearing bad news.

**Day 4 (Wednesday)**

I don't like trotting on a horse. Galloping, yes. Walking, yes. Trotting, no. I find it most uncomfortable.

I looked at Nick riding next to me as we were making our way to Ariel Ben-Chaim's and the Jewish village. He looked in pain.

'You're OK there?'

He grimaced. 'This ride is just lovely. So relaxing.'

'It takes a bit of time to get used to it.'

'My worry is the physical damage. It would be nice to check that everything works fine.'

I shot him a glance, saw his cheeky grin and quickly returned my stare to the road ahead, keeping it there.

'I'm sure it is fine. You are not the first man on a horse.' I was glad Edmund was ahead of us and could not hear.

'I have high standards. You have noticed I only provide the best services. That goes for every area.'

I bit my lips to contain a nervous laugh.

'Nick, I will take you at your word.'

We trotted in silence for a while.

'Did you have a girlfriend or someone you left behind? You never told me about how the relocation affected your private life.'

'Nothing worth mentioning.'

'Ever wanted to settle down and raise a family?'

'Nah. I am too young. Too much to experience first. Plus no one could deal with my job. That suited me fine.'

His jaw was set and his eyes had hardened. I wasn't sure if it was as fine as he just said. I called to Edmund, 'Edmund, can you tell me a bit more about Yerushaleim?'

'I am afraid I can't. I have only been a few times and always stayed at Ariel's. Yerushaleim is a little planet on its own. I never talked much with anyone else. I presume only the people trading with them have.'

'Are they that different from Lil'London?'

'They keep to themselves. They marry their children quite young, but men have only one wife. However, they seem to have a higher rate of births per woman than any other community. Many think that they have a secret. They have been asked many times over the years and never revealed anything. Some people are quite bitter about it, I am afraid. It has reinforced the animosity against them as Jews.'

So, even here, anti-Semitism existed. Sometimes, one could despair of the human race and its tendency to hate what or who is feared or not understood. Why do so many of us want to annihilate the differences, obliterate divergent opinions, and panic at stepping out of the comfort zone? It only emphasises how insecure a person, a community, a nation can be that they cannot accept an alternative to their choice of life and belief. Thinking about it, it might be more than insecurity. It might be delusion, too.

'Yoko, is everything all right? You look very stern.' I turned at Edmund's question. I had been lost in thought again. Had he been talking to me all this time? I heard Nick's horse accelerate and come closer to mine.

'Something's wrong?'

'No, no, I am fine, thank you. Just, thinking about the flaws of mankind.'

'Don't. You'll only get depressed.'

'We are not that bad, really,' Edmund said. He probably hadn't reached the First World War in the history book yet. Let's see what he thought when he reached it, and after the Nazis camps, gulags and nuclear bombs.

We continued in silence until we reached Yerushaleim. It was a very village. As we crossed it, no one looked at us directly. We received sidelong glances from the women, heads lowered, and from the children gathered round their parents. Only a few men greeted Edmund as he passed, touching their hats and bowing their heads. It didn't take long before we reached a large house, the door of which was opened with Ariel Ben-Chaim standing outside, a welcoming smile spread over his friendly face. I couldn't help thinking of Father Christmas again, so inappropriate for a Jew. Crossing the entrance, I noticed the little Jewish stick attached to the door frame. I knew about the tradition of affixing this kind of tube containing a scroll inscribed with an extract from the Torah (checking its name later on, I found out that is called a mezuzah). The room we entered resembled an apothecary's shop as described in books or seen in movies. It was panelled with wood and covered with shelves on all the walls, apart from one which had a large bay window looking onto the street. Every single shelf was packed with glass and ceramic jars, vessels and bottles of various shapes and sizes. The oldest ones were made of glass, containing herbs, seeds, powders, or some kind of liquid. I could not ascertain what the exact contents were. There was a little counter set at an angle by the window, opposite the front door. In the other corner stood a larger counter in an L shape taking up a large chunk of the room. The small one was neatly organised, with vintage scales with two copper trays and a selection of copper weights of various sizes, some wrapping sheets and empty bottles to dispense the products, and an open ledger book. The larger one was covered with old-fashioned laboratory stills, baskets, brass pestles and mortars, and all sorts of things I didn't know the use of. The smell in the room reminded me of the local market I went to with my parents as a child in the South of France. It had a large herbalist stand selling spices, herbs, honey, candles, and dried herbs. It had a wonderful medley of fragrances. I instantly loved Ariel Ben-Chaim's apothecary shop and lab.

The first thing he did was to ask me if I didn't mind sitting down for him to apply his homemade balm to my face. It stank. I don't know what was in it but it was vile and gluey and it made my eyes water. He apologised, but promised that it would help. I glanced at my reflection in the window glass and saw that I had a big chunk of my jaw and cheek covered by his thick dark concoction.

Listening to Ariel talk about his remedies, herbs, powders and so on reminded me of a father speaking about his son. He held each container fondly. He opened a few to let us discover some specific scents, taking pleasure in our reactions. There were quite a few empty pots too.

'Have they always been empty, or have you run out?' I enquired.

'Some of them have been empty for as long I can remember, and before me my father and his father. There are plenty of herbs and spices that cannot be found in England, regrettably.'

'Like which ones?'

'Any of the spices are missing.'

'Please do prepare a list. We should be able to help easily with this.'

'You are very kind. I shall prepare one and contact you when I am done.' He took out his radio and handed it to me. 'I believe I have to return this to you and you will provide me with another one, with which liaising with Edmund will be possible.'

I confirmed this and took the radio from my bag. From the other bag, I heard a yelp and it started to move. Simba was fidgeting, she wanted out.

'Would you mind if I took my cub out for a few minutes?'

'Please.'

As I pulled out Simba from her bag, Ariel looked at her gently, and then lifted her to his eye level.

'A wolf cub,' Ben-Chaim murmured as if to himself.

Simba grew quiet and stopped fidgeting. Both of them just looked at each other, before Ariel Ben-Chaim finally gave her back to me.

'She has something different about her.'

'What do you mean?' Edmund asked Ariel. I didn't comment. My silence was spotted by Ariel Ben-Chaim who turned towards me.

'I am not sure. There is something.'

'She is different.' I spoke at last. 'She has adopted a human as mother.'

'A human from another world… Yes, maybe that's it. Still, she is a very mature cub. No wolf that age would learn so soon to ask to go out and hold on. Mature and clever. And different.' Ariel paused, smiled and moved on to another subject seeing my discomfort.

'Shall I prepare an herbal tea while you are out?'

'Yes please. Thank you.'

'I understand you are also the rabbi for your community?'

'I am, Miss Salelles.'

'I am surprised. I would have thought it incompatible with being a physician, alchemist and apothecary. In other words, between a man of science and a man of faith surely one has to dominate?'

'Faith and science are not incompatible, even the reverse. God is behind the wonders of science. In any case, it is not uncommon in our faith to be both. Rabbis are scholars and as such they study the sciences as well as Jewish law, ethics and the Torah. To name but one, Moses Maimonides was one of the most prolific rabbis and physicians and his writings are acknowledged as greatly influential in the thirteenth century. Evidently, he had critics. So do I.'

I had, of course, no idea who he was referring to. I made a mental note to Google 'Maimonides' later.

Ariel Ben-Chaim, aka Ariel Son of Chaim, explained the origins of Yerushaleim to us. Nick and I were fascinated. His ancestors crossed to WII in the late eighteenth century, a few weeks after the original Fog had been created. What happened in 1782 was that the Switcher panicked after a few weeks in the house she had fogged, and fled. She must have had the help of a Facilitator or Crosser to escape, although Ariel Ben-Chaim did not talk about it. The young woman wandered in the wild for a couple of weeks before finding refuge in a Jewish village. What was bound to happen, happened: the following Saturday night she turned her refuge into a door to the Other World. She was distraught for her new friend as well as stranded in the newly fogged house or the Fog itself. The Jewish community was strongly affected. The whole village attempted to cross, not only in solidarity with the Relocated, but also in the belief that it could be an act of God leading them to a new land where they could start afresh. Apparently the ratio of one out of seven being relocated was precise for them. Indeed, the return of the Jews in England was recent and the Jewish communities were still not fully integrated or accepted. Jewish people had been expelled from England in 1290 and banned from the country for 350 years. It was only in the mid-seventeenth century, under Cromwell, that they were allowed back in under strict control and at high cost, following the petition of Menasseh Ben Israel and the support of Jews from abroad. Oliver Cromwell was economically astute: in addition to the fees paid by the community for the right to return, the Jews were bringing plenty of money with them. Their status and presence remained unclear until the early eighteenth century and only in 1753 was the so-called 'Jew Bill' introduced, enabling them to gain British citizenship. When you consider the Fog and door to the New World opened just under thirty years later, it was clear that the Jews could consider their situation as precarious in England. Furthermore, they are wanderers and not risk-adverse, ready to seize new possibilities.

Back in 1782, the Switcher, blocked in her new cage with no Facilitator or Crosser, gradually evolved from aggressive to depressive to suicidal. So despite the fear of punishment they might incur and anxious of what might happen should she die, they sent for help to her original house. Men came and took her away. The following night, the fogged house was set alight by the people who had come to take back the Switcher, or so the ancestors of Ariel Ben-Chaim assumed when they discovered the charred remains of the house. The Fog having lowered to waist level, no link was possible with their original world. They could not know what had happened as the door didn't work anymore. Any contact with their past lives had been severed. They also feared for the fate of the rest of the village, which could also have burned down. Much later, they encountered the community of Lil'London where a door to WI was still open. However, no one was able, or allowed, to give them news of their original village. They were not let through the Fog or allowed to communicate with their relatives (either because they had none left, or because the owner of the fogged mansion didn't want to help Jews, it was not clear).

Later that afternoon we rode to Lil'London to interrogate Ushi Tsou before heading home. It was a lot of riding for one day. My legs and bottom were already tender from the new regime of horse riding, but on the last trip to the house I longed for a hot bath and some ibuprofen gel. It was worse for Nick! Ushi Tsou had not been very cooperative. When I asked her who she had met, she looked me straight in the eye and said there was no one and it must have been the drugs that made me see things. I couldn't work out what her agenda was. When asked her about her allegiance to Ingis Chen, she just laughed, a loud, clear, dismissive laugh.

'What can he do for me now? Why would I work for him? I am on my own here.'

'What if he suggests some kind of arrangement?'

'I am in a position of power with him now. He will want someone on the inside of WII to run his "errands". I can negotiate the terms and he will not like that, not that it bothers me.'

'What do you want?'

She looked at me, without a smile, without any expression on her face except her icy stare. I got no answer. But when asked what she did for Ingis, she replied, 'Whatever was required. I was part of his close escort and would fly around with him anywhere in the past year. I helped him sort out a few things.'

'Have you been to Mexico?' Nick snapped.

No answer.

'Does he have a private jet?' I had noticed that Ingis seemed to travel fast.

'Yes. Jet and helicopter.'

'Do you fly?'

'Helicopters only.'

The 'tilt' in my head was immediate. We needed a pilot for the helicopter. She was a helicopter pilot. We had a match. Nick read my thoughts and frowned a 'no' at me. I took him outside.

'Come on Nick. We need a pilot.'

'I can learn.'

'How long will it take for you to learn and who will teach you? You're not going to learn on YouTube, are you?'

'They will organise a simulator and everything.'

'Nick, this is ridiculous, we have a pilot now. Yes, I know she can be dangerous, but she could also be an asset. She is a Relocated like you. She will need us for other things and certainly she will want a few things from us. We can use her to fly the helicopter!'

'I don't trust her. It would be like hanging the Sword of Damocles above our heads.'

'You don't know that.'

'She could be the one who killed my mate in Mexico.'

'Again, you don't know that.'

'Yoko, no.'

'Nick, this could be the way to have her on our side, to make her useful for something. You heard her; Ingis Chen can't do anything for her here. We can, to a certain level. Having her working with us is also a way to keep an eye on her. What is the alternative? Keep her in prison ad vitam eternam? It is a long sentence, prison for life.'

Nick fell silent. It was easy to see he was upset. As I said, I didn't like the idea either, but things seemed to be falling into place. It was logical. Also, if she had a use, she may become better integrated and if she were better integrated she could be less antagonistic and dangerous. Additionally, I really didn't want to have to say to Julia that we couldn't get her out of her solitary situation for months until Nick got a grip on flying and helicopters. We didn't mention to Ushi Tsou the possibility of her being freed and piloting for us. I wanted to talk to Leila first, as the helicopter and fuel were the Society's, so they had to agree with the idea. During the whole ride back, I had a very surly Nick next to me, sulking and sore.

**Day 5 (Thursday)**

In the end I didn't have to write or call. As I came close to the house, the FTab beeped several messages, one of which indicated that Leila would be in town tomorrow and would love to see me in the morning for a meeting and to catch up on Fog business. That suited me perfectly.

In the evening, Louise managed to drag us out after dinner for yet more drinking and dancing, Zeno and Mitch included. I really had to learn to say no, but she looked so keen and begged so endearingly. Mitch didn't do much dancing. He was more looking around, observing and sipping beer.

'What's wrong with him?' Louise asked.

'Nothing. I think it is just his nature. He is not a big socialiser.'

'Mmmm ... Yeah... Quite a mix of characters, us Foggies, aren't we?'

'Yes, we are.'

'So. Leo. He is quite keen on you. He seems nice. Do you think you ...? Or do you prefer Nick?' Louise asked, winking.

'What the hell!' I thought. 'Give me strength. I am trying so hard not to think about men and everyone keeps bringing up the subject!'

That Thursday was dedicated to home administration and brainstorming on inter-world relations. It was a fruitful day. Spending time on the development of the relations was needed, along with defining with the Italian boys what goods were required and how to organise the work and trade with Lil'London, Newtonsee and our world. It included brainstorming on our dealings with Ingis Chen. Sitting down all day at my desk, inevitably, some personal thoughts sneaked in. Working with Leo, I discovered more positives about him. Why was I torturing myself and not being with him? It just felt too much when so much was on the line right now. And I was scared, scared to mess it up or to get burnt. There was a new issue. A little demon was surfacing, it was called libido, or lust. It was called Nick. To my dismay, I had had a dream the previous night that involved him and was undeniably X-rated. The last thing I needed right now. I couldn't start up a relationship with him, not in the same way as with Leo, but the physical attraction was there! Sadly, part of the attraction might have been that it would be a fling with no strings attached. Without attachment I felt safer. Nick was not serious and it was pure flirtation. It was much less scary than committing to a relationship right now. I rolled my eyes at my own thoughts.

Leila came mid-morning and listened to the updates on my encounters with Ingis Chen, Ushi Tsou and the life in the new house. It wasn't as difficult as I feared to convince her that we could use Ushi Tsou as a pilot for the helicopter. She seemed to agree with me that it would be a faster option and a good integration method.

'She is a mercenary, after all. She can switch her allegiance to whoever makes the best offer. She doesn't need a fortune over there, she needs tactical allies,' Leila said to me.

'I am relieved you agree with me. We should take the risk, hoping for the best.'

'She needs us, and we can trust that she will try to have good rapport with us.'

'I agree. However, she is not that cooperative so far.'

'You seem to have doubts?'

'I think she is a great solution to our pilot problem and it can keep her under control, sort of. It doesn't mean I am happy about it.'

'The good thing is that she won't need clearance from any authority to travel around. Now, I have calculated that the distance between here and your family home is about 1,200 kilometres. On a full tank, our top notch helicopter can cover 1,600 kilometres. So it is feasible. What we need to do now is provide some fuel to refill at your family's house. Also, we will need a complete layout of the ground for Ushi Tsou to work out where to land. You will understand that she will fly blind. No weather forecast, no contact support, nothing. This is more dangerous than usual.'

It wasn't going to change Julia's decision to come with Eudes, of this I was sure.

**Day 6 (Friday)**

Thursday and Friday were blissful. I plunged full into the inter-world business, and even though the bin got filled with rubbish ideas, I loved it. Those two days were, all things considered, normal. There were no dramas, no diplomatic meetings, and no culture clash; no Native American scare in the US, no missing person in Kenya, Isabelle's pregnancy was fine in Marrakech, and even Christophe seemed in a good mood and positive about the future. I even had the time the night before to prepare a big batch of cookie dough, bake some and freeze the rest for future needs.

The only havoc left in my life was the damage Simba was inflicting around the new house. I couldn't leave her out of my sight for one second: if she wasn't with me constantly, the consequences were munched carpets, gnawed chair legs, torn curtains and split cushions. I had been out for less than twenty minutes to go to the corner shop to buy ingredients for the cookie dough and that was sufficient for Simba to live up to her new reputation in the living room. I didn't have the time to sort things out before Harry returned. He looked around in silence, then down at Simba, muttered 'so small, yet already a woman' and went to his room with 'always some drama with them'. I took her out saying 'London', even though we were not in the Fog house and it wasn't necessary. I didn't want her to forget what she had learned. I was also making sure to go and visit Jazz every day and practice with my wolf. So far, so good: she was amazing as my own private Facilitator/ Crosser. She wouldn't do it for anyone else though. She seemed to have accepted the others, but I was the only one who counted.

I had acquired lots of books on wolves and on people who had raised a wolf in a domestic home. A quick browse through them confirmed strong differences between wolves and dogs. I had thought my knowledge of how to train a dog would be transferable. It was not. Some basics were, but there were many adjustments to be made. First of all, wolves observe the situations they are in and assess a problem and its solution faster. In a way, I would say that Simba was not just looking at and copying what I was doing, she would look, understand, remember, and reciprocate or adjust if necessary. For example, Simba could not reach the door handle to get out of the room, but after just a few times observing my leaving the room, she had remembered how she had first got on my bed using pillows (or I assume she remembered), so she went and gathered cushions beside the door (note, not under the door as she would not have been able to then pull it open, but beside), reached the right level and she was out. She was smart, resourceful and forward thinking. She was only just six weeks old. I was in awe of what she was to become.

I had also set up in my office the largest TV screen I could find, which made conference calls quite an amazing experience. On Wednesday we had tested it for the first time with the Foggies and it really made a difference from using the FTab or computer screen. It was also excellent for communicating with Jazz, even if she was just next door. That Thursday and Friday, while working from home, I set up a connection with Jazz and even though most of the time we were not talking but dealing with our tasks at hand we felt someone else was in the room with us. It was more important for her than for me as it broke her seclusion. I made a note to add such a screen to the Society's office, where I would start working from the following week.

Working from home, away from the Fog except for my brief visits, I was also putting some distance between me and both Leo and Nick. I was re-centring myself in organising my everyday life, and dealing less with my impulses (OK, they were feelings too, but they were so new, surely they could be contained? A crush is a crush and not love, isn't it?)

We all have dreams that something extraordinary might happen to us, that we are special in some way, that we could have some adventure in our life. Even Bilbo, the most risk-averse Hobbit of Middle Earth, chose to go on an adventure when the opportunity was put before him. Still, take my word for it, when you are in the midst of such adventure, you don't see it as as thrilling as others from the outside might. Those two days at home were so welcome, I even wished they could last and be a sign of things to come. I longed for some kind of routine in this new life of mine. Routine gives a sense of normality. Looking back, I was so disillusioned: how could there be normality in a totally extraordinary situation?

The councillors of Newtonsee contacted me via their two-way radios and we agreed I would go and visit their town the next day, Saturday. So I jotted a few notes and questions down in preparation for the meeting, such as the trades they would be interested in and what they had on offer. I had the Relocated in mind, and also what kind of business would be of interest to us. Organic products were an easy trade we could get from them, even though we couldn't legally prove the origins. Again, the Society would probably be able to help with such a trivial matter by hacking whatever administration or records were necessary. I was getting pretty blasé about hacking; justifying it by the extraordinary circumstances, I felt less and less guilt. It proved difficult to determine how we could have a thriving business as Foggies with the economy of the Other World. As a consequence, and for the time being, I focused principally on the settlement of the Relocated. We could provide simple things like sugar, salt, spices, and various technologies and tools. Engineers at the Society were already working on providing a source of energy, with independent solar energy panels and storage of electricity generated in this way. This was something possibly to mention to Ingis: we would need a large supply of technology that, made in China, would be much cheaper. So far, the providers from this world, namely the Society, were financially at a loss and we received nothing from the Other World. Good inter-world relations had to be balanced in the long term, so we needed to get something in return. We especially needed to define what we were ready to give in return for the Chen Corporation's services, otherwise he would make demands we didn't really want to meet, like a fogged door in a place where he could get repayment for his support. I could imagine one by a diamond mine in Africa, or a gold mine in the States, untouched in WII. Such a door would also be a way for us to finance our trade at a loss with the Other World. Yet, it made me feel uncomfortable. First, we would have to open a door in one of those areas in Africa and they were not safe. Questions would be asked. Then, how could we prove they were not blood diamonds? Also, and probably not the last issue, we had to beware not to flood the market with new diamonds, gold, or other rare commodities from WII and affect the current markets. The whole planet's economy is a web: change one market and by ripple effect all the others are affected. Sitting down at my desk, I thought it was another bridge we would have to cross when we reached it, only preparing as much as possible beforehand. The current priority was the development of trade, and good relations with Lil'London and Newtonsee, not forgetting Yerushaleim and the other hamlets, with first and foremost, the welfare of the Relocated.

It would be misleading to think that I was a recluse for two days or that nothing happened. Certainly not! In WII, Ushi Tsou was freed, following my insistence that we had a use for her. Once she agreed to pilot the helicopter, Nick took charge of it. He told me it had been pretty easy. She had listened intently to our proposal and just replied 'OK' without a trace of emotion on her face or in her voice. He had continued, telling her it would be a long trip to pick up some people in the South of France, with no external support and so on, and again, without hesitation or facial reaction, she had replied 'OK'. A bit of enthusiasm would have been welcomed, but you can't have everything. As long as she brought back my family safe, she would have my gratitude.

I appeased my unease by reminding myself that she would not kidnap my family and keep the helicopter, as the latter would not be much use without fuel and she needed us for this. She needed us in general.

On that Friday, London lost two Foggy visitors, Mitch going back to Alaska and, Louise going back to Marrakech. Mitch's leaving was more emotional than I would have expected. Rosario was right, her brother was very much a loner, an introvert, close to being a hermit. He didn't speak much, didn't display many emotions, but he was still a sensitive man. He had come to appreciate us and had enjoyed both his stay and our company. When we parted, he gave me a big hug.

'I'll be back.'

'Any time. Come back whenever you wish. You have a room waiting for you.'

'And cookies?'

I laughed and said, 'And cookies.'

'You are doing a good job with the Foggies here and in general. I should do more, but I would be terrible at it.'

'I am not doing much. Just trying to keep things organised, really.'

'I would not have the patience.'

'You would, if you had to.'

'Do you feel you have to?'

'Yes and no. I don't mind doing it and would hate only being an observer. I need to be pro-active. That stops me over-thinking things.'

'I need action too, only not that way.'

'Well, if I understand correctly, you will have a brand new little plane to roam around in the Alaskan WII?'

'Yes! Nothing too sophisticated, that would require more training. I'll learn how to fly a helicopter too. It would be easier to land in the wild. With the plane all I can do is fly over land and land on lakes or coast. That is the only way by plane in the wilds of Alaska. Now I'm finding it too limiting.'

After lunch, Louise's farewell was more effusive. She left with tears in her eyes, bless her.

'So glad I came! I had such a good time. London is fun! I am so relieved to get along with you all. So relieved. Can you imagine, it would have been hell otherwise!'

'Yes, well, I don't know if we all get along, or if we will always agree on everything, but at least we try.'

'Like at school, when you don't choose your classmates and you're stuck with them.'

I smiled. It was exactly my thinking.

'Are you going to be OK in Marrakech? I mean, the situation is complex, to say the least.'

'I will be fine. It will be better now that Christophe can go out into town. It was difficult for him, being grounded in the house. That was harsh of her.'

'That is tough, I am sure, but one can unders ...'

'Of course I understand her! Of course I do! But the effect it had on Christophe was not making things better. A vicious circle, that's what it was. And she is impossible too. She complains all the time. She is either bossy or she moans.'

'And where do you fit in all of this?'

'I love him. OK, he messed it up. He lied to me. He lied to her. He is a typical man. He is weak with Isabelle because she is his wife and pregnant. He feels a duty towards her and the baby. But I love him and he loves me. I can't give him up. I just can't. When I think of him I have goose bumps. I have got him under my skin and he feels the same for me. I want to go back and try to make it work. I just have to. I have to. I love him.'

Now she was crying. Her tiredness from the partying of the past few days and mild hangover (probably constant since Monday) didn't help. I took her in my arms.

'Of course everything will be fine. Things will work out.'

'Do you know what Isabelle says about you?'

'Errr... No.'

'You are so positive it is annoying.'

That left me speechless.

'Just don't pay any attention,' Louise said, noticing my surprised reaction.

'Then why did you say it to me?' I thought. 'Some people...'

**Day 7 (Saturday)**

The prospect of close to four hours on a horse must have been too much for Nick for on Saturday morning he called me to say he had a surprise for me. After getting ready for the journey to Newtonsee, I crossed the Fog and entered the WII forest clearing. The surprise was evident: in front of me, Nick and Big Tom were admiring the details of a two-seater four-wheel drive quad, or ATV (all-terrain vehicle).

'Ah! Yoko. Ta-daaa!' Nick exclaimed when he saw me.

'Mate, this is really awesome. Where do I have to sign to have one?' Big Tom said to Nick who was coming towards me. He picked me up, put me on his shoulder and dropped me on the passenger seat. Simba was unimpressed, growling deep in her throat and biting his calves. Nick bent down to pat her after he put me down, approving her protecting me. Simba was having none of it. She only stopped growling when I calmed her down in a soft voice.

'I am sorry for anyone who messes with you when your dog grows up,' Nick said.

'Me too. And she is not a dog, she is a wolf.'

'Ah, yes. Sorry.'

'So, no horse ride today?' Nick was exuding both relief and joy at the thought of not having to be on a horse. I continued, 'Is that a dog chewing toy at the back?'

'Yes. Sorry, they don't do wolf chewing toys.'

Fair enough, he got me on that one.

'I meant thank you for having thought of Simba and even planned an area for her.'

'Always pay attention to the pet when you want to please the woman. She is growing up fast. Every time I turn round she is bigger. I asked for a special arrangement at the back so that she can sit neatly and have a degree of comfort and stability for years to come.'

I picked up Simba and put her on the boxed area behind the two seats. I left her carrying bag, the one I used when horse riding, next to her. She understood it meant this was her place now. Nick showed me where he had stocked up water and food for the three of us. 'Now, Nick, it's all very well, but we have never been to Newtonsee. It was agreed we would have someone accompanying us from there. How would they follow-up on a horse? In fact, where are they?'

'I talked to them. It is actually an easy journey. They have roads, you know. They are not primitive tribes. We just have to follow the road. We need to reach the one leading to Lil'London and take the opposite direction.'

'And the forest? The quad bike is not too large?'

'The path has been cleared already all the way to the Lil'London road. The Relocated and locals have been pretty active.'

I had noticed the past two days that the pre-built houses for the Relocated were coming along well and that they could already live in them. I had not noticed the roadworks though. Settled as comfortably as possible in my seat and wrapped up against the predictable cold on the drive in the open, I said to Nick, 'Shall we go?'

'Let's go.'

We left at the time we would have needed to go by horse, which was probably too early for a similar journey by quad bike. We had never tried it before. We played it safe.

'If we're making good time, maybe we could stop mid-way and have a cuppa and sandwiches by the side of the road. That must be something of a sight, the empty land and how England would have been untouched by the omnipresence of humans.'

The journey by quad bike was so easy and fast, it was undeniably a more efficient means of transport than the horses. Efficient didn't mean better. I preferred the horses. The quad bike felt somehow less authentic and more intrusive, not just because of the automatism of the machine versus the grace of the animal, but the sound was just wrong out there. I loved the tea-break it allowed though.

I was totally charmed by the town of Newtonsee. Like Lil'London, it looked more like an overgrown village than a town, with the low-built houses we can still find today in traditional English villages and not the multiple storeys of modern houses. Construction was easier without many floors and low ceilings made the rooms easier to heat. Again, as in Lil'London, the main buildings of the town were the biggest and tallest, with the town hall and the church visible from afar and from the road. A third construction was striking and seemed disproportionate: the lighthouse on the edge of town, by the harbour. I was wondering if such a lighthouse was really necessary, when foreign boats were probably extremely rare. Still, at night and during heavy weather, even locals needed a point of reference. The harbour was buzzing with activity. As soon as our presence was spotted, or heard, it all came to a halt. Everything froze. I presumed there was silence too, but I would not have known the difference with the constant roaring of the quad bike's motor.

We entered the town at the slowest speed possible. People had gathered outside their homes and on the main square. It was a repeat of the experience we had had in Lil'London. This time, they knew more about us. Some were smiling and waving, but the majority were looking pretty serious.

I had a sensation of déjà-vu on this official visit. Jack Chester (the Churchill lookalike mayor), Hugh Ashby (the tall anaemic sheriff) and William Makepiece (the hippie-like church leader) were waiting for me on the main square which was overshadowed by the church and the town hall. We left the vehicle outside and copying our experience in Lil'London we asked some of the youngsters to look after it. Nick was subdued. He wasn't there for Zeno's and my first arrival in a WII town, and had realised that the quad had been quite an entrance and certainly not welcomed by all.

The best way of describing the meeting was that Jack Chester stole the show, not by what he said – he wasn't talking much – but just by his mere presence. He let the other two do the talking and only intervened to confirm or amend the matters raised. It was obvious he was behind any decisions taken in the town's council. Mainly we discussed the possibility of having some of the Relocated move to Newtonsee and having a house fogged for them near the town. I pointed out that it was not so easy, as it involved checking what existed in parallel in our world where Newtonsee stood, as well as maintaining the Fog afterwards. In addition, we told them we aimed to keep a low profile, which would be difficult if Fog houses popped up like mushrooms everywhere.

'So how are you going to organise more people coming through, for knowledge to be transmitted to us, if you keep the doors contained and hidden?' Hugh Ashby asked. Or snapped. I wasn't sure how to take his tone.

'Hugh, I am sure Miss Salelles and Mr Baker and the other doorkeepers know what they are doing. They seem very reasonable to me,' Walter Makepiece intervened. He sounded like the stereotypical teacher or guru whose voice can drive you to want to slap them when it turned annoyingly preaching. Well, maybe it annoyed me because contrary to what he said, I had no idea what I was doing. Since waking up six weeks ago, I had been walking blind with every step.

'So you have a strategy in place, Miss Salelles?' Hugh Ashby asked and waited for an answer, which I never gave, being saved by Jack Chester.

'Hugh, I think this is still at an early stage. The doorkeepers need first to organise themselves so as not to be overwhelmed. Let's focus on the matters at hand today, shall we?' Jack Chester took two sips from his brandy-filled glass, looking straight in front of him at nobody in particular.

We discussed the Relocated. We reviewed possible trades with what we could offer in spices, iron, copper, tools, building materials, crops, and technology of course. I explained to them about the electricity via solar panels. I had done a bit of homework and it would have been possible that they knew about electricity, as multiple inventors started to develop its use in the first part of the nineteenth century in the UK and in the US. Sadly, they didn't seem aware of it.

They had a special interest in the development of ships and shipyards, notably as it was an area of no competition with Lil'London. When I explained about motors, they were very impressed. Half-consciously, I then tried to dissuade them from it, elaborating on the dependence of fuel and the mechanical support that would be needed. Bringing pollution down here was not my goal. We had already started using the motorbike, the quad, and soon there would be helicopters and planes. Belatedly, I realised we had already started the process of modernisation with its inherent negatives. It is not always easy to get rid of deeply ingrained habits.

In retrospect, the meeting was a good one. I was feeling more confident with them and about them than I had been at my first Lil'London council meeting. The day just got all ruined when we left the town hall. As we stepped out, I saw in a blur a bundle of clothes rushing towards me. I felt myself being pushed to the side where I crashed to the ground. It took me a few seconds to get my senses together and back on my feet. As I turned to check what had happened, I saw two bodies on the floor. One was of a young, very young man, 15 or 17 at best, lying in an odd posture on the floor amid a large brown cape. From the quick glance I gave to the young man and considering the angle of his arm, his shoulder was dislocated. I didn't really pay attention to him though, nor in truth did I care. The other body was Nick's, a knife protruding from his right side under the chest. I was on my knees by him in a flash, and he just had the time to whisper for me not to remove the weapon before passing out. I had to do something, but what? I didn't know anything about first aid. Simba was howling by his side and growling when anyone other than me came near.

'A doctor! We need a doctor!' I called, thinking all the while that there was no calling for an ambulance, and maybe no hospital or proper surgeon around. If someone didn't look after Nick fast, he would die. I heard Jack Chester shout for the local doctor. I thought of Ariel Ben-Chaim. I wanted him and his knowledge of the human body and plants. How long would it take him to come here? Too long, except if I went to get him with the quad bike. That would mean leaving Nick alone, with a doctor I didn't know and wasn't sure of. What if he died in my absence? Then I realised that he had pushed me. Nick had pushed me, the attack was aimed at me. No! I just couldn't let him die.

I knew the way to the village. On the road to Newtonsee earlier that day, Nick had indicated the branch leading to Yerushaleim. It was feasible that at full speed I could make the return trip in forty, maybe even thirty minutes. I had to leave now!

'Don't move him. Don't remove the knife. Just try and make him more comfortable. I am coming back with Ariel Ben-Chaim.'

I grabbed Simba, jumped on the quad, fumbled a little to make it start and left at the highest speed possible. When out of the town, I started praying.

I got lucky. I made it over there in fifteen minutes without incident. It would have been deserved, my having no idea how to drive that thing, let alone so fast. I was even luckier as Ariel Ben-Chaim was in his shop and after a brief description he grabbed a few of his products, some fabric and surgical tools (I had to bite my lip looking at them. They looked archaic, more adequate for torture than surgery) and we made our way back. All in all, it took forty-five minutes, as the return was slower.

I never stopped praying.

Thankfully, Nick was not dead when we arrived. Everything else was bad. He had lost a lot of blood, he was still out for the count and Ariel first reaction was to want to remove the knife.

'He told me not to remove the knife.'

'We must remove the knife. Bad things happen when you leave a weapon in a wound.'

'OK, I don't know much about this type of thing, but I think the worry is that if you take it out, the blood will come out gushing. I saw that in movies.'

'What are movies? Anything medically important I should know?'

'... Errr ... No. Forget movies. Just, blood gushing ...'

'Do not worry. I have seen many accidents and repaired many bodies.'

I didn't have much choice, so I shut up and let him work. It was too hard to watch him do. When Ariel Ben-Chaim started pulling out the knife, I instinctively turned my head. Simba was still on the back of the quad. She was yelping and I went to take her in my arms. She snuggled against me, her eyes fixed on Nick. I heard him moan, a barely audible sound. It chilled me as much as relieved me. As long as he moaned, he was alive. I went back to him and knelt by his head, which I put on my lap. I let go of Simba and she settled next to my folded leg. I murmured to Nick I was sorry, so sorry and tears started to flow. Not in a torrent, not with sniffing and grimaces, only silent tears. It was so unreal, me, in this place, in this world, with a man I had met so recently, who had just saved me and who might die for it.

Ariel Ben-Chaim was pushing the local doctor away. They disagreed on what to do.

'Let Ariel Ben-Chaim do his work! I have seen his books, they are correct,' I intervened.

The local doctor wrapped himself in his coat and his dignity and left the scene, mumbling to himself. I hoped I would not regret my decision and to put my trust in Ariel Ben-Chaim. He took his time. The sun was starting to drop and he was still working. Soon it would be dark.

'We need to move him from here. I need to bring him to mine,' he said.

'He won't fit on the quad bike,' I told him.

'You mean this machine we came with?' Ariel Ben-Chaim said with a look of dread. The poor guy had been on the 'machine' with an over-stressed woman who had no clue how to drive and certainly exceeded acceptable speeds. Talk about a stereotype of women behind the wheel.

'Yes. Any alternative?'

'Horse cart.'

Jack Chester said he would provide one and I thanked him. I had forgotten the three of them were still here, along with an audience of the townsfolk too. Only then did I notice the attacker was not here anymore. Ashby informed me he had already been moved to the prison, where the doctor was now tending to his shoulder, and then he would be interrogated.

'Will you join us on the cart and leave your machine here?' Ariel asked later, once Nick had been slowly raised on to it.

I was going to answer yes, when I realised it was not advisable. It was Saturday night, switching night. I couldn't go and stay any-where other than Jazz's tonight, or I would open a new door be-tween the two worlds. It was not a good idea, I had no idea where Yerushaleim was in my English homeland.

'I can't. I need to go home. It has serious consequences if I sleep anywhere other than home tonight.'

'Then let me get someone to accompany you. Your life was threatened today. We can't let you go back to yours on your own,' Jack Chester told me.

'Maybe,' I thought, 'but I will be quicker on the quad than with any of your horses. How do I know they are not behind this attack? How do I know I can trust them, or their men?'

So I answered, 'Thank you, but I will be much faster with my machine, and would be a difficult prey to catch. Ariel, I will come to your house tomorrow first thing for news. Any emergency, please use the two-way radio.'

Despite my little show of bravado, I wasn't feeling secure on my own on the road at night without any mobile or radio, in the dark and in another world. Behind every shadow, danger was looming and my imagination was not helping. As soon as I thought I would be within radio distance of the Fog, I switched on the device. Frightened, I didn't want to stop and call, but running out of fuel forced me to. Thankfully, Nick had been cautious and had attached a small tank in place of the registration plate. When at other times I loved the silence or wild sounds of that world, that night it was terrifying. My first thought was to call home while refilling the tank. However, my luck had run out, or more exactly the two-way radio battery had. It brought me close to tears.

'Simba, watch my back, will you?' She was already on the lookout. Her piercing eyes browsing around, intent on catching any abnormal sound. Good girl.

'Gosh,' I murmured to myself. 'Relying on a cub to protect me. I am so sad.'

Back on the road, I slowed down when I reached a point that I expected to be near the path leading to the forest clearing. It was dark, I was not accustomed to the road, and struggled to find my bearings. I had to retrace my way many times before I found it, dreaming of how relieved I'd be to see our little settlement by the Fog house. That led me to think that we should find a name for it, and shared my ideas aloud with Simba. I had a lot of thinking time on the road alone and didn't want to think of Nick alone at Ben-Chaim's or what might be out there in the dark surrounding me.

'Fogtown? No, too spooky. And unimaginative. New London? Boring!'

'Anyway, Simba, I shouldn't be the one choosing, I am not really living there, am I? Not at all, aside from once a week. Like today.'

'Come on! Where is this damned path?'

'Sorry Simba, I am not upset with you. I just want to go home!'

I made yet another mental note that we needed to set up some solar lighting system by the entrance to that path. It was only when one of the watchmen holding a lit lantern, appeared on the side of the road that I finally found my way home. He had heard the noise of the quad at regular intervals, and understood what was happening.

'Yoko! Thank God, Yoko! You're here!' Jazz rushed towards me from the living room as I closed the door and hugged me so tight I lost my breath for a second. She shot question after question so fast I couldn't follow and even less answer them, until she stopped in the middle of the flow and asked, 'Where is Nick?'

I couldn't talk. My serious face must have showed much more than what I had not said. She brought up her hands to her face with a sharp intake of breath. 'Oh my God! He is dead? Is Nick dead?'

Zeno, Harry, Rico, Leo and Dante were now behind her. They all had been waiting for us to return, more and more alarmed as the night went on.

'I don't know. He wasn't when I left, but he could be now. I hope not. I pray not.'

I moved to the living room. I was shaking all over and found it difficult to walk. Rico handed me a shot of grappa, which I downed in one go and he replenished my glass immediately. I told them about the attack, the race to Yerushaleim and that Nick was now with Ariel Ben-Chaim.

'You should have called as soon as you were within range. We would have made our way towards you,' Leo said half-softly, half-reproaching.

'I … I was too frightened to stop at first. The silence, the dark, after what happened, it terrified me. Then when I had to stop to refuel, the battery of the radio was gone!' Jazz, sitting next to me, gave me another big hug, accompanied by 'Ohh, sweetie.'

I went to bed soon after that. Already exhausted, the grappa had done a good job of knocking me out. I checked first where

Jack was sleeping, not wishing a repetition of last week's events, especially when feeling so weak. He was in the newly fogged Society house next door. Simba snuggled next to me and it was a great comfort to have her with me.

# WEEK VII

**Day 1 (Sunday)**

I wasted no time on Saturday. As soon as it was daylight (as far as I could guess from the colour of the Fog outside my window), I had a quick shower, dressed warmly, packed water, food, dog food and made a flask of tea for the road. Zeno arrived around 7 a.m., just as I was ready to leave.

'I am coming with you. I know Leo said he would, but I have known you longer. It's my prerogative.'

'Do you want to pack a few things for the road?'

'Do you have coffee?'

'No.' He shook his head in disbelief and went to the kitchen to prepare some, grabbing a pack of biscuits and a pot of Nutella as well. At the last minute he added a pack of carrots.

'Carrots?' I asked him.

'I like munching carrots when I'm on a road trip.'

'Ahhh. We need fuel, both in the quad and in the spare tank. I was thankful, very thankful for it yesterday.'

'Not a problem. There is a plenty on the other side for the motorhomes. Let's go.'

I left a note for Leo, who was probably not going to appreciate us leaving without him. I said he could join us later if he wished.

At the last minute, I stopped and ran to the kitchen to grab a first aid kit and upstairs to take some painkillers, disinfectant, gauze and a whole lot of different pills and balms that I just threw together in a bag. I rushed back downstairs and added a PS to my note, that if he were coming, could he first pop into a pharmacy and get sticking plasters. All the while Simba was following as best as she could, but she was still too small to keep up with me. The little thing was looking very unimpressed with the whole rush. I picked her up and put her in her bag. I put the bag of food and the first aid and medicine bag in an old rucksack and finally made my way out with Zeno.

'I was starting to wonder if you had changed your mind and decided to wait for Leo.'

'I just thought of taking some medicines.'

'I have packed a few.'

'I didn't even think about it until a minute ago. So useless!'

'Don't beat yourself up. You're stressed. OK, let's go. I drive.'

'Have you been on one of these before?'

'Nope.'

'Then maybe I should drive.'

'Nope. You woman, me man. Me driving.'

He was teasing, or only half-teasing. I couldn't be bothered to argue so laughed instead and jumped in beside him. Once Simba was settled at the back, off we went.

Zeno had a very curious mind. One day he bought a lot of smartphones just so that he could dismantle and compare them. He would check any wooden box in detail to understand how it was held together, as well as the closing and opening mechanism of different devices. He would religiously watch at least five if not twenty online documentaries on any subject, every day (at least before the Fog, he had less time afterwards). No new dish would be eaten without him analysing what went in it. We teased him all the time about it. Visiting Ariel Ben-Chaim's apothecary shop was as exciting for him as a trip to Disneyland for an eight-year-old, despite his concern for Nick.

'Do you think he will prepare something in his laboratory to help Nick in front of us? You said he has stills, didn't you? Or will he make a concoction with the pestle and mortar? Cazzo! I shouldn't be looking forward to this, because we are going for Nick. I am just curious, you know.'

'No worries, Zeno. I know both that you have an immense heart and that your thirst for learning has no bounds.'

'Do you think Nick ...?'

'I don't know. I checked online and the fact he was still alive when I came back with Ben-Chaim is a good sign. If it had been a stomach wound, he would be dead.'

'Yes, but can he survive here? There is no hospital, or nothing.'

'I guess he stands the same chance someone would have had two hundred years ago.'

'I don't know if it is a good thing or a bad thing.'

'Well, at least he will avoid the hospital superbugs.'

'That wouldn't be a problem with the Fog which would clear the bug. And if he is alive, should we try to transport him back to the house and get a proper doctor or someone?'

'I don't know, Zeno. I don't know.'

'What a mess!'

'Yep. I am with you there.'

The rest of the trip we remained silent. The clouds were low and heavy, but there was no rain. At least that was something.

When we arrived, a woman with her head covered and a kind smile led us without a word to a little room, at the back of the house. Nick was lying on a bed with his eyes closed, as Ariel Ben-Chaim tended to his wound. When we entered, Ariel said, not moving his focus from his work, 'He is alive but in a poor state. He has not regained consciousness.'

I wondered if he was unconscious, or in a coma. What was the difference? It was so frustrating being so clueless about these things.

'Do you think he will be able to make a recovery?' I asked.

'That I cannot tell at present, but I would hope so. He doesn't have a fever and the wound is clean of infection. The bleeding has stopped and from my observation the only organ affected is the right lung. He also has two broken ribs. This wound should not affect his life.'

'But the blood loss might,' I continued.

'You seem to have medical knowledge?'

'Gosh, no! I know nothing about these things.'

'You might know more than you think, especially by our standards. Here some of the most basic understanding is missing for most. If you have such basics, you have knowledge.'

'In the country of the blind, the one-eyed man is king,' I whispered, repeating a sentence I had heard many times from the mouth of my father.

'Si, we say that in Italy too,' Zeno said.

'It could be correct, but not in medicine. Here, many outside the Jewish community distrust my science as witchcraft and spells.' Ariel Ben-Chaim shook his head.

Zeno and I just stood there at first, watching the physician work patiently at cleaning the wound. Afterwards we realised we should have offered him some medicines, especially the disinfecting cream we had brought up with us. Just then, it didn't even cross my mind, because the man in front of us seemed confident in what he was doing and caring in doing so. The woman who had opened the door brought us chairs and we sat in the corner of the room. Even Simba remained in her bag on my lap without moving or asking to be let out. When he was done, Ariel Ben-Chaim offered us a herbal tea. I suggested we should have it in the apothecary room if at all possible so that Zeno could be shown round, and the physician complied. To go with the tea I offered some of my cookies, and I promptly gave the box of them as a gift when the rabbi liked them so much. The rest of the morning was spent in the shop until midday when lunch was served.

Lunch was just with Ariel Ben-Chaim. I was hoping to meet and chat with the mute woman who was kindly looking after us, so was a bit disappointed (the lunch was delicious and must have taken a lot of time to prepare). I asked him about her and if we could thank her for the lunch.

'You may. I will call her. My wife will be delighted to hear you have enjoyed your meal.'

'She is your wife?'

'Yes. I am a fortunate man, I have a good wife. She looks after me very well.'

'I noticed she was not speaking to us.'

'She cannot speak.'

'You mean… she has a speech impediment?'

'She can speak with me. She cannot speak with you. You are not Jewish.'

'We are goy,' Zeno added to my attention.

'I am surprised.' I turned to Ariel Ben-Chaim. 'I have Jewish friends, women and men and they can speak to me. They might not be deep into their religion, but I had never heard that women Jews could not speak to gentiles, or non-Jews.'

'I do not know how things are in your world. Here, to protect our faith and our women from temptation with men of other beliefs, it became common practice for them not to address people of the other communities,' Ariel Ben-Chaim explained.

I refrained from any observation to avoid entering into a discussion with him on the matter of religion. I have always tried to accept that people have beliefs that differ from mine, to keep an open mind and be aware of the differences. That didn't mean I understood or approved of them. Thus it was better not to get into a discussion that could turn into an argument. Take the Islamic veil for women: I disapproved, it being against my concept of freedom and fairness between genders, but I couldn't condemn them if it was their choice. Who was I to judge? Who was I to condemn? Mine was just an opinion.

That is why I didn't want to get on to the topic of religion with Ariel. By that time we were on first name terms. It surprised him at first when Zeno addressed him so casually. Zeno did it so naturally, Ariel smiled and went with it, and then it spread to include me as well.

The councillors of Newtonsee came to visit in the afternoon to inquire about Nick's health. They brought a few things with them: a blanket for his comfort, a large pot of vegetable and fish soup to help his recovery, and beer to help hydrate him. They also brought some medicine from their town's doctor. Ariel took it all gratefully, only to set the medicine aside when they were gone.

Jack Chester remained with us for an hour or so and informed us that the attacker was a young man of 16, from a rural hamlet of five odd houses between Lil'London and Newtonsee. For the past few weeks, this young man had been withdrawn, spending a lot time away with no explanation for skipping his share of work around the house and on the land. He had always been prone to trouble, but in the past twelve months he had found a new faith. Even though he was not attending church, he quoted the Bible often. He had become more and more agitated and extreme in his beliefs, criticising Yoko and the other doorkeepers for opening the doors to a world of evil. The parents were distraught. They did not understand the changes in their son. They were at a loss to comprehend how their son had fallen into such extreme views, believing that the Fog would bring only evil. The young man confessed to have shot the arrow that missed us and poisoned the wine. At first, he denied meeting Ushi Tsou, and then suddenly he claimed he was the one who convinced her to abduct me. Most of the time, he seemed half mad, talking to himself, saying he had failed and begging for forgiveness. Jack Chester believed him to be sick in his mind. On my part, I thought him a fanatic and psychopath. Could it be the same?

The first thing to do when back at home would be to throw away all the wine we had received as gifts from the folks of WII.

So far we had opened a few bottles and liked none of them, never finishing one. I now wondered if one of the bad hangovers we had had could have been linked to a poisoned drink.

When the afternoon turned into early evening and the sun began to set, Zeno and I argued. I wanted to stay, he objected there was absolutely no way.

'Zeno, I only left him last night because I couldn't turn Ariel's house into a door. There is no reason why I would not stay today. If there is an emergency, I could go where we have signal and ask any of you to bring stronger medicine, or communicate with a doctor. And if he wakes up, he wouldn't feel we'd left him alone. He saved my life, Zeno!'

'Exactly. He saved your life. He wouldn't want you to risk it by staying by his side in an unsecure house, unprotected.'

'I think I am safe here. And the man has been arrested.'

'We can't take the risk of you being unprotected. You are going home and that is it.'

'You can't order me around. I will do what I want!'

'You are impossibly stubborn! Don't you get it? If Nick was conscious, HE would send you home! I will stay here, OK? I will stay here and be a relay and you will go home, go to the non-fogged house and remain safe!'

'For God's sake! If danger there is, aren't you in as much danger as I am? Any Foggy could have been the target of this young fanatic, you included!'

'I can defend myself.'

'Bullshit! Don't give me the macho speech ...'

'I've been in the army. I can shoot. You can't!'

'I don't care. I am staying!'

'I am going to knock you out and carry you back home if I have to!'

'I dare you! Come on, I dare you! You think I don't know the best move a woman can use to defend herself? Hint: it involves my knee.'

'You wouldn't!'

We stood facing each other when someone cleared his throat behind me. I turned and saw Ariel looking at us both.

'If I might interrupt, we would feel more comfortable if Zeno was the one staying. We can set up a bed for him in Nick's room. We would not feel it would be acceptable for a unmarried woman to remain in the same room as an unmarried man.'

'Ariel. I could sleep on your sofa in another room,' I protested.

'Yoko, please be reasonable. Please go home. I will stay here for the night and you can come back tomorrow. We just want to look after you and this is what Nick would have wanted. Please,' Zeno pleaded.

I was angry. I wanted to stay by Nick and didn't like being told what to do. However Zeno was right, Nick would have sent me home without a doubt if he was awake. That was the only thing Zeno told me that hit home. That, plus I couldn't impose myself at Ariel's who obviously wanted to send me home too. So I had to give in and made my way home in a foul mood.

When back, I had a quick dinner with Jazz and went to my place. Simba was more and more reliably getting me from one world to the other on command so I didn't have to call for Rico and Harry and just hoped to sneak home quietly and hit my bed. I was still amazed the wolf could understand things so fast, and at such a young age.

Leo must have been watching the comings and goings between houses, and he knocked at our home within ten minutes of my arrival.

'So how is Nick?'

'He is alive, but unconscious. He lost a lot of blood. I am writing an email to update everyone. I also want to look for a trailer for the quad to drive him back home. We could organise transfusion or treatment here more easily.'

'Why don't you just take one of the mobile homes? There's a dirt road to get out of the forest now, so that would work. It would take a bit longer, but you wouldn't be able to drive fast on the quad bike with Nick on a trailer anyway. And in a motorhome Ariel could come with you as well and explain to the doctor here what treatment he gave.'

'That's a brilliant idea! I can't believe a whole day got wasted not doing that first.' I was both pleased and feeling pretty useless again. I should have thought of it.

'I also need to check with the Leila if there is a doctor or nurse we could get who would be willing to cross the Fog with the risk incurred. Maybe the one that went to Marrakech? I will contact her now.'

'Yes … Why didn't you wait for me this morning?'

'I woke up very early and Zeno was awake as well. He insisted he wanted to come with me. He said as he had known me longer he had the prerogative.'

Leo just looked at me seriously and didn't comment. He was sulking. He moved on by saying he had gone to the pharmacy and gathered more essentials, but then he couldn't come and join us because he had never been to Yerushaleim and didn't know the way. By the time he had asked for someone from Lil'London to come and accompany him, it would have been too late anyway. Plenty was happening around the house too.

First, he had informed the Foggies by video call about Nick. When I asked if there was any important news from the others, Leo kept the feedback brief. 'Same old, same old. Nothing to declare.'

Ushi Tsou came to inspect the helicopter and had made a few take-offs and landings. The goal was for her to leave on Tuesday to pick up Julia and Eudes in the South of France. In my absence, Harry and Rico, especially Rico as he had been to my parents' recently, had liaised with Leila, Julia, Mum and Dad to organise the details of the mission. Rico had also been thinking a lot about how to help Nick.

'I made a cake for him.'

'A cake? Well … That is sweet.'

'It will help him feel better.'

'Because he will feel the love?'

'It will dull the pain. It is a "special" cake.'

'No! You didn't! A space cake?'

'Yep, I did. Got him the best of the crop, too. I've got contacts, you know.'

'He is not even conscious.'

'He'll make it. And then, with my cake, he will fly through recovery with no pain and a light mind.'

'You are nuts … I bet you ate some too?'

'No, you are the nutty one. I am just off my head, and right now that is pretty literal.'

'I am not going to comment on that. I don't want to know.'

'Love you too, babe.'

**Day 2 (Monday)**

First thing in the morning, Leo and I drove one of the motorhomes to Yerushaleim. Ariel came out of the house with a big smile to inform us that Nick had woken up. He was asleep now but not comatose anymore. It was crucial that he had opened his eyes. Ariel told us he expected him to survive. He joined us on the journey back to the portal. When we arrived, he could not hide his fascination for the Fog first, then for the numerous details in the house that were alien to him. Once Nick was settled in the first floor room facing the back, we gave the rabbi and physician a quick tour of downstairs and explained the principles of the electricity, the music system and something he also used, the radio and video control corner. The Society's doctor, Susie, arrived around midday. While she was checking on Nick, Ariel remained in the room watching her work. He didn't ask any questions, but soon the doctor started to explain what she was doing and the concepts behind it, such as sterilisation, disinfection, stitching, and temperature check. She also checked the eyes' reaction to light for concussion (he might have fallen on his head), blood pressure, heart rate and the like. Ariel was captivated. I was surprised myself, understanding he had been right: even I knew those basics when some were new to him, or not proven in his world.

In the early afternoon, Nick opened his eyes and Susie called me in. He was very groggy and smiled weakly. I sat next to him and told him what had happened. He nodded that he remembered. His hand in mine, I thanked him for saving my life. I had a big ball in my throat when saying this. I had feared so much not being able to thank him. Nick tightened his fingers on mine, smiled and nodded some more. He said with a croaky voice, 'The bastard, did I kill him?'

'No. He has been arrested.'

'I was worried I'd snapped his neck by training reflex. Has the sheriff interrogated him yet?'

'I don't know … We haven't contacted them yet. You were our priority.'

'You must follow it up! As soon as I can move, I will go and …' Nick began.

'No. You are in no shape to do anything. Newtonsee and Lil'London sheriffs, Hoare and Ashby, are investigating. Let them do it.'

'Useless …' His short outburst had exhausted him.

He closed his eyes for a minute and fell asleep. I asked Susie if he had had anything to eat, or if I should prepare some soup. She said she had found some cake in the kitchen with a card and his name on it and cut two slices for him earlier, which he had already eaten. I winced. To tell or not to tell …

Monday was not just a day of good news.

Arriving in my new office next door for my first day working there ('day' is to be taken loosely here, more like afternoon), I was informed that the fireman had shown up again, this time accompanied by a friend. Phil, who broke the news to me, told me the 'friend' had said he was a photographer, but that he didn't think he was.

'Something is up,' he pursued. 'Leila has informed me that the tech team found sporadic reference to the fogged Essex house in phone conversations and emails. The people involved have had meetings about it, so we can't control what they do and say. This is not good.'

'What did the fireman say?'

'He asked me to have a look at the house with the fog problem. I said my job was to control the access to the site, not to organise visits. I played the grumpy stubborn arse that would have none of it. The other guy kept silent and was observing the whole place, the new houses, the new gate, the height of the boards around the Fog. Even worse, he noticed the helicopter landing and taking off.'

'No! But the helicopter is in World II!'

'I guess the woman pilot tested her skills on the Foggy roof and the sound travelled to here too.'

'That is bad! Could the helicopter be mistaken for a construction machine or something?'

'Not really and not if you know your helicopters. The man immediately frowned, looked towards the house, looked at me, but didn't ask any questions. He knew.'

'Argh!'

'I think there will be an official visit soon.'

'By the police?'

'At best.'

'Great!'

In the late afternoon, I went into the forest to give Simba a walk and meet the Relocated to update them on Nick. He had woken up again later and asked to eat something. By that time I had hidden the cake and prepared a chicken soup. He was less pale but in quite a lot of pain so Susie gave him some morphine and he was soon asleep again. I took the cake back out and left it in his room.

'How long will it take for him to recover?'

'It's not too bad. The issue was mainly a heavy loss of blood. The rest will heal.'

'What about the lung? I read that a knife wound could make it collapse and then they spray blood when they exhale?'

'True. He was lucky, it avoided most of the lung, only scratched it. Ariel saw the damaged side of the organ, so for him the lung was affected. Nothing in comparison to the alternative real wound. Nick will be in pain for some time, but there won't be long term damage.'

'Maybe it wasn't just luck. He was a boxer, he knows how to parry a blow.'

To raise our spirits and occupy our minds, I mentioned to the Fishers, Big Tom and Jazz that the local community of Relocated in WII needed a name. It was found by the younger ones, Maisie and Owen Fisher, who proved to have a good knowledge of the movies and a sense of humour. The new town of the Relocated was to be ... Woodfellas! I dread to think what they would have come up with if they had been vampire movies aficionados – Twifog? The Relocated, encouraged by Jazz, organised a naming ceremony of the new settlement in the evening, to which we, the Foggies, were cordially invited. Jazz planned it the old-fashioned way: at home, with champagne, canapés and a fifties crooner play-list. Everyone enjoyed it, and they were still more relaxed when the party moved outside, with guitar playing, singing and dancing around the campfire.

'I will have some adjusting to do,' Jazz whispered in my ear, listening to the country music. 'I still can't get used to wearing flats when going out. I have taken to wearing my heels inside just for the sake of it. And learning to drink beer, over champagne. That is hard!' she said, cradling a half-full bottle of champagne in her arms.

'Maybe you can compromise and stick to wine?'

'Wine would do.'

'You snob.'

'Yes, so what? You'll just have to be my drinking buddy.'

'OK. Sometimes.'

'Don't you 'sometimes' me, missy! I am thinking Saturday night is going to be girls' bonding session over drinks.'

And with this she poured me more champagne.

That evening, sitting by the fire with a bottle of beer in hand, I thought back to the Foggies Board Meeting earlier that day. The tensions between us persisted. Both Adam and Christophe had asked for Leila to join in. It sounded serious and I feared another meeting with outbursts. Adam launched a lawyer-style speech which was obviously prepared in advance.

'I think we should work with Ingis Chen, albeit undeniably within limits. No offence, Leila, I very much appreciate the Society and how you are helping us. I don't think any of us will ever be grateful enough. You will always remain our special partners. We need to be practical all the same and we need to be open to others' input.'

Leila's face was set in a businesslike manner, unreadable. She nodded, before commenting that the Society had never requested exclusivity. I thought of all they had done for us, all they had spent, without so far asking for anything apart from information, like an inter-world Greenpeace with a thirst for knowledge. Leo looked unconvinced and upset by Adam's little talk. He made an effort to contain himself in his reply.

'I just don't think we need him, or to involve private interests based on profit with the Fog. I am not anti-capitalist or communist. Anyhow, look at the economic disaster of the world today. It would be nice for once not to involve the super-rich guys who play with the other 99 percent of the population as if they were puppets ...'

'Again, no offence to you, Leila, but Leo, for all we know the Society could also be financed by a billionaire, playing his cards well by using a charitable institution as front,' Adam argued.

'No! I would not ...' Leila started.

'Leila, I am not saying this is the case. I am just saying we have only your word for it and so far we have no reason not to believe you. Still, we have no proof,' Adam interrupted.

Christophe jumped in, 'You know what, I agree! The Society is good, but maybe others can compete and help us in other ways.'

'I think the Society is really doing a brilliant job for us,' Harry interrupted, raising his voice over Christophe's. 'For all that, we aren't going to be able to hide for ever. Sooner or later we are going to have the government on our back and I bet that will include their military, secret agencies and so on. Then we will have to defend our freedom and rights and defend our interests. We could do that by threatening to go public, but I am not really keen on that. Talk about creating a mess! Plus, I have no wish to be seen a freak or an object of public scrutiny. Or we have a strong ally, or allies. It is all very well that we have the goodwill of the Society behind us and their impressive top notch technology, but it is a tough world out there and we could do with a shark or two to protect us as well.'

What Harry said was the most convincing to me and I conceded him match point. Leila remained silent, only a slight pout of her mouth betrayed emotion. Leo weakly argued a little more, 'So you think the Society is a dolphin rather than a shark? They've proved themselves to be pretty resourceful to me.'

'Do you fear dolphins?' Tony asked from Alaska.

'Err ... No ...' Leo hesitated, knowing where Tony was leading the conversation.

'Exactly. I am with Harry and Adam. I want people – including the authorities – to know that they can't mess with us,' Tony continued.

'So we'll have our own "good cop, bad cop"?' Rosario asked with a smile.

'In a way, yes,' Tony answered her, returning her warm smile. Young love.

'I hear you all, but I can't help thinking Ingis Chen just wants to use us for his own goals and benefits. The man is dangerous!' Leo persisted, shaking his head.

'Well, we are going to have to be tough with him. He may want to use us, but we can use him too," Adam stated.

Ingis Chen had a real mini business empire and ran it well. He didn't have a real impact on political powers around the globe, but he seemed to be building a strong economic network and alternative ways to connect the men in power. Now that could be an asset if we were to work with him. Please note: I referred to working with him, not for him. The latter was out of question. I decided it was my turn to say something. Against my personal feelings, I put water into my wine. Working with Sophia, I had prepared myself to make concessions. Now after Harry's speech, I was ready to accept the inevitable.

'Adam, Harry, you have convinced me too. We have nothing to lose by taking what Ingis Chen has to offer and making it work to our advantage, especially when we made it clear we already have strong back-up from and relations with the Society and have no intention of severing them.' I made this last statement while looking at Leila on the screen. She cracked a little smile at my comments. 'Unfortunately, we are moving forward blind. I wish we could have the time to get settled and organised in our new life before having to deal with whatever or whoever comes next. I fear we will need all the help we can get. We shouldn't alienate Ingis Chen and his corporation, he knows about us already, so we might as well play along with it. The way I see it, in the long term he could also be useful for his connections to protect or defend us. We are very well aware that we will not manage to remain a secret from governments for ever. When that happens, we will need some kind of official support by an entity with weight. By using Ingis Chen as a front man, the Society's protection could remain private. It would give him a status and role with the authorities, which no doubt would be satisfactory to him! Again, the details remain vague at this point and maybe this will never happen if the existence of the Fog remains hidden.'

There was no point in saying that it would be a counterbalance to the Society. It had already been raised. There was a potential conflict of interest looming with some of us working for the Society's company, and this would have to be addressed as well, and with it, the ownership of the houses. It had been too good to be true.

'Another point will be important to agree on,' I continued, 'which is what information will be given to Ingis Chen? When dealing with him, we need to agree on what and within what limits. Moreover, we will need a structure ourselves.' They all acquiesced. I suggested everyone write down their notes and ideas and email them to Sophia and me to prepare a draft on it. This is when I broached the idea of a structure and charter for the

Foggies. Everyone, either because they liked the idea or were eager to finish the call, readily agreed.

Afterwards I wrote a message to Ingis Chen informing him that our group would soon be in touch to discuss the arrangement of a partnership, or something similar, with him. It was not my most enthusiastic endeavour.

**Day 3 (Tuesday)**
Considering that in the past few weeks, I had had a rollercoaster
of a life, with heart crush, verbal abuse, threats, abduction, knife
attack, I felt the mild hangover that morning was entirely acceptable. Despite that, I was up early and ready to get on with a busy
day. I was determined that Tuesday would be a good day in both
worlds, one in the morning and one in the afternoon. The plan
was to meet with Zeno and Leo in the morning and review the
situation in London, not regarding its links with the Other World
but what was needed to organise things from that side. In the
afternoon, I was looking forward to a bit less work and a bit more
fun. Big Tom, Barnaby Sparrow and Augustus were going to have
friendly boxing matches to assess Big Tom's level and enable him
to see how boxing was practised in Lil'London. We were all invited to join in. I had never been to a boxing match, so I was a complete newbie. I would go and visit Nick throughout the day as well.
   'We are under surveillance,' Phil told me in the morning.
   'Ingis Chen?' I asked.
   'Yes and no.'
   'What do you mean? It is either him or it isn't, no?'
   'I meant yes and no. Some of the watchers are professionals,
Chen's team, and some others amateur, so not just Chen.'
   'That means we have a brand new problem! Who are the ama-
teurs, do you know? What about the Chen team, are we at least
sure that it is them? The last thing we need is more people in-
volved ...'
   'Chen's team for sure. They are not hiding themselves much.
The reverse – they are very open about it. So we were able to take
pics, match faces with databases and they are indeed mercenaries. One or two I recognised from that night at the restaurant. So
it is fair to assume they are Chen's people, although of course we
cannot confirm it except by asking him.'
   'I will! The others?'
   'The fireman and his friend.'

So Ingis Chen had located us at last. It was just a question of time, but I would still ask him how he found us. As for the other two, we needed to find out more about what they knew. The easiest way would be to talk to them. I went into my office. Everything was modern but understated. It looked like a normal office, not a high-tech centre. It had been done like this on purpose, so that if there were any visitors the company looked like a normal trading one. The security office was much more impressive, with entire walls turned into screens, as well as touch screen tables for brainstorming. That would be how I would expect the best mission operation centres of the CIA, MI5, or Mossad to look like.

'Ingis Chen's office,' a young voice picked up the call.

'Hi. Yoko speaking. May I speak to Ingis Chen?'

'Certainly. I will transfer you.'

Funny how the ego can be boosted just by getting through the PA call screening.

'Yoko. How nice to hear from you. What can I do for you?' The man with the golden voice answered.

'Good morning Mr Chen.'

'Please, call me Ingis.'

'Just a quick call, Mr Chen, to double-check a few things. I believe you have found my office location?'

'I believe I have.'

'Your team is not very discreet.'

'They have no reason to be. We are not spying on you. We are your ally now.'

'Business partners would be more exact. May I ask how you found us?'

'Ushi Tsou called.'

'We didn't know she had retrieved her phone.'

'I think you will find there is a phone in the fogged house where she landed a helicopter.'

I didn't feel very bright right then.

'So she told you where we were. Fair enough.'

'She didn't. The helicopter did. We just had to trace incredulous callers about the sound of a helicopter landing in their vicinity. That was unwise.'

I agreed but wasn't going to tell him, now was I? We had made several mistakes.

'Did you enjoy your conversation with Miss Tsou?'

'She was not as cooperative as I might have liked. Nonetheless, it was nice to talk to her.'

'I am sure. She is such a sweetie.'

'By the way, I presume you are aware you have two people sitting outside your lot who don't belong to me and look too neophyte to belong to your mysterious protector?'

'Yes, we know.'

'Do you wish me to get rid of them?'

'No, we'll take care of it, thank you.'

Before hanging up, I briefly shared with him our idea that as part of being our business partner we would like him to act as our official benefactor. He listened carefully to my arguments, including the role and powers it would give him towards the authorities, before saying that he liked the suggestion and would get back to us on it. Really, our dealings with Ingis Chen and Ushi Tsou reminded me of a philosophical concept on the notion of contract: you contract with people for one of two reasons, because they can help you or because they can hurt you. Here, it went both ways.

The call finished and, before dealing with the fireman, I called Leila to let her know of the helicopter mistake and that we had to stop landing/taking off from the house roof. It had been stupid not to foresee the noise would attract attention from locals and passers-by, including the fireman's friend. She informed me that the Society was on alert, but had not expected the noise from World II to be audible in World I as well.

Regarding the fireman, the Society had tracked down very little: a few texts had been exchanged in London, bits of conversation intercepted, making reference to a fogged house. Nothing clear at present and it could be of no importance but what they didn't like was how vague the references were and how the individuals concerned were making an effort to disclose as little as possible, as if they were aware they could be listened to. I left the office and went into the street, Simba and Phil next to me. He told me, without indicating by gesture, where the two men were, the make, model and colour of their car, as well as its registration plate. I had no clue about make and model, but colour and registration, yes. As I started walking towards them, the fireman tried to hide behind a newspaper. The other one was much more relaxed, playing with his mobile nonchalantly. I knocked on the window of the driver, the fireman.

'Hello!' I greeted him.

The fireman lowered his window.

'Hi! I am Yoko. You visited recently to view the house where we used to live? The one which had a pipe leak that created fog? I thought I recognised you!'

'Yes! Hi! Sorry, we ...'

'How are you? On a day off?'

'Well ... I am not working this week.'

'I wanted to tell you, you roused my curiosity when you last came.' Here I glanced at the friend and faked hesitation. 'When you were talking about the pipe leak and the fog. I mean, you looked pretty serious about it.'

I glanced once more at the friend, bit my lip a little and waited.

'I am serious about it,' the fireman replied. 'I have discussed it with my friend and he agrees with me that there is something wrong with this fog, that there is more about it than ... Maybe we could have a coffee and discuss it? Would you have time today? Obviously you were going somewhere now, but ...?'

'I was just going to walk my puppy. Why don't you join me?'

They both got out of the car and we headed to Kensington Park up the road. Without looking behind me I figured we were being followed and my back was being watched.

'I don't understand why you are so preoccupied by this fog? I mean, it doesn't seem linked to your job as a fireman any more. There is no fire. Is it linked to yours, sir?' I asked the third person.

'Let's say I have a personal interest in the matter,' the friend replied.

'You are doing a study on unusual pipe leakage?' I tried again.

'Not really. More on similarities in unusual occurrences of late.' The friend remained vague.

'What do you mean?' I asked naively. But the other man, who still had not introduced himself, clamped his mouth shut. The fireman took over.

'There was a similar fog in Essex ...'

'So you see it happens more often than we think then!' I exclaimed, playing the silly card.

'... And I would also make a parallel with the strange fog that happened around that hotel in Mexico and a suburb in Indonesia.'

I kept silent for a moment, then commented, 'Are you sure you're not stretching it a bit far?'

'I watch the news and read the papers religiously. They all happened at the same time and they all had some odd events around them,' the fireman said.

'Did we have odd events?'

'You had a missing person,' the other man said. He still hadn't introduced himself, so I decided to force it.

'Sorry, I don't think we have been introduced. I am Yoko Salelles.'

'Sam.'

No last name. A job for Phil then. We shook hands.

'Now, Sam, are you referring to this Westminster Council employee who never showed up at ours?'

'That's the one.'

'And you link his disappearance to the fog?'

'Yes.'

'He got lost on our front patio?'

'Now you are being sarcastic,' the fireman said, whose name, by the way, was Deepak Chattopadhyay (I would never be able to pronounce it well and wouldn't want to be insulting or disrespectful, so I entered that grey area when you talk to someone never using a name. It felt similar to when you don't remember the name altogether: pretty awkward.)

'Miss Salelles. People went missing in Indonesia. People were murdered in Mexico, yet some bodies were never found, considered missing. A civil servant went missing too around your house. And in each case, the locations had an unexplained cover of fog that would neither spread nor disappear, except very suddenly in Indonesia,' the mysterious Sam summarised. 'I have grounds to think this fog of yours is indeed hiding something.'

'In that Essex house you referred to, did someone go missing as well?'

Neither of them replied.

'So, who went missing?'

'This is not the point,' Fireman Deepak replied dismissively. 'The point is we believe this fog needs to be investigated. We would really appreciate if you would let us in and view your old house.'

'I see. And what makes you think I can? I do not live there anymore.'

'Maybe from your roof?'

'You want to climb on my roof, then climb over the new partition and look over to see if there is a strange fog?' I looked bewildered and dubious.

'Yes,' Fireman Deepak said. The other one, Sam, went mute again.

'First, it is really dangerous ...' I started.

'I am a fireman, I can deal with ladders and roofs,' Deepak cut in.

'Second, do you realise your theory about the fog is really, really far-fetched?' I continued.

'How about the helicopter?' Sam interrupted.

'I beg your pardon?' I was stalling for time, all the while trying to think of how to deal with that question.

Sam stopped walking and looked at Simba.

'What type of puppy is this?'

'Err … I can't exactly pinpoint her breed,' I offered as an answer.

He was looking at her with a frown. She didn't like it and started her throat growl, staring back at him. She didn't sound like a normal puppy, so I knelt down to caress her and make her stop.

'So, the helicopter?' Sam repeated.

'Yes, I heard about that. I wasn't home this weekend when it was heard, so I don't know. We are not far from Kensington Palace, so maybe some royalty was flying low?'

'You don't seem very inquisitive about what is happening in your neighbourhood,' Sam persisted.

'I have lots of other priorities.'

We were getting nowhere. They were not leaving with much information and neither was I. What I had confirmed from our chat, though, was that someone else had gone missing in that other house in Essex. We needed to look into that and check if the house was now properly closed off to the public or not. I was shaken from my thoughts when I noticed that Sam was taking a picture of Simba with his mobile.

'What are you doing?' I instinctively grabbed Simba in my arms in a protective way, which made him do another one of those brief frowns he seemed so good at.

'Just taking a picture of your dog.'

'Why?'

'I am a photographer. I shoot what is beautiful and intriguing.'

'Leave my wolf alone,' I thought but didn't say. It was important people did not know Simba was a wolf, it would raise more questions. I would have to check what other big dog breeds came close to a wolf, so to have an answer ready next time. I also realised my defensiveness had not been good. This man seemed an observer with a dangerous eye for detail.

Nick was now officially on the path to recovery. He remained a bit groggy from morphine, but was back to his old self and joking that the roles were reversed, me looking after him instead of him protecting me.

'I am enjoying your nursing me,' he said as I brought him a bowl of chicken soup with bread and butter for lunch.

'In addition to feeling guilty because you took the hit for me, I have ulterior motives,' I replied.

'You want to see me topless.' Nick was definitely back to himself.

'Topless is a bonus, not the ulterior motive. I am trying to put you in a good mood because in a minute you might be upset.

'Why? You have replaced me?' He smirked.

'Big Tom, Sparrow and Hoare have a boxing match this afternoon. An amicable one: they want to assess each other's levels and practice. I know you would have loved to join in.'

Nick pulled a sulking face and told me I was right, he was disappointed and would have loved to be in the ring.

'One of the very few things I was looking forward to in my new world, 'he commented.

'Well, apparently aside from the blood loss, you only have a minor flesh wound. I am sure you will be up and showing off your boxing skills in no time.'

'I will.' Nick looked up and smiled. 'But when you miss a match you miss an opportunity to assess the strength and weaknesses of the adversary. Yoko, would you do me a favour?'

'If I can, yes.'

'Are you going to attend the match?'

'Yes, I intended to only if you didn't need me.'

'Please go, and please film it for me, so that I can watch it and check out the competition.'

I laughed. The former professional was revealing himself.

Later that evening, I went to my home office for a late call to
Leila. Despite being in touch during the day, we had not had a
proper talk. I had shared my bad feeling about Fireman Deepak
and especially Mysterious Sam and she promised to dig further
on the latter. Something just wasn't right.

Leila told me that Mysterious Sam, whose last name was
traced as Riverson through his contacts with Fireman Deepak,
was indeed a photographer. He was travelling extensively and pro-
ducing little, but quality work. Leila said there wasn't much to be
found out about him. He kept a low profile, seemed to be doing
quite well selling to undisclosed collectors and had good security
on his private data.

'He appears to be a bit of a hermit. We really can't get a
proper insight into the man. Probably one of those guys who
is protective of his private life and cautious about his online
presence.'

'How do they know each other, Deepak and him?'

'We don't know. I can't put my finger on it. Yoko, I don't understand his involvement at all. It doesn't fit.'

'What about the house in Essex? Have you boarded it?'

'We have. No one can access it.'

'Could anyone see the Fog?'

'I don't see how they could.'

'How about the missing person? There must be one, that's why
Fireman Deepak and Mysterious Sam are investigating.'

'We can't find anything supporting this theory.'

'Could they be referring to Jack, Ushi Tsou, or Ingis Chen?'

'We looked and again, we can't find anything supporting this
theory.'

It was all so frustrating, and when Nick called me to go and
see him, I was in a preoccupied frame of mind. First, I had to do
a quick tour with Storm in the forest to empty my head and not to
inflict my mood on him. In Nick's room, Big Tom was there. They
shook hands as I entered and Big Tom left.

'Did you enjoy the match? I would love to have your impressions,' Nick asked. I had emailed him the video of it.

I couldn't share his excitement, being torn when it came to the boxing match experience. On the one hand I had not stopped wincing each time one of the adversaries received a blow. On the other hand, I had been taken over by the combative spirit and surprised myself cheering when a good punch landed.

'I don't know. I had never seen a match before. I am a bit disturbed by the violence and fascinated at the same time.'

'Fair enough. Hopefully you will grow to like it. I'll explain the rules and tactics to you. You'll see, when you understand it you'll enjoy it more.'

Quite honestly, I wasn't sure I wanted to understand more. One time could be enough. Maybe it was just too violent for me.

'Anyway,' Nick said, 'it was very interesting. There are obvious differences between the two worlds' techniques, but in practice boxing is boxing. I can't wait to get back in the ring! In the meantime, I am also glad because I found the solution to my main worry: your security.'

'You want to forbid me from going out of this house and to WII until you recover?'

'I did consider it. You would have disobeyed without a doubt. So I had to find an alternative: Big Tom.'

'Mmmm … Are you sure? He is a bit special.'

'Nutty, so are you.'

'Don't call me Nutty.'

'Thomas will be perfect until I am back on my feet.'

'Because he can use his knuckles?'

'And because he can use a gun.'

'He told you?'

'Yoko, the first thing I did upon my arrival was to check out everyone here and search their pads. I have known he had guns all along.'

'And what about mine, did you know about that too?'

'And Jazz's. Same type of guns, so I assumed Big Tom provided you with them.'

'Hun-hun,' I replied noncommittally.

'Thomas has agreed to look after you for now and his tough background is coming in handy. This aside, anyone calling his mother at least three times a day and playing with Owen and Maisie half the time must have a good heart deep down.'

'I don't have the choice, do I?'

'No.'

'OK then,' I sighed.

'I want to see Ushi Tsou. I want to ask her a few questions about her mysterious contact.'

'Forget it Nick. You are only now emerging.'

'I need to ask her a few questions. Now that she is out and has a role in the community, she might be more inclined to talk.'

'That will have to wait.'

'Why?'

'She is leaving first thing in the morning for the South of France to pick up my sister and nephew.'

'That was fast.'

'Not as fast as I wanted. I had told Julia it would happen today.'

'It would have been better to wait and have answers first.'

'You don't know my sister. It was better to go and get her rather than wait any longer. If not for her, for my parents.'

'That bad?'

I nodded.

'Great. I am so looking forward to having her joining us here in Woodfellas.'

He and I both.

**Day 4 (Wednesday)**

Ushi Tsou left at dawn. I was there with a mug of coffee to see her off. The Society had prepared a file for the trip, with directions and any information she may need to help her find the house in France. On my side I had prepared a file with photos and descriptions of my family. I don't know how she could have got anybody else by mistake, there was just the one Fog there, but better to be safe than sorry. It was a long trip and one without the usual backup, so I felt anxious that she would not make it back. Either that or the anxiety came from the prospect of my sister moving here and dealing with her on a daily basis.

Afterwards, I decided it would be a day for history, both in reading and in writing. It was high time to learn more about Lil'London's background and write properly about what was happening around the fogged houses. I wanted to document what I was living through and witnessing, and express my point of view. The other Foggies were probably writing their experiences too.

First, once Ushi Tsou had left, I put my trainers on for an overdue jog and headed out to London with Rico, who was going to buy some canvas and paints. Simba was still a bit too young for a full hour jog and I planned to leave her with Phil. She was having none of it and began howling. Not barking, howling. So I took her with me. I jogged slowly to start with, Simba on my heel and when within five minutes she started to show signs of fatigue, I put her in my rucksack. It is probably not good for a puppy to be shaken like that, but she was happy which was the main thing. For the last couple of minutes I repeated the slow jog and she galloped next to me. It was adorable and most importantly she was exhausted afterwards, letting me do some work without my having to check if she was eating a piece of furniture or not.

I had kept a good record of the events in London and Lil'London so far and only had the past few days to update. It didn't take me long. Then, recalling the events of the previous day, I searched how best to refer to Simba's breed in London.

The closest to a wolf was a malamute. Malamutes are a breed of large dogs, more often found in North America and traditionally used for pulling sledges because of their size and strength. Often mistaken for wolves, it was perfect for Simba. While doing the searches, I browsed for characteristics and photos of wolves at seven weeks old and updated the food and drink intake necessary for wolf cubs this age. Simba was above the average bracket. Now that she was a bit older, I should also be able to bring her to a vet for the necessary vaccinations. It may not be useful for her, what with the Fog clearing her body of viruses and diseases, but I'd rather be sure and have a proper health check. Plus, a little jab against fleas, ear mites and limes disease would be a good preventative measure.

Next I turned my focus and keyboard skills onto the Foggies bunch. Everything was getting into a routine for us all, despite the tensions between some of us.

In Nevada, Sophia was reluctantly getting used to having Native Americans from the Other World in her social network, Michelle was attempting to maintain a normal life in WI and cold-shouldering her mother-in-law, and Adam was enjoying some kind of basic trading with WII. I was getting to know Sophia more since the previous week's catastrophic FBM. She and I had been working together to prepare the Foggies meeting that evening, she being in charge of liaising internally with everyone and following it up, me working on the documents and negotiations. She was not the easiest person to work with, always in need of recognition for any comma she might add to my texts. It was all due to a high level of insecurity though, not to a bad core, and when we sorted out who would do what, she got into it and was efficient. She was to be the Foggies community Company Secretary, I would be the General Manager. She would take over all the administrative tasks and smooth running of the group, while I would be in charge of the external communications between Foggies and with the external worlds. I wasn't sure about her, but my incentives for us to get along were high. The two of us success-fully working together would be the first step towards healing the clash between Foggies and towards creating a stronger bond. We had to bridge the gap between us. We had to! In Nairobi, Mary was spending much of her time in the tribe of her beloved and adjusting her modern Swahili to the old one of WII. Putu's life had not changed much, only popping into the fogged house every other day to enable mother and daughter to get back to their original world to run their errands.

A quid pro quo had been reached between Louise and Isabelle in Marrakech, whereby they would look after Helo every other day and Christophe would stay with the person having Helo, so that he could have freedom of movement. I wasn't sure how long such arrangement could last, it seemed riddled with problems in practice, emotional ones on top.

As for us in London, Jack was the Foggy worrying me the most of late. I feared he was returning to a state of depression. He was a very sweet young man, but aside from joining us at the table for the odd lunch and dinner, Jack would spend much of his time watching TV in his room and sleeping. He kept saying he was tired and even though he would smile saying this, I found there were warning signs: empty sad eyes, drained energy and deflated demeanour. When we all tried to involve him in our activities, in either world (the Relocated tried as well), he would always find a reason to pull out, under the pretence he wasn't up for it, or he lacked competence, or something else. He seemed to lean on us, regularly calling even though he had nothing to say, just to check we were around and yet was detached from any life with us. So yes, I was worried.

Rosario, Tony, and Mitch were still the least affected by the Fog. They had not encountered any indigenous population in WII so far and they had escaped notice of the change in their home and circumstances. Mostly, Rosario was now talking about her imminent wedding to Tony, a mere six weeks away. They had invited us all to join the festivities in Alaska to celebrate with them.

'It will be the perfect opportunity for us all to meet at last and on such a happy occasion!' an excited Rosario had said during the previous video conference. She added, 'Hopefully Leila and all the other Society members we met and who have constantly been there for us will join too!'

'And as usual, the Relocated are missing all the fun,' Isabelle grunted from Marrakech.

'Maybe we could set up a big video conference on the day, so that you can participate remotely,' Tony suggested. 'It wouldn't surprise any of the other guests with how virtual our society is these days and as long as we get our story straight on how we all got to know each other, it should work.'

'You know what, I am all up for the video conference on the day,' Jazz said. 'At least I would get to dress up and make myself all gorgeous – with high heels – for the occasion. Maybe we could do some virtual shopping before, couldn't we, Yoko?' Jazz was already in planning mode.

'Isn't it a bit dangerous, all the Foggies in one place?' Harry interjected. He wasn't the only one with mixed feelings on attending the wedding.

'Yep. I think it would be a good chance to have a good catch for anyone interested in the Fog. I don't like this. Imagine if the US government knew ...' Rico added, true to himself.

'When is it exactly? Because I have a school trip coming up,' Michelle intervened in the conversation.

'We need to talk about this. I don't like the idea of you going where we can't easily keep an eye on you,' her father cut in.

'What?! Dad!' Michelle burst out.

'Let's not talk about it now, shall we?' he stopped her.

'Well, it is not as if you could stop me anyway, Dad.' She wasn't going to be shushed that easily. Both father's and daughter's faces were closed off and full of annoyance.

Sophia wanted to go because the wedding was the first important social Foggies event, and there was no way she would miss it. On the Kenyan side, Mary, Clare and even Putu were quite keen to go. They had met and liked Mitch and through him had felt a bond to Rosario and Tony.

It was clear from the discussion that we in London also had grown to appreciate the Alaskans. Also, this wedding was like a symbol of sorts, that despite our strange new circumstances life still went on and happiness could prevail. We had a lot on our mind, which is why we were all eager to go and have some fun. Except for Michelle, who grunted something unintelligible, we all agreed to go. Security would have to be high.

Leila disapproved of the general decision to attend the wedding. Her concerns were similar to Harry's and even Rico's reservations. It was not safe to have all the Foggies in one single location. She surprised me, as she often did, by her relaxed attitude despite her misgivings.

'I admire your being so cool about it, when you just admitted you don't like the idea,' I told her.

'It is not my place to make decisions for you.'

'Some people would try and influence our decisions.'

'It is not how the Society or I do things. It is not our philosophy.'

'I remember once, I think it was before we met, you wrote to me a sentence that struck me as very wise: "Try not to resist the changes that come your way. Instead let life live through you. And do not worry that your life is turning upside down. How do you know that the side you are used to is better than the one to come?" I recognised it as being a quote from Rumi, the Sufi poet and philosopher. Are you a Sufi?'

'I am not a Sufi and yet I am.'

'Oh come on ...' I sighed.

'I mean I am not a follower of the Sufism branch of Islam, of their faith and yet, I believe in their approach to life and faith. The same way I believe in the philosophy of life of Buddha, of

Christ, in the wisdom of Marcus Aurelius and many more. What I appreciate are the ideas, the concepts, the thoughts and, yes, the spirit behind the words and wisdom.'

'But if you think us going to this wedding is not in our best interest will you not try to convince us otherwise? What does it have to do with any spirituality?' I asked. 'I am all for having a good spirit and approach to life, but it doesn't stop me being practical about things.'

'I have told you my thoughts and why, and will tell the rest of your group what I think. That is sufficient. I will have made my case, then it is up to you to make your own decision. You will then be responsible for the consequences of your decisions and actions. We will set up the best security we can, plan ahead as much as possible, get organised to the highest standards. Aside from this, there is no point getting worried about something that is not yet finalised. We do not know if by then some of you will not have change your minds. We do not know if the bride and groom will elope and get married in Las Vegas. The future is not known and all things change. So why worry about it when all those worries are but illusions. We will prepare for the worst and plan for the best. The rest is not up to us.'

'I say, you are a very wise bunch.'

'So are you.'

'Not like you I'm not!'

'Really? I think you are. Not once have I heard you moan about your losses or worry about the future. You live in the present. You accept what is: you do not resist it, but you absorb it and just deal with it. Yes, you live in the present! Although you are not always happy with how things are, you accept them and make the best of it, working on what you can do to lead the boat to better current. I say that is pretty wise, don't you think?'

'I don't really have the choice.'

'You could grunt, cry, scream, sulk, snap, bite ...'

'What would be the point? Anyway, we all do the same, us Foggies, it's not just me.'

'No, you don't all react the same. Look at Jack, look at Christophe, and look at Sophia or Michelle. They have more inner difficulty in coping with the change. Although I must admit, as a group, you are doing pretty well. Maybe that is why the Fog happened to you.'

'Because we get on with things? Do you think that is the criteria that this Fog picked? Really?' I said, partly sarcastic, partly truly curious.

'I have no clue. I doubt any of us will ever know why the Fog appears and how it picks people, or locations.'

'I would love to know.'

'Why?'

'Just because it is nice to understand. It is not just Zeno who has a curious mind.'

Nick was now leaving his bed for meals. We had lunch with Jazz at hers, with a simple lamb stew and fresh bread, followed by an apple crumble I made on a last minute whim. I still felt guilty about Nick's state, and also enjoyed learning more about him while spending time in his company. Nick was a contrast, almost the opposite, to the passionate, extrovert and expansive temperament of Leo. He was always in control and seemed to have a silent inner strength that made you feel secure simply by his presence. I was more and more appreciative of him and his gentle way of teasing me. Yet, Leo was vibrant, seductive, with a confident charm and an irresistible joie de vivre. The difference between the two was made more obvious when I spent time with them one after the other. Leo showed up after lunch to take me for a walk with Simba in the forest. Within minutes of being with Leo, I was back under the spell of his Latin charm. If Big Tom hadn't been taking his role as a bodyguard very seriously and not leaving us out of his sight, I might have fallen for it. I had to get a grip. First, I wanted to stay off any relationship until my head was clearer on where I stood and the situation was a bit more settled. Then, I couldn't let myself be attracted by not only one but two men with both being linked to the Fog! It was such a classic: when I had a nice little quiet life, dating was non-existent, and now that it certainly wasn't a good time for it, two men were interested and interesting. Argh!

Aside from writing the chronicles of life with the Fog, much time was spent on preparing for that evening's FBM. It was to be a crucial meeting for the Foggies. I had worked hard on preparing a document that could satisfy everyone. In the past few days the draft had been sent to each of the Foggies around the world for their feedback and amendments. Today, we should be able to agree on the final document, a document that took most of my attention, apart from a lunch break and walking Simba.

When all the Foggies logged out from the video conference, we had been connected for three hours. I was exhausted but elated.

'We can do this,' I thought, and said to Jazz. 'It's going to work. We are going to make it work.'

She looked at me with a big smile, vehemently nodding in agreement. Indeed, we had done it! We had all agreed on a code of conduct between us.

The happiest one had definitely been Mary, though not about the FBM achievements. She wasn't the same person we had conversed with a couple of weeks before. Clearly floating on a cloud of love, there was no end to her cheesy description of how wonderful and strong and good-looking and thoughtful her new-found bushman was. They couldn't talk to each other properly yet due to the differences in the old and modern Swahili, it didn't seem to stop her pointing out how fascinating he was.

'Looks like you are always back to being a giddy 17 year old when you have a crush. Don't we ever grow out of it?' Michelle asked, to no one and everyone.

'No!' we replied in unison.

'Another hope crashes...' she commented.

The Foggies Board Meeting had established three points in its conclusions that day:

- The Foggies Ten Commandments: our code of conduct;
- The Foggies Charter: our basic rules and framework;
- The Foggies External Relations: in both worlds, including with the Society and Ingis Chen.

The application of the agreed line of actions and behaviour would not always be easy. Personal interests or preferences would sometimes need to be put aside for the benefit of everyone in the long term. So, we would need to remind each other of the long-term goals regularly. Adam Koplat had emphasised this when talking about the future, to the pleasure (not) of his wife: 'I want to continue to work hard because when I am not here anymore my daughter will be. As a father, I want to give her the most secure future possible. The other Foggies need her for her Facilitator role, but she doesn't have direct benefits from the Other World. What will happen to her when I am gone? Or when you are all gone? She is one of the youngest and when there are no Switchers left, she will have no purpose, no role and no income if she has dedicated her life to us. He turned to his daughter and continued speaking directly to her. 'Michelle, I want to make sure you will be all right. I know it all seems very far away, but I am your father, I worry. It will always be too soon the day I will not be able to be there for you and you will have to fend for yourself. I want to make sure you will be as secure as possible. And I know, if we work to-gether, all the Foggies, we can enable that for Michelle and for all of us. That is why I am in a hundred percent and you can count on me a hundred percent.'

My thoughts were also that nothing could help the migraines when the Fog disappeared with the last Switcher. What then? This subject was avoided. It would rise again too soon, especially for the younger generation of Foggies.

Conclusion no.1 – The Foggies 10 Commandments: our code of conduct.

The Foggies 10 Commandments were (and still are) as follows, in no order of importance:

1.  Trust. Do not break promises, agreements or rules. Trust is the most important link between Foggies. We are bound together by the Fog. Our lives and personal interests are now linked.
2.  Reliability. If we can't rely on each other, we are f***ed. Simple.
3.  Open Communication. All rules and decisions are up for discussion. If discussion fails to resolve a disagreement between one or several Foggies, time for a Foggies Board Meeting.
4.  Support. We are now like a new modern family. We haven't chosen each other, but we have to make do and accept each other with our good qualities and flaws. We must support each other. More and more, we will need each other.
5.  Foggies First. The interest of the Foggies as a whole should come before short-term personal interests. In the long term, we share the same ones.
6.  Discretion. What happens between the Foggies remains between the Foggies. No divulging of other Foggies personal information or any general Foggies business to outsiders without explicit agreement from all concerned.
7.  Respect. Each of us is different, we have different cultures, different ways of seeing life and different reactions. We should respect the individual differences within the Foggies and each other's boundaries. Should they clash with the interests of the group, only then should they be addressed by the board and a compromise found.

8. Freedom. As a group, Foggies shall remain free of allegiances in their decisions and actions. Personal bonds (religious, work, office, political party etc.) should not affect the interests of the Foggies as a group.

9. Responsibility. The Foggies have unique access to another world. This gives Foggies an unusual 'power' and control over access to the door or to the advantages of the Other World. Let's keep it real. We are not gods and must remain responsible and level-headed. Our actions have consequences which we must keep in mind.

10. Universal Values. A Foggy should not act in an immoral, or unethical way, or in their own interest at the expense of the rest of the Foggies or Relocated.

(These commandments were utopian, we were aware of this. We were not a family, we didn't have blood ties. Chances were this would never work. Nonetheless, we believed we could make it happen! Large families may have blood ties in common, sometimes they have nothing else, no common interest, not even real liking for each other. We Foggies, we had the Fog running in our blood tying us to each other. We might have been dissimilar in many ways, but self-protection, shared interests, survival even, bound us together.)

Of course, even as we agreed on our commandments and their importance we already knew they would not be easy in practice and hence the Foggies Charter came into play. I had already put quite a lot of thought into the matter. The discussion had been intense: some of the rules were pretty tough. The charter was drafted, imperfect and incomplete, but the simpler the better as far as we were concerned. It was for our own knowledge and use only, after all.

Conclusion no.2 – The Foggies Charter

The main points were thus:

'Fogging'

When avoidable, no fogging of a location by a Switcher unless agreed by the majority of Foggies, to avoid abuse, accidental relocation and to meet the requirement of keeping the Fog alive afterwards (which could involve other Switchers).

'Crossing'

Each Switcher and Crosser will benefit from a Facilitator's support at least once a month to access the 'modern world'.

Each Facilitator will benefit from 8 weeks holiday a year, not exceeding 3 weeks in a row and to be taken separately. No two Facilitators can go on holiday at the same time.

'Communicating'

- Foggies will attend the standard weekly Foggies Board Meeting (FBM) in person or virtually unless prevented by unavoidable circumstances;
- Foggies will keep an online 'Foggy journal' and report once a week on their location with status updates and any information that could be relevant or necessary in case of emergency;
- Foggies will share a calendar accessible to the others indicating their location;
- Communication between Foggies and private information must remain secret: identities, locations and roles must be kept undisclosed, unless agreed at least by those concerned if not by all the Foggies, depending on the circumstances. What was agreed as well was the minimum we could disclose about the Fog and the Foggies if we were in a situation that required it, and, most importantly, what we were not to disclose. The idea was for all of us to have the same story, in order not to put anyone else at risk by revealing too much.

'Foggies Board Meeting – FBM'

- A necessity: it ensures proper communication;
- Decisions on standard Fog-related matters are agreed as a majority;

- In case of breach of the 10 Commandments, the Foggies Board Meeting (excluding the one/ones concerned) will agree unanimously on the necessary punishments to avoid repetition of the breach (temporary exclusion from access to the Fog with the risk of severe migraines, temporary withdrawal for Facilitator help, temporary limited access to the FBMs and online information). Extreme measures would be definite exclusion from the Foggies community.

'Foggies Rationale'

(I had expressed a wish that everyone would agree on being a charity. In the end we compromised agreeing not to be a big business venture, but accepting that money interests couldn't be avoided.)

The Foggies Entity was to be a profitable group, with charity purpose for the Relocated. It would have to be amended in practice, but the principles were these:

For each fogged local area:

- 1/4 of the profits will be allocated for the Relocated everywhere for support and/or commerce and inter-world development (although we all knew some of the costs there would be taken care of by their relations);
- 1/4 of the profits will go to the local Foggies;
- 1/4 of the profits will be put in one big pot to divide between each Foggy equally;
- 1/4 of the profits will be put in one big pot for savings for any Fog emergency.

Any other paid activities would have to be either non-Fog-related or on a consultancy basis, for us to remain independent. In the case of the Society, we needed to revise our contracts for consultancy, not as employees anymore.

So the rationale of the Foggies was limited to the economic rationale so far. It was difficult to build a rationale on nothing existing or specific. We would also have to work out a cover for the activities of the Foggies and exchange of funds at an international level. We had no wish to have any government investigating at us for money laundering or similar.

Conclusion no.3 – The Foggies External Relations

Aside from the WII locals, the external relations were limited to the Society and Ingis Chen. Considering we had a lifetime of Fog and parallel world issues, this would expand.

"The Society"

They were to be our associates. Their preference was for discreet support, this was fine by us. It would be good in our dealings with Ingis Chen and any others in the future not to know the details of our private back-up and their not-so-legal methods. The Society could only continue to help if they were not being directly attacked, which they might be if they were considered by others to be a threat or impediment to gaining access to us. So the Society was to be the Foggies Private Support. In a way, they also represented the charitable and non-profitable branch of our activities, with their ever green spirit and longing for a balance between the two worlds and learning from each other.

"Ingis Chen"

For the time being, we considered that his corporation would enable us to set up contracts with the modern business world. Also, none of us had any illusions our presence wouldn't be known sooner or later: we would not be able to remain in the shadows forever. Ingis Chen was to be used as a kind of public back-up, helping the Society to remain hidden. To those who pointed out that he already knew we had other external help, Harry brushed the argument off saying that it would be in Chen's interest to appear to be the only one and thus the important one.

"Governments", "Religion Groups" etc.

To Be Determined.

That would be the next headache to come, but we were not there yet (Thank Goodness!).

So that was it. The Foggies were now a non-official organised entity, not just a bunch of people thrown together with no idea how to deal with each other. Well, we were still not completely sure how to deal with ourselves, but now we had a basis.

I made a call to Leila, briefed her on the new Foggies group and listened to her praises. She was pleased we were focused on building strong foundations for the future and including the Society in our plans. She added that if I needed any help to draft legal documents and other paperwork with Ingis Chen, we could of course count on her. It was a hard reminder of the next task at hand: get in touch with Ingis Chen and start negotiating with him. Adam Koplat was more appropriate than me for this and he mentioned he would start working on it right away with experts from the Society. Either he would meet with Ingis in person, or Leo and I would. Adam would be our lawyer, without divulging who he was or his involvement with the Fog. We were all in agreement: there was no need to inform him yet of the names and places of all the other Foggies. He would know soon enough.

At about 11.00 p.m., I picked up the *Lil'London Tales* and proceeded to read. I didn't read very far, feeling asleep with the book in my hands …

I was woken up by a shout from below, then another one outside my door. In the blur of my sleepy head, there seemed to be running and loud banging in the house. Suddenly my door was opened wide and shadows of men in black rushed in. Simba growled and yelped. A man grabbed her and held her muzzle, then I was grabbed too and a hand was placed on my face. The room was dark and I couldn't see the details of anything. Only the light from the parking lot through the window enabled me to distinguish the outlines of the men – or women – who had erupted into my room. Names went through my mind: Ingis Chen, Leila, Nick, Leo, Zeno and so on, all mixed and without much idea what to do or what to think. There was a strong smell with that hand slammed on my face. I briefly understood I was being drugged before I lost consciousness.

**Day 5 (Thursday)**

I opened my eyes in an unknown room, on an uncomfortable single bed with a thick white duvet and two not-that-fluffy pillows. The room itself was bare and bland. The bed was basic, but everything was clean. The window was closed tight by wooden shutters. As I woke up, I focused on finding clues to my location and what this room was. The light was coming from a single bulb hanging high with no lampshade around it. The shutters could not be opened from the inside: the handles had been removed. Simba was not with me so I was worrying. I was hoping they had left her at home. I feared for the sake of the others in the house. Had everyone been abducted, or worse, wounded? I didn't even want to consider that anyone could have been killed. I turned my thoughts back to Simba. If she was still there, new people from the Society would come and look after her, but if they had taken her, what would they do to her? She was so young! They ... Who were 'they'? There were not many possibilities, and Ingis Chen was my first choice. This bastard must have been working on gaining time and information while falsely agreeing to a partnership on our terms. Otherwise, who else? I tried to consider the other options. Could Ushi Tsou have contacted someone else on the outside? Then, of course, there was the Society. Had they lied to us all along? No. It wasn't them. They had proved many times we could count on them, and Leila had never let us down. Leila was now a friend. I trusted her. A camera was attached to the wall in the opposite corner of the room next to the one and only door. Angry, I stood up, noticing I was still in pyjamas. I walked to just under the camera all the while staring at it and rudely gave it the finger. I went back to the bed, pulled off the duvet and threw it over the camera. I missed a few times before getting it hooked. I wasn't doing anything constructive, just venting my anger and fear. However, what it achieved was to attract an immediate visit from my jailor.

The person who came into the room was none other than Mysterious Sam. He was accompanied by two other men with blank faces, one of whom, while Mysterious Sam and I had an eye-to-eye staring contest, took the duvet off.

'After you,' Mysterious Sam said, moving aside from the door to let me pass first.

I took a deep breath while calculating what my options were. There were none, other than to do as he asked, so I moved forward. One of the men walked ahead of me. Sam walked alongside on my right, holding my arm tightly and leading me forward and the last man followed behind. We walked to the end of a short corridor into another non-descript room, with a bland table, two bland chairs facing each other on both sides of the table, three bland walls with nothing on them and no windows. Only one wall was different, with a large mirror taking most of the space. There was no doubt in my mind, from the many thriller and detective stories I'd watched on the big and small screen, that we were in an interrogation room with a one-way through mirror.

'Super, ' I thought.

'Please have a seat.' Mysterious Sam indicated the one seat opposite the door. I went and sat down as instructed.

Someone I only saw partially from the open door handed a folder to Mysterious Sam. He sat down, put the closed folder aside, crossed his hands on the table in front of him and looked at me.

'So, first things first, what do you have in the morning? Coffee? Tea? Orange juice?'

'I would love some water.'

He nodded and turned to look at one of the men who then left, closing the door.

'On its way,' Mysterious Sam commented.

'Thank you.'

I was not being friendly. I was fuming inside and probably looked it. What I was trying to focus on doing was to keep control and to look in control. None of us spoke while waiting for the water to arrive. I wish I could say that my eyes were defiant on the man known to me as Sam Riverson, photographer, but they were not. I did manage to sit straight in my chair with my head up, but the eyes were down on the table, unfocused, as I attempted to concentrate on my breathing. My hands were clamped together tightly on my lap. It only took a few minutes – going on an hour in my head – for the water to be brought over. These minutes were precious to me. They helped me to compose myself. I'm not sure if it was Sam Riverson's intention, or if on the contrary the suspense was supposed to play on my nerves.

After I had a few sips of water, Mysterious Sam (as it happens, I had very aptly nicknamed him) broke the silence. 'So, Yoko, you don't mind if I call you Yoko, do you? I am afraid you haven't been totally truthful with me.'

'Ditto.'

'There is no work being done in that unusual house you lived in.'

'None? I'll ask for a refund.'

Mysterious Sam closed his eyes, took a deep breath, reopened his eyes and smiled.

'Please stop this act. This is just annoying,' he continued. I remained silent and he pursued his little talk. 'As no one would let us have a look, we had to take it upon ourselves to go and check by force. From experience, we had to use some people who had already "tested" the previous Fog and came back, the very same policemen who had been to the Essex house. As you had correctly guessed, someone had gone missing there and we couldn't take the risk of having this repeated. Now, could you explain the nature of the two people living in your previous house, both of whom couldn't be brought back with us?' He checked his folder for the names. 'Jazz Jones and Nick Baker?'

'What do you mean by "the nature of the two people"? Would you like me to define man and woman to you? It all started with Adam and Eve.'

'STOP IT!' he shouted, slamming his hand on the table. I couldn't help leaning back in my chair from surprise. Trying to play it cool didn't stop me from being terrified. Plus, my only asset was information, but I couldn't use it in full, not wanting to partake from it. However, I had already learned a lot. This guy couldn't be working for Ingis Chen who knew about the Fog. He wouldn't ask the basic questions Sam Riverson was asking. In addition, they had been using the help of the police and Ingis Chen wouldn't, or so I believed. My brain was working overtime, I struggled to keep up.

'So, Yoko. Let's start again,' Sam sat back down. 'We know Jazz Jones is a good friend of yours. We haven't worked out what brought the other one, Nick Baker, to that house, but maybe you will be able to enlighten us?'

'Sam, you don't mind if I call you Sam, do you? What makes you think I have to give you an explanation for anything?'

'Let's summarise,' Mysterious Sam continued with an obvious effort to contain himself. 'Four people are living in a house, on a lot with seven other houses and a front private parking lot. One day the house is covered by a strange fog. Within two weeks, the area is closed off, the house is walled, the whole site changes ownership to an unknown, untraceable holding company; the four residents of the fog covered house move next door into two houses knocked into one, which is not within their financial means, but somehow it happens. Jazz Jones, stuck in the fog house, sells her place remotely. Next, documents on the fog disappear from the fire station administration, both the paper copies and on the server. The local council mysteriously approves some unacceptable building work in record time and emails which no one recalls typing are found in the database. The security system surrounding the terraced houses is now reminiscent of the White House. Helicopters seem to land at will on their roofs, although there is no record of flying route and authorisation. And finally, your smartphone or tablet and online communications are impenetrable, which is most unusual for a normal person.' Sam raised his head from the file he was reading from and added, 'I will discount your sudden change of job. Apart from the fact it adds to the list of sudden occurrences, it is nothing unusual in itself, except that again we can't trace the holding company behind your current employer. So? Don't you think we'd be curious about what's going on?'

'Well, presented like that, it's hard to deny that there's been a lot going on around the houses that's out of the ordinary.'

'Thank you. I appreciate your honesty at last. Now, talk.'

'Why? Who is the "we" you include yourself in?'

To gain time, ask questions, that was my tactic. To gain time and to avoid answering.

'Yoko, my patience has limits.'

'From what you have summarised, you know we are not talking about trivial stuff. So why talk to anybody until I know who I am dealing with?'

Mysterious Sam reopened the folder and turned it towards me. He spread the documents out on the table. There was a mixture of email printouts, maps, photos, detailed information on Jazz and me, Zeno, Harry and Rico, and they were all headed with a crowned logo. Stamps with 'UK eyes only' and unknown department names were displayed on each of them. On one I read 'MI5'. I didn't have a chance to read anything, as Sam had only aimed to let me have a brief look and gathered the documents back into the folder and closed it.

'Satisfied?' asked Sam.

'I want to hear you say it.'

'Unbelievable. You really are a pain. Fine! You are dealing with the British Secret Service. You know, you're lucky I'm a nice guy, because I could use force on you to get information.'

I was totally out of my depth here. I could feel my little facade of bravado crumbling. I repeated inwardly, 'Keep cool. Keep cool. Keep cool. They can't touch you or they would have done so already. Be strong. Be strong!'

'I don't know how it all started and I can't explain most of it,' I began. 'The Fog phenomenon, for example, I can't explain it. No one can.'

'Tell me what you can explain.'

'Then will you tell me about the missing people?'

'Just talk!'

'I am warning you, this is a bit out there.'

The man took a deep breath and I decided to carry on talking before I wound him up even more.

'So, here goes. The fogged houses in London and Essex, they are passageways to what seems to be an alternative earth, or world.' Somehow, it was much more awkward to say this to a spy than to my parents. I continued, 'It seems the two worlds have the same topography and seasons, even if sometimes the weather differs. Same for the population.'

'What do you mean by "population"?'

'I mean there is almost nobody there.'

'Which means there are some inhabitants?'

'Yes. It is complicated. There doesn't seem to be a real indigenous population. The ones there, they are descendants of the Relocated.'

'The Relocated?'

'The ones who, once they have crossed through the doors, cannot come back.'

'I see. And you said the people living there are "descendants" so that means passageways have opened before.'

'Yes.'

'When?'

'Every 231 years.'

'Are you kidding me?'

'No. The last opening was in 1782.'

'How do you know all of this?'

'They already spoke English in 1782, you know. All we had to do is ask.'

'Sarcasm again?'

'Shall I continue?'

I took his silence and stare for a yes, and went ahead.

'OK, so let me guess. One person got into the Essex house, crossing the Fog as he or she did so. When that person decided to leave the house and crossed through the Fog, he or she ended up in a forest, an old-fashioned forest, with lovely little birds and red squirrels, with boars and wolves and foxes and bears. That poor person got a bit of a shock and quickly ran back inside, where they may or may not have had a cup of tea or a straight Jack Daniels, depending on what was to hand. Then that person tried to go out again, but faced the same forest. Now it was the Jack Daniels for sure. How long it took for that person to contact someone I cannot say, but it soon became obvious his or her mobile, or the internet in the house, or even the landline, was working. So was the television. That was reassuring. Unfortunately for them, it was difficult to get anyone to believe their story, wasn't it? Finally someone did. Maybe someone who tried to pull him or her out? And soon you came into play. Anyway, for your information: been there, done that.'

'So that happened to you too?'

'Yes.'

'You said 'fogged' house. Not 'fog' house.'

'So?'

'That is a subtle but important difference.' I shifted in my seat. Bugger. That was a mistake on my part. He continued, 'Fog house would refer to a house covered by fog. Fogged house means something or someone has covered it. Now, if you made the difference and your English is good enough to grasp it, I would say you know that something or someone is involved.'

'Shit. Shit, shit, shit, SHIT!' I screamed internally, all the while trying to keep a calm open face. I had to diffuse that bomb and the best I could think of was to divert the question.

'The house was not originally surrounded by Fog. It has been fogged. I cannot explain why it happened. I can't explain the Fog phenomenon, I told you, but I do believe there is something behind it all.'

'Please don't tell me you see it as a miracle of God.'

'Cynical?'

'Sceptical.'

'Pity. That would be the nicest and the easiest explanation.'

'What is yours?'

'No idea. There is a plethora of options: this planet is going towards the apocalypse and that Other World is our Noah's Ark. Or some scientist somewhere did an experiment that went pretty wrong. Or I am the victim of hidden camera jokes. Or I am dreaming?'

'Wait! If you experienced the 'relocation' to the forest, how come you are here with me now, not there?'

'I have super powers.'

'Listen, I am tired. You had some sleep, I didn't. So please don't test my patience anymore, it is at its limit!'

'I mean it though. I have some kind of powers. If I am crossing the Fog with certain people, I actually can come back,' I sighed.

There was no way around it, I would have to reveal more. The good news was that between Foggies we had discussed the eventuality of having to explain the basics, reluctantly or not. I also kept telling myself the secret services were supposedly not my enemies. Maybe on the contrary it was about time we discussed things with them. So I would give them the 'agreed' debrief on the Fog. First, how we discovered the Fog, how we discovered from the local WII there was a way for a select few to come back and the 'categories' of Foggies. I continued on how we got the support of a financier as part of a business deal. Between Foggies, we were to remain vague on the details. In no circumstances were we to discuss other locations, other Foggies, the Society and Leila. We should never fully unlock the FTab either.

'Earth to Yoko?' Sam shook me out of my thoughts.

'Sorry. I was remembering how it all started.'

'Yes, well, remember aloud. So you were saying you can come back if you travel with certain people. You are referring to the 'Crossers' aren't you?'

I frowned.

'Yes, I know,' he said, reacting to my frown. 'You see, among the persons we encountered last night was Jack. Now Jack is not in good mental shape, is he? He is a nice guy, but he is scared and scared people talk, especially to a nice government like us, an ally of the US. We learned a lot from him. The only issue is that he is pretty dazed and not very thorough in his answers. We were hoping you'd give us a better insight.'

'You have been playing with me then.'

'That's called interrogation, Yoko.'

'If you already have the information you wanted and I can't help you with more, can I go now?'

'Very funny. Now tell me more about the Switchers, the Crossers and the Facilitators. I understand Jack and you are Switchers. Zenone Grande, Leonardo Lumbrosi and Dante Bopani are Crossers, and Harry Baxton and Enrico Scelti are Facilitators. Seven people with 'special powers': one English, one American, one French/Italian/Japanese, four Italians. Pretty unbalanced. One woman, six men, including a gay one. Still unbalanced. Ethnic origins? Again, no balance. We tried to find a common thread, to understand why you were picked, but we couldn't come up with anything. We also want to know more about the help you have, how you got all the funds and fast-tracked getting the houses, and the work done, and the technology for security. Jack was very vague about them, just saying – there Sam took his notes and read from them – 'they appeared one day and offered help and they know a shitload about stuff and they are geniuses with computers. He said maybe they are Chinese mafia, or Russian, he is not sure and didn't really want to know.'

I smiled, thinking, 'Good man. He played dumb. He may be down and bluesy, but he got his lines right, the Jackny boy.'

'Why are you smiling?' Sam said, hands clasped, elbows on the table, and leaning forward in a mildly aggressive way.

'Because you seem to be as much in the fog as we are.'

'Tell me more about this Chinese guy, Ingis Chen.'

'So you know his name?'

'Jack didn't remember, but someone else did.'

'Did you try googling him?'

'We can do a little better than Google in the services. OK, between you and me, I did google him too. Big fish in his sector. He wasn't on our radar for anything until now. What I want to know is what is his involvement with you?'

'You know, I just realised, maybe now is the time I should ask to talk to my lawyer?'

'We are treating you as a terrorist and a threat to national security. Your rights are dismissed.'

'You know I am not a terrorist!'

'I don't know anything. We don't have a clue who you are, except that your super power is to "switch" those "gates".'

'Let's make a deal. If you get me some food, I'll tell you about our Fog household. Just bread and butter will do, with tea, please. And cookies. Actually, cookies first, tea second, the rest I am flexible.'

'I think it's easier to deal with terrorists. They are "bad guys", we give them hell, plain and simple. You ...' Sam sighed.

'I am easy. Just feed me.'

Sam rolled his eyes, slammed both his hands on the table and pushed himself up, shoving the chair back as he did so. He left me in that room alone for a few minutes and came back with tea and a pack of double chocolate cookies. Food at last! Now we were getting somewhere.

I was in the mood for cookie tea dipping, and enjoyed sipping, dipping and eating for a couple of minutes. Sam was drumming his fingers on the table. So the rules were to be decent with us.

'Well, you're not on a diet,' a colleague of Sam's said, who had remained in the room. He looked like a fop. Exactly the kind of player I would run away from in any bar.

'I'm hungry.'

'I have met some women who say they are hungry, eat half an apple, say they are full and keep the other half for dinner.'

'Why do you complain? That's a cheap date.'

'Most of the time they drink like fishes and usually champagne.'

'And you hang out with them because ...?'

'They are pretty to look at.'

'And I bet their conversation is fascinating as well?'

'No idea. They talk a lot but I can't be bothered to listen. I focus on my next move.'

Sam interrupted, 'Shall we get cracking on this story of yours?'

'First, are my friends and everyone alright?'

'Sure, they are all happy and cheery in their rooms.'

'Want me to eat more cookies very slowly?'

'Your housemates are all here and one by one are being interrogated. The guys that were on site for security are here too, and are staying mute. They are pro, most with army background. Their records are clear. Back on the lot, your friend Jazz is acting the damsel in distress who has no clue what is going on. Nick Baker is blaming morphine – what happened to him anyway? – for not being able to talk. The other Italian guys, also with rooms in our little B and B here, seem to have forgotten most of their English. I told you, everyone is here, apart from Jazz Jones and Nick Baker. Happy now?'

Now I had to talk and did so, speaking slowly to give me time to think twice before saying anything.

I told him about that Sunday when we woke up in the Fog for the first time, about how we discovered the differences between us and how we were affected by the Fog. I replaced the name of Leila with the name Ingis Chen for the mysterious contact and the answers we received. Sam had more questions, but I told him to let me tell my story first and he could ask for details afterwards. I explained about the accidental relocation and lack of control of the Fog effect on people. I continued talking, briefly detailing the encounters in Lil'London, Newtonsee and Yerushaleim. I related to him how we had established a positive contact with the locals and were now working together for their benefit and ours, with a large place to the Relocated. I went on about my role as an 'ambassador' dealing with the diplomatic sides of things, including the administration that went with the Relocated's role as consultants. Zeno was the commercial consultant, Dante the architect, and Leo was the project manager for both Zeno and Dante.

'What about Jack? He didn't mention any role.'

'Maybe he is still working it out and we are leaving him the room to do so.'

I talked for a long time. The cookies and the tea had helped give me some strength and revived my spirits. At half a pack I had push them away. Now I was eyeing the rest with interest, even though I would rather have proper food. I also needed to stretch my legs and was desperate for the bathroom. I said it all to Sam who called out for someone to accompany me to the ladies' room (which was also the gents' room) and then back to my room. Someone brought me a soup, a couple of slices of bread, some cheese, a small apple, and a sticky toffee pudding. Nothing exciting, but it was food.

It was a good time to think and my focus was on Simba and my FTab. I was very worried about my wolf, but I didn't want to make too big a deal of it. The last thing I wanted was to attract attention to her. On the FTab, I was surprised Sam hadn't mentioned it more than in passing and more generally referred to our technology. I was under no illusion questions were bound to be asked about it soon. My hope was that we would be able to get away with hiding the true interest of the FTab, its double identity, which had been reinforced after the Ushi Tsou episode. As with a laptop which has a guest user and a locked user, the FTab had a general use, activated with a standard pin code. For mine, it then gave access to the good old Google account, with its emails and Outlook and my good old Facebook. But if you entered an alternative password, you then had to authenticate the device with iris recognition via the front camera, combined with thumb prints on the back camera. It had been strongly upgraded with top notch personal security, but so worth it in the circumstances!

The thought cheered me up. We were ready, we had our stories worked out, our technology could face the challenge, and we had a link to the Fog that made us unique. Our so-called super powers could be turned into an asset. I just didn't want them to mess with my wolf and yet couldn't say a damn thing.

'What about the other Relocated out there? Who else is there aside from Jazz Jones, Nick Baker and, just a wild guess, James Fisher, the Westminster Council employee?'

'That is difficult for me to answer. I want to respect their privacy, you see. They have family here still and most of the families don't know.'

'Names, Yoko.'

'It isn't fair!'

'Yoko ...'

So I told them about the rest of the Fisher family. I didn't talk about Big Tom or Ushi Tsou. Ushi Tsou for obvious reasons: the less I said about her, the fewer questions would be asked about Ingis Chen's first involvement with us. She was probably not registered as missing anyway. Big Tom had asked that should anyone enquire about him we shouldn't say a thing. So normally no one would talk, but if anyone slipped up then Sam would know we were withholding information and had worked out what to disclose in advance. He probably already suspected, but it was unproven.

'What about Nick Baker? How did he get in there?'

'Personal security and he just happened to be transferred to the other side.'

'Personal security provided by Ingis Chen?'

'Who else? You think we have much choice?'

'Us. We should have been your first choice.'

'Considering you are the ones detaining and interrogating us, when the alternative was a brand new home, brand new responsibilities and our own independent lives, our choice seems to have been a good one.'

'Tell me more about Ingis Chen.'

'Again? I told you, I don't know much about him. He isn't a friend or anything. More like a business partner, really.'

Sam sighed. He took a bit of a break and reviewed his notes.

'What of Nick Baker's wound? How did it happen?'

'An unfortunate incident. With a knife. Nothing worth mentioning.'

To write that my interrogator was unimpressed was an understatement. It was obvious despite his blank, non-expressive face.

'I can't believe you would be so lacking in curiosity about it all. All of you. You remind me of ostriches, not looking further than finding little holes to hide their heads in.'

'And so what?'

'So what? This is either pathetic, or you have cooked up your story together nicely.'

'Whatever. You are not in our shoes and you don't know what a relief it was to have someone with answers and to have help to get back on our feet to build some kind of a life. Both ways: no fuss, no questions asked. Life is so much simpler now, lived on a need-to-know basis.'

Sam's pen was tapping nervously on the table besides his folder. He pursed his lips and looked down at his notes again.

'What about the helicopter?'

'We were trying to get one to pass through to the Other World for faster transport over there.'

'Flown by whom?'

'Nick has basic flying knowledge,' I answered, knowing very well that his experience was limited to planes, but Sam Riverson didn't ask me for the specifics.

'What about the Essex house?'

'What about it?'

'Why was it turned?'

'I wasn't there.'

'My understanding is that Chen wanted to open another fogged house with Jack. That was all I needed to know.' I smiled naively at him or as naively as I could.

The spy looked up to the ceiling, murmuring, 'Why me?'

He slammed shut his folder, stood up, and knocked three times at the door which then opened. While doing so, he said to me, 'Right. I have had enough. You are the most frustrating cooperative person I have ever interrogated.'

One of my guards came into the room and indicated that I should follow him.

'One last question before I leave?' I asked.

Sam looked resigned as he breathed out a barely audible 'shoot'. He was back at the table and looking down at his folder, either preparing for the next interview, or checking for the inconsistencies in my stories.

'My dog?'

'She is fine. Now leave.'

I was taken back to my cubicle with its bed. The discussion about Chen was a sensitive one: it was the weak point in our story, not just because it was not true, but also for the importance it gave him. The role of Ingis Chen in today's narrative raised him to being a key figure in the Fog story. We would need his official cover from now on. Then his weight in relation to the Fog and Foggies, and on the political and strategic platforms, would increase. However, his position with us was not secure enough for him to take the risk of alienating us by abusing his new role. His leverage was limited. We would have to make sure it stayed so.

I was tired. Very tired. I lay down on my bed and I knew I would fall asleep fast. I had no idea what time or day it was.

I wished to know more about what had happen in the Essex house after the shoot-outs, also when and why the Security Service got involved. I was hoping to ask Sam about it later, but didn't get a chance to. No one came to see me again, except to bring dinner. I was still sleeping when the man showed up with the tray of bland food. At least they added a mini-bottle of wine, the in-flight size one. It wasn't great, but it made the food go down less tastelessly.

**Day 6 (Friday)**

I woke up with a start. I had no idea what the exact time was, but clearly it was breakfast time. I knew for two reasons: first, I was hungry, second, what woke me up was someone entering with a breakfast tray. Full English breakfast, with sausages, bacon, baked beans, toast, scrambled eggs, mushrooms and tomatoes. Not my favourite being French, but I wasn't going to be fussy. I could do with a proper meal: who knew what the day ahead would hold? While I was eating, Sam entered. He just stood there looking down at me, his face unreadable. I couldn't work this man out, he was acting both nice and distant at the same time. I even tried the karma thing, thinking maybe his vibes would help give me more of an idea about him. Nothing. My instinct was drawing a blank. Maybe spies have karma control training? In any case, it was frustrating.

'Slept well?'

'I've had better.'

'I will wait outside for you to finish, then it is time for a little talk.'

Minutes later, Mysterious Sam came back and led me to the interrogation room.

'So, Yoko, interesting device you got there,' Sam said, setting an FTab on the table.

'How do you know it's mine?'

'Fingerprints. Also, your mother rang.'

'How is she?'

'She sounded a bit stressed when I answered.'

'Did you have a nice chat?'

'She wasn't very loquacious. She insulted me in Japanese.'

'You surprise me. My mother does not use bad language.'

'She made an exception for me. Does she know about you being a Switcher?'

'Yes, vaguely.'

'Everything is vague with you. Now, if would you be so kind as to log me into your phone.'

After prevaricating to avoid him being suspicious if giving in too quickly, I reluctantly told him the general pin code, grateful for the wonders of the Society technology.

For several minutes, Sam browsed my phone content. It contained the remnants of my previous life, transferred from my old phone. There were all my social contacts and friends, the odd picture and some messages and emails, not one mentioning the Fog, evidently. The Foggies outside London, Leo and Dante and the newly met Relocated were not in there.

Sam told me they had been trying to get into the phones but their attempts were halted by their technology team who had found the self-destruct virus which meant that the risk of destroying any relevant content was too great.

'You have a secret file somewhere, don't you?' Sam asked, not lifting his head from the device.

'It wouldn't be a secret if I were to acquiesce, would it?'

Sam didn't react. He didn't even look up from the FTab. Instead he asked another question.

'I want to talk to Ingis Chen.'

'Feel free.'

'Where is he now?'

'No idea. I am not his PA.'

'Telephone number?'

'Don't know it by heart and you have my phone.'

'There is no "Chen" in your address book and you know that.'

'Well, you can call it a precautionary measure linked to my awareness of the government's Big Brother attitude. I made sure not to keep what I wouldn't want to be found. We were taught a few tricks to protect ourselves from technology and digital betrayal, both here and in Woodfellas.'

Sam shook his head. 'I can't believe you called the place Woodfellas.'

'Why not?'

'It's ridiculous.'

'Why?'

'Because.'

'You can't even come up with a good reason why it's ridiculous.'

'I can't believe how annoying you are.'

'If by annoying you mean I hold my ground and may even have a point, then thank you.'

Sam looked up at the ceiling, whispering 'Why me?' and burst out laughing. He handed the phone to me with a nod indicating to call. Well, no could do, I would have to log into the secret FTab as I didn't know Ingis's number by heart. That wasn't going to happen.

'I mean it. I don't know it by heart. The card is somewhere at home. There was a time, long long ago, when I remembered telephone numbers. That was before mobiles.'

It was true the card was still at home, hidden and taped on the inside of one of my chick lit books. I desperately needed to talk to Ingis Chen before Sam and his guys did, because there was a major flaw in the Foggies plan. We had all agreed what to say and Ingis Chen had consented to be our official cover, but unfortunately we had not briefed him on the details yet. I had waited to have a proper meeting with him for this, which I now understood had been a mistake.

'Let's put Chen aside for now. Jack, Leo, Dante, they were in Italy.'

'Yes.'

'So that means there could be others like you lot out there.'

I responded noncommittally, hunching my shoulders and saying, 'I presume.'

'Maybe Ingis Chen supports the others as well?'

'You'll have to ask him.'

'We will, when we get his direct number from you or when his assistants finally let us through on the general one.'

'Keep your expectations low. Like us, he doesn't have all the answers. No one does.'

'So the man has his limits too. Good to know. By the way, where is he now that you need him most?'

Another rhetorical question. I remained silent.

'Right. Then I guess that will be it then. I'll order a search of your house for Chen's card as you don't seem keen to tell me where it is. My apologies for the mess. It would be so much easier if you'll just fully cooperate. Anyway, I'll bring your phone to the team. Now that it is open, we'll break into it and find out what you are hiding,' Sam said, bringing the interview to an end.

'A good thing I didn't keep naked pictures of me in it then.'

Sam smiled slightly, a real one, with the corner of his eyes turning upwards. I wasn't. The FTab might have a tough time ahead of it.

After this relatively short visit to the interrogation room, one of Sam's fellow spy colleagues led me back to my boring cubicle. I slept some more, which astounded me. How much sleep can one person have in one day? In such a stressful situation too?

I was not impressed when Sam showed up again in what could have been late afternoon. Not that I wanted to be alone, far from it. This room was dreadful and when awake there was nothing to do but think. Too much thinking didn't help my spirits. Nevertheless, I wasn't delighted to see him because I feared more digging for information and details I didn't want to give. I was tired of parrying his questions and not confident I could keep my story straight for long. So it was a nice surprise when Sam just sat on my bed and suggested we have a little chat, a more informal one.

Sam told me the story of the fogged house in Essex. It wasn't far from what I had guessed the previous day and it amazed me how people were connected. When the Society left the Essex house, following the shooting between them and Ingis Chen's team, the police went in. What was bound to happen, happened: one of the policemen who went to the house didn't make it back out to his original world, but was relocated to WII. The reason why it wasn't spotted by the Society's monitoring of mobile communications was because he didn't take out his mobile to contact his colleagues, he used police radio. Because it was dark and because it was in Essex and not London, he thought at first he may have inadvertently gone through the back of the house walking out into a garden with many trees. The mind always tries to rationalise, to find logical explanations when faced with the bizarre. He decided to check if someone was hiding in there. Going back over his tracks, he couldn't see the house again, it being under the Fog in the dark of the night. He finally made it inside and the place was empty. He felt something was amiss. Finally, he used his radio. Luckily for him, the one person who had remained was his partner. If anyone would have believed him, she would. She knew him well. She went back to the house, met him, went to the back and noticed there was no garden. When they tried to go to their car, after several attempts with him not showing up, she tried to pull him out herself and felt the electricity separating them. Most people would be incredulous and she knew it. She decided she ought to know more before raising the alarm or putting any of this in her report. The only person she mentioned her partner's situation to was his sister, also a good friend of hers. She visited Kim in person, hoping to be more convincing face to face. This, again, left no phone trail for the Society to pick up. Kimberley Epson was in her late twenties, her partner, Edward or Ed Epson in his early thirties. They were very close siblings and still went to visit their parents back in Nottingham once a month. Kim could not hear about her brother's odd situation and resist going to see him for herself. Doing so, she was relocated herself. She was the link to Sam Riverson.

Kim was working as restaurant manager in one of the trendiest and poshest venues in Central London, Mayfair to be exact, where she had met a friendly yet mysterious photographer, Sam. When telling me the course of events that brought him into the story, Sam said the place was his local. A posh Mayfair venue is also a classic pick-up place and as I raised an eyebrow, glancing from him to his peacock colleague and back to him, he added that no, he was not like his colleague and no, he had not tried it on with Kim. 'We just became friendly as I was there so often. She is a gorgeous woman, but too insecure, too keen on men and drinking and too easy to seduce. She has a good heart though.'

However, once before, she had bumped into him in the street by day. It was her personality to be very friendly (some would say over friendly) and she immediately hugged him, as she did to everyone she knew and liked. He was carrying his gun and she felt it. She didn't say anything, but both of them knew that a professional photographer is not supposed to carry a gun in town. Kim also thought that he was a good guy and her instinct told her he was on the right side of the law. She didn't ask any questions, but when she was stranded in the fogged house, she remembered him and convinced her brother to make contact, hoping for a discreet investigation before appearing to be fools in front of the police. She could not have picked a better person to reach out to. She called one of her colleagues in the restaurant to have a message passed on to him. He came, listened, checked he couldn't get them out and started investigating. He had an inquisitive mind and he knew he was onto something big. Was Kim aware she could have sent him to the other side too? She must have realised it was a possibility, but she might also have thought the relocation was linked to her family. There again, she didn't know it was a relocation. Sam used his work connections to dig around for news of unusual events and fogs in the United Kingdom. He studied in detail any information on the Indonesia and Mexico cases too. Then by chance he came across a new application from Fireman Deepak to obtain the fog analysis results for our house. You see, Fireman Deepak didn't like not being able to close a file. He was a bit of a maniac. The case of our house being covered in an unexplained fog was still nagging him. When he had gone to review the file, he was perplexed to find that it had gone missing. So much so, he had written to get back another copy. Sam met Fireman Deepak, heard his story, talked to the other firemen who showed a lesser interest in it all but confirmed what had happened. The photographer spy knew he had a new lead. Things accelerated from there. Sam switched his focus to our house and the sudden recent changes of the whole terraced houses, unconventionally fast. Once we and the house were on his radar, he built up a case. He must have done a good job, as despite the oddity of his report he got his bosses' interest and they decided that it was time for action.

In that room cell, I listened to how I found myself on that bed.

'Well. That's quite a story. Thank you for enlightening me.'

'Glad you enjoyed it.'

'You couldn't tell me in the other room? Not in line with your interrogation is it?'

'No. it isn't. We are supposed to ask questions and get information, not tell little stories.'

'So, why did you decide to tell me?'

'I couldn't find any proper reasons – apart from the code of practice – not to. And I want you to understand, Yoko, that we are not against you. I don't think you are the enemy here, so really, we stand more chance of getting somewhere if we treat you with a bit of respect.'

'Thanks. It's appreciated.'

'How do you say it in French ...? "Donnant-donnant", isn't it?'

'Yes. "A given for a given" although in English it's "give and take".'

Was it a new strategy, a different approach to make us open up more? I believed he meant it, but also that the FTab was holding onto its secrets. I didn't know how. It must be obvious to their technical team that a large chunk of the device's memory was in use and not by the general access they could see. I didn't know how the FTab resisted their technical experts, but I was glad of it.

'When can I see the others? When can we go home?' I switched subject.

'Not yet.'

'What day and time is it?'

'Friday evening.'

I had to be back home by Saturday evening. Sam knew Saturday nights were switching nights, Jack had told him. I was concerned they would try to keep us over so that they would have their own passageway. Worse, Jack and I would be in the same location overnight. And then one of us wouldn't wake up.

'Can I see the others at least?'

'Not today. A meal will be brought out to you later.'

He stood up and exchanged a few words with a man who was standing beside the door. Sam picked something up and came back, holding a book.

'I brought you this.' He held it out for me.

'Oh! PJ Woodhouse?'

'I think you need something light to read.'

'I'm not sure even PJ Woodhouse could make me laugh here.'

'No one can resist Bertie Wooster and Jeeves.'

'We'll see.'

Sam turned to leave but stopped at the door, holding it half open, and turned to ask me one last thing, 'By the way, you never told me your dog's breed.'

I hesitated. Jack or someone else may have revealed Simba was a wolf cub. If they knew, they would also be aware she was special, having crossed to this world. I wasn't going to take the risk and decided to bluff hoping everyone had kept their mouth shut.

'She is a malamute.'

'A malamute?'

'Big dog breed. Similar to wolves. Where is she?'

'Like a wolf. That explains it … She's with me. Jazz wanted to look after her, but I thought she'd need walks and fresh air and Jazz couldn't take her to the park, so … Good night, Yoko.'

'Good night. Thank you for taking care of Simba, Sam. She matters a lot to me.'

'My pleasure.'

As he closed the door and I heard the locks turning, I couldn't breathe. I prayed Sam was really looking after Simba out of kindness and didn't doubt me.

'Please, don't test her. Please let her be. Please, please, please,' I implored silently.

**Day 7 (Saturday)**

'What? What?' my voice cracked.

My heart was pounding, my eyes struggled to open and my head refused to compute where I was and what was happening. A woman had burst in my room and ordered me to get dressed. We were leaving in five minutes, she said. Her face was familiar. Slowly, I remembered she was working with Sam Riverson. She had accompanied me to my room once before. It took me a couple of minutes to put my clothes on in my spaced-out state. She returned soon and was standing by the door waiting impatiently for me to get my act together. I had no notion of the time of the day, not having seen daylight since being put in that room, but considering my struggle to wake up, I presumed it was the early hours of the morning. As I crossed the threshold, she handed me a dark fabric bag and indicated I should put it on my head. Once I had done as she asked, she placed a headset on top and loud music blasted in my ears. I asked if she could turn it down and couldn't hear a reply. As the volume wasn't lowered, I assumed the answer was no. It was the Beatles. It could have been worse.

Someone, most likely the same woman, led me to a vehicle. You might not be able to hear or see, but your body recognises much more than you are conscious of when you rely on sight and hearing alone. My walk felt different on the tarmac. The step to get in a van is different from stairs or the one to get into smaller cars. The seat arrangements are different. When inside the vehicle, the headset was pulled off and Sam talked to me.

'I've got news for you.'

'Somehow I guessed something was up.'

'You are going back home.'

'Really?' I wanted to believe him, hope was bubbling inside me, but I feared a trap.

'Don't get too excited, you are not fully free.'

'No kidding. I have a bag on my head.'

'We don't want you to know our current location.'

'So, are we all going back?' I still waited for the downside.

'Yes. We decided that we don't know enough about this Fog of yours to open a new location. We don't know either how the locals would react in what you are saying is another world.' I could hear a slight sniggering at the mention of the Other World. 'So we decided that we were going to move you all back to your lot. According to Jack, you have a "Fog dependency" and we don't want you to go into withdrawal.'

'When back home, what's next? Back to our comfortable little lives?'

'Yes and no.'

I bit my tongue to stop a sarcastic comment and waited for further details. He continued, 'We are taking over your security system, your data control room and your entrance/exit controls. In short, we are taking over Chen's protection and surveillance, and we are adding monitoring inside your walls as well. Plus, we are placing our men on site.'

'Jeez. Thank you for the trust.'

'You are still getting a good deal! You are withholding information and we have to find out the details. If indeed this Fog is real and that Other World exists, you really think you can keep it hidden and under control for long? Not only that, could you be that selfish?'

He might have had a point, but I wouldn't concede it out loud. Mostly, I was focusing on the meaning of being under their surveillance inside and out: freedom was relative already, but we could find a way to keep our independence. There was an issue with cameras checking my coming and going.

'What about Simba, will I get her back now?'

'Of course, she is your dog.'

'Thank you.'

'I don't think she took to me.'

'Simba doesn't accept anyone but me.'

'She destroyed my home.'

'Ah … She is young.'

'She even managed to break into the fridge. It seems she turned over a chair, pushed it next to the fridge, climbed up and opened the door.'

'Mmm … She is very clever.'

'You can say that again.'

'Let me know the damage. I'll cover the costs.' I had my pride and don't like debts.

'I'll put it on expenses.'

'Your bosses will accept that? You surprise me.'

'I think they are already pretty surprised by the whole Fog case, so a bit more won't make much difference …'

After my short chat with Sam, the headphones were put back on. The sun was only just rising when headphones and hessian sack were lifted from my head. I was back on the old parking area of the houses, with my old housemates, Jack and the Italians. Jack was very emotional, crying and apologising for having talked at all.

'Thank God you are all here. What a nightmare! They put me in that room and they were trying to make me talk and I …' he started. Harry interrupted him.

'Don't worry Jack,' Harry said. 'Let's not talk about it now. We are not alone.'

We all hugged each other as if we hadn't seen each other for months. Except Leo. Leo grabbed me by the waist, pulled me to him and kissed me passionately, taking my breath away. My first reaction was surprise, the second was pleasure. In that instant, I forgot where I was, who was around and my resolution to keep intimate relationships at a distance. When we broke free, Leo held me close a bit longer, just enough time to whisper in my ear that I hadn't left his thoughts and he liked me too much to play games. My knees were shaking. I was not a very public person when it came to displays of affection, so was grateful for the arrival of another van that created a diversion. Six men got out, their heads covered like ours had been. They were the Society's security who had been picked up at the same time we had. None of them was Phil, he had been home with his family that night. They nodded at us, we nodded at them and they walked out of the parking lot.

'They are free to go?' I asked Sam, my eyes still on the group departing.

'Yes. We can't keep them, but we'll keep an eye on them. The company you are working for has legal contracts with them and they argued they were just doing their jobs. They are pros, they don't talk. Well, they would with the right type of pressure, one not advised at this stage. Hopefully it won't be necessary.'

'Is it why we are back too? You can't actually get a good grip on us, something that holds the road properly?'

'The discovery of a parallel, or alternative world, or new planet, or whatever you call this WII, would be grounds enough. You are here so that we can work out the truth behind your theories.'

'You need us so you are being nice to us. What about afterwards?' Harry cut in.

Sam ignored the question. 'Let's go inside. Yoko, I have brought back the destructive Simba and will bear no responsibility for the state of your house.'

'First, I want to check on Jazz and Nick.'

I didn't give him or anyone else time to disagree and started towards my former home. I saw some of the British intelligence agents begin to move towards me, but they stopped after a glance in Sam's direction. I turned and said to Rico and Harry, 'Could one of you come and get me in five minutes? Thank you.' They both nodded.

Looking around as I walked in, it was strange that nothing had changed in our two days absence and yet the situation had shifted in power.

As I stepped into the Fog, an agent appeared by my side. It had not been my intention to 'escape' to World II but if it had been he was to stop me.

'So, Nameless Agent, you are braving the Fog, are you?' I enquired.

'Been there, done that. I am a policeman in Essex. I have been assigned to this team temporarily.' He stayed behind at the bottom of the stairs as I tiptoed to the first floor. I gave Jazz's door a gentle knock and pushed it open. I heard a shriek, the light went on, and I saw a dishevelled scary looking angry woman sitting up in bed, holding with both hands what looked like a samurai sword. She blinked at me several times before recognition kicked in and then Jazz dropped the sword and rushed towards me, hugging me tight and talking so fast I only heard the first sentence and the rest was blocked out.

'Yes, Jazz. We're back. Are you OK? Have they treated you well? What happened here? Where did you get this monstrous sword!'

'Oh! Yoko! You're here! This little thing... a loan from Lil'London. Gosh! I have so much to tell you!'

'I am sure. Just not now. It's just a brief visit to let you know we are back. They are all waiting for me, including the ones who took us, namely, the British Secret Service.'

'No friggin' way! So Nick was right!'

'He knew?'

'He guessed right away. Apparently they were pros, but playing too much by the book to be mercenaries or private.'

'So he isn't worried?'

'He is worried sick, mostly for your safety and sometimes he remembers the others as well.'

I went to Nick's room and opened the door an inch. He was still sleeping, unmoved by Jazz's shrieks and our babbling. I closed the door and returned to Jazz, wanting to know about the Relocated. They were all fine. They had stayed away from the house since Sam's team visited – one of his agents was there all the time. Nick had thrown them a written message attached to some books to warn them.

'Those guys control all the surveillance. I bet they're listening to us right now. Bastards!'

'Have you been in touch with our wise woman?' I hoped she would understand my reference to Leila. She did.

'Yes. I used our little super-device. Is it still safe?'

'I think so. Thanks to the updates after the Tsou Bitch events.'

I heard the door downstairs slam and Rico calling me. It was my clue to leave and I made for the door.

'OK, time to leave.' I kissed Jazz goodbye. 'Let's go for a walk when I come back.'

'Yes. Come back as soon as possible. We need to talk. Oh! And Yoko, what about Simba?'

'I'm going to see her now. Our walk will include her!' I beamed a smile at her.

'Come back soon! We really need to talk!' She looked worried.

As I left the smile disappeared. I would have to be extra careful with Simba to hide the fact that she could travel to both worlds. For the moment there was no communication from the Relocated to the spooks, so it should be fine, but after?

'Stop!' I told myself off. 'You can't do anything about it now. Keep your head clear. Deal with what you have to now.'

As the three of us came out – Rico, the agent/policeman and me –, the old gang and Mysterious Sam were nowhere in sight. They were already in the house. The agents, these men and women with new and expressionless faces, were on each corner of the lot and by the entrance gate. I hated them. It felt as if the haven of home had been tainted.

I swallowed my anger and went inside.

The house was in perfect order. The secret service team had certainly fully searched and wired the house inside and out, but you couldn't see a trace of where they'd been and their work. I could hear Sam in the dining room talking to the Foggies. Rico went directly to the kitchen to prepare coffee.

'So solar energy is in place, mobiles work in the vicinity of the Fog, and we know from the radio control in the 'fogged house' that you use radios to communicate at a wider range. Now, Ed and Kim have provided photos and video footage of their forest, but we didn't really know what we were dealing with then and didn't want to send them far.' Sam interrupted his speech when I entered the room.

He stood up and came towards me, putting his hand on my shoulder briefly before retrieving in a swift movement. Behind a general, slightly distant attitude, the man had moments of friendliness. There seemed to be warmth underneath, but he was repressing it, stifling it. I wondered if he really was a photographer and, if so, if he used photography to express what he buried inside. Or maybe it was part of the job, never to reveal himself. Pity.

'Thank you for coming back,' he said as we walked to the table where all the others were seated.

'I said it would take five minutes. You sent one of your goons with me anyway.'

'You could have disappeared in that Other World of yours and we would have lost you.'

'If I say I will be back, then I will be back.'

Sam nodded his head once. They had kept a chair for me at the front end of the table, but first I gave Simba a big cuddle and played with her. She had grown in only two days. She couldn't contain her happiness at seeing me and made a mess on the floor. I mopped it up while Sam carried on.

'So, here is what we want first: to meet the locals next door in the fogged house. We would also like to send drones.'

'You want, or you would like? Because, with one you demand, with the other you request,' Harry snapped.

'We request. We wish to have your cooperation. You know we cannot do anything without you in that … World II. Honestly, couldn't you come up with names other than "Foggies", "WII" and "Woodfellas"? It's painful even just saying them.'

'What's wrong with them?' This time it was Rico's turn to retort, joining us with coffee and, bless him, cookies and defrosted croissants. He was right. It was early morning, breakfast was in order.

'Difficult to take them seriously.' Sam looked mildly surprised as if he had to mention the obvious.

'And so what?' Rico slammed the plate and coffee pot on the table.

We were all in a foul mood with Sam and had good reason to be. The last two days had not been fun. Moreover, the food had been bland at best, disgusting at worst. That last point was unforgivable.

'We don't want to alienate the locals.' Sam switched back to his original point. 'The Mexico massacre is not something we want to repeat. You are in contact with them and you seem to have done things pretty well so far.'

'Thanks,' Zeno groaned.

Rico added in a very audible fake whisper, 'Smooth talker. Very smooth.'

'We also have a few unanswered questions,' Sam went on, unperturbed by Rico's words.

'Such as?' Harry's eyes had narrowed to two suspicious slits.

'The Fog, how it works, you. Tests must be done. It would help if you could participate too.'

'So we are going to be lab rats?' Harry hissed.

'The results might lead us to a better understanding of what is happening, which in turn could improve your situation. We could find a way to make all of you come and go as you wish, for example.'

'And what if you end up blocking us all in the Fog like Yoko?' Zeno exclaimed.

Sam stared at Zeno, then at each of the people around the table, before replying. 'Were you ever going to get in touch with the authorities? Do you have any idea of the risks linked to this Fog should it fall into the wrong hands.'

We kept silent, until I spoke with, of course, another question. 'So, does that mean you agree we are "good hands"?'

'Yoko, I think here they say we are "good eggs",' Dante corrected.

'Here I was thinking foreigners didn't have a good grasp of the English nuances. Now, let's start with your handheld tablets. As a token of our good faith, we are going to give them back to you.'

'Fantastic. I presume you have put all kind of trackers and listening devices on them?' I replied.

'What did you expect? Free reins? There is an amazing discovery on your doorstep, a surreal occurrence you have some unexplained links to. For weeks you hid it from the government and you ally yourself with a foreign entity whose purpose, methods and full identity are still unclear as far as we are concerned. You really thought all we would do is ask a few questions, give you a pat on the back on the way out and leave you be? Are you totally delusional?' Sam's voice had risen to a mixture of frustration and exasperation.

'Nope. Our heads are just a bit foggy,' Harry retaliated in a similar tone.

'Very funny. But seriously, we are trying to work with you here. Will you give us a break and just try to help us a little?'

Just then my FTab rang. I recognised my ringtone. Sam looked at the gym bag he had brought with him, opened it and dug out a plastic bag with a load of handheld tablets. He separated the one ringing, checked the label which had my name on it, and passed it to me. No name was displayed, just 'Undisclosed'. It meant the caller was a contact from the secret data of the FTab. I discreetly typed my secret code to be able to answer.

'Yoko speaking.'

'Yoko, Leila here.' I glanced at Sam. I couldn't be sure communications were still secure. I wasn't even sure there was anything left to secure anymore. Following the old adage 'better safe than sorry,' I opted for being cautious with Leila.

'Hi. I am afraid it isn't the best time to talk.'

'I know. I was informed of the latest events, being taken away, being back and being under new surveillance. First, are you OK?'

'Yes.'

'Good! Now, can I help?'

'I would love you to. I just don't know how yet.'

'For your information, communications with the FTab are still protected and private. We got notifications they were trying to do all kind of things on it. We were accessing the FTab at the same time. So what we did was let them place their little technology in and we bugged it so that we can turn it on and off when needs be, or divert it, or send edited or erroneous information. We bugged their bug. So right now we only let them hear your side, as they can anyway via the person who is with you. From our side, they will have an edited version.'

'Great! That's a relief!'

'Yoko, you are back home. I take it as a good sign. They might try to get control, but you have some good cards in your hand. They won't want to alienate you. If you need us, we'll be here.'

'I know.'

'Did you tell them about us?'

'No.'

'So you used the Ingis Chen storyline?'

'Yes. But ... I haven't had a chance to discuss it with the concerned.'

'I see. We might have an issue there.'

'Yes.'

'You know I can't contact him to let him know.'

'Yes. It's on my mind.'

'Shall I just send an email on your behalf telling him he is not to divulge any details on your connections with him until you talk to him?'

'Yes, thank you.'

'I wouldn't do it without your explicit permission.'

'Mmm ... OK then. But I want to hear it first.' It wasn't news we were under the Society's thumb when it came to technology and security and they could break into anything. It was a taste of what the Society had done to others for us, it was not that pleasant.

'I'll draft it and read it to you. It will also be in your drafts in case you can access your inbox later and handle the contact yourself.' Leila was using her soothing tone. She had noted my surly voice.

'Fine, thanks.'

'When we have managed to break into their surveillance system in and around the house, I'll let you know.'

That cheered me up somewhat and after saying our goodbyes, I hung up.

Sam looked at me. 'A bit early for a call, isn't it?'

'I am sure you will know soon enough thanks to your bug,' I grunted. He wouldn't, but he didn't know that yet.

'You guys, you make me laugh with your philosophy and talk of independence. I ...' Sam began.

'You laugh in your job?' Leo interrupted with a show of mock shock.

'And this Chen, do you really think you are free with him?' Sam continued. 'From the system in place when we came in, he clearly had access to all your communications and could see whatever happened in the terraced houses site. Not much freer than with us and more risky.'

'Except that he supports us, he doesn't control us. He is not telling us what to do or how to do it. He suggests, yet the power of decision remains with us. So, yes, we can compromise, we can set up some rules, we can do a lot of things with our "supporter". It is a proper partnership. You, or the state behind you, you will want to set the rules. The government always sets the rules with little compromise.'

'I am afraid, you are right. The state sets the rules. It has the interests of the nation, of the people in mind, not the interest of a few only. That is how it should be,' Sam concluded. He stood up, saying he had to go now and we could probably do with a few hours' sleep. It was 5 a.m., we had been awake for an hour or two, difficult to say without a watch. He left informing us he would be back mid-morning and would appreciate it if we didn't leave the house.

The boys and I just sat around the table, puffy eyed and pale. An unpleasant smell floated around us: we hadn't had a bath or shower for days now. I wanted to think the unpleasant smell was mostly from the men. We couldn't really speak, as we were being listened to, so we just sat there, looking at each other, trying to share our impressions and ideas by telepathy I supposed. It didn't work that well. At a loss on what to say, Rico picked what he thought to be a safe subject of conversation.

'So, now that you kissed Yoko openly, Leo, can we talk about your affair at last?' he asked.

'What affair?' Zeno and Harry exclaimed, immediately on the edge of their seats.

'No Rico, I didn't really intend to talk about it,' I sighed.

Harry opened his eyes wide and whispered, 'No! You mean that you two …? Oh my God! Is Leo your mysterious lover? But of course! That is why you said you connected online first!'

'Cazzo! How did we not notice?' Zeno continued.

'Listen guys, and you Leo, I am sorry, but it is too complicated. Look at what we have to deal with! It is just too much. It is not a good idea. Leo's kiss on seeing me was just a reaction of concern. We talked about it. He knows I am not ready. I don't want to add a relationship on top of everything right now, especially with another Foggy. No! So please let's not talk about it. Let's also make sure it doesn't go on the agenda of a FBM, shall we? It isn't something that would please a few of them, and that's another reason why this is not a good idea.' My tone was quite harsh from exhaustion. I saw the hurt on Leo's face, and I was sorry. However, I needed to be firm.

'But, Yoko, you ...' Harry began.

'I don't want to talk about it! It is not an easy decision.' I turned to Leo. 'I like you, you know I like you. It is just not possible right now. I can't. Please...'

Leo nodded. My eyes were brimming with tears, and I looked down at the table to hide them.

Silence settled in again. Then I thought that if we couldn't talk, we could write. If we hid the screens of the FTabs from the surrounding cameras, it would work. I grabbed mine and indicated to the others to fetch theirs. I stood up and got a large shawl and several jackets and coats for the men from the entrance hooks, using the shawl to cover myself and the tablet. The others around the table understood. Harry thanked me, but said he was going to bed and would fiddle with his tablet from there. He was right, we didn't need to all be in the living room, looking like big plotters on camera. Leo and Dante took the clue and opted to withdraw as well. They needed a room to sleep in. I offered my spare room to Jack on the first floor. Zeno and Rico played the Italian card and accommodated the Romans. In the end, nobody stayed downstairs and group instant messages gushed from all the bedrooms of the house.

First, I confirmed to everyone that our exchanges, as per my earlier chat with Leila, were protected except from the Society itself and each other. Furthermore, I confirmed I would be calling Ingis Chen next. His emails might not be safe from the British intelligence services. His line might be tapped too, so I would have to speak in code. Ingis hadn't made a fortune by being stupid, he would get it. Hopefully. We shared our thoughts and experiences on the last two days and felt confident none of us had disclosed more information than necessary, at least not consciously. Inadvertently, we could have let something slip, we were exhausted, and we couldn't remember every detail of every conversation. The one I was most worried about was Jack. His depression was blatant. In a private message he confessed he was feeling a bit down. That happened to him when he was stressed and overwhelmed. He was subject to bouts of anhedonia. I had never heard of 'anhedonia' so resorted to my usual solution, I googled the word. It turned out to be a type of mood distur-bance, the like of those commonly observed in many psychiatric disorders. It was not exactly a depression, but an inability to ex-perience pleasure from activities usually found enjoyable, with mood changes often resulting from stressful life events. It was no wonder Jack had had a prolonged anhedonia episode in the past weeks: the Fog appearance, two abductions, being in an un-known town far from family and friends ... Those were 'joie de vivre' killers all right. What mattered now was how to help him get his mojo back.

Afterwards, I intended to pencil a few ideas for the attention of Ingis Chen. I fell asleep before I had a chance to write three lines and woke up with a start in the morning just before 7.30. I opened my eyes already tired – don't we all hate it when that happens? –, hugging my FTab. It displayed a notification of new message from Leila. She just wanted to check on us and asked if I would be able to go to WII at some point today, where we could talk by phone without anyone listening in on my side. I liked the idea, ergo I wrote back that I would try at the earliest opportunity, if the secret service didn't block my way.

I popped downstairs to the kitchen for a large mug of tea. The house was totally silent, in complete contrast with the number of people currently in residence – even more counting the ones listening in and watching. Back to bed, sipping tea and writing, hidden under cover of the duvet, I was lost in thought as to how to approach Ingis Chen subtly.

'Argh!' I groaned. Tired and fed up, my eyes were getting hot and wet. A big ball was blocking my throat. I had the toughest challenge to face since the Fog transformed my life. It was one too many. Tears started to well and slowly streamed towards my cheeks and my chin. I was crying in silence, sniffing as my nose started to run.

'Dammit!' I restricted my explosion to a whisper. 'I don't even have tissues anymore! Typical!' I had the choice between going downstairs to get some in the kitchen or using my T-shirt. I didn't want to be seen in that state and I pulled a face at the idea of using my nightwear to blow my nose, so I quickly tiptoed to the bathroom, grabbed a spare toilet roll and rushed back into my room.

'Get a grip, Yoko, Get a grip!' I frowned and clenched my jaw, angry at myself. I had been doing so well holding up until then!

I had to get busy and occupy my mind. I opened my personal folder and started typing my diary for the past two days. By filling my mind with work, I intended to kick the blues out of my system. It had been a good thing my diary was typed, not written in a notebook as originally planned. I made a note to mention to the other Foggies to beware of and even destroy paper trails. It would be wisest to scan or take photos of what they wished to keep, and anything best not read by anyone else should be discarded. The problem of privacy remained with the Society. We would have to look into creative solutions to keep a minimum, which from now on a luxury for us. In general though, I trusted them.

That made me realise I wasn't fussed about the invasion of my privacy anymore. I had split freedom and independence from privacy. Could it be one of the major lessons of trusting the Society? Even with little privacy, as long as there was respect between the parties involved, you could still act of your own accord and lead the life of your choice. So long as we were treated with respect, I didn't mind the actual loss of privacy.

Respect.

After I typed that word, I enlarged it, put it in bold and underlined it.

At 8.30 a.m. I felt ready to call Ingis. Having to be cautious in case his line was bugged, there was no point waiting until I was in the forest before I contacted him.

'Ingis Chen's mobile,' his personal assistant answered.

'Hi, I am Yoko Salelles. Before you transfer me, please tell me your name.'

'Good morning Miss Salelles. You do not wish to speak with Mr Chen?'

'I do, but if you are always answering the phone for him, it would be nice to know your name.'

'Oh! I see. I am Anna. However Mr Chen has three PAs at his service. In your local time, that would be me from 7 a.m. to 3 p.m., another from 3 p.m. to 11p.m. and the third from 11 p.m. to 7 a.m. six days a week. The three of us are based in different countries, so the lines have a complex redirection system between Europe, America and Asia.'

'And you, where are you based?'

'Europe.'

'UK?'

'No. Shall I transfer you to Mr Chen now?'

'Yes, thank you Anna.'

'You are welcome.'

I waited one second for the smooth voice of the dapper Ingis.

'Yoko. At last.'

'Good morning, Mr Chen.'

'Please, really, call me Ingis.'

'I am afraid I do not have much time, Mr Chen. I am not free to talk at length.'

'I see.'

'Maybe you are not free either. Am I interrupting?'

'Maybe we should meet?'

'I think a few people would intrude. Indeed we have had to reveal you were the one watching our backs, the one organising our security, equipment, and the acquisition of the lot for a more private purpose.'

'I see. Then I should take their call soon.'

'I am surprised you haven't already.'

'I was hoping to talk to you first. Anything more I should know that you couldn't keep secret?'

'I told them how you found us that first week and how you only advise and support, but don't interfere.'

'Really? That doesn't sound like me.'

'You went beyond yourself on that one.'

'So now I am on the frontline. I guess that means you owe me one.'

'Not really. We had discussed it, now you have even more to lose.'

'I believe the terms were very vague. I think we will need to meet soon to clarify them all.'

'It will be difficult in the immediate future and really I am in no mood to argue. So I will clarify one thing for you right now. I am amazed to have to remind you: when it comes to the Fog, we Foggies are irreplaceable. You aren't. Goodbye, Mr Chen.'

'The kitten has claws. Goodbye, Yoko.'

Next, I wrote to Jazz to ask her if she could brief me on what had happened in WII in my absence, as far as she and the Relocated knew. My next visit to her and World II was not confirmed yet and kept saying we had to talk. I was eager to know more. When Jazz didn't blurt out straight away what was on her mind, it wasn't a good sign. I also took some time explaining the situation with Leo. She was my best friend, I couldn't leave her out now that the others knew, it would hurt her. I let my head do the writing, not my heart. That helped me be even more resolute and to feel I was making the right choice.

I felt cramps in my stomach, heard footsteps on the staircase and understood the signal: time for a second breakfast. When I reached the kitchen, Harry was preparing tea. I started making coffee and took out a loaf of sliced bread which was showing signs of age. After the usual morning greetings, Harry told me he had to go to the university to sort out a few things linked to his absence. It was Saturday, a non-working day, a detail that had never mattered with him. I wasn't sure he would be let out of the houses' front courtyard, but didn't mention it. Harry already knew. When he had gone, I called my parents. Who knew what Sam the spy had told them? They must be in such an anxious state.

'Mum?'

'Yoko! Thank God! How are you? Where are you? What is going on?'

'Mum, I am back at home. I am fine. We just had a surprise visit from the government who wanted to ask us a few questions.'

'The man who answered my call ...'

'He belongs to the government.'

'Are you OK? Are you sure?'

'Yes Mum. I am fine.'

'But they ... You took a long time to ...'

'They had a lot of questions.'

'Did they get a lot of replies?'

'Not as many as they hoped.'

'And me, you won't tell me anything, will you?'

'The most important thing is that I am here, at home, though the lines aren't safe.'

'So I can't really talk either.'

'That depends if what you have to say is very private or not.'

There was a little silence over the phone. I heard my mother mutter something to someone I guessed was my father, then spoke to me again. 'Your sister, she has gone off the grid. Did you know?'

'You mean she is off on a trip?'

'I mean she went on a trip, but she has disappeared during the trip, with Eudes and her guide.'

It took a moment to compute. My head went dizzy. My sister, my nephew and Ushi Tsou were missing, they had gone AWOL. 'Ushi, you bitch!' I screamed inwardly.

I received confirmation soon after from Jazz. She had replied to my message.

> *My dear Nutella,*
>
> *I hate not to tell you face to face! Serious things have happened. First, your sister and Eudes: they should have arrived by now, but they haven't. They left your parents as planned on Thursday morning. The weather was fine both at departure and arrival in WII. We don't know in between, of course, but we expected them by Thursday evening. I spoke with Nick, Leila and your parents, and we are all hoping they hit bad weather and that Tsou just stopped somewhere on the way, waiting for the rough flying conditions to pass. Maybe they will arrive today. We hope there hasn't been an accident, or worse from Tsou Bitch. I didn't tell your parents the details about her antics. I tried to deal with the situation as you would: say the minimum and don't worry them unnecessarily. Your being taken away wasn't helping. One thing for sure, I am not telling MY family about the Fog anytime soon. The longer I don't have to deal with that kind of worrying about me from them the better. It was too hard to hear their anguish and pain!*
>
> *There is more!*
>
> *Poff called on the radio network. I managed to answer on Nick's big control. I pressed buttons randomly and it worked, unbelievably. He began to say there were updates on the attack. I had to cut him short as I didn't want the spooks to hear and told him that it would be better if he*

*could speak with the Fishers. Then Maisie would be able to relay the information to me in less explicit terms in person. The spooks let her return to WII as she is young and her father is there. At least they have a heart! Anyway, here is what's up: your young attacker is dead! He killed himself in his cell, by hanging himself. He left a note saying 'I have failed you my Grace. Please forgive me.' Now to be honest, I don't care that he killed himself, but it indicated that he was not working alone. He had not just suddenly convinced himself we were the work of Satan, he had been indoctrinated by someone against us! Brain-washed, or something like that! He was also enamoured of his mentor. Yes, by a woman! And we know that because he left drawings of her, many drawings, hidden in a little shed where they were probably plotting (and more dirty stuff, if you want my point of view). Sadly, despite the efforts of the sheriffs of both Lil'London and Newtonsee to find more clues about this woman, so far nothing has come up. So danger is still out there and it has a mastermind! I am telling you. I can't wait for Nick to be up again and your protective shadow. Then I'll get Big Tom to watch mine. He is a sweetie, by the way. And the man can cook a bloody good sticky toffee pudding. Maisie brought it over just for Nick and me.*

*I miss you, Nutella.*

*And I am worried for you.*

*And scared. Having Nick in the house is great. I know right now you have other spooky matters to manage than my moods, so I have decided to ignore, play dumb and act as if everything is fine. I am trying the 'think positive' approach. Plus, they've put a camera in my room now. No way will I let them see me cry on camera.*

*Jazz xxxxxxx*

*PS They found my gun and taser and took them away. Nick's too. He has more in his trailer, he said, but left them there for now. Tell the bastards if anything happens to me it will be on their heads. Maybe at least get them to give me back my pepper spray. They even took that!*

*P.P.S. I understand you don't want to talk about the 'Leo situation'. I will respect this, and will not broach the subject unless you mention it to me. However, I know you. You are strong and very sensitive, yet you are not emotional in the sense that you do not let emotions lead you. It is a quality in the sense that it helps you not take things personally and think rationally; it is a flaw because you use it to over-protect yourself and stop you letting someone in. I love you, my friend, and I hope Leo will not give up and will tame you in the end.*

My head and body felt numb, yet I wasn't shocked, not even surprised. Maybe that was because I had reached the point when one or two more drops would not make any difference in a river I couldn't control. All I could do was keep my boat afloat and try as best as I could to avoid the treacherous currents. Hence, I bit my lips at the thought of my sister and nephew, either in the hands of the elements or in Ushi Tsou's. I frowned at the idea that whoever wanted me dead in WII was still out there, that it was a woman and she might be Ushi Tsou's ally. It puzzled me why a woman would want to kill someone who symbolises more freedom for her kind. The ways of other people's minds never cease to amaze me. I had to remain stoic, rational to face it all. There was no place in my life now for anything sentimental anyway. It was easier for now to put that side on hold. I was glad Jazz understood and would not be on my back. When Leo's morning kiss came to mind, it brought a smile to my lips. Then I froze as

Julia and Eudes came back into my mind. Putting the emotional under wraps was easier said than done. I was determined to manage, it was necessary for me to cope with the present. As for the future, we would see.

I sent a long email to the Foggies recounting the latest events and our current situation, copying in Leila and Jazz for their information. I also dropped an email to Ann Fisher, who had lost her direct access to her family in the past few days. I just hoped she was not detained somewhere as we had been. Very soon, all the Foggies replied and exchanged instant messaging as a group. The Foggies' support was absolute. From Alaska, Nevada, Morocco, and Kenya, everyone replied present immediately. They had been in touch with Jazz, offering to come and help to search for my sister and nephew (it would be like looking for a needle in a haystack, so the idea was put to one side for now), and to come to take over the crossing of materials if require. The four other Switchers promised the Fog would be maintained. If the abbreviation FU could not have been interpreted wrongly, I was tempted to call our group 'Foggies United' but Rico protested FU in short could be misinterpreted ... Instead, I suggested 'Gatekeepers'. It was adopted unanimously, with our company being called Gatekeepers Associates. Sophia had also further reinforced the group with more clarity on our roles within it. Each of us had one, more often than not linked to our professional background and competencies. Open to adjustment and changes in practice, those specialities were to be used when dealing with the Society and Ingis Chen, and now with the authorities as well. To ensure unity across the board, we had been paired to exercise them when possible:

- Harry was to be our 'in-house' history expert;
- Zeno and Leo would be the commercial gurus;
- Rico was to work with Leo and Zeno in London, and continue to develop his art;

- Dante was the architecture expert, and would aim to integrate as much modern technology as possible in WII while respecting the local traditions and needs;
- Christophe would look after Gatekeepers Associates' finances and investments, along with Tony;
- Louise and Rosario would organise events and travel between Foggies;
- Adam was to be our legal expert;
- Sophia would be Gatekeepers Associates' Company Secretary and Administrator, working with me;
- Mitch and Clare's role was to defend, protect and preserve the wild of WII. They were our Greenpeace elements!
- Putu was our medical counsel, supported by Mary, regarding the psychological help any one of us might need (she was already working on Jack's case);
- Jack, Michelle and Helo did not have a determined role yet, either because they were uncertain as to what they wished to do, or were too young.

As for me, I was to be Communication and Public Relations, working with Sophia when it related to the internal communications between Foggies. In general, everyone would work with everyone. It was easily feasible, being a relatively small group, and all our activities were intertwined. We all agreed on this. WE ALL AGREED! The Foggies were a team. I punched the air, sitting in my bed, one arm out from under the duvet. After the past couple of days, the support of the other Foggies confirmed the results of hard work along with my hopes and dreams. We were strong, we were united, ready to face adversity. It gave me strength to face the day ahead, to face what British intelligence had in store for us next.

When I finished writing and reading, the house was full of life and Simba was clearly in need of a little walk outside. I got dressed and made my way downstairs, saying a quick 'hi' to anyone met on the way. I made a swift escape when Leo moved towards me, a naughty sparkle in his eyes. I was such a coward. I both wanted him and didn't want him. Despite my belief that I knew what was best for me, at that moment I struggled to control my attraction to him, and didn't want to lose him as a friend altogether.

'I just … I am not ready. It is not the right time!' I said to myself as I closed the door.

'You are scared,' a little voice in my head corrected.

'Shut up!' I told it.

'As if,' it replied. 'You know I am right. You keep an emotional distance to cope with everything, to avoid asking yourself personal questions. You fear being involved, you stay emotionally remote so as not be unsettled, and you are terrified of getting attached, in case it didn't work, in case you get hurt. Face it, you cannot tune me out forever.'

The nagging internal voice was, happily, interrupted by one of agents in the parking lot.

'Where are you going?'

'Just walking my dog,' I replied, trying the charm strategy by adding a smile to my response. I was dealing with a woman and she was unmoved. She looked suspiciously at Simba.

'Fine. He is small, so you have five minutes. Stay away from the two boarded houses.' With her last words, she moved to post herself by the aforementioned wooden wall. I let out a sigh. Jack and I had to sleep there tonight, each in a house, otherwise tomorrow there would be a new door to WII to handle. That was a conversation to have with Sam. He hadn't shown up for his scheduled visit mid-morning.

'Can I speak to Sam?'

'Who?' she asked suspiciously.

'Sam. The agent interrogating us? The one that brought us here? Your boss?'

'Ah! Agent Riverson.' She frowned at me, not liking my familiar way of addressing her boss.

'That is so nice of you to have told me his full name. I had been wondering what it was for some time,' I retorted, even though I knew his name all along. I wanted to wipe clean that smirk of hers. It worked.

I heard our front door open and close. I turned my head. Leo was coming towards us. He stopped by my side, putting his hand in the hollow of my back, as a tender and protective gesture. I was so totally not in control. I repeated my request to be put in touch with Sam, or Agent Samuel Riverson. The agent took a radio out and repeated my request. She then abruptly said time was up and I had to go back inside. I bit back a reply, her attitude was getting me inflamed and I didn't trust myself to remain polite. She was not worth wasting my time and energy on, I needed to focus on the bigger fish.

Just before we closed the front door, she raised her voice from her watch point and informed me that Agent Riverson would be with us at 3 p.m.

Lunch was tense. We rarely did it, but for once we switched on the television while we ate. First we put on the news, then as we all got mildly depressed by the ramblings of politicians, the latest celebrity antics, the economic difficulties, or the health threats carried in our everyday shopping trolley, we changed channel to a movie. We had missed the start and it wasn't clear what was happening, but nobody cared. It was something with Tom Cruise in it. It was entertaining enough and it passed time until Mysterious Sam arrived. Jack had joined us for lunch and remained until halfway through the movie. He then declared he was going to bed. I suggested he might want to stay for the meeting with Sam, but he declined, saying he would be useless anyway. He looked lifeless and exhausted with dark circles under his eyes.

When Sam arrived, he simply sat and watched the movie with us until it was over. Only then did we get to business, cup of tea in hands, comfortable on the sofa. Any newcomer would have thought us a group of friends relaxing at home.

'I want to check everything is fine in WII,' I told Sam when the credits started to roll.

'You went this morning,' he replied.

'It was barely daylight. I only went to the house and stayed for just five minutes. What did you expect me to check? Anyway, you let me go earlier, so why not now?'

'Momentary weakness on my part. Why don't you call Jazz?'

'Because there are also Nick, the Fishers and the contacts in Lil'London to consider. Talking about the Fishers, I hope you are not harassing the poor wife? Ann has lost her all family, she doesn't need you on her back.'

'You make us sounds like the Gestapo or Russian NKVD.'

'Well ...' Rico started.

'Careful ...' Sam hissed, narrowed eyes on Rico.

'Sam, Jack and I have to sleep in both fogged houses tonight anyway. It is switching night,' I reminded him. He finally relented, although there would be an agent in the house at all times.

We talked all the way through to the early hours of the evening, sometimes peacefully, sometimes in chaos, everyone talking over each other, raising voices, making demands and threats. On Ann Fisher, Sam conceded that she could not be found. Her husband must have warned her. As the sky started to darken, I was relieved that my biggest achievement in this meeting was that Jack and I could sleep in the fogged houses that night. It was the most urgent priority on a Saturday. Sam asked a few questions about the FTab. He threatened to take it back following our secret use of it during the day. It was time to negotiate.

'What do you want from us?' The simplest question, yet the one that led to the most important part of the discussion.

'We want your full cooperation.'

'For what?'

'For research, controlling access to the Fog and access to that Other World, and complete knowledge on what is happening over there.'

'Oh … That's all?' Dante's sharp tongue let slip.

Sam ignored him and continued. 'And we want you to defend the best interests of this world over there.'

'Especially the British best interests, I presume,' Rico said in a terrible fake posh English accent, difficult to take seriously when it sounded so heavily Italian.

'If possible.'

'Why?' I asked.

'What do you mean, why?' Sam looked at me, genuinely surprised.

'You don't know what it means? I thought English was your mother tongue?' I commented.

'Yoko, don't you start again.'

There was a pause, Sam looked murderous and I gave in. 'Why would we give you not only full cooperation, as you first said, but also full control, as you then described?'

'Because you are not qualified to handle of the dangers of this high stakes game.'

'Hang on a second,' Zeno interrupted. 'You are implying you are more qualified? No one is qualified at all! No one from this world has experience about this type of thing. No one from this world has any rights over the Other World and vice versa. If we are the guardians and handlers of the door, there might be a reason. We could very well be a private entity. When the government go to public companies for the best contract, they publish bids and select the offers they consider best suited. Well, we could do the same!'

'Except that when it comes to national security then we take over.'

'If you take over, again, this is not full cooperation you want, but control and domination,' I pointed out.

'We need your full cooperation to have control and you know it.'

We looked at each other, old friends, new friends, ex-potentially-future lovers and smiled. Yes, we knew it all right.

'What happens if we say no, if we refuse to give you our full cooperation?' I asked for all of us.

'We will have to force it. Personally, I very much hope we will not reach that point,' Sam replied. He seemed to mean it, not relishing that idea.

'What about if we propose conditional cooperation?' I persisted.

'What do you mean?'

'Well, we will agree to cooperate with you under defined terms,' Zeno explained for me.

'Are you trying to negotiate with national security?' Sam looked at each one of us.

'We are not trying to. We are negotiating,' I corrected.

'You are not in a position to negotiate.'

'Yes, we are. You need us, you said it yourself. YOU are not in a position not to negotiate.'

'We have you.'

'Really? You hold us here, which is true. And that is all. You mentioned this morning when I went to check on Jazz that you had to trust me to come back, that I would be only five minutes. You also had to rely on Rico to bring me back, you couldn't send anyone else. You hold us here, but that is all you can do. Without us, World II is only a concept, a dream for you.'

Their only other recourse that I could think of was blackmail. Leila had reinforced security around all our families. Abroad, it was more difficult for the British to use that card. I glanced at Harry. He never talked about his. As a Facilitator, still fully based in London, his family didn't need to know anything about the Fog. They were under the Society's watch too. It was not bullet-proof. British intelligence still held us captive. In addition, Ushi Tsou's disappearance with my sister and Eudes could also be for blackmail. If so, on whose behalf? Herself only, or …?

'You want to bring back Kim and Ed Epcott, I am sure,' Leo added. 'It isn't fun for that policeman and his sister to be stranded alone over there in Essex. Again you will need us, to lead them here and integrate them.'

'If you want to send drones and learn about that alternative world's layout and potential, you'll need us,' Zeno broke in.

'To liaise with the local communities, to develop trade, and to understand their history and knowledge, you need to keep us happy,' Harry said, coming back from work, shadowed by an agent, and joining the conversation in a flash.

'You told us what you want. Here is what we want: for you to treat us decently and as business partners. We want a proper working relationship. You will remove the cameras from the courtyard and the terraced houses, as well as inside the houses. You can leave them outside the terraced houses' land, but not inside. If you don't trust us, we won't trust you,' I continued.

'You mean you would rather have a foreigner and unaccredited man like Ingis Chen backing you than us?'

'Inside the outer wall protecting the houses, it's private. The majority of us are foreign and our protector may have more credits that you know of. Consider it to be like an embassy: the area is Fog territory. If we need your services, we will let you know. Outside in the street, it is your domain,' Harry said, in a matter of fact voice. 'In addition, in the Other World, please remember there is a difference between exploring and exploiting. It would be nice for once not to repeat the mistakes of the past. This is not another opportunity to colonise and create a new British empire.'

'What if Ingis Chen is a dangerous man? What if he intends to use you to access a world where he can run dangerous activities with impunity?' Sam was tense and on edge, he was losing some important ground.

'What makes you think we would allow it?' Leo exploded, furious. If Sam knew how much Leo disliked Ingis Chen, he would have laughed at his earlier questions.

'For God's sake!' Sam stood up. He didn't have anything to add, our positions were clear. His parting words were intended to make us rethink our views. 'I do understand you wish to protect your private lives, it is human nature. Just take some time to think of the bigger picture. The authorities are here to set up the rules, structures and laws we comply with for the benefit of society as a whole. You've got to be realistic. It makes sense for you to abide by the laws and the power of the state like anyone else. I think you'll agree that you could have a worse state than the United Kingdom to comply with. This ...' He pointed to the window and the Fog outside. 'It is too big a discovery, too big an opportunity, and too big a risk to be overseen by you only, or by a company with no supervision. I believe we came in just in time to stop you making some big mistakes. I will pass on your 'terms and conditions' to my superiors, but again, I think you are not being realistic. You should accept that you are not private citizens anymore. You are part of national security. In fact, you are part of international security. This is bigger than you as individuals. You should not make your private lives and feelings a priority. They should be set aside.'

There was a pause after he left. His words were like a cold shower. 'You are not private citizens anymore ... This is bigger than you as individuals. You should not make your private lives and feelings a priority, they should be set aside.' I hated that part of me felt he was right. Worse, that part knew he was right. I shook my head, conversing with myself, silently, staring at the window.

'No. I refuse to do it. I will not be swallowed by the big state machine. So he, or they, believe they will take over from now on? Think again. Maud Poff didn't have tea with the state, she was chatting with an individual. Ariel Ben-Chaim didn't save the life of a state, but an individual's. What about the Relocated? Do they care about the state, or do they care about the people surrounding them and showing some concern and personal support? I will – we will! – endeavour to work 'for the greater good' as the saying goes, but I will not be annihilated in the process. You wish to set up rules, structures and laws to deal with the Fog, fair enough, I get that, but you will have to set them with us, not unilaterally and then imposing them onto us.'

We had struggled so far, yet it was nothing to the battles that were to come, it was only too clear. I looked at the others and they were as determined as me. The game was not up. In a world dominated by offer and demand, the Foggies had monopoly of the Fog. We were ready for the fight! All of us Foggies, we were united and ready! With the Society behind us, we were strong. We could and would face the challenges from both sides of the Fog gates.

Harry stood up and, even though deep in thought like us all, declared by force of habit 'time for tea'.

Rico burst out laughing, Zeno joining in within seconds. The latter stood up, opened his wine cabinet and took out a bottle of Chianti.

'Come on mate, forget tea. Let's open a bottle.'

At the same time, Harry put a pack of cookies in front of me, my favourite kind.

# ACKNOWLEDGEMENTS

This book could not have been written without the valuable help of my friends. The support I have received overwhelms me with gratitude.

I am especially thankful to Alaa Al-Essa for the years she spent listening patiently to my stories, for her analysis of my characters and their interactions, and for her constant hand on my shoulder to support me moving forward. Anna Hewitt-Jones was a truly devoted friend in her dedication and patience to proofread my manuscript and correct my flawed English. Her task was daunting and my appreciation is tremendous.

The advice, support, comments and recommendations of many friends have greatly improved my work and kept my spirits up while labouring to find the right words. To all of you who believed in my project and in me – Antoine, Alexandra, Arun, Patricia, Hiren, Stephen 'SMOX' and Ivan to name only a few – thank you!

# ABOUT THE AUTHOR

Virginie Bonfils-Bedos was born and raised in Southern France and moved to London for her studies. After reading political science and European legislation, she earned master's degrees in European public policy and management of European affairs, and went on to begin a career in strategic communication.

A lifelong writer with a passion for words, Virginie Bonfils-Bedos has always kept notebooks filled with fictional or real stories she shared with her family and friends. Along with her love of writing, she began dedicating more time to her creativity over the years, with activities such as acting, mixed media art, and photography. She is also a scriptwriter, collaborating with a movie director on a feature film.

Walking through London one foggy morning, an unusual idea caught her imagination. It paved the way for her debut novel, *Gatekeepers*, with a sequel currently in the works.